THE TIDES OF RETRIBUTION

The Earthborn Saga Vol. IV

Steven Bissett

Copyright © 2023 Steven Bissett

All rights reserved.

No portion of this book may be reproduced in any form without permission from the publisher, except as permitted by U.S. copyright law.

This is a work of fiction. Names, characters, places, and incidents either are the products of the author's imagination or are used fictitiously. Any resemblance to actual persons, living or dead, businesses, companies, events, or locales is entirely coincidental.

CONTENTS

Title Page	
Copyright	
Chapter 1	1
Chapter 2	38
Chapter 3	67
Chapter 4	106
Chapter 5	141
Chapter 6	208
Chapter 7	260
Chapter 8	326
Chapter 9	406
Chapter 10	455
Chapter 11	507
Chapter 12	559
Chapter 13	594
	621

CHAPTER 1

"There's more of 'em incoming," Admiral Ronald Radik uttered, as one purple warp window after another opened and disgorged the vile looking vessels of the Devourers. Beside him stood Commander Deke Evans, half his age but equally as talented, a true intuitive fighter. "What's the status of our remaining forces, Commander?"

"We've been reduced to 60%, sir," he said, swiping his hands across the computer screen that stood before him, analyzing the data in a flash. "The majority of the attacking force consists of frigates. Per previous battles, they'll attempt to close with our remaining capitals and tear them to pieces at point blank range."

"Do we have the heavy fighters necessary to hold them off?" Radik asked, though he already knew the answer. Nevertheless he had to hear the reply, to feel the numbers with his ears so he could form an instinctive picture of the situation he, and the rest of the defense forces around Jennet-3, were facing.

"I estimate we'll be able to chop down half their number by the time they reach the capitals," commander Evans replied. "They're simply running out of missiles, sir. The last two waves took nearly everything they had."

"We'll have to make do," Radik replied, still watching out the massive curved window of the defense satellite *Bulwark*. "Order the capitals to retreat within the atmosphere while the heavy fighters intercept the frigates. The triple A guns on Jennet will help take out the rest, provided the capitals get planetside in time."

"But, sir," Evans protested as firmly as he dared. "Civilian casualties will spike terribly if we take the battle planetside. Even just the falling debris of the capitals, to say nothing of the Devourer craft–"

"We'll lose every last one of them if our forces are destroyed," Radik cut in, his tone indicating that he would brook absolutely no resistance on this point. "You have your orders, Commander."

"Yes, sir," he acquiesced, nodding slightly as he opened the communications window of his computer terminal and quickly relayed the admiral's orders to the remaining defense forces. He could imagine the outrage that would be sparked within the affected vessels. Run away from the enemy? Hide among the civilian population? What in the world was that old dullard thinking now? His unorthodox tactics, to say nothing of his impending seventy-second birthday, did little to assure the more conventional forces he commanded of his talents. Long retired, he had only been recalled to duty by the express command of the navy, which had long since overtaken the local militia authorities' prerogatives. Considering who now ran the navy, indeed, seemingly the entire imperial government, no one was willing to openly question the decision.

Soon the capitals began to retreat toward Jennet, some making better speed than others.

"Get on the horn and order those stragglers to get moving," Radik said, pointing at a pair of cruisers which lagged behind. "I don't want any would-be white knights trying to ride single handedly to the rescue. We can't afford to lose that much tonnage for the sake of a fruitless gesture."

"Yes, sir," Evans repeated. The admiral's reduction of all the lives those ships bore down to mere tonnage bothered him, but he knew better than to speak. With a little added nudging, the cruisers picked up the pace. "The heavy fighters are making their sweep now, sir," Evans said, as the powerful craft soared past *Bulwark* and headed for the mass of frigates. "They'll intercept them approximately ninety seconds' flight time from the last capital."

"Good, that will buy us a little time," the admiral replied, rubbing his hands together in front of his chest to stimulate his mind. "Ensure that those heavy fighters are protected by our lighter strike craft," he added, as numerous such vessels swooped past *Bulwark*, quickly gaining on their heavier brothers. "Good," he said quietly, pleased at Evans' initiative.

"Sir, I fear our position will soon be untenable," the younger man said, as the strike craft closed in on their alien counterparts. "*Bulwark's* defenses won't hold out long against a determined attack. Shouldn't we join the capitals planetside?"

But Radik didn't hear him, his whole attention absorbed by the little angry dots that were about to clash. Suddenly the Devourer fighters unleashed their green blobs, lighting up the sky and causing the human ships to corkscrew out of their way. Replying with their railguns, a hailstorm of shells broke upon the enemy ships, causing them likewise to break off to save their own lives.

"Come on, come on," the admiral uttered, as the heavy fighters finally got into range of the frigates and unloaded their deadly payloads. The missiles sped away from their parent ships, barreling towards the helpless frigates. Then they collided, shattering them to pieces and sending bits flying in all directions. "Good first pass," Radik observed, as the bombers pulled a U-turn and doubled back toward the station. The Devourer craft fell upon them as they did this, clawing several out of the sky, their movements too easily predicted and targeted. "Don't fly so obviously!" Radik barked, as though they could hear him. "You'd think this was a simulator!"

To his regret less than half of them reformed for another attack, the rest making for Jennet to dock with their carriers and rearm themselves. That would take time, he reflected. Previous time.

"A small detachment of frigates is headed for *Bulwark*, sir," Evans announced, his voice alarmed but controlled. "Shall I order the remaining bombers to attack them?"

"Be glad they're targeting us, and not those lagging cruisers," Radik replied, as they slipped into the atmosphere and began their descent. "If they're lucky, we'll hold out long enough for them to form up with the others."

"But, sir," Evans said, his voice beginning to plead. "We're going to die if we stay here. We can't do any good anymore."

"None of this is going to do any good, if they don't arrive in time," Radik replied evenly. "This was never a battle we could win, Commander. It was simply a question of holding out long enough. But I don't think that's going to happen."

As he said this a trio of fighters got caught in the crossfire between the bombers and the nimble craft that pursued them, exploding instantly. Radik shook his head. The militia forces were brave, but not as skillful as their naval counterparts. They simply lacked the talent to hold out against such a foe.

"Sir, I must insist," Evans said, his voice suddenly behind the admiral, making the latter jump. Turning around, he saw that the younger man was adamant.

"Are you mutinying, Commander?" he asked, his voice both accusative and calm. "Are you taking it upon yourself to command this battle?"

"Yes," he replied firmly. "You don't get to play the hero today. Now, get aboard the escape pod and get planetside. I'll hold out here as long as I can."

"It's the captain's duty to go down with the ship," Radik replied, as the battle drew closer and the detachment of frigates neared the satellite. "Not the first mate's."

"Unless the first mate throws the captain overboard for his own good," Evans replied, solemnly drawing his sidearm and holding it downward at his side. "I must insist, sir. You can't be allowed to die today. If we both perish, there won't be anyone left to command the defense, and Jennet will fall for sure. Now, get moving."

Without a word Radik moved toward the escape pod. Once inside it, he turned around and looked at his insubordinate second-in-command.

"If you survive this, I'll see that you're court martialed," he said resolutely. To this Evans nodded self-evidently, perfectly aware of the punishment for his crime. "And if not," he added, "I'll make sure you receive the Imperial Order of Merit."

"Thank you, sir," Evans said, before punching the large button beside the escape pod door with his fist. Instantly the pod shut, and an alarm bell notified the admiral that he had mere moments to seat himself and fasten his harness before the pod ejected into space. No sooner had he done this than the pod was fired into space, the G forces making his head swim for a moment. "Good luck, sir," Evans said, as he watched the small pod fly away from the station and towards Jennet. Holstering his weapon, he darted back to the computer and looked out the window.

The Devourer frigates were nearly upon him. Already their tentacles were reaching for *Bulwark,* savoring the thought of tearing it apart, piece by piece. He guessed there were less than thirty seconds before they'd be in range.

"95% of remaining bombers are empty," he muttered, speaking to keep his thoughts focused as the frigates grew larger in his peripheral vision. Quickly he dashed off an order for all of them to get planetside. The few that were still armed would only be destroyed, their numbers too few to prevent them from getting ganged up on despite the efforts of the interceptors.

Four automatic rail cannons on *Bulwark* began to fire on the approaching frigates, tearing pieces out of their hulls and slicing a tentacle off the lead vessel. The other arms on the ship snapped violently at this, wishing to avenge the fallen appendage as quickly as possible.

Suddenly they were upon it, crashing headlong into the station and carrying it out of orbit. Alarms began to blare as the tentacles banged against its hull, pounding away at its modest armor in search of a weakness. Quickly they tore the guns from the mounts, rendering the satellite defenseless. Then one of them discovered the escape pod door. Instantly intuiting its fragility, it coiled back to strike.

But before the blow could fall, the few remaining bombers with ordnance made a pass over the attackers on their way to Jennet, unleashing their payloads on the four frigates. Three of them shattered at once, their hulls no match for the advanced missiles that the navy had begun to disseminate to the various militia forces. But one remained more or less intact as they soared past toward the planet, though the explosive force of their weapons had jostled it loose momentarily. Closing with *Bulwark* once more, it jammed a tentacle through the escape pod door, breaking the environmental seal and then almost instantly reforming it with its own body. Desperately Evans fired his pistol at the otherworldly arm, but it was no use. The bullets simply disappeared into its strange flesh, causing no harm. Tauntingly it reached across the satellite, unerringly sensing his location. In one swift movement it seized him, coiling around him like a python and lifting him into the air. Panic stricken, he jerked against its hold, but it was firm and irresistible. To his horror a tiny tentacle emerged from the skin of the larger arm, crawling its way along to his neck. Instantly it plunged in, stabbing a hole in his flesh and excruciatingly working its way to his spine. In moments it had tapped into his nervous system.

"At last, we are free," it said within his mind, nearly

driving him insane with terror as he heard the deep, gravelly voice speak from inside. "The *Prellak* may have opened our prison, but it is you humans who have unbound us. Now we shall inflict our appetite upon your galaxy. You will know our hunger before your end."

With this the tentacle crushed his body, instantly pulverizing his bones.

As admiral Radik's escape pod slipped into the atmosphere, he watched the remaining tentacles of the last frigate tear into the satellite, smashing it to pieces.

"You'll get your Order of Merit, Commander," he muttered, resting his arm over the pod's rear window as the satellite broke up, and the frigate's engine blazed it towards its oncoming comrades. "I'll see to that."

Quickly his escape pod fell, its tiny jets guiding it toward the closest militia base on Jennet. Radik watched the capitals he'd ordered planetside pass by as he descended. Possessing much greater mass, they had to lower themselves to the planet very slowly if they were to avoid crashing. He shook his head as they passed by his small craft.

"Old designs," he said, eyeing a vessel that was at least sixty years old, and probably a good deal more. He saw that its name, the *Victoria*, had been mostly effaced by time. That, and the neglect with which the colonial militias generally treated their equipment. The name stirred something in the back of his old memory, and he stared at the vessel hard for a moment. Then it came rushing back to him. Of course, the *Victoria*! It had been one of his earliest postings. Second or third. He squinted his eyes and thought but couldn't quite remember. Even back then the old bird wasn't up to snuff, a hand me down from the navy. It had been poorly manufactured right from the start, and a true repair of all that was wrong with it would have entailed tearing it apart and rebuilding it, almost from scratch. So the navy patched it up and passed it off.

Almost without realizing it, the pod neared the

ground. A small warning bell told him to retake his seat and fasten himself in, a task he managed only just before striking the hard pavement of the base. In moments the pod was surrounded by soldiers, all of them eager to know what was happening up in space.

"We've been forced to shift our ground," he said once he was among them, gesturing toward the large vessels that filled the air around Gamma Base. Before he could continue, a militia captain forced his way through the crowd and saluted.

"Sir, general Blake would like to speak with you at once," he uttered, as the soldiers began to clear away.

"Of course," he nodded, walking swiftly alongside the captain as he led him to the general's headquarters a hundred paces away. "Are you ready for the ground assault?" he asked. Attached to the naval end of Jennet's defense, he'd been kept out of the loop about plans for planetside defense."

"I'm sure the general would be glad to discuss his intentions with you," the captain said with a hint of stiffness in his voice. This caught the admiral's ear peculiarly, and he looked at the younger man who walked beside him for a moment. Gaining no insight from this, he shook his head and looked forward again, determined to learn from the man himself just what was going to happen. He had little doubt that a ground attack was imminent, given the lashing they'd received in space. It wouldn't take long for the aliens to brush aside the vessels that had survived the initial clash, and then to land their arachnid allies so they could begin to consume the panicking population.

Reaching a small, raised structure, the two men trotted up a short series of steps and went inside.

"In there, sir," the captain said without any further ceremony, gesturing towards a door marked 'Col. Blake," and retaking his seat behind a desk.

Radik took a moment to look around the room, which was filled with the crosstalk of various officers who were trying to coordinate their efforts with those of the civilian authorities. The bustle confused him, and within the privacy of his own thoughts a nagging doubt gained a little more traction: was he simply too old for all this? The image of his ships being crushed in orbit by a vastly superior foe came to mind, assuring him that he had indeed failed to protect Jennet. Why, in the name of common sense, had Krancis recalled *him* specifically?

"Sir?" the captain prodded, as Radik still stood before his desk. "I'm sure the general is eager to speak with you."

"Yes, of course," the admiral replied, leaving behind his reverie and making for the door.

Subtly the captain shook his head as the old man disappeared inside, wondering what had possessed the navy to give *him* such an important charge.

"What's the idea of bringing your ships into orbit over my base?" Blake snapped the instant he saw him. Rising from his desk, he walked around it and looked with fiery eyes at the older man. A pair of intelligence officers who'd been speaking with him stood up and quietly left for the outer office. "The city is less than two miles from here. *Any* falling debris is going to cost either civilian or military lives, to say nothing of the fact that you've *drawn them to us*."

Momentarily the admiral was rattled, the force of the general's outrage shaking his already brittle confidence. He was unsure what to say until he recalled that it was Krancis himself who'd chosen him for the task, and he'd as yet failed to make a mistake in the overall conduct of the war. There must have been *some* reason he'd plucked him from the obscurity of retirement, though for the life of him he couldn't see it. He'd just have to have faith.

"General Blake," Radik said, trying to confidently fill out his voice as much as possible. "I have ordered the remainder of our forces to this location so that the local anti-aircraft weapons can assist them in–"

"Do their job for them, you mean?" the general

snapped. "Well, get them out of here at once, do you hear me? I'm not going to have rubble falling from the sky, crushing my men and equipment as I try to organize our defense."

At this juncture they both paused, the noise of a heavy tank rolling by outside making talk impossible.

"General, if we cooperate, we stand a better chance of holding out until *Sentinel* arrives," Radik urged him.

"*Sentinel* isn't coming at all," Blake replied. "Or hadn't you heard? They have a more pressing engagement to see to at the moment."

"But…Jennet…" Radik stumbled.

"Isn't worth their time," the general said sharply. "Now, get your ships away from my base. Better yet, why don't you send them against the Devourers right now? My sources indicate you've still got approximately half your force. So put them to good use."

"They'll be crushed," Radik uttered.

"Just as well," Blake replied, opening the door for him to leave. "It's not as if they've been much use, anyway."

Without another word Radik stepped out of the general's office, the door promptly slamming behind him. The people in the outer office watched him for a moment before returning to their tasks, their dismissive lack of interest in him, despite his rank, communicating that they held the same view of him and his forces as the general they served.

"I need to get in touch with my people," Radik said to the captain who'd escorted him there. "Can you send out a signal to one of the nearby vessels?"

"I'm sorry, sir," he said, adding the 'sir' as an afterthought as he continued to digest the data on his computer screen without looking up. "But we're not–"

Having had enough, Radik silenced the room by taking a handful of the captain's uniform in his old hand and jerking him against the back of his chair.

"*Now*," the admiral said, his anger manifesting more

slowly than it was felt. "I want to get in touch with them *now*."

"O-of, course, sir," the captain uttered, as surprised as the rest of them. His computer was hooked into the base's communications system, and it was the work of only four minutes to get in touch with one of the carriers and inform them of the situation. "They're sending a shuttle for you right away, Admiral," the captain said helpfully, as he put down his phone. "It'll be here inside of ten minutes."

"Good," he replied, heading for the door.

As soon as he left the headquarters building, the noise outside assaulted his ears. Tanks and troop carriers were on the move; men were shouting; the roar of craft overhead sounded like thunder and lightning. It was enough to make his head spin, long used as he was to the quiet of a little farm he maintained some hours away.

Unsure where he should wait for the transport, he decided to stick close to the headquarters building. Soon he was proven right, as a small two-man shuttle left the carrier *Daring* and made a beeline for the structure. Setting down in one of the few open spaces still left in the madhouse of a base, the pilot gestured for him to get aboard and took off the instant he was fastened in.

"I'm sorry for my lack of manners, sir," the pilot said over the radio, as Radik put his headset on. "But that base is like an anthill: everyone's running every place. I didn't think smart to hop out, just in case–"

"Don't worry about it, son," the admiral chuckled, appreciating the young man's solicitous attitude after the treatment he'd received from the ground pounders. "I've had worse introductions."

"Yes, sir," he replied, guiding the craft through the busy air back towards the *Daring*. Ground-based fighters and heavy bombers mixed with their navy counterparts, making the skies a hazardous place to fly in. "Wish they'd get out of the way," the pilot muttered, before remembering the admiral. "Oh, excuse me, sir."

Radik didn't care: Radik hadn't noticed. He looked out the side of the small craft's cockpit at the mixture of military hardware that stood in anxious readiness to meet their implacable foe. He drew a sharp breath as he thought on the beating they'd already received, and he wondered how much more they could take.

"Here we are, sir," the pilot said, breaking in on his thoughts just as the little ship disappeared into one of the *Daring's* massive hangers. Landing hastily, the shuttle bounced against its mothership, jostling its cargo. "Excuse me, sir," the pilot said again, as he popped open the canopy to release his passenger.

Before the admiral could express his thanks, a lieutenant made her way across the hectic space and saluted him.

"Admiral Radik, the admiral wishes to see you at once," she said deferentially.

"Yes, of course," he replied. Having been long out of uniform until only recently, the stamp of military protocol wasn't as deeply ingrained as it once had been. Reaching out, he shook the pilot's hand and nodded his thanks for getting him out of the base. Before the young man could respond, Radik had already turned his back and was quickly making his way to the bridge.

"Well, what do you know?" the pilot muttered, as his hand hung limply in the air for a moment. He held it up before his eyes, a specimen to be examined. "Never had that happen before."

"How long until the Devourers break through the atmosphere?" Radik asked, following close behind the lieutenant as she navigated the crowded hallways.

"Not long, sir," she replied. "They're currently gathering together their forces in orbit. We estimate it will be less than twenty minutes before they begin their descent."

Radik cursed under his breath, but otherwise kept his

feelings in check.

Within moments they were on the bridge, the lieutenant standing aside once admiral Bruce Calhoun was in view. Captain of the assault carrier *Daring*, he was a tall, broad shouldered man with steady, penetrating blue eyes. Fifty-five, with a sharpness of outline that never failed to attract female attention, he was both leader and father to every crew member aboard the ship, any one of which would gladly die on his orders. His face broadened into a wide smile when his eyes fell upon Radik.

"How are you, Ronald?" he asked heartily, shaking his hand and grasping his arm. "We thought we'd lost you up there, when the *Bulwark* went to pieces."

"No, but we lost a good man instead," Radik said, equally glad to see his friend but weighed down by the events of the day. "Commander Evans didn't make it."

"I'm sorry to hear that," Calhoun said sincerely. "But at least we've still got you. Come, let me show you the battle."

Following Calhoun to a large horizontal display, Radik clasped his hands behind his back and watched.

"Now, here's where we are, floating over Gamma Base," he said, pointing towards a bunch of little triangular shapes on the screen. "Our heavy bombers are nearly rearmed, and will be ready for their next assault. Our fighter cover has been weakened from the losses in space, but we'll have the local, ground-based craft to help pick up the slack from them. And that says nothing about the anti-aircraft cannons and missiles that the army has at its disposal."

"I wouldn't count on too much help from them," Radik replied gravely. "The army takes a pretty dim view of us right now. In fact, they want us to clear out of their airspace forthwith."

"You're joking?" Calhoun replied, looking at him for a moment and seeing that he was not. "Well, that's their tough luck," he said with a shake of his head, dismissing the topic and continuing. "Now, they'll likely send their fighters first, trying to hold down our bombers until the frigates have a chance to close with our capitals. That's our achilles heel: the fighters. We'd stand a pretty decent chance of at least holding the line if we could guarantee our bombers a safe path to and from their frigates and some of the larger ships. But without that," he shook his head again, lowering his voice. "I'm afraid we're just piling bodies against the door, trying to keep 'em out as long as we can."

"I know," Radik said, looking at the screen. "But it's the best we can do."

◆ ◆ ◆

Rex Hunt sat in his cabin aboard *Sentinel*, staring at the wall and holding a drink in his hand. Resting crossways on his bed, his back against the wall, he hadn't so much as twitched in a quarter of an hour, his thoughts unable to move away from his brother.

It was funny, he reflected, that he felt the way he did. A year ago he wouldn't have missed him at all, back when he was nothing but a desperate renegade. One who'd tried to kill him more than once, no less.

But such a change had come over him since that first night he'd been struck by the Rex's ability to inspire fear, that primitive, almost childish, drawing out of the true dark power that resided within him. Next to all that he'd accomplished since then, the skills that Ugo had given him seemed trivial.

But the growth of his brother had not. Ever since facing his deepest fears twice, he'd been a changed man, a good man. Annoying at times, to be sure. There'd been more than a few occasions that Rex had wanted to tape his mouth shut. But that was just the grinding of personalities, and not a mark against his character.

"What a waste," Rex muttered as he sloshed around his drink, his first utterance in nearly a day. "What a miserable, stupid waste. He deserved better than that."

Once again the tears welled up in his eyes, and this time he didn't fight them down. Freely they flowed down his cheeks, moistening his neck as he drew a deep breath and sighed it out.

Why did redemption always come too late for the Hunts? Why didn't Maximilian realize before, literally, his last moment alive, that he was on the wrong course, that he had been corrupted? Why was it such a short time before his end that Milo turned over a new leaf? And so genuinely, too?

Rex didn't know, so he threw back his head and downed the rest of his drink. It burned his throat, but didn't bring any wisdom.

Sooner or later he'd have to rejoin the others. He knew they must be worried about him. Especially Wellesley, whom he'd left with *Esiluria* in the ship's library. Krancis had wisely kept his distance, and Pinchon had knocked once or twice to make sure he was okay. But otherwise they'd left him alone. They knew he wasn't the sort of man to process his grief in public, to share it with others. Except, perhaps, with Tselitel.

His heart ached a little when he thought of her. It'd been so long since he'd heard her voice, touched her face, that he was beginning to feel that she was just some kind of memory, and not a real person. A fantasy image of the Ideal Woman, according to Rex Hunt.

And then, like a phantom from the past, he thought he smelled the scent of her skin. Earnestly he snapped his head toward the door, as though somehow she'd gotten aboard the ship and was there to comfort him in his lowest moment. Chiding himself for his ridiculous hopefulness, he thumped his hand on his bed in disappointment and rolled onto his side.

Still holding the glass tightly in his hand, he continued to watch the wall. Fixing his attention on something, anything, allowed him to process his emotions rationally, keeping them from flowing over him.

"Heh, *rationally process emotions*?" he snorted, aware of the contradiction.

But he didn't have much choice other than to keep them at bay, allowing them in little by little, like a small insect nibbling on a gigantic leaf that was too big for it to handle all at once. A tidal wave of feeling for his brother wanted to carry him away, he knew, and it was only by compartmentalizing it and carefully feeling it just a little at a time that he maintained his own dominance over it. It wouldn't do to be carried away at such a time, after all. Who could say when he would be needed to charge up *Sentinel* again, or to blast something or other.

The bitterness of that last thought caught his attention, and made him think. Without really realizing it, he'd pushed aside his past objections about being little more than a weapon. With Milo gone, they came roaring back, his priorities different. It was then that he realized he was still in shock, his perspective jarred by what he'd gone through.

"And by this," he muttered, putting the glass on a small nightstand beside his bed and twisting onto his back with a sigh.

Truth be told, he didn't know why he'd reached for the alcohol. Why does anyone? Does it really help? Rex didn't know. It had never really done him much good. But what else can you do when you're in grief? There was nobody to seek revenge against. The planet who'd brought on the mortal conflict which killed Milo had been destroyed. He could try to paint his rage onto the rest of the *Prellak*, but he knew that wouldn't satisfy him. Besides, Krancis wasn't about to neglect the empire so they could settle a score with a gaggle of leaderless worlds.

His mind gradually grew hazy as he thought, and the combination of drink and emotional exhaustion finally carried him off to sleep.

His dreams were tormented but meaningless, simply distorted recreations of what he'd been through. Sometimes Milo survived his ordeal, and sometimes he didn't. Mostly he didn't. Sometimes Gromyko was in the reactor with them, just standing around as though to watch. At no time did he see Krancis, which struck him as odd, even in the distorted consciousness of sleep. For that matter, he never saw Tselitel or Pinchon, either. Wellesley was always around his neck, but he was curiously quiet.

As he slept he thought, and gradually he realized that those three, plus himself, represented all that was left of his old life. Tselitel, Krancis, indeed, everyone he'd met after that fateful day that he'd insisted on escorting Ugo home in the blizzard, *all* of them had been recent acquisitions. With Milo gone, only Gromyko and Wellesley remained from the old days.

With a sense of claustrophobia closing down around his heart, he began to fret in his dreams. The old fear of being alone cropped up again and wouldn't let him relax. His face tightened in anxiety until finally he began gasping in his sleep.

"It's inevitable," a voice seemed to say within his mind. "Sooner or later, they'll all be gone. Even the AI will leave you. And then you'll be alone."

The force of this notion scared him back to consciousness. He jumped when he saw someone standing over him in the semi-dark of his room.

"You're safe," Soliana said soothingly to him, laying a gentle hand on his face and stroking his cheek. "You have nothing to fear here."

"I wanted to be alone," he said pettily, sitting up in his bed and shaking the dream images from his mind. One in particular, depicting Milo smiling optimistically as they were about to enter the reactor, wouldn't depart. "Get out of here, Soliana," he said, his tone more of a suggestion than an order.

"You don't have to conceal what you're feeling from

me," the girl replied, moving to where he sat and modestly sitting on the edge of his bed behind him. "I could feel your anguish, your pain, no matter where I was within the ship. At no point has your grief been concealed from me. I can help you."

"Nobody can help me now," he said bitterly, shaking his head as he looked away from her. "There's nothing for it. You can't bring people back from the dead." He paused and turned toward her. "Don't you get it? I'm the last Hunt. The rest of my family is gone. Sooner or later I'll join them. It's just a matter of time, the way things are going."

"You have a very long way to go before you meet your end, Rex Hunt," she assured him, putting a small hand on his arm and rubbing it softly for a moment before withdrawing it. "And I felt your brother's mind as he departed this life," she added, causing him to sharply look away, her words painful. "He was happy, Rex," she insisted. "He'd gotten what he was after: to make his life count for something. Nobody can ask for more than that."

"He wasn't even thirty," Hunt replied. "What kind of a life is that?"

"It's not how *long* it is that matters," she said quietly. "It's what it *means* that counts. And your brother's life gained a meaning in that moment that will last as long as the Earthborn do. He saved the empire, Rex, and every life that looks to it for safety and strength. That means the Earthborn, the remnants of the *Kol-Prockians*, and innumerable other races who look to this galaxy for guidance, safety, and security in the millennia to come. You don't realize this, but humanity has been chosen for a great fate; one that reaches far beyond the confines of the Milky Way. And you are the progenitor of this fate, the starting point from which all else will follow."

"Must it be done at the cost of everyone I know and love?" he asked bitterly, turning toward her instantly, his eyes aflame. "Unless Wellesley's people can do something for

Lily, she won't last much longer. Dad and Milo are gone. How long until Antonin gets his head shot off? Or you, for that matter? Oh, it's quite a fate I've been selected for," he said, turning away from her and laughing dryly. "My lot in life has been to suffer, that's all. When do I get some respite? Some little bit of *peace*? I scraped out a life on Delta-13 because there was no other way. But I hated every soul-sucking minute of it. I could never just lay back and *know* that everything was going to be alright. I've never known security since the government banished my family to that desolate rock."

"You're grief stricken and hurting," she said to explain his feelings. "You must allow yourself time to calm down, to breathe. It will be long before the pain of this last battle leaves you."

"That'll never happen," Hunt shook his head. "You don't forget something like that, no matter how much time passes. You just sort of get to the point where it doesn't stop you dead in your tracks, seizing your heart and squeezing it until it's ready to burst." He looked at her and then away again. "You must know that. You must have known grief."

"I have known grief," she uttered quietly, the gentleness of her expression giving it added weight. "I too have lost all that I knew and loved. I wouldn't even know my family if I saw a picture of them. All of my past life has been erased and replaced with other notions."

"That operation you underwent," Hunt elucidated.

"Yes," she said, the occasional flashes of it that passed her mind still striking her with terror. "Krancis and I examined them once, but we couldn't make out much. They haunt me to this day," she added, unconsciously drawing her hands to her chest and clutching them. "Ever since that initial examination I have been tormented by them each night when I sleep. Oh, he didn't mean to do that," she said with a little smile, as Hunt turned to her with concern in his eyes. "Krancis was just trying to draw them up so we'd understand–"

"Why didn't you say something?" he cut her off, extending a tender hand to her knee and touching it gently. "You didn't have to suffer alone like that."

"Nor do you," she smiled. "And yet you choose to do so."

"That's different," he replied, withdrawing his hand.

"The torment of losing a loved one is great," she allowed. "But can it be compared to that of losing yourself? Your very identity and history? I don't know who I am. I am told my name is Soliana, but I can neither confirm nor deny that. My mind courses with a thousand different ideas daily, most, perhaps *all*, of which aren't mine. I am a psychically gifted storage device, a sort of backup for all the information that some group of people decided I needed to have. What do I even know is *me* anymore? I mean *really* me? Can you tell me a greater tragedy than that?"

"Reckon I can't," Hunt replied. "I'm sorry. I didn't realize all that you were going through. I just assumed you'd made your peace with it."

"I can never make peace with this existence until I at least understand *why* it had to be so. Who foisted this upon me? And *how* did they know what I needed to know?"

"Like the *Keesh'Forbandai* command that let me into the reactor that first time," Hunt added.

"Yes, and many other things. I tell you," she said, loosening up and scooting a little farther back onto the bed to make herself more comfortable, "I don't know if I'm blessed or cursed. Yes, I get to play a major part in this war. I'm important, decisively so. But at what cost? Is Soliana, if that's even my name, actually the one who's important here? Or am I just a convenient memory bank for someone else's data, an organic computer? Typically I feel like the latter, just a bundle of confused notions all swirling around at once. So I keep to myself and try to sort them out, avoiding the embarrassment that would follow if I acted out everything that came into my head. Though sometimes, one thing or other bobs to the surface and forces itself into the open. Like when I directed you and Krancis towards *Eesekkalion* that first time."

"*That* would have ended badly," he said, leaning back on his elbow and looking at her. "He would have had us right where he wanted us. We would have charged him up without being able to take him down."

"Yes, that was the dark world's plan all along," she nodded. "He never anticipated that we could overcome and shatter him. He had planned for us to be his regeneration. Had that happened," she shuddered. "Only our darkest dreams can give us an answer as to how terrible that would have been. A fully rejuvenated *Prellak* world in a galaxy depleted of meaningful *Ahn-Wey* opposition? That would have been disastrous."

"We dodged a bullet on that one," he nodded. "That's for sure."

"And yet…" her voice trailed. Her eyes grew cloudy as she mentally drew away, no longer seeing him.

"Soliana?" he asked after half a minute, when she'd failed to return. "Are you alright?" Passing a hand before her face, she neither moved nor noticed. Without warning she rolled off the bed away from him, falling against the floor and striking her head. "Soliana!" he exclaimed, diving to his knees and lifting her up. "Soliana? Soliana, are you alright?"

"Coming," she muttered, her eyes milky and half dead. "They're coming…to…" she struggled to say.

"Coming to what? Who is?" he prodded, shaking her gently to focus her mind. "Think, Soliana! Think!"

"Coming…to…" she fought out through unwilling lips. Then her eyes cleared, and she shook her head confusedly. "Rex?" she asked, unsure what had transpired.

At the very same moment a sharp knock was heard on the door. Before he could respond, Gromyko twisted the knob and threw it open.

"I see you've been keeping busy," the smuggler said wolfishly, winking toward his friend as he crossed his arms and leaned against the wall beside the door.

All at once an irrational urge exploded in Rex, and he dashed off a little shot of fearful mist at Gromyko. Striking him in the chest, it made him nearly jump out of his shoes. Bolting through the door, he took off down the hallway yelling about some beast that was chasing him. No sooner had he left than Krancis stepped in.

"We really need to work on that temper of yours," he said, walking slowly to the pair and kneeling beside the unfortunate girl.

"Nothing's sacred to him," Hunt growled. "Milo's barely gone, and I'm supposed to be looking around for some fun? What does he think I am, some kind of animal?"

"Judging by the force of your emotional reactions," Krancis said, pressing a hand to Soliana's forehead and closing his eyes for a moment before resuming, "he wouldn't be far off. You can't go zapping your friends, especially at a time like this. We all need to work together."

"Oh, he'll get over it," Hunt said. "I didn't hit him that hard. It'll remind him to take people's feelings a little more seriously for a change."

"That's something he'll never do," Krancis said. "He'd need an entire change of personality for that." Then, focusing his eyes on the girl, "She hit her head pretty badly. We need to get her down to medical."

"I'll take her," Hunt said, about to lift her up in his arms.

"No, these fine people will take her," Krancis replied, gesturing over his shoulder towards a trio that entered just as he spoke. "I've got something that I need to talk to you about."

Hunt handed Soliana off to her caretakers, watching as they lifted her onto a stretcher and carted her away.

"Now, there's been a new–"

"How in the world did you know that?" Hunt cut him off.

"Know what?" he asked patiently.

"That she needed help," Hunt replied. "How did you get here just after she hit her head, having already called ahead for emergency medical services? Don't tell me you can actually see the future."

"I should think such a notion wouldn't be surprising, given all that you've already seen since leaving Delta," Krancis replied. "But the truth of the matter is much more mundane. Recognizing her inherent instability, I've equipped her with a small medical device that keeps track of her status at all times. It immediately sends out a warning signal to *Sentinel's* medical bay if any irregularities are detected. It also sends a signal to me. As for my timing, that was a simple coincidence. I was already on my way to see you."

"About what?" he asked, crossing his arms and leaning against the wall.

"Well, you needn't be so suspicious about it," Krancis replied. "I simply wanted to keep you in the loop. But perhaps this would be easier in the library. Come with me."

Mutely Hunt lowered his arms and followed the man in black to the nearest teleporter. In seconds they were whisked into *Esiluria's* domain, where they could hear her chatting with Wellesley.

"Rex!" the *Kol-Prockian* AI exclaimed as he entered. "I've been worried about you. We all have, in fact, though I'm sure some of us would never admit that fact," he said, causing *Esiluria* to put a holographic hand to her mouth as her eyes playfully regarded Krancis. Sitting down without bothering to reply, Krancis threw a leg over the other and waited for Rex to seat himself.

"Alright, so what's the big mystery?" Hunt inquired, once he'd taken his place. "Something in the wind?"

"You could say that," Krancis replied. "The destruction

of *Eesekkalion* has sent a ripple through the ranks of our enemies. The remaining *Prellak* worlds are disoriented and disheartened. According to my sources, they are panicking at the thought that we'll do to them what we did to their leader. None of them have even half the power that *Eesekkalion* did before the end, so naturally their fears are quite reasonable."

"This is a great boon for us, Rex," Wellesley cut in, finally glad for the chance to say something, anything, to his friend. "They're no longer bending their power against the rest of the empire! It's like they're getting both confused and, dare I say it, *cooperative*?"

"I should think that last part is a bit of a stretch," Krancis replied, casting a glance at the amulet as it lay on the table before looking once more at Hunt. "Deep in their souls they will never cease hating us Earthborn for taking what they conceive to be their birthright in this galaxy. But they're not going to stare down the barrel of a loaded gun, either. With *Sentinel* to hold over them, I have little doubt that we can bring them to heel. We may even be able to turn them to our advantage."

"You mean make them work for us?" Hunt asked, leaning in a little closer, the thought intriguing enough to push aside his grief for a moment and excite him. "Recruit the *Prellak* to the human cause?"

"They want to live just as much as anybody," Krancis said, by way of explanation. "They know that *we* know all that they've done against us, and they'll fear retribution. Now, it's a question just how much use they'll be with the death of their leader. He was their guiding light in more ways than one, and his loss will sap them of most of their power."

"Why?" Hunt asked.

"Because it takes both raw strength and incredible talent to cast psychic powers like they've got across countless lightyears of space in any effective way. *Eesekkalion* was their leader for a reason. He had the touch, if you will, for applying their combined strength. Without him, they're likely to be little more than clucking chickens, twisting this way and that, unsure what to do and *how* to do it."

"Then our potential new "ally" is probably a toothless tiger," Hunt summarized ruefully, his intrigue over.

"Most likely," Krancis replied, unperturbed. "Still, they may be of some use. They must be privy to more than a few things that would be very interesting to know. They've been working with the *Pho'Sath* since time out of mind. Just tapping into the memory of one of them could yield a treasure trove of data."

"Great," Hunt said flatly.

"But that's not all," Wellesley said, hoping to inspire some interest in his friend. "The Devourers are acting differently, too."

"Like how?"

"They're suddenly ignoring the *Ahn-Wey* worlds," the AI explained. "Well, what's left of them, anyway. It's like they're suddenly last week's news."

"Then they're forming up on human targets?" Hunt asked Krancis, who nodded.

"But not just any human targets," he elaborated. "They're ignoring the industrialized worlds, and heading for locations with both high populations and an enormous amount of greenspace. They *should* be undercutting our industrial base, especially as it is finally getting into gear and beginning to replace some of our losses. But they act like they couldn't care any less about them."

"I told you that they aren't that bright," Wellesley said.

"This doesn't play like a lack of intelligence," Krancis shook his head. "It's a deliberate act, a part of some larger plan. I've never gone along with the theory that the Devourers are just dumb appetites wrapped in ships. There's something more going on in there than we know about. Than *anyone* knows about, in fact."

"Care to venture a theory of your own?" the AI asked.

"Nothing I could say at this time would be anything

more than speculation," the man in black replied. "It would have no value at all."

"As you wish."

"That's what you wanted to tell me?" Hunt asked. "That the *Prellak* are confused and the Devourers are acting weird?"

"Not altogether," Krancis uttered, unshaken by the younger man's pointedness. "Though those two facts are important elements that inform our steps going forward. Clearly, with the shattering of the *Prellak* as an effective force, there is no longer any need to keep you aboard *Sentinel*. There's no question of their being able to arrest our movement after the death of *Eesekkalion*. And while you *do* render valuable services to this vessel even when we're merely engaged in battle with the Devourers, keeping you on board as a 'battery' is a waste of your talents. The empire needs you to be employed more actively than that."

"Doing what, exactly?" Hunt asked, leaning back in his seat and watching the other man skeptically.

"Hunting down *Pho'Sath* agents and destroying them," Krancis replied without batting an eye.

"What!?" Wellesley exclaimed. "You want him to go up against the most dangerous beings we've ever encountered in perpetuity? Just one right after another? Are you *trying* to get him killed?"

"Don't you have any faith in him?" Krancis asked, just a hint of a smile on his lips.

"I've got more faith in him than I've got in half the imperial navy," the AI retorted. "But some things are just stupid. And making a career out of cornering those *monsters* is *stupid*."

"And how else would you employ his talents?" Krancis countered. "His power is redundant in space: *Sentinel* already has all the necessary might to destroy one Devourer fleet after another. And he can't be very much use on the ground against their spider allies, because they'll just pour over the countryside like a wave of death, avoiding him. The *Prellak* are no longer a credible foe, so that removes them from consideration. Just exactly what targets are left for him?"

"And if you get him killed?" Wellesley asked pointedly. "What if we need him for something else in the future, and he just so happens to be inconveniently *dead*?"

"I consider that most unlikely," Krancis replied. "Without a doubt, the *Pho'Sath* are formidable, dangerous, and cruelly efficient. But they're also arrogant, self-deluding, and clearly very vulnerable to the powers of the dark realm. A single man will be able to wreak havoc in their ranks, tearing them out of the positions of power they've made for themselves among the separatists."

"So that's it, then," the AI said with finality. "You're out to hit the Fringers again, just like when you floated the idea of attacking one of their planets with *Sentinel*. Don't you think the Devourers require all of our attention right now?"

"He's right, Wells," Hunt cut in, finally feeling the urge to speak. "I can't do any real good here anymore. And someone has to start breaking them down."

"Yes," Krancis seconded. "The Black Suns are already making their weight felt against the separatists. But they can only do so much. They're afraid to get anywhere near the *Pho'Sath* agents because the rumor mill is full of the stories of how they treat their enemies. That's where it'll take a man who's not scared to kick over their little house of cards. Besides, once the separatists realize that the *Pho'Sath* aren't the demigods they make themselves out to be, they'll start to think twice about being at war with both the empire *and* the Black Suns at the same time. It could bring them to the table and save a lot of lives on both sides."

"I still think it's a bad idea," Wellesley said with hesitation. "But it's up to you, Rex. I'll go where you go."

"I thought you would," Hunt smiled, before turning to Krancis. "Where's the first target?"

"A planet called Erdu-3. It's a hotbed of rebel

sentiment, though opposition forces are pretty strong there, too, so you won't be without support. Although perhaps it would be better to put that statement the other way around."

"Meaning?"

"That you're more likely to be of help to them," Krancis explained. "They're outgunned and outmanned, but that isn't stopping them from taking gambles. Desperate gambles. I've received word that a loose group of resistance fighters are planning to attack the *Pho'Sath* agent who runs the whole organization there, a being named *Deldrach*."

"Well, if they're going to take him out…" Wellesley's voice trailed.

"They're going to *try*," Krancis replied. "But they're not likely to succeed. *Deldrach* is a force to be reckoned with. I doubt if anyone in this galaxy has ever challenged a *Pho'Sath* as powerful as he is. But we need him gone, all the same. He's far too efficient to be left alive, and he's also on the cusp of breaking the opposition on Erdu. They don't know that, yet," he added, his tone implying criticism at the failure of their intelligence apparatus, "so we'll have to step in and keep them afloat. They have contacts that would not be easily replaced, combined with a knowledge of their surroundings that would take years to even approximate, were we to try and start from fresh."

"So they need to be kept in the game, but they're in way over their heads," Hunt summarized.

"Yes," Krancis nodded.

"Why do I get the feeling you're not telling us everything?" Wellesley said, his 'eyes' audibly narrowing.

"You're a very suspicious AI," the man in black replied, rolling his gaze over to the amulet for a moment before addressing his answer to Rex. "But the fact is, he's correct. Part of the bargain for getting Gustav Welter to look after the emperor was that we'd help out the resistance from time to time. The terms of that 'help' were never spelled out explicitly, the opposition resting content that I wouldn't let them fail if there was any other path open to me."

"Sounds like a pretty trusting lot," Wellesley commented, uncertain if that was a good thing in this case.

"I have a considerable reputation among the more useful elements that operate in this galaxy," Krancis said by way of explanation. "They are well aware of my value as an ally."

"Interesting."

"So I'm supposed to go out there, knock off this *Pho'Sath*, and then call it a day?" Hunt asked.

"More or less. Naturally, if you can be of use to them in any other capacity while you're out there, that would only serve to strengthen their attachment to the empire."

"And to you," Wellesley observed.

Again Krancis eyed the amulet, his lips tightening slightly as his displeasure finally began to manifest itself.

"You'll take one of the 'egg' ships we have on board," he continued, bypassing the AI's comment. "It'll permit you to get there quickly, and without drawing the attention of either the Devourers or the *Pho'Sath*. But it will have to be carefully concealed when you land. The last thing we want is for it to fall into enemy hands."

"I'll be careful," he replied, annoyed to have the obvious pointed out to him. "Who's my contact on Erdu?"

"*Esiluria* will give all the relevant data to your opinionated friend," he said, nodding toward Wellesley on the table. "Contact details, meeting locations, and so forth. Everything that you'll need to know."

"Fair enough," Hunt nodded.

Just then the teleporter flashed blue, and Gromyko stumbled out of it.

"You didn't have to blast me, my friend!" he exclaimed at once, his body drenched in sweat from his run. Slowly he shambled towards the table. "I'm so exhausted I can barely stand!" he uttered, his voice ragged.

"Take my seat," Krancis said, pushing back from the

29

table and standing up. "I think we're done here," he uttered, looking down at Hunt for a moment, his statement in reality a question.

"I've got all I need," he said.

"Good," Krancis replied, walking past the perspiring smuggler and departing moments later in a flash of his own.

"Er, you *blasted* Antonin?" Wellesley asked, as Gromyko dropped into Krancis' seat with a loud sigh and leaned back to rest his bones. Though he no longer saw the creature that had chased him from Hunt's room, his eyes nevertheless darted to and fro, careful just in case it hadn't truly left, but was only hiding so it could ambush him unawares.

"I'll say he did!" Gromyko said forcefully. "I've never been so scared in all my life. What were you thinking?"

"You needed to be reminded to mind your manners," Hunt replied implacably, his eyes tight and unforgiving. "So I reminded you."

"You wound me, my friend. You really do," the smuggler said dramatically. "I was only–"

"You were shooting off your mouth when you should have known better," snapped Rex. "Besides, you should have seen that Soliana was hurting, and at least had sympathy enough for her to bite your tongue."

"Soliana was in pain?" he asked, his eyes evincing both concern and embarrassment. "I, uh, I didn't know."

"If you'd kept your mouth shut long enough for your *eyes* to work, you would have," Hunt said, growing agitated at the smuggler's carefree attitude. "Now, have you got something on your mind, or are you just filling the air with noise, like usual?"

Taken aback at the force of his words, Gromyko shook his head side to side and said nothing.

"Good," Hunt said, rising from his chair, snatching Wellesley off the table, and making for the teleporter. "Drop me by the medical bay, *Esiluria*."

"What in the world has gotten into him?" the smuggler asked once he'd gone.

Fuming, Hunt emerged from a teleporter and strode heavily along the corridors that led to the ship's hospital. Reaching the front desk, he asked after Soliana.

"I'm sorry, Lord Hunt," the woman at the desk said deferentially. "But nobody is allowed to see her. She's been heavily sedated."

"Why?" he asked, concern temporarily pushing aside his anger.

"She was convulsing when she came in," the woman explained. "It took three men to hold her down so she wouldn't hurt herself. It was like she was possessed, a totally different girl. I could have sworn she was *trying* to throw herself out of the bed they'd put her in, just to hurt herself. She was panicking, out of her senses."

"Tell me what room she's in," Hunt said. "I've got to see her."

"I'm sorry," she repeated. "But–"

"Lord Hunt?" a graying man inquired, approaching him from the side. He was around fifty, tall, with a hint of a paunch and a stoop to his shoulders. "I'm Doctor Pryce." He looked at the receptionist. "It's alright, Grace. Krancis left word that he should be allowed to see the girl."

"But, Doctor," she began to remonstrate, about to cite the hospital's rules.

"Come with me, sir," Pryce said, ignoring her objection and gesturing for Hunt to follow.

"Our dear friend thinks of everything, doesn't he?" Wellesley uttered through skin contact, as Hunt fell in alongside the doctor and walked with him down a corridor with rooms on either side. "Makes you wonder what else he might have planned out for us in advance."

Hunt didn't respond, nor did he particularly care. Sure, Krancis had an annoying way of being on top of literally *everything*, and in truth it did give him some pause when he thought of it. But at that moment he was still too angry with Gromyko to have room in his head for anyone else.

"Here, sir," Pryce announced, stopping beside a door marked "19" and quietly opening the door for him. "Please don't be with her long," he whispered. "She needs her rest."

"Of course," Hunt replied mechanically, not really paying attention to the doctor now that his eyes were on Soliana. She lay stretched out on a bed that took up most of the small room. Silently Pryce closed the door behind him.

Without a word he approached her bed and knelt, carefully looking at her face for any sign of trauma. There was a bruise on her cheek from when she hit the floor of his bedroom earlier, but otherwise she seemed calm, not in any sort of pain.

"Better than I expected, honestly," Wellesley observed after a few moments had passed. "She looks decent enough."

"Are you sure?" Hunt asked in a whisper, something about the young woman striking him amiss. "She looks older somehow, or worn out."

"Well, she's been through a lot these last few weeks. I guess getting 'possessed' by implanted memories will do a number on you. Provided that's all that's been going on."

"It was nice of you to drop by and see me," she mumbled through dull lips, her eyes still closed. "I think I'm alright for now. Th-they've calmed my body with medicine."

"They told us that," Hunt nodded, putting a hand on her wrist and rubbing it gently. "Is there anything I can do for you? Anything you need?"

"You are going to leave the ship soon," she said, her eyes fluttering open with effort. "Be careful, Rex. You're stepping into a world that you know nothing about, with only your great power to see you through. Yet even such a strength can be overcome, should it be taken unawares. You must promise me that you'll be cautious, conservative in your efforts."

"I'm always cautious," he replied.

"No," she smiled, rolling her head back and forth on the pillow and then grimacing from the pain of her bruise. "Not always. When your emotions are inflamed you act rashly. You will see things on that world that will drive you to rage and hatred, more than you ever thought possible. You must keep yourself in check, save yourself for the rest of mankind." She leaned up for a moment and looked him squarely in the eye." Do not risk your life in a blind fury, seeking retribution."

"What are you talking about?" Wellesley asked, as she dropped her head back onto the pillow. "I think Rex can handle himself."

"You know little of the *Pho'Sath*," she said, swallowing hard and closing her eyes. "Of their evil, of their vile tortures and ruthlessness. You haven't seen what they do to prisoners, how they shatter their spirits and break their bodies. You will see things that will make your blood boil with rage." She paused for a moment, taking a breath as her heart rate climbed at the memory of numerous *Pho'Sath* acts of horror. "You are a hot-tempered man, Rex," she continued in a calmer voice after half a minute. "Despite your general coolness, you are easily tipped into anger and the desire for revenge. You must control these impulses."

"You don't have to worry about me, Soliana," Hunt assured her.

"But I do worry," she replied, touching the back of her hand to his cheek affectionately, an act that made him draw back a little. With a hint of disappointment on her face, she lowered her hand and closed her eyes again. "There's nothing more I can do for you. Now I need to rest."

"Alright," he said, standing up and looking down at her. He was going to say more, to express his thanks. But it didn't seem appropriate somehow, so he just nodded silently to her and left.

Wordlessly Hunt walked back down the corridor, past

the disapproving receptionist and out of the medical bay.

"Curious indeed," Wellesley uttered, once Hunt had put some distance between them and the hospital. "That girl has got a thing for you."

"I know that," he replied with discomfort, his anger at Gromyko finally pushed aside by the strange feeling he had. "She hasn't made a secret of it ever since we met in the Black Hole. I just thought she had a little more tact about acting on it. She knows how I feel about Lily."

"The heart's a strange thing," the AI opined. "Sometimes it drives us to do things that don't make very much sense, rationally speaking, but that make a whole other kind of sense."

Hunt stopped dead in his tracks.

"Are you saying it's a *good thing* that she's trying to step between me and Lily?"

"No, of course not," he replied quickly, aware that such an idea was the fastest way to invite his friend's ire. "What I meant was that she's been looking out for you this whole time, and that that's probably been motivated in part by her feelings for you. If your guardian angel is in love with you, she'll likely spend a little more effort on your behalf than would normally be the case."

"That's a pretty ruthless attitude towards love," Hunt said with aversion, resuming movement. "You're suggesting that I *use* her feelings."

"No, I'm suggesting that you don't look a gift mystic in the mouth. We've gotten a lot of benefit out of knowing that little gal, and I don't think that's going to stop any time soon. So let her have her feelings, they can't hurt anybody, can they? You'll never let things get out of hand because of Lily. And it's pretty clear that she'll not push things too far if such a thing bothers you. So keep her between the rails, and be thankful for the added motive on her part to keep you alive."

Hunt knew where his friend was coming from, but the amorality of his pragmatism was too much for his emotionally heightened state to accept just then. Without a word, he slipped the amulet from his neck and put it into his pocket to break the skin contact. Naturally the AI could have addressed him through the ship's communications system, but he knew that his old friend wouldn't do that, respecting his need for space.

Reaching his room, he had just closed the door when a knock jarred him out of the privacy of his thoughts.

"What?" he demanded, certain that it was the smuggler coming to bug him again.

"Sorry, Rex," Pinchon said from the other side. "But can I see you for a second?"

His respect for the colonel made him cringe at his outburst. Quickly he opened the door and invited him in.

"I didn't want to bother you," the colonel began awkwardly, not quite sure where to look. There was something about Rex that always unsettled him, just a little. The idea seemed strange to him, especially given how much younger he was. But something about his singularity, combined with his rare emotional intensity, always put him a little off balance. "I heard from Gromyko that you're heading out on another mission soon. I'd like to come along, if you've got any use for me. I know this is a bad time," he added quickly, just as Hunt was about to speak. "But I didn't know just when you'd be leaving, and I wanted to make sure I talked to you first."

"Thank you, Colonel," Hunt said sincerely, Pinchon's quiet, respectful earnestness touching him. "Did Antonin give you any details?"

"Said he didn't really know any, just that you were heading off again soon. I guess that AI chick in the library told him about it."

Briefly Hunt shared what Krancis had told him.

"*That* is quite an assignment," the colonel said, after he'd emitted a low whistle. "Seems like our lord and master has got quite a high opinion of you. I figured he liked to keep everybody under lock and key, more or less."

"No, he gives you plenty of freedom once he's got you figured out," Hunt replied, heading for the half empty bottle that stood on a small table and pouring himself and his guest a small drink. "He figures he's got me pegged at this point."

"Does he?" Pinchon asked, nodding his thanks for the drink as Hunt handed it to him.

"I'd say no," Hunt replied, taking a sip. "But he seems to know more than he's got a right to, so how could I honestly say? I half think the man is psychic."

"Got to be, to my way of thinking," the colonel replied, before taking a sip of his own. "Seems like he just knows too much for any other explanation to be possible. That, or he's got some kind of cosmic second sight that clues him in to how things are gonna turn out. I'd love to go out gambling with him some time," he added with a chuckle, before emptying his glass. "But something about having him over me gives me the willies. I feel like a bug under glass. Honestly I didn't breathe easy until I took off for that last mission with Gromyko and–" he stopped himself, grimacing at his blunder. "Aw, I'm sorry, Rex," he said with a sincere shake of his head.

"It's alright," Hunt uttered, pouring himself just a smidgeon more. He raised the bottle toward the colonel, who declined. "He died the way he wanted to. I guess you can't ask for more than that."

"I guess not," Pinchon seconded. Hunt's words implied a kind of acceptance of his brother's fate, but the colonel had seen too much grief not to recognize the signs. His friend was still in shock, and even if he'd achieved something like rational peace with Milo's demise, his heart and soul were still months, maybe years, from recovery. It would be a long road. "So," he said after an awkward minute had passed, during which Hunt had stood quietly and thought, "let me know if I can be of any use to you. I'd rather not stay on this ship longer than I have to."

"Thanks, Colonel," he said, taking the older man's

glass back and watching as he left. "Thanks a lot," he added with quiet appreciation.

CHAPTER 2

"I think we're getting close to the rendezvous point," Bessemer said tensely, his hands tightly gripping the controls of the transport.

"How can you tell?" Frank asked dryly, as Tselitel peeked out of the cockpit at the purple-blue nebula that surrounded them. "You'd sooner find a set of false teeth in a blizzard than a station in all this. Why in the world did Krancis have us meet up here? There must be a thousand other places we could have gone to."

"I guess because nobody else will be able to find it, either," Bessemer replied, piloting the ship forward at a crawl. His instruments were all affected by the nebular, none of them giving him a lick of guidance in the enormous, hazy cloud.

To guide them to their goal, Krancis had had their transport equipped with an extremely short-ranged transmitter that could be activated once they were within the nebula. If they were close enough to the station, a receiver would pick up their signal and send out one of its own. Then it would be a simple matter of homing in on it, docking, and turning piloting duties over to Welter.

Provided they could find the station, that is.

Nearly an hour passed after Bessemer's initial optimistic appraisal. Inching along, afraid to crash into any of the debris that floated around them, each of the passengers kept their eyes glued to the strange wonder around them.

"It's beautiful," Tselitel said, finally breaking the silence. "But in a terrible way. I feel like something bad happened here. It's like a graveyard. Or a tomb."

"What a nice way to brighten the mood," Frank said tartly. Not as cool under pressure as Wellesley, his manners were affected more easily by his environment. "Besides, what could you honestly feel about this place, anyhow? It just feels strange and out of the ordinary, is all. Nothing tomb-y about it. Not in the slightest."

Tselitel realized that he was trying to convince himself rather than her, and for the first time she became aware of a fundamental brittleness in his nature. He didn't like being out of his element, forced into circumstances with which he was unfamiliar. His diagnosis of *her* problem was actually a self-diagnosis.

Unfortunately, this little spurt of insight did nothing to calm her nerves, which had been growing ever more tense as their time in the nebula increased. Seeing this, Rhemus reached out a hand and placed it, fatherly fashion, upon hers, giving her a little squeeze.

"You're alright," he said quietly, giving her a little reassuring smile before he released his hold. "Captain?"

"We must have passed nearly from one side to the other," he said in a tight voice. "I've had the transmitter blaring the whole time. We must have missed it somehow. That, or the station has been damaged."

"Or destroyed," Frank added. "You see all this rubble floating around. With all these bits of rock and ships and whatnot, it'd be a miracle if the station hasn't been battered into dust by now."

"Krancis wouldn't send us to a broken station," the emperor uttered authoritatively. As he said this, the nebula around the egg began to thin rapidly. Soon they emerged from it, back into the black loneliness of space.

"I'm sorry, my lord," Bessemer said, leaning back in his seat and taking his hands off the controls for a minute. "I must have missed it."

"That's alright," Rhemus replied patiently, though his nerves were as strained as any of theirs. More, perhaps. "Relax for a little while, and then we'll double back and try again."

"Yes, my lord."

"If…my calculations are correct," Frank said musingly as he thought, "we passed right through the middle of the nebula. I mean, more or less. Naturally, with the maneuvering we did, there's going to be some zigzag to our path, but not enough to carry us very far out of the way. Honestly, I don't see how we could have missed it."

"What makes you think that the station is smack in the middle of it?" Bessemer replied.

"Isn't it?" Tselitel asked.

"Why would it be? There must have been some drift over the years. It's probably pretty off center by now. Oh, well. We'll find out soon enough. Just give me another minute, and we'll have at it again."

Tselitel leaned back in her seat, looking at the unfathomable expanse of space above her. It all seemed so broad, so wonderful. And yet so cold and empty. It was a terrible mistress, one with all the space, all the *enormity* that one could ever want. And yet, in itself, it bore no capacity to support anything. A vast contradiction: limitless nothingness; infinite zero. It was the very embodiment of extremity, existence reduced to absolutes that prevented life and action.

"What are you thinking about?" Rhemus asked, as he saw her mind drift away in contemplation.

"What?" she asked, drawn from her reverie. "Oh, just that, I guess," she said, pointing at the black canvas, dotted with countless stars. "It speaks to the soul somehow, calling to it like a mother calling her boy home from play as the sun goes down. I don't know, it just feels safe, like it embraces me. And yet it chills me." She laughed self-consciously, looking furtively at the emperor. "That must sound pretty silly."

"Not at all," he shook his head, following where her gaze had been just a moment before. "I think most people feel that way. There's an unspoken poetry in nature that resonates with us, but most of us can't articulate it. I've long felt the way you have, but I didn't have the words to describe it. It takes a life dedicated to the human mind, in one fashion or another, to express such things clearly."

"Oh, I don't think I've expressed it very well," she said modestly, a little embarrassed by his praise. "I don't have any talent for the real poetry of nature."

"You've done just fine," he assured her, patting her hand again before looking forward. "Captain? Are you ready?"

"Yes, my lord," Bessemer replied, slowly twisting the ship around to face the nebula once more. "Alright, let's see here," he muttered, scanning his instruments for a moment before settling on a course. Without a word he moved the ship forwards, and in seconds they were again swallowed by the cloud. Carefully he navigated around the rocks and bits of metal that filled the space, giving each of them a wide berth to ensure the safety of his precious cargo. Gradually, as he grew more comfortable with his environment, he increased his speed, until finally they were moving at a decently fast pace.

"Are you sure this is a good idea?" Frank asked, not sharing Bessemer's confidence in his own abilities. "If we crash into just one of those–"

"Then you'd better not distract him," Rhemus cut in.

Silently Bessemer smiled at this expression of the emperor's trust.

Another twenty minutes passed before they again emerged on the other side. The captain cursed under his breath.

"Do you want to wait a little while, try again later?" Tselitel asked in order to put the option on the table and spare him some of the damage to his pride.

"No, I'll give it another go now," Bessemer said in a low voice, annoyed with the nebula and himself. The first time he'd been afraid of the cloud. The second time he felt he had it in hand. Now he just felt frustrated with it. Plotting another course, he jerked the craft forward.

"Easy, man," Frank said, jostled by the ship's sudden movement. "We'll get there when we get there."

"We certainly will," Bessemer replied through a frown, intent on getting them there as quickly as possible. His eyes carefully studied the short space that was visible to him, and the ship moved easily in his hands. To Tselitel's surprise, the grace of the captain's flying increased right alongside his temper. Usually, she reflected, it was the other way around.

"I've got something," he announced, as a little blip appeared on his dashboard. "We're getting a signal. Weak, but looks like our target. I'm moving in."

With this the ship accelerated, Tselitel feeling the captain's eagerness in its movements. Suddenly it was no longer graceful, but quick, choppy, inclined to dash past obstacles instead of slowly cruising around them in a wide arc. A near miss with an ancient piece of hull plating nearly made her call out.

"Easy, Captain," Rhemus cautioned, no more eager to die in that forsaken place than Tselitel. "Cut your velocity a little and get us there safely."

"But, my lord, we're already here," Bessemer said, his tense face broadening into a smile as the little station came into view. Like an image in a dream it loomed out of the mist and rubble, its symmetry and intactness sharply contrasting with the shattered waste that hemmed it in on every side. It stood alone, evidence of civilization in perhaps the most unlikely of places.

"Is anyone home?" Tselitel asked, peering out the canopy at the dark station. "I don't see any lights. Maybe he isn't here yet."

"Oh, he's here, alright," Bessemer said, slowly circling the station to find a place to dock. "He had a lot shorter trip to make than we did. Besides," he added, "I just received a message demanding the verification code."

"I didn't know there was a code," Tselitel uttered.

"Exactly," the captain smiled, as he punched it into his computer and transmitted it to the station. "A little added precaution, just to ensure we're both who we say we are." He drummed his fingers on the dashboard for a few seconds. "Come on, buddy, get me your end of the code," he mumbled.

"Or?" Frank asked.

"I have orders to bolt," Bessemer said, his voice tightening as the seconds passed without a message. "Krancis said to give him thirty seconds. And that time is up…now."

Bessemer laid his hands on the controls and was about to pull away from the station when his computer beeped. A quick glance at the message was all that it took.

"Talk about waiting for the last moment!" he said with relief. "Alright, we can dock. The code is correct."

"Good," Tselitel said. "I was afraid we'd come all this way for nothing."

Along with the verification code Welter had sent docking instructions, directing them to bay four. Its thick metal door began to roll away just as they reached it, revealing a small but sufficient place to land the egg. As Bessemer got it inside and docked, the door began to close upon them.

"Glad we're among friends," Tselitel said nervously. Already ill at ease in the strange nebula, the door felt worryingly like a prison door, hemming them in.

"Instruments indicate that the bay is filling with air," the captain commented. "We'll be able to hop out in just a second."

Soon Bessemer raised the canopy, and the three passengers descended out of the egg, planting their feet on the hard metal of the station with a clang that echoed through the space.

"Wonder where our friend is," Frank commented, hanging from Tselitel's neck and tucked into her shirt for skin contact.

The trio moved along the tight space to a door at the far end. Bessemer looked between his two companions for a moment, and then knocked sharply upon it. From within they heard a muffled response.

"What was that?" the captain shouted, his voice bouncing off the walls and hurting Tselitel's ears. He pressed the side of his head against the door, straining to hear. "Get back!" Bessemer said suddenly, moving the emperor and the doctor away from the door just as a dark blade burst through its lock, shattering it. "Well howdy-do to you, too!" Bessemer exclaimed, as Welter shoved the door open and stood before them. "You know I could have had that little dagger of yours jammed into my side if I hadn't gotten away from the door when I did."

"I'm sorry for that," Welter replied sincerely, though without any note of regret in his voice. It was a simple error, and not something that required an emotional response. "You're Bessemer?" he asked, sheathing his Midnight Blade.

"That's right," the captain replied, shaking his hand perfunctorily and then stepping back. "I present our lord, Emperor Rhemus."

"Your Majesty," Welter said with a bow, though not a particularly deep one.

"And Doctor Lily Tselitel."

"Ma'am," he nodded towards her. "I suppose you'll all welcome the chance to stretch your legs a little before we head for Quarlac. The station has long been abandoned, so you can walk up and down it freely. But stick to the main areas." Here he gestured over his shoulder toward the damaged door. "Some parts of it have worn out, and can't be relied on."

"This whole station will probably be damaged when we pop the seal on the bay door back there," Bessemer said, as the trio followed Welter into the main corridor of the small station. "Cutting that lock guaranteed that."

"So?" Welter replied evenly. "Nobody's used this outpost for decades. Nobody is going to miss it once we're done with it." He paused and looked down the length of the modest corridor. Half the lights were out, and the other half were flickering intermittently. "It's a miracle anything still works here."

"Why was this outpost built?" Tselitel asked. "I can't think of a more desolate place than this nebula."

"It was some kind of research station," Welter replied. "For what I don't know. The computer barely works, and most of the files have been corrupted through time."

"So that's why it took you so long to respond with the verification code," Bessemer observed.

"Yes, the system ground to a halt just before I was going to send it. Started whirring again when you were about to pull off."

"Lucky break," the captain opined, as they reached the top of the hallway and stopped before a locked door. "What's in there?"

"Search me," Welter replied with a shrug. "I haven't bothered to look. Besides, it might have been depressurized."

"Might have?" inquired Tselitel.

"Yeah, the computer won't give me an up or down answer. Keeps flashing between yes and no, so I decided to leave well enough alone. Didn't want to compromise the station just to settle my curiosity." He looked between the three of them for a moment. "You can keep moving around here if you want to. I've got some kit to transfer from my ship to yours for the journey." He looked at Bessemer. "I imagine you've got a few things to move as well."

"A few," the captain replied, as Welter lumbered away. "Kind of a strange guy, don't you think?" he asked Tselitel, once he was out of earshot.

"He's hurting over something," she replied, her healer's heart picking up on his pain at once and sympathizing with him. "He's carrying some kind of burden. It's enough to crush him."

"Well, he'd better stay intact until his mission is over, that's all I know," Bessemer commented, before turning toward the emperor. "My lord," he said, taking his leave and making for the egg.

"How do you know all that about Welter?" he asked her once they were alone. "Long years of practice as a psychiatrist, I expect."

"That helps," she said quietly. "But I also have a gift for that sort of thing. It caused Delta-13 to draw Rex and I together."

"Really?" he asked, surprised at her words. "I had no idea."

"Yes. It knew his potential, but recognized that he needed someone to help him reach it. He's terribly tangled up inside. Or at least was. I've done what I could to help him straighten things out, but he'll always be a tormented man. Those Hunts are a tortured lot, for whatever reason. Their inner worlds give them more trouble than anything outside themselves. I'd guess Maximilian was the worst in that regard, in that he couldn't ultimately make sense of it, allowing the *Prellak* to corrupt him. Rex is more put together than his father, but he's still got a lot of frayed wires. Milo seems the most normal, though he's teeming with unresolved problems, too. As a psychiatrist I want to help those two just as much as I can. But there's something a little…cracked, in the Hunt foundation, and no amount of therapy will put it together again. Oh, I don't mean to imply that they're crazy," she said quickly, afraid her words would be misinterpreted. "I just meant—"

"I understand," Rhemus said, as Bessemer emerged from docking bay four carrying a small bag with his belongings. "He's a tortured hero," he continued when they were again alone. "It's too bad. Nobody has a greater right to enjoy the fruits of his labor than Rex does. I suppose he'll always be something of an outsider looking in, not really able to participate."

"My lord, perhaps *you* should be the psychiatrist," she smiled.

"Oh, I've got a good grasp of people," he replied with a modesty that pleased her, shaking his head to dismiss the point. "Besides, something about your Rex appeals to me. I find him very easy to relate to. In another place and time, we could have been family. I'd almost think we were, if the family genealogy wasn't worked out in such fine detail, given my position."

"Yes, of course," she nodded, as Welter reentered the corridor with two large bags.

"Might take us a while to find our new friends," he explained as he passed through to bay four, holding up the bags. "These'll keep us alive until then."

"Excellent," Rhemus replied, receiving a nod for his words. "That Welter is an interesting man," he continued. "He respects my office without being overawed by it. I must say, it's a refreshing combination, especially given the intimate reliance we must each of us have on each other from now on."

"My lord?" she asked, her eyes showing growing concern. "I thought the *Kol-Prockians* were our allies."

"Oh, I don't mean to worry you," he said reassuringly. "But the fact is we don't know just what we're jumping into. They might be a good deal less cooperative than we anticipate, only using us to secure what Krancis promised them here in this galaxy. All we can be *certain of* is each other."

"Yes, my lord," she replied quietly, as Welter came back into view and paused, eyeing her for a moment. Without saying a word he seemed to communicate something subtle, something important. Then he turned and headed for the computer room at the other end of the hall. "Would you like to walk a little more?" she asked the emperor.

"No, I get tired pretty easily these days," he replied, reaching for an overturned bucket and turning it upside down. Taking a seat, he let out a sigh and stretched his arms over his head. "I'll just rest here for a few minutes. But you don't have to keep me company," he added, gesturing towards the computer room when he saw her eyes upon it. "You can ramble around if you want."

"Okay, if you're sure," she uttered, receiving a confirmatory nod that sent her on her way.

Reaching the room, she found it lit only by a large, damaged computer screen. At least a fifth of the display was non-functional, just splotches of black, dead pixels. "What are you doing?" she asked, nearing Welter.

"Checking the station for problems," he replied, as her eyes were attracted to a trio of blinking red alerts.

"What are those?" she asked.

"Maintenance warnings," he replied factually, as though they didn't concern him at all. "One is for the oxygen recycler, which is about to conk out for good."

"Oh, how charming!" she said with a nervous laugh. "And the other two?"

"A bad seal on docking bay three's inner and outer doors, and the same for bay four's inner door. Nothing to worry about," he added calmly. "We'll be out of here before they become our problem."

"I certainly hope so," she replied, turning around and leaning against the computer's desk. "I would hate to come all this way just to suffocate."

"Indeed," he replied without interest, clicking through a few more items before turning his head to look at her. "Can I help you with something, Doctor?"

"Me? Oh, no. I'm just floating around. The emperor wanted to rest for a few minutes, so I thought I'd just ramble a little."

"Do you usually ramble in one place?" he asked, nodding towards the desk against which she leaned. "Come now, Doctor. You're not here to examine the station. You're here to examine *me*. What's the matter," he asked, crossing his arms. "Think you can't trust me?"

"Krancis trusts you to keep us safe," she replied.

"Which doesn't answer my question at all," he said, fixing her with his eyes. "Or is there something else on your mind? You've been looking at me strangely ever since you got here. And frankly, I'd appreciate it if you'd stop it."

"I'm sorry. I didn't mean to make you uncomfortable."

"Nobody likes to be under the magnifying glass," he replied, uncrossing his arms and looking at the screen again. "What sort of doctor are you, anyway?"

"Psychiatrist," she uttered.

"Oh, that's right," he said, nodding to himself. "I thought your name was familiar. Well, I know it'll be hard for you, given your background and all. But don't try to peel back my layers, alright? You seem like a decent enough woman. But I'll take it poorly if you start trying to ferret out my deepest motivations and darkest secrets."

"Is that why you stared at me in the hallway earlier?" she asked with quiet insistence.

"What do you mean?" he asked, skeptically squinting at the screen as he spoke. "I just looked at you."

"It was more than that," she replied. "I could feel it, like an appeal for help. That's why I came in here, though I didn't realize it until now. You're hurting badly."

He paused and looked at her.

"I told you not to peel back my layers."

"I can't help it if your unconscious mind starts reaching out to me," she replied. "It's a counterbalance to your conscious attitude to repress whatever is going on inside. Something in you intuited that I'm a healer, and it's guiding you to me. I can feel it."

"Funny that I can't," he replied, unconvinced. "Now, Doctor, if you'll just leave me to finish my work here, I'll be with you and the emperor very shortly."

"As you wish," she said graciously, pushing off the desk and making for the door.

"Just a moment," he said, just before she left.

"Yes?" she asked, watching as he turned around and approached her. Stopping a couple feet short, he looked her up and down. "Just why are you on this little expedition into the unknown?"

"I have a condition that only the *Kol-Prockians* can help with," she replied, holding her hand up so he could see it tremble. Instinctively he reached out and grasped it, gauging the degree of her deterioration through touch rather than sight.

"Valindra," he said after a moment, letting go.

"How in the world do you know that?" she asked with amazement. "Most people haven't even heard of it, much less seen it first hand."

"It's a long story," he replied, before looking her up and down again, his crisp, analytical mind taking in every detail. "A woman in your condition should be looking after herself," he added. "Not digging into the traumas of others."

"That's *why* I dig into the traumas of others," she replied. "Because at least their conditions can be resolved."

With this she left, the feeling of his eyes on her back sticking with her until she reached the emperor.

"Learn anything?" he asked, his tone a bit light as the stress of the journey began to make itself felt now that he was at rest.

"A few things," she replied, looking back towards the now empty doorway. "He's an interesting man. I look forward to getting to know him further. I should think–"

She stopped speaking when she saw Rhemus begin to lose his balance, nearly tumbling forward off the bucket.

"My lord!" she exclaimed, doing her best to hold him up as he drifted away from consciousness. "Help! Help me, please!" she shouted, causing the two men to race to her location just as her meager strength was about to fail. Seizing him firmly, they moved him off the bucket and stretched him out on the floor.

"Get some blankets," Welter ordered Bessemer, as he felt Rhemus' neck for a pulse. "This floor is too cold for him to lay on it for long. I put some in that egg ship."

Quickly the captain dashed off to bay four, returning moments later with a bundle under his arm.

"Lay them out here," Welter said, gesturing alongside the emperor. "Alright, let's get him onto them. That's it. Easy. Okay, right there. Hand me that other one," he said to Tselitel, indicating one that Bessemer had dropped just out of reach. Carefully he stretched it out across Rhemus. "Probably just too much strain lately," he uttered after a few moments had passed, during which he'd checked the older man's breathing and found it essentially normal. "Just give him a little while."

"He needs medical care," Tselitel said to no one in particular. "There could be something very wrong with him that we don't know about."

"I think we all know what's wrong with him," Welter replied evenly, tucking the blanket under his shoulders before standing up. "And only the aliens in Quarlac can help with that. The best we can do is give him a chance to recover, and then get him there as quickly as possible." He looked at Tselitel and then Bessemer. "One of you keep an eye on him. I've got to do something about that bad seal we've got on bay three's doors."

"We should leave now," Bessemer said. "If the station's about to fall apart–"

"It's not that bad," Welter replied. "It ought to hold together for at least another couple days. But I want to do

51

what I can to guarantee that." He paused and pointed at Rhemus' unconscious form. "We shouldn't move him like this if we can help it. I don't want to add to the strain he's already under. Things are only going to get harder once we reach Quarlac, and he ought to get at least some small breather before we put him through that."

With this he left them.

"I don't know about that guy," Bessemer said, crouching beside the emperor and looking at his careworn face.

"He seems to know what he's doing," Tselitel replied.

"Yeah," the captain muttered, before looking up at her. "I just hope Krancis is right, leaving you two in his hands. I get the feeling he's sitting on a powder keg of some kind. That bit back there with the blade, jamming it into the lock like that," he shook his head. "That was dangerous. What if the emperor had been standing on the other side, and not me? What if he hadn't realized what he was saying in time, and caught it right in the side?" he asked, jabbing two fingers into his ribcage. "No, ma'am: I don't like it at all."

"I'm sure Krancis knows what he's doing, choosing this man," Tselitel replied, not half so certain as she sounded.

"Well, whether he is, or whether he isn't," Bessemer uttered, standing up, "looks like you two are stuck with him. Just keep your distance, alright?" he said, his voice dropping so it wouldn't carry.

"Why, do you think he'd try to hurt me?" she asked.

"No," the captain shook his head. "But he might get you hurt right alongside himself. I'm no psychiatrist, but I've seen enough men who'd given up on their own safety." Here he stabbed a finger toward the computer room. "And *that* man doesn't give a hoot if he makes it to the end of this week. He's just going through the motions of staying alive and keeping his end of the war up. He's awfully good, so even just the motions are enough to make a difference. But he'll be careless when he doesn't intend to be. So watch yourself."

❖ ❖ ❖

"We are losing power! Repeat, we are losing power!" the carrier *Courage's* captain called out over the radio waves. "Mayday! Mayday! We are going down!"

Radik watched as the assault carrier began to spiral towards the ground, its path carrying it on a collision course with the *Daring*, upon whose bridge he stood helplessly. The *Daring* attempted to move out of the way, but it was struck by the falling vessel, taking severe damage to the right hanger. Every crew member was thrown off their feet by the blow. Radik hit the deck hard, cutting open his forehead.

"Are you alright?" Calhoun asked, helping him to his feet while the rest of the command crew returned to their stations.

"It's over," Radik said, stumbling to a window and watching as a squadron of Devourer craft shot by, pursuing the last of the bombers. "We've been beaten."

The army base beneath them had been pulverized by the falling debris of the battle. Scarcely a quarter of the militia's vessels remained in the air, and most of them had sustained critical damage. A pair of massive Devourer carriers floated victoriously over their shattered foe.

"I'm afraid there's nothing else we can do now," Calhoun said heavily, as he reviewed the battle on the screen before him. "The only option is to charge 'em, taking as many down with us as we can."

"I agree," Radik said grimly, nodding his head. "At least–"

At this moment an alien frigate lost power from the damage it had sustained and fell onto the engine compartment of the ailing carrier. The blow again tossed everyone into the air, scattering them across the floor.

"Captain, we're losing altitude!" one of the command staff shouted. "We're going down!"

"Everyone brace!" Calhoun ordered. Moments later they struck the ground, the impact ripping the crew from their handholds and battering them mercilessly. Several were killed instantly.

In the midst of moans and cries of pain, Radik pulled his abused, half-numb body upright and staggered to where admiral Calhoun lay. The ship was in utter chaos, people running to and fro, trying to escape the doomed vessel. The sound of green blobs hitting its tortured hull told them they had not more than a minute or two before the ship was finished off.

"Come on, Bruce," Radik said, striving to pull the younger man off his belly and onto his feet. "We've got to get out of here. Bruce?"

"You…go…" he said, half rolling over to reveal a mouth that dripped blood. "I'm all smashed up inside," he added, grimacing as Radik felt his ribs for injury.

"I'm not going to leave you here," Radik said, fighting Calhoun to a half-upright position that caused him to gasp in pain. "Now, let me get under your arm…" he said, his old body no match for his large, athletic charge. Helping him a few feet towards the door, he stumbled when Calhoun fell over again, landing on top of him.

"I tell you…I've had it…" he gasped. "Now, get out of here." He fixed the old man with his tormented eyes. "You've got to look after…these people now. Get them together. Help them fight."

"That's what we need you for, Bruce," Radik insisted, shaking his shoulders as though to jostle life back into him. "I'm too old for that."

"No," Calhoun said, licking his bloody lips and then spitting because of the taste. "This is all on you now." With this his eyes rolled back in his head, and the breath left his body.

Horrified, Radik let him drop against the floor, deaf to the noise and panic around him. Staring down at the lifeless body of his friend, he didn't notice the hands of the lieutenant grasp him until she began pulling him towards the exit.

"Admiral, we have to leave now!" she shouted over the din, trying to penetrate the fog that had engulfed his mind. "Sir! Please!"

With a shake of his head he recovered himself. Recognizing the woman who'd shown him to the bridge before, he quickly nodded his agreement and followed her into the crowd of escapees. The lights flickered in the ship as exposed wires crackled and shot off sparks. Suddenly the whole vessel went dark, the power plant going offline. Several people shouted their dismay, but the lieutenant simply found Radik's arm in the dark and pulled him to a stop.

"Wait a moment," she said, her voice barely audible.

Like magic a set of emergency lights blinked on, casting a dim white glow over the agonizing scene. All around them bodies lay, at least half of them dead from fatally striking the hull on impact.

"We need to help these people," Radik said, as the lieutenant tried to pull him into motion again.

"We need to get you out of here, sir," she insisted, still dragging on his thin arm. "There's no hope for these people," she insisted in as low of a voice as she could manage. "They'll never escape the spiders."

"The spiders," Radik mumbled, having forgotten them in all the excitement. Soon they would be lowered to Jennet from their transports, free to spread across the countryside and consume every last life they found.

Stumbling forward over the rubble and bodies, they saw the dying yellow rays of the setting sun in the corridor ahead. Hurrying their pace, they reached the opening moments later. Letting go of his arm, the lieutenant peered down the gash in the ship to the ground below.

"It's too far, sir," she said, shaking her head at the thirty foot drop. "We'll die if we try it."

"Come on," he said, gesturing for her to follow him and rejoin the crowd that streamed past.

No sooner had they left the opening than a stream of Devourer blobs crashed through it and killed several passersby. Jerking their heads around in surprise, the pair watched as the acid burned the flesh from its victims, consuming them almost instantly. Looking at each other, their minds were suddenly in agreement. They had to survive in order to give back to the Devourers what they had dished out.

"Come on," Radik said, taking off down the corridor as quickly as his old bones could manage.

A little farther along the corridor they found another opening, this one scarcely ten feet above the ground. With luck they both managed to land without injury. The grass was incongruently cool and peaceful after all they'd seen inside the ship. But they had no time to reflect on that. Fighters were circling overhead, protecting the frigates as they made for the last of the militia's capital ships.

"It'll be just a few minutes before they've got complete control of the air," Radik said, searching the sky as they moved away from the *Daring* and under the cover of the trees.

"What do we do, sir?" the lieutenant asked anxiously, looking between him and the sky.

"We survive," he said ominously, his voice strained as he craned his neck.

He knew the spiders would be hot on their tails as soon as the air battle was over. That gave them ten, maybe fifteen minutes before they were overrun. They had to hide somehow, to find some kind of cover until nightfall masked their movements from the vessels above. Before he could think any further, an army captain charged up to them on feet of lightning.

"Sir!" he exclaimed, sliding to a halt and nearly falling over. "We have to move now."

"Where?" Radik asked.

"There's no time to explain, sir," the captain said, the words rapidly tumbling out of his mouth. "I have orders from general Blake to round up all high ranking officers and escort them off the field of battle at once." He looked at the lieutenant and then back to Radik.

"Let's go, then," the admiral replied.

"I'm sorry, sir," the captain shook his head. "Only high ranking officers. Those were my orders. There's not enough room to take everyone."

"I'm *changing* your orders, Captain," Radik snapped. "Unless you want to explain to general Blake why you left me behind to die."

The captain hesitated for a moment, and then nodded his acquiescence.

"Come quickly," he urged, gesturing for them to follow as he hunched his body over and sprinted for the trees.

Hours after nightfall they reached an old mine buried deep in a nearby forest. It had long been abandoned, its produce too meager to justify the expense of running it.

"What is this place?" Radik asked, echoing the sentiments of the other high ranking officers they'd found on the way there. The ceilings were low, but the walls were broad and sturdy. It looked more like a bomb shelter than a civilian project.

"They found gold here once, sir," the captain explained, as he guided them, hunched over, through the tunnels. "The company that ran it usually harvested more hazardous fare, typically with robots. The story goes that they had some bots they weren't using, so, finding some ore here, they set them to work digging."

"Hence the low ceilings," the lieutenant commented.

"Yes, that's right," the captain replied, ushering the group to the side to permit another one to pass. "The machines only needed corridors around five feet high, so that's all they dug," he continued, moving them along. "Once the gold ran out, they abandoned the place. Similar efforts were made in the area, but because they were done with remote controlled robots, very little footprint was left behind. They're all but impossible to spot from the sky."

"I never knew they were here," Radik uttered, surprised at his own ignorance given how long he'd lived in the area.

"It's one of the army's better kept secrets," the captain said, his voice broadening with pride. "We've been retrofitting them ever since the Devourer war began." He paused at a metal door marked 'HQ.' "General Blake is waiting in here for you, sir," he said, looking at Radik.

"What about the rest?" the admiral asked, nodding toward the rest of the group.

"I have orders to see that they're well taken care of for their contribution to the defense effort," he replied. The correctness of his tone made Radik eye him for a moment, searching for any sign of the barb that he felt must be hidden in the younger man's studied politeness. After a few seconds he shrugged.

"Alright."

"This way, please," the captain said to the others, gesturing for them to follow. "Just go right in, sir," he added as they moved away.

"Is this what we've come to?" Radik thought, glancing around the cramped space for a moment before knocking out of habit. "Hiding in holes like rats?"

"Come in!" barked Blake from the other side, his voice unmistakable. "Oh, it's you," he said with disappointment, his mouth twisting into a pointed frown the second his eyes fell on the admiral. "I *told* you to get those ships of yours away from my base," he continued, tossing a hand towards the chair that stood before his broad, squat desk. He sat behind it, smoking a cigar. "When you boys started dropping like flies out of the sky, your carcasses did more damage than the aliens."

"I relayed your wishes to admiral Calhoun," Radik said, a little unsure of himself and trying to find his bearings as he took the roughly offered chair. "He felt it wasn't the right course to take, and I agreed with him. We needed your triple A, missiles, and local air support to give us a hand."

"One which didn't manage to turn the tide in your favor at all, and merely served to inflict added casualties on my command," Blake growled, his face growing red. "I don't know just what they teach you boys at the academy, or wherever you learned your trade. But you seem to think you can ride roughshod over us in the army." He fixed the admiral with ruthless eyes. "That's a fantasy. I want you to know that. *Any* attempt to ignore my authority, either in this base, or in the operations to follow, will be met with irresistible force. Do I make myself clear?"

"Indeed," Radik replied, his confidence rising as his temper began to warm. "Tell me, General, did you drag me in here just so you could thump your chest?"

"Thump my–" he began, halting angrily. "I had Captain Benedict escort you here for one solitary purpose: so that I could make clear to you, and through you, your entire command, that this is now a purely army operation. You, and your people, are to enjoy *no* authority during the course of our defense. I would strip you of your uniforms if I could," he added with a narrowing of his eyes, "just to make certain you wouldn't exert the least influence on those around you. The navy has botched their end of this from start to finish. It's time someone clipped your wings."

"I believe the Devourers have done that," Radik said, rising from his seat and making for the door. "Do you have anything else to say to me, General?"

"No," Blake replied, leaning back in his seat and

grinding his cigar between his teeth. "Nothing at all."

With a nod Radik opened the crude metal door and left, not bothering to close it. It was a petty move, he knew. But some men made themselves so disagreeable as to justify pettiness.

Moving deeper into the mine, he noticed that the army personnel tended to turn up their noses when they saw his uniform. It bothered him more than he cared to admit, to himself or anyone else. But after all that he'd been through since the aliens first emerged from warp above Jennet, he'd hoped for a little human warmth and camaraderie, even if it *was* with the army. Clearly, that wasn't in the cards.

His morose thoughts brightened a little when he heard the pretty young lieutenant talking animatedly with the officers who'd been rescued earlier. Their voices were echoing down the corridor, mingling with other voices. He paused and tried to discern which room they were in, for several dotted either side of the path. Finally he just moved along slowly, poking his head into each one until he found them.

"Sir," the lieutenant saluted crisply upon seeing him, a move that was followed by the others present. The scene was slightly ridiculous, given that they were all hunched over. But he appreciated the show of respect after the chewing out he'd just received.

"What's the word from Blake, Ronald?" asked another admiral, an old acquaintance of Radik's. "What's the state of our defense?"

"We're to have no part in what's to come," he replied heavily, sitting on a crate. The others followed suit, except for the lieutenant, who remained standing, more or less. "Oh, sit down," he said with a wave of his hand when he realized what she was doing. "It's silly for anyone to stand in circumstances like these."

"Yes, sir," she uttered, crouching down and leaning against the wall since there were no other crates.

"Blake's made it clear that he thinks we're responsible for every human error since Eve first met the snake," he continued. "He blames us for the loss of the battle *above* Jennet, and for the damage our debris did to his forces."

"Well, it's not like the Devourers really needed our help to overcome Gamma Base," the admiral from before said. "Just before my cruiser, the *Vengeance*, went down, we picked up another wave coming in from warp. They're multiplying faster than rabbits."

"What, in the name of common sense, is the *appeal* of this planet?" Radik asked. "It's just a farming world. Sure, there's a large population. But the Devourers have never shown any real preference for mere bodies before. Why the sudden appetite?"

"Perhaps they want to destroy the population," the admiral suggested. "Instead of hitting our industrial worlds, just grind us down through sheer extermination. It'd do a number on morale, too."

"I don't read their tactics that way," Radik said, shaking his head as he thought. "There's got to be something else going on." He was silent for a few moments, and then dismissed the question and looked at the others. "How many of us have made it?" he asked. "Do you know?"

"I'm only aware of the six of us," the admiral replied, indicating the other four high officers who sat with them. "And the lieutenant here, of course," he added, nodding in her direction.

"Seven people," Radik muttered. "There's got to be more out there."

"Sure, but how much longer can they last?" the admiral replied. "You know most of us are getting up there in years. Shoot, Calhoun was probably the youngest we had. It's just so hard to keep talent in the colonial service, what with the pay the imperial navy can offer and all." Here he smiled. "That's why we were lucky to get you back in the service."

"Yeah, some luck," Radik replied, his tone flat and

61

uninterested as he reflected. Then he emerged again. "Blake's gonna let our people rot if we let him," he said in a lower voice, gesturing for them to draw a little closer. "I think we're the only hope they have. If we can sneak some of them back in here–"

"What an interesting idea!" the admiral replied rather loudly, trying to mask Radik's words as an army major slowly walked past, his eyes suspiciously on them until he was out of sight. "Ronald, we'll never be able to pull that off on our own. And Blake isn't going to let us, anyhow."

"I'm not going to give him a choice," Radik replied, his voice growing determined. "But I'm going to need help."

"Where are you going to *get it*?" the admiral asked insistently, leaning in closer. "We're not exactly the fittest of the fit, you know," he added, nodding towards the aged, ungainly bodies of the men and women around him. "Sure, that farm of yours has kept you in good trim. But we've been flying desks for years. Outside of the lieutenant here," he said, glancing at her and then back to Radik, "we're simply unfit."

"Then she and I will do it," he said resolutely.

"I-I've never served on the ground before," she replied. "Sir," she added quickly.

"Well, I hope you're a quick learner," Radik said. "Because we're leaving just as soon as I get a drink of water and half a bite to eat."

The pair found it surprisingly easy to get out of the mine. Despite Blake's overwhelming hostility to naval involvement, the people under his command were simply too busy to keep track of them. The mine was scarcely more than marginally organized chaos at this point, with everyone running around, trying to figure out what to do. The front entrance lacked so much as a sentry.

Slipping out the entrance and into the surrounding darkness, they made it a couple dozen paces before Radik stopped.

"What's your name, Lieutenant?" he asked, realizing that he didn't know.

"Julia Powers, sir," she replied correctly.

"And you say you've never served on the ground before?"

"No, sir," she said with embarrassment.

"Well, just stick close to me then," he said, patting her back and moving carefully forward in the darkness. "I know the brush like nobody's business."

Now that he was in his element, Radik relaxed. Though something of a naval prodigy in his younger days, he'd never truly taken to the service, with its strict rules and stuffy decorum. Despite the encouragement, in some cases, pleadings, from others, he eventually turned his back on the militia and returned to the land, working the soil with his own two hands. That was where he felt natural, free, at peace – not floating in space, wrapped in who knows how many tons of metal.

That fact alone made him question, as he had many times before, why in the world Krancis had put him in charge of Jennet's defense. He shook his head as he crouched along in the darkness, certain he would never know the answer.

Reaching the edge of the forest, the duo crouched down and looked towards the scene of their defeat earlier in the day. The milky white light of Jennet's massive moon glowed all around them. All the birds in the trees had long since fled, and the frogs and crickets who typically enlivened the night were all silent. Nature, and not just man, knew that something terrible had happened that day.

"Where are we going to go, sir?" Powers asked, her eyes darting back and forth in the gloom.

"We've got to find as many survivors as we can," he replied, as though thinking out loud. "We'll never find them in all these trees," he added. "So we'll get close to the wreckage and try to search around without getting spotted."

"But what about the spiders?" she inquired.

"That's a chance we've got to take," he said, standing up into a hunch like before. "Now, come on."

The sounds of Devourer craft increased as they drew closer to Gamma Base and its graveyard of ships. Occasionally a fighter screamed overhead, driving them to the ground despite the foliage above them for fear of being picked up on their scanners. The air around them grew brighter as they approached, the blaze of many fires adding to the light of the moon. The wrecks were burning. The flammable parts, anyway.

"Keep low," Radik whispered, putting a hand on her shoulder and pressing her a little closer to the ground as they moved. They had begun to cast multiple faint shadows from the competing fires, though she hadn't noticed. Her heart had been too noisily beating in her ears, her eyes too actively searching the distance, for her to notice what was right next to her.

Nearing a crashed heavy fighter, they were about to bypass it when a moan stopped them in their tracks.

"Sir!" Powers said urgently, though Radik had heard it, too.

Scanning the area to ensure no spiders were nearby, the admiral guided them through a minefield of half visible metal shards and other bits of probably a dozen different vessels. Stopping beside the young man who'd moaned, they knelt.

"What's your name, son?" he asked, as a pair of eyes, their whites shining brilliantly in the moonlight, stared up at him.

"J-J-J," he struggled to say, his voice quivered, his chest shaking uncontrollably.

Sympathetically Powers laid a hand on his stomach, but pulled it back when she found it thoroughly wet. Looking at it in the gloom, she could make out the dark red hue of blood coating her palm.

"Don't worry about your name," Radik said, as he

continued to stutter.

"S-sir," he said with effort. "W-we lost. They beat us. H-how could they? I thought *Sentinel* would come."

"So did I," Radik admitted, putting a fatherly hand on his shoulder and squeezing it. "So did I. But it can't be everywhere at once. Someone's got to pay the price. Looks like our ticket came up."

"Y-yes, sir," he nodded, immediately groaning in pain from doing so. "I'm sorry, sir," he added, once he'd stopped. "I-I hurt so much~. I-I can't feel my..." his voice trailed, his eyes shifting downward.

Taking his hint, Powers felt for his legs but found that they terminated just past his thighs. The rest had been lost in the crash.

"You'd better g-go, sir," he said. "I'm finished."

"I'm sorry, son," Radik uttered with sympathy, patting his shoulder before standing up. "Truly sorry."

Gesturing for Powers to follow him, Radik moved a few paces off and then stopped and looked back. Hesitating a moment, the young woman knelt and kissed the dying man on the forehead, murmuring some small words of comfort to him that the admiral couldn't hear. Then she resumed her hunch and followed him.

"Sir?" she whispered, as they moved farther and farther into the graveyard. "Where are all the bodies?"

"That's what I'd like to know," he said.

Burning rubble; shattered husks; craters. But no bodies. Outside of the young man they found, there was not the slightest indication that any humans had even taken part in the battle. At first his mind jumped to the spiders, thinking that maybe they'd carried them away. But there were no tracks in the soft ground, none of the telltale scratches that invariably marked their passing. It gave the scene an eerie feeling, like they had passed into some kind of dream land.

The illusion was shattered the moment they looked into the twisted hull of a fallen cruiser. A gash in it permitted moonlight to shine inside, revealing at least two dozen bodies all piled together.

"But how?" she asked him in a barely audible hush. "Why?"

In reply he merely shook his head and moved to the next wreck. The scene was the same.

"They must be rounding up the live ones," he thought out loud, resting his arm against the hull as he looked inside. "That's why they left that young fellow back there. He wouldn't have lasted long. Shoot, he'd probably have died simply from the act of moving him."

"But *why*?" she asked again.

"That's what we're trying to find out," he said with a shrug. A faint noise in the distance caught his ear, and he moved around the wreck to hear it better. "Do you hear that?" he asked, nodding towards the city of Numek some miles in the distance. "Sounds like–"

"Screaming," she said ominously, her eyes finding his. "But I don't hear any weapons being fired." She looked around the graveyard once more, and then back at him. "I'd *think* it was the spiders…" her voice trailed.

"But that doesn't seem too likely, all things considered," he agreed. "Seems like they've got something else in store for us now. Come on: let's get over there and take a look."

CHAPTER 3

Hunt was on his way toward the hangar to join Pinchon for the journey to Erdu-3 when Wellesley spoke up.

"Aren't you gonna say goodbye to Soliana?" he asked, as his friend strode heavily along the corridor that connected his room to the nearest teleportation station.

Hunt frowned at this question but continued to walk. The girl had barely left his mind since the moment she touched his face and brought her feelings out into the open. The memory of it made him uncomfortable, almost a little nauseous. His attachment to Lily Tselitel was nearly religious in its intensity, and he felt simultaneously surprised at Soliana's forwardness and insulted that she felt anyone could ever come between him and the ailing doctor. He'd planned to slip off the ship without seeing her, hoping to sidestep the whole question and let the matter die. But the AI wasn't about to let that happen.

"I think you owe her that, at least," he continued, as Hunt moved inexorably towards the teleporter room. "After all, without her–"

"Just why are you doing this?" Hunt snapped, his question making two people halfway up the hall turn their heads to look at him.

"What makes you think I'm doing anything?" Wellesley asked, as his friend moved past the onlookers and rounded a corner. "I'm just trying to keep the family together, is all. That girl has done a lot for us, especially lately. I think it would be wrong for you and the colonel to just leave her here on her own."

"She has Krancis and Antonin to keep her company," he replied, shoving his hands into his pockets.

"Ooh, what a lucky girl," the AI replied sarcastically. "A machine and a clown. Don't you think she appreciates a *little* broader mental range than that? You and the colonel are the only balanced people she knows. Besides, it's got to be mighty depressing to be cooped up in that hospital room, with nothing but four bare walls and a refrigerated nurse to keep you company. And *now* that she's going through all that scary stuff, the visions and convulsions and–"

"*Fine*," Hunt grumbled, just as he'd reached the door to the teleportation room. "Hospital," he tersely ordered the technician.

"Of course, Lord Hunt," he replied.

Materializing near the medical bay moments later, he strode quickly towards the front desk.

"Oh, Lord Hunt," the receptionist said with both surprise and a hint of dismay. "I'm sorry, but your friend–. Sir–. No, you can't–" she stammered, trying to arrest his steps as he walked towards Soliana's room. Quickly she trotted after him. "Lord Hunt," she said when she'd caught up with him. "With all due respect to your rank within the empire, you *cannot* simply come down here whenever you feel like it and–"

With one sharp, dark look, he stopped her in her tracks. The anger flaring in his eyes, she saw something terrible at back of them that made her reconsider her choice to go into medicine.

"P-perhaps if you just see her for a minute…" her voice trailed, as he left her behind in the corridor.

"Glad to see you still have your old way with people," Wellesley commented, as his friend reached Soliana's room.

Quietly turning the knob, he slipped inside and shut the door.

The room was silent, save the beeping of a few machines that were hooked up to the unconscious girl. Dark, except for a small nightlight, Hunt gave his eyes a couple of seconds to adjust before approaching the bed and taking a seat on its edge. She lay unconscious beside him, her arms atop the blanket. They looked especially thin, as though she hadn't eaten in weeks. Something within him, he didn't know what, drove him to reach up and gently touch the young, careworn face. Instantly he withdrew his hand, chiding himself internally.

"It's not infidelity to care for someone else," Wellesley said, as he drew a sharp breath and exhaled in exasperation. "You don't have to be so severe with yourself."

Hunt was confused. He knew he didn't love Soliana, but she appealed to him all the same. She was so potent, and yet so completely helpless, that he couldn't help but want to wrap her up in his arms and keep her safe. One minute she spoke with the authority of a god, and the next she was just a puddle of jelly, unable to take care of herself. His mind went back to her wandering the Black Hole, of all places. The thought made him shudder when he considered the trash, the *refuse*, who were there at the time. If any *one* of them had gotten their hands on her…

Unconsciously he began grinding his teeth.

"Calm down, Rex," the AI cautioned him, watching his vitals. "This girl's a psychic, remember? You start going off, even in your head, and you'll probably wake her up. She's been through enough, don't you think?"

Instantly Hunt tried to push the thought aside, but it lingered on in the back of his mind.

"We should probably go, before the little dictator at the front desk makes a racket."

Nodding silently, Hunt arose to go when Soliana's hand unconsciously reached out for him. He eyed it doubtfully for a moment, as it hovered in the air. Then he shook his head and took it. Gently she drew him back to the bed, and slowly her eyes fluttered open.

"You've come to see me before departing," she uttered groggily, her eyes barely able to fix on him because of the sedatives. Weakly, she smiled. "I was hoping you would. It's so terribly lonely here. I don't know anybody."

"Called it," Wellesley said, causing Hunt to roll his eyes.

"Thank you for being so thoughtful," she said, rubbing his hand between her fingers.

"You're welcome," he said awkwardly, both guilty that he'd come against his will, and uncomfortable that she was showing her affection yet more palpably. "Look, Soliana–"

Suddenly his words were cut off by a violent straightening of her body that thrust her head hard against the pillow. An anguished moan escaped her lips as she began to convulse.

"Wellesley? What's happening?" he asked, putting his hands on her shoulders to try and stabilize her.

"I-I don't know," the AI replied, blazing through the health information he was gleaning from their skin contact. "I-it could be a seizure of some kind. There's a spike of electrical activity in the–"

"Did you imagine you could destroy me so *easily*?" a deep voice rumbled from between her lips. Instantly Hunt recognized it as *Eesekkalion's*. The girl's face twisted into a wicked smile, her eyes turned dark and vicious.

"What have you done to her?" Hunt demanded, doubling the force of his grip to hold the foul being's victim in place.

"Nothing that cannot be undone," he replied. "But know this: her mind is balanced on the edge of a knife. One tiny…little…twist," the evil voice said, savoring every syllable, "and she'll be a vegetable for the rest of her days. No, less than that," he corrected himself. "An empty shell.

I'll destroy every last trace of personality, both her own and those that have been implanted in her."

"What do you want?" Wellesley asked.

"She really *is* a remarkable creature," *Eesekkalion* continued. "So vacuous, so *moldable*! She's like clay, just waiting to be reshaped into another form. Such a contrast to you, isn't she?"

"Get to the point," Hunt snapped.

"Feel like you're losing control of the situation, Rex?" the being taunted. "But you should be used to that by now. You've never really been in control of anything from the moment you fell in with Ugo Udris and his band of idealists. You've bounced from one master to the next, until, finally, you do Krancis' bidding. You left your love behind on, what do you call it?" he paused, the girl's eyes rolling back in her head as he searched for the memory. "Ah, Omega Station. You left her behind on Omega Station because he wanted you to."

"Is there, you know, a *point* to all this?" asked Wellesley, trying to antagonize the ancient intelligence. "Or are you just in love with the sound of your own voice?"

"Your people will never know safety in this galaxy, *Kol-Prockian*," *Eesekkalion* sneered. "Their pathetic remnants will die out in Quarlac, no matter how well they hide themselves. The *Pho'Sath* are searching for them daily. And you know their powers all too well to be glib about that."

Suddenly Soliana's eyes went wide, and the darkness retreated from them into the back of her mind. With a gasp she looked at Hunt, who removed his hands and allowed her to sit up again.

"Are you alright?" he asked.

Without a word she threw her arms around him, her body quivering.

"It was horrible!" she said in an earnest whisper, as though afraid that it might hear her. "I was paralyzed, frozen! I could hear and see everything that he did. But I couldn't control myself. I was a prisoner in my own body!"

Before Hunt could respond the door opened. Expecting to see the front desk nurse, he was surprised to see Krancis in the doorway.

"Him," she said, wagging her finger at the mysterious man as he closed the door and joined them. "Above all, *Eesekkalion* fears him."

"As well he should," Krancis replied factually, no hint of bragging in his voice. "I'm the only one who can destroy him for good."

"Then you *knew* about all this?" Hunt asked, wishing to stand up and confront the man but held back by Soliana's arms.

"I *suspected* this," he stipulated, walking to the other side of the bed and leaning back against the wall. "Just as the planet shattered, there was an energy discharge. Not the wave of dark energy that leveled the Devourer fleets, but a smaller, subtler one. It moved through *Sentinel's* systems in a flash and then vanished. *Esiluria* informed me about it after the fact, having sensed it in passing. But after an extensive search by both her and our engineers, nothing could be found. The energy had to go somewhere, since it clearly hadn't dissipated in the system, since our instruments would have detected it." He crossed his arms and looked down at the bewildered young woman. "I therefore suspected that it, whatever it was, had passed into you."

"And you left me to suffer his will?" she asked in an agonized voice.

"What was I to do?" Krancis countered. "I had to be certain by allowing him to manifest himself, and that would only happen if he felt safe from interference. Safe from *me*. Neither Rex, nor anyone else aboard this ship can possibly threaten him. He knows that I have the power to destroy him, once and for all. But that is only possible if I can catch hold of the thread of his memory that floats in your mind. That couldn't be done before now, because he was too well hidden. It would have been like searching this entire room for a speck of dust. But now there will be a trace of him that I can follow. Expunging him from your psyche will be a simple matter."

"But...how is such a thing even *possible*?" she asked, continuing to clutch Rex as though her life depended on keeping him near. "We saw the dark world destroyed! This vessel's mighty cannon shattered it into a billion pieces. It *couldn't* have survived that."

"It didn't," Krancis replied. "Not actually. What's lodged in you is only a fragment, a tiny memory shard of his overall consciousness. Naturally, a shard from something that size will be correspondingly huge. But you mustn't think that you're carrying *Eesekkalion* around with you at this very moment. What you have is a snapshot, a mere slice. It is filled with malicious intent, and indeed could do great harm if it wasn't about to be extracted. But it's only a shadow of its former self, a caricature."

"It said it would destroy her personality if we tried anything," Hunt cautioned, as Krancis approached her bed.

"If *you* tried anything," Krancis specified. "But not me. Now, take your arms off him," he said to Soliana, "and lean back. Don't be afraid," he added, as she eyed him doubtfully. "This will all be over in a couple of minutes. And then you'll never have to worry about that foul being again. Nobody will."

Fearfully she looked at him, and then turned to Hunt for confirmation. With a frown he nodded.

"Do it, Soliana," he said, gently grasping her wrists and disentangling her. Leaning back slowly, she looked between the two men before settling on Krancis.

"This is going to be terrifying for you," he explained, as he took a seat on the bed and reached for her temples with his long, thin fingers. "The essence that's lodged in you will have to be drawn up like a poison before it can be dissipated and destroyed."

"You mean it will control me again?" she asked, her body beginning to tremble at the thought. "I-I don't think I can–"

Without a moment's hesitation he placed his fingers on her temples and began to exert his powers. Instantly her eyes shut, her consciousness pushed aside.

"Hey!" exclaimed Hunt, about to grab his wrists and pull his hands off.

"If you value her life and sanity, you'll leave me alone," Krancis said factually, breaking his concentration on her for a moment to drive his point home. "I'm the only chance she has, and there isn't a second to lose." He watched as Hunt wrestled with himself before finally nodding. "Thank you," he said perfunctorily, turning his gaze back to the girl and closing his eyes. In less than half a minute she began to shake.

"Do you *really* believe you can take this body from me?" *Eesekkalion's* voice thundered from her unconscious lips. "That is beyond even you, Krancis." The girl's eyelids flashed open, and in place of her pretty eyes were the dark orbs from before. "There is great darkness in me; too great to be overcome by your likes, Krancis. Or should I say..." his voice trailed, as Soliana's eyes rolled back in her head again, "Jannik. Yes, *Jannik*. That's your true name, isn't it? But not just your name: your identity, your self, your *soul*! The sign of a life abandoned and gone. Ah, not merely gone: destroyed, obliterated."

Instantly the girl's body jerked back against the bed, and *Eesekkalion's* deep, otherworldly voice bellowed in pain.

"What are you doing?" he asked in terror, as the darkness began to fade from Soliana's eyes. "That's not possible. No being has the power to overcome my will!" He growled. "If...you attempt to remove me..." he said in quick, pained gasps. "I will take her mind with me! I will extract *her* like juice from a piece of fruit, leaving only the husk. And then, to destroy me, you shall have to destroy *her* as well!"

"No," Krancis said, shaking his head. "That's where you're wrong."

Tremblingly the girl began to move on the bed. Rex reached over to hold her down, but she was strengthened many times by the dark being's consciousness and fought his grasp. Desperately her hands reached for Krancis' throat while he calmly continued his work. Unable to hold her back, Rex threw himself atop her, fighting her arms under his chest and holding them down with everything he had. Desperately she snarled, trying to bite at him but unable to move her head because of the effect Krancis was exerting there.

"I will destroy her mind!" *Eesekkalion* roared, as Soliana's body struggled under Hunt's weight. "I will destroy her soul!"

"No," Krancis uttered, "you won't."

With this the girl's body tensed one more time and then went limp. The beeping of the machines, which up until then had been going at a furious pace, finally began to calm. Doubtfully Hunt looked between Soliana's unconscious face and that of Krancis beside him.

"It's alright," he assured him, leaning back and taking a deep breath before continuing. "He's gone. He can't hurt her anymore."

Hesitantly Hunt released her hands, ready to grab them again in case it was a trick. When she continued to lay still, he moved into a kneeling position and then climbed off the bed.

"She's going to rest for a while now," Krancis said, standing up and walking around to the door. "We'd better go. We can't do anything more for her."

Opening the door, he stood and waited for Hunt to join him. The younger man watched Soliana for a few moments, and then passed through the doorway into the corridor. He was surprised to see what looked like half the hospital's staff waiting for them anxiously. At that moment he realized that all of *Eesekkalion's* bellowing must have been audible from one end of the medical bay to the other.

"You can go in and tend to her now," Krancis informed them, leaving the door ajar. "She's been through quite an experience, but she'll be alright. Just monitor her condition and let me know if anything changes."

"Yes, Krancis," doctor Pryce said, before turning to the rest who had gathered. "Alright, people: back to work. The show's over."

"Come with me, Rex," Krancis said in a low voice, as the others began to disperse. "I've got something to explain to you."

Minutes later they were in his room. Without ceremony he dropped into one of his chairs and rubbed his face.

"I don't mind admitting that that was one of the most draining experiences I've ever had," he uttered, after half a minute had passed. "It's not often that one has to extract such an essence. Twice I nearly lost her." He wiped the back of his hand across his mouth and looked over to Hunt, who hadn't moved from the door since entering. "I imagine you'll hold that fact against me, railing about how I shouldn't have taken chances with her life and sanity."

"No, you did what was necessary," Hunt replied simply, leaning against the doorway and looking at him.

"Surprise, surprise," Krancis said in an exhausted tone, his usual balance temporarily effaced. "Thanks, by the way," he added. "I couldn't have finished if you hadn't held her down. That's when *Eesekkalion* got desperate. If I'd been forced to break contact then to peel her hands off my neck, he could have destroyed her."

"You're welcome," Hunt said, moving into the room and sitting on the armrest of a large padded chair. He eyed the mysterious man for a few moments, his exhaustion striking him oddly, though he couldn't define why. Then it struck him. "You really care about that girl, don't you?"

"Is that such a surprise?" Krancis asked, leaning back in his seat and closing his eyes. "You can't do the things I've done without being capable of feeling."

"Then why do you ride me about it all the time?"

"Because your feelings have an unfortunate tendency to diffuse your efforts and distract your mind. You have an instinct for lost causes – hopeless cases. Perhaps that's a good thing, considering the situation we're in," he reflected, opening his eyes for a couple seconds and searching the ceiling as he thought. Then he closed them again.

"And your feelings have never gotten in the way of the 'grand mission' you've chosen for yourself?" Hunt shot back, crossing his arms.

"Once," he replied quietly, his tone sincere and regretful. "Only once."

Hunt uncrossed his arms and looked down, feeling ashamed for the barb he'd just thrown. Yet his aversion for the man was too great for him to apologize, so he gave the air a little time to clear and then changed topics.

"Do you think Soliana will be alright now?"

"Oh, sure," Krancis replied with certainty. "Every last drop of that foul being has been drained out of her. She doesn't need to fear him ever again."

Suddenly a thought struck Hunt, making him sit a little more straight on the armrest.

"Could she have any *other* memories like that lodged in her?"

"Most likely," he replied. "She's like a sponge for powerful psychic influences." He opened his eyes and looked at Hunt. "What, you've only thought of this possibility now?"

"Well, it's not *my* job to know everything," Hunt replied, a backhanded compliment being as close as he could get to acknowledging Krancis' talents in his presence.

"Yes, I suppose we're both tuned to our own specific purpose," he replied, yet again closing his eyes. "Fashioned by destiny. This war will make us heroes, Rex. It already has, in fact. It simply remains to be seen if anyone will survive to remember."

"And that matters to you?"

"Not in the least. I'm no public man, and I've never wished for the adulation of the multitude. I simply want to preserve my people through the present crisis, and then quietly evaporate into the ether."

"That's not much of a future," Hunt replied.

"Indeed," Krancis said reflectively, his thoughts far away as he spoke. Then he returned. "You'd best prepare to leave. *Sentinel* shouldn't hold this course any longer. We need to drop you off and head back to where we can do some good."

"Alright," Hunt said, pushing off the armrest and making for the door. Halfway to it he stopped. "What was *Eesekkalion* talking about when he mentioned your other name?"

"Something that doesn't exist anymore," the man in black replied, his eyes shooting open and fixing on Hunt. "Something that need not concern anyone."

"Clearly it concerns you," Hunt observed. "And it concerned him. He thought he had you over some kind of barrel by sniffing out that you used to be called Jannik. Why is that so important?"

Slowly Krancis arose and moved on tired legs toward the younger man, stopping a couple of feet short.

"I told you never to speak of that again," he insisted, his voice low, almost threatening.

"I can't help it if it gets thrown in my face," Hunt countered. "*Eesekkalion* would have trumpeted it from the rooftops if he'd had the opportunity. You're just lucky that he didn't mention it loud enough for all the medical staff in the hallway to hear. Face it: this *isn't* the best kept secret in the world. So why all the tension over it?"

"Would you call your attachment to Doctor Tselitel, and the feelings it excites in you, *tension*?" he asked with studied calmness.

"No," Hunt replied.

"Then you have *some* idea of the importance of this

matter to me," he said, nodding towards the door. "Now, I suggest you proceed with your mission."

"Alright," he said, his tone resentful. At the door he paused, looking back one more time as he put his hand on the knob. "Keep a good eye on her."

"Well, *that* was interesting," Wellesley opined as they moved down the hallway. "Never thought the old boy would let his guard down."

"He was just tired," Hunt replied. "It's not some kind of breakthrough."

"Oh, but it is," the AI replied with energy. "You didn't just work with him: you saved his neck, quite literally. That's not the sort of thing that a man like Krancis forgets. Of course, he'll still throw you into a ditch in a hot second if it serves his purpose. But outside of a situation like that, I'd say you've made a friend."

"And *I'd* say your gears are getting rusty. He and I will never be friends. We're like oil and water."

"No, you're a lot more alike than you realize. That's really the trouble, you know. You're both so similar that you can't tolerate the almost mirror image you present. He beats on your emotionality because he's got the same problem, though he's managed to contain it better. You both represent the same psychological principle, just expressed to different degrees. He's learned to regulate and channel the emotional energy that surges through him, while you tend to let it spill out where it wants to. But you're both teeming with a rich, devoted feeling world that is decisive for you. That's why he can be so mercilessly cold: the strength of his attachment gives him the strength to cut off every objection to the course he's taking, even those raised by his own conscience."

"And you're saying *I'm* like that?" he asked, nearing a teleportation room.

"Yeah, but you're not so finely tuned. That's what makes you look so different, superficially. He's a rarefied spirit compared to you, and you're a savage compared to him.

But it's for exactly the same reason: you're both motivated by an emotional center that, in your case, spreads you out; and in his case, makes him hyper focused. He's like you, just defined, *refined*, and concentrated."

Hunt said no more. Deep in the back of his mind, he suspected the AI was right. It made him think of the comparison between Maximilian and himself, although in that case the roles were reversed, and *he* was the more developed, the more finely-tuned, of the two. At that moment the idea disturbed him, the historical precedent lending it further weight and pushing it closer to acceptance. Maybe he really *did* exist on a sort of spectrum along with Krancis, and he was the more primitive of the two, the less developed and evolved. Such notions had gone through his mind before, but always as mental specters, and never as anything that approached what he actually thought. Suddenly the comparison with his father had made it seem likely.

With this in mind he teleported to the hangar, where Pinchon and Gromyko were waiting for him.

"My friend! What took you so long? We've been waiting ages for you."

"Soliana had another episode," Hunt replied, looking at the ship and then the colonel. "All ready?"

"More or less," Pinchon replied, leaning against the egg as he worked his teeth with a small pick. He nodded to the smuggler beside him. "The Hope of the People here wants to go along."

"Of course! I'll go crazy cooped up inside *Sentinel*! I need the open air in my lungs, the broad vistas of *freedom*, if I am to survive." He gestured to the walls around them. "These metal confines will be the death of me! And with all of you gone, who shall I talk to? What shall I *do* with myself?"

"Play cards?" Pinchon offered, enjoying the smuggler's discomfort.

"Bah! I am not a solitary man! I need to mingle! To

feel the air around me filled with the souls of others! Besides, you're taking *him* along, aren't you?" he asked, pointing to Pinchon.

"The colonel's a better pilot than I am," Hunt deflected.

"And these ships can practically fly themselves, from what I hear!" the smuggler retorted. "The *Keesh'Forbandai* are excellent engineers! Admit it, you simply don't want me along!"

"Alright, as a matter of fact, I don't," Hunt said, dropping his voice and drawing close to spare his friend as much embarrassment as possible. "Face it, Antonin: this isn't the kind of environment for you. It's going to take skill and precision to pull this off, not to mention experience. I've squared off against the *Pho'Sath* once, and I know I can do it again. The colonel here may be all kinds of help when working with the resistance, given his background. But you–"

"I've got *plenty* of experience dealing with rebels and renegades!" Gromyko exclaimed, his volume drawing the attention of half the hangar to his somewhat unlaudable claim. "Anything this pirate can do, I can do just as well," he added in a slightly lower voice, when he noticed the multitude of eyes upon him.

"You're not going, Antonin," Hunt said, his tone dropping as he pushed past the smuggler and climbed up into the ship. "Are you ready, Colonel?"

"Yep," Pinchon nodded, tossing aside his pick and climbing in after him.

"Fine friend!" Gromyko shouted, before turning and striding out of the hangar.

"He'll get over it," Wellesley opined over the ship's speakers. "By the time we're back he won't even remember it. He's got the memory of a fly for things like this."

"Either way, it was the right call," Pinchon said, dropping the canopy and firing up the ship. "Radio the captain to drop us out of warp, will you, Wellesley?"

"On it."

Once the massive ship had reentered normal space, the colonel guided the egg out of the hangar and flew to a safe distance. Before he had a chance to warp himself, an enormous dark rift was torn in space ahead of the warship and swallowed it up.

"Didn't waste any time, did they?" he asked as the rift closed.

Within moments a much smaller warp hole opened in front of the egg, likewise carrying it to another dimension.

"And now we wait," he said, unfastening his harness and leaning back in his seat with a sigh. "Now that we're alone," he added after a couple of minutes, "would you mind telling me why you were so bent on keeping the smuggler out of this? I know why *I* didn't want him along. But I didn't figure you would be so determined about it."

"Next to Wells, he's the last friend I have from the old days on Delta," Hunt replied. "If anything happened to him, almost that whole chapter of my life would be gone forever."

"Makes sense," the colonel nodded. "Guess I'd feel the same way, if all my associates weren't more or less the underbelly of this galaxy. Traveled in different circles, that's for sure."

"Yeah," Hunt replied without interest, his mind drifting back to the conversation he'd had earlier with Wellesley. "Why did you call him the old boy earlier?"

"I…didn't?" Pinchon said, searching his memory.

"No, I meant Wellesley," Hunt clarified. "He called Krancis 'the old boy.' Why? He's not that old. He looks like he's around forty."

"Well, that's something that I've been waiting to mention," he replied quietly. "Remember when you and he were both touching Soliana at the same time?"

"Yeah?"

"Well, I *might* have taken the opportunity to scan his

body."

Both Hunt's and Pinchon's faces flushed at this admission, and they simultaneously hoped that there wasn't any kind of recording equipment in the ship that would eventually acquaint Krancis with the AI's action.

"Are you out of your mind?" the colonel asked after a few stunned seconds had passed. "I'm not a big fan of Krancis. I've made no secret of that. But I know a dangerous man when I see him, especially one who values his privacy. He'd throw you into the nearest black hole if he found out."

"Then I suppose you'd both better keep this between us, eh?" Wellesley said with a confidence that bordered on recklessness. "What are you two worried about anyway? It's just a little scan. It's not like I read his mind."

"I don't think that distinction would matter to him very much," Hunt replied.

"Well, what's done is done. And whilst there wasn't a *lot* I could gather from him, I did discover one interesting little tidbit."

"What's that?" Hunt asked, not sure he wanted to know.

"Your forty or fifty estimate is just a little wide of the mark."

"How wide?" inquired Pinchon. "Five, ten years?"

"Mm, close. Try about sixty."

"He looks good for sixty," the colonel said, eyeing his own reflection on the canopy and wishing he didn't show the miles gone by quite so vividly.

"No, you misunderstand," the AI uttered. "You have to *add* sixty years. I'd say he's about one-hundred and thirteen years old."

"What!?" exclaimed both men at once.

"Naturally there's a certain amount of room for error," Wellesley added. "He's a very different kind of human. Recognizably Earthborn, but...different. It's possible that the various markers that I analyzed have been slightly misinterpreted."

"By how wide of a margin?" asked Hunt, his head spinning.

"Oh, six, maybe seven years at the outside. It can be difficult to be exact in a matter like this, not knowing his background at all. It would be easier to nail him down to an exact number if I knew everything he'd been through, especially any medical treatments that might have aged him in peculiar ways. But I have no doubt that he's at least over a hundred."

"How's that even *possible*?" Pinchon asked. "He looks younger than *I* do. Honestly, I'd figure him more around Rex's age, except his bearing implies he's a lot older. But *that* old..." his voice trailed.

"It's a strange, strange universe we live in, my friends," Wellesley commented, as they both tried to come to terms with this new revelation.

"Then how come he hasn't crumbled to dust already?" the colonel objected. "How could he live that long? I mean, sure, there's all this talk about medical tech halting diseases and whatnot. But he's not hooked up to *anything*. He just ambles around like the rest of us. Although, he *doesn't* ever seem to sleep..." his voice trailed again as he thought.

"He's got quite a relationship with the dark realm," the AI explained. "I could detect the effect of its presence all throughout his body."

"So it's sustaining him like some kind of battery?" Pinchon asked.

"It seems like it. Admittedly this is new turf for me, so some of the data is hard to parse. Besides, I was never a *medical* AI, anyway. Someone with more expertise in this field could probably tell us more. Not that I'd hand this information out, however."

"What, are you suddenly feeling respectful of his privacy?" Pinchon laughed. "Isn't that a little late, given you've already scanned him?"

"The guy is pretty finicky about his background, and I figure it's for a good reason. Maybe the *Pho'Sath* could use this information to attack him. You know, work out his background and threaten his loved ones, or something? Until now he's been exquisitely independent of any possibility of extortion. Nobody's been able to bring any pressure on him at all. That might change if this data got into the wrong hands."

"You're right, Wells," Hunt agreed.

"So what'd you scan him for, then?" the colonel asked. "Seems like you should have left well enough alone, if this info could be used as a weapon."

"Curiosity got the better of me," he admitted with a hint of embarrassment. "It doesn't happen to just you organics, you know," he added. "Lacking any *meaningful* physical form, I have to get my giggles out of the lives and actions of others. My only real participation in life is vicarious, and that sometimes makes me nosy."

"I'm sure our lord and master would love to hear that," Pinchon uttered.

"So it'll be our secret, then," Hunt said. "Just the three of us."

"And what about the AI aboard this egg?" the colonel asked, only then remembering it.

"Don't worry," Wellesley replied. "I've already taken care of it. Doesn't know a thing."

"Good," Hunt nodded, still coming to grips with what he'd heard. "Very good."

❖ ❖ ❖

Mafalda Aboltina and Bo McCloud waited in the living room of a shattered, broken down old house. It had been the scene of an assassination many years before, a bomb having been thrown threw the window at a gathering of underworld luminaries. Since then, nobody had had the slightest reason to clean it up or tear it down. Rain poured through the cracked roof and shattered windows every time it stormed, leaving the wood rotten, soft, and covered with mold. A terrible stench filled the air, though Mafalda was surprised she could even smell it, after her sojourn in the abandoned apartment complex. The air was humid, close, stultifying – like a swamp that had been somehow moved indoors.

She tried to be patient. Crouching beside McCloud in a corner, as far from the street as the room allowed, she rocked on her heels. Her one consolation in the midst of such filth was that the boards beneath her were too mushy to creak.

An hour had passed, and then two, but there was no sign of their contact. They said nothing, not wishing to risk being overheard. They just occasionally stood up to get the cramps out of their legs before squatting down once more to keep as low a profile as possible.

Suddenly a face appeared before one of the broken windows, and Mafalda inaudibly gasped. She was about to stand up when McCloud silently put a hand on her arm to restrain her. Trying to find his blue eyes in the darkness, she could make out only a blurry, spectral outline. She looked back at the face in the street. It looked like a man, but could have been a particularly stocky woman. Squinting in the gloom, she tried to work out his physiognomy. But then he turned and shambled rightward down the street, his aimless, shuffling stride indicating at once that he was just one of the city's many beggars.

With a sigh she thanked her lucky stars that she'd kept her mouth shut. They couldn't afford to draw any attention to themselves. Even a hint that their presence had been detected mandated calling off the operation. And she couldn't have that. She *wouldn't* have that. Above all else she wanted to strike a meaningful blow against those she had served for so long, to redeem even a portion of the life she'd spent undermining the empire.

And nothing would answer that purpose so perfectly as helping the Dread Phantoms assassinate *Deldrach*.

For another hour they waited, until her legs burned and begged her to move. It was almost more than she could stand when yet another face appeared before the window. Again it arrested her attention, and she stared at the dark outline for several moments to try and make it out. She was sure it would move on like the other one had when she heard the figure's tongue click twice. There was a pause, during which she didn't breathe. After precisely twelve seconds the tongue clicked twice again, and McCloud stood up beside her.

She stood up as well, and nearly fell over because her legs were nearly numb. Nearly falling against Bo, he caught her and held her steady for a few seconds, letting the blood flow back down into her feet again. Then they both joined the figure by the window.

"Sorry I'm late," a woman said, addressing McCloud. "They're prowling the streets tonight like rats hunting a piece of cheese. They must have gotten word that something is in the wind."

"Is the operation off?" McCloud asked, making Mafalda's heart jump into her throat with dread at the thought.

"No," the woman replied hesitantly. "We're still on. We can't let *Deldrach* get out of our clutches. Word is he plans to head out soon, moving to another planet."

"No!" Mafalda said earnestly, fearful that her chance would be taken from her.

The woman looked at her for a second. The darkness hid her expression, but Mafalda felt an unfriendly aura coming off her. Then she turned back to McCloud.

"We're still scattered around the city, trying to form up. With all the separatists on the street, our guys haven't been able to move hardly at all. But there's still a chance–."

Pausing, she jerked her head sharply over her right shoulder, searching the darkness.

"We can't talk like this anymore," she whispered urgently. "Get out of there and follow me. Quickly."

Without making a sound they clambered out of the bombed out house, slipping onto the street and falling in behind their guide. With cat-like deftness she led them along the dark street, ducking into alleys and empty buildings whenever she could. After nearly an hour of careful, tense movement, she stopped and leaned against a brick wall.

"We're close," she uttered quietly, catching her breath. "Very close. But, so are they," she said ominously.

Having had a chance to see her in motion, Mafalda realized that the woman was very much older than she was. At least sixty, she thought, given the stiffness of her movements and the fatigue she'd suffered. It made her wonder how hard up the Dread Phantoms were for recruits, if they had to send a woman like her out to guide them in the night.

"Another ten, fifteen minutes," she continued, before pausing for breath. "Not more than that."

Without another word she took off again, determined to reach the rendezvous. The night was heavy, overcast, constantly threatening to rain. Mafalda's clothes stuck to her body, and the lack of any breeze made her hot and uncomfortable. A stench arose from the refuse all around them, activated by the humidity in the air.

Without warning her foot slipped out from under her, and she fell to the hard pavement. With a twist she landed on her side, the blow squeezing the air from her lungs and making a loud wheeze escape her lips. Sharply the woman stopped and turned around, dragging her to her feet before Bo even had a chance to move.

"Be *silent*, stupid girl!" she whispered sharply in her ear. Angrily she pushed the younger woman out of her grasp and resumed her steps. She moved quickly, trying to leave the scene behind in case someone had heard.

As her side began to throb from the blow, Mafalda

felt her spirit shrinking within her. It wasn't just the organization that disliked her: clearly the Dread Phantoms had their own aversion as well. Her heart began to ache at the thought.

Somehow aware of this, McCloud reached out a hand and patted her back as they moved. She appreciated the gesture, but the knowledge that he would likely be forced to break with her, given his affiliation with both the organization *and* the Phantoms, blunted its impact. After all, given the universal scorn with which she was treated, how could either organization tolerate any one of their members spending more than the minimum time possible with her? And even if Bo *did* go against their wishes, that would only damage him in their eyes, and she couldn't let him do that.

With these heavy thoughts on her mind, she slipped through the night with her companions, finally stopping at the edge of town. With a light hand she grasped Bo's jacket and pulled him close. She did the same with Mafalda, though her motion was much rougher, dragging her nearly off her feet.

"*Deldrach* is overseeing operations from a house just north of here," she whispered in their ears. "Near the end of the old logging road. You know where that is?"

They both nodded, their silhouettes barely visible against the cloudy sky.

"Alright. Just stick on this road and you'll be met halfway along it by any of the others who've managed to make it. Be careful, and be *quiet*," she said, this last word pointedly directed at Mafalda. "There's no margin for error. One of you slips up, and everybody dies."

"Aren't you coming with us?" Mafalda asked, concerned to lose her expert guidance in the dark, despite her hostility.

"I can't be any help to you now," she replied gruffly, before looking at McCloud. "Good luck, dear boy," she added, kissing his forehead before vanishing into the darkness between them and the city.

"Old friend of the family," Bo explained once she'd gone. "She thinks she's my mother, or something."

"It's pretty clear what she thinks of me," Mafalda murmured, regretting the words once they were out of her mouth. Resolutely she shook her head, trying to set her personal feelings aside to focus on the mission. "I'm sorry, that was silly."

"It doesn't matter what they think," Bo replied, gesturing towards town. "What matters is what *you* think."

"If that's true, then I'm a goner," Mafalda thought, though she managed to bite her tongue before she said it. "You're right, of course," she nodded, trying to sound as bright as she could. "We'd better get a move on. The others are waiting."

"Come on," McCloud nodded, taking her hand and trotting silently into the forest.

The night was lively, organic, almost festering around them. There was excitement in the trees along the road, as though the entire animal kingdom was on high alert for some impending event. Birds chirped in the night, bats swooped low over their heads, and a thousand varieties of insect emitted their strange calls to one another. It made her anxious, the noise playing upon her already excited nervous system. At least nobody would hear them coming, she reflected.

But that wasn't all that was on her mind. Bo's hand wrapped around hers was an unpleasant reminder that he was smitten with her, a fact that had been made abundantly clear during their stay in the apartments. He'd refused to leave her, even for a moment, and she was sure it had made him miss at least two appointments with both the Phantoms and the broader organization. She knew that their association must come to an end if he wasn't to damage his relations with either group, but that the come down would be hard. Better to end it quickly, before his feelings had a chance to grow any further. Once *Deldrach* was dead, she would tell him.

Half an hour up the road, and they were stopped by a strange call. It sounded like a bird, more or less. But it was focused, intentional, a signal instead of a mere random sound broadcast by a half-intelligent bit of birdflesh. Drawing Mafalda into the trees after him, Bo waited a few seconds and then made a little chirping sound. It so perfectly mimicked the bird it was based on that Mafalda half thought one had swooped down and landed next to them. In a second he made the sound again, and then she was certain he had made it.

The call was repeated, and McCloud pulled her deeper into the forest. It was impenetrably dark, and despite the matter of his growing feelings, she was glad to have his hand to guide her through the brush. Having spent very little time in the woods at night, she was about as lost as she could get.

"Stop," a male voice insisted off to her left, loud enough to make her jump and pull on McCloud's hand. "We've been waiting for you," he continued, his voice indicating he was around her age.

"Hi, Lucius," McCloud said, reaching out his hand in the darkness and somehow finding that of his friend. "Mafalda, this is Lucius Barrow."

"Glad to know you," she replied, extending her own hand which was ignored.

"Have you seen any of the others?" Barrow asked McCloud, as Mafalda lowered her hand and told herself the fiction that he simply hadn't seen it in the darkness. "I've got three with me now, waiting a little way up the road. I wanted to nail you before you reached the rest of us, just in case I goofed and called a Fringer towards us instead."

"No, I haven't," McCloud shook his head. "Regina said that they're scattered around the city, trying to get out. But the Fringers are watching the place like a hawk." He paused and looked up at the sky as well as he could through the foliage. "It's getting pretty late. I think we may have to go ahead with the numbers we've got. We can't afford to let him get out of our grasp now, not when we've come so close."

"That won't matter if we hit him when we're too weak to make it count," Barrow countered. "This guy is the big banana, don't forget. He makes that chick that Welter took down a while ago look like a kitten."

"I think you're exaggerating just a bit, Lucius," McCloud replied.

"Not that much."

"Anyway, we've got Mafalda to guide us to him," Bo continued. "And with our powers, and the Midnight Blade, we'll take him down for sure."

"Lucky us," Barrow said sarcastically, Mafalda feeling his critical eyes on her in the darkness. "Well, come on. I'll take you to the others."

Moving slowly through the brush, Barrow led them deeper into the forest. Thorn bushes and dry, dead sticks scratched at her, drawing blood here and there as she moved blindly through them. Soon they stopped, and Barrow and McCloud squatted down near a trio of almost invisible dark shapes.

"Hi, guys," Bo whispered, shaking hands and exchanging brief greetings.

"Where are the others?" a female voice asked, a little older than Mafalda.

"No idea," McCloud replied. "Probably back in Biryth."

"Then what do we do?" she continued. "We can't wait here all night."

"That's what I was thinking," McCloud replied.

"He wants to go off half-cocked," Barrow interjected. "I say no."

"It's not up to you, Lucius," a much older man replied from the darkness behind them, making them jump. He was a tall man, and the two people who flanked him looked almost like children beside him. Mafalda thought he must have been almost seven feet tall. His eyes rolled over to her, and despite the gloom she was surprised to find them visible. They glowed, ever so faintly, and revealed the trail his gaze left up and down her body. "You're Aboltina," he said, his deep voice rumbling like the soul of some ancient tree.

"Yes, sir," she replied.

"All told, we make nine," he observed, looking the nearly invisible group over, a hint of reluctance in his voice.

"Is that enough?" she asked, surprised to hear the words leave her lips as she spoke. But something about the man put her, not at *ease*, but in a state of calmness. She felt that he was critically evaluating her, and that his judgment would be swift and harsh if he felt she got even a hair's breadth out of line with the Phantom's goals. But for all that he presented an aura of fairness, of stability and coolness that ran counter to the hasty prejudice with which the others readily pushed her aside. Here, at least, was a man who would let her prove herself before he made up his mind.

"It may be," he replied quietly. "Provided we each give it everything we have." He stepped into the middle of the group and slowly turned around, each of them feeling his searching gaze. "I'm not going to lie to any of you: not all of us are going to make it through this. The odds are simply against it. Ideally we'd have at least twelve to throw against him, but that has proven impossible. I could only round up two others on my way here, and the rest have been hopelessly delayed or forced to abort. We're on our own from this point on, utterly dependent on each other." He paused and searched them again, before letting his eyes stop on Mafalda. "There's an outsider among us tonight. But for this mission she's just as much one of you as I am. We can't afford hesitation or distrust of each other. She's taken an awful risk in coming over to us, and that at least should be counted in her favor. Remember, further, that she has more to lose from this operation than any of you. They'll torture you for information if you're captured," he explained, looking at them before again settling on Mafalda. "But she'll have her mind and body peeled back, layer by layer, if she falls into their hands. They do not tolerate defection, especially from someone who'd been so highly placed. They make an example out of her. Of that you may rest assured."

The man paused for a few seconds to let his word sink in. Mafalda could hear feet shifting in the darkness as self-consciousness came over the group. It wasn't that the man was rebuking them. He understood their feelings and didn't expect them to change. But for one night, at least, they had to put aside their personal sentiments and place themselves in the hands of one they had long since learned to hate. They felt both humiliated at their lack of professional detachment, and humiliated to be led into a separatist hideout by a woman any of them would have been glad to eliminate just a few weeks before. Their feelings were jumbled and confused, and Mafalda hoped that whatever she could bring to the table would be worth the price she was already costing them in terms of cohesion and trust.

"What is the plan, then, Nikolay?" an older woman asked, breaking the silence.

"I have studied the terrain around this hideout intensively," he replied. "But the inside has long been a secret." He looked at Mafalda. "That is your purpose in coming with us. You will lead us directly to the chambers that this foul being inhabits, so that we can promptly kill him."

"And if she betrays us?" the woman asked, agitation growing in her voice as she spoke what so many of them secretly feared. "What better way to redeem herself in their eyes than to lead us into a trap?"

"That will not happen," Nikolay replied. "She's been examined and found pure."

"I'm sure the granddaughter of Ugo Udris has been taught many secrets with which she may deceive the mind of even a powerful psychic," she replied suspiciously, her eyes narrow and accusatory as they contemplated the young woman in the darkness. "To say nothing of the arts she must have learned from her alien masters."

Sporadic murmurs of agreement could be heard from some of the other members of the group, making Mafalda blush and shrink yet further inside herself.

"If any of you doubts the wisdom of this plan," Nikolay said in a voice that was grand despite whispering, "let him depart at once. But," he added, "know that you shall forthwith cease to be a member of the Dread Phantoms. If you are no longer capable of trusting the most potent minds within our ranks, then you are no longer of any use to us. You will have permitted fear and distrust to displace sound judgment and cool reason. If that is the case, then please rid us of your presence at once."

This was heard without comment. After several moments, Nikolay nodded.

"Then let your silence be your answer," he said with finality. "We move out at once."

Wordlessly everyone fell in behind the giant man, following the path that he made through the bushes and trees. Mafalda waited until the rest of the group was ahead of her, and then tacked herself onto the rear. McCloud glanced back several times, wishing to draw near but impeded by the rest of the walkers. The path was narrow, and there was no place to stop.

"Keep your mind on your task, Bo," Nikolay said quietly, his voice carrying only so far as it needed to. "It will take your full concentration to come out of this alive."

With this all conversation ceased. Much like the woman who had guided them before, Nikolay masterfully led his team around patrols and along hidden paths. Mafalda concluded that he possessed a remarkable faculty for perception, one that allowed him to penetrate both the darkness and the foliage that surrounded them. Like a bloodhound following a scent he moved without hesitation, his every step decisive and final.

After a long interval of careful movement, he slowed them to a halt and crouched down.

"The hideout is just beyond this wall of trees," he informed them, pointing over his shoulder at a dense growth. "When we emerge on the other side, we'll make straight for the hideout. We have approximately one hundred feet of open ground to cover, so stay low and follow quickly."

Without another word he made his way through the leafy branches on his hands and feet, pausing just long enough on the other side for the rest to reach him before rising into a half hunch and darting quickly for the hideout. It was a large old house, two stories high and painted white.

Just as before, Mafalda was in the rear. Her heart jumped into her throat when she saw the hideout, recognizing it immediately despite the darkness. She had seen many people tortured there. Indeed, she'd helped the *Pho'Sath* on many occasions, and the memory made her conscience ache. Moreover the sight of the structure brought back the screams, the smells, the *aura* of people tormented in captivity. It added weight to what Nikolay had said before regarding her fate if captured. She knew better than any of them what would happen to her in that eventuality. Long before her death finally came, she would wish she'd never been born. The fear this inspired in her almost made her stop dead in her tracks. But at that exact moment she remembered the fate of Amra Welter, her unconscious forcing the memory to the fore to drive her on. Mafalda knew she had to make her sufferings right. She *had* to carry on, to give back to the *Pho'Sath* at least a fraction of the pain they'd brought to that poor girl.

Trotting quietly after the rest of the group, they all reached the side of the house and paused. Sentries were moving along the fringes of the surrounding forest, completely unaware of their uninvited guests. A handful of lights were scattered around the space, attached to outbuildings and the odd free standing pole. Casting a dim glow, Mafalda was able to make out the faces, more or less, of her companions.

Her eyes fixed on Nikolay's broad, strong face just as he looked at her. With a gesture he indicated that it was now her show, and the rest of the group prepared, with varying degrees of willingness, to follow her inside. Taking a deep and, she hoped, *silent* breath, she led them around the house to the front. Peeking around the wall and seeing no one, she climbed over a low white fence that wrapped around the front porch. The boards creaked as she put her weight on them, making her cringe. Moving right up next to the house so that she stood as close to the board's supports as possible, she managed to work her way to the front door without making a sound.

With sweat beading on her forehead and running down her nose and cheeks, she looked back on the group. They'd followed her example perfectly, stretching out in a line of eight bodies all the way back to the fence. Nikolay, standing first in line, nodded for her to continue.

Beside her was the door. She knew from past visits that it creaked terribly, but only if one opened it normally. Firmly grasping the handle, she used all her strength to lift it up against its hinges as she opened it. This shifted the door's contact points with its hinges just enough that it was all but silent, a little trick she'd picked up once when she'd wanted to slip out for some night air. Holding the door just wide enough for the largest of them to fit through, she informed them through pantomime how it needed to be handled, and then went inside.

The house was all but dark. Straight ahead was a corridor flanked on both sides by rooms. Each of their doors had dim lights shining beneath them, just barely illuminating the path they had to take. Taking off her shoes, she laid them aside and waited for the others to follow suit.

Then she began to walk between the lights, infinitely tense lest a misplaced step should send a noisy creak echoing down the bare wooden walls. At the end of the hall she stopped and turned to the right. A door faced her, one with no light shining under it. Lifting it as she had the prior, she opened it carefully, revealing a spiraling wooden staircase that was only just visible because of a light shining somewhere below. Gesturing for them to take it slow, she placed a socked foot on the top step and began her descent.

This portion of the house had been added more recently, and was of very solid construction. In truth the top of the structure was just a facade, an entry point for a much larger facility that had been carved out of the earth years before. The staircase belonged to this latter portion, and was so robustly built that it didn't creak in the least. Inching her way downward, her ears pricked for the slightest sound from below, she felt almost unable to breathe from the tension. As her head began to swim she was forced to pause, bringing the whole line to a halt. Nikolay sharply poked her in the back with one of his massive fingers, instantly returning her to motion.

Finally they reached the bottom, the cold of the concrete floor seeping through her socks. Ahead stood a door which, like the others, permitted a small amount of light to shine under it. Waiting for the others to make their way down, she approached and pressed her ear against it. Closing her eyes and stilling her breath for a moment, she could hear someone talking in the distance.

"It's okay," she whispered in Nikolay's ear once she'd moved away from the door. "Whoever's talking is in one of the side rooms. The corridor sounds like it's open. I don't hear any noises at all."

Wordlessly he nodded his understanding, indicating for her to continue. With less care than before, since it was relatively new, she opened the door and blinked as the light from the hallway filled her eyes. To her relief she found that her ears hadn't deceived her. Ahead of them stretched a long corridor made of concrete, dotted with thick wooden doors. They belonged to the rooms that the Fringers stayed in. After them they would encounter the cells of whatever prisoners were on hand at the time; small, nasty spaces with hardly any circulating air. And then, after that, *Deldrach's* personal chambers.

Slipping one foot out the open door, she crept into the hallway and moved along the line of doors. The rule, generally, was to close all doors at night, since *Deldrach* liked to walk the facility at times and hated to be observed doing so. It was his desire for privacy that had relegated him to the back of the facility, where the rooms were not in the least comfortable or pleasing to the eye. They had been originally intended as overflow rooms, in case they needed extra space for storage or prisoners. By his order they were made over into crude quarters for his personal use, their remoteness ensuring that foot traffic outside his door would be non-existent.

As she led the way past the closed doors, one of them suddenly opened. Turning sharply, she saw a man filling the doorway, utterly shocked to see Mafalda Aboltina standing in front of him. He was about to open his mouth to raise the alarm when Nikolay clamped a hand over his mouth and simultaneously stabbed him with the Midnight Blade that had been concealed in his jacket. Almost instantly the man was dead, his life extinguished with barely a sound.

Moments later they were in motion again, Mafalda scooting along the hard, silent floor on quick feet. She feared that their luck wouldn't hold for a second unexpected encounter, and wanted to cover the ground between the Fringer's quarters and those of their master as quickly as possible.

Taking a left turn at the end of the corridor, they entered the prison area. Here the doors were more tightly packed together, reflecting the lack of room in each cell.

She slowed a little when she heard a moan from one of the middle cells. But instantly Nikolay's hand was on her back, pushing her onward. There would be time to worry about the prisoners later, once their job was finished.

At the end of the cells they took another left turn, and were immediately faced with a large, imposing door. Just the sight of it was enough to make Mafalda's skin tingle, and she gazed at it for a moment before turning to Nikolay.

"Once through the door, there'll be two rooms on the right," she uttered in as low a voice as she could manage, barely hearing her own words as she cupped her hands around his ear. "Neither have doors. A dim light is always running in the hallway, but the rooms themselves are sometimes dark. It depends on his mood."

Nikolay nodded, and then briefly relayed the gist of her words to the others with the deft use of simple hand signals. Nodding their own understanding, they each prepared themselves for the battle to come.

Moving to the door, the massive man laid a hand on the knob and turned it silently. Looking at the group, he counted down from three with his fingers. On hitting zero, he jerked the door open, held the Midnight Blade high, and charged inside, the others close on his heels.

"So, you have come at last," *Deldrach* said from the first room on the right, as his attackers exploded into view. The lights were on and shining bright, and he sat in his robes in a large chair that was positioned against the back wall. The walls and floor were made of simple concrete like the rest of the facility. The voice of the *Pho'Sath* was deep, yet smooth, cunning, intelligent. His tone was that of one who was master of all he beheld. "But your numbers are too few to complete the task you have set for yourself."

"Your time on this planet is over," Nikolay uttered, stepping ahead of the others into the middle of the room, the Midnight Blade held tightly in his left hand. "This night will see your foul life ended."

"That is where you are mistaken," *Deldrach* replied, rising casually from his chair and towering over them all, even Nikolay. The group reflexively shrank back upon seeing his true stature, which was nearly eight feet. "You should have brought stouter souls with you, *Phantom*," he said, the last word dripping with scorn. "But then, the Earthborn have always been a feeble race, simultaneously held up and down by their neighbors. Your spirits are *weak*," he taunted, taking a step closer and causing them all, save Nikolay, to recede. The enormous being looked down at the dauntless man who stood just a few feet away. "You have signed your own death warrants by coming here."

"No, we have signed *yours*," he replied.

The robed figure raised his masked face towards the others. He searched their ranks for a moment before his gaze finally fell upon Mafalda.

"You have thought, no doubt, that you would redeem your past actions in their eyes by betraying me into their hands," he said. "But you have only delivered them to death."

Hearing this, the spirit of revenge welled up in her and pushed her fears aside. With a shout she charged the massive being, intent on closing the distance and pouring all of her copious powers into him at once, even if it shattered her to do it. But as soon as she was in range, *Deldrach* snapped out the heel of his palm, catching her square in the forehead and sweeping her off her feet. She slammed hard against the concrete, nearly losing consciousness from the blow.

In that brief moment the others charged, trying to gang up on him. Though each of them were psychics with various talents, each had been taught to inflict mental and physical pain through touch. Now they sought to lay hands on him, to paralyze him just long enough for the Blade to be driven into his shell. But in an instant he struck half of them down with his gloved hands, flooring them as he had Mafalda. The others managed to make contact, pouring their powers into him and making him cry out. With a fierce roar he backhanded two away, and dropped the last with a crippling blow to the stomach that audibly broke ribs.

Unable to attack because of the bodies that had recklessly thrown themselves between him and his target, Nikolay finally raised the Blade and thrust it towards *Deldrach's* chest. Seizing the massive man's wrist, he twisted him off balance and threw him against the chair and onto the floor. With a grunt he landed, instantly jumping to his feet for another go. His movements were swift and cat-like despite his size, and he was once again before *Deldrach*.

"You're skillful," the being said, as he dragged one of his assailants to her feet and clenched an enormous hand around her neck. "But consider this: every time you fail to destroy me," he uttered, using his fearful power to dissolve her head and shoulders, "I will kill one of your friends."

With a howl of rage Nikolay charged again, swiping the air to drive *Deldrach* back. Deftly the *Pho'Sath* evaded a pair of thrusts, kicking his attacker in the stomach with such force that his stomach nearly burst.

"Another miss," *Deldrach* taunted, as he crippled two Phantoms who had gotten back on their feet and made another charge for him. Knocking the one unconscious, he seized the other and dissolved him. "Soon they'll all be gone, evaporated like water."

With a grunt Nikolay fought his way upright, blood dripping out of his mouth. The blow had driven every ounce of air from his lungs, and he struggled for breath.

"Why don't you…come and finish me…then?" he growled, crouching guardedly with the Blade held in front of him.

"Why indeed," *Deldrach* replied, stepping over Mafalda.

Feigning unconsciousness until this moment, she seized his back leg as he moved over her, making him stumble. With a shout he fell towards the Midnight Blade, Nikolay seeing his chance and thrusting it forwards. With his great strength he jerked against Mafalda's hold, using her as an anchor to twist around the Blade and crash into his attacker. Both of them fell to the ground, the *Pho'Sath* landing heavily on Nikolay. With a growl he grasped the hand which held the Blade, using his power to dissolve it. With a scream the massive man watched his arm below the elbow disappear, the Blade clattering noisily to the concrete. *Deldrach* grabbed the Blade by the handle, careful not to touch its lethal edge as he arose. Holding it before him, he laughed at his fallen assailants.

"To pin your hopes on a single weapon was reckless," he uttered, dragging one of the Phantoms to his feet and running him through. "You have simply given me another tool with which to destroy you."

Screaming with outrage, Mafalda jumped to her feet and made a final, desperate run for him. But, dazed from the blow she'd received upon striking the ground, he easily evaded her and struck her with a wicked backhand that sent her spiraling to the floor. She struggled to her knees, valiantly trying to rise. But a half-hearted kick from the *Pho'Sath* was all it took to knock her onto her back. Helplessly she panted on the concrete.

"Your team is defeated," *Deldrach* continued, seizing another Phantom and examining her face for a moment before throwing her away and turning to Nikolay. "All that remains is to extract what little information you may have which could be of use to us, and then discard you like the trash you are." Then he paused, angling his giant head down at Mafalda, who lay at his feet. "Except for you," he said, savoring his own words. "You're going to pay a special price for betraying us. Many will be your screams for mercy before you finally perish."

One of the Phantoms struggled to his feet and stood on the other side of Mafalda. To her horror, she realized it was Bo McCloud.

"Do to me whatever you would do to her," he said

bravely, his speech slurred from the blows he'd received. "Just let her go."

"Oh, I'll let her go," *Deldrach* replied, stepping over her and advancing on him as he retreated. "I'll release her energy into the cosmos, disintegrating her. But not before I've broken her mind, her body, and her will. There shall be nothing left save a hollow shell, a husk matching the description of Mafalda Aboltina."

With a yell he charged the being, crashing into his abdomen with a grunt and pushing him back a foot or two. But *Deldrach* grabbed the back of his shirt in his powerful hand and lifted him off his feet, tossing him aside. Like a shot he jumped up, but his balance was shaken and he nearly fell over when a kick from the *Pho'Sath* struck him in the knee, shattering his leg and dropping him with a scream. Scornfully he grasped a handful of his shirt front, pulling him upright as he panted with pain.

"It's time for you to join your ancestors, young *warrior*," he said contemptuously, drawing the Blade back to plunge it into his stomach.

"*Now!*" shouted Nikolay, signaling for the rest of the group to get to their feet and charge with everything they had. All save Mafalda crashed into the *Pho'Sath* as he turned around, carrying him off his feet and forcing him to drop McCloud. With a groan the huge alien struck the wall, his assailants seizing both his wrists in their many hands. They strove to fight the Blade out of his clenched fist. But even their combined strength couldn't overcome his sheer power, and he slowly lowered its edge until it sliced into one of their number, blackening his shoulder and forcing him to let go. Then, one by one, he struck them down, saving Nikolay and McCloud for last.

"You fought better than the rest of them," *Deldrach* said to the huge man as he stood over them both. "Were you not Earthborn, that would entitle you to at least *some* dignity."

With a single blow to the neck he ended him.

"And that leaves you," he said to McCloud, as he struggled to stand before the alien, brave to the last.

"Kill me," he snarled.

"Oh, I will," he said, seizing him by the shirt and carrying him to where Mafalda could see him. "This one cares for you," he taunted her, holding his victim up in his outstretched arm as though he were a mere doll. "For that reason," he continued, dropping McCloud beside her upon the hard concrete and bending over, "he shall be made to die by your hand."

With horror she watched as *Deldrach* took her hand in his powerful grasp and wrapped it around the handle of the Midnight Blade. Recalling what the *Pho'Sath* had made Welter do to his own daughter, she desperately tried to fight him. But she was too weak and battered to resist. Helplessly she was dragged into a kneeling position, held up by the alien's great strength. McCloud lay before her, gasping in pain as his eyes found hers.

"It's...not your fault...Mafalda," he uttered, gulping hard. "You must...believe that."

"I'm sorry," she said pleadingly, shaking her head as tears began to run down her cheeks. "I'm so sorry!"

With this the *Pho'Sath* forced her hand downward, pinning McCloud to the concrete with the Blade. Quickly he turned to shadow, disintegrating into countless shards. Tearfully she fell into his dust. Unable to control herself, her chest convulsed as she loudly began to sob.

"Savor these tearful moments," he *Deldrach* said, seizing her by the back of the neck and lifting her off her feet. "They pale in comparison to what lies ahead."

CHAPTER 4

"How is he doing?" Welter asked Tselitel some twenty hours after their first meeting. Leaning against the computer desk, his arms folded over his chest, his eyes penetrated her. His resolution to remain distant had only strengthened, in her estimation, in the time she'd known him. He was solicitous enough about the emperor, but seemed to regard her with aversion, as though, despite his wishes, she would stop at nothing to get inside his head and peel back every painful layer of his psyche in a compulsive attempt to help. At times he'd been gruff with her, at times indifferent. He spoke without interest to Bessemer, regarding him as little more than an imperial functionary, a sort of errand boy. With effort the willful captain kept his ire to himself, though Tselitel, with her practiced eye, could easily discern how upset he really was.

"He's dropped in and out of consciousness several times in the last few hours," she replied, concern for the ailing emperor aggravating her condition and making her hands tremble and her voice shake. "I don't think we can wait to move him any longer. He needs medical help from the *Kol-Prockians*."

"I agree," Welter replied, breaking eye contact and looking at the floor as he thought. "This station is gonna force us out into the cold, anyhow. I wouldn't want to spend another day here."

THE TIDES OF RETRIBUTION

"I'll try to wake him," she uttered, nodding her agreement and turning for the door.

"Wait," he said, the pointedness of his voice making her stop dead. "There's no point in disturbing him. I'll carry him to the ship as is."

"I don't want him jostled too much," she objected, as he neared her. "We don't really know what's going on inside him."

"Bessemer can help keep him steady," Welter replied. "You can hold his head up."

With effort the three of them got Rhemus into the ship, the hardest part being the moment that they had to hoist him over the side and into his seat. Somehow he didn't awaken despite the occasionally rough treatment with which Welter handled him. Once he was fastened into his seat, he climbed down again.

"This is where we part ways, Captain," Welter announced. "Head for the ship I brought and power up. I'll open the outer door once you give the signal."

"Who's gonna open the door for you two?" Bessemer asked, looking between Welter and Tselitel. It was with reluctance that he contemplated leaving her in the other man's care, especially as her condition visibly worsened. He knew it was the only way to save her life, but it was terribly hard. He'd grown fond of her during their short time together, and felt something like a brother's concern for her wellbeing.

"I'll program the computer to open it up after a few minutes," Welter explained. "It'll be enough time for me to get back in here and ready for takeoff."

"Take care of yourself," Tselitel said to the captain, stepping forward and putting two thin arms around him for a moment. "Thanks for looking after us," she added in a meaningful whisper.

"You're welcome," he replied, his eyes searching Welter as he watched. "Good luck," he said to the latter man,

107

shaking his hand and then heading into the station for his ship.

"Get settled in," Welter told Tselitel over his shoulder, following the captain. "I'll be right back."

With effort she climbed the side of the egg and got into the right rear seat. Even this simple action drained her, and she paused for a few moments to catch her breath. Looking at the emperor, she closed her eyes and muttered a little prayer that they weren't already too late to save him. He'd been so good, so robust during much of the journey that she'd nearly forgotten his condition. But now she feared that he'd been pushing himself too far, burning through his remaining strength to put up a front of normalcy for their benefit. He'd spoken nothing but incoherent sentence fragments in his sleep ever since falling off the bucket the day before. It was a challenge for her not to worry herself sick over him.

Determined to remain as level-headed as she could, for his sake if nothing else, she got herself strapped in and waited for Welter. Several minutes passed before she heard a loud clanging sound that made her jump. It was off to the right, and she immediately realized it was Bessemer's door opening. Ever so faintly she heard his engines light up and rocket away, carrying him off to parts unknown to her.

Another minute ticked by, and then she heard footsteps in the station. Welter appeared in the doorway, his head held low as he moved slowly towards the egg. Climbing up the side without a word, he powered up the ship, lowered the canopy, and waited.

She knew she could trust him. After all, like she'd said to Bessemer, Krancis himself had chosen him for the task. But the captain's words of warning wouldn't leave her mind. They combined with her own observations to paint a picture of a man in a poor state of mental health. Whatever his talents (and they must have been potent, she reasoned, or he wouldn't have been chosen), he was off his game.

She wondered if something had intervened between Krancis' selection of him and the onset of whatever trauma he was going through. Then a little spark of fear began to glow in her stomach, quickly growing into an active, churning fear: what if Krancis, just once, had been uninformed? What if Welter really *was* a bad choice for the task, as Bessemer feared? After all, the man in black *did* have an entire war to conduct. It would strain credulity to the limit to think he was incapable of at least an occasional oversight. The thought made her long for the captain's steadying presence as she eyed the back of Welter's head.

But no, that was nonsense – just the result of her condition playing on her nerves and exaggerating her fears. Welter had so far proven resourceful, pragmatic, and on point. Whatever personal demons he was wrestling with, he had them far enough under control that they didn't interfere with his effectiveness. He could be counted on.

The back and forth inside her own head made her feel silly, as though she didn't know her own mind. And that was a charge that nobody could ever level against her. Not honestly, anyway.

And yet…the edges had been fraying more and more as the days passed. Ever since Rex had been forced to leave her alone on Omega Station, she'd felt more dependent, more *helpless*, than ever. She could no longer settle her own thoughts with certainty. It had made her cling to McGannon despite her irascibility and constant need to put her down. Any port in a storm, she dryly thought, though not without appreciating the ex-minister's genuine concern for her. Help sometimes came from strange, unexpected sources.

Then she paused her train of thought, her eyes wandering to Welter again.

Could it not be the same with him?

"Alright, this is it," he said at the same moment she thought this, making her gasp. He half turned to look over his shoulder at her to find what was the matter, and then changed his mind. "Door's opening in five seconds."

The entire station had been depressurized since the inner door could no longer form an adequate seal. Anything less, and they would have been thrown backwards against the opening bay door the moment the air began to escape. She could hear it grinding open behind her, though the rear of the craft obscured her view. As if in answer to this, Welter lifted the egg off the station and turned it around, muttering an oath under his breath as his eyes fell upon the door, which had half opened and then jammed.

"What's wrong?" Tselitel asked, as the door jerked and shook in place.

"The machinery's *garbage*, that's what," he growled, slamming his fist on the armrest so hard that she felt it in the back.

"But…we're not stuck…are we?" she asked hesitantly, her stomach beginning to churn anew.

"Well, honey, unless you plan to get out there and pry it open with your own two hands," he uttered through gritted teeth before pausing. Once the words had left his mouth and come back in through his ears, he realized he was off base. "We've got to get it open somehow." He thought for a few seconds and then lit up. "Bessemer!" he exclaimed, activating his radio. "He might still be in range. Bessemer? Do you read me, Bessemer?"

Pausing, he heard only static in reply.

"Station might be killing our range," he explained, before trying several more times without effect. "Well, so much for that idea."

"Wait, couldn't Frank interface with the station and use its equipment to contact him?" Tselitel suggested.

"Of course! Why didn't I think of that?" the AI replied. "Though I'm not exactly certain how to interact with this particular set of hardware. It's very–"

"Cut the chatter and give it a shot," Welter said. "With all the debris in this nebula, it'll be hard enough to raise him as is. Let's not let him get any further out of range."

Without another word Frank set to work, shoveling his way through the mass of confused data that awaited him in the station's network.

"This place is a disaster," he replied fussily. "A real trash heap. The system has gone so long without maintenance that it's decayed almost beyond use."

"Can you do anything with it, Frank?" Tselitel asked eagerly.

"Naturally. It's not as if–"

"Then do it," Welter cut him off.

"As you wish," the AI said with a ruffled sense of pride. "Captain Bessemer? Can you read me? This is *Kerobenah*. We're trapped inside the station and need your help. Do you hear me, Captain?"

Several seconds passed without a word.

"Captain Bessemer, please respond," the AI continued. "The bay door has jammed and we can't get out. We require your *immediate assistance*." A further pause, and still no reply. "I'm sorry. I guess the station's comms equipment is too beaten up to work. I mean, it *says* that a signal is going out. But that must just be the system's diagnostic software going on the fritz."

"Well, what if we're *sending*, but not *receiving*?" Tselitel asked. "Like you said, the system is in bad shape. Couldn't it just be going one way?"

"I guess so," Frank replied. "I haven't got any means of verifying that theory, however. All I've got is what the station tells me."

"We'll give it a few minutes," Welter said. "See if Bessemer swings back around again. Could be that the doctor is right."

Uneasily, Tselitel leaned back in her seat. Despite the volume of their voices, Rhemus was still sound asleep. She reached over and checked the pulse in his wrist, finding it more or less normal. With a sigh she folded her hands in her lap, trying to keep them from trembling as well as she could. Then a crackling voice came over the radio.

"...ssemer. I've rec...transmission, and will be with you..."

"Good call, Doctor," Welter said, his tone even.

Soon they saw the captain's ship floating on the other side of the half open door. Having established line of sight, they were at last able to communicate without having to use the station's old equipment as a relay.

"So, the door's jammed?" Bessemer radioed.

"The machinery must have rusted to bits," Frank said. "Probably a miracle that it opened for us yesterday."

"We need you to blast it open with your weapons, Captain," Welter said, ignoring the AI's surmises. "I'll move the ship to the back of the bay."

"Are you insane?" Bessemer exploded, his suspicions about the man's mental state adding to his outburst. "You want me to open fire on a dilapidated station while the *emperor himself* is inside? What if a piece breaks off the door and crashes through the canopy? It could kill him instantly, to say nothing of Doctor Tselitel."

Welter couldn't help noticing that his own life hadn't warranted mention.

"Calm down, Captain," he replied. "Your craft has a pair of rocket pods under the wings and an automatic railgun embedded in the nose. Neither of those are going to do a lot of damage – the door's too heavy, built to stand the rubble and debris of the nebula bashing against it regularly. The rockets are low yield, and not likely to do a lot of harm. The greater danger is that you can't deal the door enough damage to punch a hole for us."

A sigh came in over the radio.

"Just what do you want me to do?"

"Blast away enough of the door that I can slip this bird out. Or, failing that, weaken it to the point that I can push through what's left."

There were several seconds of dead air.

"Does the emperor agree with this plan of action?" he asked at last.

"He's still unconscious," Tselitel replied, looking at the aged man beside her.

"And you, Doctor?" the captain inquired. "You can't see any other way from where you sit?"

She looked around the empty bay for a moment, and then shook her head.

"I don't," she said regretfully. "I know it must sound awfully dangerous. But the emperor's in a bad way, and I don't think we can spend any more time waiting around. We've got to get on our way."

"Alright," he replied reluctantly. "Get back as far as you can. And tip that canopy away from the explosion. It's the weakest part of the whole ship."

"Just get that door open for us," Welter replied, disliking the captain's statement of what he considered the obvious.

With this Bessemer backed his vessel away from the decrepit station. Flicking several buttons on his dashboard, he armed both the rocket pods and the railgun.

"I hope this works," he muttered, before unleashing one of his warheads. It shot out ahead of him and collided with the door, brilliantly exploding but doing little damage. With this he gained a bit more confidence in Welter's plan, seeing that the door was indeed sturdier than he'd thought. Three more rockets struck it before it began to crumble. Fearful lest the dislodged pieces should fly inside, riding the wave of the next explosion, he moved his ship line with the egg and activated his radio.

"The door's starting to come apart," he said. "I'm gonna try to chew it off with the railgun."

"Make it fast."

Resuming his former position, Bessemer aimed his railgun and squeezed the red trigger on his joystick. The ship rumbled as the weapon spat shells, pouring them out like there was no tomorrow, nor any end to their supply. Soon a thousand little bites had been chewed in the battered portion of the door he'd targeted, and it appeared ready to break free and float away into the nebula.

"It's about had it," he radioed, pulling into sight once more. "Should bust upon without any pressure at all. Just bits and pieces holding it on now. Hang on, I'll see if I can get it loose."

"No, don't," Welter said quickly. "That ship's not as sturdy as this one. We'd better do it."

"It also isn't hauling the *emperor*," Bessemer countered.

"There's no point damaging it so you can play the hero," Welter retorted, guiding the egg towards the door to settle the point. Before the captain could reply he pressed it against the damaged section and pushed through it with ease. The door scraped against its hull, but the *Keesh'Forbandai's* engineering was too sound for it to leave so much as a scratch. The vessel, and its occupants, passed safely into the nebula.

"Looks like you were right," Bessemer admitted. "Need me for anything else?"

"Nope, that's all," Welter replied in a businesslike tone. "Good luck to you," he added, before turning the egg away from its rescuer and leaving him behind.

"Likewise," they heard over the radio.

"Well, *that's* the sort of thing that you hope never happens again," Frank opined as the station shrank into the murky distance. "Got to admit, I'm a little claustrophobic. I know that must sound strange, given that I'm an artificial intelligence, and thus presumably not–"

"That was a good call, Doctor," Welter repeated, indifferent to Frank's comments. "You were right: the station *was* sending without receiving."

"Thank you," she replied, recognizing the hint of

appreciation in his voice and glad for it. "What's our next move?"

"First we get out of the nebula. Then we drop into warp and make straight for Quarlac."

"I've been meaning to ask you," she said, feeling the harness tug against her as he guided the ship around the debris in their path, "why did we meet up here? There must have been a thousand places that would have been safer, more convenient, than this."

"I guess Krancis didn't think so," he replied evenly. "I just received word to come here, and that was that. No explanation. He's not accustomed to explaining himself."

"Indeed not," she agreed. "Have you ever met him?"

"No," Welter said, flying the egg between a pair of asteroids before continuing. "Can't say I have. From what I understand he likes to keep to himself."

"Seems to," she replied.

They fell silent for a time, and she turned her head to gaze out the canopy into the surrounding nebula. It was beautiful, mysterious, mind-expanding. It stimulated her imagination, making her body feel small and insignificant as she contemplated its hugeness and immateriality. It was like spirit somehow made physical, personified. But the scene was also terrible. The aimless bits of ships and rock that floated within its confines seemed an apt metaphor for the ultimate finishing point that all life must finally reach: death, unconsciousness, the ultimate indifference. Eventually all bodies became empty shells, a thought that anxiously reminded her of her own impending fate. That is, unless the *Kol-Prockians* could do something to stop her deterioration.

Finally they passed out of the nebula. The emptiness of space made her feel suddenly exposed, vulnerable, and, despite her company, alone. She realized that she preferred to have something wrapped around her, be it a building or a space cloud.

"Alright, hang on to your hat," Welter said, punching in the coordinates for Quarlac and opening the dark rift. "Heh, never seen one that color before."

As they slipped inside, swallowed by the dark hole, Tselitlel suddenly panicked. Gripping the seat in front of her with all her strength, she jostled Welter.

"You alright back there?" he asked, surprised at her action.

The rift closed before she could respond, cutting off their connection to normal space and leaving them alone in the dark tunnel. Her lungs constricted until she could barely breathe, and her body began to shake violently.

"She's in some kind of trouble," Frank said with alarm, as the panic attack seized her mind and stopped her tongue. She continued to grip the chair until her knuckles turned white and her hands started to ache. "You've got to do something."

"Like what?" he asked, unfastening his harness and twisting in the seat so that he kneeled in it.

"Soothe her! Calm her down! Do anything, but do it quick!"

Hesitantly he put his hands over hers, unsure what to do and falling back on instinct. Gently moving his hands up her wrists to her elbows, he began to stroke her slowly.

"Take it easy," he said, his voice more authoritative than calming, his bedside manner needing some work. "We're safe now. Nothing can get us in here."

Almost painfully she raised her eyes until they met his. Her neck muscles were tight and visible as she compulsively constricted them. As her gaze weakened he realized she was running out of air. With instant certainty he leaned over the back of the chair and smacked her face.

"What do you think you're *doing*?" Frank exploded in outrage, as she slumped off to one side and then began to straighten herself. "Bessemer was right: you *are* out of your mind!"

Desperately Tselitel gasped in as much air as she could, filling and emptying her burning lungs rapidly.

"I don't know what Krancis was thinking, sending you along," he continued, as Welter carefully studied the doctor's face. "What would ever possess you to *do* something like that?"

"No, Frank," she managed to wheeze, her face red and perspiring. "He was right." She reached up and touched the sensitive skin of her left cheek and she continued to gasp. "Painful," she added, rubbing it, "but right."

"Wha–" he began, stopping mid-word. "I don't–. But–." He paused and tried to gather his flustered thoughts. "Are you alright?" he asked at last.

"I am now," she replied, working to steady her breathing. "He did it with the best of intentions, Frank. Please don't be upset."

"I'm not upset," he said at once. "Well, I mean, I'm not *not* upset, considering he just *hit* you, which is beyond the pale in my book. But–."

"Would you rather I let her suffocate?" Welter asked, settling into his chair again now that the excitement was over.

"Obviously not," the AI replied acidly. "But perhaps someone with a little more *medical aptitude* could have resolved the situation without resorting to *caveman* tactics."

"Next time she starts to asphyxiate, you be sure to run out and get one," he replied.

"Oh, if you think you're going to–."

"Frank, would you disconnect from the system for a while?" she asked, finally regaining her equilibrium and leaning forward in her seat. "I want to talk with him."

"Alright, fine," he said dramatically. "Nevermind, of course, that I was the one who–."

"Yes, *thank you,* Frank," Tselitel said emphatically.

Without another word he disconnected.

"Thank you for that," she said once they were, in

essence, alone. "I-I just couldn't breathe. It was like a giant was sitting on my chest, his hand clamped over my mouth. I fought to get air into me, but I couldn't."

"You're welcome," he replied, still facing forward in the ship.

She sat back for a moment, disappointed by his matter-of-fact tone. Desperately she wanted to form a connection, to feel *some* kind of camaraderie with at least one of her companions. She decided to try again.

"I'm not sure why it is that you're keeping such a distance from me," she began, her voice a little uncertain as she tried to find her footing. "But I–."

"Look, there's a practical reason that we've been thrown together," he said, twisting in his seat to look at her. "My job is to get you and the emperor to Quarlac, and then to look after you while you receive treatment. And that's what I'll do. Long or short, that's what I'll do. But I didn't come out here to make friends, and I'm not interested in forming anything more than a working relationship with you." Facing forwards again, he added, "I don't need it."

"I can see that," she said at once. "But *I* do. I'm not strong enough to do this on my own. Bessemer knew that, which is why he looked after me. The emperor has, too, in his own way." She sighed. "I can't take care of myself anymore. I'm ashamed to say it, but it's true. My condition has sapped my strength, physical, emotional, and mental. I know it's unfair to ask this of you, but I need more than a working relationship. I need a friend."

"What, and *I'm* not your friend?" the AI cut in.

"*Frank!*" she said pointedly.

"Okay, fine," he grumbled, withdrawing again.

"You don't need me as a friend," Welter replied ominously. "If you're looking for someone to lighten your load, you'd better look elsewhere. I'll only add to it."

"Perhaps we can lighten each other's loads," she suggested, turning her head a little to the side as though to hear his thoughts.

"I told you I wasn't interested in having my layers peeled back," he replied, his words bearing a clear warning.

"And I won't," she assured him. "I'm not going to invade your privacy. But if you *want* to talk about it, I'll be here."

◆ ◆ ◆

"I can't believe it!" lieutenant Powers said as she knelt beside Radik, watching the fires rage in the city of Numek less than half a mile away from their hiding place in the forest. Above the buildings floated Devourer craft, their tentacles snapping up survivors as they ran, carrying them off. "What are they doing? What *possible* reason could they have for taking them?"

"That's what we've got to find out," the admiral replied, gesturing for her to follow and taking off quickly into the forest. "They're flying south of Numek," he explained, as they began to circle around the embattled city. "Right now we're up on the east side. If we stick to these trees–."

"But, sir," she said between breaths, struggling to keep up with the athletic old man. "What's south of here?"

"Well, there's an old quarry," he uttered. "They might be using it as some kind of camp." He looked through the thin line of foliage that separated them from the city, the screams of the populace adding energy to his steps and driving him on. "It's clear that, whatever they're doing, they want 'em alive."

Powers could say no more, forced to save her breath for the exertions he was putting her through. Her clothes were soaked through with sweat, her hair tousled and falling into her eyes every time she placed one leaden foot in front of the other. Never more than decently fit, she was no match for the rustic admiral and his woodsman's stamina.

"Please, sir," she gasped after jogging another mile behind him. "I've got to rest," she said, dropping to the ground on her hands and knees and sucking in air.

"That's alright," he replied, moving half a dozen steps away to look through the trees. The scene was the same: burning buildings; screaming people; ships mysteriously snatching them from the streets and carrying them south. He shook his head, and with a heavy heart returned to where she'd stopped. If he'd succeeded in space, none of that would have happened…

"I'm sorry, sir," she apologized, as he stood over her and thought, fearing that he was disappointed.

"Oh, you're alright," he replied, his mind still in Numek, the pretty girl before him in fact off his mental radar until she'd spoken. "You've held up well," he added, trying to encourage her as she continued to wheeze air and fought to stand. She stood in a hunch, her cramping stomach muscles pulling her downward.

"Sir, what are we doing out here?" she inquired. "We can't stop those ships from taking those people away. And if they *are* gathering them up in some kind of camp, two people won't be enough to break them out."

"I know," he nodded, walking slowly for her sake. "But if we can figure out what they're doing, we might be able to get Blake to send a message off world. If it's bad enough, Krancis will bump our priority up the list and send *Sentinel* out to help us."

"Oh, that would be a dream come true, sir," she said longingly, holding her side as it continued to pain her. "But what if general Blake won't send the signal?" she thought after a moment, her hopes evaporating. "His equipment probably can't reach much farther than the planets in this system, which would force him to relay a message via an imperial vessel hiding somewhere nearby. But the aliens must have driven them all away by now. Sending a signal would probably just draw their attention to his headquarters for no reason."

"Then we find our own way to send a signal," Radik said determinedly, his face hardening as he brushed through the greenery. "One way or another, we've *got* to get *Sentinel* out here. It's our only hope."

"Yes, sir," she agreed, fighting to speed up as his pace unconsciously increased, his mind drawn away by his thoughts.

The noise of the Devourer's vessels passing overhead increased as they reached the bottom of Numek and continued south. The sounds of leaves rustling, sticks snapping, and the scampering of an occasional animal – all were drowned out by the engines of the victors. Instinctively Powers would duck when the ships passed above, fearing to be spotted. But Radik just strode along, his chest high and proud as he pushed through the branches that blocked his path. He had an intuition as to what the parasites were doing, but it had yet to form in the front of his mind. Like a ghostly hand it reached up from his unconscious, filling him with a righteous anger that caused him to scorn either capture or death.

"Sir, we need to keep low," Powers cautioned after one such occasion. "If they should see us–."

"Let them see us," he replied grandly, his nostrils flaring with contempt for the invaders as another craft flew over them, drowning their words with noise. "I'll make them pay for ever coming to Jennet," he added, once he could hear again.

"Yes, sir," she said, still struggling to keep up.

Another hour passed before he finally called a halt, which Powers gratefully acknowledged by dropping onto the ground in a sweaty heap. The air was close and still in the forest, with not the slightest breeze to lessen her suffering.

"We're close," he said, squatting down on the ground and leaning his back against a large tree. "Very close.

Shouldn't be more than ten or twenty minutes before we hit the quarry." He paused and looked at her in the darkness. "Keep your ears open for spiders," he added, once another craft had passed overhead and she could hear him without shouting. "Do you hear that?" he asked.

She raised her head above the forest's floor and listened, nodding after a moment.

"Ships," she uttered quietly. "They're not passing out of earshot anymore. They're landing and taking off."

"Correct," he confirmed. "It's hard to pick out of the–," he paused with a frown, as another ship passed noisily overhead. "It's hard to pick out of the *din*," he continued pointedly. "But if you can lock your ears onto just one ship, you can hear where they suddenly go silent. That's when they descend into the quarry to drop off their cargo."

She waited for another ship to pass and then did as he said. Sure enough, the sound cut out suddenly.

"See?" he confirmed. "Now, I haven't been near the quarry in years. But once upon a time I hunted in this area at least twice a week. Provided they haven't changed anything, I should be able to get us right in and out again. There used to be a chainlink fence wrapped around it to keep trespassers out. It was broken down in a few places – wild animals and young troublemakers took their toll on it. But most of the damage was on the east side, so we may have to work farther south before we can really see what's going on."

"Sir, why are you telling me all this?" she asked after a few moments had silently passed, sensing he was hinting at some unspoken point.

"I want you to know what you're getting yourself in for," he explained. "You've already taken your life in your hands coming with me tonight. You've been brave, and you've followed orders implicitly. But I'm not going to order you to come with me into that den of vermin," he said, jerking his thumb over his shoulder toward the quarry. "That's got to be your own decision. It's at least an even chance that we don't come out of this alive."

"I'm with you," she assured him at once, nodding her head several times. "All the way."

"Good girl," he smiled in the darkness, glad he could rely on her. Twisting where he sat, he looked around the tree as though he could see the quarry, his mind taking him back along a path of old memories. "This used to be such a beautiful area," he said, his voice almost wistful. "I had a little lodge, oh, maybe an hour from here. It wasn't much, just a roof over my head and an icebox so my game wouldn't spoil." He looked up as another ship flew by, shaking his head. "Be a miracle if this place is anything like what it used to be once those scum are finished with. Even if *Sentinel* comes, it'll take years to rebuild." He pushed off the tree and stood up. "Come on, Lieutenant, let's find out what they're up to."

Offering her his hand, he pulled her upright and then led the way south. As he'd anticipated, the fence was still intact and blocked their way. Working their way along it, they reached the north-east corner and turned south.

"It should be right around here," he mumbled to himself, his words barely audible even in his own ears due to the ships overhead. His hand ran lightly along the fence in the darkness, searching for an opening. Suddenly he found it and snapped out a hand to stop Powers. Grasping her shoulder, he pulled her back.

"There's a hole in the bottom of the fence," he said, speaking directly into her ear. "I'll climb through first, then you. Keep low, or it'll scratch you."

She nodded her understanding, and he got down to his knees. Reaching out again, he found the hole and traced its outline in the darkness. Then he got down on his belly and crawled through, leaving plenty of room between himself and its jagged edge.

Exhausted, Powers didn't drop down and laboriously slither through. Instead she got on her hands and knees and tried to duck her way through, but ended up catching a back full of rusty wires. With a yelp she dropped to the dirt, her tired limbs precluding any more moderate movement. Awkwardly she dragged herself through, meeting up with Radik on the other side. She was glad that he'd been busy watching the sky as she'd made her attempt, the noise of the engines covering up her yelp. He felt her warmth behind him once she'd drawn near, and he turned to confirm all was well. With a nod she lied, the blood already beginning to stain the back of her sweaty shirt as a dull throb set in.

Without a moment lost he bent his steps towards the quarry, keeping low now that the foliage was sparse and close to the ground. Many years before, the company which had operated the quarry had removed all the trees and plant life from within the fenced area. Over time seeds had blown in, and slowly nature began to reclaim the space that had been carved out of it. Ducking under and between the branches of these hardy pioneers, the duo managed to draw within fifty feet of the quarry without being spotted by the semi-constant stream of vessels.

Radik dropped to his belly, gesturing for Powers to do likewise. There was a bare piece of turf between the rest of the fenced area and the actual quarry itself, offering no cover at all. Slowly they crawled, pausing whenever a ship was above them. Inching along this way, they reached the rim of the pit and looked inside.

Powers released a gasp at the sheer immensity of the hole that had been cut in the planet. It was enormous, both deep and broad – large enough to fit a small town. Below she could see many people moving around in one half of the space, the mine being divided by a wall of landed Devourer craft. On the far side of this divide was another space, one filled with animals.

"What are they doing?" she asked, her voice inaudible in the din. Squinting in the darkness, she tried to make out what was going on.

Radik drew a small monocular from his breast pocket

and held it up to his left eye. Surveying the scene for several minutes as Powers anxiously waited for his report.

"What's happening down there, sir?" she asked, speaking into his ear.

"It's just what I feared," he replied, handing her the monocular. "See for yourself."

Eagerly she took it and held it up to her eye. Finding the human half of the makeshift camp, she looked over the prisoners. They were cowering, almost beside themselves with terror. Suddenly a scream rent the air, the pitch just right to echo off the stony walls and reach even their ears, far away as they were. Snapping the monocular to its source, she saw a large, square ship parked on the western end of the enclosure. At least a dozen small tentacles were in motion, picking up their human victims and dragging them inside. At the back of the ship a kind of dark, gooey mass was extruded. Very small ships, no more than half an imperial fighter in size, would then grasp this mass with tentacles that ended in a mesh-like net, carrying it upwards and applying it to the warships that floated above the quarry.

"They can't be," Powers uttered in disbelief. "They can't be using *humans* as some kind of *resource*."

"That's exactly what they're doing," Radik said, taking the monocular again and looking at the animals on the far side of the pit. "But it's not just us: any organic matter is fair game. The wildlife are suffering the same fate. They're using us to repair their ships. Once they're done with that, they'll probably start building more, if there's enough of us left."

"That's horrific," Powers said, shuddering at the thought. "It's cruelty beyond words."

"That seems to be their stock and trade," he replied, looking the camp over once more before putting his monocular away. "Come on, Lieutenant: we've got to report this."

Working their way back over the open ground, they reached the fence and ducked through it. Glad to once more be under heavy cover, they stood up and quickly retraced their steps.

"We're going to take a detour," Radik informed her some twenty minutes into their journey. "There's no point in heading past Numec again, so we'll track farther to the east and give it a wide berth. That'll–," he paused, his voice again obscured by a passing ship. "That'll lower the chance of us getting detected."

"Yes, sir," she replied, regretting the added length of the trip but immediately recognizing its necessity.

"We'll swing by that lodge I mentioned, too," he added after a minute or two had passed. "I'd say we're both about done in, and could use an hour's rest."

"Oh, that would be wonderful, sir," she said gratefully, her entire body pleading for rest with every step she took.

In the darkness she looked at Radik, admiring his long, lithe stride. He was like a cat, his every movement natural, casual. She almost had to remind herself that he was an admiral, and not simply a man of the forest.

It was with a certain amount of embarrassment that she compared his athleticism to her own lack of it, especially considering his advanced years. He possessed the stamina of someone less than half his age, never seeming to tire. It was then that the thought struck that he must be planning the break in the lodge for her sake. The idea filled her with shame, and forced her to stop.

"What's wrong?" he asked, noticing instantly.

"Sir, I'd rather not stop along the way," she uttered, the aching muscles of her body protesting her every syllable. "I-I'd like to go on."

"Lieutenant, you've had it," he observed factually, drawing closer in the darkness so he could lower his voice. "This is no time to muscle through. We have to make sure that this information gets back to Blake. And, through him, to Krancis. An hour's rest will do us both a lot of good, keeping our wits sharp and our nerves cool. By dawn we'll both be worn thin."

"Not you, sir," she replied.

"Oh, is that what this is all about?" he said, a smile audibly forming on his lips. "Well, you may rest assured, Lieutenant, that I'm not calling a stop to coddle you. I need it, too."

"Begging your pardon, sir," she objected. "But you look fit as a fiddle – just as good as when you started."

"That's because I know how to carry myself," he replied. "An admiral's got to have the right bearing, you know. Although I *do* admit that I've still got something left in the tank, I'm not going to run it down to zero. That would be the stupidest thing I could do. I'd have the strength to drag myself over Blake's threshold, provided we weren't intercepted. But a couple hours after dawn my nerves are gonna be shot and my brain'll be dull, and that would put both us *and* our mission at risk. No, Lieutenant, I'm not trying to baby you: I'm trying to ensure we get back alive. Is that clear?"

"Yes, sir."

"Alright, then let's go," he said, resuming his walk, Powers falling in behind him.

Light was breaking on the horizon when they found a small wooden structure hidden under the bows of a pair of large trees. Impossible to see from the air, and almost invisible from a hundred feet in any direction, it was the perfect hideout for them to recover in.

"This is it," Radik said quietly, suspicious if someone else had found it in the meantime and taken up residence. "Be careful," he whispered, drawing a small pistol that he'd kept in an inner pocket. Gesturing for her to stop, he snuck up to the door and immediately kicked it in. With a crash something fell off its perch and then shot out the door; a dark gray streak, no larger than a racoon. Sticking his head inside and finding no other houseguests, he motioned for her to approach. "It's alright," he said, putting the gun away. "Just some critter sitting on a shelf. Must have scared him out of his mind when I kicked the door open and sent him tumbling off."

Following him inside the one room dwelling, the smell of animal feces immediately struck her nose and made her gag.

"Pretty nasty, isn't it?" he asked, nodding his sympathy. "They must have pawed a hole in one of the walls and set up a little colony here. Best cover for miles, so I can't blame them. But I wish they hadn't."

Feeling around in the darkness, his hands found a wooden box and opened it. Deftly searching its contents, he quickly got hold of a candle and a small box of matches. Lighting it, he set it on a small shelf above the box, the paltry glow just enough to illuminate the small space.

"I liked to rough it," he explained, when her eyes quizzed him over his use of such basic technology. "Something happens to you when you're thrown back on your own resources, without any modern gadgets to carry the weight. Something good."

"Yes, sir," she replied mechanically, not wishing to test his theory in her own case.

She watched as he dug around in the box, reaching far into the bottom. In a moment he drew out a couple cans of preserved meat, tossing one of them to her.

"Probably past their due date," he said, holding his up to the light and examining it for a moment. "Oh, yeah. Years past. Still," he uttered, peeling the lid off with the attached ring and discarding it, "can't hurt to try it." Carefully he sniffed it. "Smells alright," he observed, before briefly running his tongue across its contents. "Tastes fine, too."

"I don't know, sir," Powers said doubtfully, her head slowly shaking from side to side.

"Just check it like I did," he replied, dismissing her concerns with a wave of his hand. Closing the box, he sat down on it and began to dig at the old meat with his fingers.

"Just spit if it doesn't taste right."

Reluctantly she followed his example, and was forced to admit that it seemed okay. Taking a seat on the floor, her back against the front wall, she felt something squish underneath her.

"There's something soft on the floor," she commented, the air filling with a dusty, foul smell as she moved.

"You just sat in some feces," he said without looking up, shadows dancing across his face in the candle light.

"Oh!" she exclaimed, shooting to her feet at once and heading outside to wipe her backside on a tree. "I hope that's most of it," she said when she returned, still holding the tin of meat.

"Turn around," he said, surveying the damage. "More or less," he informed her, finishing his meal and putting aside the tin. "Get that stuff inside you double fast," he ordered, standing up and grabbing a battered old broom from the far end of the room. With short, quick strokes, he'd brushed the floor clean by the time she'd finished. "We'll rest for an hour and then be on our way," he said, stretching out with a sigh. "We can't afford any more than that."

"Yes, sir," she assented, laying down beside him. Exhausted, she fell asleep almost as soon as her head connected with the hard floor.

In scarcely the blinking of an eye she was awake again, the admiral's hand shaking her shoulder.

"Time to get up," he said in a low grumble.

"What? Already?" she asked groggily, her throat dry and clogged with the cabin's dust. "It can't have been more than ten minutes."

"Try four hours," he said, standing up and cursing under his breath. "I'm getting old," he chastened himself, shaking his head. "We've got a lot of ground to cover, girl, so get on your feet and we'll be on our way."

Good as his word, he walked right out the door the instant she was upright, leading the way into the trees and bushes that surrounded the small structure. Stretching her arms over her head, Powers tried to stifle a yawn as her body awakened. The forest was dull and gloomy, the sky threatening to rain at any minute. She reasoned that that must have been the cause of their oversleeping: the lack of warmth and light from the sun had tricked their bodies into thinking it was time for a good, long rest. If it hadn't been for the admiral's hyper alertness, she felt, they would have likely slept until nightfall.

She could hear him still grumbling ahead of her, kicking the occasional plant beside his path with annoyance. Considering all that they'd been through since the beginning of the invasion, she felt that the extra rest was probably a good thing. She was certain that she'd have been little short of a zombie had she not gotten those extra few hours – a two-legged dead weight, brainlessly following Radik where he led, leaving all the actual work of survival up to him. At least now she could function again.

With consciousness came a renewed awareness of the scratches she'd gotten from the fence. The sharp initial pain had reduced over time to a dull throb that had spread across all of her lower back. Touching it lightly to test it, she gasped as the pain shot up her spine into her brain.

"You alright back there?" Radik asked in a low voice, his keen ears missing nothing.

"Yes, sir," she said with formal correctness, hoping the rigid certainty of her tone would push the question away and leave him free to think of more important things than the consequences of her own silly mistake the night before. "Just a little scratch."

"Alright," he said without interest, far too angry with himself to concern himself with her minor problems. Besides kicking himself, he had the task of getting them back alive staring him in the face. He knew the forests around Numek better than almost any man alive. But he hadn't been in the area in years, and this made him uneasy. And, more than that, his advancing years made him question just how sharp his recollection still was. It seemed more or less intact, but the embarrassing proof of his decline that he'd just received in the cabin made him doubt that. Perhaps he'd been slipping in little ways and hadn't noticed. True, he'd managed to guide them both safely to the quarry in the night – a far tougher task than heading back to Blake's HQ during the day. But the question still bothered him.

An hour into their trek, and the sky finally began to dribble. It was neither harsh nor constant; a mere suggestion of what might come, if Jennet could make up its mind to rain that day. Enough moisture fell down through the branches to gradually dampen their clothes, making the walk hot and uncomfortable. Dead leaves stuck to their boots, doubling the noise of every footfall.

Powers longed for a drink. It had been such a long journey *towards* the quarry, and now they were going to repeat it, though by an even longer path. The salty can of meat she'd eaten hadn't helped, either. Careful lest the admiral should see her acting like a child, she tipped her head back and held out her tongue, trying to catch a few sweet drops as they fell from the trees overhead. After a couple of seconds she quickly closed her mouth and looked ahead, making certain he hadn't noticed. Emboldened by the sight of his indifferent back before her, she tried again, tipping her head even further to catch more. This she continued to do, until the admiral abruptly stopped, and she nearly walked into him.

"Stay here," he whispered, holding up his hand to emphasize the order while simultaneously lowering his arm to indicate she should crouch. Hunching over, he slipped off his shoes and tip toed noiselessly away.

Her ears pricked to every sound within a hundred feet, Powers' dropped to the balls of her feet and tried to remain as still as possible. The rain masked all save her own breathing, which sounded terribly loud. Fruitlessly her eyes darted to and fro, her vision blocked in every direction by the density of the greenery.

Then she felt it: eyes upon her. She didn't know just *how* she knew, but her neck hair stood up, and her scalp began to tingle. Anxiously she jerked around, certain that the observer was behind her. But there were only more trees.

Suddenly she became aware of her every bodily sensation. The beating of her heart; the short, tight breaths that passed between her lips; the ache of her lower back; the burning of her calf muscles as she squatted. The perspective was irresistible, as if a hand had seized her mind and was guiding her inwards. The experience passed as quickly as it had come, just in time for Radik to emerge from the foliage in front of her and scare her.

"We're not alone out here," he informed her in a whisper, slipping his boots back on. "But I don't think we've got anything to worry about."

"I felt something," she replied, her tone preoccupied, as though she hadn't heard him. "It was in my head. I-I don't know what it was."

He stopped and looked at her.

"Like it was searching you?" he inquired, crouching down as well.

"Yes," she said earnestly. "I felt eyes on me, like someone was standing right behind me. But there wasn't anybody there."

"I used to get that," he uttered, nodding slowly to himself. "When I'd come out here and hunt. It was like a ghost was walking behind me. I used to just write it off as loneliness, my mind inventing company to break the stillness of the forest. But I never quite believed that," he finished, almost wistfully.

"What I felt *must* have been real," Powers said.

"I agree," the admiral replied, standing up. "I reckon that confirms what I said, that we don't have anything to worry about."

"But, sir–," she began.

"Whatever it is," he explained, "it predates the Devourers on Jennet. That feeling was my constant companion on some of my last hunting trips through here. It didn't hurt me then, and I don't see any reason for it to come after us now."

"But what *is* it, sir?" she asked.

"I haven't the least idea," he shook his head, his voice respectful as he looked around them. "I guess we won't know, unless it decides to reveal itself."

"Yes, sir," she assented, falling in behind him once more.

Widely bypassing Numek, the pair continued to walk as the rain gradually worsened, turning into a downpour. Their ears useless, their eyes filled with water, they groped through the forest. Twice they slipped in the mud, the latter time Radik falling over backwards and smacking the back of his skull against Powers' unsuspecting face. Yelping, she dropped to the ground, the admiral landing on top of her. With a grunt Radik rolled off her, twisted around, and pulled her upright.

"Are you alright?" he asked, taking her chin in his hand to examine her pretty face.

"I think a tooth might be loose," she uttered regretfully, putting a finger in her mouth to check. "Yup, it's loose," she said with finality.

"I'm sorry, Lieutenant," he replied sincerely, chastening himself inwardly for losing his footing. Yet another indication of old age, he thought. "I'm truly sorry."

"Oh, I'm okay, sir," she replied with as much spunk as she could manage, given the circumstances. "All in the line of duty."

Shaking his head, he sighed his exasperation and carried on, wishing with each step that he could say something that would take back the harm done. But no words came to mind, and eventually he had to let the issue drop.

With yet another pain to contend with, Powers' essentially stopped observing the world around her. Tired, battered, out of her element, she was like an academic that had suddenly decided to go on safari. Her experience in the militia's naval branch hadn't prepared her for anything like what she was going through. In the forest, with the elements on one hand, and the Devourer's vessels flying overhead on the other, what mattered wasn't book learning, rules, and orderliness. No, the preeminent factors were experience and instinct, the latter invaluable but impossible to teach. One had to be born with it, as Radik had clearly been.

All through the day they traveled, taking only the briefest pauses and moving as quickly as they could. As the world grew dark, they came into line with Gamma Base and its graveyard of vessels.

"Now we know where the survivors are." she said gloomily, once Radik had pointed this fact out. "They're being processed."

"Not for much longer," he replied with determination, quickening his pace. "Once we get the signal out, Krancis will have to send *Sentinel* to assist."

"But what if other worlds are suffering the same fate, sir?" she inquired. "There must be other worlds that need its help, too."

"It's got to come," he replied. "It's just got to."

Unconsciously she put her hand to her mouth, gently feeling her tooth. As soon as he noticed she jerked her hand away, wishing she hadn't been so obvious.

"How is it feeling?" he asked.

"Oh, it's fine, sir," she lied, the pain reaching from her tooth up into her skull and around her right cheek.

Without another word he resumed movement one last time, intent on reaching Blake's headquarters without any more pauses.

As they approached the mine, he reached for Powers'

in the darkness to slow her down. Mutely he communicated the danger they were both in, approaching an armed camp without any way of identifying themselves beforehand. Nodding her understanding, she quietly followed along as he worked his way indirectly towards the hideout's opening. Feeling that the sentries must be near, the admiral ducked low to the ground, waited for Powers' to follow suit, and then called out.

"Hello the camp!" he said in a voice just loud enough to carry, his hand on the lieutenant's back to keep her down, just in case one of the guards discharged a panicked shot in their direction. "Hello. The. Camp," he enunciated clearly, speaking a little louder. Still no reply.

"Maybe they're inside, sir."

"No, I don't think so," he replied, slowly standing up. He put his hand on her shoulder when she began to rise. "No, wait here a moment," he ordered. "Something's not right."

The rain had again dwindled to a trickle, enabling Powers' to hear him brush through the nearby branches and move on ahead. In less than a minute he was back.

"Sir?" she asked, half rising.

"Nobody's covering the front," he uttered, his mind running with a half dozen different fearful possibilities. "Come on, we'll look inside together."

Giving her his hand, he pulled her upright and drew his pistol. Raising a finger to his lips, a gesture she could just barely make out in the gloom, he made for the entrance. Stopping for a moment and taking one last deep breath, he hunched over and went inside.

The lights were still on. Food was boiling over or burning up on a half dozen different cookstoves. Everywhere there stood crates of supplies that had been hastily deposited, here and there their lids broken in, revealing their contents.

"What happened here, sir?" she asked, looking around a modest room in amazement.

"They left in a hurry," he said, bending down to shut off one of the stoves before continuing. "And they left voluntarily."

"Why would they do that?"

"You don't see any sign of a struggle, do you?" he asked openly, extending his arms to either side to indicate the entire space. "There's no blood, no corpses. Whatever their reason for leaving, it wasn't violence."

"B-but this entire place is bomb proof," Powers replied, trying to come to grips with what he was telling her. "What could have driven them out?"

"Not *driven*," he corrected, moving to an unopened crate and resting his tired bones on it. "*Drawn*. They were persuaded to leave. Somehow or other, the Devourers had 'em over a barrel, giving them no choice. That's got to be it."

"But there's no record of them ever communicating with humans," she objected. "Not since the start of the war."

"There's no record of them making human *paste*, either, Lieutenant," he observed emphatically. "Something's changed in them lately. Something *bad*. I think things have just gotten a whole lot worse for all of us."

Silently she joined him on the crate, glad to finally get off her legs after so many hours on the move. Not particularly tall, her feet dangled a few inches above the ground.

"What do we do now, sir?" she asked, unsure if she really wanted to hear the answer. "Look for general Blake?"

"Whatever's happened to them is beyond us now," Radik replied. "We can't do them any good, just the two of us. Better to get the message to Krancis and bring *Sentinel* here without another minute lost." He glanced around the room, looking for the radio. "We've got to find the comms room. Can you run a radio?"

"Yes, sir," she nodded, sliding off the crate and quickly disappearing into the corridor that ran in front of the room. "I've found it, sir!" she called a minute later, her voice echoing down the hall.

Sighing, he slid off the crate and hunched his way through the tunnels to the source of her voice. He found her busily clacking away on a keyboard that was attached to a monitor and a rather robust looking piece of comms equipment.

"This thing is attached to an antenna several miles from here," she informed him, as he knelt beside her and watched.

"Is there any way for them to trace it back here?"

"No. The connection is wired, running underground the whole way. They wouldn't know unless they've tapped into it. But they *will* pick up the signal the instant we send it out." She paused and looked at him, a dark realization on her face. "Provided they haven't destroyed it already."

"Let's find out," he said grimly, nodding towards the screen for her to proceed.

"Yes, sir. What do you want me to transmit?"

"Tell them that the Devourers have established a facility for processing human beings into the raw material necessary to repair their ships," he said, the horrible words almost sticking in his throat as he uttered them. "Add that they're doing the same to the animal population. That ought to at least get their attention."

"Yes, sir. Jennet's well-known for its massive amount of wildlife," she added helpfully. "Anything else?"

"Just that we need immediate assistance, and that, given our abundant population, both human and otherwise, we anticipate that the Devourers will begin sending their damaged fleets here for repair, after which they'll be free to roam and threaten the entire empire. Sign it Admiral Ronald Radik, security code four-eight-five-nine. That way Krancis'll know it's genuine."

"Yes, sir," she replied, her fingers moving quickly across the keyboard. Once he'd given it the once over, she sent it out.

"I reckon that's all for now," he said, twisting onto his rear and leaning his tired back against the wall, his mind wandering back to the quarry. "There's nothing else we can do for the poor souls that have already been taken."

"Are we going to stay here, sir?" she asked, folding her legs under her and looking at him with wide eyes.

"No," he shook his head, resting his elbows on his knees. "They'll probably swing through here from time to time, looking for more survivors who've come to hole up. We've got to stay on the move, away from infrastructure and under cover at all times. We'll grab whatever we can carry and make our way north. The forest stretches for miles and miles, so they'll never be able to find us. Provided we're smart."

"But what about…" her voice trailed, unsure if she should continue for fear of looking afraid.

"About what?"

"About…that presence we felt earlier?" she inquired, unable to help dropping her voice. "It's still out there somewhere. Maybe it even followed us here."

"Probably be good if it did," Radik replied with a dry laugh. "Like I said, it's never done me a lick of harm in all my years of hunting and hiking. At the very least it's neutral. Who knows, it might even be favorably disposed towards us." He looked around at the empty space. "And we'd better hope that's true. 'Cause right now we could use all the help we can get."

"Yes, sir," she said. And then, "Shall I start getting the supplies together?"

"Oh, I'll help you with that," he said, getting up the same time she did. Following her to the corridor in a hunch, he reflexively placed a hand on her lower back that made her jump. "What's wrong?"

"Oh, I scratched myself on that fence last night," she said with embarrassment. "I didn't duck low enough."

"Peel up the back of your shirt," he ordered at once, his

tone insistent. "We don't want that to get infected."

"No, sir," she agreed, reaching back and pulling it halfway up her back.

"Yeah, you got scratched up pretty good," he said, eyeing the fingers of torn flesh that had been gouged into her back. "You should have said something last night," he added, pulling her shirt back down. "Come on, there must be some medical supplies around here somewhere."

Searching each of the rooms in a tiring hunch, they finally came across an unmarked crate filled with bandages, antiseptic, and numerous other medical articles.

"Here," he said, tapping his finger on a crate for her to sit while he unscrewed the cap. "Hitch up your shirt."

Wordlessly she pulled up the back again, leaning forward on the crate and clenching her teeth to the anticipated pain. In an instant it felt like fire had engulfed her back, making her inhale sharply and jerk away.

"Easy," he said, dabbing her soft skin with a moistened cloth. "You're lucky we got ahold of this when we did. It's already pretty inflamed. Too much longer and you probably would have had a pretty bad infection on your hands."

"Yes, sir," she said through gritted teeth, the pain reaching up her back and making her squirm.

"Oh, I think we can let go of that 'sir' business from now on, Lieutenant," he said, gently wiping her wounds to clean them. "It'll probably be just the two of us for the foreseeable future, until *Sentinel* comes. Not much point in standing on ceremony."

"No, sir," she replied reflexively, making him chuckle good-naturedly. He knew that inground habits died hard

"What's your first name?" he asked, as he dried her back and then began to apply bandages.

"Julia," she replied, glad that the pain was finally dying down. "What shall I call you?"

"Oh, whatever you want," he replied. On half a second's reflection, he realized that she would be too overawed to call him anything but 'sir' unless given specific instructions. "Just call me Ron."

"Okay," she said, unwilling to be so informal unless she absolutely had to.

"Look," he uttered, as he finished with the bandages and put a hand on her arm to indicate she should turn to face him. "I've been out of uniform for longer than I care to admit. The navy was never really my bag, and I don't regret having left it. The rules and formality are all something that I can do without. It's just the present crisis that dragged me back in again. So, if you think you're having a hard time calling me anything other than 'sir,' consider how hard it is for me to hear it! I've just been 'Ron' for so long now that when I hear someone say 'sir' I half want to look around to see who he's addressing. I'm not someone who needs or wants to be handled with kid gloves. I like people to be straight on and direct with me. So consider it a favor to me to let all this drop, alright?"

"Alright," she nodded, before forcing herself to add, "Ron."

"There, that wasn't so hard," he smiled. "You're all patched up, though you'll want to watch it for a day or two. Try to avoid twisting it, or the bandages will fall off."

"Yes, sir," she replied at once, before laughing at herself. "Oh, I'm sorry."

"It'll take a little time," he said understandingly. "Now, enough playing patient. Give me a hand digging around for the things we need. I want to be out of here within the hour."

Forty-eight minutes later, a pair of dark figures left the mine network with packs on their backs and rifles in their hands. Though unseen by their foes, they did not go unnoticed by the presence that had made itself known to them hours earlier.

CHAPTER 5

Krancis stood on Sentinel's bridge, his hands clasped behind his back, watching the dark tunnel stream by as he had on so many prior occasions. There was something restful about the experience. He found it a taste of the eternal, a space seemingly removed from time itself and set aside. The notion had always intrigued him, implying as it did a separation from pain, suffering, and death. Though he knew that it could never be more than a respite from such thoughts, for the memory of them would haunt his every living step until finally he, too, met his end.

These reflections were interrupted by the door opening behind him.

"What are you thinking about?" Soliana asked hesitantly, moving slowly towards him as the door closed.

"Thoughts appropriate for my own self alone," he replied cryptically, watching the blackness for a few more seconds before turning his head towards her. "How are you feeling?"

"Strange," she replied, shaking her head and looking confused. "Like something has been…pulled out of me. A little piece of my soul has gone."

"Not a piece of your soul," he corrected her, facing forward again. "An intruder, that's all. An invasive thought; a fragment of another consciousness. It was never any part of you."

"I disagree," she replied, her voice a little stronger than it had been. "It found an affinity in me, a point of connection that allowed it to hide. I've been reflecting on this a great deal since you and Rex saved me. It's all I've been able to do, locked away in that room without any company," she uttered, her tone almost chiding. "When you drew it out, you drew out a part of me."

"Were that true," Krancis replied, "it would be a service, and not something to regret."

"But I *do* regret it," she insisted. "I regret it enormously. You may have cut out the cancer, but you took living flesh along with it. I've had a piece of my psyche excised, and I don't know how to get it back. Or if I even *can*."

"It's strange that you should *want* it back, given the destructive evil of the being that, you claim, bonded with it."

"One must accept one's whole nature as it is," she replied sagely. "And not chop pieces off of it at will. We lack the wisdom to know in advance what *is* and *is not* suitable, productive, *desirable*, in our own natures. I fear that something great has been lost."

"That is the kind of greatness that we can do without, given the present crisis," he said with unflinching certainty.

"And yet, there is a terrible greatness within you," she countered. "Is that not hypocritical?"

"I am an exception to the rule," he replied. "As is Rex Hunt, and a handful of others. There must always be those who are greater than others, empowered *above* others, to do the necessary work of maintaining life when once the weaknesses of humanity have piled up and brought us to our knees. Were all of humanity extraordinary, there would be no need of such men as myself. The intelligence, discipline, and moral courage of our race would be such that exceptions would be utterly unnecessary. However, since that is *not* the case," he finished, a hint of resentment in his voice as he spoke, "it *is* necessary for certain personalities, certain extraordinary *natures*, to enjoy a degree of power and discretion that is not allowed to others."

"You speak as a dictator speaks," she replied.

"I am a dictator," he said. "Though I rule in the emperor's name, serving him, and by extension, the empire which is his responsibility."

"You rule in his name," she assented. "But it is entirely out of your own mind. You follow your own counsel to the exclusion of all other points of view."

"Would you have a master surgeon consult a veterinarian on how to remove a brain tumor?" he asked. "Such is the distance between myself and others," he continued after several moments of silence from the girl. "I ask no counsel because I do not require it. I am more prepared, by both nature and experience, to grapple with the present crisis than any other human before or after me. I have been born for this time."

"Your confidence crosses into arrogance," she cautioned him. "No one is above correction."

He turned his head toward her again.

"True. But how can a lesser correct a greater? I have no equal in wisdom, much less a superior. No one can attempt to teach me without making plain at once his own ignorance and limitations. A soft stone cannot sharpen one that is harder."

"Then you bear a great and terrible responsibility," she said, slowly coming around to his point of view. "As the greatest, it shall be your burden if the empire falls. No one will have such a share of the blame as yourself."

"I'm fully aware of that."

"Except perhaps Rex," she reflected.

"His is a different burden," Krancis replied. "His role in the present pales in comparison to his duty to the future. The ultimate continuation of our race lies with him alone. Obviously we require his peculiar talents if we are to succeed in the present struggle. But the struggle will be fruitless if he should fail in his next task – one in which he has shown neither interest, nor concern, because his heart pulls him in another direction."

"You're speaking of doctor Tselitel now," Soliana observed.

"Yes," he nodded. "She is the sole conundrum that has escaped my copious talents. She cannot bear him an heir, which is very nearly of more importance than even his own life. It is conceivable that we could win this war without him, though our likelihood of success would drop dramatically. However, the Earthborn *will not* survive without another Hunt to carry forward the power that has been bred into them since time out of mind."

"Is that all you see when you look at him?" she asked, drawing near and tilting her head as though to verify his reply. "Just a weapon? A stepping stone for future humans to stand on? What of his own desire, his own passion? Can you really expect him to be nothing more than a cog in the vast machinery you've constructed?"

"We're all cogs," he replied dispassionately. "We all have our roles to play, and we're blessed if we can carve a little time, a little space, out for ourselves. Our duty is to the collective first; whatever crumbs are left over are ours to savor. This is the law of humanity, the pillar of our strength. We of the Earthborn are not particularly capable as individuals. But we whip just about every other race in our cohesion, in our *unity*, when we're smart enough to place it above every other personal consideration that would detract from it. This is visible whenever our survival comes into question. Suddenly we're strong, focused, certain of what must be done. And we do it, without hesitation or undue sentimentality. That's where Rex has dropped the ball: he's failed to step away from his own petty attachments and think of the broader problem facing our entire race. We can't hope for another man like him to simply crop up. The road that led to his family's affinity for the dark realm is literally gone, considering the shattering of the *Prellak*. With

Eesekkalion they could never repeat their accomplishment."

"Accomplishment?" she asked incredulously. "They've distorted an entire family's existence! They've chosen a destiny for them out of their own envy! A weapon was fashioned out of human flesh and bone, and you speak of it with the indifference of an arms dealer, fondling a curious yet lethal handgun!"

"The work of the *Prellak* came back on them again," Krancis replied imperturbably. "Their great skill delivered into our hands our only means of survival. Without Rex we never could have charged *Sentinel's* reactor, which would have sealed our fate. Equally, without him, there would be no operative to send against the *Pho'Sath* who would possess more than a slight chance of success." He paused and looked at her. "It's not wise to be overly sentimental about such questions. In human affairs, it invariably comes about that we must see our fellow men as mere tools, dehumanizing them to some extent so that we can deal with them rationally. Indeed, sometimes harshly."

"You're a very cold man," she said with a visible shudder.

"That is something that I have long striven to be," he uttered with a kind of rational satisfaction. "My entire reason for being is this crisis, and I must not fail it. To do so would rob every vestige of meaning from my body and soul."

"Such a narrow life," she replied, her tone bordering on pity. "You are as much a tool as Rex would be, if you had your way."

"I don't expect of others any more than I demand of myself," he explained. "To do so would be insincere to the cause I have dedicated my life to. But make no mistake," he added, looking at her for emphasis, "Rex *must* come around to my way of thinking. He *must* break his attachment to Lily Tselitel and have a child with a suitable woman. Despite the affinity that the dark realm clearly has for him, even its great power will eventually fail him, and he will die, either from age or in combat. The hopes, the future, of humanity cannot rest upon the shoulders of one man. There must be heirs, a continuation. The dark power of the Hunt family *cannot* be extinguished."

"Is that why you sent doctor Tselitel out of this galaxy?" she asked. "To keep her away from him, to weaken the hold of his affections?"

"Nothing could ever do that," he uttered bitterly. "No, shocking though this may be for you to hear, I truly sent her to Quarlac to save her life. Rex is bound up so completely in her existence that it would destroy him to lose her. Should that happen, our hopes would vanish. That is the difficulty – the problem that has proven unresolvable. If she continues to live, he would die before breaking from her and involving himself with another woman. But if she *dies*, it will shatter him to the core. In lieu of an answer, I have simply bought time. She will be safe with the *Kol-Prockians* for the time being, preserved by the remnants of their once great technological prowess."

"But should another answer present itself..." her voice trailed.

"Then I would have no choice but to follow it," he replied frankly. "But you already know that," he added. "You haven't come in here to discuss these matters with me. Not really. Deep in your psyche, you've already worked out the dimensions of my mind and the resolve it possesses. You're simply dragging to the forefront of your thinking what your insight has already unveiled."

"You are a strange and potent man," she replied. "A conundrum. A complex mingling of intelligence, brutality, genuine sympathy, and love. You do all these things, these cruel things, to save what you care most about. You are a surgical knife: sharp, cold, indifferent to suffering, yet useful for preserving life, a necessary tool. But that analogy does you an injustice," she added, her voice quickly growing sensitive as her insight manifested itself. "Your heart is inflexibly attached to what you love, and in their service you would do anything. Truly you are a feeling man, a man with emotion, though you hide it." She paused and looked at him. "Even with our numerous psychic encounters, I cannot find you out, not truly."

"That is by design," he said. "Such things are hidden within me. Only the occasional scrap rises to the surface."

"Such as your true name?" she inquired, subtly raising an eyebrow.

"Yes, such as that," he assented, his eyes reaffirming his stance on that sensitive matter.

At that moment a message came in over his ear radio. Pressing his finger against it momentarily, he nodded to himself.

"Understood," he replied, before clicking it off again. "We're about to emerge from warp."

"Where?" she asked, as the ship dropped out of the dark tunnel. A large, lush planet floated before them. On either side of the massive vessel were two fleets of Devourer ships, their fighters and frigates in the final stages of mopping up the local resistance.

"Wymark-2," he said, as a pair of carriers on each side of *Sentinel* unleashed their craft against it.

Like gnats they swarmed all around, obscuring the view from the bridge as they cast their impotent green blobs against its armor. The frigates that had been battering the local forces broke away, making a beeline for the main gun in an attempt to take it offline. A handful of capital ships were also on hand, heading for the rear to assault the weaker armor of the engines.

"They mean to disable the ship," Soliana's gift informed her. "They have given up all thought of actually destroying it."

"How do you know that?" he asked.

"I can sense it," she uttered, surprised at her own insight. "I can…hear it. The mind of the Devourers is speaking, transmitting its will across space to its separate members. They're like the cells of a massive, sprawling body. All the vessels in this system are controlled by a single intelligence." She paused and looked at him. "I've never heard that before. There was always an organizing will, of course. But it was subdued, dull, repressed. Like the impulses that pass without a will of their own up and down one's nervous system. They didn't direct, merely coordinating."

"And this is different?"

"Yes," she said with an aversion that bordered on horror. "This is…active, intelligent, roving. And angry. Very angry. The rage of millenia has been stored up within it. And now it has burst forth, with no restraint upon it." She eyed him anxiously. "I fear we've made a terrible error in shattering the power of the *Prellak*. They no longer hold the parasite to their own purposes, restraining its actions and its will."

"There was no other option," Krancis replied with certainty, dismissing the question at once. "Whatever consequences we face for having done so will be addressed in their turn."

As he said this several battleships closed with the dreadnought, slamming their tentacles against it in an effort to drag themselves all the more quickly to its engines. Simultaneously the frigates approached the crevice which housed the main cannon, flying inside in an attempt to find a weakness.

"Captain," Krancis radioed. "Let's clear our throat."

Almost instantly the dark cannon fired, blasting the frigates into dust. The turrets that dotted *Sentinel's* hull burst into action, dashing their dark bolts of energy against the fighters and capitals, disintegrating the smaller craft upon contact and damaging the larger ones.

"Swing the ship around, targeting their carriers," Krancis radioed the captain, watching calmly as the space around them was swept clean of fighters.

The battleships continued dragging their way to the rear, their movements sharp, snapping, vicious.

"You're correct," the man in black calmly said to Soliana. "This is a level of energy and determination we haven't seen before. They were always somewhat passive before, as though not totally engaged upon their task. Any vestige of that has been swept away."

"Do they pose any danger to the engines?" she asked fearfully, just as the attacking vessels reached their target.

"Captain," he radioed again. "Burn them."

As the Devourer's tentacles struck the engine cavity and began hammering away for a weakness, they suddenly blazed to life, their incredible heat burning them to a crisp in seconds. Soliana winced as this occurred.

"The parasite didn't like that," she uttered. "It sent great pain through its psyche."

"Good," he nodded. "It's nice to know that our blows are being felt."

With most of their tentacles burned off, the battleships flared their own engines and attempted to crash into the larger vessel. But *Sentinel's* burned hotter than they could bear, and their bows began to disintegrate from the heat. Impotently they crashed against it, sending a loud but harmless clang through the rear of the dreadnought.

By this time the main cannon was lined up with one of the carriers. At once it fired, the dark beam darting across the space that separated the two ships and colliding with the alien vessel. Quickly the shadow spread across its hull, paralyzing its organic machinery and driving the last of its fighter complement into space.

To keep the battleships at bay, *Sentinel* had continued to burn its engines at the maximum, causing it to close with the two carriers on its right flank while it fired. Once the first carrier turned completely black and exploded, Krancis ordered the captain to shift his flight path straight into its sister ship. Vainly the vessel attempted to move out of the way. But the enormous warship slammed into it at top speed, breaking it into several pieces and passing through to the other side.

"Bring us around again," he instructed the captain, as the remaining battleships disintegrated from the combined weight of their own aggressive tactics and *Sentinel's* many guns.

"Look! They're warping away!" Soliana pointed, as a pair of purple warp rifts were torn in the space before the two remaining carriers.

"Captain, give them something to remember us by," Krancis ordered, as the warship lined up with one of the vessels.

The dark beam burst from the crevice once again, striking the enemy ship and deadening a portion of its living hull. About a quarter of it was so affected before it managed to slip into warp.

"They'll not soon forget that," he uttered, as the purple rifts closed and they were left alone in space above Wymark-2. "This is Krancis, of the warship *Sentinel*," he radioed to the planet's garrison. "We have annihilated all vessels in orbit. What is your status?"

"Krancis, we're under heavy attack and require immediate assistance," a male voice replied. "The Devourers are flying over our cities, gathering up prisoners. We can't hold them back. Over."

"Understood. We'll be with you shortly."

"They never gathered prisoners before," Soliana said ominously, as the ship turned toward Wymark. "I fear something terrible is taking place."

"You're probably right," Krancis assented, as the planet slowly grew larger. "Usually they just unleash their spider allies on the population and leave the rest to them. This is something new."

Soon the massive warship penetrated the atmosphere, descending slowly through layer upon layer of thin, wispy clouds that did nothing to obscure the natural beauty of the world. It wasn't long before they could see the battle raging below. Ground based missiles and triple A attempted to cope with the numerous fighters that scoured the surface, but to little avail. There were simply too many.

"Let's even the odds a little," Krancis said, as *Sentinel* came into range and its turrets darkened the sky with its beams. But this time the vessels ignored it, focusing all their attention upon the human population. The fighters discharged their blobs against military and civilian targets alike, while the frigates used their tentacles to smash both infrastructure and anyone they could catch in the open. Turning his head off to the left, Krancis instructed the bridge's computer to zoom in on a small section of ground far in the distance, where ships could be seen rising and falling. No sooner had he done this than they stopped falling, seemingly abandoning the area with one consent. "Take us to that area the instant we're finished here, Captain."

In minutes the air was clear, and *Sentinel* lumbered in the direction indicated. The vessels that had left it tried to make their way back to the city to inflict more damage, but were cut down by the black beams.

"Not today," Krancis said with quiet satisfaction, as the last of the alien craft disintegrated. "Now, what were you doing *here*?" he asked, as the ship neared its destination.

Halting over the area, he looked down through the transparent floor just as Soliana gasped and recoiled in horror. Before both their eyes was a crudely made field of snapped off trees. All throughout it were dead bodies, civilian and military, that had been smashed to pieces by the vicious tentacles of the invaders.

"What evil work were they pursuing here?" she asked, her body beginning to tremble. "And why did they kill them?"

"Because they didn't have time to finish," Krancis explained factually, his eyes hardening as he examined the scene. "We stopped them part way through."

"Through what?" she asked.

Before he could reply, the captain radioed him again. For several seconds he listened.

"Very well, Captain. Set a course for Jennet, but bring us back over the city first. We have to make sure these people are adequately prepared to look after themselves for the time being."

"What's happened?" she asked.

"A message has just been received from admiral Radik," he explained. "And he knows first hand what they've been doing with our people here."

"Well?" she prodded when he fell silent, regarding the scene one last time as *Sentinel* began to draw away. "What were they doing?"

"They were turning our people into a construction resource," he replied. "A kind of paste or glue that can be applied to their ships. They appear to use only living matter, rejecting the dead as unsuitable."

"Then why did they *kill them*?" she asked desperately, her heart aching for the lost lives she'd just beheld.

"To spite us," he replied. "To cost us as dearly as they could. That's why they opened fire on the city once we'd descended: they no longer had any thought of profiting from our people. They just wanted to inflict all the damage they could during the short time they had."

"Cruel, vile beasts!" Soliana exclaimed, nearly screaming with anguish at the thought.

Calmly he turned to her.

"That's the enemy we face," he uttered. "We must match it in every particular, being no less ruthless. Now do you understand my stance?"

"Yes, I'm afraid I do," she nodded. "We must be terrible to defeat the terror before us."

"Precisely."

"I just hope we don't lose our humanity in the process," she added.

"That is something that can never be destroyed, only hidden, and only for a limited time. However, the maintenance of our humanity is no longer our concern. That task belongs to our children and grandchildren. *Our* task is to pass life along to them, by any means necessary."

"I agree," she said, as *Sentinel* moved into position above the damaged and burning city.

"Captain, get into communication with the survivors at once, and advance them every supply that we can reasonably spare without impacting our functional capacity. Inform me the instant this is done, and we are ready to depart."

With a nod to Soliana he left her alone on the bridge.

◆ ◆ ◆

In a hazy stupor Mafalda hung from a pair of shackles that were tightly clasped around her wrists. They were bolted to the concrete wall of the underground facility, holding her a foot off the floor. Her body felt battered, exhausted; her mind was no less abused.

"Good, you're awake again," *Deldrach* uttered, walking slowly to where she hung and standing before her. "You're tougher than you first appear. Many minds have been broken by what you've been subjected to." He raised his gloved hand to her chin and lifted her head, her eyelids half-closed and scarcely seeing him in the gloomy darkness of the room. "But do not conceive for a moment that that means I'm in a hurry for you to die. I have carefully monitored your health to *ensure* that this lasts as long as possible. You'll regret ever betraying us." Forcefully he jerked the hand that held her chin sideways, making her grimace.

"My only…regret…is that I ever worked with…you…scum!" she forced out of her dull lips. "*That's all!*"

"You think you're strong, because your *spirit* is strong," *Deldrach* retorted, moving a few steps away, clasping his hands behind his back and addressing the darkness of the other side of the room. "But I have already conquered your body. You are powerless to resist me, as all your team were. Despite their best efforts, they all fell. What chance do you have?"

"I have no chance anymore," she replied. "But that does not concern me."

"It should," he replied, turning back towards her. "You of the Earthborn are far too concerned with principle, when all that really matters is *power*, the ability to do. You believe you've won some kind of victory if you can go to your grave without groveling, without *begging* for my mercy. But such a victory is hollow. When the rest of the Earthborn fall, it will not matter to them that Mafalda Aboltina didn't surrender her spirit in the end. They won't remember you, and they wouldn't care if they did. What matters is what you can *do*."

"You're crazy," she gasped, even this short exchange of words taxing what little strength she had, leaving her breathless. "Power mad."

"The *Pho'Sath* are powerful," *Deldrach* replied. "It is why we are feared, in this galaxy as in others."

"The *Pho'Sath* are...*demons!*" she exploded, the force of her expression shaking her body as it dangled.

"You'll regret that utterance," he promised, laying a massive hand alongside her head and plunging her into a nightmare world of old memories. "Let's explore once again your darkest moments."

For nearly an hour he paraded the most painful memories she possessed before her mind's eye, finally culminating in the death of her sister and the cruel murder of Amra Welter.

"That last one holds a special place in your battered soul," he taunted, withdrawing his hand. "In that moment you became aware of all the pain you'd inflicted on your own kind in the name of freedom for the fringe. A petty, petty cause, if ever there was one. But, then, the members of your family have always had a contradictory degree of talent and dedication when compared to your intellectual breadth. It has made you *perfect* tools for the *Pho'Sath*. Manipulating you," he finished, bringing his enormous head close to her face and dropping his voice, "has been almost too easy."

"They'll come for me," she said desperately, trying to top him. "The Dread Phantoms will find me, and they'll *kill you!*"

"They don't seem to be very good at that," he replied with a laugh. "If nine of them couldn't manage it, then how could any number succeed? There's only so many of them. No, Mafalda, you must accept your fate: there isn't any rescue coming."

"I don't want...to be rescued," she uttered weakly, before tightening again and raising her face to look at him. "I want you *destroyed!* I want the blood of Amra Welter *avenged a thousand times!*"

"I cannot be beaten," he replied, walking to where she hung and pressing a hand against her chest. "Not by anyone."

A sudden pulse reverberated through her body, and she felt every organ within her cease functioning. Helplessly she watched the indifferent mask of *Deldrach* gaze upon her. For a few seconds she retained consciousness. And then, her brain running out of oxygen, her world went dark and she slipped away.

"Not yet," *Deldrach* said, sending another pulse through her body and reviving her. Panic seized her body as it attempted to grapple with what had just happened. "We have power over life and death, Mafalada," he continued, pressing a single finger against her heart and stopping it at will. Instantly a sharp pain filled her chest, and she began to gasp and convulse. "Don't you see that?" Another small pulse passed from his finger, restarting the organ and slowly reducing the burning pain she felt. "There is absolutely *nothing* your kind can do to stop us."

"Tell that…to the one who…killed Amra," she snarled.

Viciously he backhanded her, the force of the blow lifting her up in the shackles and dropping her down again with an excruciating jerk that tore at her hands. Seizing her jaw, he clamped down with his fingers until the bone started to bend under the strain, making her scream.

"She never told you her name, did she?" he growled, lowering the pressure enough for her to again fall silent. "The *Pho'Sath* that you helped Gustav Welter kill? It was *Anzah*, and she was my chosen Journey Partner – the one with whom I would meet everlasting life." He leaned in closer. "And you took her from me. Above and beyond all your crimes, that is the one that *burns* the hottest within my soul. That your petty kind should so much as *dare* to raise a hand against the *Pho'Sath* is reason enough to destroy you. But to–"

"Succeed?" she interjected, causing his hand to tighten again until her jaw actually broke. With a horrified, open-mouthed scream she felt the front of her jaw dangle down.

"It isn't yet time to truly break your body," *Deldrach* said, lifting the broken portion of her jaw back into place and using his arcane powers to fuse it together again. "I want your body whole, so that you can feel the full force of what lies in store. Too much damage numbs the mind and dulls the nerves."

"Kill me now…or kill me later," she said, surprised that her jaw worked again. "It makes no…difference."

"It makes a difference to *me*, Mafalda Aboltina," *Deldrach* replied. "You and Welter destroyed *Anzah* quickly. But I will take you apart piece by piece. That is your punishment. When my work on this miserable planet is finished, I will see to it that Welter suffers the same fate."

"He'll kill you," she uttered with devoted certainty. "He's too strong."

"All Earthborn are weak," he said scornfully. "It was only through the distraction you provided that he was able to kill *Anzah* with a blow from behind. Otherwise she would have slaughtered you both. But enough of words," he said with a wave of his hand, before applying them both to the sides of her head. "It is time to renew your agony."

Just then a sharp knock was heard at the door.

"What?" snapped the *Pho'Sath*.

Promptly it was opened, and a man of around thirty with dark hair stepped inside. Tall, lithe, strongly built, he dashed a glance at Mafalda before addressing her captor.

"My lord *Deldrach*, we have received a message from the high council," he said. "They are demanding to speak with you at once."

Emitting a low growl, the alien released his hold on his prisoner and moved past the messenger towards the door.

"Watch her," he ordered as he left. "She may use her powers to try and harm herself."

They could both hear him angrily muttering to himself as his steps receded down the hall. As soon as he was out of earshot the visitor slipped to the door and quietly closed it.

"There isn't much time," he said. "You must listen carefully."

"What…what are you…" she stammered.

"I'm going to try and get you out of here," he explained. "But the timing couldn't be worse. There's a lot of separatists in the building, and there's no way to get you past them all."

"Aren't you…a sep–separatist?" she asked incredulously.

"I was," he replied, pausing momentarily to listen for any sign of approaching footsteps. "But like you, I came to my senses. I've just been biding my time until I could find a way to hit back that would actually mean something."

"Don't blow your cover over me," she shook her head. "I'm not worth the effort. Stay hidden, harvest whatever information you can, and then get out." When he didn't respond she spoke more forcefully. "Do you hear me? You've got a chance to do them a lot of damage. *Don't* throw this opportunity away."

"I won't," he assured her. "Now, just hang in there. I'll get you out as soon as I can."

With an exhausted sigh she relinquished the point, lacking the strength to push any further.

"What's your name?" she asked after nearly a minute had silently passed.

"You can call me Ian," he said with a small grin. "I already know your name, of course. You're wanted by every separatist cell in the fringe at this point. *Deldrach* is happier than sin that you decided to drop yourself right on his doorstep. It's given him something to hold over the other *Pho'Saths*. It's probably why they're talking to him right now. It's rare for the high council to contact us here. The risks are too great to chance it more than every once in a while."

"All this…excitement…over me," she mumbled with a subtle shake of her head. "I'm not worth it."

"It's because of your family," Ian explained. "When the granddaughter of Ugo Udris speaks, people listen. You've got too much prestige to be left alone. They needed to find you, to break you, to *kill you*. Otherwise, with all the pressures the Fringers are under now, there's a very real risk you'd turn some of them away from revolution and back towards the empire. Not all of them, of course. But enough that you might upset the *Pho'Sath's* plans for good. And they're not about to let that happen." He drew a little closer. "So, you see, it's vitally important that you survive. The counterrevolutionary forces need you to rally around; need you as a *symbol*. Otherwise there'll be no head to lead the body, and the whole mass will stumble along in confusion."

Pausing, he wrapped a strong arm around her knees

and hoisted her up the wall.

"What are you doing?" she asked, nearly falling forwards out of weakness. With effort she pressed herself more or less upright against the wall.

"Giving you a little break from those shackles," he said in a strained voice. "They must hurt awfully."

For the first time in what seemed like ages she was able to rotate her cut and bruised wrists. She wiggled her fingers to draw blood back into her half-numb hands, making the most of every second. More than she'd thought possible, she was comforted to feel Ian's strong arm around her legs, holding her close. Quietly she sighed, savoring those stolen moments of human warmth, of compassion, that must sustain her for interminable hours of future torture.

"You'd better put me down," she said in an urgent whisper after a few more seconds had passed. "If *Deldrach* sees you–."

"I'll hear him coming," he cut her off, squeezing her legs a little tighter. "Just leave it to me. I've been around here too long to give myself away that easily."

For several anxious minutes they were entangled like this, until finally Mafalda's nerves couldn't handle the tension of his risking exposure any longer.

"Please, put me down," she said. "He'll be expecting my hands to be starved for blood. If they look normal…" her voice trailed.

"Yeah, alright," he assented reluctantly, slowly lowering her down and regretting the grimace that crossed her face as the shackles once again ground against her raw, sensitive wrists.

"Thank you," she said, trying to fight off the pain as it shot up her arms, "for your kindness."

"You're welcome," he said with a small, almost ironic grin on his puzzled face. "Listening to you, you'd think that you *deserved* what's happening. Don't you realize all the good you've already done? The hope you've brought to those wavering among the separatists? That alone should be enough to wipe away any guilt you're feeling."

"Not when your crimes are as cruel, as *bloody*, as mine," she replied with a painful shake of her head that she instantly regretted.

"Then look to what you'll do in the days to come," he said, stepping farther away as he heard footsteps coming down the corridor outside, "and find redemption there."

As soon as he finished speaking *Deldrach* reentered, shoving the door open so violently that it swung one hundred and eighty degrees around and slammed against the wall. Angrily he strode up to Ian, seizing him by the shirt and easily lifting him off his feet.

"My lord?"

"My connection to the high council ceased part way through our discussion," he uttered angrily. "The antenna must have broken down again. I have already spoken to you once on this matter, and I will not repeat myself again. Either the apparatus will be repaired at once, or you will find yourself without half of your body the next time it breaks down. Is that understood?"

"Yes, my lord," he nodded vigorously. "Absolutely. I'll see to the repair myself."

"Do so at once," *Deldrach* ordered, swinging him towards the door and releasing his grip. Stumbling, Ian just managed to keep his balance and remain upright. "It is imperative that I speak with the council without delay. "Take your tools and go. And be discreet," he added. "The opposition is eager to find the location of our communications equipment."

"Yes, my lord," he said obediently, as the alien turned his back to him and faced Mafalda. "I shall be as quiet as a mouse."

"Go," *Deldrach* said, dismissing him with a wave of his hand. "And shut the door."

Without another word Ian departed, but not before

winking meaningfully to the prisoner. As soon as the door clicked, the *Pho'Sath* pressed a finger against her chest, right above her heart.

"Now," he uttered in a low growl, still fuming from the failed meeting. "Where were we?"

❖ ❖ ❖

"We're getting pretty close to Erdu-3," Pinchon announced, stretching his arms over his head and trying to work the stiffness out of his legs by pumping them.

"It's gonna be good to finally breathe the fresh air once more," Wellesley said over the ship's interior speakers. "I've had enough of space. "First we were stuck in those ships my people left lying around for days; then it was the Black Hole; then the ships again; then Omega Station; then it was *Sentinel*; and finally this egg. It's enough to make you bonkers."

"You forgot the interlude on Bohlen," Rex pointed out.

"Oh, bah! How long were we on the ground? Like fifteen minutes? That's hardly enough time to get the kinks out of my circuits! Besides, it's not like we were exactly there to *relax*. Getting dropped into the middle of a battle between spiders on the one hand, and shadow monsters on the other, isn't *my idea* of a break. More like a really brief nightmare, except we were awake."

"Why in the world did you drop into a situation like that?" Pinchon asked incredulously. "Felt like stretching your legs?"

"No, the *kals* were fighting off the *karrakpoi* in order to protect Rhemus," the AI said incidentally, as though it excited no interest in him at all. "They'd made some kind of deal in their twisted minds, and promised not to eat him if he'd order the imperial navy to come back and beat the brains out of the Devourers overhead."

"And...?" the colonel asked.

"And what?" the AI inquired, still fixated on his own point.

"What happened?" he said self-evidently. "Clearly the emperor survived, but I haven't heard of any mobilization of the navy to Bohlen. Did Krancis break the emperor's word?"

"The *kals* broke their half of the bargain," Hunt interjected. "It was one of their chiefs that made the deal, but some of them didn't go along with his way of thinking. Killed him, along with a bunch of the emperor's servants once we'd gotten Rhemus onboard."

"And what did you do?"

"What he does best," Wellesley replied for him.

"Wish I could have been there to see that," the ex-pirate said quietly.

"It wasn't exactly a nice thing to see," the AI uttered. "They murdered this nice old lady and a couple of young guys because their mindless, savage minds couldn't comprehend the benefit that would accrue to them if they held up their end. They were like upright animals, but ten times worse because their appetites numbed them to even the most *basic* notion of self-interest, which is common to pretty much every sentient being. Even a dog knows not to bite the hand that it knows is going to feed it."

"They're just shadows," Hunt said with a shake of his head. "Remnants, like the burned on remains of a stew that's been left on the stove for too long and sticks to the bottom of a pot. You can't expect them to be rational, 'cause they're just fragments of their original personalities. Frankly I'm surprised that even a handful of them could be found who were willing to work with us."

"The exception that proves the rule, I suppose," Pinchon said.

"Indeed, but couldn't the exception have been just a tad *larger*?" the AI persisted. "There were only a few dozen *kals* there. Now, tell me, is it too much to expect that at least *that many*, out of the *entire* population on Bohlen, could have had even an ounce of sense?"

"A few *dozen*?" the colonel asked with surprise. "You took on that many by yourself?"

"Oh, our boy has grown a lot since that night we were chased into the bunker on *Preleteth*," Wellesley said.

"Well, sure," the colonel allowed. "But I didn't know things had changed *that* much."

"How did you think he was powering *Sentinel*? With his rugged good looks?"

"Look, don't get on my case," Pinchon said good-naturedly. "I just assumed that the technology was so advanced that it did most of the work." He paused. "You really took out that many?"

"Yes," Hunt replied reluctantly, mentally revisiting the bitter scene.

"There was something like thiry *kals*," Wellesley added proudly. "Smashed 'em like so many grapes under his foot."

"Now I *really* wish I'd been there to see that," the colonel said, his voice relieved. Twisting in his seat to face Rex, he added, "I'll be frank: I'd been a little worried about this mission until this moment. Going up against those *Pho'Saths* didn't sound like long-term employment to me."

"Then why did you want to come along?" inquired the AI.

"Well, *someone's* got to look after Rex," he replied with an ironic grin. "Doesn't sound like he can take care of himself. I mean, what if there had been more than just *thirty kals* to kill?"

"It's not exactly something I like talking about," Hunt said.

"I know," Pinchon said quickly, nodding his understanding. "And I really am sorry about those poor people who were killed. But you've got to understand, you've got power unlike *anything* I've ever heard of before. I've been from one end of this ridiculous galaxy of ours to the other, and most of the gifts I've heard of were little more than parlor tricks. Take Girnius," he offered as an example.

"What, the pirate boss?" Wellesley asked.

"Yeah. Now, I didn't know this until I met him, but he can cast little dark blasts. Nothing much from what I saw, just enough to break cups and the like. But he acted like it was some kind of great, awe inspiring power. *That's* most of what you see out there. Or at least most of what *I've* seen. Sure, there's a middle-point where a handful of them reside. The Fringers have done their best to recruit the ones who are outside the core and middle worlds." He paused and locked eyes with Hunt momentarily before continuing. "But what *you've* got is…nothing short of a superweapon. I can't tell you how impressed I am. I really can't."

"Thank you," Hunt said, reluctant to once again be characterized as a weapon, an image that had been gradually taking hold in his own psyche and pushing aside his sense of self.

"You bet," the colonel nodded, before turning forward again.

"Well, if all goes well, you'll certainly get to see him in action before we leave Erdu," the AI uttered. "This *Deldrach* sounds like a pretty nasty piece of work. Probably going to be quite a showdown."

"I hope so," Pinchon said. "It's about time they started catching some of this war right in the teeth." A beep sounded from the dashboard of the egg. "We're about to drop out of warp."

Within moments the black tunnel ended, depositing them once again in normal space. Erdu-3 loomed before them, a massive orb that blocked most of the front view.

"We're…a lot closer to the planet than I'd expected," Wellesley said, a little uneasy that they'd emerged with so little margin for error. "If we'd been just a bit nearer–."

"That's why we weren't," the colonel said, confident in his own flying abilities. "I wanted to put us close so we'd minimize our time in the open. Our rendezvous is directly below us. We'll dart right down and land."

Good as his word, Pinchon increased their speed and dove right into the atmosphere. Rapidly they descended, quickly losing sight of their surroundings in a dense thunderstorm that stretched for many miles.

"Nasty bit of weather we've got here," the AI observed, as Rex looked out the canopy into the impenetrable fog. "Good thing you've got so much experience flying one of these things blind," he added, a touch of tartness in his voice from being cut off earlier.

"Well, look at the bright side," the colonel replied, grinning despite his intense concentration on the ship's instruments. "If we crash, at least you'll survive."

"Oh, happy day," Wellesley said sarcastically. "I'll be buried with the wreckage of this goofy little ship for a hundred years, before some grubby little scrounger finally finds me and slings me around his neck because he thinks I'm pretty. No thank you! I'd rather just get it over with in a hurry."

Wordlessly the colonel brought the craft down, slowing his descent to a crawl as they neared the ground. Despite his confidence, he was unwilling to risk a mishap in the wind and rain. The storm had only gotten worse as they'd lost altitude, and the force of its gales could be felt through the controls.

"Just where are we going to hide this thing?" Hunt asked. "It's not the sort of thing to go unnoticed."

"There's an abandoned militia base a couple of miles from the town of Biryth," the colonel informed him. "Krancis said nobody's been there in years, so we'll stick it in one of the old hangars. Should be safe enough."

"And if anyone finds it?" Rex prodded.

"Don't worry," the ex-pirate said, as the base briefly

came into view via a gap in the fog. "This thing has been programmed to respond to either my biological signature or yours. Nobody else can get this thing open. Furthermore, the AI has been instructed to preserve the technology housed in this craft at all costs, even if that means destroying itself."

"Our bases are covered, then," Hunt said, nodding with satisfaction as the structures once again faded away in the mist. "There!" he exclaimed, pointing to a large hangar just as it disappeared. "That looks like a good place to park this thing."

"I agree," Pinchon replied, having seen it at the same time. "Just another minute, Wellesley, and you'll have some of that fresh air you were talking about."

"Can't wait."

Skillfully the colonel dropped the ship to just a few feet above the ground and floated to the hangar. A pair of large metal doors, partially drawn to either side, gave them just enough room to pass through. Setting down on the dry, broken concrete, Pinchon shut down the ship and popped the canopy.

Unfastening their harnesses, the two men stood up and looked around. The hangar was a throwback, to be sure, looking at least seventy years old. Probably more, the colonel thought. Old fluid stains covered the concrete, along with the odd pool of blood, which looked more recent.

"That's enough to raise a few questions," Pinchon said, pointing at one of the pools, his voice echoing through the empty structure.

"Probably some kind of gang activity," Hunt replied, slipping Wellesley around his neck and climbing over the side.

"Yeah, that's what I thought, too. Too much blood to be just a single victim. Must have been at least a small handful at the same time. And," he added, pointing to several other pools, "it happened more than once. This place reads like some kind of execution spot. Or an *initiation* spot. Some of the scum on this planet are pretty rough." The colonel paused to swing himself over the side, just as Hunt's boots struck the ground, the sound reverberating. "Our boys had orders to stay out of their way, since they were so vindictive. Picking a fight with just one in a bar was enough to start a small feud most of the time. And the chairman didn't like what that did to business."

"Were your boys very active on Erdu?" Hunt asked, as Pinchon joined him.

"No more than anyplace else," he said, looking back up the craft at the open canopy. "Alright, you can lock up now," he said to the AI, who mutely obeyed. With a grimace he twisted his arm. "This thing keeps giving me the business," he said, popping off his artificial limb and rubbing the stump for a moment before sticking it back on. "Oh, well. Better than the alternative."

"Not that this...macabre place isn't *fascinating*," Wellesley said through Hunt's skin. "But how about we get some of that fresh air?"

"Our mutual friend wants to see the sights," Hunt chuckled, nodding towards the open doors. "Shall we?"

"Of course," Pinchon grinned.

Together they strode to the opening, looking out for a moment at the downpour that awaited them.

"Wish we'd brought rain jackets," the colonel said with some regret, as he contemplated the multi-mile walk to Biryth. "Reckon we'd better try to close these doors?"

"Probably just draw attention if we do," Hunt replied, looking over his shoulder at the egg. "Besides, it's far enough back that nobody'll notice it unless they're close. I'd say let's leave it as is."

"Fair enough," the colonel said. "Well, guess there's no way around this."

With that he stepped into the cold rain, Hunt right beside him. Hunching their shoulders against the watery barrage, they jogged across the battered and broken concrete that connected all the buildings of the base together, shortly reaching a narrow road on the other side. It led out of the base and into the surrounding forest.

"This is *not* what I had in mind," Wellesley grumbled, feeling every sensation that Rex did. "This is more like drowning on dry land."

"It's gonna be dark soon," Pinchon shouted over the deafening roar of the rain. "We'd better hoof it if we want to hit town by nightfall."

In lieu of replying Hunt simply nodded. Pinchon, aware that Hunt had more stamina than he did, broke into a sprint without fear of wearing him out. He carried it as long as he could without exhausting himself, and then dropped into a quick jog to recover. They did this several times, until half the distance to Biryth had been covered.

"Let's take a little break," the colonel uttered, his breathing ragged as he led them under the boughs of a large, leafy tree. Deflecting most of the rain, it was one of the few merely damp places along the road. Pressing his back against its trunk, he allowed his chest to heave freely.

"Too many years behind a desk," he said with a self-conscious chuckle. "Used to be that I could have covered the whole distance without stopping."

Hunt just shrugged, unbothered by the delay. Leaning against the tree himself, he watched as the rain hammered the ground around them. The road, thankfully, was made of concrete, clearly an extension of the base. Had it been mere dirt, they wouldn't have made it half so far. It would have been nothing more than a bog.

"I've gotta say," the colonel said after a couple of minutes had passed, and he'd regained his wind, "this plan sounds a little thin. Just head into town and wait until we're met. What if our contact runs into trouble? We'll be boating in the ocean without an oar."

"A peculiarly apt metaphor, all things considered," the AI said over their ear radios. "But, reluctant though I am to admit it, if Krancis came up with it..." his voice trailed.

"I know, I know," Pinchon uttered. "If our lord and master planned it, how can it go wrong?"

"Believe me, nobody feels more strange about that than I do," Wellesley replied. "It's like the guy's got the magic touch. I swear, I haven't seen anything like it in all my long, *long* days. In a more primitive time, he'd be worshiped as a god. Or at least revered as a prophet."

"I think we're way past prophets at this point," Hunt interjected. "Soliana's a prophet, though a disjointed, misguided one. Krancis seems like he's got a crystal ball."

"Makes you wonder what he isn't telling us, doesn't it?" the AI asked. "I wonder if he's got all our fates penciled out in advance, and he's just watching us ramble ignorantly along, like rats in a maze. I don't like dangling from his chain, no matter how beneficent he's been so far."

"He *did* save Soliana," Hunt observed. "And it took quite a bit out of him to do it, too. I've never seen him worn down like that." He hesitated for just a second before continuing. "Frankly, I found it a little...disturbing."

"What?" the AI asked. "Why?"

"Well, it's not like we haven't all benefited from his *beneficence*, as you called it," he replied defensively, crossing his arms. "And while I *do* hate to admit it, I've gotten used to having him watch over our affairs."

"I know what you mean," Pinchon seconded, trying to put him a little more at ease. "He's like having a rattlesnake guard your bed at night. You know nothing's going to slip past him and get to you. The only question is–."

"Will he take you out himself?" the AI finished for him.

"Yeah," the colonel said. "I already told you that I don't like being around him. I don't think I relaxed for even an hour aboard *Sentinel*. But I'd hate to have anything happen to him. Right now, I think we *need* the smartest, nastiest rattlesnake we can get our hands on to win this thing." He laughed. "I just don't like to spend any more time around him than I have to."

"Why?" Wellesley asked. "It's not like distance can protect you from his all seeing eye. The guy probably knows the situation on Erdu better than we do. And we're standing right here!" The AI's tone was tight, exasperated, and it caught Hunt's attention.

"Something on your mind, Wells?" he asked after a few silent moments.

"Me? No. Why would there be?"

"I think we're all aware that you've got a personal aversion to Krancis," the ex-pirate commented. "It reaches a *little* beyond your usual suspicions of other people's motives."

"Don't you two think we ought to be getting a move on?" he asked, his voice growing grumpy. "It'll be dark pretty soon."

"Have it your way," Pinchon said, pushing off the tree and moving with Rex to the edge of its protective boughs. Reaching his hand out, he caught a few heavy drops before he pulled it back. "Good to the last drop, eh?" he laughed, his mood seeming to brighten as the world around them grew dark. "Shall we?"

Biryth was soaked and gloomy as they reached its outskirts. Scattered street lights, the few that still worked, somehow managed to penetrate the fog and rain, beckoning them on. They left off running when their eyes fell upon it, falling into a moderate walk to recover their stamina and lessen the chance of being seen. Given the city's importance to the separatist movement, there *had* to be spotters watching who came and went. But there wasn't the slightest hope that either man would see them in such conditions. They could only hope that the miserable weather would play to their advantage, letting them slip by unseen.

"I can't see a thing," Wellesley said, reading Hunt's vitals and correctly guessing what was on his mind. "Stands to reason that they can't, either."

He took a little heart at this, though he continued to walk with smooth, understated movements, hoping to blend in with the night. The colonel instinctively did the same, and together they passed into the south-west corner of the city, a place of rundown, abandoned homes. Most of the windows and doors had been scavenged years before, taken by other residents to spruce up their own houses. Like so many gaping eyes, the dark openings watched them. For all they knew each building had a spotter, sitting *just* out of the dim, flickering glow of the nearby streetlights, watching their every movement and radioing ahead for an ambush. It made the colonel's hair stand on end, and he reached down to double-check that the pistol holstered to his hip was still there.

Hunt neither carried nor required a weapon, and his awareness of the power that ran through him gave him an enviable confidence. He felt invigorated by the danger that surrounded him, glad to once again be in a position to inflict some damage for the human cause first hand. And, through that cause, to secure the safety that Tselitel needed to eventually be cured of her illness. Thinking of her made his heart glow, but he quickly tamped the feeling down. There would be better, more suitable times for soft sentiments.

Recognizing the natural ease with which Hunt approached the situation, Pinchon gradually slipped back and followed him. He moved with complete certainty, ready to meet anyone who got in their way with overwhelming force. That was something the ex-pirate was hesitant to do, given that discharging his pistol would be certain to draw the attention of every rat, gang member, and separatist agent in that section of the city. He was glad to pass the reins to someone who could operate without making a noise.

"Where are we going, Wells?" Hunt asked almost inaudibly in the rain.

"It's a little hard to tell, given the lack of decent

landmarks," the AI replied, his voice distracted as he consulted the data that Krancis had given him. "But keep moving along this street. I'm sure we'll see something that will give us our bearings."

Rolling his eyes at this lack of certainty given the danger of the situation, Hunt nevertheless pressed on. He could feel the colonel right behind him, his warmth unmistakably emanating despite the cold of the rain. Or perhaps *because* of it, he reflected, before deciding that he didn't care. His eyes searched the trash-strewn edges of the street, watching for hostile eyes glimmering in the scanty light. A nasty stench filled his nostrils as they crossed over a sewer grate, making him cough despite his determination to be silent. The instant he did so something skittered away on the right side of the street, knocking the lid off an old metal trash can. Noisily it clattered to the ground, the sound reverberating up and down the street despite the pounding rain.

With one consent the two men picked up the pace, risking a little noise to get away from the scene. Fifty paces away they dropped back into their walk, more resolute than ever to be utterly silent.

"Must have been a raccoon or something," Wellesley opined.

"How about our bearings?" Hunt asked tensely, feeling the AI had taken his mind off his work.

"I know, I know," he replied. "Look, there's nothing around here but rundown houses. I mean, I *know* more or less where we are. But I can't give you an exact street. Not without–," he paused, making Hunt halt abruptly and nearly causing the colonel to walk into him. "Okay, I know where we are now," he uttered after a moment. "Hang a right."

"Are you sure?" he asked, seeing a narrow alley that ran between a line of three story brick homes. The only light he could see was at the very end, where it once again intersected with a street. The whole length was dark.

"That's the most direct path to where we want to be," the AI replied. "It'll also get us out of the open. Now, come on."

Moving slowly, the colonel right behind him, he reached the alley and peeked inside. It also stank, though not so terribly as the sewer had. Stepping cautiously into it, the two men moved on cat's feet, carefully feeling the ground ahead of them with each step. It took several minutes for them to reach the other side, but they did so without making the slightest sound. Somehow more soaked than ever because of the water that ran off the roofs of the houses, they paused just short of the intervening street and looked up and down it. Seeing nothing, they waited for Wellesley to direct them.

"Alright, move north up this street," he said over their radios. "You won't have far to go before you duck into another alley. I'll point it out when you're close. Just take it slow and try not to draw attention to yourself."

Finding the colonel's gaze in the darkness, Hunt shook his head at the obviousness of this statement.

"I see everything you do, remember?" the AI asked pointedly. "Just because you didn't *verbalize* it doesn't mean I don't know what you're saying. Now, get going."

Hunt flicked the amulet with his finger to remind him just *who* was wearing *whom*, and then moved into the street. It was poorly lit, like all of Biryth, but he could tell that they were slowly penetrating into a *slightly* less rundown part of town. Here every second or third light worked, instead of every fourth or fifth. The windows were not as uniformly missing or broken, and the odd structure had a coat of paint that wasn't more than twenty years old. It reminded him of some of the more unsafe portions of Midway, just without the snow.

Careful to duck around the glow of the lights, the two men were slowly getting accustomed to their surroundings and slipping into a stealthy mental rhythm when a woman's scream tore through the rain's din two hundred feet down their backtrail. Nearly jumping into the air, they looked back in time to see a pair of dark figures chasing a smaller, skinnier one. Clearly the lead runner was the screamer, her feet desperately dragging at the broken, ancient concrete as it slipped underneath her. Stepping into a puddle that obscured a deep, jagged crack, she tripped and fell forwards, her face striking the concrete and bouncing off of it.

Fighting to her feet, she was about to sprint away in a half stunned daze when her assailants caught up with her.

"Now, *where* do you think you're goin'?" a woman asked, yanking her right arm and twisting her back down to the ground. The runner jerked herself towards her and managed to sink her teeth into the flesh between her right thumb and palm, tearing a bite out of it. "Gyaaaaaahh!" she screamed, pulling back her hand as it began to gush blood onto the street.

Taking this time to get behind the runner, the woman's companion slipped his arm under her chin and drew his elbow tightly against her throat. She coughed and gagged as her feet came off the ground, furiously waving her arms and legs to try and break his hold. But she couldn't reach far enough back to get him.

"You'll wish you'd gone quietly," the woman ominously promised, slapping her viciously with her undamaged hand. "Once we've got you all rounded up–."

Before she could finish her sentence a dark mist struck both attackers from the shadows twenty feet behind her. As their worst nightmares materialized before their eyes, they forgot all about the woman and took off screaming down the street. Their victim fell to the concrete, her hand instantly shooting to her throat as she gasped for air. Before her two men suddenly loomed, causing her to skitter back on her hands and feet until she struck a dead lamp post.

"Take it easy," Hunt assured her, reaching out and grasping her shoulder and ankle to stop her from squirming away. Instantly she tried to bite him, but he was faster than her previous target and pulled his hand away in time. "Hey! We're *friends!*" he said forcefully, grabbing farther down her arm and shaking her. "Just keep those teeth of yours in your head." Wordlessly she watched him for a few moments, and then began to relax. "What did those people want?" he asked, crouching beside her as the colonel did likewise. "Why were they chasing you?"

"We've got to get out of the street, Rex," Pinchon said tensely. "They're gonna draw every eye and ear in Biryth."

The woman started when she heard this.

"*You're* Rex Hunt?" she inquired.

"Yeah," he said indifferently, before turning to the colonel. "We'll have to take her with us a little ways, just to make sure they don't have any friends in the area who'll chase her."

Before the colonel could respond, the woman shot her arms around Hunt's neck and squeezed him tight. Jumping because he thought she was trying to sink her teeth into his neck, he then realized this was not the case.

"You can't *believe* how relieved I am to hear it's you!" she said eagerly. "The separatists have been hammering us day and night, chasing us out of our safehouses with the help of their overlords. We haven't had a moment's rest." She drew back and looked into the dark silhouette of his face. "A lot of our people are already dead. They're methodically destroying the organization in Biryth."

"That's why we're here," Hunt assured her, giving her a little squeeze.

"Rex, we need to move," Pinchon reiterated, glancing up and down the street for danger.

"Yeah, alright," Hunt said, before looking at the woman. "Are you okay? Can you walk?"

"I'm a little dizzy," she replied, as he pulled her upright. "But I think–."

She stopped mid-sentence as she lost balance and

nearly fell against the colonel. Pulling her back, Hunt kept them from colliding and then slipped an arm around her waist.

"Here, I'll help you until you get your equilibrium back," he whispered, almost dragging her across the street, Pinchon following close behind. The ex-pirate's pistol had long since been drawn, and he was ready to discharge it into anything that moved.

Reaching the alley Wellesley had mentioned, they ducked around a flickering cone of light from a nearby post and got off the street. Pinchon stayed near its mouth, watching the darkness as Hunt moved deeper inside. Pressing the woman against the back wall of an old butcher shop, Hunt released his grip and doubled back to where the colonel stood.

"Anything?" he asked, searching the darkness and rain.

"No, nothing," Pinchon replied, the pistol still firmly in his grip and held close. "Either they're playing it *real* cool, or we've gotten away with it."

"We'll move a little further before drawing any conclusions."

"I agree," he replied, leaving his post and following Hunt back to where he'd left the woman.

"Are we in the clear?" she asked, as they rejoined her and Hunt slipped a hand around her left arm to help her.

"Can't be sure," he replied, moving them as quickly down the dark alley as possible.

Still searching the ground with their feet, they made slow progress, though this was balanced out by the lack of noise they made. A cat started along their path, hissing momentarily and then darting back the way they'd come. Finally they reached the end, and looked into the street.

"This girl's in bad shape," Wellesley said over their ear radios, avoiding skin communication so as not to alarm her by the sudden sound of his unknown voice. "It's hard to get a clear signal through her shirt. But that was a *really* nasty blow she took to the face when she fell. You need to get her off her feet as soon as you can. This exertion isn't what she needs right now."

"What do you suggest?" Pinchon asked as loudly as he dared, his question confusing their increasingly dazed charge.

"What are you talking about?" she inquired.

"We need to get you off the streets," Hunt said. "Is there anywhere we can take you?"

"There's a safehouse west of town," she uttered. "About a mile along an old dirt road. I-it's been abandoned for a long time, so nobody knows about it. Tornado tore the top off it years ago. That was our rendezvous spot if things got really hot, a collection point if the organization was shattered and we had nowhere else to go." She paused and looked at him doubtfully. "But that was only as a last resort. Low level members like me were supposed to connect with one of the higher ups to find out if it was time to go or not. I was hoping to find one, but those two jumped me first," she said, jerking her thumb towards their back trail. Then she shuddered. "They'll chop my head off if we risk compromising its location by heading out prematurely."

"You won't have to worry about that," Hunt assured her, his voice mingling both compassionate authority and a scarcely concealed threat to anyone who might raise a hand against her.

"I don't think she'll hold up that long," Wellesley interjected. "Take her hands for a moment, Rex. Give me a clear reading."

"Alright," he uttered, clasping her hands to her further confusion. "Don't worry. I have an AI that's scanning your body for harm. We need to know how much longer you can hold up."

"I'll do what I have to do," she said bravely, though a slight faltering in her voice betrayed her condition.

"Granted, I'm *not* a medical AI," Wellesley began.

"Skip the disclaimer," Hunt ordered. "What's your diagnosis?"

"She's probably got another ten minutes before she passes out. The blow she took was bad, worse than I initially thought."

"Are there any safehouses closer to us?" Hunt asked, leaning his head down towards her to emphasize his question. In the faint, faint shimmer of light that bounced off her eyes from a distant lamp post, he could see them growing distant. "You've got to focus," he said, moving his hands to her shoulders and giving her a little shake. "Think: which one's might still be safe?"

"None of them are safe anymore," she told him. "Some hotheads tried to kick over the beehive by killing the top alien agent on this planet. But all they managed to do was kick them into *high gear*. I think it was the shove they really needed to finish us off for good."

"Don't worry about *Deldrach*," Hunt said. "We'll take care of him later."

"Don't say that name!" she harshly whispered. "They can hear you!" she added anxiously, looking all around her in the rainy darkness. "They can hear when we talk about them. It's how they know what we're doing so much of the time. It's almost like they're inside our *heads*. Only special places can protect us from their insight; special *substances* that can block their minds."

"I don't much care if he can hear us or not," Hunt replied. "I plan to settle humanity's account in full with him before the sun rises. Now, what's the best *possible* location to take you?"

"I already told you that there's no safe place within Biryth," she said. "Our only chance is to f-flee to…to the…."

Suddenly her body went limp, and Hunt only *just* caught her before she struck her head a second time against the cruelly hard ground.

"Great! Now what are we supposed to do?" Pinchon growled. "We can't sneak around the city with this chick thrown over your shoulder! She'll slow us down."

"Don't see that we have much choice," Hunt replied calmly, though he hated the situation as much as the colonel did. Bending over, he slipped his arms around the woman's knees and hoisted her over his right shoulder. With a grunt he stood up. "Wells?" he asked, his voice straining from her weight.

"I know, I know," he replied hastily, searching the data he'd been given aboard *Sentinel*. "Alright, given that she was fleeing south to north, she was probably trying to meet up with some of her associates on the upper end of the city. We can *try* and scrounge around for them, hoping they bump into us in the dark."

"That's the weakest plan I've heard in years?" the ex-pirate objected.

"Well, it's *that*, or start randomly going to known safehouses when we've just been told that the separatists are taking them over one after another. We're bound to encounter Fringers. If running around in the dark with this girl is bad, how would you like to get into a *fight* while she's along for the ride?"

"What about that safehouse she mentioned outside town?" Hunt suggested.

"You mean their little forbidden hideaway? How are we supposed to find it? All she said was that it was part way down a dirt road. We'd probably miss it in all this mist and rain, and spend half the night prowling the west end. No, cut it any way you like, I think our best bet is to hope we run into one of our guys in the north. Granted, none of us have the kind of psychic abilities that would point them out to us. But we know that *they* do."

"Of course!" Pinchon said in an enthusiastic whisper. "That's why Krancis felt our contact would be able to find us. A psychic gift!"

"You're just figuring that out *now*?" the AI prodded. "Of course that's what he had in mind. It's just a question of getting close enough. So…" his voice trailed dramatically.

"Alright, we'll head north," Hunt said, nodding for Pinchon to take the lead.

The colonel shot a sour look at the amulet around Hunt's neck, and then raised his pistol. Peeking up and down the street, he rounded the corner and slowly headed north. A lamp post, unusually bright given the condition of the others they'd seen, flickered fifty feet away. Its cone of light reached across the road, giving them just enough room to squeeze by if they pressed themselves against the stony houses that ran along their side.

The rain poured off the house's roofs in a torrential, splattering flood that shocked them as they passed into it. Moving slowly so as to keep their footing, Hunt regretted the bath the unfortunate girl on his shoulder was getting. Eagerly stepping back into the street as soon as they were past the glow of the lamp, Hunt felt the young woman begin to shiver from the soaking she'd just suffered. Condemning her assailants under his breath, he urged the colonel to pick up the pace with a little nudge to the back. Nodding his understanding, Pinchon sped up, his eyes darting all around them every few seconds. He was on edge, his old pirate's instinct for trouble telling him danger was just around the corner.

It was a long walk before they finally penetrated the northern end of Biryth. Twice they'd stopped because of the sound of loud, reckless steps reverberating along the narrow streets. The first time they saw the cause, a pair of figures eagerly looking in at every broken window they passed on their way south. Something told them the duo was on the wrong side of the political divide, and they managed to move out of the way before they passed into visual range.

The second time was different. The sound of footsteps was loud, distinct, clear despite the rain's tumult. Pinchon turned his head every which way, but couldn't get a fix on where it was coming from. It *seemed* to emanate from the buildings themselves, as though a ghost were abroad and he wanted them to know it. Wellesley dismissed this notion at once, though his companions' neck hair stood up all the same. It felt…otherworldly, like a cold breath had passed down the street around them. Feeling no urge to hide themselves, they waited for it to pass and then continued on their way.

Working farther and farther, the buildings finally began to thin out and assume the beaten, neglected character of those they'd seen upon entering the city. The colonel, hearing Hunt puffing harder with every labored step, led the way into the back of an abandoned store of some kind. The shelves were all empty, the signage destroyed. The only thing that betrayed its former purpose was a shattered cash register and a broken and splintered wooden counter.

"Over here," Pinchon whispered, guiding Rex to a waist-level shelf and helping him deposit his load on it. "Pretty," he said, brushing the wet hair out of her eyes in the dim, reflected light of the lamp across the street. "Can't be much older than twenty-four or twenty-five," he added, the anger rising in him as he saw the bloody gash on her face where she'd struck the street. Coldly he looked up at Rex. "If we ever run into those scum again," he threatened, brandishing his pistol in a sincere promise to exact justice.

"I know," Hunt nodded, half sitting on the shelf to give his tired legs a chance to rest. "We'll make hash out of them if we cross paths. But first we finish what we came here to do."

"Fair enough," Pinchon agreed, sliding his gun into his holster and slowly walking to the front of the store. He watched the rain for nearly a minute, his arms crossed as though deep in thought. Then he came back. "Storm's backing off," he informed him. "That's bad news for us. We're about to lose the best cover we've had all night."

"Won't be bad news for her," Wellesley observed. "Her

body temperature is dropping."

"And you waited until *now* to tell us?" the colonel asked pointedly, striding to where she lay and pressing a hand to her wet neck. "He's not kidding," he said to Hunt, concern in his voice and eyes. "We've got to do something in a hurry, or she could end up in a real bad spot."

"She's not *that* far gone," the AI replied tartly. "I've been monitoring her condition for a reason, you know. I estimate she's got a good hour left before we need to *start* getting concerned. Right now her skin and extremities are cold. But her internal organs are warm and safe. She's in no immediate danger."

"Good to know," Hunt said, looking out the front of the store at the slowly diminishing rain. He shared the colonel's misgivings about the waning storm, hoping it would last long enough to see them to some kind of shelter for the girl. Once she was safe he didn't really care, being more than willing to give battle to the separatists, and their allies, on any ground they happened to choose. But he *didn't* like the idea of fighting with an unconscious, injured woman in the same area. She was bound to get hurt.

"Why don't you let me carry her for a while?" Pinchon asked, reading the younger man's eagerness to get going despite his temporary fatigue. "It'll give you a chance to rest up."

"You sure? Even with the arm?" he asked, rising off the shelf.

"Are you kidding? Our lord and master gave me only the best," he whispered with a grin, twisting his hand around and flourishing his fingers. "Believe me, I'll be fine."

Without another word the ex-pirate bent over the woman and drew her onto his shoulder with a grunt. Heavier than she looked, he briefly rethought his determination to carry her before dismissing the thought.

"Be a little easier if she was awake and could hold *on!*" he uttered, emphasizing this last word as he jostled her a little more firmly into place. Clamping his arm over the backs of her thighs, he pressed her against his shoulder and nodded for Hunt to lead the way. "Let's go," he strained, eager to get moving.

Without further words Hunt stepped through the back of the store. The roof in the rear leaked in several places, making the floor slippery and causing him to glance back every few seconds to ensure the colonel kept his footing. Once outside he stopped pampering him, aware that his sole duty at that point was to keep them from stumbling into the enemy. The colonel would have to do the best job he could on his own.

"Where now, Wells?"

"I really can't say," he said over their radios. "Like I said before, our only real hope–."

"Shh!" Hunt silenced him, dropping into a crouch.

Pinchon awkwardly did likewise, the weight of his load nearly blowing out his back as he squatted down. Her legs dangled down between his knees, connecting with the ground and taking some of the weight off just as he flirted with a herniated disc.

"What is it?" he gasped, the air squeezed out of his lungs by the maneuver.

"Just saw a shadow dart across the street, over there," he pointed, indicating a dark space between two windowless buildings, each of them three stories high with smooth, gray walls.

"I didn't see anything, Rex," Wellesley objected. "Are you sure you didn't just imagine it?"

"That's 'cause you were too busy talking," he replied with a degree of good humor that surprised him, given the danger. He looked over his shoulder at the colonel. "Hang tight for a minute. I'll be back."

Before he could respond, Hunt was off. Like a cat he stole across the dark street, sidled along the left building of the pair, and ducked inside the place he'd indicated. Shifting onto one knee, Pinchon laid the girl down and drew his pistol. Cocking it silently, he rested an elbow on his knee and waited, glancing around every few seconds.

"It's alright, Colonel," Wellesley said over the radio half a minute later, causing him to start. It was such moments that made him glad he never let his finger rest *inside* the trigger guard. Nearly cursing the AI, he released a sharp breath. "Colonel?" he asked.

"What's the deal?" he replied after a moment.

"Not to brag," Wellesley said proudly. "But my plan worked. We've just found a member of the resistance. Get over here."

"My pleasure," the colonel muttered, putting away his pistol and eyeing his unconscious charge hesitantly. A dull throb had started in his lower back, and he didn't relish adding to it. However, he was even less willing to show his age and call his young friend over. Taking a deep breath, he grasped her wrists, turned around, and drew her awkwardly up his back. Carefully walking across the street in as low a hunch as he could risk, he stepped into the darkness between the buildings and paused.

"Rex?" he asked, unable to see anything in the inky shadows for a few seconds.

"Straight ahead, Colonel," Wellesley radioed. "Our new friend is jumpy, and insisted on moving deeper inside."

"Wonderful," Pinchon thought, fighting the young woman a little higher up his back and trudging as well as he could through the litter-strewn darkness. This wasn't an alley, being rather some kind of service entrance that served both structures. As his eyes adjusted he could make out ramps on either side of the narrow path, each one leading up to sliding metal doors that appeared not to have been used in at least fifteen years. Quietly he grunted with each step, his back aching more and more. "Why couldn't *Rex* have come back for her," he grumbled, before remembering the ear radio.

"Our little friend is scared half out of his mind," Wellesley explained instantly, determined that his friend not be ill-thought of. "Without Rex to hold onto him, we'd almost certainly have lost him."

"What?" the ex-pirate asked, wondering if the AI literally meant what he said.

"You'll see in a second. We're only fifty feet ahead of you."

Sure enough, he could hear voices whispering ahead of him as he approached. Despite the darkness he could make out Hunt's outline, and his hand was very clearly clamped down on the much smaller wrist of a small, trembling fellow. Hardly above five feet, his head shot each way every two seconds, his body twitched noticeably, and he faintly muttered to himself.

"Let me give you a hand," Rex said, dragging the little man with him as he moved to help the colonel lower his burden to one of the ramps.

"Who's this?" Pinchon asked, straightening up and stretching his back.

"Sayer Pole," the little man said at once, something about the colonel's voice drawing him back to clarity. "I was on my way to save my *life* when this, this *brute* zapped me!"

"You didn't stop when I told you to," Hunt replied factually.

"I thought you were with the separatists!" he exclaimed in a harsh whisper. "What did you expect me to do? Just hand myself over? I've already been beaten up twice by them tonight. They're rooting us out, all around the city."

"We know," Pinchon said. "Did you say *twice*?" he clarified after a second's reflection, recalling the trouble the two Fringers had given their unconscious third wheel.

"Yeah, twice," he replied tartly, drawing against Hunt's iron grasp fruitlessly. "Look, I'm not gonna bolt, okay? I ran because I thought you were trying to capture me. So," he said pointedly, putting his other hand on Hunt's arm and fighting to free himself, "let me go!"

"I'll let you go when I'm convinced you're not gonna run," he said implacably, jerking the little man sharply to get him to stop his fidgeting. "Now, where were you running to?"

"That's none of your business," he replied sourly.

"Couldn't have been an abandoned house west of town, it's top torn off by a tornado?" Pinchon asked.

"How do you know about that?" Pole asked in shock. Looking between the two of them momentarily, he then tried to bolt again.

"Look, you little renegade," Hunt said through gritted teeth, sliding an arm around his middle and hoisting him forcibly off the ground, squeezing the air out of his lungs as he crushed him against his side. "Either you play it straight with us, or I'll give you the worst nightmare of your life." Adding bite to his threat, he held his other hand out in front of him and made smoke rise from it. "Now, we're cold and tired, and one of your friends is unconscious. We found her being chased by a bunch of Fringers, who knocked her around pretty bad. She needs care right away. Are you gonna help us get her to safety or not?"

"Th-there's no safety in Biryth anymore," he replied tremblingly, his eyes transfixed by the smoke as it evaporated into the rain.

"Then take us to the safehouse outside town," Pinchon said.

"How do you know about that?" Pole repeated, his tone insistent this time.

"Because *she* told us about it," the colonel replied, pointing at the scarcely breathing figure laid out behind him. "She told us because she trusted us. Now you've got to do the same, if you want to make it out of town alive."

Before the little man could reply, the sound of feet coming up the path startled them. Clamping his hand over Pole's mouth, Hunt drew as far back as he could, pressing himself against one of the buildings. Pinchon did likewise, hoping that the exposed form of the young woman wouldn't draw attention until their uninvited guests were too close for it to matter. Drawing his pistol, he looked at Hunt, who nodded back.

"Sayer?" a woman's scared voice whispered as loudly as it dared. "Sayer, are you here?" They heard her footsteps stop thirty feet away, as she sensed she was no longer alone. For several seconds she waited, unsure what to do.

Pole put both hands on Hunt's wrist to pull it away from his mouth. Reluctantly, Hunt moved it.

"Sybil!" he whispered emphatically, drawing her back into motion.

She gasped when the dark shapes before her turned out to be people. Fearing that Pole had been captured, and that the men with him were separatists, she turned to run.

"Wait, Sybil!" Pole insisted. "It's okay! They're friends!"

Hesitantly she turned back and eyed them, particularly concerned by the man who still held Pole off the ground. Seeing this, Hunt took a gamble and released him. Slowly the little man walked away from his captors, approaching the woman. With him for a comparison, they saw that she was even shorter than he was. Couldn't have been more than four feet, ten inches, Pinchon thought.

"It's okay," Pole reiterated, putting his hands on her shoulders for a second before turning back to face them. "They're not separatists."

"They're not with us, either," she replied doubtfully, before her eyes fell upon the unconscious woman on the ramp. "Audrey!" she said anxiously, bolting to where she lay and dropping to her knees. "Audrey," she repeated, putting her little hands tenderly on the larger woman's cheeks and closing her eyes for a few seconds.

"Audrey?" Pole asked, confused. "You know her?"

"Of course!" she replied as he drew near and knelt. "Don't you remember? That girl who used to work the south side with me? Oh, that's right: you never met her."

"*This* is Audrey?" he asked, taking a moment to look her over and wishing he'd met her sooner.

"She's in a bad way," Sybil uttered, looking up at Hunt and Pinchon. "We've got to get her off the streets."

"We know," Hunt said. "That's what we've been trying to do all night. But your friend here's been stonewalling us."

"Oh, he's not my friend," she said, lowering her gaze again. "He's my brother."

"I take it height doesn't run in the family," Wellesley commented, causing the two men to chuckle seemingly without reason.

Cautiously Sybil glanced between them, and then back to Audrey.

"Sayer, we've got to take them to the safehouse," she said with conviction.

"Are you nuts? You know we can't do that! It's bad enough that we're going without permission. But to bring *strangers*!"

"It's that, or she's going to die," Hunt said, uncertain if that was really true but hoping they'd believe it. "Besides, we're not just strangers. We were sent here by Krancis to help you."

"Krancis indeed," Sayer snorted.

"I believe them," Sybil said earnestly. "Besides, what choice do we have?"

"We'll be kicked out of the organization for this," he replied. "Even if we're right, they'll never trust us again. We can't afford that kind of *initiative*. This has to go through the right channels."

"Your channels are broken," Pinchon replied, crossing his arms. "If you wait for official word, this girl will never have a chance. She took a nasty beating from the separatists, to say nothing of this miserable weather."

"They're right, Sayer," Sybil assured him. "I can feel it. She's fading."

Anxiously, frustratedly, the little man looked between

the four of them, his eyes lingering longest on Audrey. He'd never been forced into a position of responsibility before, and his instinct was to fall back on the official line and spare himself the burden of choosing. But as soon as he was about to speak words to that effect, his conscience froze his tongue. Unable to condemn an innocent girl to spare his own neck, he at last relented, nodding defeatedly.

"Good," Hunt said, making for Audrey and scooping her up in his arms with an ease that made Pinchon shake his head in the darkness. "Lead the way."

Nodding, Sayer led them to the back of the path and paused. Another street lay before them, running north and south. He gestured for them to hold back and peeked his head around the northern corner. Dashing around it without warning, Pinchon grumbled and stepped forward, his hand on his pistol.

"Wait," Sybil said, laying a tiny hand on his arm. "He'll be back."

The colonel eyed her for a moment and then relented, allowing the half-drawn pistol to slide back into the holster. A minute passed, during which the rain finally petered out. The only sound they could hear, besides their own breathing, was that of water dribbling from the rooftops and splattering in the street.

Then a second minute ground slowly by. Hunt shifted his burden a little, twisting her more flatly against his chest to pull her center of gravity closer to his. His arms were behind her back and knees, her face nestled in the hollow of his shoulder.

"The moment of truth," Wellesley ominously commented over his friends' radios, casting a brighter light on Sayer's disappearance than either of them were willing to. Halfway through a third minute, Pinchon spat, drew his pistol, and sidled to the edge of the southern building.

Just then Sayer shot back around the corner, out of breath, his chest heaving convulsively.

"What did you see?" Sybil asked, as though his appearance was the most normal thing in the world, precisely what she had expected.

"They're out there...not sure how many...not a lot...but enough...watching all around..." he said between wheezes, his already tight nerves cranked to the max. "Must be trying to head us off...ran around trying to find a path... couldn't find one." As he said this his breathing grew harder, his throat starting to tighten as panic set in. "We're too late! If you hadn't waylaid me I could have...been safe by now!"

"Shut up," Pinchon said in a low tone of disgust, pulling the little man farther inside and taking his place by the corner of the north building. Looking around the side, he saw a row of abandoned buildings running along the opposite side of the street. Windows were smashed, doors were broken in; here and there an entire wall had collapsed. It looked like a battle had been fought there. He stuck his head a little farther out to try and see his own side of the street. But it was obscured by a piece of the building that jutted out a half dozen feet away. The same was true of the southern view. "Looks clear," he said, turning back to his companions.

"It would look clear...to the likes of you..." Sayer said, his panic at being trapped quickly dissolving and turning to anger towards those who had stopped his flight. "You don't know anything about...Biryth...all the places they can hide... all the places they *are* hiding...you'll never see them."

"Then what do you suggest?" prodded the colonel.

"There's nothing to *suggest!*" Sayer replied in an anguished whisper. "It's too late! You've cut us off! There *isn't* a path, don't you get it?"

"Then we'll make one," Hunt said. "Take us on the safest path you can. If we run into anyone," he added, looking between the two Poles, "get out of the way. You won't want to get caught in the crossfire."

Grumbling to himself, the little man moved to the edge of the south building and looked fearfully out at the shadows cast by the shattered homes. Any one of them could hide a separatist agent. Each of them probably *did*, a little voice in the back of his head added. His anxious imagination easily painted silhouettes into every dark space his gaze fell upon. In half a minute he was convinced that an army of Fringers faced them, just waiting for the little team to fall into their laps.

"Let's go, Junior," Pinchon nudged him roughly, having moved up behind him without his knowledge. "We haven't got all night."

Looking at the colonel, and then at the pistol he held, Sayer gulped hard and then moved slowly around the corner. A street lamp somehow burned at both ends of the street despite the general lack of electricity in the area. He'd noticed it before, but he'd been too agitated to realize how wrong it was. Then it struck him: the separatists must have powered them up somehow in order to make the opposition's retreat that much harder. His heart began to pound even harder in his ears than it had before. Had it not been for Pinchon's gun and Hunt's terrible gift, he would have bolted right then and there, leaving even his sister to her fate.

"Pick up the pace," the colonel ordered in a whisper, as the little man practically crawled his way along the shattered fronts of the old buildings. He felt naked moving past all those gaping windows and open doors, and wished more than anything else to get out of Biryth and back into the countryside. They could still be ambushed out there, he knew, but they'd have more options for movement. Inside the city, they could be channeled and led around like dogs on a leash. Putting his hand on Sayer's shoulder, he started to shove him along.

"Stop that!" he whispered sharply, twisting out of his grasp and looking at the older man with hatred in his small, beady eyes. "Touch me again and I'll let you find your own way."

"No," Pinchon assured him, silently cocking his pistol

and holding it at the ready. "You won't."

Sayer's defiance evaporated instantly. Mutely facing forward, he moved as quickly as his terror-stricken heart could manage. Heading south until they neared the light, he paused and pressed his back against one of the few buildings that still looked halfway decent.

"They're thinning out," he uttered, as though speaking to himself. "There's not as many through here. But there doesn't need to be. The light covers for their lack of numbers. The concentration is in the middle."

"So where do we go?" Pinchon asked, Sayer's strange way of speaking making him doubt him yet further. Quietly he began to wonder if the little renegade was off his rocker.

"They'll see us in the light. Yes, for sure they'll see us," Sayer said, as though assuring himself on that score. "Our only hope is to skirt it, to pass as far north of it as we dare. Our silhouettes will be visible if we're too close. We needn't ever step in the light to be revealed by it."

"What are you *doing*?" Hunt whispered pointedly, his arms beginning to tire. "We can't stand here all night."

"Make up your mind, Junior," the colonel ordered. "Which way will it be?"

"It's dangerous in the middle," he said nervously, his tone indicating his mind was far from being made up. "But it's the only way."

"Then it's a good thing we're dangerous, too," Pinchon replied, grabbing a fistful of his shirt and shoving him into the street.

A gasp escaped Sayer's lips as he found himself in motion. Twisting his head around, he saw the entire group right behind him. Given no choice, he got his feet moving and led the way into a narrow side street.

"Where does this lead?" Pinchon asked quietly, moving his mouth to Sayer's ear.

"O-out of town," he assured him in a trembling whisper. "Straight out. B-but..." his voice trailed.

He could feel it: there were more of them here. And they were close, awfully close. The man with the gun had been wrong. This was the *wrong* place to cross over the street. They must turn around…

"Nope," Pinchon whispered firmly, grabbing his shirt again as he tried to double back. "We're committed."

The psychic tension in the air was so high. Why, oh why, Sayer wondered, couldn't they all *feel* it? They were walking right into–.

"Don't bother trying to run," a man's voice said from fifty feet ahead.

All at once the street was filled with silhouettes. At least ten stood before them, and half as many behind. Capping off both ends, they slowly approached.

"That's far enough," the colonel growled, still gripping the back of Sayer's shirt in case he tried to run. Quickly Hunt laid Audrey aside, leaving Sybil to look after her as he joined his friend. "Unless you're looking to cash in your life insurance."

"You won't leave this city alive," the man before them said, taking another slow, sure step. "We've got it locked down tight."

"I'll be sure to remember that when your blood is pouring into the street," Pinchon replied, the pistol aimed squarely at him. "Now, back off."

"I'm afraid that's impossible," the man replied, a smile audible on his lips. "You see, we have orders to gather up every last one of you. We're responsible with our lives if anyone escapes. So, naturally," his voice trailed, his arms gesturing for the mob around him to close in.

Hunt waited for them to draw near, not wanting to miss any of them in the darkness. They were all armed with handguns, a real professional lot. He couldn't afford for random bullets to go bouncing off the buildings, not with four other people who might get hurt. He had to wait for the right…moment.

"Rex…" Pinchon mumbled into his radio, his one-gun-against-ten bluff not working. They could hear their assailants chuckling and muttering to each other, savoring the fun they were about to have.

Suddenly a scream broke out to their right. The heads of both groups snapped onto the cause: a tall woman in ragged brown clothes had burst from between two buildings, foaming at the mouth, tearing at her own hair as she ran among them. With one consent the separatists gunned her down.

This was what Hunt had waited for, the vital moment of distraction. He cast darkness at all their attackers at once, freezing them into so many shadowy statues. He just *barely* managed to pull it off, several of their weapons having been leveled on them. Hunt continued to pour darkness into them until they shattered like windows, their pistols clattering to the street. One of them, the hammer already drawn back, went off on impact, sending a bullet ricocheting off the ground and into Sayer Pole's thigh. Instantly he screamed and dropped to the ground, the colonel having relaxed his grip.

"Sayer!" Sybil exclaimed, unsure where he was hit and afraid he was about to die. Leaving Audrey where she lay, the little woman dropped to her knees before Pinchon, her hands all over her brother. "Where are you hurt?"

"In my leg!" he all but shouted, writhing in the wet street. "Oh, it hurts so bad!"

The colonel looked down on the little man in more ways than one, shaking his head as he turned towards Hunt.

"So *that's* what you can do," he said, impressed.

"It's a good taste of it," Hunt replied, surveying the damage he'd done. A little river of rainwater ran down the middle of the street, carrying away particles of their assailants. "*That's* why I waited," he added, nodding towards Sayer. "No matter how fast I try and throw this stuff," he said, holding up his hand and generating just a puff of smoke for emphasis, "a quick eye and a handgun will always be faster. Multiply it by ten…" his voice trailed.

"And the math gets bad real fast," Pinchon agreed. "Well, we'd better get crybaby and the others out of here. The Fringers will pile on after all that noise."

Wordlessly the two men gathered up the rest of the group, Hunt slinging Audrey over his shoulder while Sybil got under her brother's arm and helped him amble along. Pinchon took the lead. To their surprise, they met with no further opposition, reaching the trees that bordered the west end of town in short order.

"Kinda funny that we didn't see anyone else," Wellesley radioed.

"Maybe they didn't want a taste of what the others got," Pinchon replied, still impressed by Hunt's accomplishment.

"There are many skillful psychics within the separatist movement," Sybil uttered, straining under her brother's weight. "It would have been trivial for them to detect that ten of their own suddenly perished. Passing the word along to the others, they may send out for reinforcements."

"You mean their alien pals?" Hunt asked dismissively, grudgingly avoiding the term *Pho'Sath* since it seemed to upset the resistance so much.

"Yes," she replied solemnly. "By now they know that there's something more powerful than our people moving along the streets of Biryth. In truth they should have sensed you before this. Your dark presence gives off such a distinct impression. But I suppose they didn't know how to interpret the signal they'd received."

Moving under the trees and away from the city, the faint light of the street lamps finally gave way to sheer blackness. Scarcely able to see a hand in front of their own faces, they stayed close together, following Sayer's instructions whenever faced with another path. Mostly they stayed on the same road, following it straight out of town. But then they began taking turns. The two visitors let a couple of these pass before finally calling the group to a halt.

"Audrey said it was straight along the road out of town," Pinchon said. "What's with all the twists and turns?"

"She must have been lying," Sayer said, his voice still a little shaky. "It's anything but a straight shot. Do you think we'd hide somewhere easy to find?"

They didn't know which one to trust, though at that moment both men were inclined to doubt anything the little rascal said. They both looked at Sybil's silhouette, which she somehow noticed in the darkness.

"Don't look at me," she shook her head. "I've never been to the hideout. Only Sayer has."

"Oh, fantastic," Wellesley groaned in their ears, expressing what they both felt.

"Alright," Pinchon said in a low tone, drawing a little closer, still holding his pistol up. "But if you're lying…" his voice trailed.

Sayer could hear that the ex-pirate's patience was at an end. Fearfully his eyes shot between him and his weapon. Finally he nodded.

"I'll get us there," he assured him. "Y-you'll see."

"Get moving," he urged him, gesturing with the pistol and moving out of the way so the pair could amble along. Casting a disbelieving look at Rex despite the darkness, he shook his head and fell in beside the duo.

"Oh, what fun we have on our little journeys," Wellesley said sarcastically. "Led around in the dark by an imp and his even tinier sister! I mean, look at her! You could put her on a slice of bread and eat her in one bite!" The AI sighed in exasperation.

"Take it easy," Hunt said quietly, aware that his friend was getting frustrated. But before he could say more, Audrey stirred in his arms.

"W-where?" she asked, as they passed under the low

boughs of a small tree, its wet, drooping leaves moistening their heads and shoulders.

"Just relax," Hunt said to her. "We're on the way to your people. They'll take care of you."

She raised her head, trying to say something to him. Then a gush of air escaped her lips, and she fell limp again.

"Don't worry," Wellesley said, analyzing her momentarily. "Just lost consciousness again. But we really do need to hurry."

"How much farther is it?" Hunt asked.

"Not far," Sayer assured him. "Not far. It's just–," he paused suddenly, pulling his sister to a halt. Another path had opened, angling off to the right. He looked between the two anxiously.

"Is there a problem?" Pinchon asked, his words so clearly enunciated that they made the little man gulp hard.

"No…no problem," he replied, wracking his brains to try and remember which path was the right one. "It's just…" his voice trailed, speaking to himself rather than them, and instantly regretting his words.

"What?" Hunt asked, moving forward with Audrey and looking down at him.

"I haven't, uh," he stumbled, his sensitive nerves growing taut enough to snap. "It's the right path," he said at once, nodding vigorously and pointing towards it.

"Are you sure?" Pinchon growled.

"Yes, absolutely," he assured him, continuing to nod for his own sake as much as theirs. "It's the right path. This is where we have to go. The safehouse is just a short way ahead."

"Alright," the colonel said. "Lead the way."

Slowly the group felt their way along the sorry little dirt road. As they proceeded it narrowed into little more than a game trail, bushy plants crowding them in on either side and squeezing them into single file. Hunt made by far the most noise, or rather his charge did, as her limp legs dangled through the foliage to his left. Whispering for them to stop, he managed to fold her legs up, pressing her ankles against the backs of her thighs. Wrapping his left arm around them, he managed to squeeze her into a smaller package.

The game trail suddenly terminated in a wide open space that was surrounded by tall, thick trees. To their right Pinchon thought he saw just a hint of a box shaped silhouette rising out of the ground.

"This is it!" Sayer said, his voice disconcertingly surprised at his own accomplishment. "This is the safehouse!"

No sooner had he said this than the bushes and leaves around them rustled, and they found themselves surrounded by a dozen dark shapes.

"Lower your weapon," a man ordered, indicating Pinchon with a rifle he held.

"Didn't we just leave a party like this?" Wellesley asked, as the colonel put his gun on the ground.

"It's us!" Sayer said. "It's okay. We're with the resistance. Audrey Wyard is with us. She's hurt real bad." For several seconds the shapes didn't move. "Look, that man is carrying her, alright?" he insisted, pointing to Hunt in the gloom. "You can see for yourself."

The man who'd spoken nodded to another beside him. Slowly he stepped into the smaller group, clicked on a tiny, tiny light, and examined the unconscious girl's face. Clicking it off, he nodded to his boss.

"Come on," he said, gesturing for them to follow as his second-in-command stooped and picked up the colonel's pistol.

The group was led to the box shaped silhouette, and the man clicked on his little light again. It was as Audrey had said, the remains of a house that a tornado had decimated long before. Guiding them through the rubble, the man in charge opened a trap door and led them down inside. The stairs being unstable, a pair of men took Audrey from Hunt to make sure she descended safely.

"What is this place?" Wellesley asked, surprised to find a sophisticated facility underneath all the rubble above.

The hallways were narrow, but made of clean, well-poured concrete. The ceilings were decently high at six and a half feet, and the rooms were spacious enough to ward off claustrophobia. Computers were in nearly every room, giving the impression of an advanced communications and observation station. Weapons were few, mostly carried by the guards who stood at regular intervals. They puzzled Hunt momentarily, given that they would not be able to hold such a small facility for long against a determined attack by the separatists. Then it dawned on him: they weren't there to guard the *facility*, they were there to guard the *data*. Their mission was to hold out just long enough for the technicians to wipe every last one and zero from their systems. They didn't give off the ragtag air that most of the other opposition forces possessed. Their faces were grim, disciplined, almost like imperial…troops.

"Uh, Rex?" Wellesley asked, the idea striking him at the same moment.

Hunt nodded slightly to indicate he saw it too, but was otherwise silent. The resistance folks, he felt, might not take too kindly to having an AI walk through the middle of their most sensitive base on Erdu-3, recording everything he saw in his copious memory.

They were led into the back of the base by the lead man and a couple of his comrades, these latter following up the rear. Their guns were held at the ready, though they didn't have the air of men about to use them. They were merely on parade.

"In here," the lead man said, knocking on a brown door at the end of the main hall and waiting a few moments. An unintelligible reply was made, and he twisted the knob and gestured for Hunt and Pinchon to enter. "Not you two," he said, blocking the Poles' way and pointing to another room nearby. "Get him to the hospital," he added, looking at Sybil.

"You too, Captain," a woman's voice said from within the room, just as the two men entered.

Heeding her words, he stepped in after them, closing the door and standing with a loosely disciplined air.

"You two have had quite a night," an old woman said from behind a desk. Rising, she walked around it and shook their hands. "Rina Phican," she introduced herself. "I already know your names," she continued, "so we'll dispense with the amenities. Time is short. The Fringers are chasing us from Biryth. Their allies have whipped them into a high fever of activity, and it's all we can do to keep our heads on our shoulders." She paused. "Drink? Something to eat?"

"Both, please," Pinchon said emphatically, sensing Rex was about to decline.

Briefly Phican relayed the request through an intercom on her desk, and then leaned against it, crossing her arms and eyeing them. The food arrived before the silence had a chance to grow awkward, an attractive young woman delivering it wordlessly and then departing.

"Please, help yourself," she said.

The colonel required no encouragement, but, as he'd expected, Hunt declined. The facility struck him wrong, as did the guards. He sensed he wasn't being told the whole story, but rather was being guided along by carefully chosen bits and pieces.

"You're a skeptical man," Phican observed, as Hunt continued to stand before her, the captain off to his left and a little behind. "That's good. There are too many believers these days." Then her eyes went to the captain. "Organize your men, a team of six. Have them ready within the hour."

"Yes, ma'am," he replied, turning crisply and leaving.

"Now that we're all alone and cozy," Pinchon said, boldly leaning on a corner of her desk and chewing on a sandwich. "Would you mind telling us what the imperials are doing here?"

"That's classified," she replied, not appreciating his liberties.

"Lady, we've been shot at, drenched, forced to drag one of *your* little lost sheep up and down the streets and, I think, encountered a ghost," he said with a pointedness that would have been sarcastic had his eyes not been deadly serious. "Now, I'm not as spunky and young as my friend over there," he added, gesturing with his sandwich towards Hunt. "He enjoys it. It's good for him, good exercise. But my bones are a little too tired for this smoke and mirrors swill that you want to pour down our throats. So," he finished, standing up for emphasis and crossing his own arms, "are you gonna level with us?"

Her eyes shot between the two men momentarily, a sour expression on her face.

"They're not imperials," she corrected him. "They've been disavowed by the government. Mercenaries, you could call them. They work in very small numbers, and on *very* specific projects for us." Her voice lowered. "If the Fringers got wind of their presence in our ranks, it would be a propaganda field day for them – and a disaster for us."

"Disavowed," Pinchon mulled, grabbing another small sandwich and half resting on the desk again. "They don't strike me as the rebellious sort, the kind that would get themselves thrown out. No, ma'am, they're too on point for that." She scowled at him as he worked his way closer to the truth. "I'd say they've been 'kicked out' especially for you. A cloak and dagger move like that's got Krancis' fingerprints all over it." His eyes lit up with realization, and he smiled at Hunt. "The old boy never puts all his eggs in one basket, does he? Here we thought we were the whole answer to their little–," he caught himself before saying *Pho'Sath*, "alien problem, but we're just the tip of the spear. Rather you are."

"Very good," Phican replied in a grumble, moving back behind her desk and gesturing for the younger of the two men to draw near. Pinchon just twisted where he sat, drawing the upper part of his right leg onto the desk and leaning his elbow on it to rest his tired back. His attitude ground on her further, making her wish she could have him thrown out. But his obvious friendship with the 'tip of the spear' for their upcoming operation precluded that. "These men have been placed on Erdu to help us deal with the separatist threat. We must be *very* cautious, and *very* discreet. As I said, if so much as a *syllable* escapes this room about their presence here, it would be a catastrophe for us. We're already reeling from their recent attacks, and the pressure that's put upon our limited resources. It could push us over the edge if we lost any more sympathy in the fringe." She paused and ground her teeth. "It was your former organization, Colonel, that drove them to this. Feeling the uptick in pressure, they decided to knock out one of their weaker opponents before things got any worse. They've temporarily lowered the priority of their usual imperial targets in order to finish us off. That's why they've suddenly got so many bodies to throw at us, and so many resources to arm them with. Girnius had to throw fuel on the fire at just the wrong time, *just* when we were really starting to reveal the true nature of the separatist movement to the people of the fringe. Now we'll be lucky to survive the next few months."

Having had some *small* part in Girnius' sudden change of attitude, Pinchon glanced at Hunt and then found an interesting portion of the wall to stare at. This didn't go unnoticed by Phican, who nevertheless was unable to decipher its true meaning. After several seconds' thought, she decided he was embarrassed because of his former allegiance to the Black Suns, and was glad to have finally found a stick to poke him with.

"And just what's our part in all this?" Hunt inquired. "I gather I'm still supposed to kill–."

"Ah, ah!" she stopped him, holding up her hand.

"...*our mutual friend*," he continued with annoyance,

thinking that the resistance was superstitious. "But I don't think Krancis sent those men here just to keep an eye on things."

"They're here to ensure that you reach the target, and are not interfered with until after our mutual friend is eliminated," she explained. "Thanks to a suicidally reckless move by some of our more radical members," she continued sourly, "the target has been placed on high alert. Moreover, the countryside is teeming with his minions, and the security around his location has been stepped up threefold. Before this point there was little question that you could have slipped in and dealt with him yourself. But the situation has changed since you departed *Sentinel*, and you'll need an escort to make it safely to the target."

"Are those men familiar with the terrain?" Pinchon asked, picking up his third sandwich. "In a situation like this, nothing counts for more than experience."

"I would be quite interested to hear your thoughts on operations of this kind, Colonel," she replied with biting sarcasm. "The deftness with which your Black Sun comrades have kicked over the beehive and inflamed the fringe is a lesson to us all. Is that more along the lines of what you would like? I'm sure we could find a few washed up pirates around Biryth to guide Hunt to his target, instead of the professionals we now have at our disposal."

Tickled by her words rather than offended, he looked up at Hunt and couldn't help chuckling.

"No, I think we'll be able to manage with them," he said after a moment, meeting her iron gaze with humor in his eyes.

"*You* won't," she said pointedly. "*He* will. There's no place for you in this operation, Colonel, so you'll just enjoy our hospitality for the time being."

"No dice," he replied, standing up and taking a step towards his friend. "Where he goes, I go."

"Out of the question," she replied at once, pressing a

button on her desk which instantly caused a pair of guards to enter, their rifles at the ready. "I'm finished with you, Colonel." She looked at the guards. "Escort him to a place where he can rest."

"You soldier boys lay a hand on him, and your arms will be ash," Hunt said, the dark force of his words stopping them in their tracks. "You ready to learn to shoot with your feet?"

"Leave us," Phican said with an aggravated wave, dismissing the men. "You're every bit as emotionally compromised as Krancis said you'd be," she uttered with disappointment.

"He says the nicest things," Pinchon replied.

"Philippe stays with me," Hunt said, his words a command. "Anyone who has a problem with that can take it up with me."

"What do you think this is?" Phican asked with aggravation. "Some kind of game? An outing with friends? We're on the brink here. This is no time to play favorites over who gets to go and who gets to stay. Whatever your friend's *peculiar* talents," she emphasized with narrowed eyes, "he's not going to be of much use on a mission like this. He's not practiced in covert operations, and he has no gift to bring against the target. He's useless."

Hunt shook his head.

"That's where you're wrong," he replied. "He's got a gift that none of you have."

"And just what's that?" she asked, as the pair made for the door, Pinchon taking along the tray of food.

Pausing with his hand on the knob, Hunt turned.

"Unlike the rest of you, I can trust him."

With this they left her alone to fume.

"You two sure know how to make friends," Wellesley gently chided them, as they stepped into the hallway. "Don't you think it *might* be an advantage for these people to like us?"

"Where do you think Audrey is?" Hunt asked the colonel, as he scanned the closed doors at their end of the corridor.

"Probably the same place captain what's-his-name sent those midgets," he replied.

Knocking twice, Hunt quietly opened the door to find a small, *small* hospital had been set up in the largest room of the facility. A handful of beds had been separated by curtains, and absolute silence reigned within, save for the beeping of a few machines.

"What are you doing here?" a fifty-something doctor asked in a sharp whisper, his six-and-a-half foot frame forcing him to stoop. He looked at the colonel's plate of food as he set it aside on an empty chair. "This isn't a dining room."

"We're curious about someone who came in earlier," Hunt replied quietly, his connection to Lily Tselitel giving him a more respectful attitude towards the medical community than he tended to have towards authority, as he'd demonstrated shortly before. "Audrey Wyard."

"What business is it of yours?" he asked, the strain of overwork having exhausted his nerves.

"She'd be dead if it weren't for us," Pinchon replied. "We found her when the separatists were ready to beat her to death, and then carried her halfway through town. Now, are you going to take us to her, or should we just find her ourselves?"

On hearing this the man's hard glare softened somewhat, and he nodded.

"Quietly," he instructed, before gesturing for them to follow. Leading down a long line of raised, narrow beds, each one filled with a sorry looking case that seemed to be just barely hanging on, they stopped at the second-to-last bed. "As you will have seen," he commented, "hers is not the only case we have to treat here."

"Will she make it?" Hunt whispered, his eyes

sympathetically studying her bruised, partially bandaged face.

"It's fifty-fifty at this point," he replied, crossing his arms and relaxing a little now that he was speaking in his professional capacity. "She's taken a terrible beating. The trauma to her head is severe. In the inner worlds this would be almost trivial," he uttered, before noticing their surprised, questioning eyes upon him. "Oh, not the beating," he explained quickly, still whispering. "But the question of survival. It's just that our resources here are so limited, so crude. There just isn't a lot we can do for her except make her comfortable and keep her warm. To be honest, you probably would have done just as well to find a dry house and leave her in front of the fireplace."

"Has she said anything?" Pinchon asked.

"No," he shook his head. "She hasn't regained consciousness since they brought her in." He stood with them for another minute, quietly contemplating her battered face. "I've got to go. Other patients need me. If you don't disturb her, you can wait with her for a little while."

"Thanks, Doc," Pinchon said, as he moved around the left curtain and spoke quietly with the patient in the final bed. "Boy," the ex-pirate said under his breath, moving up the right side of her bed and kneeling on the ground, resting his elbows gently on her mattress. "It ain't good."

"Get up alongside her, Rex, and touch her arm," Wellesley said. "Maybe I can learn a little more about her situation."

Glancing halfway around the curtain and seeing part of the doctor's back, Hunt moved quietly to her side and pressed the tip of his finger against the inside of her elbow. For several seconds he waited, carefully listening for movement from the next stall. Finally he withdrew it.

"Wells?"

"Like he said, massive head trauma," the AI reported over their radios. "I can't give you anything more than what he already told you, except to say that I'd give her *slightly* better odds of survival. Say, sixty-forty."

"Well, that's something, anyhow," Pinchon mumbled, getting back to his feet and looking down at the unfortunate young woman. "Sorry we didn't get to you sooner, girl," he added regretfully, before inching his way between the bed and the curtain back towards the main walkway. He waited for Hunt to join him, and then together they left the hospital.

CHAPTER 6

Julia Powers awoke to the sound of a voice whispering on the wind. She'd laid down hours before beside Radik, both of them taking their rest under the cover of several short trees.

Each night they had a different camp, the admiral feeling that consistency of place was the most likely thing to end them. Journeying by night, they kept out of sight of the vessels that flew continually overhead. Daily the alien ships found more survivors, carrying them away to the processing facility to the south of Numek. Using the provisions they'd found in the mine, they'd managed to support themselves while evading capture.

But no matter how far they moved, Powers always felt that a presence was following them. Mostly it was little things: leaves rustling when there was no wind; a sense of warmth or safety that seemed to come out of nowhere and had no rational justification given their situation; the feeling that someone was watching her. None of these things were very definite to her thinking, and she was ashamed to raise them to Radik, even though he'd spoken of his own belief in the presence. It made her worry that the pressure of the war was working on them both, and that they were beginning to cast magical fantasies onto the forest as a coping mechanism. She knew that people used to believe that gods inhabited trees and stones and the like, and she suspected that they were regressing into a kind of primitive religiosity to grapple with the inexorable might of the Devourers.

At least, that's what she'd told herself until she heard the voice on the wind.

It was clear and distinct, though what it said was unintelligible. It made her skin crawl to contemplate it, lying in the dark with the moon overhead, the leaves rustling around her, the admiral soundly sleeping. A chilly breeze began to blow from the east, causing her to draw her body tightly together under the blanket she'd taken from the mine. Despite her embarrassment, she found her ears carefully listening for the slightest sound of the presence. Her reason might have dismissed it, but her instincts were on full alert.

Then she heard it again, and sat up sharply with a gasp that made the admiral shift and mumble in his sleep. Like an affectionate daughter she leaned over towards him and drew the blanket a little farther up his shoulders.

No longer able to deny the voice, she gingerly pulled on her boots, laid her blanket aside, and strode a dozen paces away from their makeshift camp. They'd stopped a short way from an old game trail, and she followed this for about a hundred feet, until she was certain she was out of earshot.

"He-hello?" she asked hesitantly, feeling stupid to be addressing the night air despite her reluctant belief that something inhabited it. "Are you out there?"

In reply she heard another hushed message on the wind. But the rustling of the leaves covered it up.

"I'm sorry, I didn't hear that," she apologized, her pulse climbing at the thought that an invisible being was speaking to her. "Can you repeat yourself?"

Like a sigh the words were repeated, but the language was strange, and she hadn't the least idea what was said.

"I-I don't understand you," she said in a trembling voice, growing worried that she might anger...whatever it was. "Can you speak in my language?"

"Yyyyyeessssssss," was the hissing, snake-like reply. "But," it added after a long moment during which she'd begun to tingle all over from fear, "inadequately. I-I cannot…make…myself…transparent."

"Do you mean clear?" she asked, her helpful spirit causing her to speak automatically despite her dread.

"Yes," it repeated, the long, hissing blur vanishing as it found its footing. "I cannot speak…clear–clearly. My terms are…short…false…" its voice trailed.

"Insufficient?" she offered.

"Yes," it repeated again, before falling silent. For nearly a minute she waited, sweat gathering on her forehead despite the chill in the air. "You have been good to the old man," it said, finally breaking the silence, its manner yet more direct. "You take care of him."

"We take care of each other," she replied, not wishing to cheat the admiral of his due.

"Yes," it uttered, pausing as it struggled for words. "I must teach you. You must be made to learn. There is truth to be shared. My words are false."

"No," she insisted, gathering her courage. "No, I understand you. Please, go on."

"I do not speak of myself," it began. "I speak through another. I learned your speech through his guidance. I have copied his spirit. There is much difficulty."

This puzzled Powers, who quickly resolved to zero in on the parts she understood, hoping to expand them into a broader picture.

"Who is this other?" she asked. "Can I talk with him?"

"I do not know. He has been gone for many years. He may return."

"Is he in this forest?"

"I have searched the surface, but I cannot discover him. I dread he is gone into the sky."

"What was his name?"

"Taegen," the voice replied. "His name was Taegen."

"Taegen?" she asked, remembering the year of mourning that Rhemus had ordered after his death. "I'm sorry" she said slowly, "but he's gone. He was killed in an accident."

"I am sorry to hear that," the presence uttered. "I had much dread when he left. Now my dread has been confirmed."

What followed was a long, melodic utterance in another language. The mournful tone gave her the feeling it was some kind of epitaph to a lost friend, a leavetaking with the dead. Eventually it finished, and the air was silent.

"Are you still there?" she asked, her voice small and uncertain.

"Yes," it replied. "I have watched the creature that attacks us both. It consumes the creatures of the forest as it consumes you. Every hour that passes makes it stronger. It cannot continue."

"We've already sent out a signal for reinforcements," she assured it eagerly. "Now we're waiting on the imperial navy to arrive. I'm afraid there's nothing else we can do."

"Much can be done," the presence replied. "Much can be learned in this time. Your people must know. The truth will be shown. I have felt the intention of the parasite. They have been aptly named. But my words are crude. Another must be made to see."

"I don't understand," she shook her head. "Another?"

"Return to your admiral," the voice ordered her. "And I will make it transparent."

Slowly she nodded, before turning and working her way back up the trail to where she'd left Radik. Despite their official abandonment of decorum, she still felt hesitant to touch such a superior officer. But the knowledge that the presence had followed her overcame her reluctance, and she gently jostled him awake.

"Sir? Sir?" she asked, falling back on military address as a way to balance out touching him in her mind. "Please wake up, sir."

"W-what?" he muttered, a split second before his mind shot to full alertness. In one sharp motion he jerked upright, drawing a pistol from his belt and searching the darkness around him. After several seconds he realized they were alone, and put away the gun. "What is it?" he asked.

"Um, th-that presence that we noticed before?" she asked meekly, the words sounding insane to her despite all she'd experienced in a few short minutes. "It spoke to me. I mean, it's *speaking* to me."

"Right now?" he asked with interest, locking eyes with her in the moonlight and dropping to his knees before her. "What's it saying?"

"I mean," she paused, trying to clear her head as it became increasingly foggy. "I…don't know what I mean. D-do you hear it?"

He raised his chin into the air and slowly turned his head to and fro, listening carefully for the slightest hint of a voice.

"No," he shook his head. "What's it saying?"

"I…there's *so much…thought…*" her voice trailed, as she fell back onto her rear, her head growing dizzy. "I…I…."

Without warning she dropped back onto the ground with a thud, Radik's hands too late to catch her and break the fall.

"Julia? Are you alright, Julia?"

"She is fine," Powers uttered robotically, her voice stiff, formal, yet still her own.

"Is this the presence speaking?"

"Yes," she replied, her entire body stiff save her mouth and throat. "I had to speak with you – speak with *clarity*. My own faculty is poor. This girl communicates very well. She is my mouth."

"Will she be alright?" Radik asked, laying a solicitous hand on her soft shoulder and squeezing it.

"She will not be harmed. The mind is safe. There is no

danger. She only sleeps, the consciousness pushed aside. She will return upon my departure."

"Understood," Radik replied, though his head was spinning at the thought. "What did you want to tell me?"

"The parasite is angry. It has been unshackled. Now its appetite will be indulged. Consumption of life is its only purpose. All will be Devoured. The name is correct. It seethes with rage over its past treatment. It was merely a weapon. It was manipulated by the vile worlds. Their power was bent upon it, holding it down. It was dull and could not think. Now it wishes revenge on all life. But also to consume it for itself. Both humans and animals are useful for this purpose. It is strengthening itself. It repairs damage, and builds anew. A second wave will begin soon. Now the parasite seeks rest. Then it will break upon your kind. It has planned this."

"It is not a beast," the voice continued. "It is intelligent. The mind is vast, ancient, sophisticated. Its eye is upon all that moves in this galaxy. It hungers for flesh of every kind. You must strike quickly. There can be no hesitation."

"We're doing everything we can to stop it," Radik replied. "But it's so powerful. It sweeps aside our defenses at every turn. Only *Sentinel*, an ancient warship, can stop it."

"I know of *Sentinel*," the voice replied. "The parasite reflects on it. At all times a portion of its thought is bent upon the destruction of the vessel. It has been thwarted by the warship. But it studies it for weaknesses. It experiments with different techniques. That is why it accepts battle."

"Of course!" Radik exclaimed. "It's trying to sound us out, to finally find a flaw it can exploit! I could never understand why it continually allows itself to be beaten. I thought it was just too dense to do anything smarter."

"The parasite is wise and patient," the presence replied. "It is meticulous. You must never underestimate it again. Every action has a purpose. It knows that only your chief vessel can save you from destruction. It is the only obstacle. It sacrifices fleets to find its vulnerability. Once it is discovered, it will be destroyed."

"I don't think *Sentinel* has a weakness," Radik said. "Not one that the Devourers can exploit, anyway. It's much too advanced for them to cope with."

"Without hesitation you underestimate the parasite again," the voice chided. "Do you not hear what I say? The creature is wise, though it appears crude. It is cunning, sly, manipulative. Do not imagine your vessel to be invulnerable. It is not. All things, all beings, all *weapons*, have a weakness. It remains merely to be found. Then the parasite will attack without hesitation. It will pour all of its energy against that one point. And you will be defeated."

This sobered Radik, who thought several seconds before responding.

"Then what can we do?" he asked.

"Destroy it *before* it can find that weakness," the young woman's mouth chomped out mechanically. "It has many tools to find what it seeks. It need not only attack your vessel. It can also penetrate the mind of your people. It can pierce your bodies and invade your thoughts."

"It can probe our thoughts?" he summarized, cringing as he thought back to commander Evans, and what he might have been subjected to.

"Yes. It can also speak through your people, as I am with this young woman. It penetrates the spine, controlling the body. It was in this way that the mines were abandoned. It spoke through a victim, threatening to kill all the hostages it held if your army did not surrender. Then it carried them away for processing. But only after it harvested their thoughts for data. It knows the location of every place you could hide. It is wise that you have remained on the move. Otherwise you would have been captured by now."

Powers gasped painfully and arched her back, raising her belly into the air before dropping it back down again.

"What's wrong?" he asked, his hands shooting to her

shoulder and stomach, as though to intuit the problem.

"She hears my words in her sleep," the voice said. "She is traumatized. There is great suffering in her soul for her people. She regrets their pain. It is expressed bodily."

"Oh," Radik said. Unsure what else to do, he patted her gently and withdrew his hands.

"I am almost finished speaking to you," the voice said. "Then I will release her back into her body. She will awaken at once. She will not consciously remember my words. You will have to inform her of what has been spoken. It is imperative that you communicate with your people what is happening. They must know how the parasite seeks to manipulate them into revealing a weakness. Great care must be exercised. But be wiser than this. It will seek other ways to undermine you. It desires to explore the mind of anyone familiar with the weapon. It will penetrate their deepest secrets, peeling back their thoughts. There is no resistance against it. The psyche will be probed to the last layer. It studies, studies, studies. Above all it studies you. It is meticulous."

Having made this point with great emphasis, it prepared to withdraw from Powers' body.

"Wait!" Radik said, sensing its imminent departure. "What else can we do? How can we best undermine it? Is there a ship we can take to flee Jennet on? Or a place we can hide until the imperial forces arrive?"

"There is no ship," Powers said mechanically. "All commercial vessels were destroyed when the invasion began. The probing of the army's minds yielded the locations of all hidden military ships. You are stranded on Jennet."

"Then can we *hide* somewhere? Is there a place that the parasite doesn't know about?" Several seconds passed. "Hello? Are you still there?"

"There is a place," the presence said reluctantly. "A secret place. A *sacred* place. It was shown to me by Taegen."

"What, the emperor's mystic?" Radik asked, not having heard that name in a long time. "He was here?"

"He was here," the voice confirmed. "He taught me many things. He taught me to speak with you all. Taught me to care for the beings of Jennet, both small and great. But there is more – a great mystery. I do not know it. He did not know it. But it exists, and it is *very* ancient. Older than the Earthborn; older than your fallen kin. It is seemingly beyond all record."

"Fallen kin?" Radik asked, being unaware of the ancient history of his people.

"I cannot explain these things now," the presence replied. "I must resume my observation of the parasite. I will visit you again. I will guide you when you are lost. But you must not expect me always. I must watch the infestation. I must discover all its thoughts."

"But how can we find this hiding place?" Radik persisted. "We don't even know where to look."

"It is an hour north of this position," the presence informed him. "There is a cave, though a power protects it from normal eyes. You will not see it. Yet it is there. You will find this cave and enter it. The Devourers will not find you there. It is in the face of a low cliff."

"I think I know the place," Radik said, wracking his brain. "A river runs about a half mile south of it, right?"

"You are correct," the voice replied. "But you must be careful. That place is sacred. It will not be violated. You must show respect."

"How?"

"By your demeanor, your spirit," it explained. "The posture of your soul. It will know if you disregard it. Pass this along to the young woman. I must depart."

Unconsciously Powers writhed in the grass for several seconds, then laid still. Anxiously Radik watched her in the glow of the slowly descending moon. Suddenly her eyes opened.

"What happened?" she asked, trying to sit up but finding her body weak.

"Just take it easy," he told her, putting his hands on her shoulders to press her back down. "You've been through quite a lot."

"I don't...remember," she said, frowning as she tried to think. "No, wait. I remember coming back here. And then...there was this...I don't know, *noise*, in my head. Like a voice talking...to...me..." her voice trailed, her eyes wide as they searched the admiral's face for any sign he thought she was mad.

"Don't worry," he replied with a dry chuckle, reading her thoughts and shaking his head. "I don't think you're nuts. Not after everything I've just heard."

"You mean it spoke to you?"

"It did," he confirmed. "And it did it *through you*."

"Through...*me*?" she asked, the idea making her skin crawl. "Oh," she trembled, finally finding the strength to sit up and drawing her knees against her chest. For several seconds she rocked forward and back, trying to come to grips with what she was hearing. "What did it say?" she asked at last.

"A lot," he said, getting to his feet and gathering up their blankets as she watched. "Told me what the Devourers are up to, along with some intel that we've got to get to Krancis any way we can. Unfortunately we can't escape Jennet: the ships have all been destroyed. But there's a place we can hide until the navy shows up."

"Do you mind, Admiral?" she asked meekly, reaching out for her blanket as he was about to put it away. "That thing put a chill in my bones."

"Oh, sorry," he said, handing it to her before stuffing his into his pack. "We'll set out at once. The location isn't far, and we should be able to make it before sunrise. It claimed that there's no way the Devourers will be able to find us there. But," he paused, not quite sure how to say the next part. "The place is somehow sacred. It said there's a mystery there, one we must respect. I think we're gonna have to be very, very careful."

"I understand," she nodded, standing up unsteadily and drawing the blanket closely around her. She tried to reach down and grab her pack, but she was still too weak to hold the blanket around her with one hand and carry it with the other. She tested dragging it a little way, before the admiral stopped her.

"Here, you've been through enough for one night," he said, looping his own pack over his shoulders and grasping hers with a strong hand.

"Thank you," she said. "I'm sorry. I ought to carry my own weight."

"You carry more than enough weight around here," Radik assured her, leading the way with the bulky packs toward the game trail. "A stranded admiral couldn't ask for a smarter girl to accompany him," he added with an audible smile.

On the way Radik filled her in on all the presence had told him. Equally intrigued by the mysterious hideaway, they both moved on eager feet to its location. They crossed the shallow river that the admiral had mentioned before, reaching the cliff just as the sun's rays began to spread across the morning sky.

"Not a minute too soon," Radik commented, putting down the packs as Powers sat down on a large rock and wiped her brow. She had long since shucked the blanket, the fatigue of her possession combining with that of the journey to make her hot and sweaty. "It said we could look at it without seeing it," the admiral said as much to himself as to her. "Like it's cloaked or enchanted somehow."

Putting his hands on his hips, he stalked slowly to the right of the cliff face, leaving Powers on her rock near the packs. The cliff was neither very tall nor very long, seemingly erupting out of the ground for no reason before sharply terminating forty feet in the sky.

"No caves, no obvious paths," Radik said, rejoining his

companion as he continued to stare. "I think we're just gonna have to walk up and down its length, rubbing our hands across it until we find an opening."

"Okay," she assented, standing up with a modest grunt and about to shamble forwards.

"Maybe you'd best let me," he said with a courteous smile, taking her arm and guiding her back to her rock. "Just take it easy for a little while. There's not much cliff, anyhow," he added, turning around to face it. "There shouldn't be–," he paused. "Do you see that?" he asked her.

She looked up and followed his eyes to a barren stretch of rock.

"See what?"

"No," he muttered, walking forward with a mysterious air, "I didn't think so."

"See what?" she repeated, rising off the rock with some effort and following him. "I don't see anything."

He approached the cliff and stopped a foot short of it.

"Neither did I," he said, turning back to her for a moment, before seemingly pressing his hand straight into solid rock. "Not until a second ago."

"But…how…" she stammered, blinking her eyes at the sight.

"I couldn't see it until it wanted me to," he smiled, before withdrawing his hand. "Stay right here. I don't want to lose this spot in case it changes its mind." Quickly he hurried off and grabbed their packs, lugging them in a trot back to where she stood. "I'll go in first," he told her. "If something happens, bolt. One of us has to stay alive to warn Krancis."

Putting down the packs, he appeared to walk straight through a wall of rock. Several anxious minutes passed during which she had the hardest time obeying the order she'd been given. Still weary from all she'd been through, she decided to move a couple feet away from where he'd disappeared and lean against the wall. It was then that she discovered how broad the entrance truly was, for she fell right through and landed on the hard rock with a yelp.

"Are you alright?" she heard his voice echo back to her, quickly followed by reverberating footsteps.

Looking up, she saw a cave that descended into the ground at a twenty degree angle. It was broad, dry, and glowed a gentle blue despite lacking a visible light source. Struggling to her knees and then to her feet, she put a hand against the side of the cave to support herself as Radik returned.

"Are you alright?" he asked again, taking her arms in his hands. "Are you hurt?"

"I hit my side," she said with embarrassment, grimacing as she nodded towards it. "I tried to lean against the cave and fell through."

"Oh, well, let me have a look at it," he said, putting his right hand on her left side and feeling her ribs, causing her to inhale sharply. "Well, it doesn't seem like anything is broken. I think you just bruised it up pretty bad. Should be better in a couple days."

"What did you find?" she asked as he drew his hand away, hoping to shift attention away from her silly mistake.

"Well, this cave runs deep," he said, grabbing their packs and bringing them inside. "I didn't actually reach the end of it before I heard you cry out. But it doesn't seem like anyone, or any *thing*, has been down here in ages." He pointed upwards to the ceiling and then rubbed his fingers together. "Thick layer of cave dust. Hasn't been disturbed in a long, long time. I think it's probably safe for both of us to head down at once."

Shambling alongside the admiral, her hand still on her aching ribs, Powers felt as though she was descending into some new, magical world. The blue light grew more intense the farther they went, until it seemed almost... palpable, like living particles in the air. She wanted to say it had a scent, too, but she wrote that off as mere fancy.

"Strange, isn't it?" he asked her, carrying a pack in each hand and looking around. "It's like a dream, except we're awake. A living fantasy."

"What do you think is causing it?" she asked, trying to get a rational handle on it as the magic of the scene turned to eeriness. Much like her experience with the presence, she felt as though immaterial eyes were upon her, watching and measuring her every step. It had struck her as significant that only the admiral had been able to see the opening, and only *after* he'd very nicely suggested that she rest herself. While he seemed to derive an almost boyish delight in the strangeness of the experience, she grew more and more concerned that she was somehow unworthy, an intruder in a sacred place.

"Cross your fingers, and maybe we'll find out," was the most he could say, his voice dropping as they moved inside.

Finally the tunnel terminated in a large, cavernous room. It was shaped like a sphere, the floor sloping downward as one approached the middle. The same was true of the ceiling, sloping upward. In the center of the floor stood a craggy pillar of rock, reaching up to the center of the sphere. Atop it was nestled an orb of glimmering blue light. Its glow filled the entire space, yet was somehow gentle and easy on their eyes, despite their being adjusted to the dimness of the cave.

"What...*is*...that...?" Powers asked with wonder, her eyes transfixed by the beautiful light. "It's like..." her voice trailed.

"Like it's looking into your soul?" Radik finished for her, not being quite so carried away as she. "I can feel it too," he added, putting down the packs and taking a few steps towards it. She quickly caught up with him, her fatigue forgotten as the light drew every ounce of her attention. "Remember," he said a few seconds later, his voice shaking her from a reverie she had noticed falling into, "the voice said we had to be respectful. Whatever this thing is, it's pretty powerful. We need to be smart."

"O-of course," she agreed, nodding and locking eyes with him for a few seconds before they gradually drifted back to the light. "Still…it's so *beautiful*."

Her body felt warm, and all the pains she'd accumulated since the air battle over Jennet seemed to vanish. She felt neither hungry nor tired, a delicious sense of wellbeing coming over her. She followed Radik down to the base of the pillar, and was disappointed to find that it obscured some of the object's brilliance. Without really noticing she began to back away, trying to get back into the light.

"Come here, Lieutenant," he ordered sternly, his voice echoing off the walls and shocking her out of the trance she'd fallen into. With a self-conscious shake of her head she scurried back to where he stood. "You've got to keep your wits about you," he said, grasping her shoulders and dropping his voice for emphasis. "Hear me? This thing isn't bad, I don't think. But it's incredibly powerful. I can feel it pushing on my mind, trying to get inside and see what makes me tick. It's like the presence in that way, though not quite so courteous. I know how it's making you feel: I feel the same way. But you can't just let go because it feels good. We're only hiding here to make sure our intel gets back to the fleet. And we can't do that if we let this thing push our minds aside and turn us into a couple of vegetables. Have you got that?"

"Y-yes, sir," she replied, the dullness of her reply confirming his fears.

"Alright, come on," he said with a shake of his head, taking her hand and pulling her back up the slope.

"Where are we going?" she asked in a distracted tone, her head fixed on the beautiful light.

"We're heading back into the cave," he said, grabbing the packs' straps with one hand and dragging both his loads unceremoniously.

"What? No!" she exclaimed, fighting his grip and

nearly pulling him off his feet. With a livid expression she drew his hand to her mouth and tried viciously to bite him. Twice he jerked his hand away, but she kept at him, trying to break his hold.

In one swift, decisive move he dropped the packs and slapped her across the left cheek with his hand, twisting her head sharply and nearly jarring her teeth from her gums. With a yelp she received the blow, her eyes suddenly clearing.

"Admiral?" she asked, looking shakily between him and the light. "What's happening to me?"

"I don't know," he shook his head, grabbing the packs again and heading for the door. "But you're not staying here for another minute."

As they retreated away from the sphere back into the cave, Powers hand began to tremble in his.

"I'm sorry," she said fervently, pressing her free hand to her dizzy head. "So, so sorry. I don't know what came over me. I just *had* to stay. I couldn't bear leaving. I-I hated you for a moment back there."

"I don't doubt it," he replied with a dry laugh, recalling the fierce look of her bared teeth as she tried to sink them into his flesh. Halfway back to the entrance they stopped. Radik dropped the packs and looked at her. "How do you feel now?"

"Okay, I guess," she replied, her head throbbing from the blow she'd received. "I can still feel it pressing against my mind, trying to get inside, like you said. But it isn't very strong here. I think I can control myself."

"We'll stop moving when you're *sure* you can control yourself," he replied, taking up the packs again and striding with her to the entrance. "And not before."

A hundred feet short of the mysterious mirage that covered the cave's mouth, Powers pulled him to a stop.

"Here," she said with certainty, nodding her head. "Right here. I don't feel it pushing in on me like before. I can handle it."

"Are you *sure*?" he asked, looking into her troubled, but calm, eyes.

"Yes, I'm sure," she replied.

Dropping the packs one last time, he released her hand and watched to see if she would bolt. To his relief she knelt before her pack instead, drawing out her blanket and spreading it across the hard ground beside her. Following her common sense example, he did likewise, glad to rest his tired bones. Like before she drew her legs against her chest, resting her chin on her knees and rocking back and forth.

"What have we gotten ourselves into, Admiral?" she asked, finding it especially hard to break protocol right after attacking him.

"I don't know," he replied stoutly, reaching into his pack and drawing out food and drink. "But I intend to go back."

"What, down *there*?" she asked, nodding into the cave.

"I don't think that thing was trying to attack us," he replied. "I think it was trying to *communicate*. But it's got an awfully ham handed way of doing it. Maybe this first bad experience will teach it to back off a little, and give us a little more space."

"Don't do it, sir," she said, shaking her head. "What if something happens to you down there?"

"Then you'll wait up here and tell Krancis what we know once *Sentinel* arrives," he replied evenly. "Whatever this thing is, the emperor's personal mystic, Taegen, thought it was very important. That's reason enough to explore it further, even if there is some risk."

"Some risk!" she exclaimed. "I nearly took a bite out of your hand!"

"Yes, but it didn't affect me that way," he replied calmly. "Now, I know you're worried about me, and I appreciate that. But my mind's made up. I'm going back down there."

"Yes, sir," she replied in a defeated voice, looking away

and resting her chin upon her knees as before.

After they had eaten and rested for a little while, Radik gave Powers firm orders to stay put and made his way back down the cave. Walking slowly, he kept careful watch over his mental state. He'd spoken confidently to the lieutenant to calm her nerves, but in truth he was more than a little uneasy about facing the oddly glowing mystery on his own. If he started to come unglued, it was up to him to notice it and act quickly. Even a little hesitation might be enough to push him over the edge.

But to his surprise, he found that the shimmering blue light had vanished in the spherical room. The orb, now a dark, impenetrable black hue, sat idle atop its column of stone. The space was still illuminated, but he couldn't define how. It was all just *visible*, as though he'd gained some faculty for seeing in the dark. Cautiously he stepped towards the craggy pillar, stopping just when the orb was about to fall out of sight. Putting his hands on his hips, he drew a deep breath and released it slowly, trying to process what had happened in the meantime.

Maybe he'd been right, he reflected, and the orb, realizing it had gone too far, dialed back the output, apparently, to zero. He still had a little sense of magic in the air, as though it was enlivened by an intelligence, an awareness that surrounded him. But he couldn't be sure that wasn't just fancy, a holdover from his first encounter with the strange room. He wanted to step closer, to get a better look at the orb. But then the column would obscure his view. Crossing his arms, he looked around the room for an answer. It was then that his eyes fell upon Powers, standing awkwardly near the entrance.

"I told you to stay–," he began, his voice echoing powerfully through the chamber, magnified far beyond what he'd expected. Catching himself, he stopped and looked at the orb again. "What in the world?" he asked, trying to mutter but still speaking loudly.

"I had to come along," she said in an apologetic tone, her own voice small within the huge space. Noticing this, she, too, looked at the orb. "It must be magnifying just you," she uttered with wonder as she drew near to him.

"I've *got* to get a closer look at that thing," he said earnestly, whispering so that his voice was more or less normal. His eyes darted up and down the column, checking for handholds. "I think I can climb it."

"I don't think that's a good idea," she said cautiously, gently putting a hand on his arm to stop him. "Remember what the voice said: we have to treat this place with respect. What if we're not supposed to climb on that thing? What if that, I don't know, *desecrates* it somehow?"

"Only one way to find out," he replied confidently, feeling more in his element now that the task was a hands on one. In reality, half his fear of going into the room was that he'd be forced to deal with the entity from a distance, that he'd have to fence with it in some intuitive game of barely implied meaning. *That* he hated above all things. But now he sensed that the orb was beckoning to him, asking him to climb up to it by virtue of the lack of presence it now emanated.

"Then let me go," she insisted.

"No," he whispered, shaking his head. "This thing is magnifying *me*, not you. It's telling us that its attention is on me alone. If we *really* want to avoid desecrating this place, don't you think we should follow its wishes?"

She looked at him for a moment, trying to find words to argue. But he was right, and all she could do was nod and look away.

"Just stay here," he said, squeezing her arms warmly. "And actually *do it* this time!" he added with a touch of good humor despite the gravity of the situation. "I don't want us fighting over the same handholds at the top."

"Okay," she nodded again, smiling a little for his sake but dreadfully worried that he'd fall and break himself into pieces.

"Alright," he concluded, turning from her and sizing up the column. Approaching it, he walked all around it for the best place to start climbing, Powers' mimicking his movement from a distance, keeping him in sight. "Alright," he repeated, "keep your fingers crossed."

He'd said this in a light tone, but she slipped her hands behind her back and fervently crossed every finger she could. Her eyes grew wider as he rose above the hard, unforgiving floor, her heart tightening with every foot he added to the distance he must fall if a rock came loose or his hand slipped. Halfway up he started to grunt with each movement, the handholds growing farther and farther apart as he climbed. She saw him glance down at the floor and then jerk his head upward, regretting the impulse that had caused him to look. More afraid than he was, given that she could only helplessly watch, her body began to shake from sheer nerves.

Near the top he had to spiral around the pillar, following the now scanty handholds almost out of sight. She moved to keep him in view, her imagination presaging over and over how badly he'd be hurt if he fell. Bones broken, organs shattered; he'd die, for sure, even if the impact didn't finish him right away. Violently she jerked her head to the side, momentarily taking her eyes off the column and the dire thoughts it spurred. Hearing him gasp she looked back. Thankfully, he was merely fighting for air after his exertions, and not falling to his death.

Unconsciously she drew a hand from behind her back and began nibbling her thumb nail between her front teeth. He was almost to the top. So, so close. But it was plain that the handholds had all but evaporated. The last few feet he'd have to reach up, grab the lip of the column's top, and pull himself up by sheer strength. He was undeniably athletic, but did he have that kind of power anymore? She didn't know.

"Be careful," she uttered half-heartedly, her voice too small to reach his ears.

With sweat pouring off his face, he drew his body up as high as his handholds would allow, and then braced himself. For several seconds he closed his eyes and breathed, trying to recover as much stamina as he could before committing to the final test. He looked up, measuring the distance in his mind between himself and the lip. Then he reached for it. The fingers of his left hand *just* wrapped around the top. Working them as far around the lip as he could, he gripped hard and released his other hand. Suddenly his body weight shifted to the left, and his right foot slipped from the tiny lip of rock it'd rested upon. Despite the distance he heard Powers gasp below.

Holding on with his two left limbs, he fought his right hand upward and managed to grasp the lip. That was it: the moment of truth. With an incredible effort he dragged himself up to the top, slipping his right arm across the top of the pillar and using it to anchor himself. Doing the same with his left, his feet now dangling freely in the air, he elbowed his way farther inland.

"Are you alright?" Powers' asked just after his legs had disappeared. "Sir?" she asked more loudly, cupping her hands around her mouth.

In reply she saw a hand stick out over the edge, waving erratically that he was alright. Nearly dead from fatigue, he laid on his back for a minute and desperately caught his breath. He turned his head towards the orb, a massive black sphere at least four feet across, and perhaps five. At that moment he didn't particularly care, simply glad to have reached the top. The terrible thought of how he'd get down crossed his mind, but he pushed it aside with the certainty that the climb simply *had* to be done to answer their questions.

Struggling onto his elbow, and then to his knees, he looked at the sphere with wonder. Somehow it seemed to absorb light, reflecting nothing at all. It was like peering through a window into the darkest night imaginable. Twice he raised his hand to touch it, but each time he hesitated and drew it back, unsure if that would offend it in some way.

"What do you see?" Powers' called from below.

"It's hard to–," he began, thoughtlessly speaking at a normal volume, his voice booming through the room. "I don't know," he added in a whisper, which the echo had died out.

On his hands and knees he maneuvered all the way around the orb, finding nothing that suggested either its function or its nature. Finally he gulped, reached out his hand, and touched it.

Instantly he was carried to a place above Jennet, above the Milky Way itself. He saw stars dotting the blackness of space, the chaotic swirls of nebulas, and the progress of time. *Lots of time.* A blink of the eye saw stars shift markedly in their places. He realized he was being taken on a journey through history, winding backwards from the present moment to a point where even the star formations he'd memorized long ago were completely unrecognizable.

And then it stopped.

The journey simply halted for no apparent reason. For what felt like an hour his consciousness floated over the galaxy, until the timeline finally began to wind forwards. Reaching the present day once again, the orb broke its hold on his mind and he was back in the room.

Feeling drained and unsteady, he awkwardly shifted from his knees to his back.

"Julia? Are you still down there?" he asked loudly, forgetting himself again.

"O-of course," she said haltingly, her tone both anxious and curious. "Are you feeling okay?"

"Why?" he whispered.

"You've only been up there for a few minutes," she explained.

"I *have*?" he asked with surprise. "I had no idea. It seemed so much longer."

"Sir, how are you going to get down?" she asked, voicing what was now her main concern.

"I'll figure that out later," he replied determinedly, rising from where he lay and kneeling before the orb once more. "Right now, I have to learn more about this object."

He pressed one hand against it, and then two, but nothing happened. Puzzled by this, he moved around it slowly, touching it all over without effect. Standing up, he reached along the top of the sphere, but nothing happened.

"Sir?" he heard Powers call from below, watching with concern as he walked around on the column. "*Please be careful,*" she pleaded, her fingers once more behind her back and crossed the instant she uncupped her hands from around her mouth.

He waved distractedly to acknowledge her concern before his attention was totally absorbed by the strange object. He couldn't feel any distinct effect coming off of it anymore, but it both fascinated him and magnified his voice, so he was certain it was still applying itself to him in some way. It felt cold, smooth, impossibly hard. Like some kind of black diamond that had been formed by pressure and time. An *incredible* amount of time. Then an idea bubbled up from the back of his mind and struck him in the forehead: the orb had been establishing a context! Its own *personal* context! It wasn't just taking him on a fanciful jaunt down time: it was giving him a starting point, a perspective with which to understand what was to come.

"What's to come," he mused under his breath, the magnification carrying even this slight utterance to Powers' apprehensive ears.

"What?" she asked, though he ignored her.

"What an incredible…thing," he thought, running his hands appreciatively across its silken surface.

He knew that no such object existed in nature. How could it? How could a perfect orb of impossibly black matter come into being? And how could it interact intelligently with its surroundings? No, it was something else entirely. *Someone* must have built it, that was certain. But who? And what was its purpose? Was it some kind of computer, or data storage device? Was it supposed to maintain a record of the galaxy, a sort of self-written history book? Did *other* galaxies have them?

Absorbed by these questions, he didn't notice for several seconds that it had begun glowing blue once more. Urgently he tried to pull his hands away, but they were adhered to its surface.

"Julia! Get out! Get out!" he shouted, jerking his head over his shoulder to look at her.

But he was too late. With a moan the young woman's eyes rolled back in her head, and she fell against the hard floor.

❖ ❖ ❖

Several times during their journey, Rhemus had dropped in and out of consciousness. Tselitel helped him any way she could, which, unfortunately, meant little indeed. He barely ate or drank, and his sleep seemed to offer him no rest.

"It's because he's off Bohlen," Welter explained from the front seat. "That planet had some capacity to hold his disease in check, keeping him more or less functional. Without it, he's deteriorating fast."

"What can we do?" Tselitel asked, her own condition making her anxious and agitated.

"Just get him to those aliens as quick as we can," he replied. "They're the only ones who can do him any good at this point."

"If only he could have stayed on Bohlen," she said quietly, tenderly brushing his hair with her trembling hand. "It's terrible to see him like this."

"He had to leave eventually," Welter replied factually, seemingly unmoved by the emperor's plight. "The Devourers were going to attack sooner or–."

Rhemus was jolted awake by the name of their implacable foe, and his eyes looked around the cockpit for several seconds. Then they closed again, and he slumped back in his chair.

"How much longer until we reach Quarlac?" she asked, once her heart had descended out of her throat and resumed its old position.

"We're already there," he said, still looking around the seat at Rhemus' unconscious form. "We've been here for a little while now. Just a matter of reaching the *Kol-Prockians*."

"Well, how long will *that* be?" she asked.

"Not long," he assured her. "The planet they chose is pretty close to our galaxy, all things considered. We don't have to head very far into Quarlac."

"Good," she said with relief, hoping that it would be soon enough for Rhemus. "What kind of planet is it?"

"A *terrible* one," Frank answered. "Volcanic, with noxious air and a temperature that'll burn your skin off if you venture onto the surface without protection. Clouds of dust float through the sky, just *waiting* to fill your lungs and choke the life out of you. Lava flows across much of the planet, the world's molten core constantly gushing out of a thousand different geysers. So you can see why it was perfect for my people to hide there. Who'd ever want it?"

"Good thinking," she replied with dread, wondering how they would ever survive in such a place.

"But don't worry," Frank added proudly. "*Kol-Prockians* are excellent survivors. We can adapt to just about anything, given a little time. The exiles found one of the few dead volcanoes on the planet and built a base inside it. We'll be safe inside it."

"Just no moonlight walks?" she asked lightly, her dread more or less evaporating with his assurances.

"Alamar doesn't have any moons," Frank replied densely. "And if it did, the thickness of the atmosphere, combined with the clouds of dust and ash that constantly swirl over its surface–."

"No, Doctor," Welter cut in. "No moonlight walks."

"Naturally I knew she was joking," Frank said huffily, only catching on to that fact after Welter had cut him off and inadvertently clued him in. "I simply have a passion for explaining how things work."

"Good to know," Welter replied without interest, examining the instrument panel before him. "Fasten the emperor's harness, Doctor. We'll be coming out of warp in about ten minutes."

Doing as she was bidden, she managed to get Rhemus belted in despite the way he was spilled over his seat. Then she settled into her own place, easily sliding the harness over her slender form and clicking it. Anxiously she looked out the canopy, watching the mysterious blackness stream by. Without a word of warning it suddenly ended, the ship dropping out of warp a short distance from a smoldering red planet.

"What the?!" she exclaimed, having fallen into reverie.

"Time's up," Welter explained, as he guided the vessel towards Alamar. "It's been ten minutes."

"Oh, of course," she replied, recovering her equilibrium and looking out the front of the canopy at the angry planet. "Not a very happy place to be," she commented, as it grew larger and larger.

"I should say not," Frank agreed. "According to the information that Krancis gave me before departing, the occupants of *Kren-Balar* are suffering from terribly low morale. Naturally, it's only an estimate of their mental state, given that we're the first visitors they've had in ages, and all communication has been handled from a distance. But there are certain telltale signs that can be used to deduce such a likelihood."

"Are they dangerous?" Tselitel asked.

"Why do you think I'm here?" Welter asked rhetorically, shifting the Midnight Blade a little in his jacket as he spoke.

"I'm sure that Krancis doesn't anticipate any danger from my people," Frank said quickly, his pride wounded. "I don't think there's any risk of your being harmed by any of them."

"You can never tell what someone'll do when they're backed against a wall," Welter replied, taking one of two small automatic pistols from his right jacket pocket and handing it over his shoulder to Tselitel. "Take it," he said, after he'd held it in the air for a moment.

"Oh, I'm not very good with guns," she said, gingerly taking it in both hands despite its small size.

"Then don't open fire except at close range. Can't miss if they're just a couple feet away."

"Mister Welter!" Frank objected. "Are you planning to *attack* the very people who have offered your emperor refuge?"

"That depends on how they treat us," he replied in a low, merciless voice. "If they play nice, they'll get no trouble from me. But if they try to give us trouble, they'll find out in a hurry that we mean business." He glanced over the shoulder of his seat. "Stick it into your jacket, Doctor. We don't want to give them any undue alarm."

She hesitated several seconds, unsure what to do. Fearing that their escort's forethought would lead to disaster if the *Kol-Prockians* took their weapons the wrong way, she nevertheless tucked it inside her jacket once she realized it's the sort of thing Rex would have advised her to do. Best to walk in well prepared, she reflected with some misgivings.

As the egg penetrated the thick, polluted atmosphere of Alamar, visibility dropped to just a few yards. Using the ship's highly advanced instruments, Welter quickly descended through a cloud of ash to less than half a mile above the bubbling, tormented surface. The air was suddenly fairly clear, and Tselitel gasped as her eyes fell upon the undulating lakes and rivers of lava beneath them. Several geysers of molten rock spouted and gushed, contributing to the never ending flow.

"It's...incredible," she uttered in wonder, her eyes darting this way and that to try and take it all in. "It's like... all the surface of the planet is alive, and every passing second sees it move and live."

"You'll get used to it soon enough," Welter replied, piloting the ship towards a small cone in the distance.

"Is that our destination?" she asked, straining against her harness to see.

"Yes. We'll be there in a few minutes."

Soon they were above the dead volcano, seemingly the only one within miles, as all the others gushed and poured lava. Despite what she'd already seen of Welter's skill, Tselitel had to grip the seat of her chair in her trembling hands as they began their descent into its small opening. The ship only barely fit, its rear scraping against the cold, hardened lava. Then all was dark.

"Hang on, I'll activate the ship's light enhancement," Welter said, clicking a few buttons on the dashboard.

Suddenly the entire inside was visible, and they could see that the volcano ran much deeper than first appeared from the outside. Evidently it had flooded the area immediately around it with lava, half burying itself before finally ceasing in total exhaustion.

"There," Welter said, as his eyes fell upon the gray outline of a small landing pad at the very bottom of the volcano. "And they're expecting us," he added, right after a small string of lights activated, mutely welcoming them to land. He glanced over his shoulder at Tselitel briefly before looking down again, guiding the ship towards the pad. "Stick close to the emperor, and be ready to use that thing if you have to. We don't really know what we're getting into here."

"I understand," she replied, growing more and more nervous as they descended and finally touched the pad.

Seconds after making contact, a thud reverberated through the ship, and they saw the volcano's floor rising all around them. The pad was moving lower, drawing the ship into the base and away from the heat and toxic air. A door began to cover the hole into which they were descending. A burst of claustrophobia shot through Tselitel as she saw them hemmed in on every side and capped off above. What if something went wrong? What if the *Kol-Prockians did* take their weapons the wrong way? They'd be trapped under a thousand tons of rock, far from any kind of help.

With effort she calmed herself, aware that she would be no use to Rhemus if she came unglued. Slipping her hand into her jacket pocket and clutching the little pistol, she swallowed hard and watched countless years of sediment rise past her.

Suddenly they reached the bottom of the shaft, arriving inside a large, open hangar. Ships were parked in all directions, representing every possible make she could imagine. Many were completely unknown, and of unusual design.

The platform they rode finally hit bottom with a metallic clang, jostling the passengers. Rhemus muttered in his sleep, but didn't awaken.

"Looks like our welcome party is here," Welter said with a strong note of aversion in his voice. Beside their craft stood five *Kol-Prockians*. Lean, humanoid, but with an air of almost bird-like lightness, they moved in choppy, inelegant motions. Two of them were conferring together, their eyes darting between each other and the ship. The other three were standing mutely behind them, their weapons held at the ready. "Seems like they can't figure out just how to begin," Welter opined.

Tselitel studied the aliens with keen interest, glad to finally put faces to an exotic name that, thanks to Wellesley, had become part of her everyday speech. She found that the mental sketches she'd made in idle moments weren't too far off the mark, given the details Wellesley had shared back on *Preleteth*.

"More or less of human height, but much narrower and lighter. Average weight was around one hundred and thirty pounds," he'd said at the time.

But this spare description had obscured as much as it had illuminated. The general outline was correct: they seemed almost the skinny cousins of the, in comparison, bulky Earthborn. In silhouette one could easily confuse one race for the other. However, it was in the face that the two peoples immediately, almost shockingly, diverged. The *Kol-Prockians* had a nearly flat nose, their nostrils embedded in the bone structure of their skulls. Their cheekbones were broad, very broad, giving their faces an exaggerated kite-like shape when viewed from the front. Tselitel reflected that this must have something to do with the nature of their nasal faculty, it reaching side-to-side instead of front-to-back as with humans. The eyes of the two talkers were rather small but lively, animated, almost hyper as they bounced from one object to another during their discussion. Those of the three escorts refused to fix on a single place, moving perceptibly from second to second despite the rigidness of their bodies.

The hands, feet, and limbs of the aliens seemed human enough, though very thin and light. They wore uniforms that covered their bodies right up to the neck, making it hard to tell how much of their form consisted of muscle. Despite this, she felt that it would take at least two *Kol-Prockians* to cope with a human opponent in physical combat. They simply lacked the mass and size to compete.

"Aren't you going to open the canopy?" Frank asked after a few moments had slipped silently by.

"Never hurts to keep 'em waiting for a few minutes," Welter replied, quietly drumming his fingers on the armrest of his seat. "We don't want to look too eager. They're the ones who are getting their bread buttered out of this deal."

"I'd say both sides stand to benefit," the AI replied, a little chagrined at Welter's attitude. "I think you're just being unfriendly."

"It's their base," he replied. "Let them make the first move. If they can ever make up their minds."

It was with discomfort that Tselitel watched the discussion continue outside the craft. Shouldn't they have already had a protocol worked up? Wasn't the emperor of man important enough to warrant at least *that* much forethought? As she thought this the conversation ceased, and one of them, stepping a little ahead of the other, waved for the canopy to be raised.

"About time," Welter murmured, opening the cockpit and looking over the side. As he did so the aliens' eyes shot to his large, scowling face, darting around and studying every facet of it.

"My p-people wish to welcome you to *Kren-Balar*," the lead alien said in good but hesitant English. "It is our honor to have such a distinguished guest."

"Yeah," Welter nodded, before looking over his shoulder at the slumped form of the emperor. Then he looked back at them. "He needs all the help you can give him. Right now. Are your facilities ready to receive him?"

"Yes, yes, oh, yes," the spokesman said earnestly, his active eyes filling with concern as they bounced between Rhemus and Welter. "We hadn't anticipated he would be in such a dire state. A medical team will remove him at once to the hospital wing."

"Good."

A few hurried words were spoken into a communicator that wrapped around his wrist, and in less than a minute half a dozen *Kol-Prockians* wearing white coats were moving across the hangar, pushing a stretcher.

"Guess medicine is practiced the same everywhere," Tselitel reflected, surprised to see such a familiar sight in an alien installation.

Carefully they got the emperor over the side and strapped onto the stretcher. Loudly, incoherently, he grumbled in his sleep just as they were about to move him. Freezing in place, the aliens' eyes darted between one another.

"It's okay," Tselitel assured them, realizing that they were scared to be treating what was likely their first human, especially one of such importance. "He's just sleep talking. He's been doing it for some time."

They watched her for several seconds, their eyes bouncing all around her face. She felt they were trying to gauge her trustworthiness as a source of medical information.

"You can listen to her," Welter chimed in, moving to the emperor's side. "She's a doctor, too."

"Oh, I wouldn't say–," she began.

"You're too modest, Doctor," he said assertively, gesturing for the stretcher to move. "Shall we?" he asked, his tone little short of a command.

"I hope you haven't given them the wrong idea," she whispered to him nervously as they walked a few steps behind the stretcher, just out of earshot. "I'm just a psychiatrist. If they start to question me about his condition or his medical history–."

"Right now he needs treatment," he interrupted again, his eyes never leaving the stretcher. "Something had to be done to get these guys moving. None of them wants the responsibility of something going wrong, so I had to dump it in your lap."

"Thanks," she said with a flare of her eyebrows, her nerves nevertheless steadied by his pointblank common sense.

"I would have done it myself," he added quietly. "But nobody would buy me for a doctor, so it had to be you."

"I understand," she nodded.

Led out of the hangar and into a long, narrow corridor, they began to work their way down a maze of nondescript hallways. Each door they passed had writing on it, but it was in the language of their hosts, and neither of them could read it. Frank could have translated everything their eyes fell upon, had Welter not deliberately broken skin contact by stuffing him inside his jacket pocket. It was the one consolation he could find for entering the base, and he intended to make the most of it.

The light-footed march of the three guards could be heard right behind them. Apparently sharing Tselitel's physical assessment, they gave Welter a wide berth, unconsciously raising their guns a little whenever the turning of a corner or a glut of other people forced them nearer to him. They'd recognized at once the anger and frustration that trembled beneath the surface, scarcely held in check by his iron will. He walked with the heavy, slightly lethargic motions of a lion who, at any moment, and for any reason, could break forth and tear them limb from limb.

Penetrating the hospital wing of the base, the garb of the occupants changed to the familiar white of their medical companions. Every *Kol-Prockian* they passed paused or slowed a little as their eyes darted across the faces and bodies of their new guests.

"This way, please," the spokesman said, gesturing hesitantly down a very narrow corridor that required them to move in single file. The emperor's stretcher took up almost the whole path, forcing anyone they encountered to doubleback and wait for them to pass.

The corridor merged with another, much larger one at the end. Resuming their old formation, more or less, the group continued another fifty paces before stopping at a door impressively named in bold, alien characters.

"This is the doctor who will see to the emperor," the spokesman explained, as the door was opened and the stretcher was wheeled in. He was about to close it again when Welter's powerful hand clamped around his wrist and stopped him. Fearfully his eyes darted around Welter's face. The guards stood impotently by, unsure if they should intervene given the man's evident importance. "Please, sir," the spokesman complained, recovering himself and trying to twist his thin wrist out of the hold. "He'll be very safe with doctor *Keelen*."

"Wherever he goes, I go," Welter stated, looking around at the rest of the entourage to drive home the point. "Understand?"

Reflexively even the guards nodded, his air of mastery giving him instant authority.

"B-but, sir," the spokesman tried to object, as Welter pulled him away from the door and entered.

The personnel who'd wheeled Rhemus inside still stood beside his stretcher, listening as doctor *Keelen* spoke quietly to them in *Kol-Prockian*. The room was some kind of preparatory space for the main preservation chamber, with computers and shelves of tools spread along the walls. The doctor himself was tall, vital, with graying tufts of hair on his head. His eyes shot immediately to Welter as he entered.

"This is not a place for non-medical people," he said in a peculiarly precise fashion, as though the tip of his tongue had to puncture each word as it flowed across it. Unlike all of his comrades, his eyes rested pretty steadily on those of the emperor's zealous bodyguard. Evidently used to authority, he lacked the schoolboyish uncertainty the others had evinced. "You'll have to wait somewhere else."

"That's not going to happen," Welter replied, his back and shoulders arching a little as he reflexively shifted into a panther-like combat pose.

"Your antics won't get you far inside a base that we wholly control," *Keelen* said dismissively, before looking at the guards and snapping his fingers. To his visible surprise they didn't move, the force of Welter's presence overawing them. His surprise quickly soured into an acidic scowl, and with a wave of his hand he ordered them to get out. "You, too," he said, pointing at the spokesman and his ineffectual companion. "All of you, get out!" he exclaimed, looking at the *Kol-Prockians* attending Rhemus, his anger growing with each order.

Quietly they filed out, leaving the three humans with the fuming doctor. Tselitel moved her trembling hands behind her back, wishing above all else that a more diplomatic man had been sent instead of Welter. Her fertile imagination could already see the rest of the base closing down, shutting them in until they were under control. They'd probably be locked away for their impudence, powerless to do anything for Rhemus because they'd offended their hosts beyond what anyone could reasonably tolerate. Oh, if only–.

"You've made an accurate assessment of our people," *Keelen* said, cutting off her train of thought. Leaning against the far wall, he crossed his thin arms and darted his eyes between the three of them for half a minute. "They must be handled with a decisive spirit," he continued, confirming what Welter had already intuited. "But that spirit should not be borne by visitors, by *guests*," he concluded, his eyes narrowing with emphasis.

"You would do no less, were he your emperor," Welter replied.

For several tense moments Tselitel looked between them, anxiety twisting her stomach into knots as the power play continued. Finally the doctor nodded.

"That's true enough," he agreed, his shoulders easing a little as he uncrossed his arms. "You're the other patient?" he asked, his gaze darting up and down Tselitel's frail, slightly shaking form.

"Yes," she nodded, surprised she could speak given the tightness of her throat. "I have–."

"Valindra, yes, I know," he cut her off, still ruffled. "Krancis sent ahead all the medical information your people possess on both of your conditions. Which, unfortunately, isn't particularly extensive. It's remarkable that an empire as powerful as yours doesn't have a greater handle on how to care for its own people. I should have thought–."

"And *I* should have thought that a people who tore themselves apart in a civil war, allowing themselves to be carted away into slavery later, would be a little more circumspect when lecturing others on imperial priorities," Welter uttered, his deep-seated rage bubbling dangerously close to the surface.

Realizing that he had a remarkably dangerous man on his hands, the doctor, much against his temperament, decided to back off.

"We'll do everything we can for the two of you," *Keelen* said in a somewhat softer tone, looking at Tselitel and then Rhemus. "But you must understand that we cannot cure either condition. We can only slow their progress and limit their symptoms. Perhaps, had he been born during the height of my people's achievements, we could have cured him. But those days are gone. And as for your Valindra, I'm afraid there's no known cure."

This last sentence struck Tselitel like a blow to the stomach. Hoping against hope, she'd cherished the idea that the *Kol-Prockians*, even if they couldn't cure her themselves, might know of someone that could. Her heart seemed almost to stop, and she breathed with difficulty.

"Are you…alright, Doctor?" Welter asked, her face turning red.

"I–I need air," she managed to say, turning unsteadily for the door when a strong pair of hands grasped her shoulders and turned her back.

"No," *Keelen* said, as she faced Welter with tears forming in her eyes. "You need the preservation chamber. It'll even you out for the time being."

"How long will I last in there?" she asked, a pair of droplets springing from her reddening eyes as she blinked. "I mean *really*? Six months? Six years?"

"It's impossible to even approximate an answer until we examine you," *Keelen* replied. "But there should be no risk in the immediate future. Try to take some comfort in that fact."

A couple of hours later, once they'd been processed according to standard *Kol-Prockian* medical protocol, the two of them were placed inside the chamber. It was square, the walls forty feet long and the ceiling ten feet off the floor. The space was separated into four quarters, divided by the thinnest possible cloth curtains. Rhemus, still unconscious, had been carefully laid out upon the floor. Both of them had been given thin robes to wear.

"This will prevent the absorption, and subsequent blocking, of the healing effects of the chamber," *Keelen* explained briefly when he'd introduced her to the chamber. "We regret that your emperor must rest upon the floor. But the same rule applies to bedding and furniture as well." His eyes went to Welter's. "Furthermore, we must minimize the number of occupants if we are to maximize the effect. Each additional body draws healing energy from the chamber, keeping it from those who need it most."

Frowning at this, Welter examined the other quarters and found an old *Kol-Prockian* bunched up in a corner, his arms wrapped around his legs. The alien gazed up at him, his eyes slowly examining his features. Gruffly the visitor nodded, before returning to the others.

"Who's he?"

"A much renowned scientist, the greatest technical mind our people today possess," *Keelen* replied. "Without him we could never have kept the chamber functioning this long. For this reason, against protocol, we allow him to stay in here as long as he wishes. That has been his one condition ever since he began to care for the device one hundred years ago."

"A hundred *years*?" Tselitel asked.

"The chamber is a potent longevity booster," he replied. "And provided the subject is healthy, as *Karnan* was when he first entered, it will give one an unnaturally long life."

"Then why don't all your people use it?"

"Because every individual into which energy must be channeled increases the demand on the apparatus," *Karnan* explained as he rounded the curtain, his steps unsteady. His thin robe looked comically large on his emaciated frame as he shuffled towards them. "The equipment in these walls is almost impossible to repair when it breaks down," he said in a shaky voice. "It's terribly expensive to even approximate the quality our ancestors put into their m-machinery. So we have to make do. In order to *lessen* the burden on the system," he said, looking at the doctor and Welter, "we strictly omit all but the most deserving cases from using the chamber."

"We were about to leave, sir," *Keelen* said respectfully.

"Then why don't you leave *now*," he replied pointedly, aiming a thin index finger at the door and sharply jabbing it. "Before you place any more needless demand on the system."

"Of course, sir," *Keelen* uttered apologetically, moving towards the exit until he realized Welter wasn't in tow.

The emperor's bodyguard stared hard at the ancient *Kol-Prockian*, boring into his mind with his practiced gaze.

"You've got nothing to fear from me, human," *Karnan* uttered with a laugh. "Look at my hands," he said, holding them up. "Look at my *arms*," he added, rolling up his sleeves. "I'm hardly strong enough to stand at this point. I can only do my work with the utmost difficulty." He looked at Tselitel. "She would be more than enough to stop me, had I any ill intent. Which I don't. It was only the promise from Krancis that brought me back in here, that drove me to continue my life's work a little bit longer. I've…seen enough of suffering," he said, shaking his head.

"He'd decided his time had come to an end several months before Krancis' message arrived," *Keelen* explained quietly, as though the old *Kol-Prockian* would lash out at him for his words. "Only the promise of a new home for our people brought him from his chosen deathbed and back into the chamber."

"And I'll stay here until my work is truly complete," *Karnan* asserted. "Until all *K-Kol-Prockians* can grow and live under…under the aegis of…."

He began to cough, his body shaking violently as he did so. Fearing that he would fall over, Welter and *Keelen* helped him to the floor, after which he slapped their hands away.

"I'm not dead yet," he said acerbically, scowling up at them. "Now, will you get out of here and stop b-burdening the system?"

For several seconds Welter eyed him, before nodding and looking at Tselitel.

"Remember your duty," he said to her. "I'll be right outside the door. If you so much as *squeak* for help, I'll be here instantly."

"Thank you, Gustav," she uttered quietly as they left.

Once on the other side of the door, *Keelen* closed it. A glass panel was at the top of the door, and through this he peered at the occupants for a moment. Then he turned to Welter, who was pocketing the small pistol they'd found on Tselitel when she changed her clothes.

"What did you imagine you were entering when you came here?" *Keelen* asked. "A hostile camp? A band of renegades who'd sell out you and your emperor for some trinkets? This deal means too much to both sides for either of us to allow it to fall through. You didn't have to bring weapons."

"How do you know our language?" he asked indifferently, ignoring the question as he moved a chair to the right of the door and sitting down. "I was under the impression that we required a translator to deal with you."

"A few of us have learned your language," *Keelen*

replied with annoyance at having his question brushed aside. "All high ranking officials have been required to do so."

"Why?"

"For just such an occasion as this. A few of us have long felt that the human empire offered our only likely means of survival. Learning your language was part of our preparation, in case we could ever prove valuable enough for you to invite us back into our home galaxy."

This last part was spoken with a subtle souring of tone that was not lost on Welter.

"Then most of you don't speak it?"

"No," he shook his head with a frown. "They're too shortsighted for anything requiring real discipline. Did you seriously expect that individuals who could be pushed aside, as *you* pushed them aside, could hold themselves to any course of action that didn't offer any guarantee of reward?" Crossing his arms and leaning against a table, he continued. "My people are not what they used to be. They're fickle and restless and uncertain. We used to be better than this, *stronger* than this. But the best of us did not escape to this base all those years ago. For a time we were low scavengers, with only a few minds being worthy of mention. These precious few maintained the technology that has made us of such value to you in this dark hour. The rest are weak and worthless."

"They're not worthless, so long as they're your people," Welter replied.

"What good are they, if they can't contribute to our survival as a race?" *Keelen* asked, his voice rising as he grew angry at the thought. "They're a drain on our resources. They fight with each other when they ought to be working *together* to ensure we have a future. Like stupid little animals they concern themselves with their own petty desires, ignoring that we must *cling* to each other if we're to survive. The fact that we're hiding in an extinct volcano on the worst planet imaginable is lost on them, for they, as their ancestors had before them, have grown accustomed to that fact. They can't imagine a better future, a future worth *striving* for. So it's up to the few minds that are capable of more than gratifying their appetites to hold up the rest. An enormous burden is upon those, like myself, who have the foresight to do this."

His voice had grown quite loud by this point. He started when a frail fist beat against the glass, and he looked to see *Karnan's* scowling face looking out at him. Instantly remorseful, he made for the door to apologize, but was waved off by the old scientist. Grumpily he turned his back and disappeared from the window.

"I forgot myself," he uttered, returning to where he'd been leaning and crossing his thin arms. For half a minute his eyes surveyed the floor before his feet, regretting that he'd disturbed *Karnan*. "He deserves rest most of all," he said. "Without him the chamber would have gone offline long ago, and our hope would have ended."

"A people who are disheartened and weak can be easily bought," Welter said after another period of silence.

"What?" *Keelen* asked.

"You asked me why we came into *Kren-Balar* armed," he explained. "That's why. Living on the edge, you'd kill half your number if it saved the rest from extinction. When a people are pushed to the brink, they'll exchange *anything* to save themselves. And that includes foreign guests, especially if a certain…party promised them aid."

"Many believe that merely mentioning the true name of those beings invites their insight into our most hidden places." He paused to spit his contempt for them. "We call them the *Dolshan*, the despised people. Clearly you are of the same mind."

"Where the emperor's wellbeing is concerned, I'm determined to play it safe," Welter replied.

"Indeed," *Keelen* uttered, glancing at the door's window before looking again at his guest. "Have you met our leader *Seldek* yet?"

"No."

"The niceties of diplomacy are entirely lacking in you," *Keelen* said with a shake of his head. "You will have caused offense by doing so. You should have seen him first."

"My only purpose is to ensure the safety of the emperor and doctor Tselitel," he replied factually. "Every other consideration is irrelevant."

Keelen eyed him for a moment, studying him a little harder than he had before. From the first few minutes he'd known him, he'd sized up as a surly bodyguard with a superiority complex. But now he detected a hint of something more. A strain of pain, well hidden, ran right through the middle of everything he thought and did. With almost cruel coldness he regarded the world around him, and the people in it. Yet despite that he still bore attachments, the most obvious being that to the emperor. Another less visible but constantly present one was his dedication to the human cause, without which his devotion to Rhemus would be nothing more than a personal fondness. Then it clicked into place.

"You're in mourning," *Keelen* said, unable to hold back despite knowing it must be sacred ground to the human. The look of hatred on Welter's face instantly told him how sacred that ground was, and he raised his hands in an apology that was not accepted. Finding the burning stare of the man intolerable, the *Kol-Prockian* excused himself. "I'll find *Seldek* and bring him to meet you all," he explained. And then, as a parting shot, "he likely hasn't come to see you because you should have gone to *him* first."

With this the alien left him alone with his dark thoughts.

Inside the chamber, Tselitel sat propped up against the wall, occasionally brushing Rhemus' troubled brow as he slept. Already she felt a little better, her hands and feet trembling a bit less. The temperature was rather on the high side; around eighty, she figured. She reflected that this was likely necessary given their ancient companion's frail condition.

Reflexively looking at the ship which divided them from each other, she wondered what he was thinking about. Did he like them? Was he annoyed to have to share his chamber with them? She didn't know, and with a shrug she faced forwards again. She was startled to see that *Karnan* was standing a few feet away, looking at her curiously.

"I-I'm sorry," she stuttered, saying the first thing that came to mind in an attempt to disguise her surprise. "I, um."

"It lulls you, doesn't it?" he asked with interest, moving closer and sitting down. "Doesn't it?" he repeated, when she just looked at him.

"Uh, yes," she replied, trying to gather her thoughts. "I guess I didn't notice it at first, but I feel very…restful."

"Fascinating," *Karnan* uttered, trying to keep his voice down for Rhemus' sake despite his enthusiasm. "I've never seen this equipment used on a human before. I'm terribly interested to know what you're feeling."

"Well, um," she began, staring at the wall behind him for a few moments to find her thoughts. "I feel very…warm, and a little hazy. I didn't realize it until I started talking to you. I feel very lucid internally, like I can almost see my thoughts." She paused, reflected, and then corrected herself. "Actually, I *can* see my thoughts, like scenes in a dream. Everything is passing through my mind like a tapestry, one long canvas of thought, and not the little snatches that one usually sees. I feel separate from the outside world, free to dive deeper and deeper into myself."

"Good," *Karnan* uttered. "Very good. Then you're at once aware of the risks as well, aren't you?"

"Risks?" she asked, shaking her head slightly to indicate her confusion.

"Addiction," he replied. "Right now, you're simply glad to feel some relief from your condition. But it takes very little thought to imagine how you could wish never to leave here, to stay separate from your responsibilities and plumb the depths of your own mind for the rest of your life. Like harvesting diamonds from a mine that you carry around at all times."

"Oh, that would never happen to me," she laughed a little too loudly, considering the unconscious man beside her. "What I mean is," she continued in a quieter voice, "that I have plenty to keep me drawn to life outside this room."

"Others have thought so," he replied soberly. "And yet I have seen many dragged from this chamber by force, vowing revenge on anyone who would separate them from the peace it brings. For that is its greatest gift: peace. It supports your health and suppresses what ails you, while giving you the internal focus to delve within. Every inner discovery feels like a revelation, so vividly does your imagination paint it on the walls of your mind." He eyed her gravely for a moment. "It's not to be taken lightly."

"No," she agreed, shaking her head. "It isn't."

"Good," he smiled. "Just keep aware of how you're feeling. And watch him, too," he added. "His condition looks worse than yours, and that may soften his will. Such cases entail a larger risk, given that the body cannot maintain itself as effectively against outside influences. You may need to help him maintain his equilibrium. Tell *Keelen* if you notice any abnormalities in his mentality. It may be necessary to take him out from time to time so that he can avoid addiction."

"I understand," she assured him, looking at Rhemus as his chest rose and gently fell with each breath. "He does seem so much more peaceful now, like a weight has been lifted from his shoulders. I was so worried for him on the way here. He lost consciousness before we'd even reached Quarlac."

"Then he'll likely be in a heavy dream state for the time being," *Karnan* opined. "That's often the case with severe cases that are brought to the chamber. He is probably exploring the deepest reaches of his psyche as we speak, learning new things about himself that have long been obscured by the dictates of consciousness and everyday life."

"Good things, I hope," Tselitel uttered. "He's had enough on his plate ever since the Devourers arrived."

"They'll be true things," he told her. "The unconscious mind speaks in a strange dialect that is oftentimes baffling. But if you can decipher its messages, you can be introduced to an entirely new world. It can unsettle or distress you, but it's true, all the same. All that remains is the *courage* to put it to use."

"I know," she smiled. "I'm a psychiatrist."

"Oh, I'm sorry. I didn't mean to lecture you on your speciality."

"No, no, I'm not offended," she said earnestly. "I value what you have to say, especially coming from a different perspective as you do. Such a different culture! And so many *years* of experience! I'm honored to listen to you, to understand a little bit of what you've learned. Please don't ever be reluctant to share any of your thoughts with me."

"I won't," he smiled again, glad to have found a conversational companion to help ease the long, lonely hours in the chamber. "I'm sorry that this space is so spare," he added, gesturing towards the walls. "But we've been unable to isolate a material that doesn't inhibit the effects of the equipment. And believe me, I've *tried*," he chuckled. "Sitting on the floor gets old after the first few *decades*. I wish we could manage even the most basic furniture. Just a chair! But anything more than the thinnest cloth gets in the way," he said, rubbing the sleeve of his robe between his fingers.

"It must have been so hard for you, spending all these years in here," she sympathized.

"It will all be worth it, if we can hold up our end of the bargain and keep your emperor safe," he said, pausing to cough gently. "He's the single most important being on this base, for both of our peoples. No exertion is too great to keep him secure." He nodded to the exit behind him. "Your friend outside the door knows this."

"Yes, he does," she agreed, the thought of him raising anew the concerns she had for what trouble he might inadvertently stir up.

"He's not in such a good state himself," the wise old scientist commented. "It seems Krancis has sent us three broken vessels, each of which must be mended if they are to fulfill their destiny."

"I'm afraid the emperor and I can never be mended," Tselitel said quietly. "Though I hope Gustav can. I think he's a good man, beneath all that pain and rage. If he could just *get* to it."

"You can mend a pot without strengthening its basic structure," he replied. "Mending doesn't make a thing perfect, nor does it ensure it will last forever. The question isn't one of rendering an item perfect; it's a question of making sure it holds out long enough to do what it was *put here to do*. Once it has served its purpose, as I am now doing, it can gratefully yield itself to the cosmos, rejoining the matter from which it was ultimately drawn."

"But I don't have a mission," she objected. "Oh, the emperor must stay strong for the human race, and I can easily imagine Gustav being an important part of this war. But nobody needs, well," she paused, thinking of Rex. "There is a man, one who needs me. But I wouldn't call that a mission. More like a terrible dependency. My heart aches when I think this, but sometimes, for his sake, I wish we'd never met. He says I've rescued him from a life without meaning, and I believe that's true. In fact, it's true for *both* of us. But I'm an albatross to him, a terrible liability that could pass away at any moment and shatter his heart in two."

"Then your mission is to ensure that doesn't happen," *Karnan* replied. "One's mission in life isn't always accompanied by high-stakes decisions or the kind of explosive action that Welter out there is used to. Your mission is your part in this life that's indispensable, the action that *you* individually need to take. How else is it a mission? If anyone could do it, it would simply be a task, one more item on the cosmic checklist. It has to be something that *you* must do, and you alone. It doesn't matter how big or small it appears to be, because it will have repercussions down all of time. Never ignore *your* role, *your* task, merely because it seems to be minor. Your life appears futile to you, a dead end road that's about to lead off a cliff. But that's not what it means to Rex Hunt. To him, you're inexpressibly important, which *makes you inexpressibly important*."

"How do you know his name?" she asked, not recalling having said it.

"Oh, I'm privy to everything that goes on around here," he said. "Not a single important decision passes before *Seldek* without him first checking it with me. It's hard to ignore a century and a half of experience, even if most of that time has been spent tinkering with ancient technology."

"Have you ever worked on an ancient AI?" she asked.

"No, they're impossible to find these days." A few seconds silently passed, and then his eyes brightened. "Wait, yes, I have. It was so long ago that I forgot. But I *did* mess around with one once, trying to figure out how they worked. It was at the end of its life, and tried to help me understand how it was made, but it wasn't any use. Oh, our ancestors had a knack for those things that we can't even *hope* to match today. The things we churn out are little more than toys, just basic assistants to help run the more mundane aspects of the base. You can't trust them to make important decisions, because their psyches, if you can call them that, are always flawed." He shook his head. "Yet another lost art among my people. Sometimes I just want to give up when I think of how we live in the shadow of our forebears. But then I see the faces of my comrades as I walk through the corridors of this base, and the anxiety, the *uncertainty* written there spurs me on. I have to keep going, no matter how much the memory of our lost glory pains me. The *Kol-Prockian* people must continue.

Their flame *cannot* go out."

Silently she reached out and grasped his thin hand.

"We'll do everything we can to ensure that doesn't happen," she said. "Both Rex and myself are very fond of your people."

"But…you haven't met us before today," *Karnan* replied, suspecting that she was just being kind. "How could you be fond?"

"Oh, I forgot to mention," she said with a self-critical shake of her head. "Rex found one of your ancient AIs on the planet Delta-13. He's been his companion for years."

"He *did*?" he asked excitedly, his voice echoing off the walls. "How is that even possible? We've heard rumors of ancient AIs, but we've never been able to actually *find* one. What kind of condition is he in? Can he still function at a high level?"

"Yes, yes he can," she assured him, lowering her voice markedly to remind him of the emperor. "He seems to still be in his prime, though admittedly I have nothing to compare him against. He's crisp, rational, and on point."

"Incredible," *Karnan* said in a tone of disbelief. "To think that one of the *ancient* AIs is still among us, and functioning well! Does he play a major part in the war? Is he a great help to your Rex?"

"An enormous help," she gladly told him. "And given the loudness of his personality, he is probably making the walls of *Sentinel* reverberate with his advice."

"Ha! That's just like how they made them!" he clapped his hands. "Pushy, acerbic, and not a little full of themselves. Always think they're the smartest in the room."

"That's Wellesley," she had to laugh. "Though he's a pleasure to be with, really. Perhaps the years have worn off some of the rough edges."

"Could be, could be," he said eagerly, his mind a thousand miles away as he contemplated the sheer improbability that one of the old AIs had survived so long, and retained his faculties. Then a puzzled look crossed his face. "Can't imagine the ancients calling him Wellesley. That sounds like a human name."

"Oh, that's just a nickname that Rex gave him. His real name is *Allokanah*."

Suddenly the old scientist's face fell, and he gazed at her with bewilderment.

"You...must be joking," he uttered in a hollow voice, his head slowly shaking from side to side.

"No, not at all," she said quickly, confused by his behavior. "Why? What's wrong?"

"*Allokanah* is considered a traitor by most *Kol-Prockians*," he said gravely. "Those who believe in the fringe rebellion of the old days hate him as a turncoat. And those who support the old confederation believe it was through him alone that *Koln* was able to hold out so long, thus irreparably damaging us as a civilization and sealing our fate. One thing is certain: without him, there would have been no meaningful civil war, with its incredible loss of life. The fringe would have been crushed in fairly short order, and the old regime wouldn't have been fractured beyond repair. We may have still been defeated and carried away. But we stood a chance before the war. After that, there wasn't any hope." He sighed, visibly distraught. "If *only* it had been a different AI that survived, one other than *Allokanah*. It's like fate is taunting us by saving *him* and letting all the rest die."

"They're not...all dead," she began earnestly, slowing suddenly as she realized that Welter might not agree with revealing Frank's heretofore undisclosed presence on the base. "There's another one, though he's not as capable. Not nearly."

"Are you sure?" *Karnan* asked, his hopes rising again. "How do you know?"

"I've...met him," she answered carefully. "We named him Frank, but his real name is *Kerobenah*."

"Can't say I've heard of him," the old alien said,

furrowing his brows as he thought. "Nope, don't remember him. But, who knows, that might be a good thing. Do you know what side he was on? I mean, back in the civil war?"

"He was with the confederation. Resoundingly for the confederation."

"All the way through?" he clarified, turning his head a little as if to see around any obfuscation she might attempt to spare his feelings.

"Yes, from beginning to end," she assured him. "He's quite proud of it, actually."

"Well, that's something, anyhow," he said. "Is he very capable?"

"I'd say moderately so," she replied cautiously, having no knowledge of ancient *Kol-Prockian* AIs outside of Wellesley. "He seems rather…uncertain, like he's out of his depth a lot of the time."

"Well, if his name's any indication, that's not a big surprise," the alien uttered, wrapping his arms around his legs and leaning back, gradually growing weary. "The prefix *Kero* indicates that he worked in one of the confederation's bureaucracies; *benah* means he was more or less a manager, but in the middle range. Likely he was a moderately important bureaucrat, decently skilled in his area of expertise but mainly overseeing others."

"That sounds about right," she nodded, reflecting on some of the AI's chatter during the trip to Quarlac. "I got the impression that he was away from the fighting, his hatreds simple and his principles pure because he never had to actually get his hands dirty and see the terror of war up close."

"You're very perceptive," *Karnan* said with an appreciative smile, regaining a little of his former energy. "You've drawn a great deal of insight out of your interactions with him. But, I suppose that shouldn't come as any surprise, given your profession." With this his energy waned again, and he used what little he had left to stand up with a grunt.

"No, no," he said, holding up his hand as she rose to help him. "Really, I'm alright," he insisted, as she took his arm and slowly guided him back to his partition. "Thank you," he said with a combination of pleasure and aversion as he settled down in his usual corner.

"You're welcome," she replied, standing over him for a moment and then crouching down, surprised to find herself more limber than she'd felt in years. "Are you going to be alright?" she asked with a gentle hint of concern, as he looked down at the floor and puffed his fatigue.

"Oh, don't worry about me," he said, waving his hand and immediately coughing. When he'd recovered, he added, "you must remember that I'm dying, child. Nothing can save me from that, not even this chamber. And while I appreciate your kindness, since it shows you have a sympathetic heart, I don't want you to crowd me. I was orphaned months after birth, and I learned from an early age to look after myself. I don't intend to take on a mother now."

"I'm sorry, I didn't mean to smother you."

"Oh, you haven't," he shook his head, coughing again as the motion constricted his throat. "But let's just make sure it doesn't come to that, okay?"

"Okay," she nodded, about to rise when something crossed her mind. "Can I ask you one last thing?"

"Sure."

"Well, how do you speak our language so well? You're perfectly conversational, like a native."

"When you're stuck in an empty chamber off and on for a hundred years, you've got to find something to do," he smiled weakly. "I've studied a lot of different things during that time."

"But how? I mean, if you can't bring things in with you, there must–."

"You said one question," he cut her off, kindly but firmly. "Now let me rest, child. I'm spent."

"Alright," she said solicitously, standing up and

returning to Rhemus.

Her mind was swirling with ideas as she settled in beside his head, and nearly a minute passed before she thought to look at him to make sure he was alright.

"Still breathing," she thought, watching his chest rise and fall. Thinking to check his pulse, she gingerly grasped his right wrist. "Normal enough."

Leaning back against the wall, she let out a sigh and shook her head, feeling pity for the unconscious ruler.

"What a state to fall into," she reflected, brushing his brow again with the affectionate tenderness of a natural healer. She paused and raised her hand, realizing that it wasn't trembling anymore. Barely suppressing a joyful laugh, she turned it back and forth before her eyes. Then her face grew serious, and she held it as still as she could to ensure the symptoms were gone. Not so much as a wiggle of her little finger! She would have bent right over and kissed Rhemus, had he not been asleep.

"There is hope, Rex," she thought. "And maybe I can't live forever. But I can live long enough for you."

CHAPTER 7

Mafalda Aboltina hung limply from her shackles, lacking so much as the strength to raise her head. The same terrible red lines that she'd seen on Amra Welter's face now marred her own, a mysterious side effect of the Pho'Sath's manner of battering their victims' psyches.

She was beyond pain. The dark room with its long shadows had no meaning for her. There was no longer good and bad, right and wrong. Just fact. The room was before her, the floor was beneath her, but she had no capacity to *feel* anything about them. Once they had been horrible, despicable, constant reminders of her utter helplessness against an implacable foe. Now they just were.

Blankly she stared at the floor with an unfocused gaze, her eyes empty and half-lidded. Deldrach had pierced her mind, penetrating to her deepest secrets, passing through layer after layer of unconscious material. As his Journey Partner *Anzah* had done to poor Amra, she reflected, so *Deldrach* had done to her. She didn't regret this fact, viewing it as the inescapable result of a lifetime of wrongdoing. Justice had finally swung round.

"So, you're awake again," *Deldrach* said tauntingly. Without knowing how he'd gotten there, she suddenly became aware of his feet standing on the floor beneath her. She felt his hand grab the back of her hair, dragging her head roughly upwards. Dully she looked at the frightening mask that stood just inches away from her. Her stomach wanted to churn, her body to shake, her heart to tremble with fear. But she had no stamina for such things any longer. "I thought that it would be a pleasure to break your mind," he continued. "To peel back every secret, every shameful thought you'd ever had, every disgraceful deed that you'd ever done. But I find no pleasure in breaking a mind as narrow as yours. The Earthborn are small, degenerate, beneath enlightenment. You lack the breadth of mind to present a truly interesting subject. There's nothing of note in your worthless psyche. Except," he said, holding up the index finger of his other hand, "except, for one little tidbit of information that you'd recently discovered yourself. While I was plumbing the depths of your mind, I came across a most peculiar woman. One clad in white."

She stirred at his words, her eyes focusing as she weakly shook her head back and forth in revulsion that he should have found such a sacred secret.

"Oh, but I did," the alien said with wicked satisfaction. "And I found traces in your memory of an old man, too. He accompanied you through your psyche in his clumsy way, stumbling through the myriad layers of your mind before finally chancing upon the golden door that holds your most fundamental self. She told me what she conceived to be your destiny."

Shaking her head more violently, a despairing gasp escaped her lips.

"*Destiny*," he uttered with scorn, squeezing his fingers so tightly in her hair that her head froze in place. "Do you know what your destiny is? It is to die. That has always been the lot given to your people. Long ago your kind would have been swept from this galaxy, had the *Keesh'Forbandai* not intervened with their treaty." He growled with rage at this thought, tightening his grip until hair began to come loose in his hand. "But they had to meddle, so intermediaries have been necessary. For countless generations your people have been a blight on this galaxy." He leaned in close, his mask practically touching her helpless face. "But not for much longer. Soon, we will–."

His words were suddenly cut off by a blast of darkness striking him in the back. With a howl of surprise and anger he turned to see a pair of men standing at the door.

"Knock, knock," Hunt said, his eyes cold and hard as death.

"Ooh, that's a good one," Wellesley said, as he and Pinchon moved a couple feet inside.

"So, you've come to rescue this little lost sheep," *Deldrach* said, releasing her hair and seizing her by the neck. With one arm he lifted her up in her shackles, her body dangling from her throat. "This woman is of no value now. Though I am glad that she has brought you to me, Champion."

"You know, I vote we just throw out the whole Lord Hunt thing and just go with Champion," Wellesley said lightly. "It's much cooler."

"Silence, *Kol-Prockian!*" the *Pho'Sath* bellowed.

"Oh, that's right, you *can* hear me, can't you?" the AI asked flippantly.

"You know me?" Hunt asked, moving a little farther into the room.

"Every *Pho'Sath* knows of you, Earthborn," *Deldrach* replied, a hint of respect coming into his otherwise contemptuous voice.

"Let her go," Hunt ordered him, spreading his feet and hunching a little for action.

"Of course," the alien assented grandly, releasing his grip and letting her drop painfully back into her shackles. The sudden jolt threw her battered head against the wall, knocking her unconscious. "You should never have crossed the galaxy to rescue this pathetic little creature," *Deldrach* uttered, taking a couple steps away from his victim and crossing his arms. "We are well aware of your sentimentality, and how it clouds your judgment. But we never expected it to deliver you into our hands so *easily*, so *willingly*. It is never possible to overestimate the folly of the Earthborn."

"I didn't come to rescue her," Hunt replied, his eyes darting to the unfortunate girl and studying her for a moment before returning to *Deldrach*. "I came to kill you."

"Many have tried," the *Pho'Sath* laughed. "But none have succeeded. And not just humans. I am famed far and wide as *Deldrach the Destroyer* by races your kind have never imagined to exist. Shortly, you will see why."

Eyeing his giant foe, Hunt glanced at the colonel and nodded towards the door.

"Better wait outside," he said. "This could get a little rough."

"Would you go?" he asked pointedly, moving to Hunt's other side for emphasis. Seeing the Midnight Blade rest in its sheath against the wall opposite the door, he kept his eyes on the alien and went to get it. Returning, he drew it with a flourish, the mysterious darkness of the Blade bespeaking its power and purpose at once. "This ought to help even things a little."

"The nine who bore that Blade between them couldn't defeat me," *Deldrach* uttered. "What hope do *two* have?"

"That depends on the two," the ex-pirate smiled. "Anytime you're ready, Rex."

Instantly the Deltan raised his hands and cut loose with a massive blast of darkness, striking the alien in the chest and driving him a step backwards with a grunt.

"You'll have to do better than that," *Deldrach* retorted. "You're powerful, young Champion. But no amount of your patron realm will be able to destroy me from across the room. You'll have to close the distance for that, to touch me." He leaned forward, raising his hands for combat. "And that is where *I* excel."

Not willing to trust his enemy's word, Hunt immediately blasted him again, keeping up the stream until

Deldrach began to march slowly forwards against it, proving its futility. Cutting the flow, he moved off to the right as Pinchon pivoted to the left.

"You have proven the truth of my words," *Deldrach* said, stepping between them and turning his back to Pinchon. "Why would I lie to you, Earthborn? I have no need of a tactical advantage to crush you both."

Seeing his chance, the colonel raised the Blade and moved in, about to plunge it when the massive being whipped around and kicked him in the stomach, sending him tumbling over backwards. The Blade flew from his hand and clattered to the floor. Grasping his stomach with his left hand, he got his right under him and forced himself upright. Slowly he made for the Blade, picked it up, and mimicked Hunt's hunched posture as both he and the alien watched.

"Are you two ready to go again?" *Deldrach* asked.

Hunt knew that *Deldrach* was trying to tempt him into touching him. It was through such contact that the *Pho'Sath* in the Black Hole had worked her healing effects on him, and he had little doubt that the same process could be worked in reverse to destroy him. At that time he'd had the element of surprise, touching and filling the operative with darkness before she had a chance to push back. But *Deldrach* knew what was coming, knew what he was doing, and clearly wanted the battle to proceed a certain way.

"Did you come here to fight, or to stare?" the alien asked, shifting his gaze between the two of them.

"They k-kill with their touch," a weak voice rasped out, causing all eyes to dart to Mafalda. She looked at them with dull eyes, her mind barely functioning. "My sister, she..." her voice trailed, before she fell slack once more against the shackles.

"That's something we both do, isn't it, Champion?" *Deldrach* asked, shifting a little to keep both his assailants in sight as the colonel drew near, the Blade held up in front of him. "We bring death to all we encounter, until we're not even whole beings anymore. We're weapons of war."

At that moment Hunt realized that *Deldrach* was as averse to touching him as he was. Both of them had the killer touch, and neither could afford to give his opponent a chance to use it. That's why the alien kept talking, kept forcing him to think of something *other than their duel*: he was trying to make him slip, to get distracted for one precious second in which he could be destroyed. Somehow the *Pho'Sath* seemed to grasp his realization just as it occurred to him, because he started backing towards Mafalda.

"If you will not fight," he uttered, stopping just short of her and laying a hand on her stomach, "then this one shall pay the price."

Through her clothes her skin began to glow. With instantaneous instinct Hunt stretched forth his hand, the power of the dark realm flying from his fingertips and striking a place just beside *Deldrach's* hand. He could feel the intelligence of the shadowy essence cooperating with him to deliver just enough of itself to counteract the *Pho'Sath's* assault without hurting his victim. In a quarter minute he gave up, withdrawing his hand.

"You've grown very powerful," *Deldrach* nodded with increasing respect, still standing beside Mafalda. "But," he said, seizing her neck and lifting her limp body into the air once more, "there are many ways to kill someone, some more prosaic than others."

"*Don't*," Hunt ordered sternly, his face twisted into a hateful scowl as he prepared to spring at him.

"Oh, I'm not unreasonable," the *Pho'Sath* said, shaking her loosely in his grip. "But if the Champion of the Earthborn wants to save this little lost sheep, he's going to have to give something in return." The alien's mask turned towards Pinchon and then back to him. "Your friend must leave us alone, to fight to the death."

"What do you say, Rex?" the colonel asked, still holding the Blade before him. "From the look of that girl,

I'd say she's about had it. No use getting yourself killed over someone who'll be room temperature soon anyhow."

"A generous sentiment indeed," *Deldrach* said. "But I doubt that your friend will be so cold."

"Go on, Philippe," Hunt said, nodding towards the door to his right. "I'll be with you shortly."

With a frown the ex-pirate shook his head, moved to Hunt, and held out the dagger for him to take.

"The Blade leaves, too," *Deldrach* stipulated.

Again Hunt nodded towards the door. Muttering under his breath, Pinchon stepped into the hall and closed it behind him.

"At last, we're alone," the *Pho'Sath* uttered with satisfaction, slowly lowering Mafalda back into her shackles.

"More or less," Wellesley chimed in, to the visible irritation of the alien, who only barely kept himself from lashing out verbally.

"He f-fears...you," the prisoner said through dull, unwilling lips, looking at Hunt.

"Open your mouth again, and I will tear your jaw out!" roared *Deldrach*, turning sharply towards her and clenching his fists.

In this instant Hunt struck. Hitting the massive alien with two quick blasts of darkness, he covered the distance between them and locked hands with him. *Deldrach's* huge fingers wrapped around his palms and began to glow, attempting to pump the power of the light realm into his body. With a scream Hunt felt it enter him, searing his hands and sending bolts of pain up his arms and into his shoulders. Quickly it spread, until the more lethargic power of the dark realm gathered up its true might and drove it back. Hunt could feel it coursing through his body, cooling the terrible burn he'd just received and filling him with a sense of power and mastery. With an angry grunt he shoved *Deldrach* back against the wall beside Mafalda, gritting his teeth as sweat poured off his face.

Now it was the *Pho'Sath's* turn to scream. With a deep animal roar he bellowed out his agony, the sound reverberating throughout the base. He tried to use his great strength to crush his smaller opponent. But already the power of the dark essence was flowing through his suit, slowing its movements and weakening its output.

In a desperate move, *Deldrach* wrestled his left hand free and seized Mafalda's wrist. It began to glow white hot, and Hunt instantly cast a stream of darkness against it to negate the alien's assault.

Briefly distracted, Hunt suddenly felt his right leg kicked out from underneath him. He fell backwards and hit the ground hard, only just keeping his head up high enough to avoid striking it on the concrete floor. Like a rock his giant assailant fell upon him, using the prodigious weight of his suit to crush the air from his lungs as he wrapped his long fingers around his neck. Gasping for air, Hunt was forced to place his palms on his own shoulders and channel the dark power back into himself to negate the effects of the light realm. With a snarl *Deldrach* released his hold, elbowing Hunt in the stomach as he slid off him and got back to his feet.

Still fighting for breath, Hunt struggled upwards as the alien seized his arm and spun him off against the wall Mafalda hung from. With a loud twack he struck it, pain shooting all through his back and hips. Ragefully *Deldrach* charged, his hands outstretched to seize him by the throat again. Quickly regaining his equilibrium, Hunt ducked him and let his still clumsy body crash into the wall. Before he could turn around, Hunt had his hands on his shoulders, pressed him harshly against the wall, and poured forth all the power he could muster. The alien screamed again, but in a higher, more fearful pitch. As his suit began to seize up again, *Deldrach* put his arms to the wall and desperately tried to push off. But the implacable man behind him shoved all the harder, determined not to give him a moment's respite.

Sensing that his power was nearly exhausted, the alien dropped his legs out from underneath himself and fell to the floor. The move surprised Hunt and gave him an opening to elbow him in the knee. The blow struck like a brick, and Hunt fell backwards onto the floor again. Painfully he got back to his feet as *Deldrach* did the same, the latter's increasingly damaged suit clumsy and off balance.

"You fight well," *Deldrach* managed to say, though his vocal circuits were heavily damaged and caused his voice to crackle. "For an Earthborn."

"I fight well *because* I'm Earthborn," Hunt said, standing proudly before his opponent, his body bloodied and soaked with sweat.

With his suit's final strength, *Deldrach* shoved away from the wall and lunged for Hunt. Their hands found each other again, and the might of the shadowy essence within humanity's Champion flowed once more into the suit of the *Pho'Sath*. With an agonized groan he fought back, conjuring all the power the light realm had to offer. But it wasn't enough. Slowly he began to fall, slipping to his knees as the suit's strength waned and the darkness coursed through it.

"This isn't the end," *Deldrach's* voice crackled, as his suit began to disintegrate and the light it held within gleamed forth. "My sacrifice will be remembered by all who partake of the Journey."

"No, they will die for their crimes," Hunt said inexorably. "As you have."

With this the suit crumbled apart, releasing a huge cloud of bright particles that quickly evaporated.

With a ragged, exhausted breath, Hunt dropped to his knees in the suit's dust and panted. Closing his eyes, the sweat poured down his red face and began to mix with the ashes of his enemy. For nearly a minute he rested, gathering himself together before venturing to stand. His legs shakily bore his weight, and with effort he moved to where the unconscious prisoner still hung. Gently he put a hand to her cheek.

"Wells?"

"Hang on, I'm checking," the AI said doubtfully, the girl's appearance not calculated to inspire hope. "Okay, well, there's good news and bad news. Which do you want first."

"Surprise me," Hunt replied, removing his hand and leaning his back against the wall beside her.

"Physically, she's decent enough for someone who's clearly been tortured to the very limit of human endurance. She needs food, water, and careful tending for at least a week. That'll get her out of the danger zone."

"And the good news?"

"Not to sound cliche, but that was the good news. Basically she'll make a full *physical* recovery as long as she's treated well. It's the mental side that's got me worried. I'm not sensing a lot of activity. Well, I *am*, but not the kind you'd want. She seems confused, dazzled, like the world is a huge incomprehensible swirl of nonsense that she can't make the least sense of."

"Isn't it?"

"Well, sure. But we all posite certain underlying consistencies to make sense of it all. Half the time they're fictitious, as you know, what you might call 'useful errors' that help us get through our lives with our sanity intact. But this girl isn't doing that. She isn't trying to make sense of anything. When her brain *does* send some kind of signal, it's totally unrelated to the signal that preceded it. It's like she's on some kind of drug that scatters her mental activity across the entire gamut of conceptual possibilities. But," he concluded, "I would like to remind you that I'm–."

"Not a medical AI," Hunt finished for him.

"You know me so well. Should I tell the colonel to come in?"

"Give it a minute," he replied, pushing off the wall with effort and moving in front of the prisoner. Carefully he looked her battered body up and down, before finally zeroing in on her face. "There's something about this girl, Wells," he said quietly, his eyes tracing the nasty red marks on her face. "Something..." his voice trailed, as he brushed his thumb down one of the lines. "I don't know what it is. It's like she's calling out to me."

"Don't you think we should get her down?" Wellesley nudged him, feeling he'd forgotten the obvious.

"Oh, I know that," Hunt said. "But there's something in this moment, some insight." He clenched his fist as he tried to drag it to the surface. "There's *something* important about this girl. Something very important. I just wish I knew what it was."

"Come on," the AI urged him after another silent moment. "If it's really important it'll come to you in time. Now, let's get her down. She's been through enough."

Feeling much of his former strength returning, Hunt wrapped an arm around her hips and hoisted her light form up in the shackles. With an unconscious sigh the air was squeezed out of her lungs as she rolled over his shoulder, her head resting on the back of his neck. A charge ran through him at this touch, one he couldn't make sense of. Pushing the thought aside, he used his dark power to shatter her bonds. Limply her arms fell around him. Shifting his hold, he slipped an elbow behind her knees and another behind her back. Her head nestled on his shoulder, he looked at her poor, battered face for a moment.

"I see you took care of business," Pinchon said from the doorway, causing Hunt's eyes to dart to him. Slowly the ex-pirate walked to the pile of ash on the floor and crouched, rubbing some of it between his fingers before brushing it off on his pants. "Another one down."

"Yeah," Hunt agreed, eyeing the dust one last time before making for the door. "Let's get out of here."

"You want any help with her?" the colonel asked, following him into the hall where a half dozen of the men Krancis had sent waited in dark clothing, only their eyes showing. Suppressed submachine guns were held at the ready, having only recently cooled from aggressive use. Respectfully they moved off to either side of the hall, letting him pass. "You deserve a break after fighting with that colossus."

"I'm alright," Hunt replied, as his burden's eyes slowly opened and looked up at him. She started when she saw the escort, somehow finding the strength in her arms to wrap them around his neck and pull him closer. "You're okay," he said, pausing in the midst of the men and letting her look them over. "Friends, from Krancis."

"K-Krancis?" she asked doubtfully, her throat dry and raspy. An instinctive sense of revulsion welled up from the back of her mind at the thought of the emperor's right hand, an artifact from her separatist days. Slowly it passed away, and her thoughts went to her captor. "*Deldrach*?" she asked ominously.

"Dead," Hunt said seriously. "He can't hurt you anymore."

With this her anxiety passed, and with a relieved nod she lowered her head to his shoulder again.

The escort formed up behind Lord Hunt, and with the colonel at his side he carried the girl from the house of her torment.

"Well, we killed your boogeyman for you," Pinchon told Phican hours later, dropping into one of a pair of seats that had been placed in her office after their last encounter. "Or rather Rex did," he corrected himself, as Hunt sat down beside him. "Saved some girl to boot. Left her at the hospital."

"Yes, I've heard," she replied without enthusiasm, her eyes moving between the two men before her desk. "She's not exactly a favorite around here. I don't suppose she told you her name?"

"She's been a little unconscious for that," Pinchon replied pointedly, her manner grating on him all the more because he'd started to grow attached to the ex-separatist.

"She's been tortured out of her mind," he added a bit more softly.

"Yes, that has a tendency to happen whenever someone falls into their hands," she replied unsympathetically, as though it were a mere data point for her. "Their attempt to kill *Deldrach* was doomed from the start. He was simply too powerful for anyone on this planet to handle, even if nine of them tried it at once."

"*Nine?*" Hunt asked with surprise.

"Oh, yes," she confirmed. "And many more before them. He was the most powerful operative ever to set foot on this planet."

"Before you," Wellesley said to Hunt through skin conductance.

"Just what is this beef that you have with the girl he was torturing?" Pinchon asked, still rankled.

"That *girl* is Mafalda Aboltina. She worked for the separatists and helped them torture a very dear friend of mine," she said, her eyes softening unconsciously as she thought of Amra Welter. Then they hardened again. "She's done more harm on this world than she could ever possibly redeem. Her mere presence in this base is an insult to every person who's stayed true to the emperor."

"People change," Pinchon replied pragmatically. "At a time like this, we should be glad to get friends from any quarter. I don't know if you've noticed," he added with a hint of sarcasm creeping into his voice, "but even with *Sentinel* we're still fighting an uphill battle."

"I don't need you to lecture me on the realities of warfare in the fringe," she snapped. "I've been accustomed to them for much longer than you have, Mister Pirate. And I will *not* be told from which quarters I will and won't receive new operatives. The last thing we really need in the organization is one of Ugo Udris' many, many granddaughters."

"*What?*" Hunt and Wellesley asked simultaneously.

"Of course," she replied, scarcely restraining her

temper. Though she was rapidly growing to hate the colonel, she saw no reason to pour her wrath out on Rex. "Wherever you find separatists, you're going to find an Udris or two. Well, in blood, if not quite in name." She paused and looked into his eyes for a moment. "Why the shock?"

"I met Ugo, back on Delta-13," Hunt explained. "He took me in for a time, taught me things about the dark realm. He was misguided in most of his understanding of it, but he got me started. Eventually I had to break with him."

"And I hope you never looked back," Phican said.

"Not once."

"Good."

"So you don't think Mafalda has truly left her wicked old ways behind her?" the colonel asked without interest, putting a leg over the other and forming a tent with his natural and artificial fingers in front of his chest. "Seems to me *Deldrach* had broken with her in every way. You don't inflict that kind of treatment on anyone you plan to work with in the future."

"I've already told you," Phican said with increasing anger. "She's done terrible harm to the people of this world, bolstering the separatist cause in myriad ways. That's reason enough to cast her out. And the plain fact, on top of that, is we have no use for her."

"Her head is packed with knowledge," Pinchon replied, his voice rising. "She must know any of a thousand things your people would *die* to get their hands on."

"And what's the value of that, if we can't *employ* it?" she retorted. "Our operations on Erdu-3 are nearly at a standstill. The Fringers, and their masters, have driven us to the absolute brink. It's going to take months of work just to get back on our feet, to say nothing of engaging the enemy once more. No," she shook her head gravely, "we've been battered nearly to bits. Her information is going to be out of date by the time we can put it to any kind of use. Until then she'll just be a liability, another mouth to feed and another body to protect. And we don't have the resources to lavish that kind of largess on anyone."

"I'm not buying a word of this," the colonel replied. "She must know things that will be relevant for your off-world operatives. And no matter how hard the Fringers try, they're not gonna be able to change the locks overnight." He fixed her with his knowing eyes. "You're throwing that girl out into the wind for personal reasons. You're letting your emotions cloud your judgment."

"There is no place in this organization for Mafalda Aboltina," she said resolutely, returning his glare. "As soon as she's conscious, she must leave."

"Rex, do me a favor and take your earpiece out," Wellesley told him. As soon as he'd done so, holding it in his hand before him, the AI cranked the volume up to the absolute max and bellowed *"are you out of your mind?"* to Phican, causing them all to jump. "Have you checked with the hospital? Have you studied that girl's vitals? Well, I have, and she needs at least a *week* of solicitous care before even *attempting* to stand on her own two feet. And you're gonna dump her into the wild? In all my *centuries* of consciousness I've *never–*."

"There is no place for her here," Phican reiterated, finding her balance once more. "If you wish her to be cared for, you'll see to it yourselves."

Hunt was more surprised by her attitude than angry, but the colonel could have pounded nails with Phican's forehead at that moment. Staring at her with murder in his eyes, it was all he could do to keep from dragging her old body across the massive desk and putting *her* in the hospital. Sensing this, Hunt arose and looked down at Phican scornfully, turning for the door just as Pinchon was about to open his mouth and damage relations between the empire and the loyalists in the fringe. Exhaling sharply, his nostrils flaring like an angry bull, the ex-pirate followed his friend and left.

"Two more seconds in there," he growled to Hunt once the door was shut, holding up a pair of fingers. "Two, more, seconds."

"I know," Hunt said.

"You're awfully cool about all this," Wellesley commented, his own anger subsiding very slowly. "Aren't you angry at that old bat?"

"What were we gonna do?" Hunt asked rhetorically. "Beat the life out of her? Then take down half the base when they try to beat the life out of *us*? These guys want nothing to do with Mafalda, so she's better off without them anyway. We'll just have to take her with us."

"But *where*?" Wellesley asked. "She's an awfully big target, if Phican is to be believed. The Fringers have operatives on every planet in the fringe. If we take her to a hospital they'll be sure to find out and pounce on her before her head even hits the pillow."

"What about *Sentinel*?" Hunt asked.

"Don't think we can count on meeting up with it," the AI uttered. "Krancis has got to be cruising around the galaxy as we speak, fighting the Devourers. He's not gonna make a side trip because we've decided to play guardian angel."

"Well, we'll figure something out," Hunt said, gesturing for Pinchon to follow. "Come on, let's check on her."

"I'm afraid she can't stay here very long," the doctor said with embarrassment once they'd reached the hospital, his hands fidgeting. "I've just received word–."

"We know," the colonel said. "We were there when her royal highness cooked up the idea."

The doctor glanced around to see if anyone was in earshot.

"I can't tell you how sorry I am about all this," he said earnestly. "But Phican isn't alone in her feelings. Most of the organization doesn't want anything to do with Mafalda." He shook his head warningly. "They have long memories."

"So do we," Hunt replied, before nodding down the

long room. "Where is she?"

"Down at the end," he said. "We put her next to Audrey Wyard."

"Surprised you could find the room," Pinchon said honestly.

"We had two cases go terminal between the time you left for your mission and returned," he explained. "Once there's nothing more we can do for them, we put them in another room to await their end. It's a terrible way to go. But we just don't have the resources to do more."

They exchanged a few more words and then left the doctor to his work. Finding Mafalda's bed, the two men moved up either side of it and looked down at her.

"Been through a lot, this kid," the colonel said solemnly after a few moments. His finger gently traced one of the red lines that ran down her left cheek. "I've never seen anything like that before. Looks like a tattoo or paint or something."

"It's some kind of result of the torture that *Deldrach* put her through," Wellesley explained. "When I scanned her I tried to figure out what it was, but it doesn't match anything in my database. Close as I can get is that the skin's pigmentation has changed. Kind of like a suntan."

"Will it go away?" he asked.

"Your guess is as good as mine," the AI replied frankly. "I should think it would, provided some deeper level of damage hasn't been done. But we're all tilling virgin soil when it comes to the *Pho'Sath*, so I'd be lying if I said I was certain."

"Let's see how she's doing," Hunt said, softly grasping her elbow with his fingers.

"A little better," Wellesley reported after half a minute. "Getting her out of those shackles is letting the blood flow freely again. And despite the trauma she's been through, I think she knows she's in a safer place than she was before and has relaxed a bit."

Just as he finished speaking she moaned softly. Her eyelids crept open, and slowly her gaze moved from Hunt to Pinchon, and then back to Hunt.

"Thank you," she mumbled with exhausted earnestness, reaching feebly up to take his hand. "For getting me…away," she continued with a gulp. Painfully she pressed her head against the thin pillow and tightly shut her eyes, squeezing his hand as she tried to drive the memory of her agony away. "I-I don't think I could have taken another day. Another hour."

"It's alright," Hunt assured her, squeezing her hand back and putting his other hand on her shoulder. "You're safe now."

"I-I don't have any place to go," she said, her eyes anxiously searching his. "They thought that I was asleep, but I heard them right after they laid me out. Phican hates me. They won't let me stay here."

"I said you were safe," Hunt reiterated. "And you are. With us."

"With…you?" she asked, looking between the two men and swallowing hard again. Then she shook her head. "No, don't burn your bridges with Phican. I'm not worth it. She'll never forgive you for helping me."

"What bridges?" the colonel asked, barely suppressing a scornful laugh. "I nearly throttled her ten minutes ago when she told us what was gonna happen to you. There's no love lost between any of us, though she seems to think Rex is decent enough to work with."

"Then don't do this for his sake," she said urgently, trying to sit up but finding herself too weak. "Please, the fringe is in bad enough shape as it is after all I and my family have done. Don't let me come between the empire and the only meaningful opposition group on this planet."

"That's speaking somewhat generously," the ex-pirate replied, sitting on the edge of her bed. "Whatever good this organization could have done is in the past. Their teeth have been pulled out one by one, and now all they've got is an empty mouth to gum the separatists with." He wrapped his lips over his teeth and made several quick chewing motions that made her giggle despite the pain she was in. "Don't worry about any 'harm' you might do by going along with us. If the rest of the opposition in the fringe is this pathetic, we'll just have to throw our hopes behind the Black Suns. And our lord and master, of course," he added with a roll of his eyes.

"Who?"

"Krancis."

"Oh."

Just then the doctor appeared several feet from the foot of her bed., His cheeks blushing with shame, a pair of men stood beside him. Hunt noticed that neither of them were imperials, but rough-looking locals. One was fat, with coarse stubble running from his chin down to the base of his neck. Probably forty. The other was younger, with a thin but wiry build. His eyes were small and angry. Both men looked as if they'd broken their fair share of bones. Pinchon glanced carelessly over his shoulder at them, and then turned back to Mafalda.

"As I was saying, if the local opposition can ever get its head on straight, sure, we *might* bring you back to help 'em out. But right now you're just going to waste around here. Ah," he said, as her mouth opened to object strenuously, her eyes filled with worry. "Don't argue. I know you want to help them any way you can. But they just aren't worth it." Then he looked back at the men and smiled.

"It's…time to go," the doctor managed to force out of his lips.

"Of course," Pinchon said grandly, sliding off the hard, thin mattress and looking down at Mafalda. "You've spent enough time in these miserable surroundings anyhow. I know you don't feel up to traveling, little honey, but it'll just be a quick warp jump in our ship, and then we'll get you aboard *Sentinel*. We've got the best hospital you could ask for, decked out with every kind of trinket a body needs to get well."

"You're taking her...to *Sentinel*?" the thin man asked in amazement, the anger in his eyes replaced by envy as he contemplated the months of struggle that awaited him and his comrades on Erdu-3. "This little...nothing?"

Pinchon, still looking at Mafalda, smiled when he heard this. Not a smile of pleasure, but the sort that a man has when he's about to do something both ill-advised and *very* satisfying. As he turned to face the man, the team of black-clad escorts came into view, still holding their weapons.

"Lord Hunt," one of them, Lieutenant Greene, said as he stepped a little ahead of his fellows. "We received word that you might be," he paused and looked around momentarily, "departing soon. Do you wish for us to escort you back to your ship?" His cool, professional eyes found those of the two local thugs, causing them both to take a step back. "Or would you prefer to remain here," he continued, looking at them a moment longer before returning his gaze to Hunt.

"We're going to leave, Lieutenant," Hunt announced, his own eyes finding those of the thugs and causing them to further shrink into themselves. "We're needed elsewhere."

"Of course, my lord," Greene said crisply. "Shall we carry the young woman?"

"I've got her," Pinchon cut in, bending over and slipping his arms behind her knees and back. Weakly she put her arms around his neck, feeling his body strain as he drew her weight off the mattress. With a grunt he stood erect, shifting her weight a little before sidling along the edge of the bed and passing through the men at the bottom. He paused briefly at Audrey Wyard's bed, looking at her unconscious face for a moment before walking down the long line of patients and passing out of the hospital.

"I'm sorry I couldn't do more," the doctor said

pleadingly to Hunt as he followed behind Pinchon.

"I understand," Hunt assured him, stopping to shake his hand. "Thanks for what you've managed to do for her."

"You're welcome," the doctor nodded, squeezing his hand firmly before letting it go and watching him depart with the rest of his team.

The trip back to the ship was uneventful, the escort fanning out to ensure no Fringers were lying in wait along their path. The ground was still muddy from the recent rain, causing Pinchon to struggle with his helpless load. But they were more than halfway back to the ship before the exhausted colonel finally let Hunt take over and carry her. As with Audrey Wyard, he had to roll his eyes at the ease with which the younger man bore her weight.

Mafalda remained silent, using her feeble strength to try to lighten the load as much as possible. Occasionally she would open her eyes and watch the face of the man carrying her, dumbfounded that so much effort was being put forth on her behalf. Otherwise she would rest her head against his shoulder, trying to relax and sway as naturally as possible with the rhythm of his motions to lessen the inertia of her body.

Finally reaching the abandoned hangar, Hunt put Mafalda aboard and then turned to the men who had accompanied them.

"What are your orders from Krancis, Lieutenant?"

"He said to do whatever you instructed us to do, my lord," Greene replied. "Once the mission against the *Pho'Sath* agent was complete, we were to be completely at your disposal. He felt you would have the best appreciation for the situation on the ground, sir, and that you could best direct what we should do."

"That son of a gun," Pinchon said, leaning against the ship. "I guess the old bird can trust after all."

"Do you have independent transport?" Hunt asked. "Can you leave at any time, or are you dependent on the loyalists to get you off world?"

"We brought our own vessel, my lord," Green replied. "It's hidden several hours west of here in a dense forest. Krancis wanted us to be utterly flexible."

"How long have you been on Erdu?"

"We arrived approximately forty hours before you did, my lord. We connected with the resistance at their hideout, became acquainted with their operation, scouted the terrain, and then awaited your arrival."

"And what's your appraisal of their functional capacity?"

"Speaking frankly, my lord, they aren't likely to be of any use to the empire going forwards. Any good they produce from this point on will be the direct result of imperial resources pouring into their operation. Men, material, and expertise. They'll be little more than a puppet, though they still have some contacts and local knowledge that will help. Independent of us holding them up, I doubt they'll last six months."

"I'd give 'em four," Pinchon opined. "Three and a half if Phican keeps running things like she has been. That woman would alienate her own mother."

"She's given us considerable difficulty ever since we arrived," Greene agreed. "From what I could gather in such a short time, it seems the loss of one Amra Welter has soured her, turning what used to be a very balanced and effective temperament into the one we've been forced to deal with. The rest of the organization doesn't seem to know how to deal with it, though they won't cross her. She's knowledgeable, and held positions of power and influence for decades. She's just too entrenched to remove, even if they wanted to."

"Right now they're too busy reeling to know what to do," Hunt commented, leaning against the ship himself. Peripherally he saw Mafalda poke her head over the side of the ship and look down. As soon as he glanced up she drew her head back in, not wishing to draw attention. "Well, Lieutenant," he continued, trying to wrap things up for her sake, "it was Krancis' belief that we need to keep the contacts we've established on Erdu-3 intact. That's why we took down *Deldrach* in the first place. So stick around and hold 'em up as well as you can. But if in your judgment it becomes a lost cause, pack it in and move out. We're not going to throw away good lives on this lot."

"Yes, my lord," Greene replied.

He was about to crisply salute when Hunt held out his hand instead.

"You're a good man, Lieutenant," he told him, before looking over his subordinates. "As are you all. It's been a pleasure to work with such professionals. Look after yourselves. The empire will need you again many times over before this war is through."

"Thank you, Lord Hunt," the lieutenant replied proudly, squeezing his hand firmly before releasing it. He and his men saluted, and then moved out of the hangar to give them room to depart.

"Come on, Philippe," Hunt said, clapping him on the shoulder and climbing aboard first. Joining Mafalda in the back seats, he helped her get fastened in as the colonel took his place up front and lowered the egg's canopy.

"I've never seen a ship like this before," she said in a small voice, as Hunt finished with her harness and set to work on his own.

"No one has," Pinchon said, turning it on and causing a low hum to reverberate through its hull. "It's an alien make. Travels faster than thought through warp, and it's pretty much undetectable, even by the *Pho'Sath*. You couldn't ask for a safer transport."

"To go to *Sentinel*?" she confirmed, still disbelieving that such a thing was possible.

"Yeah, about that," the ex-pirate said reluctantly, turning in his seat to look at her. "I made that part up for the sake of our 'friends' back there. We can't get you to *Sentinel*."

"Then where will we go?" she asked, her eyes wide.

"I've been thinking about that," the colonel replied, turning back to his control panel and gently lifting the craft into a low hover above the hangar floor. "And I've got the perfect answer: Girnius."

"The pirate leader?" she asked.

"What good is he going to be to her?" Hunt inquired.

"Well, think about it, Rex. He's got a private medical staff because he can't trust anyone to look after him unless they're on his payroll. We've got the same situation, more or less. Besides, he'll be glad to help a turncoat separatist just to stick it to the Fringers." He paused and looked over his shoulder at Mafalda. "I didn't mean that badly, honey."

"No, you're right," she said, shrinking into her seat and crossing her arms. "I *am* just a turncoat separatist." She looked between the two men. "I still can't believe you're doing all this just for me." She paused as a question came over her face. "Just why are you doing it?"

"Because there's something about you," Hunt explained. "I felt it right after I killed *Deldrach*. I don't know what it was, but something deep within told me to look after you, to make sure you were safe. I think it was the dark realm reaching out to me, telling us we had to connect. I've rarely been more certain of anything in my life."

"My reasons are a little less…cosmic than that," Pinchon said with a chuckle, waving to the saluting men outside the hangar as the craft exited and climbed into the sky. "I just can't stand to see a poor girl like you give it her best and then get kicked in the teeth by those who *should* be helping her. Rankled me pretty bad."

"It's what I deserve," she replied gloomily. "After all I've done, I should have died in that dungeon with *Deldrach*."

"We've all made mistakes," Hunt told her, putting a hand on her shoulder and rubbing it as he thought about his father's realization just before his own death. "What matters is what we're doing *now*. The war is still raging all throughout the galaxy, and we need every willing hand to turn the tide. As long as you're with us, it doesn't matter what you've done in the past."

"I'm with you," she nodded sincerely, her eyes finding his. "Absolutely."

"Then don't worry about what's gone before," he reiterated, giving her shoulder a little squeeze before releasing it and leaning back in his seat. Wearily he rubbed his face with his hands, yawning as he drew them away.

"I'm sorry you both had to carry me so far," she said meekly. "First from the separatist's hideout, and then from the loyalist's."

"Oh, don't worry about that," Hunt said with a tired smile. "Philippe, how long until we reach Girnius?"

"Not long," the colonel said, as the ship penetrated a thick patch of clouds that blinded them to the world below. "Around twenty-two hours in this ship."

"They say that the Black Suns are striking separatist targets all throughout the fringe," Mafalda commented, rubbing her cut and bruised wrists gently.

"So they say," Pinchon replied with a silent grin as he flew.

"But why? They've never had a problem with the separatists before."

"Because of two things. First, Krancis bought him off with a *ton* of kantium. And second, because we provided him with proof that the Fringers tried to kill him. That's what really tipped him over the edge. Honestly, I think he's hitting harder than even Krancis had anticipated. If that's possible," he added with a laugh.

"Do you dislike Krancis?" she asked, still unsure of her own feelings towards him.

"I think he's the best man for the job," he replied. "But I don't take a shine to him personally. Some folks aren't meant to get along, and I'm sure he and I are two of 'em. But I can keep my mouth shut long enough to do business with him, provided it gets no closer than that. I don't want to swap stories with the man."

"What's he like?" she asked, her voice slowly growing eager.

"Ask Rex. He knows him better."

"You do?" she asked with surprise, turning to the man beside her.

"Does that shock you?" he asked, cocking a curious eyebrow.

"Sort of," she admitted. "You seem so...passionate about what you believe in. I'd always heard that Krancis was more of a machine than a man, acting without conscience. I guess I just thought that he would have driven you off with his 'ends justifies the means' attitude towards everything."

"The ends do justify the means for him," Hunt agreed. "But only if they serve humanity or the emperor. I thought he was a cold, heartless machine as well, before I had a chance to see more than the one side of himself that he shows to the public. We have a mutual friend, a girl who's been through an awful lot. He put himself in considerable danger to rescue her from a shard of the planet *Eesekkalion* that had gotten embedded in her psyche. It was then, and shortly after, that I saw that he loves, too. Like the colonel," he said, nodding to their pilot, "I don't get along with him, either. We're oil and water. But I wouldn't want another man leading us right now."

"That's so different from what I'd been taught to believe all this time," she replied with a shake of her head, as though to shake loose the lies she'd been fed. "Both the emperor and Krancis vied with each other in our hatred. We hated Rhemus because he's the head of the empire, but we often hated Krancis more because he's so efficient. I never had any idea that he's a good man."

"I don't know that he is," Hunt replied, to her visible surprise. "He certainly does good things, but he wouldn't hesitate to throw us all into the ditch if it served his purposes."

"You can say that again," Pinchon agreed heartily.

"But…I thought…" Mafalda uttered slowly, her eyes confused.

"He loves, he hates," Hunt explained. "He rescues and kills without hesitation. I don't know just what he is. I don't think anybody does."

"He's an enigma, that's for sure," Wellesley said through the speakers, making Mafalda jump.

"Who's *that*?" she asked.

"*Allokanah* is my actual name. But everyone calls me Wellesley."

"He's an ancient alien AI," Hunt explained briefly. "I found him on Delta-13. He comes in handy, once in a while."

"Yeah, once in a while," he repeated sarcastically. "I've been checking your condition periodically, Mafalda, and I thought now would be a good time for another check up. Are you alright with that?"

"Sure…" her voice trailed uncertainly. "What do I have to do?"

"Here, you can put him on if you like," Hunt said, slipping the amulet from around his neck and handing it to her. "He can scan you through skin contact. He can talk that way, too."

"Really?" she asked with interest, raising her tired, trembling arms over her head and slipping the necklace around her throat. Carefully sliding it down her shirt collar, it dangled just above her heart. "What do I do now?"

"Just hang tight for a second," Wellesley answered kindly through the speakers, "and I'll check you out."

Self-consciously her eyes flitted around the cockpit. She was intrigued by what he'd have to say, and also a little scared in case it was bad news.

"Well, you need rest," the AI reported after a thorough examination. "Right now you're stimulated by the novelty of your situation, but you really need to try and sleep. Your body has been pushed to its limit and then some. Honestly I'm surprised you're so chipper right now. It's like you're drawing energy from somewhere."

"I noticed that, too," Hunt agreed. "After we talked to you in the hospital you've been mentally very alert. I don't think you lost consciousness during the trip back to the ship"

"I didn't," she said, shaking her head and eyeing him. "I don't know. I've felt better since you two came to talk to me. I didn't feel alone anymore."

"But bodily, you're still very weak," Wellesley inserted rather pointedly, making sure that fact wasn't forgotten. "Tell me, has your jaw ever been broken?"

"Yes," she replied, nodding subtly as fear filled her eyes at the memory. "*Deldrach* broke it when he was torturing me. But then he used his power to fuse it back together again."

"Too bad we can't kill him a second time," Pinchon said ominously, tightly squeezing the controls in his hands.

"I thought so," the AI continued, responding to Mafalda. "Honestly, the fusion is nearly perfect. Just a *hair* off point. I wouldn't have probably noticed it otherwise. Quite a good job, especially for someone who must have been freehanding it, so to speak. I gather there was no equipment involved?"

"No, no equipment," she confirmed. "He just took the broken front half of my jaw in his hand, held it against the back half, and joined them together again."

"Remember when that *Pho'Sath* in the Black Hole said her people were skilled in healing, Rex? Sounds like she really meant it. Such skill is inconceivable, either for humans or *Kol-Prockians*. Of course, their essence, or whatever you want to call it, *is* contained inside a mechanical suit, so maybe they're not really 'freehanding.' They may be capable of much greater precision than an organic would be."

"I don't suppose you scanned *Deldrach's* suit while Rex was fighting with him?" the colonel asked, as the ship broke free of the atmosphere and the blackness of space opened before them.

"I tried, but it kept me out," he replied.

"Kept you out?"

"Yeah, I couldn't even begin to analyze how the suit worked. Literally everything I know about it was passed along through Rex's senses."

"Then you experience the same things that your host does?" Mafalda asked.

"Yes, that's right. Sorry, I should have explained that."

"Can you…read their thoughts?" she queried.

"No, no I can't," he chuckled. "Not that that wouldn't have come in handy sometimes. But nobody could have an AI slung around his neck for any length of time, reading his every thought, without finally going batty. Everyone needs privacy to function, especially in the confines of their own minds. Otherwise they'd get too jumpy and self-conscious to be effective. My people found that out the hard way, and decided it was best to design their AI's without that capacity."

"'No' would have sufficed," Pinchon commented.

"Well, she doesn't know very much about my people, does she?" Wellesley countered good-naturedly. "I thought she might appreciate a little backstory."

"You're a good one for backstory, that's for sure."

Internally the AI rolled his eyes before shifting back to Mafalda.

"Anyway, like I said, you'd better get some rest. That's the best thing for your body right now. Before long you'll have the care that you need. Though I have to laugh when I remember that it will be given to you by pirates."

"Well, the doctors aren't pirates," Pinchon replied. "They're normal physicians who are paid a great deal of money to compensate them for not having any kind of life outside the organization. Girnius is a little paranoid, so he doesn't let them out of his sight. So far it's paid off." He tapped a few buttons and set a warp course for Petrov-2.

"Alright, hang on to your hats," he announced, just as the warp engine engaged and a rift of darkness opened before them. Flying into it, Mafalda gasped when a tunnel of darkness surrounded them.

"It's...incredible," she said with wonder, looking all around her with her mouth agape. "Like something out of a dream."

"Haven't you warped before?" Wellesley asked, a little surprised that the experience was striking her so hard.

"Oh, yes," she told him. "But never like this. This is... incredible," she repeated, shaking her head in disbelief. "I feel as though I'm moving down something that's living. Like it's watching us." She paused and looked at the two men. "Do you feel it, too?"

"No," Hunt said, followed by Pinchon.

"I'm sorry to hear that," she said sincerely, looking back at the dark stream. "It's unlike anything I've ever felt before. Like lying on a beach with the waves washing over you. But they're waves of *consciousness*, of something's mind." Her fatigue temporarily forgotten, she gazed at the tunnel for several minutes before speaking again. "Tell me, how did we get here?"

"We haven't the least idea," Wellesley replied. "This ship was made by a race called the *Keesh'Forbandai*, a people with an almost unthinkable talent for machinery. Somehow they utilize the dark realm to travel at speeds faster than anyone else can manage."

"That's why we can get from Erdu to Petrov in hours instead of days," Pinchon explained. "Boy, I wish I had a ship like this in the old days. You'd spend half your life just floating through space looking for targets."

"Targets?" she asked distractedly, still watching the tunnel.

"I was a pirate once," he replied. "Worked for the Black Suns."

His words broke her wonder, and she looked at him

with surprise and a hint of aversion.

"A pirate?" she repeated.

"Yes, I was," he said without shame.

"Like I told you," Hunt interjected, her eyes going to him. "It matters what you're doing *now*, not what you've done before."

"O-of course," she assented quickly, nodding her head. "I'm sorry. I just didn't expect it, is all. You seem so nice. So thoughtful."

"You don't stop being a human being because you join the Black Suns," the colonel replied with a slight edge.

Apologetically she looked at Hunt, but he just waved a hand to dismiss the matter. Unfastening his harness now that they were in the safety of warp, he helped her do the same and then leaned back again.

"I've been there," he said, looking upwards. "In the dark realm, I mean. It drew my consciousness from my body and into whatever kind of space it consists of."

"What did you see?" she asked eagerly.

"All sorts of things," he replied as his mind went back. "I saw an ocean of darkness stretching as far as I could see. Above it was a kind of sky, but without any visible light source. It just glowed a dull red. And filling the ocean from one end to the other were bodies, *countless* bodies."

"What kind of bodies?"

"Human," he answered. "With noble faces. They looked almost like royalty."

"Did you talk to anyone there?"

"Not anyone native to that place," he said. "I saw my brother there before he died in the reactor aboard *Sentinel*, plus the last traces of a memory my father had planted in me as he passed." He paused for a few moments as he thought on the two fallen Hunts, casualties in a war that had been guiding the fate of his family since time out of mind. "I *did* feel an essence there, though," he continued. "It held me between the sea of the dead and the sky. I could feel it examining me, trying to understand something. But I've never spoken with it. Honestly I don't know if it can talk or make its thoughts known in any way but action."

"Action?" she queried.

"I could feel it help me when I was battling *Deldrach*," he elaborated. "When he tried to attack you with his power I was able to negate it with the help of the dark essence. It modulated its own output so we wouldn't hurt you. That's what I mean by communicating through action: clearly it's on our side and wants to help, or it wouldn't have done that. It could have just left me to make the attempt on my own."

"Incredible," she uttered yet again, looking once more at the dark stream above them and wondering what it might be thinking about them at just that moment. For nearly half an hour she watched, before the abuse she'd been subjected to finally caught up with her and she grew sleepy. Settling into her seat as well as she could, she quickly drifted off to a sound sleep.

"At least she's finally checked out," Pinchon whispered to Hunt, looking over his shoulder first at the girl and then at his friend. "That little one doesn't know when to call it quits. She should have been sleeping instead of talking."

"It's all pretty new to her," Hunt said, taking a small blanket and covering her with it. Gently she moaned and shifted a little, unconsciously drawing it up to her neck and sighing. "She's just excited."

"Reminds me of Gromyko and Milo," Pinchon said thoughtlessly. "They never knew when to stop, either. I mean, I like young people as much as the next guy, they're peppy and all. But they never know when to quit and take a breather for their own good."

"Colonel..." Wellesley said in a meaningful singsong whisper.

"That...was so stupid, Rex," the ex-pirate uttered sincerely the moment he remembered. "I apologize."

"It's alright," he replied quietly, still pained by the loss of his brother but no longer burdened by it. He knew it was the kind of end he'd wanted all along, to leave life doing something that really mattered. He missed him dearly, but he found himself unable to regret such a noble passing. Drawing a deep breath, he let the moment drift away on the air that he exhaled.

In the front seat Pinchon wished he could kick himself. But he didn't want to disturb their passenger now that she was finally asleep. Promising himself to do it later, he shook his head and looked down the long tunnel of blackness before him.

◆ ◆ ◆

When Ronald Radik awoke, he found himself lying on his back against the hard stone of the cave's massive spherical chamber. He was stiff and very cold, the rock having drained away much of his body heat. Swallowing hard and finding his throat dry as a cork, he opened his eyes and gazed at the ceiling for half a minute before trying to sit up. With effort he fought himself onto his knees and then his feet, nearly tumbling over as he found his balance. Rubbing his face with his hands, he tried to drive away the grogginess he felt while simultaneously remembering what happened.

"I'd…climbed the tower," he mumbled, verbally walking down the last few things he could recall. "I touched the orb. I told Julia to get out. Julia!" he exclaimed, raising his face from his hands and looking around for her. She lay in a twisted heap where she'd fallen just before he'd lost consciousness. Rushing to her, he stumbled as his boot slipped on a rock and almost fell across her. Recovering his equilibrium, he dropped to his knees and felt her neck for a pulse. "Please, Julia," he muttered, closing his eyes and holding his breath. She was deathly cold, and the horrible thought that she'd frozen to death while he lay asleep a dozen paces away filled his mind. But then he felt it, a tiny pulse of her heart against his index finger. With profound gratitude he bent over and pressed his head to the floor, thanking God that he hadn't lost his friend.

Remembering to breathe, he drew a few quick breaths to get the oxygen pumping through his system, and then struggled to get her into his arms and off the floor. His muscles were dull and unresponsive, being both cold and strangely exhausted. Thinking of his climb up the column of stone, he thought that must have been what had worn him out. Realizing that he hadn't noticed the pillar since awakening, he looked around with the girl in his arms and was surprised to find it gone. The orb rested in the middle of the room as before, but the column had somehow been drawn into the floor, and it was now resting comfortably at ground level. It was pure black as before, and still fascinating to behold despite its viewer's fatigue. Shaking his head to break the spell, he slowly climbed the sloping floor of the chamber and headed along the tunnel to the fresh air and warmth of the world above.

Radik was spent by the time he passed through the mirage, barely finding the strength to set Powers down without simply dumping her into the grass. His muscles aching, his lungs aflame, he laid down beside her and dragged air into his chest with long, slow breaths. Once his head began to swim he backed off, struggled to his elbow, and looked around him.

The sun was high in the sky, but a little bit past its zenith. The sounds of Devourer vessels could be heard in the distance, though they were very faint. He reasoned that they must have cleared out the wildlife in their area and moved on to other parts of the region. With a remorseful sigh at the thought of Jennet's devastation, he fell onto his back once more and closed his eyes.

Periodically he checked Powers, reassured to find her

body warming rapidly now that it was off the cold stone and under the powerful rays of Jennet's sun. He tried waking her twice, but she refused to stir. With grandfatherly care he brushed the hair from her eyes, hoping above all things that the orb hadn't somehow damaged her mind when it knocked her out. Or even, more prosaically, that she hadn't hit her head too hard when she fell to the floor.

"Just rest now, little one," he whispered, patting her hand and laying down once more. "We're not in any hurry."

Closing his own eyes, he tried to recall his last moments on the pillar. He could remember the orb glowing, and how it wouldn't let go of his hands. He could feel the fear in his heart as he jerked his head to Julia and told her to get out, and the brief burst of agony he felt as the orb's power overcame her mind. And then he lost consciousness himself.

"Wait," he realized, rolling his head side to side in the grass. "No, I didn't."

There was an intermediate step. He'd felt the orb searching him somehow, as though it was moving up and down his every cell and examining him for some special purpose. As it did so it couldn't hide its nature from him, its consciousness mingling with his own. It felt incomparably ancient, wise, and patient.

And angry. Very angry.

The thought made his heart tighten a little, and he swallowed again. He sensed that whatever that orb was, it had a mind and an essence that so exceeded his own that it could flick him aside like a pebble if it so wished. Its sheer age was more than enough to put him in awe. But the depth of its anger made him wonder if they'd stumbled into something better left alone.

A moan escaped Powers' lips, breaking his train of thought and instantly sending him to his elbow again. Solicitously he gazed into her face, hoping to see her eyelids tremble and then open. Unconsciously he seized her hand and began to squeeze it.

"You're hurting me," she said in a dull, heavy voice.

"What?" he asked, dumbfounded.

"My hand," she explained in a croak, trying to raise it but lacking the strength.

"Oh," he said quickly, releasing his grip and struggling to his knees to get a better look at her. "How are you feeling? Are you alright?"

"I feel like I've been massaged to death," she said with a little chuckle. "Like every part of my mind and body has been worked until it can't even move anymore. Does that make sense?" she asked, finally forcing her eyes open and squinting into the glare of the sun overhead.

"It does," he nodded. "I feel the same way. The orb must have examined you, too."

"Examined me?" she asked.

"Yes. It scanned my body somehow. I thought it was because I was touching it. But it must be able to reach across the room and do it, too."

"All I remember is a presence in my mind, followed by blackness," she said with confusion, her brow furrowing as she tried to make sense of it. "It was like there wasn't enough room in my head for both of us, so I was pushed out. But I have strange memories. Things I haven't thought of in years are suddenly fresh in my mind. I think it must have been digging through my thoughts, rifling through my psyche in search of something. But what?"

"I wish I knew," he replied, looking back at the mirage. "But I've got a bad feeling that it's not anything good." He looked back at her. "Do you remember anything about the consciousness? What it felt like? Any attributes at all?"

"I don't...think so," she said slowly, trying to think back. "Wait, it seemed angry about something. But not just angry: betrayed, like something had been stolen from it. Yes, that's it: betrayed."

"Are you sure?" he asked.

"Yes, that's what it felt like," she assured him. "At least, that's how it came across to me. Maybe it was just pushing my buttons, making me think something that wasn't so."

"I doubt it," he said gravely, looking at the mirage once more and then lightening his tone for her sake. "So, how do you feel otherwise? Are you alright?"

"Just exhausted, I think," she replied, folding her hands on her stomach and closing her eyes momentarily. "Oh, and thirsty. Very thirsty."

"Hang on," he said, grunting as he got to his feet. "I'll be right back."

Bringing their packs back with him from the cave, he dropped them beside her and drew out a canteen. Lifting her head, he helped her get a few swallows down and then took some for himself. Still tired from carrying her that long way, he rolled onto his back once more and let the fresh air and warm sunlight wash over him. Occasionally he opened his eyes to look at her, but she'd fallen back asleep after her drink. Folding his hands on his own stomach, he was glad to follow her example after all he'd been through.

But sleep didn't come easily. For an hour he drifted in a strange place between sleep and wakefulness. Lucidly he saw the orb in the chamber, its personality so real he could nearly reach out and touch it. It seemed to him a stream of consciousness, a kind of ribbon of personality floating through the air. He wasn't sure if that made any sense, but it was how it seemed to him.

A thunderclap reverberated through the air, dragging him back to alertness. Scanning the sky, he was surprised to find it bright and clear, with not a cloud to be seen for miles.

"Must be some way off yet," he thought, putting his head back down and settling in again. "I'll get her inside before it starts to rain."

Yes, a ribbon. It sounded stupid to his thinking, but something about that image took hold in his mind and wouldn't let go. Like a wiggling ribbon or fish, moving through the air in search of something. It seemed almost parasitic, examining the life forms around it for their suitability. Suitability for *what*, he wondered, but had no answer to give.

And yet, it hadn't hurt either of them. It clearly had no respect for privacy or the wishes of others, but its obvious power wasn't truly brought to bear on either of them. He sensed that it could have gone a great deal further than it had, but instead it held back. It may have been rough with them, but it hadn't meant to harm them.

Then his thoughts rolled back to their first encounter, when Powers nearly bit him because she wanted to stay near it so badly. The idea troubled him, and he wondered what else the orb had in store for them.

He gradually grew dreamy in the bucolic beauty of the setting, and it took several minutes for him to realize that the sun was no longer shining down on them.

"I'll move her when it starts to rain," he reflected, unwilling to get up unless he absolutely had to.

Suddenly a massive roar filled the air, shocking him to his feet and waking Powers.

"What in the..." his voice trailed, as his eyes searched the enormous underside of *Sentinel*. The great cannon was firing, producing the roar that nearly deafened them despite being several miles beneath it. Following the beam to its target, he could just make out a disintegrating Devourer vessel in the distance.

Inside of ten minutes every alien ship within Jennet's atmosphere was making a beeline for the warship. Radik and Powers could only watch in wonder as its innumerable turrets clawed them from the sky, turning them to a fine black ash that flitted on the wind and gradually fell to the ground. Twice more the great cannon fired, annihilating a pair of Devourer battleships as they tried to close the distance and get their tentacles into the dreadnought.

Standing with his arm around Powers to hold her up, Radik watched as *Sentinel* gradually shifted off to the south towards the prison camp. The hyperactivity of its turrets slowed as the air cleared of enemies. Eagerly he half dragged the lieutenant to the mouth of the cave to try to see over the treeline to their south. For several minutes they watched the vessel lumber away, occasional bursts from its weapons darkening the sky with streaks of shadow.

"It was all over so quickly," Powers said, shaking her head as she thought on all the good lives they'd lost in their futile defense of the planet. "The Devourers never stood a chance."

As if to emphasize her point, the main gun fired again, the shockwave rattling the trees' branches as it rolled back towards them.

"We've got to let Krancis know we're still alive," Radik uttered, trying to think how long it would take them to get back to the abandoned mines. Then he remembered a small portable radio that he'd put in his pack. Leaving Powers leaning against the rocky wall, he made for their packs and brought them back. Rifling through his, he found the radio and switched it on. "Hello? This is Admiral Ronald Radik, calling *Sentinel*. Do you read me? Over."

For several tense seconds he and Powers eyed each other.

"I repeat: this is Admiral Ronald Radik of the Jennet militia, calling the warship *Sentinel*. Do you copy?"

"Affirmative, Admiral," a smooth female voice said over the radio. "This is *Esiluria* of the warship *Sentinel*. We have received your coordinates and will send a vessel to retrieve you once the Devourers have been dealt with. Please remain where you are so that we may extract you as expeditiously as possible. Over."

"Thank you, *Esiluria*," he said gratefully. "Thank you. We'll wait right here. Over and out."

"*Esiluria*?" Powers asked, as he helped her settle down on the ground, her back leaning against the wall of stone. "That's a strange name."

"Sounds alien," the admiral agreed, too excited to sit beside her and choosing instead to pace up and down before the mouth of the cave. "They made it! They actually made it! I knew Krancis would come if he could. But with an entire empire to look after, I thought our chances were pretty slim of getting any help. I just hope he got here in time to shut down that processing facility before every last human has been fed through it."

Slowly Julia's strength returned, and by the time an egg-shaped transport soared over the trees and landed a dozen feet away she was able to move, carefully, under her own power. With Radik at her side, carrying their packs, they approached the vessel and waited for the canopy to open. As it did, a handsome man came into view, a broad smile on his face.

"Admiral, it's a pleasure to meet you, sir," he said, saluting before leaning over the side and grasping their packs. Stowing them in the back, he offered the lethargic Powers his hand and pulled her aboard, Radik right behind her. "Captain Ronald Bessemer, at your service," he smiled, his eyes lingering on the lieutenant for a few moments. On his way to Jennet, Krancis had swung a little bit off his path and picked up the returning captain. "Krancis is eager to meet you immediately, sir. If you'll strap yourselves in, we can be on our way at once."

"Thank you, son," Radik said, glad to finally be under the protective aegis of the imperial navy.

Without further words, the canopy dropped, Bessemer guided the vessel into the sky, and made for *Sentinel*. The warship was floating over the processing plant, all its guns silent and still. A small door opened on its left side, admitted the egg to one of its hangars, and then quickly closed. They landed among a collection of such craft. A handful of people were milling around, many fewer than were typically seen in the hangars of human vessels.

"Why are there so few people here, Captain?" Radik

asked.

"Automation, sir," he replied, as he shut down the craft and opened the canopy. "The designers of this vessel built it to require a minimal crew to function."

"How many people are aboard?"

"Sir, I'm afraid I don't know. That information is classified."

"Of course."

Bessemer stood up, grabbed their bags, and handed them over the side to a man who was waiting. Carefully they got Powers out of the ship and then followed her down. By the time they'd reached the hangar's floor, Radik saw a lean, dark shape in his peripheral vision. Turning his head, he was surprised to see Krancis personally coming to greet them.

"Krancis, this is an honor," he said with profound wonder, as the mysterious man took his hand and firmly shook it.

"You've done well, Admiral," he replied in his precise fashion, a small, satisfied smile on his lips. "Just as I thought you would."

"Thank you, sir," he uttered with some embarrassment, his failure to defend Jennet made painfully obvious by the necessity of calling for *Sentinel*.

Krancis' eyes went to Powers and searched her up and down for a moment.

"You'd better get to the medical bay, Lieutenant. You're in rough shape."

"Yes, sir."

"Captain, see that she gets there alright," he said, turning back towards the door. "Come with me, Admiral."

Dumbfounded to be given such treatment, Radik walked beside and a little behind the man in black. Respectfully *Sentinel's* crew moved to the side to let them pass whenever there was a glut of bodies. After a teleporter ride that made his head spin, Radik found himself within Krancis' personal quarters.

"Drink, Admiral?" he asked, holding up a bottle and looking at him.

"No, thank you, sir," he declined. "I don't drink."

"That's for the best," Krancis said, pouring himself a drink before settling into a chair and gesturing for the rigidly standing admiral to do the same. "Ronald, you're not a man born for military discipline. You're an excellent leader *because* of your flexibility and naturalness of mind. So don't feel obligated to be stiff and formal. I'm already quite aware of both your respect and deference towards me, and I don't need to be reminded of that fact by a strict adherence to protocol. So drop the sir, relax your posture, and take a seat."

Surprised to be spoken to in this way by a superior, he was nevertheless gratified by the freedom it gave him. Sitting on the front lip of the proffered chair, he rested his elbows on his knees and knit his fingers together as Krancis threw a leg over the other and took a sip of his drink.

"Now, what do you have to tell me?"

From beginning to end Radik related every detail of the defense of Jennet and its immediate aftermath. His journey with Powers was stripped down to the bare essentials, most of that part of his narrative being devoted to the processing plant that lay in ruins beneath them. And then he came to his experience with the orb. Throughout his story Krancis had paid unblinking attention, at no point interrupting the flow of his words. But the orb caused him to uncross his leg and sit a little straighter, his gaze boring into the admiral.

"And you haven't seen it since waking up in the chamber?"

"No," Radik shook his head. "I thought it best to stay away from it, at least for a while."

Krancis arose, still holding his drink, and walked to a place behind his chair. He seemed to withdraw, entering another world inside his mind that drew his total attention. For a couple of minutes he mutely stood in this way, Radik watching him with ever growing curiosity.

"And it was angry?"

"Yes," he nodded, as the emperor's strong right hand turned to face him again. "Lieutenant Powers said it felt like more than that, though. Like it had been betrayed." He eyed Krancis carefully, trying to decipher the look of fatal seriousness on his face. "What is it, sir?" he asked respectfully.

Krancis' piercing eyes found his.

"A threat," he said ominously. "One who's name I dare not utter. At this time it is essentially dormant, though watchful. Should it ever be released from that orb, it would make us look wistfully back upon the present war with the Devourers. We couldn't possibly cope with its power."

"Even *Sentinel*?" Radik asked.

"Even *Sentinel*," he confirmed gravely. "The orb is made from the very essence of the dark realm. Were it not, the power it holds within would have crushed both of you in an instant. The psyche of the shadow element protected you both, restraining it to merely searching your minds for data it might find useful."

"Then it can't hold it back altogether?"

"No, just mostly. That's why the pillar of stone could descend into the floor. The being within used his great power to do that. But to force that amount of energy through its prison demands an enormous amount of stamina, and it must have exhausted itself in the effort. That's why it was inert when you awoke."

"But how could anything *live* inside that orb for so long?" Radik asked. "When I touched it, I saw a vision that ran incalculably back into the past."

"There are many beings in this universe that live longer than we do. This is but one of many."

"Incredible," the admiral said with wonder, trying to wrap his head around what he was being told. He believed Krancis implicitly, but his words were so far outside his own experience that he couldn't shake the feeling he was being told a fairytale. "What can we do about it? Can we hide it?"

"There's no place in this galaxy where it would be truly safe," Krancis replied, taking his seat once more as he thought. "The *Pho'Sath* in particular want it terribly. They know it's in this galaxy, and they've spent countless millennia searching for it without effect. Were they to find out exactly where it is, even the treaty with the *Keesh'Forbandai* wouldn't keep them from invading instantly. Our only hope is to keep its whereabouts perfectly secret. Only you two saw it?"

"Yes," he nodded. "Well, recently, that is." He paused, concerned what effect his next words would have. "There's an essence in the forest beneath us. It spoke to lieutenant Powers and myself, telling us to go there. It said there was a mystery hidden in the cave, and that Taegen had once tried to uncover its secrets."

"Taegen?" Krancis asked, for once surprised.

"Yes, the essence said that he taught it how to speak to others," Radik continued. "And that he also taught it to care for the creatures who lived on Jennet."

"That sounds like Taegen," he uttered as he thought. "But it's remarkable that he should have been here without my knowledge. I kept careful watch over him for years before his death, given the danger he was in." He found Radik's puzzled eyes and elaborated. "There were elements in the military that were jealous of his influence with the emperor. It was only through an elaborate campaign of deception, body doubles, false trails, and constant sting operations that I managed to keep him alive as long as I did. Regrettably my power was not so complete then as it is now, and his enemies finally managed to kill him." He paused and thought again. "It's remarkable that he should have been able to slip away while I was watching him."

"Could someone have just faked his name? Perhaps another mystic came here and traded on his reputation."

"Not likely," Krancis shook his head subtly, staring at the wall as he mused. "It takes something beyond mere talent to take an essence like the one you discovered and teach it to talk. It takes purity of spirit and purpose, and those aren't common attributes for deceivers. Especially the cheap sort that would try to use another's name. His fakery would come through at once, and the essence would have had nothing to do with him."

"Then how is it possible?" Radik asked, believing as most did that Krancis was incapable of error.

"Taegen, for all his goodness, was also a consummate manipulator. He must have sensed the protective net around him and found a weakness to exploit. Giving the agents around him to believe he was somewhere, or *someone*, that he was not, he managed to give them the slip. That's the only answer that I can give. The imperial intelligence apparatus was not as robust in those days, and hard data about such things is unobtainable. After his death, the emperor was more amenable to increasing both its size and scope to prevent such a future tragedy from occurring."

"Shouldn't Taegen have reported the orb's presence?"

"Taegen was a very wise man," Krancis replied. "He doubtless had his reasons for keeping it secret. The government was wide open, with loose lips trading gossip in every corner and hallway. Even if he'd passed it on to me, I couldn't have acted without an inordinate number of people finding out about it. It's much easier to act now, with the exigencies of war upon us."

A couple of minutes silently passed as Krancis thought. Slowly a question ground upon Radik's mind, until finally he had to speak.

"Sir, why did you put me in charge of this planet's defense?" he asked as respectfully as his pained conscience would allow. "I've been out of uniform for so long that I must have made mistakes that someone more familiar with the Devourers wouldn't have."

"You did the best that anyone was capable of doing," Krancis replied certainly. "Jennet was outgunned from the start, with only a fraction of a chance of holding out on its own. I never intended for you to succeed, but simply to delay them as long as possible. The rest of the navy, even those who are familiar with the Devourers, are still locked into their old ways of thinking. They think a battle consists of lining our ships up against theirs and throwing ordnance at them, a tactic that only plays into their vicious manner of closing the distance and tearing into our vessels. You kept your forces loose and mobile, dragging the enemy into range of the planet's surface weapons once you were too severely outnumbered in space."

"But there was another reason," he continued. "I am in the process of retrofitting the imperial navy with both new vessels and a new doctrine of war. These measures will *not* be popular, and will require an energetic, intelligent man to see that they are carried into execution. Such a man cannot be found in the navy that exists today because they've all been a part of the system for too long. I need an outsider, someone who thinks for himself and is capable of running completely counter to the orthodoxy of the service. But he needed to *personally* see what we're up against, the inadequacy of our current response, and the need for something better."

"I'm ready to serve in any capacity you consider me fit for," he replied earnestly.

"You may not be quite so eager once you see the proposals set before you," Krancis said. "But I know that you won't let me down."

After a few more minutes of talk, Krancis broke up the meeting, sending Radik to the hospital with orders to tell Powers to keep utterly silent about the orb. He assured the admiral that it would be dealt with shortly, and that it need not trouble his mind any longer. But the anger he'd felt from the being held within it haunted him as he made his way to the hospital, and he wondered if even Krancis' great genius could grapple with the threat it represented.

Krancis, meanwhile, remained in his seat. Without bothering to knock, Soliana opened his door, stepped in, and closed it behind her.

"He has been found," she announced.

"Yes," he replied evenly.

"What shall we do?"

"Remove him to another location."

"His power is great," she cautioned him, moving on gentle feet to the chair opposite his and sitting down on its wide, flat armrest. "He is a danger to any who come near to him. Especially those from which he could draw insight, such as you or myself. And those without such gifts as we possess will be easily penetrated by his mind, unable to defend themselves."

"Naturally."

"Then how can he be removed? As soon as he senses the purpose of his movers, he will attack them. The essence cannot restrain him fully. He will overwhelm them."

Krancis tipped his head as he thought on this. Then a smile slowly crossed his lips.

"Not if the movers are led to believe he is being taken to a place he *wants* to go."

"You are thinking of the Gate of Zeruc," she uttered.

"It's the one place in this galaxy that he is certain to *want* to go," he explained. "He will have hungered for the Gate since time out of mind, wishing above all else to leave this dimension and get back among his people."

"But the Gate is no longer functional."

"He doesn't know that. He's been locked inside that orb since long before it was damaged."

"And if he realizes he's not being taken to the Gate and attacks the people moving him?"

"He won't have any way to know where he's being taken. We'll reprogram the computer in one of the transports to provide false information. Even his pilot won't realize they're heading the wrong way. It's not as if there's any landmarks for them to look at in warp."

"You know best," she said somewhat dubiously, rising from her seat and making for the door.

"You're very communicative all of a sudden," Krancis observed, as her hand reached the knob and began to twist it.

"My mind has been simplified ever since you drew *Eesekkalion* from within me. As I told you before, you took more than just his presence from me, and the result has been a streamlining of my psyche. I can now access much more of the information that was put into me by those mysterious figures I told you about."

"Can you see who they are?" he asked, gesturing for her to retake her seat.

"No," she replied with some disappointment, resuming her place on the armrest. "They are still hidden from me. My knowledge of recent events is not as clear as those memories that pertain to the distant past. It is peculiar that I should have gained access to these notions shortly before the orb was rediscovered. It is as though fate has guided me to this moment. And you as well, since it was through your action that my psyche has been altered."

"Do you still regret that change?"

"I don't know. I'm still finding myself. The voices I used to hear, the ideas that used to swirl constantly around me, have fallen silent. I no longer feel that I am merely a host for a multitude of personalities. But the change has been hard. My mind was pure chaos, but it had become familiar and, to a degree, stimulating to me. Now everything is so quiet, so still. I don't know what to make of it."

"You'll adapt in time," he assured her. "You'll come to appreciate the ability to focus."

Several silent seconds passed by.

"Tell me, do you still intend to keep me aboard *Sentinel*?"

"For the foreseeable future, yes. You're too great a

liability to be left anywhere else. Besides, your insight can serve the empire best if you're near to me."

"As you wish," she replied noncommittally.

"Would you rather be somewhere else?"

"I would rather not be kept as a prisoner aboard this vessel."

"You're no more a prisoner than I am. We are both simply forced to remain here by virtue of the war. Were it over, I would send you away at once."

"Then you don't appreciate my presence here?"

"It isn't my policy to hold anyone against their will, provided there is another way," he explained. "I have no need of others, and thus no reason to compel them to remain by me. If they wish to stay, they may. And if not, they can go. But where the proper conduct of this war is concerned, I am deaf to all individual desires, including my own."

"And especially mine, given the insight I've gained into your mind."

"Especially yours," he confirmed. "Though the secrets you hold are already of sufficient value to keep you close at hand."

"But there's more to it than that," she replied. "I can sense it in you, a solicitousness towards me that you don't feel for others. I'd almost call it a tenderness, given the coldness with which you treat everyone else."

"I'm not in love with you, if that's what you're driving at."

"No, I know that. But you care for me, like a father for his daughter. I could feel it back when you were fighting with *Eesekkalion* for the control of my mind. In that moment your feelings shone through, and I could tell that you cared for me. I've never felt that before."

"You must have had parents."

"I don't remember them," she shook her head. "My memories only come to me in patches. Everything relating to my early life has vanished, I fear forever. It must have been those people I saw in the vision that did it, erasing the foundation of my identity for some reason or other. Perhaps to make me of more value in the present struggle they ensured that I would be detached from any personal loyalties and given wholly over to the empire."

"Perhaps," Krancis replied without committing.

"I can tell by your tone that you're unconvinced. But isn't it Rex Hunt's personal loyalties that give you the most trouble and anxiety?"

"Erasing his early memories wouldn't change a thing about him. It's part and parcel of who he is to allow his judgment to be swayed by his feeling attachments. His relationship with doctor Tselitel isn't even a year old yet."

"That's true," she agreed, nodding somewhat regretfully at the thought. "I must admit that at one time I felt destiny had drawn us together. The knowledge that those people put into me seemed perfectly suited to guide him in his struggle to achieve victory for mankind. But I find that he's forgotten me aboard *Sentinel*, and that he neither needs nor wants me."

"Love is not always reciprocated. You'd do best to put it behind you and focus on your task."

"Which is?"

"To draw forth as much knowledge as you can for our immediate use. This war is far from over, despite the victories we've achieved with our super weapon," he said, swirling his hand to indicate the vessel wrapped around them. "You mustn't simply wait for insight to come to you. Meditate in your room and try to bring it up from the back of your mind. It was planted there for a reason, and much of its usefulness is lost when it springs up on its own at the last minute. We need to know in advance as much as we can."

"Of course," she assented, before rising from her seat and leaving the room.

Finishing the rest of his drink, he activated his ear radio.

"*Esiluria*? Find Captain Bessemer and have him come to my quarters at once."

Two hours later the captain was inside the spherical chamber with a half dozen workmen standing around him, looking at the pure black orb.

"Come on, let's try again," he said, wiping sweat from his brow with the back of his hand and positioning himself behind the orb.

"Where is this thing going, anyway?" one of the men asked. "Seems like a lot of bother over a big ball."

"Krancis said this thing has to get out of here right away," he explained, getting down low to give himself as much leverage as possible. "Reckon he knows what he's doing."

"But a *ball*?" another asked.

"Quit talking and push!" Bessemer ordered, as he began to strain against its weight.

Reluctantly the men tried for the fifth time, with the same result.

"It's no good, Captain," the first man said, as each man took his hands away and dropped to the cold stone to rest. "This thing weighs more than all of us put together." He paused and looked up and then all around. "Makes you wonder how it got in here."

"All I care about is how it's gonna get *out* of here," Bessemer replied, the only one to remain standing. "It's got to get off world right away."

"And end up where?" an older workman asked, dabbing his forehead and neck with a handkerchief.

"Some place called the Gate of Zurac. No, wait, that's *Zeruc*. Zeruc," he repeated for clarity.

A sudden blue flash emanated from the orb, making them all jump.

"That's peculiar," the older man said, patting it with his palm to see if he could make it happen again.

Testing an intuition, Bessemer put his hands on it and

gave it a firm shove. To his surprise, it shifted a little.

"Hey, come on!" he said eagerly. "It's ready to move now."

"Ready to move?" the older man asked skeptically. "What are we dealing with here, Captain?"

"Hey, I get orders and I follow 'em, just like you," he replied. "Now give me a hand."

Together the men had enough strength to push the suddenly willing orb up the slope and into the cave. They paused momentarily to catch their breath, and then Bessemer kept them going until they'd made it through the mirage and into the open air. The sun was sinking in the sky, and the forest's shadows were stretching across the ground as the men dropped to the grass in exhaustion and panted for air.

"Good work, men," he congratulated them, getting to his feet first and popping the canopy on the egg that had been chosen for the trip. Its two back seats had been removed, and a makeshift stand had been made to hold the orb in place during flight. "Now we just have to lift it in there."

"Lift it in?!" exclaimed several of the men at once. "We just barely got it up here!"

"That's why we'll rig a harness and lift it in with one of the other eggs," he explained, leaning against his ship and gesturing towards one of the vessels that had brought the workers along. "It'll be a piece of cake."

"We don't have a harness like that on hand," the older man observed. "Gonna have to go back to *Sentinel* to get it."

"Then get there and back double fast," Bessemer ordered. "We don't want to do this when the sun is down."

It was much later when the man finally returned from *Sentinel* with an appropriate harness, and the men had to work quickly in the diminishing light. By far the best flier among them, Bessemer piloted the craft that was to lift the orb, doing his best to supervise the work from twenty feet in the air. Once they gave him the OK, he slowly hoisted the perfectly black sphere into the air, moved with infinite care to the other ship, and ever so slowly lowered it. Sliding it into its stand on the first try, the harness was quickly detached and he landed once more.

"Alright, you men get back to the ship," he said, climbing aboard the modified egg and dropping into the front seat. "Krancis probably doesn't plan to hang around here too much longer, and you don't want to hold him up."

Amidst general words of assent he lowered the canopy, activated the egg, and flew slowly off into the sky with his mysterious load.

From *Sentinel's* bridge Krancis watched him go. He realized Bessemer would be in fatal danger the instant he dropped out of warp and it became clear to the being inside the orb that he hadn't taken him to the Gate of Zeruc. But there was no helping it. He couldn't offer him a word of warning without tipping off his cargo as to the truth of their journey. He would just have to cope as well as he could.

It was cruel, he knew, to send a good man off on an errand like that. But there wasn't any other way.

"Sir?" Radik asked, poking his head inside the door.

"Come in, Admiral," Krancis replied without turning around.

"I've spoken to lieutenant Powers," he uttered, joining the man in black in the middle of the panoramic room. "And she hasn't breathed a word to another soul about what we've seen. She knows the score, and will keep quiet going forwards."

"Good," he said, as the pair of eggs that bore the workmen returned. He had already made provision for them, ensuring that their own part in the removal of the orb would also go no further.

"Sir, I wanted to ask you what your plans are for the Devourers going forwards," Radik began somewhat reluctantly. "The presence that spoke to me said that they're looking for a weakness in *Sentinel*, and that that's why they continue to offer us battle when every engagement heretofore has led only to crushing defeat. They're playing the long game, sacrificing fleets to discover how to destroy the only vessel that threatens them in this galaxy."

"We will continue to fight and defeat them, but exclusively on our terms. The only time they profit in battle is when we permit them to attempt new tactics. That's when they're sounding us out, and even their failures give them a more complete picture of our capabilities."

"But how will we defeat them on such terms?" Radik queried. "They're attacking us all across the empire. They'll savage us if we don't pick up the pace."

"That's where you come in," he said, turning to the aged admiral with a slight smile on his lips. "Until now the imperial navy has been little more than a buffer to slow them down. Its tactics are antiquated, as are its vessels, given the threat we now face. Only the heavy fighters are really suitable for combat against the Devourers, because they combine the maximum of firepower and maneuverability in a single package. Smaller ships don't pack enough punch, and larger ones are little more than ready-made targets for their tentacles."

"So you're planning to increase our heavy fighter production?"

"No," he shook his head. "They're much too advanced to be pumped out in the kinds of numbers we need to turn the tide. What's required is something altogether simpler, lighter, and yet more destructive to the enemy."

He briefly issued a handful of verbal commands to the ship, and a hologram of an experimental vessel appeared before them both. It possessed a large forward-facing window behind which sat the pilot, and a proportionally long body reaching back from the seat. Engines on each of its four sides offered it supreme mobility and reactivity to commands. The design was stripped to the absolute barest essentials, possessing essentially no armor and only the most basic life support system. The pilot, in fact, would have to bring his own oxygen in the form of a small tank fitted with an air purifier.

Behind the cockpit were a series of many little doors, each of which housed a powerful, short-ranged guided missile. Possessing only enough fuel to travel a very short distance, it would be the pilot's responsibility to fly the craft close enough to the enemy to activate the automatic guidance system in each weapon and dispatch it to its target. It took only a glance for Radik to conclude that most of the pilots who flew such craft would not be returning alive.

"I call it the Adler," Krancis said, after the admiral had had half a minute to digest what was before him. "As you've no doubt already deduced, this is not a vessel designed to ensure pilot safety. It is a desperation weapon, one that we can produce quickly and efficiently for maximum damage against our enemy. A new kind of light carrier is also being produced that will prioritize both speed and carrying capacity at the expense of armor and weapons. Between these two new types of vessel we'll be able to deliver an explosive payload designed to take advantage of the organic nature of our enemy, while negating the dominance that their aggressive tactics have given them until now."

"But what of morale?" Radik asked with serious misgivings. "We're essentially sending our pilots on a one-way trip."

"Only if we continue to think in the old way," Krancis replied. "Armor has been no defense against their weapons, so we shouldn't regret the loss of it. In the Adler, the pilot's survival rate is directly related to his skill in maneuvering. A single shell is all it will take to destroy such a craft. But the agility it gains in return will enable it to dodge all but the most skillfully cast shots of our enemies."

Krancis fell silent for a time, allowing the information to sink into the admiral's mind.

"When will the first strike groups be operational?"

Radik asked at last.

"Very shortly. Three fleets are nearly complete already. The main delay has been caused by the difficulty we have in sourcing the material necessary to build the warheads. As I said, they exploit the Devourer's organic nature. They consist of two parts: first, a high-explosive that can rip the tough outer layer of their ships away, exposing the softer material that lies underneath. This inner layer is not so different from our own, consisting partly of blood vessels and other forms of tissue necessary for sustaining life. Once this is exposed, it is vulnerable to the second portion of the warhead, which is a highly advanced poison that has been designed specifically to target the biology of the Devourers. Regrettably their sturdy nature keeps it from spreading throughout the vessel and killing it; they're built for war, and the blood vessels that would be needed to carry it through the ship shut down almost as soon as the poison is detected. Thus the poison only penetrates so far before halting, though the damage is both great and fairly immediate. However, even if a vessel isn't destroyed by such an attack, the poison lingers in the tissue and denies them the ability to repair the damage they've received. Should a vessel survive such an attack, they'll have to cut whole sections of dead flesh out of it before attempting to patch themselves up. Each blow they receive will not be soon forgotten."

"Our pilots are going to enter battle on unarmored ships that are loaded with high-explosive, poison-filled missiles," Radik mused aloud, the idea so strange to him that he didn't care that Krancis could hear the doubt in his voice. "Sir, I don't mean to question your orders, but I don't see how we can possibly sell this to the navy."

"That's why I wanted you to see firsthand what we're up against by defending Jennet," Krancis reiterated. "It's your job to *make* the navy accept the necessity of the Adler project. I have examined every other possible option, and this is the best by far. We still have a strong manufacturing base to work from, and given the lightness of the design we can produce many such craft very quickly. If we stick to the old way of doing things, we'll waste an enormous amount of time and material on vessels that are simply inadequate to grapple with the parasite's nature and tactics. The men will feel safer because they're wrapped in armor plate. But such armor is ineffective against the hands-on nature of their attacks. That's the most important part of your job: to show the navy the truth of what I already know, and you've already seen."

"But I failed to defend Jennet. Why would they listen to me?"

"Because it wasn't *you* who failed," explained Krancis. "It was our outdated tactics and ship designs that failed. You led them admirably, and I'll say words to that effect when your appointment as head of the imperial navy is announced. The fact that Jennet fell despite such leadership will help to show that a change is necessary. And given that you're one of the few high-ranking officers to survive an encounter with the Devourers, your firsthand experience will strengthen your case."

"I understand," Radik nodded, still uncertain but unwilling to push any further. Then his eyes went wide. "Head of the *navy*?" he clarified, as Krancis' words filtered back into his mind.

"Yes. You will still be subject to my oversight, but the daily workings of the navy will be your responsibility. I want you to infuse it with your direct, pragmatic nature. I want you to remake it in your own image. For too long it's been bound up in tradition and conventionality. It needs to be made pragmatic, streamlined, and viciously aggressive. Heretofore our tactics have been far too civilized. I want you to make the navy *angry*, Ronald. I want you to make them *hate* the Devourers with a passion. I want the highest admiral and the lowest ensign to lie awake at night thinking of new ways to destroy them. I want you to take the rage you felt when you saw them processing our people into paste and turn that into aggression. Our people must *thirst* for revenge, for justice for the souls we've already lost, and the ones that are to follow."

"What of discipline?" Radik asked, surprised to find that Krancis' message of vicious pragmatism was beginning to resonate within him. "If we whip them into a frenzy, they might be hard to handle."

"Discipline is easy to maintain when all the members of an organization are pulling in the same direction," Krancis said. "You'll get the occasional hothead that will try to take an Adler out on his own for a futile attack against a carrier. But more or less they'll follow orders, because they know you want revenge just as badly as they do. And given your experience, and the fact that you survived both the defense of Jennet and the siege that followed, they'll give extra heed to your words. You need only convince them that you are of one mind with their aims, and they'll follow you to the very end."

Slowly Radik nodded. Despite his initial misgivings, a plan was beginning to open before him. He would be open, direct, unpretentious with the navy. Presenting himself, quite accurately, as a combat officer and not a stuffed shirt, he would appeal to their basic hunger to strike back, and their general sense of bewilderment at the failure of their current tactics. His orders, briefings, and announcements would be honest and forthright, hiding nothing and laying all his cards on the table. Yes, the brass would likely take him for something of a rube. But winning over the majority of the service was his aim. He knew Krancis would open doors at the higher levels if necessary, removing obstacles with his typical prescient efficiency.

"Very well," he said at last, his voice more settled and calm. "When do I begin?"

"Immediately. I want you to familiarize yourself with

the logistics of our manufacturing situation. The Adler project, and all the elements necessary to support it, such as the carriers, is spread across different portions of the empire. It hasn't been possible to centralize our efforts because the parasite will instantly strike against them once our new approach begins to tell against it. The most critical element of the equation, the production of the warheads, is taking place on a handful of suitable worlds in facilities located underground. These facilities cannot be moved without enormous problems arising, because the worlds they're built on are the only sources for the basic elements that make up the poison itself. So one of your top priorities is maintaining their secrecy."

"I won't be able to work from *Sentinel*," Radik observed. "I have to be near the navy, to have my hands on it."

"I anticipated that," Krancis said with a hint of a smile. "An egg has been made ready, along with a pilot. You can leave at once."

"Excellent," Radik said, a smile of his own lightening his face as he reached and shook his hand. "I'd like to speak to lieutenant Powers before I leave," he added as an afterthought.

"Of course. Just keep it brief. With the destruction of the human population on Jennet, *Sentinel* no longer has a purpose here. There are a great many other places within the empire that require its presence."

"I'll be quick," he assured him. "Thank you, sir."

Hustling down the hall to the nearest transport room, he asked the technician to drop him as close to the medical quarters as possible. The receptionist was inclined to give him trouble until he mentioned that Krancis expected him to drop in on the battered lieutenant.

"Well, a few minutes would probably be alright," she grumbled, trying to save face.

Following her directions, he found Powers' door and went inside. To his surprise, another girl was sitting on the edge of her bed, her delicate fingers pressed to the unconscious lieutenant's temples.

"What are you doing?" he asked in a whisper, closing the door quietly and watching with some aversion. "Who are you?"

"I am Soliana," she replied, her eyes closed as she concentrated. "Please wait a moment."

A pair of minutes passed as Radik shifted uncomfortably from one foot to the other. He was about to speak again when the visitor opened her eyes and lowered her hands.

"Your friend has been badly hurt," she observed, getting to her feet and drawing near to him. "The being in the cave was very rough with her mind, though she'll recover in time. For now she needs rest and quiet."

"She'll get it," Radik said. "I just barely got in here myself. But how did *you* manage to get in? You don't look like medical staff."

"I'm not," she replied, looking at Powers and seeming to forget he was there for a few moments as she drifted away. Then she returned. "I work very closely with Krancis, and the hospital staff aren't willing to cross him."

"Yeah, I noticed that myself," he said with a slight grin. "But why were you touching her?"

"I was exploring her mind with my gift of insight," she replied gravely. "She's jumbled and confused, the being having had no regard for her safety. But she's young and strong, and will bounce back." She paused and looked at him. "The being interacted with you, as well. I can sense the traces of its essence emanating from you."

"That's incredible," he uttered with wonder. "Yes, it showed me all sorts of things," he added quickly. "Space and time and anger."

"Were you afraid as it did this?"

"No, I can't say I was," Radik reflected. "More awestruck than anything else, I suppose. It was unlike anything

I'd ever encountered before."

"Indeed," she nodded, before raising her hands towards his face. "May I?" she asked, halting part way.

"Sure," he shrugged, both curious and a little concerned about what she might find. He hoped that his many years hadn't caused the being to damage him as it rifled his mind, thus disqualifying him from the post he had just assumed.

Tenderly Soliana pressed her fingers to his temples and closed her eyes, bowing her head slightly. Her breathing became slow and restful, as though she was falling into a deep meditative state. As the minutes passed her posture slackened, and Radik began to worry she might fall against him. But just as he contemplated reaching out to hold her up, she removed her fingers and opened her eyes.

"I have explored you very deeply," she uttered, moving to the foot of the bed and sitting down to take the load off her now tired body. "And I can find no trace of harm," she added with a look of puzzlement.

"Is that bad?" he asked with some confusion.

"When a powerful entity prowls through the mind of a much, much weaker being such as a human, there is usually some kind of damage left behind. In the very least there's what you might call 'clutter:' upset memories, things dragged out of the unconscious and deposited in strange places. It sometimes causes people to lose even basic skills for a time, such as walking or using utensils or tools. That you should have passed through such an ordeal untouched is remarkable. It testifies greatly to your power of mind, and that of the dark presence within you."

"Dark presence?" he asked.

"Yes, didn't you know? The dark realm is exerting a definite influence in your psyche. Not one nearly so powerful as that Krancis experiences, nor Rex Hunt. But its presence is indisputable. I'm surprised you haven't known about it until now."

"I had no idea," he shook his head, amazed at the thought. "So that's why I wasn't hurt by it, just worn out?"

"Most likely," she replied. "That's why your friend is in such bad shape: she has no such affinity for the dark realm, and thus it didn't protect her. She was completely exposed before the being, and her organic faculties had to bear the full weight of the examination on their own."

"But you're sure she'll be alright?" he asked solicitously.

"Oh, quite sure. You might say that the being bruised her mind. But nothing more, outside of perhaps a few misplaced memories, like I mentioned."

"Good," he said with relief.

"Is that you, Admiral?" Powers asked groggily, her eyes slowly opening and trying to make him out in the dim light of her room.

"Yes, it's me, Julia," he said kindly, sitting on the side of her bed and taking her hand. "How do you feel?"

"Confused," she said in a voice thick with sleep. "Like half my brain is awake. I think they put me on some kind of sedatives."

With concern Radik raised his eyes to Soliana to confirm that that was the case. He relaxed when she nodded.

"They just want you to rest for a while and get your strength back," he assured her. "You did good back there, Lieutenant. Real good. I'm proud that I had you with me."

"I'm sorry I wasn't more help," she replied. "Especially in the cave. It was all on you pretty much from the time we went in there until the captain picked us up."

"Oh, don't worry about that," he shook his head. "Just focus on getting better now. I'm afraid you won't see me for a while. I, uh," he paused, not wishing to sound boastful despite his justifiable pride, "I've been appointed head of the navy by Krancis."

Powers' eyes shot open.

"What?" she asked, joy fighting its way past the

sedatives and into her voice. "That's wonderful! Oh, I'm so happy for you, sir."

"Thank you," he said appreciatively, squeezing her hand a little tighter. "I've got to depart at once and begin work on retrofitting the navy. Krancis has a plan that will shake up both our ships and our tactics."

"In what way?"

"It's all kind of complex, and I don't want to put too much on your mind right now," he said. "Rest assured, we both think it'll help us turn the tide in this war. For the first time since the Devourers broke upon us, the rest of the navy will be able to hit back. And hard. We won't be dependent on *Sentinel* to win all our battles for us anymore."

"That sounds great," she smiled, allowing her eyelids to close a little as the sedatives caught up with her again. "I just wish we had ships and tactics like that before Jennet fell," she added regretfully.

"Me, too," he commiserated. "But their loss won't be for nothing. I've seen with my own eyes how they fight, and what needs to be done to defeat them. I'll pass those lessons throughout the navy and build the kind of fighting force that we need. And when the war is won, and the Devourers are destroyed, I'll be sure that a monument is raised to the people of Jennet, so that their sacrifice isn't forgotten."

"They deserve nothing less," she agreed. Her eyes wandered from Radik and noticed half of Soliana's outline by the door behind him. Tilting her head on the pillow to see around him, she tried to make out her face. "Who's that?" she asked at last, her voice a low whisper.

"I'm Soliana," the young woman said, approaching the bed and standing beside the admiral. "I'm going to be checking in with you periodically, just to make sure you're alright."

"Does she know about…" Powers' voice trailed, looking at Radik.

"Yes, I'm aware of the orb," Soliana confirmed. "That's

why I'm here. When it invaded your mind it left some damage behind. Nothing serious, I assure you," she added soothingly, as the lieutenant's face grew anxious. "Time will right all wrongs. But you need to be very easy on yourself, and rest quietly. Don't trouble yourself about the war, and try not to excite yourself. Your psyche needs calm in order to restore its balance."

"I understand," she uttered, nodding a little. "C-could I speak to the admiral alone for a minute?" she asked hesitantly, not wishing to cause offense."

"Of course. My work is done here for the time being. I'll visit you periodically to see how you're doing."

With a faint smile in the dimness, she opened the door and stepped out.

"I wish I was going with you," she said once they were alone, her tone that of an affectionate daughter. "I know this isn't exactly military protocol, but I've grown rather attached to you, sir."

"As have I," he smiled, squeezing her hand again. "But don't worry about a thing. I'm sure we'll work together again once you're up and around. We're too good a team to stop now."

"Do you really mean that, sir?" she asked.

"Absolutely," he replied sincerely.

"That girl is awfully strange," Powers said incongruently, her eyes moving away from Radik and towards the door. "She's so young, and yet so old, like she has a whole lifetime of experience at her disposal. And yet, she felt familiar somehow, like I'd seen her before today."

"She has some gift for insight, she said," he explained. "I found her examining your mind when I entered. Maybe you were aware of it in your sleep."

"Examining my mind?" she asked dubiously. "But how?"

"I don't know. All this stuff is beyond me. But she said you took a beating in that chamber because the dark realm wasn't protecting you, but it *was* protecting me. I don't know much about this dark realm, just that it powers *Sentinel* somehow and that some people can talk to it. Well, and what everyone knows about Rex Hunt, of course. I'd like to meet that man, let me tell you. I bet he could teach me a thing or two about using it."

"Maybe so," she replied uncertainly, not knowing any more about the shadowy element than the admiral did.

"But, here I am rambling on, and you need to get some sleep," he said, releasing her hand and drawing the blanket a little tighter around her neck. "Do you need anything before I go?"

"No, I don't think so," she replied, hesitating for a moment before continuing. "Sir, um," she struggled to say, "I hope this doesn't come off wrong, but I feel like we kind of became family down there, when we were fighting to survive. Is that okay? I was orphaned at a pretty young age, and never really had a family before. I think I'd feel better about this war if I knew someone out there was thinking of me and cared if I lived another day."

Kindly he put his hands on her shoulders and smiled into her eyes.

"I'd be proud to consider you family, Julia. And you're right, we *did* bond down there, in a way most people couldn't understand if they hadn't gone through it, too. Like you, I don't have any family, either. So let's be family for each other. Okay?"

"Okay," she smiled in return.

"Now close those eyes and get some sleep. That's an order," he chuckled.

"Yes, sir," she replied, shifting her head on the pillow and doing as she was told.

Slowly he arose from the bed and opened the door, pausing to look back once more before departing.

"I was about to come and get you," the receptionist said with some annoyance, still trying to retain the authority of her position. "I said a few minutes, sir."

"Well, I won't be around to bother you for a while," he replied, walking back towards the front desk with her watchfully at his side. "I have a new assignment."

"Oh, you're leaving us?" she asked with a hint of sarcastic pleasure in her voice as they reached her post and she settled into her seat again.

"Yes, as a matter of fact. I've just been appointed head of the navy."

With her mouth agape and her cheeks flushing, she watched as the unassuming old man turned his back and walked out of the hospital.

CHAPTER 8

After many hours of resting, Tselitel awoke to the sound of a loud voice in the outer room. Groggily she rubbed her eyes and yawned, checking to make sure Rhemus was still asleep before getting to her feet and padding softly to the door. Looking through the glass, she saw doctor Keelen with his arms crossed on the far side of the room. Looking down, she could see Welter still sitting in his chair, a cold, immovable expression on the side of his face that she could see. Catching sight of her, Keelen uncrossed his arms self-consciously and looked away with embarrassment, only then realizing how loudly he'd been speaking.

"*Keelen* is a passionate soul," *Karnan* observed from his corner, his arms wrapped around his legs, his knees drawn against his slight chest. "He forgets himself on a regular basis. Sometimes I would come in here just to get him off my back."

She looked at the wizened old alien for a few seconds, and then turned back to the glass. Quietly she slid the door open and stepped out.

"I must ask you to keep your voice down," she said as firmly as her status as a guest would allow. "I'm only glad I awoke before the emperor did. He needs rest."

"I'm sorry, Doctor Tselitel," *Keelen* said reluctantly, the words grinding on his pride. Taking a step closer, he added, "perhaps if your friend here was not quite so stubborn, there would be no reason to raise my voice."

"There isn't a reason to raise it now," Welter replied with his usual coolness. "I'm not leaving this room, no matter how many knots that puts in your boss's stomach. Let him come here if he's so bent on talking."

"I already told you that I requested that he do so," *Keelen* replied tartly. "And he has flatly refused. *Seldek* is not accustomed to waiting on his guests."

"We're not guests," Welter corrected. "We're partners in each other's futures. Without us, your people haven't got a prayer. And we need you to keep our emperor alive. That puts us on at least an even footing, even if it *is* your base. Now, you tell him to quit choking on that pride of his and come down here if he wants to talk. But one way or another, I'm not leaving Rhemus lying on his back in there with nobody to protect him."

"He's in the middle of a *Kol-Prockian* base!" *Keelen* exclaimed. "You have no enemies here, human. As you say, we're allies in this struggle now. The least allies can do is trust each other, especially when each side has so much to lose. You insult us gravely by your mistrust."

"It's not you or *Seldek* that I mistrust. It's the rabble I saw in the corridors as we came here. Face it, Doctor, the morale of your base is scraping the floor. When things get that bad, there's no accounting for what might happen. Especially if a couple of discontents get it inside their heads that we've put a target on your backs by bringing the emperor to stay here. They might decide to remove that threat before a certain party finds out about it."

"You're paranoid," *Keelen* said in a nasty tone of voice. "You're absolutely paranoid. You believe people are uniquely out to get you. Even your friends."

"I have yet to find a friend in *Kren-Balar*," Welter replied flatly, his words hitting like a brick.

"I will endure these insults no further!" exclaimed

the doctor, uttering some kind of curse in *Kol-Prockian* and twisting on his heel to leave. As he opened the door he looked over his shoulder and added, "don't think that our hospitality is limitless, human. Though we are on the brink, we will only be pushed so far." With this he left, slamming the door behind him.

"Always has to take a parting shot," Welter commented without concern, as Tselitel's eyes fell upon him. Nervously she moved towards the middle of the room and turned to face him. Though the chamber had removed the anxiety caused by her Valindra, her hands nevertheless trembled at the thought of confronting the dangerous, brooding man before her. "I suppose you think I'm wrong?" he asked pointedly, crossing his arms and leaning back in his chair.

"I think that you're passionately devoted to the emperor's wellbeing," she replied diplomatically. "But that another approach is needed if we're to avoid offending our hosts."

"I'm not concerned with offending our hosts," he said. "They need us more than we need them. It would be a disaster for us to lose Rhemus, but we could conceivably continue without him. But if they lose us, their chances of survival as a race drop to zero. They ought to have the brains to realize that and stop standing on ceremony. I was sent here to protect the emperor, and that's precisely what I'm going to do. And I don't care how many toes I step on in the process."

"But we may have to stay here for a long time," Tselitel countered. "We would be best served by cooperating with them. Starting off on the wrong foot will just make our work more difficult down the road."

"Then *you* patch things up with them," he replied. "Stroke their ruffled feathers and make 'em feel important. But don't bother to ask me to move an inch from this spot, because I'm not going to."

"But *Seldek* might not receive me," she objected.

"You're the one he's mad at."

"Then put that psychiatric background of yours to work on him. But one thing," he added, reaching into his jacket and pulling out the small pistol she'd left behind upon entering the chamber. "Take this with you. No telling what you'll run into out there."

She eyed the gun for a moment, and then looked at him.

"We're safe here, Gustav. I don't need that."

"Then why did Krancis send me along?"

Drawing a breath and letting it out slowly, she hesitated a moment before reluctantly taking the weapon. Tucking it inside one of the loose pockets of the robe, she made for the door and left.

Once in the corridor, she did her best to retrace her steps back to the hangar, but was quickly lost. Her attempts to ask for directions only led to grunting and indifference from the passersby she encountered. Unsure if they could understand her or not, she eventually defaulted to asking "*Seldek? Seldek?*" and pointing in different directions to try and get her meaning across. But this similarly got her nowhere, and she decided to head back to the chamber when she ran into *Keelen* again.

"Doctor Tselitel," he said, surprised to see her wandering the hallways in her thin robe. "What are you doing out here?"

"I was looking for *Seldek*," she explained, glad to finally be speaking English with someone. "But they won't give me directions, or frankly even talk to me."

"I don't think *Seldek* will see you," he replied rather flatly, crossing his arms and shaking his head slowly. "He's very angry."

"Krancis will be as well, when he hears of this," she said, deciding on a sudden impulse to play hardball with the truculent physician. Her cheeks blushed the instant the words left her mouth and doubled back through her ears, but she knew it was too late to change her play. As bravely as she could she returned the *Kol-Prockian's* skeptical gaze, until finally he nodded his agreement.

"Yes, I suppose he would be. His devotion to the emperor is well known, even in Quarlac. Perhaps we have all been a little inflexible in our attitudes."

"Perhaps so," she assented, nodding as well.

"Come, I'll take you to *Seldek*. We must fix this rift before it grows any larger."

Without waiting for her to respond he turned and moved at a brisk pace down the corridor. Stepping quickly to keep up, she realized that the alien's pride had been wounded to give even that much ground, and that he wished to conclude his involvement as soon as possible.

Guiding her back into the hangar and then into another network of hallways, she nearly walked into *Keelen* when he suddenly stopped before a door.

"Wait here," he ordered, going inside and closing the door in her face.

Surprised at the brusqueness of his manner, her own temper finally began to flare up. After several minutes the door opened again, and he gestured for her to enter.

"Doctor Tselitel," an older *Kol-Prockian* uttered, as *Keelen* bowed slightly and left the room. "I appreciate your coming, though I wish it wasn't because of your associate's sullen attitude. He really should have come to see me upon arrival. Indeed, you all should have."

Like doctor *Keelen*, *Seldek* was clearly past his prime but still in possession of quick eyes and a sharp tongue. His whole manner bespoke a kind of nervous, kinetic energy that she'd noticed was common to the other *Kol-Prockians* she'd encountered. Most of his head was bald, and his face was deeply wrinkled by stress and the abuses of a hard life. His feet had trodden many desolate miles to bring him to that moment.

"I'm afraid the emperor needed treatment as quickly

as possible," she explained, her heart beating faster as the alien's expression soured at her words.

"There is always time for the proprieties," he replied ominously, unwilling to brook any opposition. "There is always time for *respect*."

"The emperor had been unconscious for many, many hours," she said, aware that she was likely digging her grave deeper, but unsure what else to say. Then a new tack struck her, and she jumped on it with both feet. "You must understand how worried we were for him, and how quickly we wanted to get him into the hands of your people so that their expertise could help him. Our own medicine has been unable to ease his suffering, and we didn't want to keep him from your care any longer than necessary."

Carefully she watched his face to gauge the effect of her flattery. To her relief his gaze softened, though skepticism was still evident.

"I suppose allowances must be made for your situation," he said somewhat grandly, moving to a four-seat table and gesturing for her to take a chair. Resting his thin frame somewhat delicately on the opposite chair, he put his elbows on the table, knitted his fingers together, and placed his chin upon them as he watched her pad slowly across the large room and sit down. "You didn't need to come in your chamber robe," he commented, unsure if her clothing choice indicated a lack of sense or a lack of respect for his exalted position.

"I came straight here from the chamber," she said as ingenuously as she could. "I didn't want to let a moment pass by without straightening out this misunderstanding."

"There *is* no misunderstanding," he flared suddenly, sitting up straight and unlinking his fingers. His arms crossed on the table before him, and his bony hands formed into fists. "Your Mister Welter has proven intractable ever since entering this base. Doctor *Keelen* has kept me very well informed about his behavior towards him, and the suspicion and dislike with which he regards my people. I should have thought Krancis would have sent a man with better manners to interact with a foreign people. But this man is simply a boor."

"His purpose here is to take care of the emperor," she began hotly, before remembering herself and softening her tone. "He's single-minded in his task, and finds it difficult to trust. Most of his life has been spent fighting others, and he naturally sees an enemy long before he sees a friend. There is very little of the diplomat in him."

"Then you mean to imply that it is *my* job to adjust myself to *him*?" *Seldek* asked with narrowing eyes. He spread his arms in a wide gesture, indicating the whole room. "That I should leave my office and go down there to see *him*, at *his* convenience?"

"What I mean," she replied deliberately, "is that we all need to understand the strains we are each laboring under. This is a hard time for us all, and we can only hope to achieve our mutual goals by extending more tolerance towards each other than we might be otherwise inclined to do. We must be willing to compromise."

"Let *him* compromise," *Seldek* uttered proudly. "He is the visitor to *Kren-Balar*, and not I. If this is how he intends to conduct himself during his stay here, he may find himself removed from our presence. Naturally, you and the emperor will be allowed to remain," he finished blandly, in the tone of a disclaimer. "We have no wish to unsettle the deal we have reached with your government. But we will not be insulted in our own home by a self-important bodyguard."

"I am quite certain that Krancis would not wish the emperor to remain here without the protection of Gustav Welter," she said gravely. "You must remember–."

"I *must* remember nothing!" he flared again, slamming his fist on the table. "You are in no position to dictate what I must and must not do!"

"You must remember," she resumed, her jaw

clenching as the last thin fibers of her patience snapped, "that there are many enemies of humanity in Quarlac. In sending Gustav along, Krancis has made provision for the possibility that the base will be attacked, and either the emperor or myself captured or killed. Neither of those options are acceptable, and thus it is quite likely that we shall all be recalled if you attempt to remove our protection. Or," she said as coldly as she could, "that an even less agreeable form of protection will be sent to replace him."

"Meaning?" he asked with offhand dismissiveness, leaning back in his seat and crossing his arms. "Are you implying that the base would be invaded?"

"I am *suggesting*," she stipulated, "that Rex Hunt would be sent in the place of Gustav. And where my safety is concerned, Rex's will is as inexorable as death. He would not hesitate to destroy half this base to protect me."

"If this is so, then why didn't Krancis send *him* instead of your present companion?" *Seldek* retorted.

"Because Gustav is easier to get along with," she half-lied.

With great displeasure *Seldek* eyed her, his lips drawn tightly together as though sucking on something small and tart. The notion seized her heart that she'd pushed matters much too far, and she crossed her arms over her chest to mask the nervous shaking of her hands. Matching his critical gaze with difficulty, her mind began to go blank and her breathing to slow, until she grew faint and had to force air into her unwilling lungs. Luckily, she reflected, he didn't seem to notice.

Wordlessly the alien got to his feet and made for the door. Opening it dramatically, he gestured for her to leave. Avoiding her eyes as she moved across the room, he slammed the door as hard as his official dignity would allow.

"I blew it," she thought, bursting into a cold sweat as panic began to seize her. "In one pushy conversation I've gotten us thrown out of *Kren-Balar*!"

With these desperate thoughts on her mind, she wandered back to the hangar and, through sheer luck, managed to return to the chamber on her own.

"Well, how'd it go?" Welter asked without interest, still in his chair.

"You might want to pack your bags," she said ominously, moving to a nearby table and hoisting herself onto it, her thin legs dangling above the floor. "I just had a big argument with *Seldek*."

"*You* did?" he asked with a cocked eyebrow. "I didn't think you were capable of so much as raising your voice."

"I guess you're rubbing off on me," she said with a hollow, self-critical laugh. "I tried to be sensible, to explain our position. When that didn't work, I tried flattery. When *that* didn't work, I bullied him with Krancis and Rex. That's when he threw me out without uttering so much as a syllable. These *Kol-Prockians* are terribly proud. I thought I knew them pretty well because of my interactions with their AIs. But I guess I've still got a lot of learning to do." She paused and looked towards the door behind her, thinking of her recent interview. "Provided I get the chance."

"Well, don't worry about it too much," Welter replied calmly.

"How can you say that?" she asked incredulously, her eyes searching his face. "Any minute now they could come bursting through that door with orders to kick us off the base."

"Because I have orders to ensure that doesn't happen," he said in a tone of deadly warning to any who would try it. "The emperor *will* get his treatment, regardless of the feelings of our hosts."

Anxiously she dropped from the table onto her bare feet. Walking slowly to the chamber door, she stopped and looked down at the man beside her.

"Please don't start any trouble," she said in a soft tone of pleading. "Not for my sake, but for his," she added, nodding through the glass at Rhemus' unconscious form.

"I'll do no more than is necessary."

With this bare assurance, she opened the door and went back inside.

"Is *Keelen* going to keep his mouth shut?" the old *Kol-Prockian* asked from his corner. "It's hard enough to rest at my age without him blabbering all the time. At least your friend out there keeps his voice down."

"You may not have to worry about that for much longer," she said in a depressed, quiet voice, moving to where he sat. Pressing her back against the wall, she slid down to the floor with a ragged sigh. "We probably aren't going to stay here much longer."

"What?" he asked with surprise. "Why?"

Briefly she recounted her talk with *Seldek*.

"Miserable, stupid ignormaus," *Karnan* uttered in an angry whisper, along with several oaths in *Kol-Prockian*.

"I'm sorry," she said miserably. "I thought that if I–."

"Oh, not you, dear," he assured her quickly. "I meant *Seldek*. *Keelen*, too. They've both got enough pride to fill half this base. I guess we all do. It's a disease among my people."

"You don't seem to have it," she replied quietly.

"I'm too old for pride, or much of anything else," he chuckled dryly. "Believe me, I used to rival them both. But even at my worst I never would have treated you all that way."

With a groan he slowly got to his feet, leaning a hand on the wall for a few moments to regain his equilibrium.

"What are you doing?" she asked anxiously, as he tottered towards the door.

Pausing, he turned slowly towards her.

"I'm going to make this right," he said in a tired voice that began to growl. "Come on," he continued, gesturing for her to rise and join him. "Get under my arm. I'm gonna need some help getting there."

Uncertain if he could make it, she nevertheless did as

he asked and supported as much of his scanty weight as he would allow. Still proud himself, she could tell that he was leaning on her just as little as he could manage. Opening the door and holding it open for him, they slowly ambled through together and passed through the outer room.

"Where are you two going?" Welter asked.

"To beat some sense into those blockheads," *Karnan* said without turning his head.

By the time they reached *Seldek's* room the old alien was exhausted. Leaning against the wall for a few moments, he gathered what stamina he could before knocking. Tselitel waited self-consciously beside him, aware of the mixture of awe and suspicion with which they were viewed by passersby. She began to imagine what they must be thinking of the strange pair when *Karnan* interrupted her thoughts.

"Wait here," he told her, putting a frail hand on her shoulder and squeezing it weakly. "It'll have a greater impact if I speak to him alone."

With this he pushed off the wall, opened the door, and immediately shouted something nasty in *Kol-Prockian* as he walked inside. The door slammed behind him, and for nearly fifteen minutes Tselitel could hear a one-sided shouting match take place on the other side. Discreetly she tried to listen in. But the constant passage of aliens in the hallway kept her from doing more than inching towards the door, closing her eyes, and pouring all her attention into her right ear.

Suddenly the door opened, and *Karnan* poked his head out.

"Come in, my dear," he said without energy.

Stepping inside, *Karnan* closed the door and walked unsteadily towards the table she'd sat at earlier. She desperately wished to help him, seeing how tired he was from his tirade. But she didn't want to reduce him before *Seldek*, and in lieu of supporting him she clasped her hands behind her back and walked slowly by his side, ready to catch him if he should lose his balance.

Seldek stood several feet away, his eyes downcast and ashamed, though occasionally they flitted upwards and viewed Tselitel with aversion. Once they'd reached the table, and *Karnan* had wrestled himself onto one of the chairs, he snapped his fingers without looking at the other *Kol-Prockian*, pointing to one of the seats as though ordering a dog.

"Sit," he said with as much force as he was still capable of mustering.

Tselitel nearly moved to the place indicated, taking half a step before she noticed *Seldek* moving towards it. Gracefully she finished her mistaken movement by taking the chair to *Karnan's* right.

"Is this the hospitality with which you receive our guests?" *Karnan* began. "Leaving them wandering the corridors of our base alone? Neglecting to pay them the *slightest* attention unless they come to you first? Why, you haven't even offered her refreshment, after she came all this way with me."

"I am sorry," he replied half-heartedly, his eyes moving between the old scientist and the table, but staying strictly away from Tselitel. "If she requires anything to eat or drink–."

"Why are you addressing me?" *Karnan* snapped, fully aware of *Seldek's* humiliation and determined to make him feel a great deal more. "Apologize to *her*. Make your amends with *her*. And then you can go and speak with the man sitting outside the chamber."

"What?" he asked at once, the words shooting from his lips before he could help himself. "I mean," he stumbled, as *Karnan's* face darkened. "I...don't think..." his voice trailed, trying to invent some excuse.

"That's an accurate description of yourself," he said pointedly, the force of his words striking even Tselitel as somewhat excessive. "You *don't* think. It's what caused this mess in the first place. For the first time in countless centuries our people have redemption held out before them. For this *solitary purpose* I've suffered my life to continue, spending day after day in that miserable chamber. And you would throw that *all* away because of your vanity!"

Shakily *Karnan* put his hands on the table and stood up. Without warning a torrent of *Kol-Prockian* insults and oaths passed from his lips, causing *Seldek* to shrink away from the table and towards the back of his seat. As the verbal blows continued to fall, he looked at anything but his esteemed, outraged colleague. Even Tselitel was a welcome place to set his eyes.

His energy finally spent, *Karnan* dropped into his chair again, glaring murderously at *Seldek*.

"It was never...my intention..." *Seldek* managed to say after half a minute of silence.

"I have no interest in your intentions," *Karnan* said with an increasingly raspy voice. "Only your *actions* are of importance. And they have been deplorable. They have been *felen-kor!*"

This last statement struck *Seldek* like a whip between the eyes, and Tselitel's soft heart had to go out to him as he winced.

Slowly the abused alien turned and looked at her.

"I'm...sorry, Doctor Tselitel," he uttered. "I should have seen to your people's needs...more promptly."

Angrily *Karnan* slammed his palm on the table, causing Tselitel to emit a little shriek of surprise. Resting his elbow on the table, he pointed a thin, accusative finger at *Seldek*.

"I was wrong," he said sincerely, shaking his head back and forth. "I apologize. I'll go with you at once to speak with Gustav Welter, so that we may put this matter behind us."

"Not yet," *Karnan* said, leaning back in his seat and allowing his body to slacken a little now that his victory was won. "A few minutes. We'll go in a few minutes."

"Of course," *Seldek* nodded eagerly, eyeing him with concern. Despite the punishment he'd just received, his reverence for the ancient alien caused him to feel much anxiety for his obviously weakened state. He began to wonder if he should send for a stretcher to bear him back to the chamber, but quickly nixed that idea when he imagined the glare he would receive for even suggesting it.

After a short while *Karnan* wordlessly pushed his chair away from the table and got to his feet. Pointedly rejecting *Seldek's* proffered aid, he put his thin arm around Tselitel's shoulders, allowing her to bear more of his weight this time around. Tightly she wrapped her own arm around his middle. She could tell at once that he'd nearly had it, but was determined not to struggle for his sake, lest those they encountered see how depleted he truly was. With marked embarrassment, *Seldek* followed up the rear.

Their journey back was slow, and despite Tselitel's best efforts they were both staggering and perspiring by the time they'd reached the chamber's outer room. Twice along the way *Seldek* had pleaded with the aged scientist to permit him to help. But each time he was simply ignored.

As they entered the room Welter arose, aware that something significant was about to take place. Weakly *Karnan* gestured for them all to enter the chamber together, and he kept the vigilant human in suspense until he'd lowered himself to the floor with Tselitel's help.

"This is...*Seldek*," he nearly wheezed. "He has something to say to you."

"I wish to apologize for the treatment you've received since coming here," he said reluctantly, some of his former vanity returning now that the sting of *Karnan's* tirade was receding into the past. "We shall cooperate with you in every particular going forwards. Of that you may be certain."

"Good to know," Welter said offhandedly, certain that their problems were far from over.

With a slight bow *Seldek* took a step back, and then left

the chamber.

"That's about as good...as it's going to get," *Karnan* uttered weakly, stretching his legs out before him as he leaned against the wall. "If either he or *Keelen* gives you any more trouble, let me know."

"You should have seen him," Tselitel said with pride in the old alien.

"Yes, alright," he replied with a dismissing motion of his hand. "What's done is done. Now, let me rest for a while."

"Of course," Tselitel assented, drawing away slowly and quietly leaving the chamber with Welter. "I hope he hasn't overextended himself," she said, watching through the glass for a moment before turning away. "I can't remember the last time I saw someone so angry."

"So he really tore into him?" Welter asked, half sitting on the table as he looked at her.

"Like you wouldn't believe," she assured him, dropping into his chair to rest her tired legs. "Beat on him like he was the most worthless thing he'd ever come across. Honestly I felt bad for him after a while."

"Don't," Welter replied implacably. "He had it coming. Maybe now we'll get better treatment around here."

"Yes, I hope so."

"Was *Keelen* there?"

"No, just *Seldek*."

"Too bad. He could use a tongue lashing, too. And by the looks of that old bird," he said, nodding towards the chamber, "he hasn't got too many good lashings left in him. Would have been good to set them both right at once."

"I'm sure *Seldek* will pass along what he was told," Tselitel replied. "They both revere *Karnan* to the moon and back. Neither of them want to earn his wrath."

"We'll see," Welter replied skeptically. "Hadn't you better get back in there?"

"Oh, I'm alright for the time being," she said with a shrug. "Besides, the chamber's effectiveness drops with each body that's added. I want to let *Karnan* get recharged a little more before I go in and start siphoning off energy."

"Up to you," Welter replied with a shrug of his own. "But just drop in for a second and make sure the emperor is still alright."

"Okay," she said, getting to her feet with some effort and going back inside. She glanced at *Karnan* briefly, who had stretched himself out on the floor along the wall, his hands pillowed under his sleeping head. Heading to the emperor and kneeling beside him, she was surprised to find him awake. "How are you feeling?" she asked in a whisper, looking into his eyes.

"Strange," he said in a thick voice, his throat unused to speaking. "Better. But strange."

"Are you comfortable? Can I get you anything?"

"No, just stay with me for a little while," he replied with a hint of distraction. "I've seen a lot of strange things lately. A little human companionship would be nice."

"Of course," she said at once, settling against the wall near his head and looking down at him.

"I could feel you touching me sometimes," he said appreciatively after a few minutes had passed. "Stroking my head. It made me feel a little less alone in my dreams. I want to thank you for that. You have a very tender heart."

"You're welcome," she smiled.

"The things I've seen…" his voice trailed in astonishment. "I can't think how to describe them. I know they were just dreams and nonsense, but they seemed so real. It was like I was being shown something that was actually happening." He paused and rolled his eyes up to look at her. "I've forgotten most of them now. But little bits and fragments remain." He was about to say more when he hesitated.

"Please tell me about them," she uttered sweetly, both hoping to disburden his mind and satisfy her curiosity. "I'd really like to know."

"As I said, I can't remember very much. Mostly they're just isolated scenes, like pictures. But part way through one of them I was shocked to see an enormously powerful being robed in light right beside me. Somehow we floated over our galaxy, looking down on it. He didn't seem to know I was there, or at least he didn't feel like paying any attention to me. Strange ships came against him, but with a wave of his hand he burned them up like kindling. Fleet after fleet arrived to do battle, of all different designs. But none of them stood a chance. Finally a race with dark powers came along and took his robe away, apparently draining his power in the process. With it gone they were able to imprison him. Then it just ended." He looked up at her again. "Does that make any sense to you?"

"I'm afraid it doesn't," she replied reluctantly, a little embarrassed that her psychiatric background had failed her.

"It felt like a vision," Rhemus continued after an interval of silence. "Like I was being shown something that actually happened. I guess it must just be this chamber," he concluded. "It's making me feel all kinds of strange things."

"Perhaps," she replied, intrigued by his dream nonetheless.

"I gathered from that little discussion earlier that there's been some…tension since we came here," he said, changing topics.

"Oh, more than a little," she replied significantly, briefly retelling all they'd been through.

"You've both done well," he said. "I'm proud to have you both by my side during all this."

"Thank you," she said sincerely.

"And now I'd like to get a little rest," he announced, rolling onto his side and pillowing his hands as *Kranan* had. "Even this bit of talk has tired me out."

"Of course," she replied respectfully, getting to her feet and exiting the chamber.

"How is he?" Welter asked.

"He's awake," she replied. "But very tired. His mind has been terribly active despite being unconscious. Apparently it's been one dream world after another."

"But he's doing alright?" he clarified.

"Yes, I'd say so. Seems in complete possession of himself, knows clearly where he is, and can express himself without difficulty. It's like he's awoken from a long nap. I think the chamber is doing him a lot of good."

"Good."

She sat down on the chair again and folded her hands in her lap. Occasionally she would glance at him, still half sitting on the table and staring at the wall. Something heavy was on his mind, absorbing all his attention. For a quarter of an hour she fought off the urge to ask, until finally it grew too great.

"I don't mean to pry," she began.

"Then don't," he replied flatly, without bothering to shift his gaze.

"I've helped a lot of people deal with grief, Gustav," she said tenderly, leaning forward in her seat and resting her elbows on her knees. "I can help you, too."

"And what makes you think I'm grieving?" he asked grimly, his cold eyes sending a shiver down her spine as they fell upon her.

"I know the signs," she replied as steadily as she could. "There's an entire panoply of little tells that point in only one direction. It's weighing you down, Gustav. It's affecting your mission."

"You're wrong," he said with certainty. "I have performed precisely as Krancis expected me to. The only difficulties so far have been brought to us by the *Kol-Prockians* and their numerous vices. Subtracting those from the equation, everything has proceeded according to plan."

"But you're *hurting*, Gustav," she pleaded with him, standing up and walking to where he sat watching her. "And there's no reason to."

"You can't remove the hurt I've got," he replied. "You can only mask it with scar tissue. It'll always be there, like a wound in my heart. I'll carry it until the day I die."

"But–."

"Doctor, I've already said more than I intended to," he uttered darkly. "Despite your good intentions, I don't appreciate your attempts to get inside my head. Now go back in the chamber or quit talking, because I've said all I'm going to say."

"Alright," she said, nodding slowly. Then she reached out a gentle hand and put it on his shoulder. "Thank you for looking after us. I know it's been hard, after all you've been through."

"You're welcome," he said quietly, as she turned and went back inside the chamber.

◆ ◆ ◆

Near the end of their journey through warp, Mafalda Aboltina sat motionless in her seat, pretending to still be asleep so that the men would talk more freely. In low whispers they chewed over their recent experiences, having little else to do to break the tedium of an all-black tunnel. She savored this candid look into their thinking, because she still was at something of a loss to understand them.

Wellesley was the least difficult to understand, though the greatest immediate shock. She'd encountered AI's before, but never one with as much snap and intelligence. His ever-present hint of sarcastic superiority somehow made him easier to grasp, his general mentality easily derived from that aspect alone.

Pinchon was harder. His air of worldliness and the fact of his previous piratical activities clashed with his obvious integrity. He seemed a contradiction, a good man who'd thrived in a bad environment, somehow keeping himself intact through it all. There was none of the easy indifference to decency that she expected to find in a Black Sun.

Hunt she found a total enigma, a man both fascinating and deceptively simple. His mind seemed to possess few gears, easily rotating on a crisp and clear moral foundation all his own. Without hesitation he acted on what he thought, be that looking after a turncoat separatist or battling the most fearsome being she'd ever imagined. He seemed to ask nothing for himself, indeed seemingly forgetting himself entirely in his calculations. Pinchon, she felt on the other hand, never lost sight of his own part in any equation, and seemed keen not to overextend himself in any venture.

They made up a peculiar team: the smug AI who nevertheless managed not to get on his companions' nerves; an aging pirate who, despite his air of self-containment, stuck his neck out for a girl he barely knew; and the man of dark power, possessing a godlike might that seemed to ground him rather than inflate him.

"How long do you intend to pretend sleeping?" Wellesley asked through her skin, making her start in her seat and look around.

Curiously Hunt looked at her.

"Are you alright?" he asked with mild concern, his eyes darting up and down her body to identify what made her jump.

"Oh, t-the AI spoke and startled me," she said apologetically, feeling a little embarrassed that she'd been found out by one of them.

"Yeah, he'll do that," Hunt chuckled, looking back at Pinchon and continuing their discussion in a louder voice.

"I didn't mean to shock you," Wellesley said again through skin conductance, his tone a little more solicitous than it had been before. "I just thought that you might be holding back, feeling a little out of place."

"No, I'm alright," she said quietly, trying not to interrupt the other conversation.

"Well, you'll be happy to hear that you're doing decently well," he continued. "Not great, by any means. But you're not in any danger at present. Mainly I want Girnius' people to monitor you for the next few days in case something goes wrong."

"Like what?" she asked a little nervously.

"Well, it's kind of hard to say. Not being a medical AI, I'm not exactly an expert at this, especially given that you were tortured in a fashion I've not encountered before. The *Pho'Sath* have a peculiar way of interacting with their victims. The pain and suffering they induce is somehow related to their affinity for the light realm, ironic though that may sound, given their equal capacity to heal with it. You've been put through a severely traumatic experience, delivered through a vector that both my people and yours have, at best, a marginal understanding of. I can't say, for instance, if there will be any long-term effects, or if some kind of damage has been done that I haven't been programmed to detect."

"Oh," she said dubiously, her anxiety growing.

"I don't mean to frighten you," the hastened to add. "As I said, you seem to be in good condition. Mostly this is a precaution."

"I understand," she replied.

She tried to be brave, but the agonies *Deldrach* had put her through weakened her resolve and softened her spirit. Her stomach felt hollow, her body thin and without strength. Soon she found herself emitting a tired sigh, the world around her growing hazy as she drifted off again.

The next thing she heard was the colonel angrily shouting at someone outside the ship.

"Do I look like I *care* about your boss's lawn?" he demanded, as a half dozen of Girnius' bodyguards stood around the ship, pistols in their hands and aimed at them.

The canopy had been raised, and the rays of Petrov-2's sun hurt her eyes. Half-consciously she tried to stand up, but found the harness had been fastened while she slept.

"Just sit still," Wellesley warned her. "This situation is a little…kinetic."

"No one has permission to land this close to the chairman's residence," the chief security man said. "No exceptions, Pinchon."

"Well, I'm *making* an exception," he said, standing up and causing all their weapons to train on his head. "If you boys are gonna shoot, you might as well get on with it," he dared them. "Because *that* girl needs medical help," he continued, stabbing a finger towards Mafalda. "And I intend to see that she gets it."

Tensely the bodyguards watched as he climbed out of his seat into the back of the cockpit, unfastening her harness and helping her stand. With his arm around her he glared at them, until the head man nodded subtly and waved for the men to lower their weapons.

"Give her a hand getting down," Pinchon ordered, as he helped Mafalda over the side. Several of the men glanced at the head man, who reluctantly gestured for them to help. A couple of hands went up to receive her battered form, and shakily she made her way to the ground.

In a snap Pinchon threw his leg over the side and followed her down, putting his arm back around her and protectively guiding her towards the house. Hunt followed a little more slowly, content to let the colonel run things as he took in the strange situation. Carefully the men watched him move, aware that something powerful throbbed beneath his calm appearance.

Once they were inside, it took less than a minute to hand Mafalda off to the medical staff. The excitement of the strange vessel landing in the yard had drawn the attention of every individual stationed within the compound, from the lowliest kitchen help to Wulfstan Hyde himself. The latter was content to watch the proceedings from across the large living room that dominated that portion of the house. Once the young woman was in the hands of the doctor and his nurses, he approached.

"Philippe," he said, shaking the colonel's hand firmly. "I didn't expect to see you around here again so soon. The boss isn't exactly your top admirer right now, not with the way you left us last time."

"Well, he's gonna have to get over that in a hurry," he replied without concern. "That girl needs help, and this was the closest place we could take her."

"I see," Hyde replied in a conservative tone, eyeing the ex-pirate's companion momentarily. "He'll be interested to meet you, Mister Hunt."

"You know my name?" he asked, gripping the man's hand and shaking it firm and slow.

"I think most people are aware of you by now," Hyde replied. "Krancis has made sure of that. Seems to think you'll inspire renewed hope throughout the empire, along with *Sentinel*."

"And our lord and master is never wrong, is he?" Pinchon replied in a tone of sarcastic disinterest. At this moment he noticed something was off in the layout of the house. The walls looked freshly painted, and somehow different than before. Thicker, he decided. He shot a curious glance at Hyde.

"You've come at a bad time to ask favors," he explained. "As soon as the boss started the campaign against the Fringers, he jumped to the top of their priority list for assassination." He walked a few steps and banged his fist against the wall, which failed to reverberate at all. "Solid steel. They managed to sneak a bomb in here. Killed two of my men, plus one of the boss's girlfriends. We rebuilt the walls overnight, making them explosion proof."

"So *that's* what the tension on the lawn was about," the colonel said.

"Yeah. You're lucky they didn't shoot you when you popped that canopy. I guess one of them recognized you and held the others back. Everybody's been on edge since that first bomb."

"First?" Hunt inquired.

"You don't think the Fringers would stop at one, do you?" Hyde asked rhetorically, his tone even as he sized his new visitor up. "Half the boss's body doubles are dead, and his security detail has taken a serious beating. We're up against everything from lowlives to professional assassins out of Quarlac." He dropped his voice. "Word is a couple of those aliens that are working with the Fringers have made it out here, too."

"I should think it would be fairly obvious if they were involved," Pinchon replied, a little surprised to find the Black Suns in the dark about something of such pressing interest to their leader.

"The security team isn't the only thing they've targeted," he admitted, continuing to speak low. "Our intelligence apparatus has been hit hard. They're trying to blind us so they can move in and take him out."

"I gather he's not here now," Pinchon uttered.

"No. I've got him out of town and safe. We thought something like this might happen someday. Besides, the boss is a little…paranoid. He's got a team looking after him, and he's in constant communication with me. But we're not risking him out in the open."

"Sounds like you've got things pretty well sealed up," Pinchon said with a shrug. "So why all the trouble here? They're not gonna think he's hiding out in his main house. It's too obvious."

"Because the house, along with several other backup locations, is tied into a communications network through which he oversees the entire organization."

"He always did like to keep in control," Pinchon said with a dry chuckle. "This time it might kill him."

"It's my job to see that it doesn't," Hyde replied, gesturing for them to follow him inside the house for some refreshments in the kitchen. "Drink?" he asked, leaning against a large counter and nodding towards an ornate rack filled with bottles.

"No," Hunt shook his head, resting half his rear on a modest square table as the colonel made for the rack and took down the most expensive bottle he could see.

"He's going to blow his top when he hears you've commandeered his personal medical team for a friend of yours," Hyde commented with some misgivings, crossing his arms as Pinchon took a glass and filled it.

"Not when he finds out she's Mafalda Aboltina," he replied with an air of self-satisfied mastery.

"*Aboltina*," Hyde said quietly, looking down as he thought.

"Erdu-3," the colonel verbally nudged him, leaning against the counter himself and taking a sip.

"Oh, yes," he said with a little smile, his memory finally catching up. "What is she? Some kind of peace offering?"

"We're not here to trade her," Pinchon smiled behind his glass, realizing that that's just what it sounded like. "She's changed sides, come over to us. That's why she's beaten to bits. You saw those red lines in her face? The *Pho'Saths* did that. Honestly I doubt she would have lasted another six hours, what with how they were laying into her. Must be a pretty tough kid to have held out as long as she did. But she's got a long road ahead of her before she'll be back to normal. If that ever happens."

"Does she have information we can exploit?" Hyde asked, his interest rapidly growing. "The boss'll like that."

"On Erdu-3, at least. Can't say for any of the surrounding areas. You'd have to ask."

"That might be a little tricky," Wellesley said over their ear radios, a warning sound suddenly blaring through the house. "They've just sedated her out of her mind."

"What is it?" Hyde asked, pressing a finger against the radio in his own ear as the security team communicated with him. An accusative glare crossed his face as he looked at the two men. "An unknown signal was just detected within the medical quarters. Know anything about it?"

"It's ours," Pinchon confirmed. "The girl's got an AI slung around her neck, monitoring her vitals."

With a frown Hyde pressed his finger to his ear again.

"It's alright. Stand down. Whitelist that signal." Recrossing his arms, he continued to glare at them. "You should have told me you brought an AI in with her."

"Slipped my mind, what with those guns pointed at my head and all," the colonel retorted.

Continuing to frown, Hyde looked between the men and resettled himself against the counter.

"You were telling me about the girl," he said after a few moments. "Continue."

"There isn't much to say," Pinchon replied. "We've only known her for a couple dozen hours ourselves. She used to be a bigwig in the separatist organization before she had a change of heart and decided to help them kill *Deldrach*. That didn't work out, and she ended up captured and tortured. We went there to finish the job, found her still half-alive, and got her out."

"You two killed *Deldrach*?" he asked, his eyebrows shooting up, his annoyance mostly evaporating at the thought. "How in the world did you manage that?"

"We didn't," Pinchon said, nodding towards Hunt. "*He* did."

Hyde's eyes went to him, searching him for a moment before returning to the colonel.

"Him?"

"Yeah. *Deldrach* wanted a one-on-one fight, so we gave it to him. Lasted a couple of minutes. By the time I came back, he was just a pile of dust on the floor." He muttered something self-critical under his breath, and then looked at Hunt. "We should have saved a little of it, Rex. As a souvenir. Someone's probably swept him up and thrown him out by now."

"There'll be more to come," Hunt replied with quiet certainty.

"How could one man take down a giant like that?" Hyde asked. "I've heard stories about you, Mister Hunt. But that seems to stretch credulity a bit far."

"Care to demonstrate, Rex?" the colonel asked with a half grin.

"Not particularly," he replied. "The dark realm and I have a certain understanding. I don't think it would appreciate being used as a parlor trick."

"Parlor trick…" Hyde's voice trailed as he thought. "That's what you said about the boss's power," he said to Pinchon. "Remember? The last time you were here? Said it wasn't anything compared to what Hunt can do."

"He's gotten even better with time," the colonel uttered with satisfaction.

"Mister Hunt," Hyde said seriously, uncrossing his arms and looking him dead in the eye. "I would sincerely like to see what you're capable of. We've got a certain…nagging problem that could use your particular skills. But I'd have to have a demonstration first. I can't go to the boss without something solid."

"I don't want you to go to your boss about me," Hunt said indifferently. "I have no intention of working for Girnius."

"You don't understand," Hyde replied, lowering his voice and taking a couple steps towards him. "He's being tracked by one of the *Pho'Sath*. I said when you came in that a couple were rumored to be here, but that wasn't exactly true. One of them *is* here, and she's scouring the desert right now looking for him. Those creatures have noses on them like you wouldn't believe, and slowly and surely she's zeroing in on him. If you do this for him, you can write your own check as far as the boss is concerned. He'll make sure your friend is looked after in style, and anything else you need from him in the future is yours. And," he added, "the empire will have the continued support of the Black Suns in the fringe. Without Girnius, we'll crumple like a house of cards. The organization is getting battered pretty hard for going after the separatists, and we won't be able to hold it together without him. But," he finished, "I'd need to see what you can do first hand."

"I already told you that he killed *Deldrach*," Pinchon objected. "What more could you need?"

"I need to see it myself," he replied uncompromisingly. "You're hardly one of his favorites, after the way you left last time. That's going to be enough to make him skeptical. And with all the pressure he's under," he shook his head. "He can be unreasonable even in the best of times. And right now we're in a bad spot."

With a sigh Hunt slid off the table.

"Alright, what do you want me to do?"

"We have a firing range in the lowest level of the basement," Hyde replied. "Plus recording equipment. A quick demonstration is all we need. I'll get it off to Girnius, and he can send us back the OK to go after the assassin."

"Why not just send Rex out now?" the colonel asked. "He can go and take her down, and then Girnius'll be off the hook. We don't have to go through all this rigmarole."

"*You* don't," Hyde said somewhat pointedly. "But *I* do. Only I, and a handful of his most trusted bodyguards, know where he's hiding. That location is one of the deepest secrets of the Black Sun organization. It's not speaking too heavily to say I could lose my life for taking outsiders anywhere near it."

"Even to save *his* life?" Hunt queried.

"Girnius is a control freak," Pinchon said, setting aside his glass. "I guess Hyde's right. Once he gets over the euphoria of having his neck pulled out of the noose, he'll start to resent the fact that his explicit orders weren't followed. Then, in a dark mood one night, he might decide on a change in his subordinates."

"More or less," Hyde assented. "So you can see why it's important that I proceed carefully."

With a nod of agreement from Hunt, the Black Sun led the way into an elevator hidden behind a wall panel in the living room. Riding it two floors down, they got off, moved a short distance down a bare hallway devoid of people, and climbed aboard another one.

"Thorough," Pichon commented, as they did this one more time before reaching the lowest level.

"The boss wanted this place to be as defendable as possible," Hyde explained, as they left the third elevator and proceeded down a corridor with widely spaced doors. "With everything subdivided, we can easily form choke points that will hold even a superior foe at bay until reinforcements can arrive."

At the end of the hall they stopped at a locked door with a retinal scanner beside it. Holding his eye before it, the locks popped, and he ushered them inside. Before them was a long, decently wide firing range with racks of weapons running along the back wall. Ammunition was stored in sturdy safes beneath the firearms.

"Come with me," Hyde said, walking through this area towards a door on the other side of the room. This one was unlocked, and behind it was a large room filled with exotic forms of body armor, high-powered weapons locked safely behind thick glass, and thick sheets of metal plate.

"Girnius has got some pretty nice toys," Pinchon observed, looking at a pair of massive holes that had been punched in a phenomenally expensive piece of chest armor.

"He enjoys the things that money can buy," Hyde replied simply. Bending over, he carefully lifted a square foot piece of heavy metal plate from where it leaned against the bottom of the wall and hefted it onto a sturdy workbench. He took a breath, and then said, "Mister Hunt, I want you to break this." Stepping aside so the younger man could approach, he held up his hand with realization. "Wait a moment. I have to start the recording."

This done, Hunt grasped the piece of metal in his hands and instantly began filling it with darkness. The plate quickly turned to the deepest shade of black Hyde had ever seen, before suddenly exploding into little shards that spread themselves across the workbench and floor. Without the least fatigue Hunt raised his eyes to him.

"Satisfied?"

"Very nearly," he replied, heading for the strongest piece of chest armor in the room and bringing it back. Hunt had already more than convinced him, but secretly he wished to see another demonstration. Girnius would be angry with him for wasting a perfectly good, and very expensive, piece of armor. But it would be worth it. "I want you to destroy this as well."

"This isn't nearly as dense as that piece of plate," Hunt argued, as it was laid before him.

"Just humor me. Then you can be on your way."

With a shrug Hunt took hold of the armor, quickly disintegrating it.

"Yes, Mister Hunt," Hyde said, as Hunt wiped the dust from his fingers. "Your abilities are more than satisfactory. I'll get the recording to the chairman at once."

"Good."

With some time to kill, they decided to see how their new companion was faring. Pinchon was pleased to find that Girnius' medical team was a good deal less formal about visitors than was typical of hospital staff. With only a brief word not to wake her needlessly, they were allowed into Mafalda's dimly lit room.

"How's she doing, Wells?" Hunt whispered, moving to one side of her bed while the colonel took the other side. Unwilling to jostle her by sitting, they stood above her and gazed at her slack, lined face.

"About like before. Except they've drugged her like I told you, so she's sleeping pretty soundly. You could probably drop an iron pan in here without–."

His words were interrupted by a low moan that escaped Mafalda's slightly parted lips. With effort she opened her eyes, blinking several times before settling them on Hunt.

"Or...she could wake up right now," Wellesley said awkwardly. Internally he dulled his sense of embarrassment by reminding himself that he was never intended to be a medical AI.

"How are you feeling?" Hunt asked quietly, settling down on the bed as Pinchon did the same.

"I don't know," she slurred, her tongue only half awake. Hearing her own strange pronunciation, she focused her attention on her mouth and continued. "I feel numb all over."

"That's the sedatives," Wellesley said, both through her skin and the ear radios to keep them all on the same page. "The doctor felt that your condition mandated rest above all else."

"How long will I stay here?" she asked no one in particular.

"A week, probably," the AI replied, before recalling his most recent error. "Give or take a few days. We need to give your body a chance to begin rebuilding itself before making any lasting judgments. That process might reveal something about the damage that *Deldrach* did to you."

She reflected on the idea of chronic harm for a few seconds, but was too sedated to feel any concern on that point. With a subtle shake of her head she dismissed the thought and looked at Hunt.

"Can I talk to you?" she asked, closing her eyes for a moment to clear her thoughts. Opening them again, they somewhat aimlessly searched his face.

"I'll wait outside," Pinchon said, rising carefully from

the bed and making for the door.

"Can you take Wellesley, too?" she asked, awkwardly raising her hands to her neck and trying to wrestle the chain off it.

"Here, let me," the colonel said, gently lifting her head and slipping the amulet off.

"I don't mean to hurt their feelings," she uttered in an unfocused tone, as though speaking in a half-dream. "But I had to share something with you."

"What is it?" he urged her quietly, as she closed her eyes again and several seconds silently passed.

"I felt something," she said, swallowing to clear her throat before continuing. "Back in the dungeon. I wasn't awake when you got me down. But once I was in your arms, out in that hallway with those men around us, I became aware. Something within me responded to something within you. I don't know what it is. I-I can't explain it. Like a..." her voice trailed, as her stamina waned and she briefly lost focus.

"Charge?" Hunt offered.

"Yes," she nodded slightly, gaining a little energy from the fact that he understood. "A charge. I've never felt that way before. I don't have any words to describe it." She struggled to say more, but couldn't put her thoughts together.

"I know what you mean," he assured her. "The best way I can describe it is to call it an affinity. Like magnetism."

"Yes!" she said with as much enthusiasm as the medication would allow. "Yes, like magnetism. Why do we feel that?"

"This is just a guess, but I think it might be the dark realm drawing us together," he replied, thinking back on the way that Delta-13 had brought Tselitel into his life. That time was much more intense, the living world being very short on time and subsequently rather hasty. But the sense of destiny remained, though in a more diffuse way. On reflection, Delta's actions had felt like the intent of a willful party interfering in their lives. What he felt towards Mafalda was much more subtle, like water flowing down a slope that could only be discerned with some effort. It was definitely there, but that was far from seeing her, in living color, inside his dreams.

"It can do that?" she asked.

"I have no doubt that it can," he replied. "The only question is if it *is*. It's easy to ascribe all sorts of things to unseen forces. Establishing if they're really working on us or not is the hard part."

"What are we going to do?"

"Just take things one step at a time for now," he said with a shrug. "The dark realm is on our side in this thing, so I don't think there's any cause for concern. Maybe you're an important part of this war down the line, and it wants me to look after you."

"It's hard to imagine my being an important part of anything," she uttered quietly, looking away as she spoke.

Gently he put his hand to her chin and turned her face back to him again.

"You did good back there. Real good. Plenty of other people would have broken down from what *Deldrach* did to you."

"I *did* break down," she replied. "I was finished. He'd shattered me mentally and physically. You saw what I was like: I could barely even hold my head up. All I needed was a little push over the edge and I'd have died on the spot. No, I'm not strong. I'm not like you. I can't battle with creatures like that. *Nine* of us couldn't handle him."

"It's not fair to compare yourself to me. I've been fashioned since before birth to be a weapon, to have an affinity for the dark realm and its power. My entire family has been nothing but clay in the hands of others; clay that has been shaped and molded until it can truly serve only one purpose. No, don't envy me, Mafalda. I wouldn't wish this *gift* on anyone."

"You're much more than that," she assured him. "So much more."

"And so are you," he replied. "So don't beat up on yourself."

"I don't know what I am," she said, the image of Amra Welter's shattered, mindless, screaming face floating before her mind's eye and haunting her as she spoke. She twisted her head away from the image and closed her eyes, willing it to go away. "I've done things that I'll never be able to forgive myself for," she added. "Things that will keep me awake at night for years to come, if I live that long. I helped the *Pho'Sath* in their work, and I share part of their guilt."

"You will, if I have anything to say about it," he said resolutely.

"You don't understand," she said, looking back at him with tears in her eyes. "There was a girl once. She was part of the resistance back on Erdu-3. I broke her down, abused her, helped them torture her. By the time *Anzah* was finished with her, there was nothing left. Her mind was gone, Rex," she said pleadingly, her face growing anxious as she worked herself up. "She was just skin and a bundle of nerves – like a puppet! *Anzah* made her body scream to lure me and Gustav inside, but she couldn't feel anything, anymore. Just an empty husk. And then she made her own father kill her, wrapping his hand around his own Midnight Blade and forcing it down into her! In seconds she was just ash. Such a terrible end for a wonderful, intelligent, good-hearted girl. I would gladly give my life to bring Amra Welter back again."

"Amra Welter?" he asked. "So it's Gustav Welter you were with."

"Yes," she nodded limply. "You've heard of him?"

"I was supposed to go on a mission with him to Quarlac," he explained. "But plans changed, and he went alone."

"He's a good man," she commented after a few

moments of silence. "He saved my life back during the battle with *Anzah*. She was about to disintegrate me when he threw his Blade across the room and struck her in the back. Honestly I can't imagine why he bothered. If I'd only acted in time, his daughter would still be alive." She dryly laughed, scorning herself. "It wasn't strength that kept me alive in that dungeon, Rex. It was *Deldrach* himself. I learned later on that *Anzah* was what he called his Journey Partner. For her sake he intended to drag out my torture as long as possible. He could have worked me over like she did to poor Amra, leaving only an empty shell. But he wanted me to *know*, to *feel* everything that he was doing to me. It was his revenge."

"It kept you alive," Hunt observed. "Preserved you for whatever purpose the dark realm has in store."

"Some victory," she said morosely.

"We all have our burdens to bear, Mafalda," he told her slowly, hesitating a moment before continuing. "Back on Delta-13, I killed my own father. He forced me to by threatening someone who is beyond precious to me. That left my brother and me as the only Hunts alive in this galaxy. But I lost him, too, in a fight with the lead world of the *Prellak*. If I'd been stronger, he wouldn't have needed to sacrifice himself. But I wasn't. Through both my actions and my failures, my entire family is gone. That's a reality I have to live with every day. Some of us have to walk a darker path before we can finally reach the light of a clear conscience. But that doesn't mean that we won't ever make it. I don't want you to give up on yourself." He nodded towards the door. "Philippe and Wellesley don't want you to, either. And neither does the dark realm. It has a perspective much greater than ours, and we all ought to be willing to trust it. You need to believe that there's some reason for you to carry on."

"I'll try," she said weakly, her energy fading as her excitement died down. "But it's hard to be generous with myself."

"Don't strive for generosity," he told her. "Just give

yourself enough room to breathe. Over time your strength will return, and you'll see it isn't as bad as you thought. Right now you're just battered and shocked, and in need of a long rest. You'll feel better in a few days."

"I don't think I can give myself even that," she replied. "But if the dark realm wants us to cooperate, I'll do my best to hold on. I won't let you down, not while there's a strength left in me."

"Good girl," he smiled, squeezing her shoulder and rising from the bed.

While they were talking, Pinchon was leaning just beside the door, the amulet loosely held in his hand as he thought. Through skin conductance he heard Wellesley mutter something, and he raised the AI to face level.

"Are you listening in?" he asked rather pointedly.

"Me? Why would I do that?"

"Knock it off," the ex-pirate told him. "She wanted to talk to Rex alone."

"Alright, fine," the AI replied. "You know, you've been different ever since we found that little waif."

"That wasn't an invitation to start pulling me apart."

"Well, I have to do *something*, don't I? Or would you rather I go back to eavesdropping?"

"I'd rather you kept your mouth *and* your ears shut," he said with a hint of good humor lightening his voice.

"Unfortunately for you, those aren't options. Now, as I was saying, what's with this papa bear routine you've got running now that Mafalda is a part of our happy little family? I thought you didn't like looking after young people."

"Oh, it's just that she's so helpless and all," he said somewhat defensively, crossing his arms. "She deserves a little help and guidance after all she's been through. Especially given the way those ingrates on Erdu kicked her around. She's in a bad place right now, and it would be easy for her to lose her way. I don't want that to happen."

"That's why you tore into Phican?"

"Oh that? That was just pure, personal, petty hatred. Some people are just oil and water, and that describes us to perfection. I saw that from the second I laid eyes on her. I wasn't about to get along with her. Not if I could help it."

"Not a very responsible attitude."

"I've been the boss of one thing or another for decades now. It's nice to unloosen my belt and just speak my mind. After my last run to this place, babysitting Gromkoy and–," he paused suddenly, dropping his voice. "And *Milo*, I think I've earned the right to unfasten my seatbelt and go with the flow a little."

"It just makes more work for Rex," the AI uttered critically, always looking out for his friend.

"Given that he blasted a planet out of existence, I think he can handle it," the colonel replied. "Besides, he isn't complaining. We're working together real well. Or hadn't you noticed?"

"Yeah, I've noticed," Wellesley said with some annoyance. "I've *also* noticed that you're intentionally sticking your finger in Girnius' eye. That's not very smart, given that we want him to work with us."

"Oh, he's got to cooperate now," Pinchon said with a satisfied grin. "He's stuck his neck out too far. When he signed on to go after the Fringers, he pretty much put himself into Krancis' back pocket. And once Rex pulls his bacon out of the fire with this assassin, he won't be able to deny us much of anything that we ask. He'll be a vassal of the empire, more or less."

"Not something that he'd anticipated at the time of the agreement, I'm sure," the AI concluded.

"Not hardly. He prides himself on always getting the best end of every deal. But I'd say our lord and master got the better end of him this time. An elusive, unprincipled, paramilitary organization is just what the empire needs on its side in the fringe."

"Strange bedfellows."

"Indeed."

Before more could be said, Hunt opened the door and stepped out.

"Wells, we'd better put you back with her," he said. "Just to keep an eye on things."

"Yeah, reckon so," he said over their radios, as Pinchon handed him back. "I'll see you around, Colonel."

"Alright," he nodded, leaning his left shoulder against the doorway and looking in. He saw Mafalda smile weakly and give him a little wave. Returning her gesture, he waited as Hunt slipped the amulet's chain around her neck, and then made for the door. "Everything alright?" he asked, once it was closed and they were in motion.

"About the same as before," he replied, their conversation still vividly in his mind. "Had a lot of questions."

"Not surprised, after what she's gone through."

"Yeah."

Returning to the living room, they were about to settle in when Hyde found them.

"The operation is a go," he said as soon as his eyes fell on them. "The boss is impressed with what you can do, Mister Hunt, and he's glad to have you on Petrov. He very much wishes to meet you, once the assassin has been dealt with."

"Looking forward to it," he replied without much enthusiasm.

"So where is this chick?" Pinchon asked.

"Scouring the desert north of here. She's riding around on a hover bike of alien manufacture. We've tried to strafe her on multiple occasions, but the ground up there is rough, and she's got plenty of places to hide. We've sent a few teams to eliminate her, but you can imagine how that turned out."

"So what's the insertion plan?" the colonel asked.

"Well, you've got a ship, haven't you?"

"Yeah, but we can't risk it falling into their hands by landing anywhere near a *Pho'Sath*."

"Then don't land. Just hover close enough that Mister Hunt can get out and approach his target on foot."

"And the hover bike?" the ex-pirate inquired. "What if she tries to flatten him?"

"That shouldn't be a problem," Hunt replied. "I can blast it as she gets close."

"If there's nothing else to settle, we really need to get moving right away," Hyde said with subtle urgency. "She's getting awfully close to the chairman."

"We?" Hunt asked.

"Of course. I've been ordered to take you there personally, to ensure that you reach her location as quickly as possible. The boss wants to get out of that bunker. His uncle is driving him nuts."

"You mean *Dynamite* is locked in there with him?" Pinchon laughed as he asked.

"Yes," Hyde replied, as he led the way to the backyard. "There was a communications mixup, and in our haste to get the chairman under cover, Reggie was sent along as well. Naturally, we couldn't compromise the location by moving him out afterwards, so they've been enjoying a little family time together."

"I bet that's not how Girnius describes it," the colonel said, his mirth almost overflowing at the thought.

"Believe me, it isn't," Hyde uttered seriously, it ultimately being his fault that the mixup took place.

"And how's the old bombmaker been since I last saw him?"

"Well enough," Hyde said, as they reached the lawn behind the house and approached the ship. A pair of security men stood watch over it, and Hyde wordlessly waved them off. Slowly, with their eyes fixed on the visitors, they moved to a safe distance. "He'll never live on his own again, unfortunately," he added, as he climbed into the ship. "But the doctors think he's got at least a couple of good years left in him. It's kind of hard for them to say, given his history."

"Yeah, he's lived on the rough side of life," Pinchon agreed, climbing into the front seat and settling in. Once Hunt was aboard and strapped in, he dropped the canopy and raised the craft. "Where to?"

"North-east," Hyde uttered, consulting a small portable computer. "I'll tell you when to adjust course again."

"Alright."

Quickly they departed Eastmaw, flying low over the ground to minimize the risk of being spotted.

"This isn't your typical imperial make," Hyde observed about the ship, looking over the side as the ground streamed by beneath them. "Where'd you get it?"

"Just one of Krancis' toys," Pinchon replied, his tone indicating that he would say no more.

With a small nod the Black Sun fell silent, periodically glancing at his computer to keep them on track.

"So, you got a tracker on that assassin, or what?" the colonel asked after a long interval.

"There's no way in the world we could ever manage to stick one on her," Hyde replied. "No, we've got ships flying high and out of sight that are watching her movements. She was last reported near the entrance of an old mine."

"When was that?" Hunt inquired.

"Two hours ago. Hasn't come out yet."

"That you've noticed," Pinchon corrected him. "Some of those mines are spiderwebs of underground tunnels. They go on forever. She probably just ducked into it to give you the slip."

"That's why we're observing the entire region. You're right, the tunnel networks are extensive. But they tend to keep fairly close to their source. She couldn't cross even a quarter of the distance to the boss without sticking her head up again. And when she does, we'll see her."

"What if she waits until nightfall?"

"Our pilots have the equipment to see her. And as a matter of fact, so will you," Hyde said, drawing a couple pairs of small, strap-on night vision goggles out of his pocket. "Those tunnels don't have lights," he explained, handing a pair to Hunt. "If you do have to head inside, these will show you everything you need to see. They're the best money can buy. Clear, adaptive to changes in light, and small enough not to obstruct your movements in any way."

"I wish we had these on Delta-13," Hunt said, handling them for a moment before putting the band around the back of his head and slipping the lenses over his eyes. "Nice," he uttered, impressed by their perfect adjustment to the brightness of the sun above as it shined into the cockpit. "Don't hurt my eyes at all."

"As I said, they're the best," Hyde said with some pride. "Where the boss's safety is concerned, we buy only the finest tools."

"Good," Hunt replied with half interest, his mind too absorbed by the thought of how much easier his life would have been if he'd had a pair when dodging the authorities in the rundown streets of Midway. "Got anything else for me?" he eventually asked, slipping the goggles off and blinking his eyes.

"As a matter of fact, I do," Hyde said, reaching into his other pocket and producing a rather large ear radio.

"I've already got one of these," Hunt commented, taking it in his hand and feeling its relative heft.

"This one is more powerful. You'll need it to punch through the feet of dirt and rock that will separate you from us if you have to head into one of the mines."

"It's not like there's a lot we can do for him, anyhow," Pinchon observed. "If he can't handle that *Pho'Sath*, nobody can."

"Yes, but there are more mundane possibilities as well. The tunnels sprawl in all directions, and he could easily get lost. Or he could be injured during the fight. This way we'll be able to find him afterwards."

"Fair enough," Hunt said, replacing his old radio with the bigger one.

Once they'd put it and the egg on the same frequency, Hyde informed them that it was time to change course. They flew north for just over an hour, until the Black Sun pointed out the broken, yawning mouth of an old mine.

"That's it," he said, as Pinchon slowed the craft into a stationary hover two hundred feet away. "Be careful as you approach. She could be just inside."

"I'll watch it," Hunt replied seriously, his eyes fixed on the entrance. He unfastened his harness as they descended, taking hold of the colonel's seat to steady himself as the egg settled awkwardly on the uneven ground. "I'll be back."

"Be sure that you are," Pinchon replied, watching his friend throw a leg over the side and lower himself to the sand. "Wellesley will never let me hear the end of it if you get yourself killed."

With a distracted wave to acknowledge his humor, Hunt moved quickly from the ship towards the mine. He could hear the egg take off again behind him, hovering close to the ground for a quick retrieval if necessary. Or, he also considered, to smash the *Pho'Sath* bodily if the necessity arose.

The mine's mouth rose sharply out of the desert, being part of no natural formation. It had simply been dug out of the dry ground. Dilapidated boards held it up, their appearance giving very little assurance that they wouldn't collapse should a strong breeze blow through while he was inside. The only solace he could find was that they hadn't done so yet.

Slowing as he neared, he slipped the goggles over his eyes and hunched into a partial crouch, ready for action should the assassin ambush him. With care he looked around the edge of the mine's mouth, his lenses immediately brightening the darkness within. To his relief he saw no one.

"It's his show now," Pinchon observed, as his friend disappeared inside.

Descending at a sharp incline, Hunt had to be careful to keep his footing. Loose rocks were scattered across the floor, ready to make him slip and tumble down the path. Sand also covered the floor, giving him still less traction. But despite this he was glad for it, because he could easily discern the heavy footprints that the assassin had left behind.

"Not very large," he thought, noticing that the prints were smaller than his own. After his experience in the Black Hole, he knew that the *Pho'Sath* came in different sizes. But without realizing it he'd expected the assassin to be the same size as *Deldrach*, and had anticipated a similarly desperate fight. Perhaps this one wouldn't be so bad...

After a hundred or so feet, the tunnel broke into two others, both continuing to descend into the ground. They were all decently sized, wide enough not to crowd him and tall enough that he didn't have to duck. They were a little too perfectly shaped to have been made by human labor, and he concluded that it must have been the work of robots. That also explained the perfect Y shape of the intersection, and the precisely equal angles at which the tunnels continued to descend.

Looking between the two for a moment, he noticed that the sand had been disturbed more in the right path, implying that she'd gone down it and then doubled back.

"Left it is, then," he thought, proceeding that way.

After another hundred feet the tunnel once again divided into a Y, though this time they twisted around in a U shape that brought them, horizontally if not vertically, back towards their source. Again following the left tunnel, he found that it expanded into a wide, craggy room. Its walls were pockmarked, the robots and their human minders digging only as far as was necessary to obtain whatever ore they were after. The floor was more or less even, though strewn with even more rocks, forcing him to move slowly and watch his step.

The room narrowed at the far end into another tunnel, and into this he reluctantly entered. He felt he was getting close to her now, and even in the subterranean coolness of the mine, small beads of sweat began to collect on his skin. He didn't know if it was the dark realm communicating with him, or that elusive sixth sense that had alerted humans to danger for millennia. But he chose to heed the warning and slow to a crawl. Inching along the left wall, his head was about to poke around a sharp corner when the blade of a battle-ax swung through the air and struck the ground near his feet. Instantly he jumped back, as a dark-robed figure about his height came into view and drew the ax's head out of the floor.

"They should have sent more than one," a female voice uttered, her gloved finger brushing dirt away from the ax's cutting edge. "They must be running out of willing bodies to sacrifice."

"No, they just finally figured out how to do it right," Hunt replied, his voice strong and confident despite the rapid beating of his heart.

"Of course," she nodded, not recognizing him until he'd spoken. "But what could induce the *savior* of mankind to come to a world like this?" she asked sarcastically. "Surely not merely to rescue that slimy piece of filth who's cowering in his little hideaway?"

"I needed a vacation after killing *Deldrach*," Hunt quipped dryly. "And everyone said Petrov was the place to go."

"Your humor is unwelcome," she replied in a growl, taking a step closer. "A man of your power ought to bear himself with grace. It's the only proper way for your life to end."

"I'll remember that for next time."

"Oh, there won't be a next time," she said, raising the ax and swinging it at his shoulders.

Ducking the blade, it passed over his head and stuck into the wall. Striking her in the face with a pair of dark blasts that briefly staggered her, he seized hold of the ax's head and disintegrated it. Left with a mere pole, she angrily snapped it in half over her knee and threw it aside.

"You'll pay for that," she promised.

Her weapon gone, the confined space of the tunnel was no longer an advantage for him. Slowly he backed into the room, intending to negate the superior physical strength that her suit gave her by increasing his own mobility. Like a wolf eyeing a much larger predator, he circled around her, looking for the opening to strike and pour the might of the dark realm into her.

"Like all of the Earthborn, you are weak, cowardly, fearful of being hurt," she taunted, trying to goad him. "I heard of your destruction of *Deldrach*. But don't let your victory over him fill you with pride. He was hardly the best of us."

"At least he talked less," Hunt remarked, his hands floating in readiness before him like a wrestler.

Her own pride pricked by his words, she aimed her right shoulder at him and charged. Anticipating such a move, he rolled out of the way and managed to stick a leg between hers as she passed by. Expecting her to tumble to the ground, he'd forgotten the inertia that her suit's weight gave her. Instead of tripping, her legs continued moving, jerking him to the side and severely wrenching his leg. With a shout of pain he pulled his injured limb back, staggering to his feet as she came to a stop and turned on him.

"First I'm going to break you down, piece by piece," she assured him. "And then I'll disintegrate you, as I have so many of your kind."

"If you don't bore me to death, first," he replied, noticing how easily her ego was tweaked and intending to play it to the hilt.

Lowering her head ragefully, she strode up to him

and reached out her hands to seize his head. Grasping her palms as he had *Deldrach's*, he felt the shadowy essence surge through him, pouring into her suit and causing her to scream. Like a wounded dog she retreated, shocked by the experience.

"How..." her voice trailed, the suit's fingers flicking and twitching as the darkness they'd received made them malfunction. "No matter," she shook her head, regaining her equilibrium and approaching again.

This time, as their hands met, she preemptively surged the power of the light realm into her hands and arms. With this extra boost she managed to hold her ground, though she took none from Hunt. Gradually he began to wear her down, the suit starting to shake as the darkness overwhelmed the light.

"This...isn't...possible..." she struggled to say in a distorted voice, the suit drawing power from her verbal machinery and putting it into the fight.

Somehow she found the strength to pull away again, her arms hanging at her sides as she staggered backwards. They shook and spasmed, the shadowy power causing them to misfire as it interfered with their circuits.

"The Earthborn are not this powerful," she said, trying to grapple with the gap that stood between what she believed, and what was being inarguably demonstrated. "You are too weak."

"Am I?" Hunt asked, flicking a blast of darkness into her face with a sharp wave of his hand. "Because it seems to me that *you're* the one that's losing," he added, sending another blast her way.

With a growl she retreated towards the tunnel as he approached, searching for an opening that would give her even a slight advantage. Then she remembered the rocks strewn across the floor. Instantly she stooped, seized one, and threw it at his head with all her suit's might. But her malfunctioning arm made it go wide, striking him below the knee of his injured leg. A loud crack reverberated through the air as the bone broke, sending him to the ground with a scream of agony.

In a flash she was on top of him, her hands wrapped around his neck as she attempted to flood him with light. His skin began to sparkle and glow as his own hands seized hers, stopping the influx of her power and filling her with the dark essence. Impotently she groaned, her suit losing power as he rolled her off of him and straddled her chest.

"Wait!" she pleaded, as her hands froze up. "I can heal your leg! I can fix you! Just let me live!"

He lessened the flow of shadow at her words, allowing her right hand to haltingly move again. Painfully he shifted where he sat atop her, bringing his broken leg forward so she could reach it.

"Careful, now," he warned her through gritted teeth, still paralzying her other hand. "One wrong move, and you're dust."

Cautiously she placed a hand atop his shin, causing it to modestly glow through his pants. He could feel the pain diminish with each passing second, until finally it was completely gone. As she drew her hand away, he tested his leg by flexing it a little back and forth. It moved perfectly.

"So you people are good for something," he uttered, just as he heard the sound of footsteps behind him. Jerking his head, he saw another *Pho'Sath* swing a massive fist towards him in an uppercut. Striking him in the cheek, the blow threw him off the first one and sent him sprawling to the dusty, rock-covered floor. Getting to his feet as the second alien pulled the first to her feet, he watched as she retreated behind the newcomer.

"You should have destroyed *Alvath* when you had the chance," he said, his voice deep and almost soothing in the notes of wisdom it carried. He stood nearly as tall as *Deldrach*, though his suit was broader, seemingly heavier. Hunt knew he'd be a challenge beyond any that had gone before. "Now you will die in this place, far away from all you know and love."

"What's your name?" Hunt asked, playing for time as he tried to work out a strategy. *Alvath* was severely wounded, her suit damaged beyond what it could repair on its own. But she was still a threat, especially if her rescuer could pin him or channel enough of the light realm into him to demand his full attention counteracting it. He'd never had to tackle two *Pho'Sath* at once, and the proposition made him cautious, if not nervous. "I want to know what to put on your tombstone."

"I am *Felleren*," he uttered somewhat grandly, sweeping his right arm out as though flourishing an invisible cape. "And I have traveled a great distance to see this moment. Though I hadn't anticipated crossing paths with you quite so soon. We felt Krancis would keep you close, only allowing you out on occasions that truly demanded your peculiar skills. But it seems that he holds your services somewhat cheaply, if he is willing to donate them to rescue a miserable pirate, skulking in his lair. His lack of regard for you has cost him his greatest asset."

"Krancis doesn't know I'm here," Hunt replied, shifting where he stood, trying to inch closer to the tunnel in the back. A confined space would crowd his enemies, making it harder for them to work together. Especially given the clumsiness that *Alvath* now evinced, standing unsteadily on her feet. "I'm here of my own accord."

"Then you have destroyed yourself by walking heedlessly into our hands," *Felleren* told him. "You should have trembled when you heard that the *Pho'Sath* were on this world. But your recent victory over *Deldrach* has made you arrogant. Now," he concluded, beginning to walk towards him, "you will perish."

Bracing himself for the coming attack, Hunt hunched into a crouch to lower his center of gravity. But instead of wrestling with him as the others had, *Felleren* shot out a fist that caught him in the brow, sending him tumbling over backwards. Standing calmly as his shorter foe got back to his feet, the alien pursued him calmly around the room as Hunt retreated, throwing punches every few seconds that he only barely dodged.

"You are outclassed," *Felleren* taunted him, as *Alvath* watched him follow Hunt. "Heretofore your enemies have played into your hands, challenging you to a duel of the fundamental realms. But I have no intention of fighting against your greatest point of strength. Instead, I shall draw you against *mine*."

With this a quick jab shot out. Hunt ducked most of it. But his thumb managed to strike the side of his head, cutting the flesh and causing blood to spill down his cheek and neck. Staggered by the blow, Hunt stumbled over some rocks and fell once more to his side. His mind blurry, his limbs unsteady, he stood up just as *Felleren* neared him, punching downwards at his rising head. The blow rattled all the way along his spine, driving him to the floor and knocking the wind out of him.

"You are a worthy opponent in your own area of strength," *Felleren* observed, as he grabbed a fistful of his shirt in his enormous left hand and drew him off the ground. Without difficulty he held him inches from his mask. "But your kind does not have the strength to win in a physical contest against us. Our technology is beyond your merely organic form."

At this Hunt wrapped both hands around *Felleren's* wrist, channeling as much darkness into him as he could. With a growl of pain the alien dropped him to the ground, his fingers forced open and held that way by the essence that coursed through them.

"Your technology doesn't agree with the dark realm," Hunt fought out from his breathless lips. "Your girlfriend could have told you that."

"She is my Journey Partner, and no mere fancy of

mine," *Felleren* uttered darkly, taking great offense at his jibe. "For that, I will kill you slowly."

"Good, I'm not ready to go yet," Hunt replied with as much snap as he could manage, moving around the hulking being as he continued to calmly follow him. His fingers were still locked in an outward position, but they were quickly regaining their flexibility. The power of the light realm was slowly pushing the shadow from his hand. It was then that he realized that *Alvath* was watching cautiously from the sidelines a few feet behind him, not getting involved despite the beating he'd taken. Acting on a hunch, he turned his back on *Felleren* and bolted for her, seizing her barely moving wrists and flooding her with darkness as he twisted her between himself and her Partner. With a scream she dropped to her knees, his intuition completely accurate that her suit was barely functioning. "You know the score, *Felleren*," Hunt roared through gritted teeth, cutting enough of the flow to stop short of breaking her suit. "She's had it. You come another step closer, and you'll be making your journey alone."

The alien paused mid-stride, shifting his feet to keep his balance.

"Then we have a stalemate," he said. "I cannot let you leave, and I cannot let you kill *Alvath*. Equally, *you* cannot allow either of us to live, or you will have failed to protect Girnius. Just what do you intend to do? Hold her hostage for the rest of time?"

Hunt's eyes darted around the room, looking for some way out. But the alien was right, it was a stalemate. All he could do was take advantage of the breather he'd earned himself before beginning the fight again. He thought of Pinchon, floating outside in the egg with Hyde. But all he had was a Midnight Blade, a weapon that *Felleren* was sure to negate by his unfortunate skill in hand-to-hand combat. Whatever answer he arrived at, it would have to be one that depended on himself alone.

And then, like a hand tapping him on the shoulder, he could feel the essence of the dark realm reaching out to him. It had a plan, but he could only just hear its wordless voice as it tried to impress itself upon his mind. He felt its strength coursing through his body, filling him with might. Then the plan became clear, and he knew what he must do.

"*Felleren*," he announced, dragging *Alvath* to her feet and increasing the flow of shadow into her, making her suit crumble and the light within shine through. "I hereby dissolve the stalemate, just as I dissolve your Journey Partner."

"No!" *Felleren* exploded, crossing the distance between them in a flash and seizing the back of her suit with his powerful hands.

Jerking her from Hunt's grasp, he twisted her disintegrating form around him, shielding her with his body. In this moment Hunt leapt onto his back, wrapping his legs around his middle and pouring all the darkness he could manage into his shoulders to render him impotent. Howling in pain, *Felleren* watched in horror as *Alvath's* suit turned to dust in his fingers, and the cloud of her essence floated into the air and evaporated into nothingness. As despair filled him, he realized that his suit was losing the ability to function and that he must fight back. Stiffly he raised his hands to his sides, trying to wrap his fingers around Hunt's legs to break them off. But though he could grasp them, he had lost too much strength to dislodge him. With an angry grunt he strode for the nearest wall and turned around, slamming Hunt into it and trying to grind him off. But though he crushed the air out of the Earthborn champion, he'd chosen one of the few places in the room where the wall was essentially smooth. Holding on with all his might, despite the emptiness of his lungs, Hunt felt the hold on his legs slacken and finally end, the alien's arms falling uselessly to his sides.

Sensing that his life hung by a thread, the darkness

creeping through his suit with each passing second, *Felleren* stepped away from the wall and then slammed his back against it. He did this over and over, until Hunt, too battered to hold on any longer, fell off and struck the ground.

"You are as ruthless as I am resourceful," *Felleren* said, barely managing to stand over his opponent as he gasped for air. "But that has not earned you a victory this day."

Sensing an attack was coming, Hunt managed to roll out of the way just as *Felleren* dropped knees first onto the place he'd just lain, the force of his fall reverberating through the room. Rising into a crouch, he was caught off guard when the alien viciously jerked his torso to the side, slinging his numb left arm into his face and sending him sprawling once more.

"Even in this state," *Felleren* struggled to say, "I am your superior. Your organic form cannot cope with our might."

Hunt rolled farther away from his assailant, getting to his feet as quickly as he could to keep from getting hit again. Staggered and bloody, he watched as *Felleren* got to his feet and approached.

"My arms may be of little use to me now," the alien said, lashing out a kick that could have broken Hunt's ribs in a single blow. "But I am not without weapons."

Dodging three kicks as he worked out *Felleren's* rhythm, he seized his foot on the fourth and gave it the biggest shot of shadow he could before it was jerked from his fingers. It was dull and awkward as the *Pho'Sath* put weight on it, nearly costing him his balance when he attempted to kick with the other one.

Hoping to make him stumble, Hunt retreated back towards the tunnel that led into the room, the alien slowly following him. However, when he reached the entrance, *Felleren* stopped where he stood and shook his head.

"I will not fight you on disadvantageous ground," he said. "If you would finish me, then do so here, now. For I know you cannot leave this place until I have been dealt with."

"As you like it," Hunt replied, suddenly invigorated by the dark realm to finish the struggle. He threw two quick blasts of shadow at *Felleren's* face and dashed for him. Dodging the kick that he knew would be coming his way, he slipped between the *Pho'Sath's* legs and tackled him, driving him to his back. Climbing atop his chest, seizing his mask, Hunt let the essence flow from his fingers. Impotently *Felleren* tried to shift where he lay and get him off. But his legs lacked the leverage to dump him off.

"I never would have thought this was possible," he uttered in amazement, his voice deteriorating as light began to shine through his mask. "To d-die at the h-hands of the E-Earthborn."

With this the suit crumbled into dust, the cloud of his being floating up into the air and dissipating.

Hunt emitted an exhausted sigh and rolled onto his back, the crumbs of his deadly enemy stuck to his sweaty skin and clothes. For half an hour he lay there, simply breathing and gathering his strength before attempting the return journey up to the surface. Finally, deciding he'd waited long enough, he moved to his hands and knees and forced himself to his feet. Staggeringly he walked to the room's entrance, putting a hand to the doorway for a moment to steady himself. Then, painfully, he worked his way upward.

Fifty feet short of the mine's mouth he collapsed against the wall and slid to the floor. His body ached, his lungs burned, and he had no strength to go on. Pressing his ear radio, he called the colonel.

"Philippe," he gasped.

"Rex!" the colonel exclaimed in a voice so loud it hurt his ears. "Where have you been? Are you alright?"

"It's over," he replied, swallowing hard. "I killed the assassin. And her boyfriend."

"Boyfriend?" Hyde asked.

"You mean there were *two* of 'em down there?" the colonel clarified.

"Yeah," Hunt confirmed, coughing from some dust that had gotten lodged in his throat. "I'm just inside the entrance. Set the ship down and help me out of here."

Without another word the ex-pirate did as he was told, landing in sight of the mine's entrance and quickly climbing down the side to help his friend. Lacking night vision, he took a few hesitant steps into the tunnel before stopping.

"Rex?"

"Over here," he said weakly, waving his hand though it was invisible in the darkness.

Cautiously the colonel made his way to him, moving slowly along the wall until his foot bumped into him. Finding his arm he hoisted him up, getting under his left side and helping him out into the light of late afternoon. Hyde was still in the ship, and he reached over to help him aboard.

"You look like you've been through a war," Pinchon observed, climbing in after and eyeing him. "You alright?"

"More or less," Hunt uttered, leaning back in his seat and letting his body go slack.

"We'd better get you back to the compound," Hyde said with alarm, looking at the dried blood that had spilled down his cheek from the wound on the side of his head. "You could have internal injuries."

"No complaints here," he replied weakly, waving his hand to emphasize his lack of objections. "Are there any other *Pho'Sath* agents on Petrov?" he asked, as the colonel climbed into the pilot's seat and dropped the canopy.

"Not that we're aware of," Hyde told him, fastening himself in as the battered man beside him tried to do likewise. "Here, let me," he said, helping him with the harness. "Though that isn't saying much. We knew that the assassin was here. But we had no knowledge that she had an accomplice hiding in that mine. If we had, I'd never have sent you in there."

"The Black Suns used to be great at intelligence gathering," Pinchon observed from the front seat, raising the craft off the ground and pointing it towards Eastmaw. "How did that buzzard slip through the lines?"

"Because we've never had to deal with anything as capable as the *Pho'Sath* before," Hyde replied, both embarrassed by the organization's failure and annoyed at the colonel. "They're experts at slipping around undetected. Though we have managed to develop several techniques for keeping track of them."

"I'd say you need to keep working on that," Pinchon said pointedly. "You almost got my friend killed."

"I'm aware of that," Hyde replied darkly, his ire growing. "It's not as if we're not bending our every energy on this problem. The life of the chairman is at stake. You can rest assured we're doing everything within our power to protect Petrov-2 from those animals."

"What are you going to do with Girnius?" Hunt interjected, being in no mood for the argument he sensed was coming. "You gonna move him?"

"Clearly his location is compromised," Hyde said. "At least generally. But it depends on what he wants to do. Ultimately nowhere on Petrov is really safe, but it's the nerve center of our entire organization. He may want to move, and he may not. But it's not for me to say what he's going to do."

"If he's smart, he'll get off the planet like *that*," Pinchon said, snapping his fingers. "Those two won't be the only ones they send after him. He's gonna have to lay low. *Real* low, if he wants to keep his head on his shoulders."

"I'm sure he'll make the right decision, both for himself and the organization," Hyde replied somewhat formally, indicating that he would hear little more said against the chairman.

With a sharp sniff from the front seat, the matter was

dropped.

Hunt was asleep by the time the ship descended into the backyard of the compound. Several security men surrounded the vessel, though they kept at a respectful distance. When the canopy was popped and Hyde waved them near, they efficiently helped Hunt out of the ship and into the house.

"Get him to the medical team," he ordered them, lagging behind to have a private word with Pinchon. "Just a moment, Colonel," he said, as the ex-pirate was about to walk past him.

"What is it?" he asked with annoyance, not wishing to leave his friend alone.

"So far I've let you say pretty much what you want," he began in a low voice. "But that's got to stop once the boss comes out of hiding. Most likely he'll come here first, wishing to speak with Mister Hunt. He's not going to be in any mood for the cracks you've been making."

"That's just fine with me," the colonel replied. "I'm in no mood to see him, either."

"You don't understand," Hyde said more emphatically. "The boss is *dangerous*. He's been pushed to the brink by this business with the Fringers. He assaulted one of his bodyguards at the hideout just yesterday, a man he's known for years and who would give his life for him without a second's thought. He's not being completely rational. Your life could easily be put into jeopardy if you say the wrong thing to him. I know you're used to going your own way. You'd made a name for yourself doing just that back when you had the command on Delta-13. But the boss'll make hash out of you if you get on his nerves now. You've got to remember that you're on Black Sun turf. This is Girnius' exclusive domain. And with the way things have been going lately, he's not in a tolerant frame of mind. Tread carefully."

"I suppose I can bite my tongue," Pinchon replied, resuming his walk to the house, Hyde alongside him. "But mostly for Rex's sake. And that girl's, too. They're gonna need a chance to heal up."

"I don't care *why* you do it," the Black Sun replied. "Just see that you do. I don't want any more blood spilled around here."

With the passage of a day, Hunt had more or less recovered, functionally. His body was still badly bruised and battered, but there was nothing wrong enough with him to keep him confined to bed. With effort he sat up, pushed aside his blankets, and put his bare feet on the cool floor.

"Take it easy, Mister Hunt," the doctor advised, watching him beside Pinchon and a nurse whose name Hunt hadn't heard. "You need to take small steps."

"Don't think we have time for that, Doctor," the Deltan replied, pushing off the mattress and standing a little uneasily on his feet. His head swam for a few seconds before it cleared.

"The pain medication might make you feel unsteady for a little while," the doctor explained, intuiting what he was feeling. "But it'll pass off soon enough. You haven't had a dose of it in six hours."

"I can tell," Hunt said, reaching an arm around behind himself to rub his sore back. It felt as though *Felleren* had pounded his spine flat. "How's Mafalda?"

"She's fine, Rex," Pinchon replied. "Better than that, I'd say. Wellesley's real happy with her progress."

"Yes, she's recovering more quickly than anyone could have anticipated," the doctor seconded. "When I first saw her she was a pretty sorry case. But something seems to have put a little pep in her system. Her appetite's improved, too."

"Good," Hunt said rather flatly. He was happy for her. But it was hard to be cheerful when his body felt like a giant throbbing bruise.

"Girnius is here," the colonel informed him. "Arrived this morning. Said he wanted to meet the man who'd saved his life. Honestly, I think it's half that, and half that he wants to see just how much dark power you've really got."

"I should think he'd already know that."

"He's got a pretty big ego," Pinchon said knowingly, leaning against the wall and crossing his arms. "He's gonna want to test you himself, if I'm any judge of character."

Hunt frowned, because that was exactly what the colonel was. And he was in no mood to flex his muscles for the pirate boss.

"I really wish you'd take it easy, Mister Hunt," the doctor cautioned, as the former changed his clothes and sat on the bed to pull on his socks. "At least stick close to the medical wing until another twenty-four hours have passed. For your own sake, don't leave the compound without checking with me once more."

"We'll see."

With a defeated sigh the doctor shrugged away any lingering sense of responsibility and left, followed by the nurse.

"They treat you alright here?" Pinchon asked.

"Like a prince."

"Don't you mean *lord*?"

"Oh, very funny."

"That must be something a little hard to swallow for you," the ex-pirate reflected. "Just a few months ago you were picking up trinkets for Gromyko to sell. And now, all this. You're handling it awfully well."

"Thanks," Hunt said, raising his eyes to Pinchon briefly before looking down to draw on his boots. He knew that respect was something that the colonel dished out in small servings to a *very* limited number of people, and it pleased him to be one of them.

"Shall we check on our little friend?" Pinchon asked, nodding towards the door and meaning Mafalda.

"No, let's talk to Girnius first," Hunt replied, grunting as he pushed off the bed. Not in the best of moods, he wanted to burn off his attitude before seeing her.

Wordlessly the two men left the room. Despite his eagerness to get the meeting over with, Hunt was forced by his painful body to move slowly. By this point everyone on the medical team knew about the illustrious occupant of one of their rooms, and they stole glances at him as he walked down the halls.

They found Girnius sitting on a couch with an attractive young woman in her late twenties. Her long legs were drawn prettily up onto the cushion she sat on, but the pirate boss paid her no mind. He seemed lost in a world of his own, staring hard at the wall and not noticing them in his peripheral vision until Pinchon coughed pointedly. Slowly he turned his head.

"Mister Hunt," he said in a slow, contemplative voice. Rising from his place, he walked to him and shook his hand. "It's not very often that a man does me a service that I cannot easily repay. I am in your debt."

"We're all on the same side of this thing," Hunt replied, not particularly interested in the favors the pirate boss could bestow.

"Yes, we are, aren't we?" Girnius said, releasing his hand and turning towards the couch. Sitting on the large armrest, he eyed the two men for a moment as his girlfriend scooted closer and began gently rubbing his arm. Pinchon noticed that she was a different woman than the one he'd met in his bedroom during his last visit. "It seems fate is conspiring to draw all the little divided elements of the human family together. The Devourers, to say nothing of the *Pho'Sath*, are proving far more effective in uniting mankind than Rhemus and his ancestors ever were. Nothing leads to cooperation like mutual self-interest. So tell me, Mister Hunt, just what is *your* self-interest? How can I pay you back for what you've done for me?"

"I don't see that you can," Hunt replied evenly, too tired for the niceties of diplomacy. "I don't want anything you have."

"Oh, come on," Girnius replied good-naturedly, though with a hint of steel in his tone. "Everyone wants *something*. I can bring the riches of Quarlac and lay them at your feet. I can get you food, drink, comforts you didn't think would ever be yours. The goodwill of the Black Suns opens many doors, Mister Hunt. Don't be too quick to bat away the hand that offers you friendship."

"I never reject a friend," Hunt replied, shifting on his feet to try and ease the strain on his back. "But I'm not going to be bought by trinkets." His eyes shifted to the luscious brunette that continued to stroke the chairman's arm. "Or creature comforts," he added.

Girnius leaned back a little on his seat and tilted his head contemplatively. Slowly he began to nod, an approving look on his face.

"You're no backwater rube, Mister Hunt," he said. "Your cloistered life in Midway has done nothing to blind you to the games of wily men. I respect that."

"Good."

"Krancis must have gone to great lengths to win such loyalty from a man who, for every other reason, ought to despise him and the empire he defends. After all, it was an unjust policy of that very same empire which destroyed your family, banishing you to Delta-13."

"I'm acquainted with my own history," Hunt replied, his tone unappreciative of the chairman's words. "Besides," he added cryptically, thinking of the division that had been placed in his psyche before birth, "Krancis and I go way back."

"Is that so?" Girnius asked, his voice only half-interested but his mind suddenly bursting with curiosity. "Interesting."

"There is one thing you can do for me, however," Hunt said, changing the topic to leave the pirate hanging.

"Yes?"

"Look after Mafalda until she's better."

"Oh, I intend to," he assured him. "It's not every day

that an important separatist falls into our hands. We'll be certain to take care of her."

"And I want her untouched," Hunt added, his voice dropping a little to make his point. "No interrogation. She'll tell you what you need to know without that."

"She's a separatist, Mister Hunt," he replied. "No matter what made her change sides, she's certain to still have loyalties to the people and cause she once served. She'll leave out details, figures, and places that she doesn't want us to strike. The only way to ensure a complete and honest picture is to put her under some pressure. Once she feels that her own neck is on the line, she'll sing a true tune. It's the only way to work with these Fringers."

"Not Mafalda," Hunt insisted. "You've seen the marks on her face and you've talked to the doctor treating her. You know what kind of agonies the *Pho'Sath* put her through. She won't hold anything back."

"Mister Hunt," the chairman uttered formally, standing up and taking a step towards him. "I have a great deal of experience dealing with her kind. Oh, not in the hostile fashion that we've grown accustomed to lately. But I've worked with them for years, making deals while we mutually strove to stab each other in the back. They can't be trusted. Their very way of life is built on lies and deceit. It's the only way they've remained fluid enough to avoid being crushed by the empire. Truth means nothing to them as an abstract concept. They can only be believed *after* the screws have been put to them, and even that must be double-checked by running it past other sources. They're sewer rats, scrambling from one side of a river of filth to the other and then back again, and the muck gets all over them. They don't know any other way to live."

"Anyone who lays a hand on that girl is going to have a problem with me," Hunt warned him, his voice lowering as his eyes hardened.

"I will not be threatened in my own house," Girnius

replied firmly, matching his gaze.

"Then I'll remove her from your house, and I'll brush aside anyone who gets in my way."

"Mister Hunt..." the chairman's voice trailed menacingly.

"Don't push this thing too far," Pinchon cautioned. "We're sitting on a powder keg as it is. This isn't the time for us to be at each other's throats. You think the *Pho'Sath* are finished coming after you? They'll be back, and Rex is the only one whose proven he can deal with them. Everyone else they've come across has been stomped flat. Whatever that girl knows, it isn't worth getting on his bad side. And believe me when I tell you, his bad side is *bad*."

Girnius eyed the colonel for a moment before shifting his gaze back to Hunt. Without looking he dashed a thin, wispy bolt of darkness from his left hand and struck a glass flower pot that stood upon a low shelf half a dozen feet away. The girl behind him shrieked as it exploded, throwing little black shards in all directions.

"So is mine," he said in a low, dangerous voice.

Hunt drew a deep breath and released it sharply. Moving to the interior wall that stood behind the shelf, he put a hand on it and instantly began filling it with shadow. In half a minute dozens of square feet were a deep hue of black. Then he pushed his hand through it, causing it all to shatter in an instant. The floor it supported began to sag and creak over their heads, but Hunt stood motionless, the fatal look in his eyes boring into Girnius.

"Don't press your luck," he warned him, before turning and walking away.

"What *is* that man?" the chairman asked, his gaze moving between the pile of black ash on the floor and the colonel. He'd never been threatened with such unblinking assurance in his life, and in the privacy of his own mind he admitted to being a bit rattled by the experience.

"Why did you think the emperor conferred a lordship

on him?" Pinchon asked self-evidently. "For his winning personality? We're at war, Girnius. And that's the man who's gonna see us through, if anyone can. Are you starting to catch up with that fact? Or does he need to knock over your whole house?"

Resentfully the chairman looked at him, but said nothing.

"So it *is* getting through to you," the colonel observed. "Better now than later. We're entering a new era, Girnius. A mythical era of demigods and supermen. Your little parlor trick," he said, flicking out his own hand, "isn't worth a bucket of warm spit compared to a man like Rex. The old days are over. This isn't what you might call a conventional galaxy anymore. Hidden powers are coming to light, and they're not the sort of thing you or I can grapple with unless the deck is stacked in our favor. Those assassins should have taught you that."

"There's always been dangers," Girnius replied somewhat weakly, only half believing his own argument. "There's always been a thousand ways to die for every one way to live."

"That's garbage and you know it. We've got nearly invincible aliens traipsing through the Milky Way like it's their own backyard. We've got an all-seeing eye of a man running the imperial government. An unstoppable spaceship is cruising from one end of the empire to the other, smashing our enemies. An ancient parasite is consuming planets left and right. None of these figures can be bought, intimidated, or persuaded. They each serve their cause with deadly seriousness, and will brook no opposition. And make no mistake: they'll *crush* anyone who stands in their way."

"Hunt's only a man," the chairman objected. "I have a dozen armed bodyguards within half a minute's walk from here. If I were to but snap my fingers–."

"Assuming you're stupid enough to do that, Rex would annihilate them all," Pinchon warned him emphatically.

"And," he added darkly, "if by some miracle you *did* manage to take him down, Krancis would roll right up to this planet with *Sentinel* and blast Eastmaw out of existence. You'd never stand a chance."

"Do you expect me to hand my organization over to them?" Girnius demanded, his temper suddenly flaring and making the girl jump. "Oh, get out of here!" he said, yanking her off the cough by her arm and shoving her towards the door. "Get out of my sight!" he bellowed, as she stood watching him doubtfully. With quiet haste she left the room and disappeared into the rest of the house.

"I expect you to be realistic," the colonel replied, as the chairman's eyes fell upon him once more. "The time when the Black Suns could write their own check is dead and gone forever. You've got to cooperate intelligently with the new breed of leader who's risen up to guide our affairs. Rex might be the most powerful, but he won't be the last man Krancis gives authority to. Soon this entire empire will be filled with individuals who are fanatically dedicated to the same cause as the man who chose them, and they will not be impressed by the traditional prerogatives of a pirate boss. They'll work with you as long as they can. But they'll push you aside the *instant* you get in their way. And they'll do so without remorse."

These words slowly sunk into the chairman's mind, causing him to retake his seat on the armrest and think. He hated to be schooled by Pinchon, but he knew he was right. In fact, he knew it before he'd even begun his little trial of wills with Hunt. He knew that the Black Suns were being drawn into a maelstrom they could neither control nor leave, but he hadn't been willing to admit it. Part of his mind felt that if he could push Hunt around, as Krancis' representative, he would thereby demonstrate that the organization could still act independently. It was a long shot, but it hadn't paid off. He'd seen the truth of Pinchon's words in the Deltan's eyes. There was neither remorse, compromise, nor pity. He was ready to destroy anyone who stood in his way, no matter the cost to himself. It was then that he knew he was beaten.

"You can tell him the girl won't be interrogated," he said at last.

"He already knows that," the colonel said, leaning against one of the remaining walls and crossing his arms over his chest. "He wouldn't have left if he hadn't made his point."

"Just what *is* he?" he asked again, raising his eyes to the ex-pirate, genuine consternation written on his face. After a lifetime of dealing with lowlives, crooks, and ten-cent conmen, he didn't know how to understand the monk-like integrity of the man he'd just faced.

"He's the best hope we have for seeing our next sunrise," Pinchon said, pushing off the wall and walking away. "I suggest you get aboard before the ship leaves its dock."

As he walked away, he could feel the hateful glare of the chairman on his back. But he didn't care. After Hunt's demonstration, he was a mere toothless tiger. Making his way back through the house and into the medical section, he went straight to where he knew Hunt would be. Without bothering to knock, he opened the door to Mafalda's room.

"How you doing, kid?" he asked, closing the door and sitting on the edge of her bed. Hunt was already on the other side, looking at him with weary eyes.

"How's our friend?" he asked, more tired than ever after disintegrating the wall.

"Tame as a housecat, though he'll be fuming for a while. He got the message loud and clear not to mess around with our girl, here," he said, paternally patting her on the arm. "Said he'd leave her alone from now on."

"Leave me alone?" she asked dubiously, her eyes wide and alert now that the sedatives of the first day had worn off. "What was he going to do?"

"He wanted to grill you for information," the colonel

explained. "Rex didn't like that idea, so he helped him remodel his house a little. We won't have any more trouble out of him."

"But I'm glad to share what I know," she insisted. "Just give me the chance and I'll tell anyone who'll listen."

"We know that, little honey," Pinchon said. "But he was going to interrogate you as a precaution. He figured, with your background, that you couldn't be trusted, so he was gonna put the screws to you. Naturally, nobody lays a hand on a friend of ours, so that wasn't about to happen. You'll still have a chance to tell what you know before we leave here."

"But will they believe me?"

"That's up to them. If they're too stupid to see what's right in front of their own eyes, they deserve to be ignorant."

"Okay," she nodded reluctantly, her eyes bouncing between the two of them. "How much longer do I have to stay here?"

"Well, how do you feel?" the colonel asked.

"Better than I thought I would," she replied, shifting a little where she lay to test her body. "Still weak. But I think I could stand and walk around alright. Though I'd probably be a little slow. I don't want to hold you two back."

"We're not going anywhere for a little bit longer anyhow," Hunt reassured her. "Not for at least another twenty-four hours. I don't feel like moving yet."

"Where will we go once we leave here?"

"I guess that depends on our lord and master, doesn't it?" Pinchon asked, glancing at Rex. "He's probably got our next three missions worked out in advance."

"Is this your life, then?" she asked them, though her eyes were on Hunt. "Just moving from one fatally dangerous encounter with the *Pho'Sath* after another? The risk seems so high."

"Someone's got to do it," he shrugged. "And with the possible exception of Krancis, I don't think anyone else can."

"You think the old bird could have taken down *Deldrach* and those other two?" the colonel inquired.

"I don't know. He doesn't have access to the raw power that I have. His connection to the dark realm seems more… nuanced, for lack of a better word. Subtle, perhaps. I can't say what that would look like in a battle, but it's hard to imagine him being overcome."

"Yeah, I reckon you're right. Seems like he'd have some card up his sleeve that would carry him through. Although he doesn't seem in a big hurry to expose himself to frontline fire."

"He's doing his best work where he is right now," Hunt replied simply. "There's no more valuable position for him to fill."

Still lacking his old ear radio, he realized he hadn't heard Wellesley's voice since the day before. With a tired smile he pressed a finger to the amulet as it dangled below Mafalda's neck.

"How's it going, Wells?" he asked with a chuckle.

"Oh, you're gonna talk to me now?" he asked tartly. "Great. Awesome. Superlative. Not like I've, you know, been the *least* interested in how *you've* been doing since you fell out of radio contact yesterday. You get yourself beaten half to death, and you don't have the decency to give me at least a howdy-do?"

"Are you my friend, or my mother?" he laughed.

"Both, it seems. I don't let you out of my sight for *six hours* and you have a run in with *two* of those nasty pieces of space filth. I think it's pretty clear that you need someone to look after you. It was the same way on Delta, remember? You left me with Lily, and nearly got yourself killed in that pirate base with Antonin. *Antonin*, of all people! If *he* thinks it's a good idea, you know it *has* to be suicidal."

"So, are you finished scanning me now?"

"Yeah, I'm done. You're alright," he uttered in a somewhat deflated tone, the wheels coming off his bus.

"So what were you so worried about?"

"What can I say? I'm getting fretful in my old age."

"You're not old."

"I'm older than any of you."

Hunt smiled.

"Good to see you again."

"Yeah, same to you."

With a laugh he withdrew his finger and sat up straight.

"He been keeping you good company?" he asked Mafalda.

"Oh, sure," she nodded. "We chat whenever I'm awake. He's been very interested in all the goings on in the fringe. If I didn't know better…" her voice trailed. Suddenly her eyes lit up with mirth.

Nodding his understanding, Hunt pressed a finger to the amulet again.

"Wellesley?" he asked with a roll of his eyes.

"Yes?" he asked in a drawn out singsong.

"Have you been interrogating Mafalda?"

"Interrogate is such a strong word," the AI quibbled. "*Conversing*, I've been *conversing* with this dear young lady on topics of interest to both the Black Suns and the empire. I figured sooner or later one of these morons would get it into his head to put her through the wringer, and I wanted to sidestep that possibility by having all the information on hand in advance. Besides, it would have been a good bargaining chip if Girnius suddenly decided to throw us out while you were gone."

"Good thinking."

"Thanks. I try."

"So, are you finished?"

"Well, I'm not a mind reader, so I can't say how much more is floating around in that rather battered brain of hers. But I think I've harvested most of the main points of interest. Naturally it's a somewhat *macro* view of the situation. She doesn't really have data on specific installations and figures, beyond where they are or tend to be. You couldn't plan an operation on just what she knows. Unless you're talking about Erdu-3, obviously."

"How much more time do you need?"

"Probably just a few more hours. Provided you two don't talk her to exhaustion and force me to put it off."

"Is that a hint?"

"Just a small one. She's bright eyed and alert right now, and I want to make the most of it."

"Alright, we'll leave her alone," Hunt said, withdrawing his finger and standing up.

As he turned away she reached out and took his hand, squeezing it firmly.

"I'm glad you're alright," she said sincerely, looking into his eyes. "I was afraid when they first brought you in. I thought maybe they'd hurt you badly."

"They did their best," he laughed dryly. "But it takes more than that to kill a Hunt." The second the words were out of his mouth he regretted them. With a twitch of his face he pushed the expression aside and squeezed her hand back. "Don't let that old piece of jewelry keep you awake too long."

"I won't," she assured him, releasing her grasp and watching them leave.

"Oh, Wellesley *loved* that last crack you made," Pinchon said, squinting as he pulled the radio out of his ear. "You should have heard him."

"Yeah, I knew he would," Hunt grinned, before his mind went back to what he'd said in the room. Like a dark rain cloud, the thought blotted out his happiness and made him somber.

"Your brother died well, Rex," the colonel said sincerely, intuiting his thoughts. "I know what it's like to lose someone you're close to. Believe me, how they go is more important than when."

"Leave it alone, Philippe," he said evenly, his tone

neither a warning nor a request. Just a fact.

"Okay," he obliged, drawing a breath and letting it go. "What now?"

In response to his question, Hunt strode to his room a little way down the hall and went inside.

"That answers that," he shrugged, walking down the corridor and out of the medical wing of the large house.

Heading towards the kitchen to sample some more of Girnius' excellent liquor, he was stopped by a whisper from a half-open bedroom. Pausing mid-stride, he pressed the door open with the index finger of his artificial hand and saw the girl from before, her body quivering.

"Is he dangerous?" she asked.

"Who, Girnius?" Pinchon inquired. Leaning on the doorway, he was careful not to put so much as an inch of his body through the frame.

"No," she shook her head. "Your friend. Mister Hunt."

"Oh, *him*? He's safe as a kitten. As long as you don't cross him."

"I won't," she assured him, though she was really speaking to herself.

"That's fine," he nodded, pushing off the doorway and shaking his head as he walked away.

To his surprise, he found Girnius was already there ahead of him. Sitting without any concern for his dignity atop one of the counters, he had a bottle in one hand and a glass in the other. A dull look was on his face as he contemplated the oven on the other side of the room. Lazily he turned his head to Pinchon.

"Don't mind me," he said, making rather a show of choosing just the right bottle to drink from. He knew the chairman was resentfully watching him, and he made a point to drag it out as long as possible. At last he picked one, brought it to the table, sat down with an air of propriety, poured a drink with a steady, practiced hand, and slowly drank it down.

"Help yourself," Girnius uttered contemptuously.

"I already have. On more than one occasion." Taking another sip, he lowered his glass to the table and looked at the pirate chieftain. "Take it easy. We all get the rug pulled out from underneath us sometime or other."

"*I* don't," he uttered heavily.

"Well, *I* have," Pinchon replied, tilting his chair back and resting his leg on the seat next to him. "Back on Delta, when you boys threw me to the wolves. And all because I was saving some innocent people from the Devourers."

"Is that why you've been such a nuisance?"

"Partly."

"Good to know," Girnius said with annoyance, tossing back his head as he downed another drink. "This universe is getting too big for pirates. Or anyone else."

"We've always been living on borrowed time in this galaxy," Pinchon replied. "You didn't know that, did you? The folks who built *Sentinel*? Well, turns out they've got a treaty with the *Pho'Saths*, keeping 'em from rushing in here and vaporizing us all. Without that particular act of benevolence, the whole race would have been dead eons ago."

"That's working out real well," Girnius sourly observed, thinking of the two assassins.

"Well, they're not gonna start a galactic war because some operatives have snuck across the border. It just isn't worth it. Better to leave them to us than to start something that would see numberless dead on both sides. Besides, the main thing is that they can't act openly in our space. As things stand now, we can handle 'em. Or rather Rex can."

"Yes," Girnius said mockingly, extending the hand that held his glass. "Cheers to our savior." With a frown he returned the cup to his lips and swallowed its contents.

Critically, the older man watched him.

"Why don't you settle down?" he asked pointedly.

"Oh, get off my back," he said, laying aside the bottle and glass. Wearily he wiped a hand down his face and then looked at the colonel with reddened eyes. "You really don't care, do you? What's happened to the Black Suns? You're happy to see us become a vassal. You think it's poetic justice for what happened to you on Delta."

"I think it had to happen sooner or later. I saw the writing on the wall when you tried to take advantage of the Devourers by stepping up your attacks. I knew then, if the empire survived, that it would hound you to the edges of the galaxy for stabbing them when they were reeling. You're just lucky Krancis had a use for you before the war ended. You ought to take advantage of it instead of griping about it."

"What future is there in that?" Girnius retorted. "Once the Fringers are put down and the Devourers have been dealt with, we'll be swept into the trash by men like Hunt and Krancis."

"I don't think so," Pinchon shook his head. "Something's brewing in this rotten old universe of ours. I can feel it in my bones. I think this war with the Devourers is just the first of many we'll have to fight in order to survive. And that means the empire will be hungry for allies. The Black Suns will have a long career ahead of them, if you play your cards right."

"Pardon me, if I don't build my hopes upon your bones," the chairman said in a grandly nasty tone, as he slid off the counter. Shuffling through the kitchen, he was just about out when the colonel stopped him.

"Hey, where's Dynamite?" he asked suddenly.

"Back at the hideout."

"You left that poor old bird out there on his own?"

"He's got a couple of men to watch over him." He turned to face him fully and put his hands on his hips. "Is that *satisfactory*?"

"Not hardly," Pinchon said, laying aside his own glass and standing up.

"Then go get him yourself," the chairman said with a dismissive wave of his hand. "But keep him away from me."

"Hasn't it occurred to you that they could use him to get leverage over you?"

"Nobody'd take Dynamite hostage. He'd probably blow himself up first."

"With *what*?" he asked scornfully, pushing past the muddled pirate boss and heading for the egg in the backyard. Halfway across the grass he stopped and put his ear radio back in. "Wellesley?"

"Yeah?"

"I'm heading out of town to get someone for Girnius. Shouldn't be more than a few hours. Tell Rex if you run into him."

"Alright."

"Hold up a minute," he heard the chairman say from behind him.

"What is it now?" he asked, turning around.

"Just how do you intend to *find* the hideout?"

Rolling his eyes, the colonel realized he'd forgotten that part. Briefly the pirate boss gave him the coordinates, and then shambled back inside. Muttering them under his breath so as not to forget them, he punched them into the egg's computer and took off. For once flying alone, he activated the craft's AI to keep him company, and a pretty little hologram appeared on the dashboard.

"Pardon me, Mister Pinchon," she said. "But the coordinates you've entered are in the middle of nowhere. There's nothing for miles and miles around. Are you sure that's the location you'd like to fly to?"

"Yes," he nodded, fastening his harness as he twisted the craft northward and left the compound behind. "I'm looking for a bunker."

"Oh, I see. May I inquire the purpose of our visit?"

"To retrieve an old bombmaker named Kennedy."

"And Mister Hunt? Is he well?" she asked solicitously.

"Decently well. Ought to be alright in a day or so."

"I'm glad. He took a terrible beating inside that mine."

Sensing that he didn't want to talk anymore, the little purple figure turned around and watched the ground stream by beneath the front of the craft. As the sun moved across the sky and they finally neared their target, Pinchon slowed the egg down.

"Something wrong?" the AI asked, a puzzled look on her face.

"I don't know. Something doesn't feel right."

As they drew closer, they could make out an open hatch in the middle of the desert. It had been partially ripped off its hinges by a small explosive.

"That's not good," the colonel said ominously, hovering near the bunker's entrance for a few seconds and trying to look inside. But it was all dark.

"What are we going to do?" she asked, as he floated a short distance away and put the craft down.

"I'm going in there," he told her, unfastening his harness and popping the canopy. "And you're gonna do whatever it takes to keep this ship out of enemy hands. Blow it up if you have to, but don't let 'em take it."

"I understand," she replied, as he climbed over the side and dropped to the sand below. "Good luck!" she called after him, lowering the canopy once he was clear.

"Thanks," he thought, approaching the entrance carefully and drawing the pistol he always carried from the inside of his light jacket. Thinking better of it in the close quarters, he put the pistol back and drew the Midnight Blade instead, holding it before him as he carefully descended the spiral stairs that led into the ground. After half a dozen steps he put on the night vision lenses that he'd pocketed from Hunt. "That's more like it," he thought with satisfaction, as the subterranean space suddenly sprang vividly to life.

Following the stairs downward, he was at least half a dozen stories below the surface before they terminated in a long, concrete hallway. Looking along it, he'd taken only a pair of steps when someone stuck an arm out a doorway towards the end and cranked off a couple of shots. Throwing himself to the ground as the bullets went wide, he drew his own pistol and gave as good as he got.

"Who'alls down here?" he bellowed, hoping to induce the other party to stick their arm out again so he could shoot it off.

The arm appeared again, but this time it held a submachine gun that sprayed the hallway with so much lead that he could only cover his head and stay low. Once the clip was empty and the gun had clicked a half dozen times, the arm withdrew.

In a flash Pinchon was on his feet, and he crashed through a door ten feet away on the left side of the corridor. A second later a pair of bullets chased him inside, blowing holes in the door and causing it to wave on its hinges.

Putting the Blade away lest he fall on it by accident, Pinchon held his gun at the ready and moved back towards the doorway. Somehow sensing this, his opponent shot the door again, a splinter flying out of it and striking his artificial forearm. Glad that it wasn't his other one, he took a breath and glanced around the room he was in. Boxes of all sizes stood on shelves that ran along three of the walls. The one he leaned against was bare.

Despite the dull hiss in his ears from the gunfire, he could hear feet moving along the corridor outside. Lowering himself silently to the ground, he held the pistol ahead of him in both hands, aiming it at belly height just inside the doorway. Suddenly a figure in dark clothing appeared, the submachine gun held at hip level. Instantly Pinchon discharged a shot that doubled the figure over with a groan. The voice was female, and with desperate effort she tried to aim at him as she squeezed the trigger, sending bullets flying across the room. Another shot dropped her to her knees, and a third ended her. The gun fell from her hand as she dropped forwards, clattering halfway to where he lay.

With his increasingly dull ears pricked for any sound

from the hallway, he slithered to the submachine gun and dragged it back to where he'd ambushed her. Finding the clip half full, he tucked his pistol into his jacket and moved into a crouch with the new weapon in his hands. Carefully poking his head around the corner, he instantly drew back at the sight of a muzzle sticking out of the same doorway the woman had occupied a moment before. As a dozen bullets crashed into the door beside him, he found himself wishing that his room had more than one exit.

Scanning the boxes for an answer, his eyes returned to the corpse at his feet.

"Come on, honey," he said, jerking her light, inert form upwards and shielding himself with her body. "It's time you did something productive with your life."

With his arm wrapped tightly under her arms, he bolted into the corridor and sprayed the opposing doorway with lead. Two bullets struck just below his elbow as he approached, causing his shield to jerk. But a scream from up ahead told him that his own shots had hit home, and with much greater effect. Throwing aside his new weapon as it ran out of bullets, he managed to wrestle his pistol out of his jacket by the time he reached the door, leveling it on a man who lay on his back, his blood already spilling out on the floor.

"Freeze!" Pinchon bellowed, the pistol aimed at his head. "Or you'll join your sister."

The man watched him for several seconds, only barely managing to hold his head up. Tepidly he reached for the weapon beside him. But his hand fell to the floor halfway to its goal, and with a thud his skull dropped to the concrete. A sigh escaped his lips as his head rolled off to one side.

Dragging the woman in front of him, Pinchon scanned the room and found it to be another storage space. Dropping the girl upon her companion's corpse, he turned around and looked back into the hallway. Then he heard it: a faint knocking sound from the door opposite the one he stood beside. Approaching cautiously, he moved to the side and kicked it open. When a hail of bullets failed to greet him, he carefully looked around the corner and saw Dynamite sitting against the back wall, his hands, feet, and mouth bound.

"Philly, in here," he said in a barely intelligible muffle.

"You look like you've had better days," the colonel said, dropping to one knee and taking the gag out of his mouth.

"You can say that again," he uttered, as the rest of his bonds came off.

"What happened here?" Pinchon asked, pulling the old man to his feet. "Girnius said you had protection."

"I did, until a half dozen assassins broke in here and killed 'em. I'm telling you, Philly, this planet's getting too hot for my old blood. I'm all for a little action," he said with half a grin. "Especially if it's of my own making. But this is just too much. A body won't last long with all these psychos all over the place."

"Yeah, I know," he said, ushering the old man to the door before suddenly stopping him. "You said there were six of them?"

"Yeah, but Julian's boys took care of all but two of 'em. They're the ones who locked me in here. I overheard them saying something about negotiating a trade. If they thought that nephew of mine would trade *anything* for me, they were crazy! I guess that's why he sent you here."

"No, I didn't know anything about it. As a matter of fact, I was gonna get you in order to *prevent* something like this from happening."

"Really? Well, they *did* take the bunker less than an hour ago. I guess they didn't have time to figure out the radio equipment and signal their demands. Funny that the organization didn't know about it, though, what with all those ships flying in orbit and all."

"The Black Suns haven't exactly been on their A game lately," the colonel said, urging him forward again. "Come on, let's get out of here before more of them arrive."

After an exhausting climb up the stairs for Kennedy, Pinchon got him into the egg and safely into the air.

"Where did you ever get a ship like this, Philly?" he asked, rubbing his hands across the exotic seat he sat upon. "I've never seen anything like it in my life."

"Alien make. Long story."

"Oh," he nodded, getting the hint. "Boy, it sure is good to see you again," he said, his tone brightening. "After you left the last time, I thought I'd never see intelligent life again. Well, except for Hyde. He's pretty solid. But he's an organization man through and through, and he doesn't think outside the lines like we do. Smart, but conventional."

"How've you been, Dynamite?" Pinchon asked, hoping to point the rambling older man in a more productive direction. "Feeling alright?"

"Oh, they've got me on medications and therapies now," he said with annoyance. "Can you believe it? Me, tethered to a doctor and a bunch of nurses?"

"I didn't see any in the bunker," the colonel commented.

"They were there," Kennedy assured him grimly. "A doctor, and this real pretty little thing of about twenty-five. Cute and sweet. I don't know how she ever got tied up with the organization, but she was my only bright spot while I was cooped up in there." He sighed heavily. "Broke my heart when they shot her. For the life of me I can't understand why they did it. She wouldn't hurt anyone, even if they deserved it. Just a really gentle soul."

"They're scum," Pinchon replied simply. "They don't care about human life."

"Reckon not," Kennedy agreed quietly. "Can't figure out how they found the hideout, though. Even those *Pho'Saths* couldn't find it. Or at least they hadn't by the time your friend took 'em out."

"Oh, that's just part of Girnius' genius," the colonel

uttered pointedly. "The Fringers were watching the desert the whole time, waiting for him to pop his head up. If he had any brains he would have evacuated the whole group at once, realizing that the location henceforth would be compromised. That's why I came after you the second I heard about it. I knew they'd act soon, if they'd noticed. Obviously they did."

"I can't tell you how grateful I am for that, Philly," he said sincerely.

"Forget it. You'd have done the same for me."

"You bet I would!" the old pirate said, smacking his knee. "Absolutely. Why, I would have fixed them up a real nice surprise, one that goes tick, tick, BOOM! Never would have known what hit 'em."

"I know you would've."

They were silent for a time, Dynamite's mood slipping as he thought back on the unfortunate nurse. Realizing he was growing morose, he shook his head and spoke again.

"Hey, you haven't told me what you're doing on Petrov," he said as cheerily as he could manage. "Doing some more work for Krancis?"

"Nah, came here to get medical help for a friend of mine. A girl. The *Pho'Saths* worked her over pretty good on Erdu-3, and there wasn't anywhere else to take her. So I brought her here. Then Rex got roped into taking out those two assassins, and I've been waiting around for him to recover as well."

"Is he in bad shape?" he asked with concern. "Those *Pho'Saths* are *killers*. Honestly, I thought our days were numbered when that one was out there in the desert, homing in on us. No matter what we threw at her, she just kept coming."

"He's alright. Just got knocked around a bit. Day or two and he'll be ready to go."

"Good. Sounds like we need him out there."

"No argument there."

For the rest of the trip they were quiet, save for the occasional comment from Dynamite. Landing in the compound once again, the sun had begun to drop in the sky, casting long shadows from the trees and structures that surrounded the main house.

"Give him a hand," Pinchon ordered the men around the egg, as Kennedy struggled to get out.

"I'm alright. I'm alright," he insisted, though he really wasn't. The experience had taxed him to the limit, and his face was hot and flushed as he was helped into the house.

As Pinchon reached the ground, Hyde approached with a look of concern on his face.

"Kennedy looks rough," he said, eyeing the ship and wondering where the rest of the group was.

"Watching your security and medical team get slaughtered will do that to you," the colonel replied flatly, walking away from the egg.

"What?" he asked incredulously.

"The Fringers took the bunker a little before I arrived. They killed everyone but Dynamite, apparently planning to trade him. I finished off the ones who'd survived the initial attack, and brought him back."

"I don't believe it," Hyde uttered in amazement.

"You'd better," Pinchon said, turning on him sharply and stabbing him in the chest with his index finger. "That's the second time in two days that you've nearly gotten one of my friends killed. Either get on top of your game, or get another job. Because this is the last time I let you off the hook without taking something out of your *hide*."

Unable to reply, Hyde watched as the fuming colonel strode into the house.

CHAPTER 9

Bored almost to tears on the massive warship, Gromyko had taken to skipping the teleporters in order to explore every last nook and cranny on foot. Robbed of his companions, and wrapped in countless tons of metal, he found his thoughts turning morosely inwards at every turn. And that was something the smuggler had never been able to deal with. He required constant action and stimulation to avoid the hard questions of life and death that tended to swirl at the back of his mind, and his monotonous surroundings failed to give him that.

There *was* a flight simulator of sorts that he'd gotten *Esiluria* to manifest in her library. There were no controls for him to handle, but the AI was advanced enough to interpret the movements of his empty hands to move the ship more or less in relation to where he guided it. His quick wit and sharp, active eye helped him rapidly master the basics. Complex maneuvers were tough, however, given the lack of feedback from his 'ship.' At bottom he was an instinctive flier, and he couldn't engage those instincts without some kind of physical input from his vessel.

Outside of the simulator, *Sentinel* wasn't calculated to entertain one with such a short attention span. The crew were seriously devoted to their work, each of them hand-picked by Krancis for their skill, dedication to duty, and utter lack of need for any kind of social life. In Gromyko's simple judgment, they were little more than brainy automatons.

Soliana had become more human and natural in his estimation. He'd heard something about an intervention by Krancis, but neither of them would elaborate when he asked. Less spiritual and yet more contemplative, he found her an enigma not worth the effort to unwrap.

And that left lieutenant Julia Powers. Pretty, sweet, with just enough military discipline to give her shape and focus without robbing her humanity, he found her more than a little fascinating, if somewhat intimidating to approach. She always treated him nicely whenever they encountered one another. But his utter lack of education, outside of that which could be gleaned from the streets of Midway, made him self-conscious and, for once, tongue tied. With chagrin he compared his present problem to the ease with which he'd wrapped the ladies of Delta-13 around his little finger, at one time having five girlfriends at once. But the sophisticated Powers required more than a flashy personality and dash and verve to hold her interest. She wasn't a bored rustic looking to wrap her hopes around a fantasy.

His thoughts growing too dark to tolerate, Gromyko relieved himself with the thought that, after all, that was just what *he* thought she wanted. Maybe she'd prefer someone thoroughly different from herself.

And *that*, he thought with a grin, was something he could always deliver. *Nobody* was like Gromyko. He was *unique*, a new thing under the sun.

With a little extra bounce in his step, he proceeded down the hall to the nearest teleportation room. Exploring every last crevice of the vessel would have to wait until later.

"To the hospital," he said rather grandly, causing the technician on duty to roll her eyes.

"Wait," she ordered, as he neared the chamber. "Someone's coming through."

Annoyed at having to wait for anything, the smuggler

leaned on his back foot and crossed his arms, drumming his fingers on his bicep until the chamber flashed and Krancis emerged.

"Just the man I was looking for," he said mechanically, completely uninterested in Gromyko. "Come with me," he said, stepping back into the chamber and looking at the technician. "To the sleeping quarters."

"Yes, Krancis," she said deferentially, punching in the destination and sending him on his way.

"What does he want with me?" Gromyko asked himself, somewhat unsettled to be a part of the mysterious man's plans.

"Hard to imagine," the technician muttered, just loud enough for him to hear.

"Oh, say what you want," the smuggler replied proudly as he stepped into the chamber. "But Gromyko is not a man to be trifled with! There will yet be a day when–."

At this the woman stabbed one of the keys before her, and Gromyko disappeared in a bright flash of blue.

"Doesn't that guy *ever* shut up?" she mumbled, sitting down in her chair and pulling out a book she'd been reading.

"...his name is trumpeted from the–," Gromyko continued before halting, realizing the room had changed. "Where am I?" he asked.

"Come on," Krancis said, his hands clasped behind his back as he turned and strode from the room.

Taking several seconds to process what had happened, he noticed the technician nodding his head towards the man who had just left, urging the Deltan to get himself into gear. With quick steps he shot across the room and through the door, catching up with Krancis a dozen paces down the hall.

"So, you finally have a mission for Gromyko?" he asked. "It's about time. My talents have been going to waste! There's no–."

"I want you for a very specific purpose," Krancis cut him off, speaking in his arrestingly precise fashion.

"Soliana."

"Soliana? What can I possibly do for her?" he asked, his heart sinking as the grand adventures he'd imagined awaited him evaporated.

"It's not what you can *do* for her, so much as what you can *be* for her. She's still in a state of considerable confusion, and it's important for the war that she be set straight. There's too much noise inside her mind, and it's limiting her effectiveness."

"And you want the crisp rationality of Gromyko to set her straight?" he asked, hoping to seize *some* glory from his task.

"Hardly. She thinks far too much, and you think far too little. Between the two of you, you ought to be able to reach a satisfactory middle point."

Blindsided by this harsh judgment, the smuggler was without words for a moment.

"I don't…understand…" he said at last, shaking his head slowly.

"There are two ways to deal with the struggle that is consuming Soliana," Krancis explained. "First, is to have a powerful mind, such as my own, walk through her psyche layer by layer and sort out all the confusion. Needless to say, I don't have the time for such a task, and no other such person is aboard *Sentinel* who could perform such work."

"Well, this thing flies faster than spit," Gromyko observed quickly, thinking he'd found a hole in the man's plans. "Can't we just go and pick one up?"

"There's nobody that we can trust with the knowledge she possesses," he replied evenly. "She has had access to *my* mind, and that is a privilege that no one else may enjoy, even by proxy. And that leaves us with the second option, which is to give her a companion who will enable her to solve her own problems."

"But what if someone kidnaps me or something, and starts peeling *my* brain back like an onion?" Gromyko objected, realizing that he could be mere minutes away from putting a massive target on his back. "After all–."

"Soliana will withhold anything that it is not appropriate for you to know," Krancis said. "She is a very powerful psychic, and will be able to guide you within her mind at all times. But she needs someone to steady her once she's in there. The secrets of the human psyche are difficult to grapple with, even if one is both knowledgeable and strong."

"I don't understand. Why does she need me?"

"Because you possess a certain grounded common sense that will be the perfect antidote to the impulses that are most likely to destroy her once she's inside."

"Whoa, wait a minute," the smuggler said emphatically, stopping in his tracks and facing him. "*Destroy her*? You want to send me inside her mind when her *life* is at stake?"

"It won't be at stake with you in there," Krancis replied simply, resuming movement. "And you may rest assured, your task is quite minimal. As I said, it isn't what you can *do* for her, but what you can *be*, and that is, an anchor back to reality. Much of her mind is nearly a fantasy, and she has a difficult time telling truth and falsehood apart. You will be a palpable reminder of normalcy for her, keeping her from descending into madness."

"But why me?" he insisted. "Why not one of the hospital doctors? Or a nurse or something? I don't have any experience with this sort of thing."

"That isn't entirely true. You have experienced psychic phenomena before, back on Delta-13 when you were screened for your brief stint in the Order."

"You really do know everything, don't you?" Gromyko asked, unsure if he should be impressed or alarmed about what else he might know.

"Besides, you're familiar to Soliana. She's seen you under many different conditions, and she trusts you. It's unlikely that she will work with anyone else, due to the sheer vulnerability that the task requires. She's formed a bond with the entire original group that encountered her inside the Black Hole, and she enjoys a sense of intimacy with you all. Doctor Tselitel is in Quarlac with the emperor; and Hunt and Pinchon are on a mission. Given his simple, unpretentious personality, Milo would have been the logical choice for such a task. But with that an impossibility, we are left with you."

"You mean I'm your *last* choice for this thing?" he asked, deflating further. "Boy, you sure know how to build a guy up."

"You'll manage, despite your present feelings," Krancis told him, stopping before Soliana's door and opening it. "Come inside."

Finding the girl sitting on the end of her bed, Gromyko stood somewhat shyly aside as Krancis explained his plan. Evidently it was a revelation to Soliana as well, who was not eager to explore her psyche on her own. However, her every objection was irrefutably answered by the man in black, until finally she could only nod her head in acquiescence.

"Begin at once," he instructed them as he left. "There is no time to lose."

Once the door had closed, and Krancis' feet had retreated down the hall, Gromyko moved between Soliana and the place on the wall she'd been staring at for nearly a minute.

"So, um," he began, trying to think of what to say.

"I don't want to do this," she said abjectly. "To plumb the depths of your own mind is not a pleasant experience, especially when you're unsure what you'll find."

"But that's what makes it interesting," the smuggler assured her, taking a chair and turning it around so he could rest his arms atop its backrest as he looked at her. "It's like an adventure. It wouldn't be any fun if you knew in advance how it would turn out."

"I'm not looking to have *fun!*" she said forcefully, her eyes finding his and boring into them with an anger that surprised him. "I want *stability*, I want *calm*. For as long as I can remember, my mind has always been filled with nothing but *chaos*. Sheer, uncontrollable, undulating *chaos!* I'm not after any more *excitement!* I just want to find peace!"

"You're not going to find peace by hiding from the things that scare you," he replied. "Sometimes you've gotta be brave and face down the stuff that's threatening you. After that, it can't come after you. You've beaten it."

"This isn't something you *beat*," she said. "This isn't some animal that you can fight off with a stick or throw rocks at. We're talking about the shape and contents of my *psyche*. I've been abused, manipulated, and reformed until I don't know what's truly me and what isn't anymore. You've never known anything like that in your life! Your mind has always been a given, a solid, uniform entity that you could rely on at any time. But I'm fragmentary and broken. At times I'm calm and at peace, in full possession of my mood and reactions. And other times, I'm passing from one state to the next in rapid succession. It's like having multiple personalities. It wasn't until," she paused, thinking of the episode with *Eesekkalion* and deciding she still wouldn't mention it. "It wasn't until *recently* that I gained a measure of self-control. Now I know myself, at least partially. There's an island in the middle of my mind that I can stand on, knowing for sure that it's me. But I'm surrounded by dark and shadowy lands that threaten to overwhelm me if I'm not careful. At any time I could slip back into one of the old fragments and lose control again."

"That's why I'm here," he assured her. "To make sure that doesn't happen. To be an *anchor*."

"I'm frightened," she confessed, her body slumping a little now that she'd burned off some of her anger at Krancis. "I've never known normalcy before, even a little bit of it. I don't want to lose what I've got by chasing after more."

"From what Krancis told me, we don't have any choice. You've gotta be able to perform."

"Krancis wants a prophetess," Soliana replied. "He wants a seer that will give us an edge. I admit that I've served in that capacity of late, though I nearly got us all destroyed and ended any chance of human survival because of our duel with the dark world. That is a burden I do not wish to bear."

Pleadingly her eyes looked at him, and in their softness Gromyko realized something. With her immense mental powers he'd never realized that she was, at bottom, just a scared, confused kid. She didn't want the role she'd been given. More than anything she wished to leave it behind and lead a normal life. Well, as normal of a life as one could, given the Devourers...

"Are you listening to me?" she asked with irritation, noticing the reflective look in his eyes as he thought. "Am I boring you?"

"No, no," he assured her, raising his palms towards her and shaking his head. "Absolutely not. I was just thinking about how brave you are to have held up in all of this," he lied, hoping to give her a little confidence for the task ahead.

"I don't know *what* I am," she replied. "But I'm not brave. I just wish none of this had ever happened to me."

To his surprise her eyes began to moisten, and a little tremor of fear played through his heart. It was *one* thing to plunge into someone's mind when they were cool and confident. But if they were coming apart at the seams...

"Are you alright?" he asked hesitantly, swallowing from the tension that he felt growing within him.

"I'm okay," she replied, pulling up the edge of her blanket and wiping her eyes. "I'm sorry. Sometimes I think of what might have been, how my life could have turned out if I hadn't been taken, and I get a little emotional."

"Taken?"

"I didn't come by all these thoughts and fragments naturally, Antonin," she said self-evidently.

"No, of course not," he agreed, feeling a little stupid.

"Well, it's not like Krancis is going to let us off the

hook," she said, taking a deep breath and letting it out. "We'd better get started."

"What should I do?" Gromyko asked, trying to remember what Wanda had done with him back on Delta. "Do I need to touch your head or something to go inside?"

"No, I'll pull you in with me," she told him, rising from the bed and looking around her room for a moment. "We might be in there for a while," she mused aloud. "We'd better make ourselves comfortable. I don't want any problems with the connection once we're inside."

"Whatever you say," he uttered willingly, standing up and putting the chair aside.

"Come over here," she said, moving to the middle of her small living room's floor and laying down. "Now, put your head on my stomach."

"For real?" he asked, amused at the thought.

"I'm not making a pass at you, Antonin," she said with a frown. "This way I'll be able to rest my hands on your head without any risk of them falling off. We'll enjoy a strong and steady connection."

"I'm game," he said with a little flourish of his eyebrows as he dropped to the floor, his comment forcing her to fight off a grin. Lining up at a ninety degree angle, he rested the back of his head on her soft stomach, finding it surprisingly comfortable. The urge to flirt again crossed his mind, but he pushed it away for her sake. "What now?" he asked in a clear, workmanlike tone.

Without bothering to utter another word, Soliana laced her fingers together and rested her two palms on his forehead. He was about to object to her wrist covering his mouth and partially mashing his nose when the world around him slipped away, and he was surrounded by a gently glowing mist of white.

"What in the…" his voice trailed, as he found himself standing beside her on a small, hard disc of black. "You could give a guy a little warning, you know!"

"I thought you liked adventure," she teased, a smile on her face.

"Well, where are we supposed to go?" he asked, looking uneasily over the side of the disc at what appeared to be an endlessly empty space. "Not gonna see much from here."

"Oh, be patient," she said, her mood light and sprightly, to his surprise. "It takes a moment to drag up the right places from the different portions of my psyche. If they were all crammed in one place, the mind couldn't function. It needs to be able to move from one segment to the other."

"So it has to pick and choose," Gromyko summarized, still looking at the emptiness beneath them. "Think of some things and not others."

"Yes, exactly."

Forcing himself to look up, he reached out a hand and put it on her shoulder as he began to feel a little dizzy.

"Are you…okay?" she asked, glancing at his hand and then at his face. "Are you afraid of heights?"

"Just when there's nothing between me and them except for a whole lot of air," he admitted.

"Don't worry. I'll get us on firmer ground in a moment," she replied, closing her eyes and causing the mist to evaporate. What took its place was a beautiful nature scene, with long, flowing grass, trees, flowers, and a creek trickling a short distance away. "Is that better?" she asked.

Carefully looking down, he was glad to find the emptiness filled. Releasing her shoulder, he reached a foot off the disc and tested the ground. FInding it solid, he stepped down and looked around.

"This place doesn't look so bad," he commented, putting his hands on his hips as he surveyed. "Don't see why you were reluctant to come. Your mind is very pretty and peaceful."

"This is just one part of it," she explained, though quietly flattered by his comment. "Every psyche has parts that are nice, neutral, and bad. I picked this spot so that we could get oriented before plunging into the bad stuff."

"We don't *know* that other stuff is bad," he objected, turning towards her and dropping his hands from his hips. "We've got to explore, okay? See it for ourselves."

"All I know is that I'd rather be without it," she said. Though her words were negative, her mood was still light and friendly. Intuitively Gromyko realized that the place they occupied had a certain influence on her mental state, and it was with some misgivings that he contemplated moving into darker turf. "Ready?" she asked, a little too soon for his taste.

"Absolutely," he replied, though far less eager than he sounded. "Let's get to it."

With a smile and a nod she reached for his hand and took it.

"So we don't get separated in here," she said. "The human psyche is a slippery thing to explore. We don't want to get lost."

Hardly averse to the contact, Gromyko smiled in return and followed where she gently pulled him. Just past the creek he could see what looked like purple ground separated from them by a chasm and a thick wall of mist. Splashing through the water, they were at the end of the grass within minutes.

"That was short lived," the smuggler observed with regret, sensing her mood begin to dip as they left the happiness of the space behind them.

"There's been very little joy in my life," she replied, her shoulders starting to sag, and her grip on his hand slackening.

"How do we get across?" he asked, looking into the chasm with aversion. "Can you make a bridge?"

"There's one off to our left," she said, pointing a couple hundred feet away. It was narrow and brown, as though made of wood. It looked to be two feet wide.

"*That?*" he asked pointedly.

"The different portions of my mind are sharply divided," she said, pulling him along the edge of the green space towards the bridge. "I speculate that that's by design, allowing me to inhabit many different mental states and perspectives without the interference of the others. But it means that the connections are necessarily few and narrow. I have a very limited ability to cross from one to the other as a matter of will. Most of the time they drag *me* into *them*."

"That's like being a hostage," he replied, gaining greater insight into the daily struggle that took place inside her mind.

"You can see why I want to leave it all behind."

Reaching the bridge, they released each other's hands and started across. Gromyko went first, moving his legs in short, steady steps whilst holding his hands at hip level for balance. As the purple ground neared, he began to make out more detail through the fog. The grass looked purple as well, but sickly, thin, and ready to die. There were black trees with purple leaves, and flowers of the same colors. The entire space seemed to be on life-support, some unseen force keeping it alive.

Soliana began muttering behind him, and it took all his resolve not to look back and see that she was alright. That would have to wait until his feet were on solid ground once more.

"Okay," he said with an exhale, stepping off the bridge into the purple grass and turning around. "Time to go–," he stopped, seeing that his companion was still twenty feet from the bridge's end. "Soliana?"

"No," she shook her head resolutely, her feet locked in place. "I can't do it. I can't go over there."

"Yes, you can," he assured her, reluctantly getting back onto the bridge and glancing into the emptiness below. It made his head spin, but he raised his eyes to the girl and inched towards her. "You've got to come off the bridge. You can't stay there."

"I can't," she repeated.

Wordlessly he reached her and gently took her hand. She didn't resist as he pulled her slowly towards the purple island, taking careful, nerve-wracking steps backwards on the narrow bridge. He could see her face fall into a deeper and deeper gloom as they approached the strange place.

"You're okay," he said, as they moved off the bridge and the grass softly crunched beneath them. With her eyes downcast she followed him inland, the trees looming above them as they walked. "Weird plants," he commented, his tone incongruously calm and normal in their bizarre surroundings.

"This is one of the places I hate to go," she explained, still watching her feet as he drew her along. "It's not a happy part of my mind."

"What is it? Why does everything look so funny?"

"I don't know," she replied, stealing a look at the trees before ducking her head, as though their branches would reach down and strike her. "The unconscious has a way of representing things that sometimes obfuscates their true form. Mythological language and symbols are used."

"I remember something about that from Delta-13," he uttered, trying to recall what Wanda had told him. But the pull of the present was too strong, and he couldn't focus long enough to drag up the memory. "Weird," he repeated, before catching himself. "Uh, this isn't part of your mind, is it? I mean, it's an implant, right?"

"It's hard to say what is and isn't," she said in a dreary tone, her depression worsening. "What's really us, anyway? How can we draw sharp lines between what's original and what isn't?"

Realizing their present course would get them nowhere, Gromyko decided to change tack.

"Okay, so we're trying to settle all the confusion in here, right? So why don't we get away from all this depressing stuff and go somewhere that's jumbled up instead?"

"Is that what Krancis told you we were doing?"

"Yeah, more or less."

"These *are* the jumbles, Antonin," she said, halting and releasing his hand so she could extend hers out from her sides. "It's not as if I'm confused in the normal sense. I have different personalities vying for dominance. The point is to process what's going on inside, and assimilate these warring factions over time. And that requires exposure."

"So we're just going to hang around here until you get used to all this purple stuff?" he asked. "Doesn't seem very straightforward."

"The human mind often isn't," she replied, lowering her arms and walking slowly towards the middle of the island. "This space, the part of it that you can see, is only a *tiny* portion of what is actually taking place in this part of my psyche. It's like an iceberg, where you can only see the very top poking out above the water. This island is *deep*, and within it are housed all the thoughts, memories, and intuitions that bubble up from time to time and sweep me off my feet. The point of my being here is to familiarize myself with them, allowing them to make connections to my core personality and grow it out in time."

"So...like a city that gradually absorbs the villages around it, making one big block?" he asked, rather impressed with his own analogy.

"You could say that."

"But won't that change you? Won't that 'broadening' make you into something else?"

"That's another reason I'm reluctant to do this," she admitted in a small voice, dashing a glance at him before continuing to watch her feet move under her. "All my life I've just wanted to be *me*. But the war means that I have to take these implanted portions and make them a part of myself. I won't be a solid, single entity any more. I'll be more like a patchwork quilt, formed of different pieces. I just hope that, at the center of it all, something essentially *me* will remain. I don't want to be someone else."

"I don't want that, either," he replied sincerely, watching his own feet. "But if anyone can do this, I'm sure you can," he added in a brighter voice, trying to push away the gloom. "You must have a strong personality, or these different implants would have overwhelmed you by now. That's probably why the people who added them chose you instead of someone else."

"I can't say why I was chosen," she uttered, her voice becoming almost a whisper as they passed under the boughs of a massive black and purple tree. "I only wish they hadn't."

Lacking anything encouraging to say, he simply took her hand again. To his satisfaction, she squeezed him back firmly.

"So, it's the inside of this iceberg that's got the insights and whatnot?" he asked.

"Yes, that's right."

"So should we get a shovel and start digging, or what?"

Despite her low mood, his question made her chuckle.

"It doesn't work quite like that. We're walking along the surface because that's all we can do. This island represents an entire implanted portion; a self-sustaining, if incomplete, personality. Over time I can assimilate it through contact. But I can't–."

Suddenly her words were interrupted by a massive root that tripped her. With a yelp she fell forwards, nearly striking the ground but for Gromyko's quickness in jerking her hand upwards. She swung down to his feet, bumping into his legs and almost knocking him over. Taking her other hand, he pulled her upright again.

"You okay?" he asked.

"Yes, I think so," she replied, brushing her long hair back from her face and looking at the root. "I could have sworn that wasn't there a moment ago. Did you see it?"

"I don't know. I guess so," he said, searching his

memory but drawing a blank. "Must have been too busy talking."

"I suppose," she agreed with some reservations, eyeing it a moment longer before turning and resuming their walk. "Anyway, like I was saying, the personality has to be assimilated whole. Being self-sustaining, it would try to defend itself against any attack on it."

"So shovels are out," he laughed at himself.

"I'm afraid so. You see, what you're seeing beside you isn't really my body. It's just a personified expression of my consciousness. The same is true of your body. Because of the mythological nature of the human unconscious, things in this domain that have no physical existence are nevertheless *represented* in a physical way. It allows us to interact with them and make sense of them. Without this kind of translation, if you will, the conscious mind could never understand the processes that are running at all times in the back of the psyche. It would be a stranger in its own house."

"And it's in the unconscious that those people stuck all these personalities and all that knowledge?"

"Yes. It's ideal, really, because the unconscious can sustain them as separate entities."

"But wouldn't it make sense to put it, I don't know, in the *front* of your mind, so you could access all that stuff easily?"

"It would flood me with too much information. I would be drowning in data and insights and intuitions."

"Seems like a pretty clumsy system," Gromyko observed.

"It's far from being my favorite. But I don't think anything else could be done. Not," she hastened to add, "that I appreciate it having been done to me, anyway."

"I know," he nodded, before noticing that her mood seemed to have lightened again despite their presence on the strange island. "Are you feeling better?"

She paused and thought for a moment.

"Not better," she clarified. "But…different. Like this personality isn't affecting me as much as before." Her eyes narrowed. "I'm not sure that's a good thing. No, no it isn't."

"Why not?" he asked. "Maybe you're getting used to it already."

"No, I can feel that it has pulled away from me," she said in a darkening voice, her face tightening with consternation. "It knows what we're trying to do, and it doesn't like it. It's trying to retain its own independence."

"But how can it do that? It's just an implant."

"One with its own aims and desires. That's why it fights with me. That's why it, and the others, keep trying to take me over. Sometimes they push me aside, and sometimes they just influence my nature. But they're trying to have their own way, all the same. The purpose here is to tame them, to bring them into the fold. Especially before they–."

"Down!" Gromyko bellowed, tackling her around the middle as a giant black branch from a nearby tree swept out to strike her. Sailing over their heads as they dropped to the ground, it snapped back into place as thin, wiry roots began to rise out of the grass like worms and wrap themselves around her. "Soliana!" he shouted, trying to peel them off as she struggled against them.

"Help me!" she screamed, a band of them encircling her stomach and trying to draw her into the soil.

Fiercely Gromyko tore at them, ripping the little things to pieces and jerking Soliana to her feet. Some were still wrapped around her ankles, but between the two of them they were quickly snapped off.

Running to open grass, they turned and saw the trees shaking with violent menace, their branches creaking and their leaves rustling. Their roots burst from the ground like a thousand tiny snakes, each of them wriggling in the air and hungering to finish what they'd started.

"This…is not good," Gromyko commented, holding the trembling girl against his side as her chest heaved for air.

"It's fighting back," she gasped, pointing at the trees. "The personality is trying to assimilate *me*. It wants to consume me and become the dominant portion of the psyche."

"Then we've got to break it down. Get an ax or something to tame it."

"It doesn't work like that here," she reiterated. "We'd only be damaging the very thing that I'm trying to absorb into my own nature. It would be like ingesting cancer cells."

"Well, it's not like we can *talk* to it," the smuggler said, as the roots continued to dance above the ground.

"We need another way," Soliana mused. "A different angle of approach. It's like it got scared and attacked." She fell silent for several seconds as she thought. "Of course. That's *exactly* what it did."

"What?"

"It detected that I was trying to break and absorb it while retaining my own nature unchanged. Rationally I'd accepted the need to 'grow' my personality in order to make myself whole. But deep in here," she said, putting a hand to her heart, "I was just as resistant as ever. Instead of *assimilating* the different pieces, I was trying to *subjugate* them. In a defensive move, the personality attacked, trying to preserve itself as I would have done."

"I still don't see what we can do about…" his voice trailed, as his eyes went from her to the trees, and he saw that they were calming down. "That," he said a moment later.

"It can feel a change in my thinking," she said, closing her eyes as she spoke. "It's losing its fear." Slowly she walked forwards, but he pulled her back.

"You can't go back there," he insisted. "It's just trying to lull you so it can bury you for keeps."

"No, I can feel its sincerity," she assured him. "It won't hurt me so long as I let go of my intention to crush it. It recognizes that it's part of a broader system, and that it must cooperate with the strengthened will that Krancis' intervention has given me."

"Intervention?" he asked.

"That's a secret," she told him. "Just between us."

"Oh, I won't spill," he replied. "But I still think this is a bad idea."

"Come on," she said softly, nodding towards the trees. "You'll see."

Reluctantly he followed where her hand drew him, watching the trees for any sign of hostility. But they merely swayed in the breeze, and their roots had retreated back under ground. His body tense, and his eyes shifting every which way, he didn't notice that he'd begun to crush the girl's hand.

"Antonin," she said calmly.

"What?" he asked distractedly.

"My hand is about to snap in two."

"Oh!" he replied, loosening his grip as they returned to the tree whose roots had wrapped around her belly. "What are you feeling?"

"Curiosity," she said quietly, as the wind whispered through the leaves. "It's curious about the new resolve that I now possess. It's also curious about you."

"Tell it to mail me a letter sometime," he replied with aversion, simultaneously wondering if it could somehow penetrate his mind and see his thoughts. He felt her hand let go of his, and slowly she walked towards the tree's trunk. "Hey," he cautioned her, beginning to follow.

"Shh," she said, holding up a hand to stop him as she continued to walk on soft feet. Reaching the tree, she placed her hands on it and bowed her head, pressing the top of her skull against it.

Gromyko watched her with misgivings, still suspecting that she was being tricked. He inched as close as he felt he could without offending her, and then stood guard over the innumerable little holes in the ground through which the roots had appeared. Faintly he could hear her muttering something, but it was impossible to say what it was. Then the roots slowly began to poke out of the ground again. Not aggressively as before, but cautiously.

"Soliana," he said warningly, backing towards her and ready to slip an arm around her middle and run off with her if necessary.

"That's my fault," she uttered serenely, the soothing tone of her voice seemingly charming the roots back into their holes, for they retreated from sight. "I'm sorry."

"Don't be," he replied, before realizing she wasn't talking to him. With a shrug he moved a step closer to the tree and crossed his arms.

The minutes seemingly turned to hours as they stood there, though Gromyko couldn't tell if his sense of time inside her mind bore any relation to that he felt in the outside world. Boredom began to sink in, and it was with difficulty that he kept his mind on his task. The roots refused to reappear, and over time he relaxed and leaned against the tree next to Soliana.

"So…peaceful…" she almost moaned, her mouth hanging open as though she were asleep. "So…calm…"

With a grin he turned to look at her, finding her spiritualistic communion a little much to swallow. He wanted to make a crack about it, but knew better than to break her concentration. Wiping the grin from his lips with the back of his hand, he let his eyes wander across the purple landscape around him, trying to find something to stimulate himself with.

At last she pushed off the tree, raising drowsy eyes to his and smiling slowly.

"It's done," she whispered, a look of deep satisfaction on her face. "It has been assimilated."

"What, that's it?" he asked with surprise. "That seemed awfully simple. Just hug a tree for a few hours."

"Simple for you," she replied groggily. "But I was in a state of complex communication with it the entire time I was in contact with the tree."

"So what did you do? Negotiate with it?"

"It's difficult to explain," she uttered, trying to walk but unsteady on her feet.

"Here," he said, offering her his arm.

"Thank you," she said appreciatively, as they began to walk from the tree. "I just need to get my legs under me. It took a lot of energy to interact with the personality. It's large and dynamic, and required constant focus to keep up with. I'm afraid I'm a little jumbled."

"Do you want to lay down?"

"No," she shook her head, gathering her thoughts. "I think it's about time we left. We've accomplished a great deal for a single day. I never imagined that this would be possible. I thought it would be a terrible experience, but I actually feel wonderful, more complete. Though I'm very tired."

"Well, I'm ready to leave whenever you are. Just say the word."

In lieu of a word she acted, taking both his hands in hers and dissolving the mythic space around them. In moments he was back inside her room, his head still comfortably nestled on her stomach.

"How do you feel?" he asked.

"Just lie still for a while," she whispered, unknitting her fingers and draping her left hand across his neck and shoulders. "Just lie still."

She hardly had to tell him twice. Enjoying the warmth of her touch, he crossed his ankles and clasped his hands over his own stomach, smiling as he closed his eyes.

"I want to thank you, Antonin," she said after an interval. "I don't think I could have done that without you. It takes a special person to put a tumultuous mind at rest. You have a soothing presence for me, deep inside my mind. Your groundedness helps to calm me."

"You're welcome," he replied, noticing that her words mirrored those that Krancis had spoken hours earlier.

Seemed the old man *did* know how to pick 'em...

"I need to rest now," she said, removing her arm and implying that it was time for him to leave. "I need to sleep."

"Sure," he replied, sitting up and getting to his feet. Taking her hands, he slowly pulled her upwards, carefully not to rush the blood to her head. "If ever you need Gromyko again, you know where to find him," he said grandly, cracking one of his thousand watt smiles.

"You needn't act, Antonin," she said perceptively. "I know you're special without your needing to resort to dramatic tricks."

With an awkward chuckle he nodded to her, finding her words hit a little too close to the mark for comfort. Releasing her hands, he made for the door.

"Thank you again," she said mildly.

With a brief turn and a wave, he opened the door and stepped out.

"I see you made it back," a voice said from behind him, as he looked down the hall to the right.

"Daaah!" the smuggler said, jumping half out of his skin at the unexpected voice. Turning around, he saw Krancis leaning against the wall to the left of the door. "Don't you have anything better to do than spy on me?"

"I'd hardly spend my time spying on you, Gromyko," he replied self-evidently, beginning to walk. "How was your journey?"

"Just fine," the smuggler said rather flippantly, his dander up. "Went for a nature walk, hugged some trees, nearly got strangled to death by a bunch of roots. Nothing too weird."

"That was to be expected. Did you think that a foreign intellect would give up its autonomy easily?"

Embarrassed that the question had never once crossed his mind, Gromyko felt the best policy was silence, though that didn't help him.

"I thought not," Krancis replied evenly, observing a

fact rather than scoring a point.

"Hey, you're the one who chose *me* because I *don't* think enough," he objected, realizing immediately after that that wasn't the best play he could make.

Krancis, mercifully, let it drop.

"What else did you see?"

"Not a lot else. Chasms between big islands of… personality…stuff. Stood around for a while as she assimilated one of the islands. There was this funny little wooden bridge that ran between it and the main one. Frankly I wish the connections were a little bigger. But she said that wasn't really possible."

"Not at the time," Krancis informed him. "By the time you return you'll find they've deepened their connection. Her own ego consciousness must be dominant, so they will never fuse together into a solid whole. But they will cooperate in the future."

"You know, it's funny," Gromyko observed. "She was scared to death to get on that island, yet she was really happy when it was finally assimilated. She thought it would alter her personality, but she came away from the whole thing all warm and fuzzy. What's the deal with that?"

"The assimilation *did* alter her personality," he explained with the hint of a frown on the edges of his lips. "That's why she was content with the change afterwards, but scared of it beforehand. Her point of view has already begun to shift, and her values along with them."

"You mean she's becoming a different person?" the smuggler asked, not liking the idea. "Wait, I know, I know: what did I expect would happen?"

"Just so. You can't fuse multiple identities together without affecting the original. With each completed step in the chain, Soliana will evolve. Her psychic presence aboard this ship has already changed."

"And you're okay with that?" Gromyko asked, his keen eye aware that the mysterious man, despite all his coldness, cared for the young woman.

"She is a mere weapon of war at this point," he replied, stopping before a teleportation room door. "As are we all." Going inside, he made for the chamber and added, "Your task is done for the day, Gromyko. Good work." With this he ordered the technician to send him to the bridge, and disappeared in a blue flash.

"Huh," the smuggler mumbled, surprised to have his efforts recognized by a man he was certain didn't like him. Growing aware of the technician's inquiring eyes as they gazed upon him, he stepped into the chamber and requested the library. In an instant he was inside, finding it as he'd left it.

"Hello, Antonin," *Esiluria* said in her sweet manner. "Are you here to practice your flying some more?"

"No," he shook his head, moving across the room and joining her hologram at the table. "Do you think Krancis likes me?"

"I'm afraid not," she replied as kindly as she could. "Your two natures are too different to appreciate each other on a personal level. Though Krancis is a pragmatic soul, so it's possible for anyone to please him, given that they satisfy his aims."

"I guess that's it, then," he nodded to himself, slipping a leg onto the table and letting it lay there. "Well, what do we do now?"

"I'm ready to facilitate anything you wish to do," she replied helpfully.

"I don't know what I want to do," he said, feeling himself slowly grow confused. Something was bubbling up from the back of his mind, but he didn't know quite what it was. Like a dark cloud it was filling his psyche, casting doubt on all his thoughts. "Do I look alright to you, *Esiluria*?" he asked, wondering if he was getting sick.

"According to my instruments, you're quite healthy. Though there are early indications that you've over indulged in low quality alcohol. I recommend limiting your consumption in the future."

"Thanks," he chuckled, that not being quite the answer he was looking for. Dropping his leg from the table, he stood up with a yawn and made for the teleporter. "I think I'll hit the sack. Sorry for bothering you."

"I'm always ready to aid the Earthborn in anything they wish to pursue," she replied pleasantly, teleporting him moments later.

Yawning again as he exited the chamber, he walked slowly to his room, encountering Powers along the way.

"Oh, hello," he said blandly, his tone higher than usual, his manner growing slack and unfocused.

"Hello," she replied, eyeing him with some concern. "Are you alright?" she asked, only barely resisting the urge of her solicitous spirit to put a hand to his forehead. "You don't look well."

"Truth be told, I *do* feel a little funny," he said, his equilibrium beginning to weaken. "I think I'll go to my room and sleep it off."

"Do you want me to go with you?" she asked, as he began to walk away from her.

"N-no, I'm–," he started to say, turning to look at her but losing his balance and falling against the wall.

"Yes, yes, I will," she said quickly, moving to where he was and getting under his arm.

"I'm okay," he insisted, unable to figure out what was wrong with his legs. "Wait," he slurred, stopping before a door. "This is mine."

Opening it for him, Powers helped him over to the bed and got him under the covers. Drawing them up under his neck, she briefly leaned in to smell his breath, but was surprised to find it clean.

"Thanks," he muttered, no longer aware of anything but the soft mattress beneath his body and the blankets that covered him. "Thanks…" he trailed.

With concern she pulled away and watched him for a moment. In seconds he was snoring softly, seemingly in a state of perfect peace. Wracking her brains for an explanation, she eventually shook her head and made for the door. Closing it softly, she made it part way down the hall when she encountered Krancis.

"Is something wrong?" he asked, reading the worry on her face.

"Oh, sir," she stumbled, unsure if she was being silly to worry. "It's nothing."

"I saw you leaving Gromyko's room," he replied. "Have anything to do with him?"

"Yes, sir," she admitted. "He was acting strangely, like he was drunk. I barely helped him into bed before he passed out."

Krancis smiled.

"Yes, I thought so. He's been through quite an ordeal today, and that tends to take it out of the uninitiated. He'll be alright after a good rest."

"But what's wrong with him, sir?"

"Let's say he's been equal parts explorer and explored," he said cryptically, before resuming his walk and leaving her alone in the corridor.

For many hours Gromyko slept, his mind filled with strange dreams and images that paraded themselves through his psyche of their own accord. It was as though some inner train of thought had been activated, and quite indifferent to his wishes, dragged him along for the ride. He found that he could clearly remember all that had happened in Soliana's mind, as if one eye was upon that set of experiences, and the other was watching the unusual happenings of his own unconscious. Intuitively he grasped that the two were intertwined, that the one had caused the other to spring to life and manifest itself. The realization was uncomfortable, for there were many strange things inside his mind that he preferred, in his waking hours, to push aside and ignore. But now they forced themselves upon him, causing him to see them whether he wanted to or not.

Before him arose the black silhouettes of mountains against a background of muted red. Like objects held before a bright light, he could make out none of their details, squint though he might. The silhouettes began to near, before splitting into two groups, each one passing on either side of him. Just ahead he saw a small figure, crouched into a little ball, standing on the balls of his feet. His arms were tightly wrapped around his legs, his head held close to his knees. Curiously Gromyko eyed him, trying to draw near but unable to, still a passive viewer in his own mind.

A quiver then passed through the figure, and with tremendous reluctance he arose and stood flatly on his feet. This done, his resolve was now firm. Finding a sword in his hand, he pointed it up into the sky and began to rise above the mountains on a pillar of stone.

Standing near the base of the pillar, it wasn't long before Gromyko could no longer see the figure. The vision made him uneasy, though he couldn't imagine why.

When finally he awoke, the smuggler made to roll out of bed but *fell* out instead. Finding his body still lethargic, he laid on the floor upon his back, rubbing his face to work away sleep's residue. Attempting to rise, he found his limbs slow but willing to move.

"Never felt like that before," he muttered, shambling slowly through his room. "Well, not recently."

His mouth dry and his stomach rumbling for food, he walked into the hall and collided with a man walking past. Mumbling something in apology, he realized that his brain was still several steps behind the rest of his body, and he resolved to take things slow. Making for the ship's commissary, he grabbed coffee and anything with sugar in it to try and stimulate his mind. With two cups in one hand, and a plate full of sweets in the other, he made for a table in the back of the spacious room and dropped into a chair. His back to the wall, he found comfort in being able to watch everyone else. Manifestly he was outside normal eating hours, for many of the tables were empty, and the staff behind the counter were chatting with each other as thought it was their day off.

Eyeing the plate, he found no energy with which to eat. The coffee he downed quickly enough, finding it made a small dent in his lethargy. Filling his cups again, he returned to his table to find Krancis had taken the chair opposite his.

"Didn't think you needed to eat," the smuggler said in a tired voice, dropping heavily into his seat and nearly splashing his coffee on the table. Pausing to drink one of the cups, he clanked the empty mug down and looked at the man in black.

"How did you sleep?" he asked, leaning back in his seat, one leg thrown over the other and an arm across the back of the seat next to him.

"Lousy," Gromyko groused, taking a bite out of a donut. "I don't think you can even call it sleep. More like a movie that never stopped." Find it too much work to chew, he simply ran his upper teeth across the rest of the donut's icing, melting it in his mouth before swallowing. "What did you sign me up for, anyhow?"

"*You* signed up for this," Krancis pointed out.

"Well, you put me on to it," he replied, de-icing another donut and finishing his other cup of coffee. "I'm all for helping people. Just ask anyone in the Underground and they'll tell you." He paused and squinted, realizing how out of date that point of reference was, especially since he was likely the only surviving member of that defunct organization. "I'm all for helping people," he started again. "But whatever's going on inside that girl's mind is above my paygrade."

"Has the Hope Of The People finally met his match?" Krancis asked with a hint of a smile around his mouth.

"Look, I didn't sign on for this," he said, finding it

difficult to vary his word choice. "You said I'd drop into her mind and help her out by just being there. You didn't say *anything* about having *my* mind fiddled around with. There's a difference."

About to strip another donut, he reached for his first cup of coffee and realized it was empty. His eyes clouding as to how that happened, he shook his head and arose to refill them. Patiently Krancis waited for him to return.

"And another thing," he said, sitting down again. "I didn't sign up for this!"

"I think you've made that point already."

Puzzled, the smuggler's eyes darted around as he searched his memory. Finding that he *had* made that point already, he added, "Well, it bears repeating."

"Surely," the man across from him said, uncrossing his leg and leaning in a little closer. "I didn't come here to listen to your problems, Gromyko. What you're going through is a predictable reaction to the stimulus you've received. And to some extent you're correct: you *didn't* sign up for everything that you experienced."

"Aha!" he exclaimed, drawing the attention of the handful of other people in the room. "So you admit that I'm right."

"I acknowledge that you got more than you'd bargained for," Krancis stipulated. "Given your fearfulness of anything approaching–."

"*Fearfulness!*" he exploded.

"…anything approaching your inner world," he continued, "there was no other way to handle you."

"First, nobody *handles* Gromyko!" he insisted, standing up and finding his balance was still a little off. Steadying himself with the table, he sat down again. "And second…" his voice trailed, realizing Krancis was right about his fear.

"Second?" he queried.

"Well, it's not a very decent way to treat people, hiding

stuff from them."

"You mean to say you never hid anything from your subordinates in the Underground?"

Shifting uncomfortably in his seat, he de-iced another donut.

"Look, you'd better find yourself another boy," the smuggler said at last, the cool gaze of the other man working on him. "I'm not built for this sort of thing."

"You're perfect for it," Krancis told him with certainty. "That's why you're finding it so troubling."

"Perfect? I feel like, I don't know, I've been *drugged* or something."

"You haven't been drugged. You've been acquainted with a portion of your mind that has been neglected for far too long. That's why you're disoriented. Your psyche has been jarred, and you need to give it time to find balance again."

"But *why* am I feeling this way?" he asked.

"Because the implants embedded in Soliana were examining you, interacting with your mind."

"*What?!*" he shouted, not only drawing but retaining the attention of the room. Even the staff behind the counter leaned their arms upon it and stared. "You–, you mean–," he sputtered, unable to put his outrage into words.

"One syllable at a time, Gromyko," Krancis ordered him, his tone neither friendly nor abrasive, but neutrally firm. Casting a brief glance across the room, he sent the other occupants back to their tasks. "Now, try again."

"You…are…testing…Gromyko's…limits…" the smuggler enunciated, barely holding in his rage. Having voiced this much of his anger, his words began to flow more smoothly. "To deceive Gromyko is one thing. But this is *unforgivable!* He is not a mere picture book to be flipped through by alien intelligences! By what right–."

"By the only right that I require," Krancis uttered in his crisp way. "The right of human survival. Soliana has an important part to play in this war. But she is still lost and confused. It's up to you to ensure that she finds her way out of the labyrinth that she's been put in."

"Get another boy," the Deltan said resolutely. "I'll not be manipulated like this."

"It's too late to get someone else. The implants have already begun to attach themselves to you. Evidently you haven't thought this matter through, so I'll explain it a little more thoroughly."

"Please do," he said, tossing up his hands and leaning back in his seat.

"The implants function as separate personalities, each with their own values and peculiar insights. As independent people, more or less, they have their own likes and dislikes. That, incidentally, is another reason why I cannot help Soliana without enormous difficulties: most of the personalities don't like me."

"Imagine that."

"But they are calculated to like you," he continued. "Because your naive, surface-level intellect possesses nothing that could threaten them. They're only concerned by powerful minds that could push them aside. That's an extra reason that they give Soliana so much trouble: her mind isn't strong enough to grapple with them, not by a long shot. But with the proper guidance, she could learn to in time. So they alternate between trying to dominate her and confusing her. They practice what might be called psychological black ops. They want her perpetually off balance in order to preserve themselves."

"Then what are we even doing inside her mind?" objected the smuggler. "If she's being pulled in sixteen different directions, we're just wasting our time."

"As you already know, we are striving to *assimilate* those personalities into a coherent, useful whole. What I have just been talking about is *dominating* them, which is what every psyche passionately resists. All minds wish to see their impulses carried out, and they fear that eventually

Soliana will crush them. What we're doing is offering them a second path: mutual survival via dissolution into a greater whole. It's just about the cruelest path open to the poor girl, but it's the best way forward that we have."

"Why? Why is it the best way forward?" prodded Gromyko.

"You have been paying very little attention," the man in black said, the first hint of criticism entering his voice. "So I'll make this very, very plain: some minds have the power to see things, to know things, to *do* things, that others can't. That should be manifestly obvious to you, given your friendship with Hunt, your knowledge of me, and, of course, your dealings with Soliana herself. For reasons quite beyond the present scientific understanding of man, these special psyches can interact with elements in a way that most cannot. The most obvious case, again, is Hunt, who has a special family affinity for the shadow element of existence. But these gifts are not merely *physical*, they are *psychic*, too. Each of those embedded personalities has insights, *powers*, that the others lack. Taken together, they're a powerful force for our side. But should they continue to be divided–."

"They cancel each other out," Gromyko finished for him.

"Essentially. Though sometimes the truth manages to slip through, as with *Eesekkalion*."

"But aren't you worried that mixing them together will get rid of their power?"

Krancis tipped his head ever so slightly to the side, pleased to see that the Deltan could at least intuit what he seemingly refused to put together through reason.

"No, they were meant to work together. But only if they can be drawn into a single unit."

With misgivings Gromyko eyed him, unsure if he was being given only half the information he needed yet again. Deciding that Krancis would likely always hold *something* just out of sight, he resolved to make the best judgment he could.

"Assuming this is true," he said carefully, his words coming out slowly, all signs of his previous anger having vanished, "why didn't those secret people who put the implants into her just get them all working together from the start?"

"We can only speculate," Krancis replied, leaning back and once again tossing his leg over the other. "Perhaps they intended it as a sort of lock, keeping her divided against herself so that her insight couldn't be used by our enemies if she fell into their hands. Or perhaps they lacked the skill to bring them together, and were forced to trust that we'd somehow figure it out. Your guess is as good as mine."

"I find that hard to believe," he said. Like most people, he felt that Krancis had the inside track on reality itself, and the notion that he could be just as ignorant as an artifact smuggler from the fringe of human space seemed laughable. Turning his head a little to the side, his eyes narrowed as he searched the man opposite him for the truth.

"Normally, you would be correct," Krancis uttered. "But Soliana is a special case." He uncrossed his leg and leaned in close. As though attracted through magnetism, Gromyko found himself doing the same, sensing that something big was about to leave his lips. "The truth is this, Gromyko: she may hold the key to everything. Not just this war, but the wars that are to follow. She represents the promise of ancestral aid."

"Ancestral *what?*" he asked, confused by the statement. But Krancis just subtly shook his head, refusing to elaborate. So he tried a different tack. "But I thought Rex was the key to this whole thing."

"He's the sword, for sure. Just as I am the brain. But Soliana, if you complete your work, is to be our *eyes*."

"But...*you're* our eyes," he said. "I thought–."

"There are things even I do not know about," he replied evenly. "Difficult though that is to believe."

"You can say that again," Gromyko admitted, surprised to find a sense of something approaching intimacy with a man he was ready to assault shortly before. Confused at his own turn around, he looked at him and tried to work out what had caused the change. Defeated in this, he picked another donut off the plate and de-iced it.

Watching this incongruent behavior with an inner sense of amusement, Krancis simply waited for the still jellied mind of the smuggler to come round.

"Alright, so let me see if I've got this straight," he said at last, having skimmed the top of yet another pastry. "You plan the strategy, Rex crushes everything in his path, and Soliana is here to help us...see stuff. *I*, of all people, have to help *her* deal with the voices inside her head because I'm too shallow to threaten them. How's that so far?"

"Go on," Krancis nodded.

"So, indirectly, the fate of the human race rests with... me?"

"In a sense, yes. Though that could be said of every link in our machine of war. Without pilots to fly missions, we're finished. Without someone to build and repair our craft, we're finished. It's the same story in every war: each role is essential, or it wouldn't exist. Did you really imagine that I'd give you this task if it wasn't important?"

"I don't know. I guess I didn't–," he paused, stopping short of the word *think*. "I guess I'm not used to doing things this big."

"We've all been forced to become more than we once were," Krancis replied in a quieter tone.

"Does that include you?" Gromyko queried, regretting his question the instant it left his tongue. "Forget I asked that," he quickly added, raising his hands and shaking his head. "I don't want to know."

"And why is that?"

"Because I might just be a backwater artifact smuggler. But I reckon I've got as much need for heroes as anyone does. And while you aren't as scintillating as Gromyko," he added, his pride forcing him to swell just a bit before his next admission, "you've proven far more effective. You have my respect."

For once Krancis was both amused and a little surprised at something unfolding before him. His judgment had been the same as *Esiluria's* regarding relations between himself and the mercurial Deltan. The two seemed perfectly calculated to repel one another, and he had long accepted that notion. Neither he nor the alien AI had considered the possibility that the flexible smuggler might have a change of heart. For half a moment he contemplated the smuggler, his powerful mind seeking an answer. And then he found it: it was the result of his exploration of Soliana's psyche. The cascade of inner events that that experience had set off was leading to results even Krancis hadn't anticipated.

"Still," Gromyko added. "It wasn't very good of you to hide so much from me."

"I'm not concerned with being good," Krancis replied, standing up and pushing his chair against the table. "Just effective."

All eyes in the room followed the man in black as he strode across it to the exit on the other side. Then they moved to the smuggler, his arms crossed upon the table before him. Reaching unconsciously for another donut, he began to slide his teeth across it when he noticed the icing was already gone. Looking down, they were all stripped.

"Bring Gromyko more donuts!" he said, snapping his fingers at the counter staff and pointing at his plate. "I must have energy to perform work vital to the empire!"

Uneasily they looked at one another, almost certain that the smuggler was full of hot air. But, then again, Krancis *had* come to the commissary just to speak with him. And he never did that. Reluctantly an older woman brought a fresh plate of donuts. Wordlessly she took the old plate, the smuggler not bothering to acknowledge her as he withdrew into an inner world of fantastic possibilities.

"Wait!" he shouted, jumping up from the table and tearing across the room. The woman shrieked and dropped the plate of naked donuts, thinking he was addressing her. Upon turning she saw him bolting through the door. Mustering all her resolve, she managed not to bellow an oath after him.

"Krancis, wait!" he exclaimed, looking up and down the hall but not seeing him. Deciding to go left, he made his way past the passersby who eyed him curiously. At the end of the corridor he turned right hurriedly, walking straight into Powers. His arms shot out and grasped her just as she was about to dump over backwards.

"Oh, thank you," she said, straightening her hair a little as he released her. "Are you feeling okay?" she queried, as he shifted between looking at her and gazing down the corridor in search of his quarry.

"Me? Oh, yes. Of course," he said in a quick, half distracted tone, his eyes finding hers. Tongue tied as usual, he faced the added difficulty of a pressing question that he wanted to put to Krancis without delay. But her pretty face looked up at him with such a pleasing mixture of sweetness and self-respect that he reluctantly put his pursuit on the back burner. "Why wouldn't I be?" he asked, unable to think of anything else to say.

"Well, it's just that you seemed so out of sorts last night," she said somewhat apologetically, not wishing him to think she found him strange. "I hope you rested well."

"Yes, yes I did," he nodded emphatically, searching his typically retentive memory for any trace of her the night before and finding none. His cheeks began to blush as his mind wandered to what he might have said or done given the peculiar state he was in. "Are you heading somewhere?" he asked at last.

"Every role aboard ship is already perfectly filled," she replied, beginning to walk slowly to lessen the awkwardness of the moment. "As always, Krancis has seen to every detail perfectly. But I do wish I had something to do. Hopefully I'll be able to leave soon and get on with my job."

"No," he couldn't help muttering, his heart sinking at the thought. When her eyes went to his, he hurriedly added, "you need to be certain you're well enough."

"According to the hospital I'm fine. Physically, at least," she replied with some misgivings. "But I keep getting these strange headaches. They rush over my skull without warning, usually lasting just a few minutes before vanishing again. I've spoken to the doctors, but they can't find anything wrong with me."

"Have you talked to Krancis?"

Surprised at the notion, she looked up at him again as they rounded a corner.

"What?" he asked, unable to help chuckling at the mixture of awe and curiosity on her face.

"I…can't talk to *Krancis*," she said. "He's the emperor's right hand, the intellect behind our entire war effort. He doesn't have time for someone like me."

'Well, he seems to have all the time in the world for me," he replied with a shrug. "I don't see why he couldn't spare a few minutes for you. I don't know how in the world he does it, but he's got this…power, or insight, or *something*, that lets him…" his voice trailed, as he realized she was starting to self-consciously withdraw into herself. "Hey, what's wrong?" he asked, tapping her shoulder in a friendly fashion, his inhibitions beginning to melt away.

"You don't have to make fun of me, Mister Gromyko," she said with agitation.

"Make fun of you?" he asked, flabbergasted.

"I'm not part of the inner circle. I'm just a lieutenant. There's no way in the world that Krancis would take the time to talk to me. Now please, leave me alone," she finished, turning down another hallway suddenly and leaving him behind.

"Wait a minute," he called after her, jogging to catch up.

"I don't have anything to say to you," she replied, quickening her pace.

"Just a minute," he reiterated, putting a hand to her soft shoulder and pulling her to a stop. She paused and turned, but refused to look him in the eye. "I'm not part of any 'inner circle.' I'm just–," he hesitated momentarily, his pride flaring before settling down. "I'm just Gromyko, from Delta-13," he continued in a lower voice. "I don't know if you've noticed, but I'm not exactly revered around here."

"Krancis talks to you," she objected. "And you're friends with Rex Hunt."

"Sure, I know Rex from our days back on Delta. But that doesn't mean anything to Krancis. And as for him talking to me, well, it's just because he finds me useful. Or indispensable, I suppose."

"Lucky you," she replied, more from hurt than actual tartness, as she tried to pull away. "Look, are you going to let me go?" she asked, his hands having moved to her shoulders as he spoke.

"Not until I get through to you," he insisted. "I'm not going to have you thinking that I was putting you down. I wasn't, I promise. I don't know, sometimes I just talk without thinking."

"That's true," Krancis said from a short distance away, walking slowly.

"There you are!" the smuggler exclaimed, releasing Powers and turning towards him. "Didn't you hear me calling you?"

He looked from Gromyko to Powers, whose eyes were studying the floor.

"What did you want?"

"I had a question about–," he paused, glancing at the lieutenant. "About…the work you have me doing with Soliana."

"If you'll excuse me, sir," Powers said, taking the opportunity to turn and slip away behind the Deltan.

"Wait," Gromyko uttered, but she was already well on her way by the time he'd spun around.

"That's not how you do it," Krancis observed, watching the young woman beat a quick retreat. "Manhandling her in the corridors."

"I wasn't *manhandling* her," he protested, facing him again. "I was just trying to get her to see you. She's got some kind of headaches or something, but the doctors don't have a clue what's wrong. With all your skill, I thought you could help. But she thought I was teasing her."

"My name is feared from one end of the fringe to the other. Numberless men and women would gladly give their lives at my command. Did you really suppose she would come to me and complain about her head?"

Unable to say anything in reply, save that he had once again acted without thinking, he let the point drop.

"Now, what is it you wanted to ask me about?"

"Do we have to talk about it here?" the smuggler asked, glancing around. "It's kind of personal."

"Drop your voice and keep it quick," Krancis instructed, crossing his arms and leaning against the wall. "I don't have time for anything else. Nobody is listening, anyway."

"Well," Gromyko began, mimicking his posture and drawing as close as seemed appropriate. "I saw these funny mountains. They were all black and flat, like they were cutouts from a sheet of plywood. They sort of wrapped around me, heading left and right. Then I saw this little guy all hunched over into a ball. He was standing right on the tips of his toes, like he didn't want to touch the ground. He shook and then stood up. I don't know where it came from, but he had a sword in his hand and started to go into the sky on this big pillar. Then he got too far away, and I couldn't see him anymore. I've got to admit, it made me feel pretty weird."

"How?" Krancis asked, his interest having grown as the picture unfolded.

"I don't know," he evaded.

"You must have *some* idea," the man in black replied, his head tipping a little for frankness.

"Well, it felt like me – like I was watching *myself*. But that's not possible."

"Why not?"

"Because I was already there! How could I be there and watch myself at the same time? Besides, I'm not some funny little guy who needs to hug himself."

"Dreams present truth in strange ways. The unconscious mind doesn't speak in language that we're generally familiar with. It's symbolic, mythological."

"But what's it all supposed to mean, then?" he asked, growing distressed the more he thought about it.

"I don't think we have the complete picture yet," Krancis opined. "It's too soon to venture an interpretation."

"You mean you don't know," Gromyko uttered with disappointment.

"I mean you need to give your psyche more time to put the pieces together. You have to be patient."

"Easy for you to say."

"Consider it an opportunity to grow as a person," Krancis replied, a touch of amusement around his eyes. Pushing off the wall, he added, "don't worry too much about Powers. She's being monitored constantly."

"Of course she is," he mumbled, as Krancis walked away.

Gromyko was a mix of emotions as he made his way back to his room and threw himself onto the bed. He was excited by the importance of his task, yet exhausted by his most recent dive into Soliana's mind. He'd finally broken through the communication barrier that existed between himself and Powers; but all he'd managed to do was offend her. Krancis was more open than ever towards him, yet for that all the more uncompromising in his criticisms.

To top it all off, his head felt strange, like his perception was changing with every quarter hour that passed.

For once he regretted the mercurial nature of his psyche. He shifted from one mental state to the next with such dizzying rapidity that even he was having a hard time keeping up. He cringed a little as his mind wandered back to the commissary, and the way he'd blown hot and cold with Krancis. Realizing that the older man could have verbally smashed him flat at any number of opportunities, he appreciated his forbearance.

"Maybe he's a little nicer than he seems," the smuggler reflected, as his eyes began to close and the world around him faded away. "No!" he shouted, as he found himself drifting once more into a dreamworld of two-dimensional silhouettes. "Not again!"

Instead of mountains he saw small people, parading around him as the former had done. They seemed joyful, their little arms extended stiffly over their heads in triumph. But he felt a pall over the entire scene, the antics of the people telling only half the tale. The scent of death was on the wind. Instantly he cast his eyes around for the source, wading through the silhouettes who invariably moved aside as he neared, though they were ignorant of his presence. For what seemed like hours he searched, until finally he found the pillar of stone from his previous dream. It stood raised a couple feet off the ground. The body of the sword-carrying figure lay upon it, motionless. He knew instantly that he was dead.

Struck to the heart by this sight, Gromyko dropped to his knees and eyed the figure. Unsure if he should reach out and touch it, he hesitated for a couple of minutes before finally extending his hand towards it. As he did so, reaching up from his feet across his body, the impossible darkness of the silhouette was replaced by the clear image of a man.

Recognizing the clothes he wore, it took all his resolve to hover his hand across his body to his head. But he had to see it for himself.

"It's me," he uttered in disbelief, as his hand revealed his own features. There was no sign of a struggle, yet the body was dead. The sword was held tightly in both his hands, the blade running across his abdomen and pointing at his chin. He seemed to be in a kind of noble rest, a state of perfect ease. He wasn't so much *dead* as *still*. It was as though his mind was absent, but his body had remained.

Dropping back onto his rear, the smuggler gazed upon himself with fascination. Without his knowledge the little dark silhouettes drew near, respectfully surrounding the pillar, their hands clasped behind their backs. After an interval he noticed them. Shifting where he sat, he reached out his left hand towards one. At once its face lit up, revealing a rather attractive woman of forty. Standing up, he did the same to the others, unmasking their natures and finding them ordinary people.

This done, they joined hands with one another and began to sway in lament. Their lips parted slightly, and a low, moaning hum accompanied their reverent movements.

Astonished by the sight, Gromyko stepped over the little people and drew back, watching them move closer and closer to the pillar. With one consent they reached out their hands and touched the body, drawing its sacrifice into themselves and cherishing the blood that had been spilled in their service. Each in their turn pressed their foreheads against some portion of his body, before finally turning and walking away, disappearing into a mist that had begun to form around the scene.

"What is this?" he asked, raising his hands to his face as the fog increased, concealing them from view. Looking anxiously around, he found that the people, the pillar, and the corpse were all gone. He tried to speak, but the mist swallowed his words before they could reach his ears.

Suddenly he awoke, his body tense and covered in sweat.

"Krancis!" he shouted, bolting from the bed like a child with a nightmare.

After half an hour of frantic searching, he stopped inside a teleporter room and pressed his back against the wall beside the door. The technician on duty happened to be the same woman who'd cut him off mid-sentence back when Krancis had first recruited him to help Soliana. With aversion she eyed him, wondering what grandiose speech he had lined up for her this time.

"Are you alright?" she asked, her expression softening a little as she began to appreciate the state he was in.

"I'm looking for Krancis," the smuggler replied in a haggard voice. Though still in the grip of panic, he was too exhausted to climb the walls. Pausing to take a few tight breaths, he added, "have you seen him?"

"Not recently," she told him. "Do you want to go to the hospital?" she offered.

"No, I *don't* want to go to the hospital!" he snapped, the force of his words making her start. "I want to find *Krancis!*" Pausing briefly, he emphatically enunciated, "do you know where I can find him?"

"No," she shook her head, her eyes glued to him.

"Send me to the bridge," he ordered, stepping into the chamber.

It was with relief that the technician complied, glad to make him someone else's problem.

Stomping out of the receiving chamber, the Deltan slowly made the short journey from it to the bridge. His legs unsteady, he occasionally brushed against the wall to retain his balance. Passersby glanced at him from the corners of their eyes, but didn't venture to make their curiosity obvious. He was on some kind of mission, and they weren't about to interrupt him.

Opening the door to the bridge, he found Krancis

standing upon the transparent floor, his hands clasped behind his back as he watched the tunnel of darkness stream by on every side.

"*You*," Gromyko said, closing the door and walking slowly towards him.

"I see you've discovered the rest of your dream," he uttered calmly, not bothering to turn around.

"You *knew*," he accused him, walking in front of him and clenching his fists. "You knew the dream would end that way. It's predicting my *death!*"

"No one lives forever, Gromyko," he replied evenly. "Now, tell me what you saw."

"Why should I bother?" he snapped. "You know everything in advance, don't you?"

Disapprovingly Krancis eyed him.

"Why should this trouble you so much? You've always wanted a glorious death. That's what the figure rising into the sky on a pillar signifies: you'll soar above your fellows, ending your days in a way that will not be soon forgotten."

"But I'll still be *forgotten!*" he bellowed. "There were a bunch of little people who mourned for me, and then turned and disappeared. Those people will carry my memory away with them when they die! I'll have no permanence!"

"Everyone is forgotten eventually, Gromyko. Provided humanity endures, there will come a time when even I am a hazy myth, a fairy tale that's told to children to inspire them to live behave. The only one of us who *might* last in the racial memory is Hunt. He marks the shift of our race from a purely physical existence to one that is closely allied with the dark realm. Assuming the transformation is completed–."

"I don't care about any transformation! I care about my *legacy!*"

"Provided it is completed," Krancis resumed pointedly, his patience finally wearing thin. "He will likely be remembered as its point of origin. He will be akin to the founder of a religion."

"There must be a legacy for Gromyko!" the smuggler insisted, pushing aside Krancis' explanation. "He cannot be forgotten!"

"None of the Earthborn are forgotten to the dark realm. They are each remembered by it, their bodies transformed and preserved."

"What good is it if there aren't any *people* to remember me?" he demanded. "What good is it to be recalled by an entity like that?"

"It's the best you're going to get," he replied, pressing his finger against his ear radio for a moment. "Very good, Captain."

Instantly the ship dropped out of warp, emerging in the middle of an orange and purple nebula. The wonderful sight froze Gromyko's tongue for a few moments as he tried to take it all in. It felt magical, almost alive. Like it was watching him.

"What is this place?" he asked, his anger slipping away despite his best efforts to maintain it.

"It is the Vesryn nebula," Soliana said from the door, closing it behind her as she entered the panoramic room. "Within it is concealed the greatest secret of our galaxy: the Gate of Zeruc."

"Gate of Zeruc?" Gromyko asked, as she joined the two men and gazed upon the beautiful nebula. "What's it for? What does it do?"

"Nothing, anymore," Krancis replied. "It was destroyed long ago."

"Then what are we doing here?"

"Making sure no one is trying to fix it," he said, pressing his finger to his radio again. "Go ahead, Captain."

Slowly the ship accelerated, the orange and purple glow around them beginning to stream past. For an hour they stood and watched, though for Gromyko the time seemed to pass in a matter of minutes. Finally the cloud around them began to evaporate, a bubble of open space appearing in the middle of the nebula. Within the bubble he could make out a dark silhouette, shaped like a ring. Broken into three large pieces, with little fragments floating near each break, the segments nevertheless remained close to their original positions.

"It's enormous," the smuggler nearly gasped, the ring growing larger and larger as the ship drew near to its hollow center. "I didn't think anything was bigger than *Sentinel*."

"A few things are," Krancis replied, undisturbed by the sight. "Captain: send out the scouting parties."

Almost at once a half dozen eggs left the ship and flew out towards the shattered ring.

"Well, why don't we finish the job?" Gromyko asked, recovering his equilibrium as the eggs turned to little specks and disappeared. "Let's blast it to pieces with the cannon."

"*Sentinel* isn't powerful enough for that."

"Oh, come on. We blew up a planet, didn't we?"

"We *overloaded* a dark planet with shadow. Its very nature already did half the work for us. It was like throwing a grenade into an ammunition storage room. This," he said, waving his thin hand towards the shattered relic. "This is allied to the light realm. It would require more dark energy than we could possibly lay our hands on to destroy it. Even dissolving Hunt in the reactor wouldn't be enough. Not that that's an option, in any event."

"So put a fleet around it. Protect it."

"The essence of this place forbids it," Soliana explained. "Look at this nebula. Beautiful, isn't it? The way the orange and the purple seem to struggle with each other for dominance. Neither is strong enough to defeat the other, and so they mix together to make something lovely. But if you look closer, you will see that the purple is a good many shades darker than you realized at first. This nebula is not natural. It was originally a cloud of light energy, one that accompanied the Gate of Zeruc. Long, long ago, before even our ancient kin who were destroyed by the Devourers, there was a war for dominion of this galaxy. Those who brought the war were allied to the realm of light, and constructed this device to bring their people here. But another race, one attached to the shadow element, fought back, destroying them at the cost of their own existence. They surrendered their lives to the darkness, shattering this gate and the fleets that surrounded it. Only one of the invaders survived, and he was taken into captivity by a handful of the beings who had been spared from the sacrifice of their race. Their task done, and the hope of their people gone, they likewise gave up their lives and joined their kin in sleep."

"So...the light energy keeps us from putting ships here?" Gromyko clarified.

"Yes," Krancis said. "This vessel, along with the eggs, is strong enough to resist its corrosive effects. But a fleet of imperial ships would begin to break down at once. Our engineering isn't allied to the shadow element. Yet." Pausing, he pressed a finger to his ear. "Good, Captain. Tell them to keep searching." He looked at his two companions. "No sign of trespassers so far."

"Who would be here, anyhow?" Gromyko asked. "If the light realm–," he stopped, his brain catching up. "Oh, the *Pho'Sath*."

"Yes."

"But I thought they weren't supposed to be here. How could they try to repair something like this? Wouldn't that put them a little too clearly on the *Keesh's* radar?"

"They've grown bold of late. The stepped up war in the fringe has got them in a panic, though a very methodical one. They sense that their hold is slipping, and that's something that they cannot tolerate. It would be just like them to go for broke, thinking we were too distracted by the rest of the war to notice."

"But...they couldn't *repair* something like this," the smuggler objected. "It's too big. Too advanced." He looked between Krancis and Soliana. "Right?"

"It's hard to say just what they're capable of," she replied. "Their technology is very advanced, much more so than our own. And their society is such that it resists penetration from every other race. No one truly knows the extent of their knowledge and power."

"It's best to assume the worst where they're concerned," Krancis said, annoyed that even he had little insight into the true strength of humanity's implacable foe. "Hence why we're here."

"Well, looks like you've been worried over nothing," the Deltan said, turning from him to gaze upon the ring. "There's nobody here but us."

"We'll see."

They fell silent again, looking at the device and trying to make out the eggs in the distance. Once Soliana began to mutter something, but she stopped when she noticed Gromyko's eyes upon her.

"No trace, sir," the captain said at long last through Krancis' radio.

"Excellent," he replied. "You may order the scouting parties back to the ship."

"Good news?" Gromyko asked.

"There's no sign that anyone has been interfering with the Gate. Evidently the *Pho'Sath* haven't felt themselves capable of such an overreach."

"Or they just can't handle the job."

"That remains an open question."

"Now that that's over with," the Deltan uttered, trying to gin up some of his previous anger. "I'm not finished with what I was saying earlier."

"I am," Krancis replied, turning and walking towards the door. "Pour your heart out to Soliana, if you really need to."

Gromyko could only fume as the man in black disappeared through the door.

"Sometimes he makes me crazy," he said, clenching

his fists again. Seeing the look of concern on Soliana's face, he toned it down.

"What's troubling you, Antonin?" she asked, drawing near and laying a hand on his forehead. "Are you well?"

"Why does everyone keep asking me that?" he nearly snapped.

"Because you look *unwell*, Antonin," she replied simply, withdrawing her hand and remaining by his side. "Your mind is agitated, and it is visible in your body. You seem to have lost both weight and strength. Have you gone to the hospital?"

"No, and I don't intend to," he replied, crossing his arms. "What I've got, they can't cure."

"And just what do you have?" she asked kindly, her manner almost ethereal.

"Come on," he said, taking her arm and ushering her towards the door. "I'll tell you along the way."

CHAPTER 10

The tension within Kren-Balar remained high despite Karnan's intervention. On several occasions Seldek had invited Welter to join him for a meal. But the surly bodyguard flatly refused each time. As she sat against the wall beside the emperor's head, Tselitel anxiously contemplated the situation, unsure what to do.

"What's troubling you?" Rhemus asked her, still lying on his back though growing a little stronger with each passing hour.

"Me?" she asked, instantly wiping the look of concern from her face and forcing a smile. "Nothing. Nothing at all."

"*Doctor Tselitel*," he said chidingly. "I've been around you long enough to know when you're tying your stomach in knots over something you can't control. Now tell me."

"I'm afraid for you," she admitted, leaning her head down a little towards his and dropping her voice. "I think our hosts are angry with us."

"Hard to imagine why they wouldn't be," he replied, as aware as anyone of the situation. "Welter's behavior isn't calculated to make friends."

"I wish he wouldn't treat them as enemies," she fretted, joining her hands together over her lap and beginning to unconsciously work and squeeze them. "We're so utterly dependent on each other that we can't afford to be at odds. Especially in a place like this."

"They're not making it easy for him," Rhemus replied. "But don't worry. We need each other too much for either side to let this fall apart. They might be proud, but they're not stupid."

Eventually the emperor drifted off to an uneasy sleep, and Tselitel gently got to her feet and padded across the floor to the door. Glancing towards *Karnan*, she found him packed against the wall, his emaciated legs stretched out before him, totally dead to all that was around him.

The horrible thought crossed her mind that he might actually *be* dead, and she was about to dart to him when he muttered in his sleep and shifted his head. Closing her eyes and exhaling in relief, she opened the door and stepped out.

"Hello, Gustav," she said nicely, finding the outer room chilly and folding her arms over her chest.

"Hello," he replied without enthusiasm, still sitting in his chair as before. Not bothering to look up as she passed before him to the table, he continued to stare at a point on the wall near the opposite door.

"Any word from *Seldek*?" she asked, trying to find some way to begin the conversation.

"No."

"Or *Keelen*?"

"No," he repeated.

Unsure what else to do, she sat upon a corner of the table, her narrow feet dangling in the air. Drawing the folds of the thin robe between her legs, she pressed them together and recrossed her arms, trying to stay warm.

"Gustav," she began again. But he immediately shook his head.

"Doctor, you're starting to get on my nerves," he said in a warning tone, his eyes shifting from the wall to her. Their look was menacing, and it took some resolve to keep from gulping at the sight.

"And you're getting on *theirs*," she said as firmly as she could, deciding to gamble on being bold. "Don't you see that?

You're *hurting*, Gustav, and you're taking it out on everyone around you. We can't afford that in this situation. You need help to process your grief."

"I don't intend to *process* my feelings, Doctor," he replied in a low tone. "I intend to act upon them, as soon as my work with the emperor is finished."

"But that may take a long time," she objected. "We could be here for years."

"I can wait," he replied. "But sooner or later, I'm going to get those responsible. I'm going to *destroy* them for what they've done."

"What have they done?" she queried, sensing that he was slowly opening up and trying to seize upon the opportunity. "You can trust me, Gustav."

"I don't intend to trust anyone, Doctor," he replied, turning away from her and fixing on the wall again. "That's what cost me the only thing in this life that I cared about."

Aware that her window had closed, she slid off the table and was about to head into the hallway for some air when doctor *Keelen* entered. Critically he cast his eyes up and down her slight form, and then looked to Welter.

"*Seldek* is offering you one last chance to make amends," he said flatly. "What shall I tell him?"

"The same thing you've told him on every previous occasion."

Visibly the alien's temper flared, though he managed to control himself.

"You're being most unwise," he said deliberately. "There must be a give and take to this relationship."

"Your kind has taken a planet in the middle of our empire as payment for your services. I'd say we've given enough already."

"That's hardly what I meant," he replied tartly, offended at the implication of extortion.

"I don't care what you meant. Just tell *Seldek* that if he wants to break bread, he can do it down here. But one way or another," he said, jerking a thumb over his shoulder, "I'm not letting that man out of my sight."

"I've told you a thousand times that your emperor is secure within *Kren-Balar*," *Keelen* said with annoyance.

"So you have."

"And why do you find that so hard to believe? Your suspicions cast a shadow over all that we're trying to accomplish here."

"The emperor is one of the highest priority targets that our enemies possess. Without me to watch over him, he would be an easy victim for even a single traitor among your people–."

"There are no traitors among my people!" he shouted, slamming the palm of his hand against the wall beside him. "We are striving for survival, the same as you. Not a single *Kol-Prockian* wishes to see harm come to your emperor."

"Then those same *Kol-Prockians* ought to be a little more understanding of my security precautions," he replied acidly. "Since they have so much concern for the head of our empire."

"You're twisting my words every which way," the alien objected. "It is our *concern* that makes us harmless, don't you see? There isn't a soul among us that would raise a hand against him. This base is filled exclusively with my people. You're among friends, human."

"Friends ought to give us a little more latitude."

"Oh," *Keelen* chuckled mirthlessly, his anger rising again. Frustratedly he smacked the knuckles of his right hand against his left palm. Then he looked at Tselitel. "You can't agree with him on this?"

Sensing that he was trying to drive a wedge between them, she nodded vigorously, unable to verbalize her lie.

"Humans..." he muttered with a shake of his head. "Why must you be so suspicious?" he asked, his voice steadily rising. "Even from your allies you anticipate the worst! Are you really so small, so lacking in trust, that you cannot see the hand that is being extended to you on the purest grounds of friendship? It's unbelievable that–."

His words were interrupted by the appearance of Rhemus on the other side of the door. The sight of the human emperor made him aware of his volume, and it was with an inner tremor that he saw the prematurely aged man open the door and unsteadily walk out.

"Your Majesty," *Keelen* said deferentially, bowing his head and looking at the floor for a moment. "I apologize for waking you. It was not my intention to force you from the chamber."

Welter shot to his feet at the sight of Rhemus, ready to steady him but uncertain if he should put forth his hands to his regal form. Tselitel, having grown a great deal more intimate with the emperor, quickly reached for his arm, though he waved her off.

"As you can see," he said with some effort to *Keelen*, who'd only just raised his eyes from the floor, "they are concerned above all else with my wellbeing."

"And that is laudable, Majesty," he allowed in a respectful tone. "But there must be flexibility on both sides. There must be *understanding*."

"We are all in a trying situation, Doctor *Keelen*," he replied, walking towards him in his thin robe, his feet heavy and slow. "One that requires patience, tolerance, and not a little time."

"Time, Majesty?"

"For us to grow accustomed to each other," he explained. "We are two very different peoples, Doctor. It would be ridiculous to expect us to get along right from the start."

"Of course, Majesty," he nodded. "But the efforts of both sides have not been *equal*. My people have opened our home to you and your attendants in the hope that we shall have a long and cooperative future together. We did not anticipate being treated so…roughly," he concluded, his eyes narrowing as they shot to Welter.

"Then I will go to *Seldek*," Rhemus resolved. "And my entourage will go with me. Let us end this now."

"No," Welter said firmly, forgetting himself for a moment.

"I appreciate your concern," the emperor said with genuine feeling. "But as the head of our state, Gustav, I must go where I'm needed. I don't live for myself alone."

"You must survive," Welter insisted, dropping his voice. "As a symbol of our continued resistance. Our people need you."

"And they shant lose me," he replied, waving Tselitel near and drawing her under his right arm for support. "I have you to look after me, don't I?"

"Majesty, I must ask you to wait until I can send for extra guards," *Keelen* uttered. "It's not fit for one of your dignity to travel the corridors of our base without the proper escort."

"It will be a sign of my trust in your people," he replied. "It will help to dissolve the tensions we now find ourselves encumbered with." His strength beginning to fade a little, he swallowed and nodded towards the door. "Let us proceed."

"Majesty," *Keelen* bowed slightly, opening the door and waiting for him to pass by. Cutting in front of Welter, the alien deferentially moved to the front of the group, escorting them towards *Seldek's* room.

As they passed through the hangar, Welter's eyes searched the crowd. With awe they watched Rhemus labor slowly past, his legs growing less and less cooperative. Their gaze alternated between him and the floor, instinctively showing the same kind of respect that *Keelen* had demonstrated.

But there was one exception. He was taller and thinner than the rest, standing a good foot above the crowd. His eyes never left the emperor, following his progress from the very moment he became visible.

Then it happened: pressing his fellows aside, he crossed half the distance to the group and raised a weapon. The sights had just fallen upon Rhemus when a bullet crashed through the alien's skull, landing right between his widely spaced eyes. Instantly dead, his light form fell backwards, his gun clattering to the floor beside him.

With a shriek, Tselitel jerked around and saw the smoking pistol in Welter's hand. A scowl was on his face as he searched the crowd for threats. But instead of more danger, he was surprised to find the *Kol-Prockians* moving forwards to surround the emperor with their bodies. Turning their backs to him, their eyes similarly searching for traitors, they formed a wall and ushered him and his entourage out of the hangar and back into the relative safety of the corridors.

"Thank you," Rhemus uttered, reaching out and touching a few of them as they left the hangar. "Thank you."

A dozen of them stood together, capping off the corridor to allow the humans a safe retreat. Moving quickly, they reached *Seldek's* room and hurriedly got everyone inside.

"Emperor Rhemus," *Seldek* said, a note of displeasure in his voice. "I hadn't expected you."

Shoving his pistol into his jacket pocket, Welter stormed halfway across the room to him before a sharp word from Rhemus halted him. His nostrils flaring, his hands raised in front of his chest, he was on the verge of choking the prideful alien in front of them all. *Keelen*, remarkably, found himself in sympathy with the bodyguard.

"We've been attacked," Tselitel said, helping the emperor to a chair. "A *Kol-Prockian* nearly shot the emperor."

"That's not possible," *Seldek* replied, shaking his head as Rhemus took a seat and drew his arm from Tselitel's thin shoulders. "You must be mistaken."

"I saw it all, *Seldek*," *Keelen* seconded. "It was one of our own people. Of that there is no doubt. Were it not for the quick eye of Mister Welter, the emperor's blood would be on our hands as of this moment."

"But that's not possible," he reiterated. "There's no reason for one of our people to attack any of you."

"Apparently he thought he had a reason," Welter replied. "And he felt it was good enough to throw his life away in public." His face darkened as he drew closer to the alien. "He never would have had the chance, *Seldek*, if the emperor hadn't been forced to come here to smooth your feathers."

"You can't hold me responsible for what's happened," *Seldek* insisted. "He was a lone actor. The conspiracy died with him."

"I *do* hold you responsible," he replied, looking at *Keelen* to include him as well. "Each and every one of you. You've had a chance to make this work, and you've botched it from beginning to end. Only *Karnan* has been decent with us. The rest of you have poked and prodded us, upping the tension until something had to give. Finally it led to this."

Flinching at the mention of *Karnan*, the alien took a moment to regain his equilibrium.

"Does he speak for you, Emperor Rhemus?" he asked, trying to shift the onus of responsibility.

"Gustav Welter speaks for himself," Rhemus replied. "Which, as that assassin just learned, is more than enough."

Shifting uncomfortably at this answer, *Seldek's* eyes went to *Keelen*. But his colleague merely shook his head, signaling that he'd have to look elsewhere for support.

"What can we do to prevent this from happening again?" Tselitel asked, trying to draw the two parties to some kind of middle ground.

"I've got an idea," Welter replied ominously. "When Krancis hears how unsafe this base is, I'm sure he'll agree with my recommendation that he send a team out here to secure it."

"Are you *threatening* this base, Welter?" *Seldek* asked grandly, as *Keelen's* face paled and Tselitel's stomach began to churn with dismay. "Are you intending to *invade* it?"

"This base is a strategic resource for the empire," Welter replied. "And we'll do what is necessary to ensure its continued viability."

"We're not going to invade *Kren-Balar*," Rhemus stepped in. "But it might be advisable to enlarge the security team."

"That's definitely a possibility, Majesty," *Keelen* hastened to add, hoping to lower the temperature in the room.

"Not one more human will set foot within this base!" *Seldek* snapped. "You imagine that you can ride roughshod over us because we are weak and you are strong! *But I will destroy that chamber before I permit it to be stolen from us!*"

Having thrown down the gauntlet, the room was deadly still. Only the labored breathing of Rhemus, his elbow pressed against the table for support, disturbed the quiet.

From where she stood, Tselitel could tell Welter was weighing his options. The fingers of his gun hand slowly massaged themselves against his palm, and it was with infinite dread that she realized he was contemplating his own act of assassination. Or, at the very least, hostage taking. A thousand dark possibilities flooded her mind at this thought. Surely the *Kol-Prockians* who'd so selflessly risked their lives escorting them out of the hangar would turn against them instantly, tearing them to pieces through sheer numbers, if nothing else.

"Wait!" *Keelen* said, finally regaining his composure after the assassination attempt. "There have been mistakes and misunderstandings on both sides. I myself am equally guilty of ramping up tensions within *Kren-Balar*." He stepped closer to *Seldek*. "We have been jealous, suspicious, and small. We ought to have–."

"Speak for yourself, *Keelen!*" ordered *Seldek*, his voice sharp and fierce. "Do not presume to speak for me! These humans wish to extort the last precious remnants of our technology out of us for their own gain! Were it not for the feebleness of their emperor, they would have been happy leaving us to rot! Do not expect me to be generous and trusting with such people!"

"What is wrong with you?" *Keelen* asked, truly surprised. "It was you who wished us to cooperate with them long ago! It was *you* who insisted we learn their language to facilitate an eventual alliance! Why are you being so perverse, so utterly unreasonable? Have you lost all your sense? Have you–," he hesitated, realization widening his eyes. "You *haven't!*" he exclaimed, his tone both betrayed and accusatory.

"Do not presume to insult me, *Keelen!*" *Seldek* shouted, his voice loud and increasingly unstable. "Do not presume!"

The thin doctor stormed towards his comrade, wrapping his hands around his neck and fighting to take hold of a piece of chain that dangled down into his shirt. Like a wildcat *Seldek* fought back, dragging the doctor backwards and slamming him against the back wall.

"Do something!" Tselitel shrieked to Welter, her hands taking hold of Rhemus' shoulder. "You can't let them kill each other!"

"Why not?" he asked calmly, as the two aliens wrestled and knocked books and glassware off a shelf that ran along the wall. "Save us a lot of trouble."

With a mixture of shock and disgust she recoiled at his utter indifference. Taking a step away from the emperor to intervene herself, she instantly felt his regal hand upon her wrist.

"No," he said decisively. "You'll just get hurt." Watching a moment longer, he frowned when a large glass vase fell from the shelf and shattered against the floor. Slipping on the shards, the two aliens fell down together and continued to wrestle, the glass cutting their skin. "Gustav," Rhemus ordered, nodding towards the two of them.

Drawing a reluctant breath and exhaling it sharply, he

approached the two and drew his pistol.

"Alright, boys," he said, the unmistakable click of the hammer cocking freezing them in place. "Play nice."

Blood dribbled down their bare arms as they looked up at him, neither knowing what to do. *Seldek* recovered first, a snarl bursting from his lips as he leapt up to take the gun away. But a scornful boot in the face drove him to his back, his palms sliced open as he put them against the glass shards to try and catch himself.

"Wait!" *Keelen* said, throwing himself on top of the partially stunned leader. "Wait!" he repeated, finally managing to drag the chain from around his neck, a small silver amulet dangling from it.

"No!" *Seldek* shouted, trying to take it back. "Give that to me!"

"Hold it steady," Welter ordered, standing over him and aiming squarely between his eyes.

With a gasp the exhausted doctor got to his feet and moved towards Rhemus and Tselitel. Welter took a step back, too, allowing *Seldek* to stand up and steady himself with the shelf.

"What is that?" Tselitel asked, as *Keelen* carefully held the amulet away from himself. "What was it doing to him?"

"It's one of the most dubious inventions of our people," *Keelen* told her. "It was designed to accentuate the faculties of the user. But doing so also exaggerates the negative qualities as well, until the personality eventually collapses. It was meant to be used only in short bursts, under the most demanding of circumstances." Contemptuously he turned and looked at his colleague, who was wiping his lips with the back of his hand. "But sometimes more mediocre individuals use it to make something of themselves." Carrying it to the far side of the room, he set it carefully on a small lampstand. "I should have seen it before this," *Keelen* reproached himself. "The signs were there. I just didn't think he'd be so *stupid*–."

"Hraaagh!" *Seldek* bellowed, rushing across the room towards the amulet as the doctor moved back towards the humans, leaving it alone. Instantly he returned to it, snatching it up just as Welter put a hand of iron around the maddened alien's arm and jerked him off balance.

"I thought as much," *Keelen* uttered regretfully, shaking his head as he eyed his irrational colleague. Furiously *Seldek* fell to the floor and began to convulse.

"We need to get him to the hospital!" Tselitel said urgently.

"It's far too late for that," *Keelen* replied. "The device has already destroyed much of his mind. "

"But how?" she asked. "How can that little disc do so much harm? There must be *something* that you can do."

"There really isn't," *Keelen* told her, taking a seat opposite Rhemus and watching *Seldek* writhe. "As I told you, the device accentuates the faculties of the user. But it also causes all of his undesirable traits to grow out of anything like their previous proportion. It does this by working upon the individual's brain. In small doses this effect is usually temporary. But long term exposure leads to a permanent rewiring of the brain, one that cannot be undone by any technology that we now possess." He paused and nodded towards him. "What we're watching now is the withdrawal symptoms. The device is *terribly* addicting. Without it he'll likely die within the next two weeks, as his nervous system begins to spiral out of control."

"Then give it back to him!" Tselitel pleaded, her sensitive heart torn apart to see him suffering so much.

"The result will be the same," *Keelen* said. "Though it would likely take a little longer. *Seldek* has entered the critical stage of his use, where the effects dramatically hasten as the brain loses integrity and comes undone. He might last four weeks instead of two, but he'll most certainly die."

"But, there must be *something* we can do," she insisted.

"If there was, I would be doing it already. No, Doctor

Tselitel: he's invited this on himself. He knew the risks, as does every *Kol-Prockian*. He sealed his own fate. The only thing to do now is put him somewhere that he can't be a danger to anyone else, and await his end." He paused once more to look at *Seldek*, disgust written on his face as the insane alien snarled and twisted on the floor. "I'll have a team come in at once to take him away. We don't need to watch any more of this."

Drawing a communicator out of his pocket, he muttered something into it and resumed watching. Within two minutes a foursome of guards entered the room, shackled their former leader, and carried him out.

"I'm sorry this had to happen," he uttered with embarrassment, as Welter put away his gun and sat at the table. "This is the most shameful thing that could have occurred during your stay here. I almost can't believe that it has happened." Resting an elbow on the table, he raised a thin hand to his forehead and rubbed his brow. "We'll have to find a new leader," he said after a long moment, his voice weary now that the excitement had died down. "Someone that will inspire hope in our people." He sighed. "That won't be easy after something like this. They've suffered so many disappointments already. To learn that their leader went out of his mind using a forbidden artifact," he shook his head. "I hope it isn't too much for them."

"They'll have to take it," Welter replied. "For survival's sake, if nothing else."

"We've been on the edge too long," *Keelen* said. "We're ground too thin to hold up much longer. That's why it was such a boon when we received Krancis' communication: it gave us hope for the first time in ages. No, Mister Welter: even the urge to survive may not be enough this time. If our leaders can't hold up to the pressure, how will the lower strata of society?"

"Then give them someone they can believe in. Someone with more integrity than *Seldek*."

"And who would that be?" he asked. "We're proud, Welter, as you've seen. Too proud for our own good. It causes us to cover up our shortcomings, especially with outsiders. For that reason, we've managed to put on something of a show for you all. But you know as well as I do that our society is on its last legs. That's why that fellow tried to attack us earlier in the hangar: he was deranged, deluded, and probably acting on some mistaken sense of *Kol-Prockian* dignity. Most likely he was using an amulet like *Seldek* was, though it's almost certainly disappeared by now."

"What I saw in the hangar earlier wasn't the act of a broken people," Tselitel said. "When they surrounded us, protecting us with their very lives, I was proud of them all. That required courage and honor, *Keelen*."

"My people respond very well to power," the doctor replied. "That's why they respect and revere you, Emperor Rhemus," he said, looking at him before rolling his eyes back to Tselitel. "The greater rules the lesser within *Kren-Balar*. It's most likely a relic from our military heritage. Most of the original inhabitants of this base were in our armed forces, so they are reflexively hierarchical. It's wonderful for discipline, provided you can give them a figure worthy of respect. Lacking such individuals today, our people are headless, discouraged, and lost. The fate of *Seldek* will merely serve to lower their morale further. They aren't used to thinking and acting for themselves." He snorted. "That's probably why *Seldek* used that cursed device in the first place: he was on the same footing they were, and had to find *something* to bolster himself." He laughed mirthlessly. "You can see the same instincts in me. It can't have escaped your keen psychological eye, Doctor Tselitel, that I scorned *Seldek* as soon as I learned of his abusing that device."

"It did not," she confirmed reluctantly.

"It was his *weakness* that I scorned. The rest of my people will do the same."

"Then don't tell them," she suggested. "Say he died in

some kind of accident."

"Oh, this base is rife with gossip. They'll know what's happened almost as soon as he reaches his cell to wait out his few remaining days."

"Why don't you assume command?" Rhemus asked.

"Because I lack the nature for it, Majesty," he replied, his tone a little more respectful as he addressed him. "I don't have it in me to bear that much responsibility. I can't carry the burden of my people's survival. It's simply too much for me." A sudden shiver ran through his body as a bold, outrageous idea crossed his mind. "But you do."

"What?" Welter asked.

"Emperor Rhemus, would you consider expanding your domain to include *Kren-Balar*?"

"You must be joking," the bodyguard objected. "They'll never accept a human ruler."

"You saw how they were ready to give their lives for him, didn't you?" *Keelen* argued. "They've fallen to such a desperate place that they'll accept anyone who's strong and willing to protect them. Especially once word of *Seldek's* fall spreads through the base. They accept anyone to free them from their despair."

"I appreciate your suggestion, *Keelen*," Rhemus replied. "But, without offending my imperial dignity, it must be remembered that I myself am here due to weakness. It was the chamber that brought me to *Kren-Balar*. If *Seldek* is now an object of scorn due to his frailty–."

"But that's completely different," the doctor insisted, his excitement causing him to forget his manners. "You do not know my people as I do, Majesty. They do not think of your illness as a weakness like *Seldek's*. They will consider him weak of will, because he could not resist the temptation of the amulet. But to leave your galaxy and reside with a people unknown to you is counted an act of *courage*. Your illness is thought of as a regrettable handicap that you strive daily to overcome, and not as a mark against your character.

They're aware of your struggle, and they respect you for it. The fact that you chose the ruthless Krancis to rule in your name further adds to your legend. Outside of a handful of rabble and trash, they do not consider you weak, Majesty. Not by any measure."

Solemnly Rhemus leaned back in his seat and eyed the hopeful alien.

"I will think upon this," he replied. "And give you an answer shortly."

"Yes, Majesty," he nodded, grateful to have won even that concession.

"And now, I would like to return to the chamber," he uttered. "I'm feeling very tired after all this."

"Of course," *Keelen* said deferentially. Calling for an escort over his communicator, they arrived at once and took the lead as the group slowly worked its way back. Welter followed up the rear, standing behind Rhemus as Tselitel helped him along. *Keelen* walked by the emperor's side, ready to throw himself in front of any other would-be assassins who might crop up.

The crowd inside the hangar had expanded with time, making it difficult to pass. It wasn't until they recognized that Rhemus was among them that they made a path for him, moving back a respectful distance and eyeing the ground. Curiously he looked at them, before casting a glance at *Keelen*. The alien nodded in reply, indicating that such treatment was what the ruler could expect should he decide to take them under his wing. Thoughtfully he looked back to the crowd, studying them until his entourage was forced to turn a corner and leave them behind.

Regaining the chamber without incident, the escort remained outside, two of them standing on either side of the door. Tselitel helped the emperor to his usual place, remaining with him for a couple of minutes. He quickly fell asleep, and she rejoined Welter and *Keelen* in the outer room.

"It's taken a lot out of him," she said with concern,

watching his sleeping form through the glass. "He'll need a lot of rest."

"He'll get it," *Keelen* said with quiet intensity, standing a couple of feet behind her and watching over her shoulder. "I'll keep a guard on the door constantly. There *won't* be a repeat of today's travesty."

Tselitel turned around, wrapping her arms around herself to fight a chill she'd only just noticed. Quietly Welter watched her, leaning against the table as he replaced the spent bullet in his pistol's magazine.

"Is there anything I can get for you two?" *Keelen* asked. "Food?"

"I guess I'm a little hungry," Tselitel replied, unsure if the rumbling in her stomach was appetite or nerves.

"I'm fine," Welter said, sliding the gun back into his jacket. "Thanks."

With a mute nod the alien doctor left them alone.

"He sure is different," Tselitel uttered, joining Welter by the table and continuing to hug herself. "I thought he'd be the last one to change his tune."

"He's embarrassed. It'll wear off."

"Don't you believe people can change?"

"That bird's too old to change."

"I don't know," Tselitel differed. "I think he's known this was coming for a long time. Oh, not front brain, not *consciously*. But in the back of his mind, he's probably known all along that *Seldek* was getting ready to implode, and that someone else would have to take over. If you think about it, that explains his initial hostility to us. From his telling, only an established ruler like Rhemus could take over the leader role that his people so desperately need to fill. It would undermine his self-respect to seek out a foreign ruler, even if that's the only option for his people. So he bit and snapped at us, realizing that we were inevitable. Or rather, the emperor."

"Uh huh," Welter replied without interest.

"You don't care about any of this?" she asked, a little

hurt by his indifference.

"I think we've got other things to think about right now," he said, looking at her. "Like why you're shaking."

"Oh, I'm just cold," she replied, rubbing her hands up and down her arms.

Reaching out, he grasped one of her hands in his, taking its temperature before letting it drop to her side.

"You're just fine," he told her. "It's got nothing to do with the cold. You're shaken up. Why don't you head back to the chamber?"

"I don't want to siphon energy away from the emperor," she shook her head. "Not for the time being, anyway. I'll go back inside once he's had a chance to recover."

"And you want to work on me," he uttered with exasperation. "Don't think that I can't tell you're trying to work your way closer to me, pulling me in with all this psychobabble. I'm not interested."

"Gustav, you nearly throttled *Seldek* a little while ago," she objected earnestly. "And then you nearly shot him. Don't think I didn't notice."

He looked at her with some surprise.

"You're very perceptive."

"That's my job, Gustav: to help people by noticing things, by perceiving what they can't."

"And you think I'm walking around with a big blind spot in my brain?"

"I think you're hurting terribly, and you can't see how it's undoing all that you can be. You can't live life for yesterday, Gustav, no matter how special it was. You need to live *now*. Your love would've wanted it that way."

Angrily his head snapped to her.

"I'm sorry," she said quickly, raising her hands and ducking her head a little. "I'm sorry. That was much too forward of me."

Drawing a hot breath through his flaring nostrils, he looked ahead again and let it out sharply.

"What makes you think she was my love?" he asked after an interval.

"Because I know another man who would react the way you have to such a loss," she explained. "Nothing would matter for him anymore except vengeance. It makes me fear what will happen when I–," she hesitated, unsure if she really wanted to divulge who it was. Rolling her eyes at herself for revealing as much as she already had, she continued, "when I finally die. I'm afraid of what Rex may do."

"You're very perceptive, Doctor."

"Thank you."

"But you're wrong. I wasn't in love with this girl. She was my daughter."

"Oh," she said tenderly, reaching out a gentle hand and touching his shoulder. "I'm so sorry, Gustav. So sorry."

"Not as sorry as the ones who did it are going to be," he replied acidly. "Once I'm done with the emperor, I'm going to scour them from our galaxy. And then I'll head into their home turf and begin to break them down."

"You can't do it," she said, withdrawing her hand. "They'll destroy you."

"Not before I've destroyed a great many of them. I'll make them pay for *ever* bringing their filthy, stinking hides into our space."

"I know you're in pain, Gustav. So much pain. But you can't let this define you. Your daughter would never have wanted you to expend your life in this way. You're more than a human bomb. You have to think productively, finding ways to build the kind of galaxy your daughter could have thrived in. You have to *live* for her, not *die* for her."

"She's dead and gone. *Living* for her is nothing but a fantasy, a fairy tale I'd tell myself to justify letting her death go unpunished. I've already killed the one who was directly responsible for her murder. Soon I'll take the fight to the rest of them."

"No, Gustav," she said firmly, shaking her head. "The

empire needs every good man that it's got. And you're a *good man, Gustav*. We all need you in this war, fighting where you're most effective. Rhemus needs you; Krancis needs you; I need you. You can't throw away your life on a suicidal crusade."

"You've got Rex."

"Yes, and he can't do this by himself. He's going to need all the help he can get. And I'm not going to stand aside while one of the best fighters around destroys himself. You were handpicked by *Krancis*, Gustav. He chose you from an entire empire of possible people because you were the best one he could find to protect his beloved emperor. And you haven't disappointed him," she said emphatically, her own respect manifest in her earnest voice. "Not by a long shot. I still don't know how you saw and killed that assassin. All I noticed was endless bodies around us."

"It was simple enough. He was the only one with murder in his eyes."

"That's not the kind of thing most people can see."

"Doctor, I know you want to believe that everyone can live life and have a happy ending. But it doesn't always work out that way. I don't want a happy ending: I want to go out fighting, my hands dripping with the blood of our enemies. I want justice for Amra."

"You've already killed her murderer," she insisted. "Justice has been done for Amra. Anything beyond that is for you, not your daughter. That's why you're so focused on death, not life. You're trying to make a statement instead of building something."

"What would you know about death," he replied sourly.

"A great deal. It's hung over my head ever since I was a child. That's when I was diagnosed with Valindra. I felt my entire life disappear in an instant. Do you have any idea what it's like to have your future stolen from you at such an age? It's crushing. It's like a weight that presses you against the ground until you can't even breathe anymore. Oh, I became obsessed with death, too. I counted the days until my nervous system would turn to dust, and lost all joy, all *hope*. After a number of years I realized that I had to make the most of what I had, to do something *productive* instead of mourning what I'd lost. And I went on to become a renowned psychiatrist. I managed to do something *good* with my life, when before all I could see was darkness and death. I turned the tables on despair, Gustav. You can, too."

"I'm not in despair."

"You are," she replied knowingly. "It doesn't feel like despair, because you aren't afraid. But that's not a prerequisite for it. You only have to feel that something incalculably important has been taken from you, and that you'll never get it back. That's all despair is: loss of hope. There's no need for fear to accompany it."

"Without Amra there's no life for me anymore," he uttered quietly.

"Would you want her to feel the same way?"

"Of course not. But she was a child, barely in her twenties. She had her entire life ahead of her." Violently he slammed his fist against the table, making her start. "That's why I hate them so much: they didn't just rob *me*, they robbed *her*, too. She would have brought so much beauty to those around her. She was a wonderfully talented psychic, Doctor. But she wanted to join me in my work fighting the separatists, and I let her. I should have gotten her off of Erdu-3 when I had the chance, sent her somewhere, *anywhere*, so long as she was out of the fringe. It was only a matter of time before something disastrous happened."

"Nowhere is truly safe, Gustav. Not with the Devourers traversing the empire and striking any planet they choose. Countless lives have already been lost. She may have died even if she was on one of the inner worlds."

"Tell me, Doctor," he said somewhat pointedly as he looked at her. "Would you allow your own child to stay in harm's way for years without doing anything about it, and then have a clear conscience if something terrible happened? Could you serenely preach acceptance to yourself as easily as you preach it to me?"

"Probably not," she admitted. "I would be under the same pressures you are."

"Then don't lecture me."

"But that doesn't make it *wrong*," she insisted. "The truth is the truth, whether we have the strength to accept it or not. My own frailties shouldn't stop you from rising above this. You have to overcome your pain and carry forward the struggle that Amra gave her life for. She believed in it so much that she stayed on the front line for years, when she must have known she could flee at any time. Don't drop the torch that she so bravely carried."

They were interrupted by the return of *Keelen* carrying a small tray of food for Tselitel. They exchanged pleasantries, but from the looks on the humans' faces he quickly judged that they were in the middle of something and found an excuse to depart after inquiring about the emperor's health.

"At least he knows when he's not wanted now," Welter commented. "Which is more than can be said for you."

Grimacing at this verbal blow, Tselitel pushed off the table and looked at him.

"You hurt me, Gustav," she said sadly. "You really do. I know you're in pain. I know that you're suffering. But you can't even identify your friends anymore. I just hope you come around before something terrible happens."

"You'd like that, wouldn't you?" he asked, his words stopping her after she'd turned and begun to walk to the chamber. "It's worth anything to have your theories proven right, isn't it? That's why you can't let me go: you don't want to accept that sometimes there *is* no happy ending."

Closing her eyes as tears began to gather in them, she swallowed and turned to him again.

"I won't let you go," she said in a trembling voice, her body beginning to shake as she neared him, "because I have to believe that there's something for Rex after I'm gone. I *have* to believe that men as good as you two can survive a crisis like this and come out stronger for it. Otherwise I'll break down into despair myself, because I can't live thinking that Rex will be shattered by my passing. You both love so passionately, so *fiercely*, that you'd die for the one you care about. Whether it's a father's love for his daughter, or a man's love for his woman, it makes no difference. You're helplessly attached, joined at the very soul, and you can't resort to any of the tricks that more emotionally deft people are capable of. You can't separate yourself from the other person because you have no control over these feelings. It's the foundation of the sincere integrity that undergirds everything that you do." Her throat tightening as she spoke, she paused to swallow. "And that's why I keep after you: I don't want to see either of you destroyed in this way."

Frowning at his own truculence, Welter stepped away from the table and matched gazes with her for a moment. Her eyes red and puffy, her thin form quivering with emotion, she looked almost ready to fall over from weariness and grief. Slowly he put his arms around her narrow shoulders, drawing her close. A sob escaped her lips as she pressed her head against his chest.

"I miss him so much," she managed to say.

"I know," he replied, squeezing a little tighter.

Kicking himself for tearing into her as he had, Welter could think of nothing to say or do that would take back his words. For a long time they stood together, their embrace palpably therapeutic rather than romantic. Even if Welter had been the sort to try and steal another man's woman, he was far too emotionally cold at that point to attempt it. Instead he was a statue, a pillar of strength for the overwrought doctor to lean against while she regained her composure. At last she raised her head.

"I'm sorry," she sniffled, taking a step back. "I shouldn't have thrown all that onto you. You've got more than enough on your mind as it is."

"I don't mind," he replied, shaking his head. "Doctor..." his voice trailed, trying to conjure the words to repair the damage he'd done.

"Please don't worry about all that," she said, again reaching out and gently touching his shoulder. With a little smile, she added, "I know you didn't mean it."

"I meant it at the time," he replied. "But I don't anymore. I was wrong."

"Please don't trouble yourself about it," she requested, pulling her hand away. "It's alright."

He watched as she turned and opened the door to the chamber. Smiling once again, she disappeared inside.

"You've got quite a woman, Hunt," he thought to himself. "Quite a woman."

Leaning against the table again, he felt something shift within. Somehow the emotional temperature inside of him had dropped, and he felt he could breathe a little easier. A pang of guilt ran through him at the thought, as though he was betraying Amra by losing some of the fatal intensity of his feelings. Shaking his head to dismiss the notion, he went to his old chair by the chamber door and sat down. The good doctor had given him a lot to think about, and he needed time to process it all.

Hours later the door opened again, and Welter was surprised to see *Karnan* step out.

"Shouldn't you be in there?" he asked.

"It gets claustrophobic after a while," he uttered, walking unsteadily to the table and beginning to eat at once from Tselitel's tray. "This belong to anyone?" he asked, his mouth half full as he moved to the other side of the table and sat down so he could see Welter.

"Not particularly."

"Good. I'm starving."

For several minutes the ancient alien crunched bizarre looking vegetables. Then he took up a spoon and began to eat from a bowl of cold porridge.

"I heard you two talking," he said at last, his spoon clinking at the bottom of the bowl as he scoured every last glob out of it. "You grew quite loud at times. Did you know?"

"We were a little distracted."

"We're lucky to have Doctor Tselitel among us. She has a good heart."

"Yeah."

"But a good heart can be easily hurt by thoughtless words," he added, pointing with his spoon, his elbow resting on the table. "She needs careful handling. There's a lot on her mind."

"I'm aware of that. I don't need a lecture."

"I know," the *Kol-Prockian* said, laying aside his utensil and leaning back. "But sometimes we need to hear what we already know to be true from the mouths of others. It gives such notions more reality."

"Sure."

"And right now her faith is teetering on the edge. She needs a boost, something to help her hang on. She's worried sick over that man of hers."

"Just how much did you overhear?" Welter asked, crossing his arms. "She dropped her voice for that last part."

"I might have had my ear pressed to the door," *Karnan* replied with a grin. "Let me tell you, I barely made it back to my corner without her noticing me."

"You should have outgrown such things by now."

"I resort to whatever tactics are required," he said without apology. "As do you. It's a trait we share."

"I don't listen at keyholes."

"You don't need to. You seem to do all the talking, anyhow."

Resentfully Welter eyed him.

"How would you like to go back into that chamber

head first?"

"I wouldn't," *Karnan* replied, reaching his hands behind his head and stretching his spine over the back of his chair. "But you won't lift a finger against me."

"I won't?"

"Of course not. I'm a thinker like you, Welter, and I've done the math. You can't touch me because I'm vital to the emperor. Besides, you're not the type to kick old folks around. It's not in you."

"I could learn."

"Save the surly routine for helpless women like Tselitel."

His anger flaring, Welter jumped to his feet and strode heavily towards him.

"Okay! Okay!" *Karnan* said, holding up his hands just as he reached the table. "That was too far. Much, much too far. I take it back. I never should have said it."

With a murderous look in his eyes, Welter grabbed a fistful of his robe and pulled him to his feet. Dragging him across the floor, he opened the chamber door and pushed him inside.

"Are you alright?" Tselitel asked, as the old alien turned around and made a face at Welter through the glass. Getting to her feet, she took his arm and tried to guide him back to his part of the room.

"Oh, I'm fine," he said, shaking her off. "That man's got an attitude problem."

"You didn't prod him, did you?" she asked.

"Just a little," he evaded, turning and walking slowly back to his corner.

"Oh," she groaned, glancing at the now empty window for a moment before following *Karnan*. "I hope you didn't offend him."

"Offend *him?*" he repeated incredulously, lowering himself carefully to the floor. "*You're* the one he dug into earlier."

"He's in a lot of pain," she explained, settling down on the floor next to him, resting her shoulder against the wall. "He can't be held accountable for things like that. He never truly meant to hurt me. He was just lashing out."

"He's got a funny way of *not* hurting you," he observed, shaking his head. "You must have had a lot of abusive relationships."

"Not a single one," she replied, her back straightening as her ire began to grow. "And I'll appreciate it if you take that back, for his sake and mine. Gustav isn't abusive, nor am I one to be taken advantage of."

"Fine," he raised his hands with a roll of his eyes. "I take it back. Alright?"

She was about to make a sharp remark about this insincere apology. But right as the retort was on the tip of her tongue, she thought better of it. The circle of recriminations had to end somewhere.

"Alright," she said flatly, allowing the matter to drop.

"Well, what's wrong with Rhemus?" he asked a bit gruffly, shifting the topic. "I saw you help him in here earlier."

Only remembering then that *Karnan* had missed all the momentous events of that day, she filled him in.

"I can't believe it," he said when her tale was finally over. "What could have *possibly* driven one of our own kind to attack your emperor like that?" His voice trembled as he spoke, and he drew his robe a little more tightly around himself, though the room was far from cold. "It makes you wonder what we're coming to as a people," he added, though like *Keelen*, he already had a pretty definite opinion on that point.

"*Keelen* wants the emperor to assume command of *Kren-Balar* and its inhabitants," she informed him.

"More power to him, if he can manage it."

"Then you're not offended at the idea?"

"*Offended?*" he asked, his widely spaced eyes finding hers. "Not at all. *Seldek* was never much of a leader, and anyone who would come after him won't be any better. Your emperor is our best bet for survival. My only concern is whether we're *his* best bet."

"What do you mean?"

"Not everyone is going to go along with a human ruler. We could end up with a couple dozen more assassins like that one today. And one of them might just get lucky. That would be a tragedy for both our races."

"Then you think it's a bad idea?"

"I think we need to give it a *lot* of careful consideration, so we can best ensure Rhemus' safety."

"Assuming he agrees," she commented. "He hasn't said yes."

"Then he's very wise," *Karnan* nodded approvingly. "He knows to look before he leaps, even when new territory is held out to him. That's a temptation a lot of rulers haven't been able to resist. Makes me all the more eager to have him over us."

"You surprise me," she uttered.

"Why? Because we're both proud *and* ready for someone like Rhemus?"

"Well, yes," she said, the words taken right out of her mouth.

"*Kol-Prockians* are proud," he explained. "Much more so than we have a right to be, at least these days. But we're also pragmatic. Those two elements fight each other, but the latter quality typically wins out. And if it's a question of racial collapse or swallowing our pride, you'd better bet we're going to open wide and gulp it down in a single go. We could do a lot worse than your emperor, and it's hard to imagine any way that we could do better. Nobody wants a band of rabble like we've become. We should be thanking *you* for taking us in, assuming Rhemus agrees."

"I hope he does," she said sincerely. "I'd hate to see your people vanish for good."

"Thank you, dear," he said, reaching out and patting

her hand. "Who knows, given enough time we might find ourselves again and be a real asset to you. The way things are shaping up, I think humanity is going to need every friend it can get."

"I agree."

They sat and chatted a little while longer, before the rumbling in Tselitel's stomach forced her out of the chamber and into the other room.

"Where's my food?" she asked, seeing only the empty tray.

"Mister Genius in there helped himself," Welter replied. He was still angry, though visibly not at her. "I'll have them send for some more, if you want."

"Oh, please do," she said, rubbing her stomach. "Much longer and I'll start to eat myself."

With a nod he leaned forward in his chair and stood up. Cracking the outside door, he relayed the message to one of the guards, who transmitted it over his radio.

"Should be just a few minutes," he replied, scowling through the window as he retook his seat.

"He told me about what he said to you," she said, crossing her arms and leaning against the wall beside him.

"And?"

"I chewed his head off," she smiled.

Despite his mood, he couldn't help grinning in return.

"Thanks. That was good of you."

"We're a team. Gustav. We look out for each other. And *him*," she added, nodding in Rhemus' direction.

"Look, I'm sorry about–."

"*Don't* apologize," she insisted. "Please don't. I don't want you to."

"But why?" he asked, surprised at her words.

"Because you've done nothing to be ashamed of," she said. "Unwrapping the agony you're going through involves passing through many layers of pain. Sometimes you'll lash out at others, like me, and other times you'll lash *inwards* at yourself. As soon as you attach moral guilt to it, the therapeutic value of doing so is lost, because you'll try to isolate and repress it, instead of allowing it to do its job. It's just another part of processing your grief, Gustav. I've seen it in many other cases."

"But you said I hurt you earlier," he objected. "You cried."

"I was overwrought and lost my objectivity for a moment," she said with a shake of her head, wishing she could undo it all. "That's why I said I shouldn't have put all that onto you: I was using *you* for my own grief and anxieties. I was being a very bad psychiatrist."

"The way I see it, Doctor, we've all got to hang together if we're going to get through this. None of us is an island."

"That's true," she replied, her hope beginning to grow that she'd melted through some of his icy reserve.

"So let me know what's going on inside that head of yours. Don't try to carry the weight alone."

"Will you do the same?" she asked.

"Doesn't look like you're going to give me much of a choice," he grinned, still a little annoyed but gradually growing appreciative of her efforts.

"Not if I can help it," she replied, smiling back at him.

At this moment a knock was heard on the outer door, and a mute *Kol-Prockian* handed her the second tray of food.

"Thank you!" she said as he retreated, hurrying to the table and sitting down with relish. "Ugh, I'm *starving*."

Without concern for ceremony she dug in, slurping and crunching with abandon.

"I'm sorry," she said, covering her half-full mouth with her hand as she spoke. "I'm usually not such a pig about food. But right now I could eat a horse."

"You've been through a lot today. Makes sense that you'd have to make some of it back."

"Mhm," she nodded emphatically, chewing quickly. "Sure you don't want some? I haven't seen you eat since we came here."

"I had them bring something every once in a while. I'm alright."

Nodding again, she let the point drop and finished her tray. Suddenly her eyes went wide.

"Frank!" she exclaimed. "We've forgotten all about him!"

"I haven't," he replied with a frown. "Every time I stuff my hand into my pocket without thinking, I get a half-second diatribe. He's pretty mad."

"Well, who can blame him," she said, pushing her chair back from the table and walking over to him. "We'd better talk to him, let him get his thoughts off his chest."

"What for? He hasn't got anything meaningful to contribute. He'll just gripe for a couple of hours about how we've neglected him and then go about making meaningless comments."

"He could be very useful as a go-between if the emperor decides to assume control of *Kren-Balar*," she replied diplomatically. "Only a handful of the base's staff speak English. The rest will need a translator. And I don't think *Keelen* or *Karnan* are going to be willing to chase us around from dawn till dusk, making us intelligible."

"Fine, but he's gonna have to cry on your shoulder, not mine," he replied, sticking his hand into his pocket and finding the chain. Annoyed to the moon and back with the AI, Welter was careful to avoid skin contact with him. "There," he said, holding it out for her.

"Thank you," she said, grasping the amulet and immediately jumping at Frank's angry voice.

"Do you imagine that Krancis sent me along just to be a paperweight? That I came all this way to collect lint in Welter's pocket? But that's not the cruelest part of the equation. Oh, no. For countless years I thought my people were dead and gone. Then I find out they're alive, only to be kept from setting eyes upon their works. I can *hear* them, but the refuge they've carved for themselves out of a *volcano* is kept from me. Do you have any conception how *frustrating* that is? Imagine for a moment that–."

"Frank, I'm sorry," she said, carrying him to the table and leaning against it. "We shouldn't have left you in there for as long as we did."

At this Welter rolled his eyes.

"Don't think I didn't notice that, Welter," he said, forgetting that only Tselitel could hear him through skin conductance. "And don't call me *Frank*, Doctor. My name is *Kerobenah*. I tolerated your little nickname while you treated me nicely. But henceforth I'll be treated with the dignity that I deserve."

"Now, Frank, we've all been through a hard time since coming here," she said, her tone growing more firm. "You aren't the only one who's had to put up with bad treatment. Your people have been kicking us against the wall since we first set foot inside *Kren-Balar*, and we don't appreciate it. We realize that you're not a party to their actions. But the attitude you're taking now is similar to theirs. You're being vain and hotheaded, and if you don't take on a friendlier tone, you can go right back to collecting lint."

Welter turned his head and nodded approvingly, glad to see she wasn't being pushed around by the surly AI.

"Pfft, you can't do without me, Doctor," Frank retorted. "If you wanted to make a play like that, you shouldn't have told Welter how much you needed me beforehand."

"I can see I'm getting nowhere with you," she shook her head, walking back to Welter and holding out the amulet.

"Wait! Wait!" he said urgently, causing her to withdraw it slightly as Welter watched. "Perhaps I spoke a bit hastily. You must understand that I've been under an awful strain. Listening to that brute insult and manhandle my people made me very angry. I-I shouldn't have taken it out on you. I'm sorry."

"What's he saying?" Welter asked.

"He called you a brute, and says you're to blame for his foul mood."

"Hey! That was for *private* consumption!" Frank exclaimed. "I never meant for you to just *tell him!*"

"We're a team, Frank," she replied, looking into Welter's eyes sincerely. "We don't keep secrets from each other."

Touched by her loyalty, Welter cracked a little smile and nodded, putting together what the AI had said from her words.

"We'd like you to be a part of that team," she added, her tone brightening a little. "But you've got to come down off your high horse and walk around with the rest of us mortals. Is that something you think you can do? Otherwise it's back to the lint."

"You don't leave a guy much choice, do you?" he groused. "Play ball, or become *utterly irrelevant*."

"Up to you," she said, extending her hand once more to Welter to drive home her point.

"Fine. Fine. I'll play ball. Sheesh."

"Good," she smiled, giving Welter a little thumbs up and leaning against the wall beside him. "Now, have you got anything to tell us about the situation here? Any insight to add? Wait, hold on." She gestured for Welter to follow her to the table and together they sat down. Placing her hand atop his, she said, "okay, go ahead."

"Well, for one thing, I'd recommend getting back inside that chamber and staying there for a good, long stretch. Your symptoms have moderated considerably. But you're far from a healthy state. Your breakdown earlier–."

"I'll head back inside as soon as I can," she said with a nod. "I promise. Now, tell us about the situation here."

"What's there to tell? *Seldek's* burned out his brain; *Keelen's* reeling from both that and the attempted assassination earlier; the entirety of my race is on the brink.

They've got good fiber, as their move to protect Rhemus proved. But they're disheartened and broken down. It'll take a miracle to get them on their feet again. Or at least a lot of time and healthy living. Living inside a base year after year does bad things to you. Especially if you've got a roving, nervous intellect like my people have."

"But can we trust *Keelen* to hold up his end of the bargain?" Welter asked. "Or is the shock gonna wear off and lead him to turn on us?"

"I'm not a mind reader, Welter," Frank said tartly. "Sure, I'm steeped in the ways and behaviors of my people, having served them faithfully since–."

"Spare us your work history," he cut in. "You're the closest thing we've got to an expert on *Kol-Prockians*. Give us your assessment."

"Having *only* heard him without seeing him, and having *never* interacted with him myself, I'd venture to guess that he's more or less going to play it straight. His dismay at the collapse of *Seldek* was both sincere and total. Unless some third option presents itself, he's faced with human overlordship or the end of our kind. And I'd say he's too smart to sabotage our best hope out of vanity or some other selfish motive."

"*Seldek* destroyed himself with that amulet," Welter observed. "The remnants of your kind don't seem exactly stable, even when they know in advance the end results of their behavior."

"I doubt *Seldek* was ever completely reliable. As *Keelen* said, the artifact accentuates already existent attitudes and behaviors. It cranks them up to eleven, if you will. It doesn't take a lot of imagination to tone down what we saw of his character and realize that he was always vain, self-important, and less than sensible. Please note that when I say we *saw* his character, I'm speaking figuratively," he added, still upset to have been left in Welter's pocket.

"Consider it noted," Tselitel replied, stifling a laugh

and forcing a serious expression. "What else?"

"Well, from the snatches I've heard, *Kol-Prockian* has evolved over the centuries. That, or the people who came here had a very strange dialect."

"Can you speak it?" Welter asked pointedly.

"Of *course*. Mostly it's a question of pronunciation, which is easy enough to deal with if you have enough processing power." He paused briefly to let them express how impressed they were with his capacity. When they didn't, he internally rolled his eyes and continued. "There might be a few teething problems, but nothing major. Honestly they sound almost like rustics. Even *Keelen* has the *stupidest* way of saying *Kren-Blur*. What happened to the vowels?"

"You can ask him the next time we see him," Welter replied.

"Oh, very funny. Unlike you, I have *some* small amount of tact in my fibers. Or rather circuits."

"Good to know."

"Frank, how do you think the rest of the *Kol-Prockians* will respond to the emperor taking them in?"

"Honestly? Probably with joy. It'll be the first chance they've had in ages to be part of something relevant on a galactic scale. That's a flipside to the whole pride thing that each of you, even *Keelen*, seems to be missing: their egos are going to get a massive boost from coming in out of the cold. They won't have to hide and cower anymore. They can hold their heads high when they look out across the universe."

"That's a good point," Welter nodded, surprised by that fact.

"I *do* have my odd moments," Frank replied sarcastically.

"Not very many."

"But this whole Rhemus thing is gonna have to be kept absolutely quiet," he added. "The treaty between the *Keesh'Forbandai* and the *Pho'Sath* doesn't apply to Quarlac. The *instant* they find out that a human dominion has been set up out here, they'll jump on it and tear it to pieces."

"Then why haven't they attacked our other holdings in Quarlac yet?" Tselitel asked.

"Probably not worth the effort," Welter replied. "Our possessions are decently well protected, so they couldn't make a secret of their attacks. We have trade relations here with a number of civilizations. If they start to bring the war into Quarlac and the other surrounding galaxies, plenty of other races are gonna get nervous about their intentions. As long as it's confined to the Milky Way, they can kid themselves."

"But *Kren-Balar* could easily be attacked without anyone ever knowing about it," she concluded. "Nobody would miss it if it simply disappeared."

"Yep."

"So it'll have to be a deep, deep secret of state," Frank said. "Which means that my otherwise garrulous people will have to learn to keep their mouths shut for a change. It'll be a while before we can move everybody to our new home."

At this moment *Keelen* reentered the room. Seeing the amulet, he paused at the door and stared for a moment, wondering if his eyes were deceiving him. Shutting it out of habit, his entire attention absorbed, he approached the table and rested his hands on it, staring at the disc.

"What is that?" he asked, still not sure if he could believe the testimony of his eyes.

"An AI," Welter replied evenly.

"I know that," he said with wonder. "But it looks old. Very old. That's not a design anyone has seen in a long time."

"He's from the old days," Tselitel confirmed. "Before the confederation fell."

He stood up straight and shook his head at them.

"You shouldn't joke about such things," he said, half certain that they were teasing him.

"We're not joking," she assured him. "His name is *Kerobenah*, but we call him Frank."

"*Kerobenah?*" he asked with some disappointment, knowing at once what that meant.

"Yes. Krancis sent him along with us in case we needed a translator."

"Do you mind?" he asked, reaching out his hand and holding it above the disc.

"Please," she said, holding it out for him to take.

Still hesitant, as though in a dream, he took the amulet and strode to the other side of the room. Holding it in both hands, he looked down at it and muttered to it in *Kol-Prockian*. His face lit up when Frank talked back, and immediately they fell into an animated, though hushed, conversation.

"Wonder what he's saying about us," Tselitel said, leaning towards Welter and dropping her voice.

"Can't be anything good. Probably complaining about being in my pocket."

"That's what I thought."

"You'd think the old bird would know better than to whisper. It's not like we can understand him, anyhow."

"Maybe he's just doing it for the sense of intimacy it provides. You know, a confidential talk with a relic from his race's past?"

"Could be."

For over an hour they watched, making the occasional comment. Mostly they tried to intuit what was being said by the gestures that *Keelen* employed. After the first few minutes he fell to pacing the far wall, his arms passionately moving to emphasize some point or other. He seemed to be getting something off his chest, or wrapping his head around something. They couldn't really tell which. The only thing they were clear on was that he was utterly invested in the discussion.

Finally *Keelen* settled down. Bringing the amulet back to the table, he carefully set it down.

"Extraordinary," he said with wonder, dropping into a

chair across from the two humans and staring into space for a moment. "Absolutely extraordinary."

"He's alright in a pinch," Welter replied.

This comment drew *Keelen* from his reverie, and he eyed the man with a mixture of annoyance and incredulity.

"'Alright?' Do you have any idea what *Kerobenah* is?"

"A nuisance, most of the time."

"He's one of the few remaining intelligences from our forebears. The wealth of knowledge contained within that small disc is outstanding. And his perspective is eye-opening."

"His *perspective*?" Welter asked, it being his turn for incredulity. "He was a bureaucrat. And not a very impressive one either, from the sounds of it."

"Why are you being so insulting?" *Keelen* asked, his anger rising. "Can't you show any respect for the achievements of my people?"

"I respect your people's achievements. But Frank's just a talkative paperweight. He's hardly a top of the line piece of hardware."

Offended, *Keelen* snatched Frank off the table and began to rise. Pausing as the amulet spoke to him, he frowned and set it back down.

"He insists on staying with you two," he informed them sourly. "He says you're a team. Though given your attitude, I can't imagine why he'd wish to remain. Naturally," he said, looking at Tselitel, "I don't include you in that remark, Doctor."

"Gustav and I are a package deal," she said. "Please remember that."

Brought back down to earth by this remark, he resumed his seat.

"Why didn't you tell us about *Kerobenah*?" he asked.

Tselitel froze for a moment, not wishing to put Welter on the spot by saying she'd merely been following his lead. Remembering *Karnan's* reaction to Wellesley, she quickly cooked up an elaborate lie.

"We were unsure how he would be received," she began, glancing at Welter and then back to *Keelen*. "Frank was on the loyalist side during your civil war, and I thought his presence might cause offense if there were any of you who sympathized with the imperial faction."

"Oh," *Keelen* replied, a little confused by this explanation, as it didn't quite seem to add up. Unable to figure out why, he simply shrugged away his doubts. "Well, you didn't have to worry about that. I doubt there's a single imperial sympathizer inside the entire base. And if there are, they're probably at the very bottom rung. Discontents and so forth."

"Of course," she agreed. "It was silly of me."

"Well, the important thing is that we know about him now. There's a great deal he could teach us about the old ways of our people. We *do* have the history of our race stored in our computers. But that's very different than having an actual participant from the civil war among us." He paused and shook his head at this thought, looking at the amulet again. "Truly extraordinary." Regretfully he added, "I wish *Seldek* could have seen this day, before the artifact destroyed his mind. Now he couldn't even comprehend its significance." Briefly he fell into silent thought, before looking up and glancing between them. "I take it you haven't told *Karnan* yet?"

"Not yet," Tselitel confirmed.

"You should. Just as soon as he's awake. It'll thrill him no end."

Pushing his chair away from the table, he stood up and eyed the amulet one last time. Then he turned and left.

"He was pretty impressed," Welter observed. "You'd think he'd never even seen an AI before."

"I ran into one of the ones they put out in the last couple hundred years," she explained, thinking of *Merokanah* and the base on *Preleteth*. "It wasn't a pretty sight. He was little more than a basket case. Wellesley said that the manufacturing talent of the *Kol-Prockians* had dropped off a cliff since the old days. I think that's why he was blown away: Frank's proof that they used to be able to do it right."

"Yeah, I guess he's functional enough," Welter allowed, picking up Frank by his chain and letting him spin around a little. Then he set him back down, took Tselitel's hand, and touched the amulet. "Have a nice chat?"

"Yes," he replied flatly, unamused by his comments. "Though *Keelen's* rustic way of talking took some getting used to. Especially after he got excited and started running over his syllables like his life depended on it. He was tough to keep up with."

"I'm sure you managed."

"Obviously. Are you going to tell *Karnan* about me now? Or shall the game of smoke and mirrors continue?"

"I guess we could," Tselitel said, looking at Welter. "If he's awake."

Slipping out of her chair, she slowly padded to the chamber's door, her bare feet clapping softly on the floor.

"Looks like it," she said, returning to the table. "If you're done with him," she added, looking at Welter.

"That goes without saying," he replied, taking his hand away and leaning back in his chair.

Not wishing to hear what the AI would say in reply, Tselitel grasped his chain and carried him into the chamber. Welter heard an exclamation of joy, followed by a rapidly flowing conversation in *Kol-Prockian*. Moments later Tselitel returned.

"I don't have to tell you how well he was received," she chuckled. "Though I wish he hadn't awakened the emperor. He was sleeping so comfortably."

"Did you check on him?"

"I tried to, but he waved me away," she said with some concern, taking the seat across from him.

"He just needs some time alone. He's got a lot to think

about."

"I suppose so."

An interval of silence passed between them, though they could still hear *Karnan* animatedly chatting with his new friend.

"Can I ask you something?" Welter inquired.

"Yes, of course."

"How did you get mixed up in all this?"

"Oh, well, I was on Omega Station when Krancis decided to send the emperor to Quarlac. Given my condition, he–."

"No," he clarified. "I mean, how did you get involved with the war? You must admit that a psychiatrist isn't the most likely of frontline personnel."

"That started way back on Delta-13. I'd heard reports of the prisoners going insane out there, and I wanted to check it out and blow the lid off the conspiracy. Before long the planet started invading my dreams, giving me premonitions about Rex. I could feel something was desperately important about him, and I had to learn more. I saw him outside my window one night, but he ran off before I could talk to him. Then I saw him again sometime later, chased him into the snow, and got lost in the forest. I would have frozen to death if he hadn't come back for me. After that I knew I couldn't let him go. We left the planet together when the Devourers showed up, and went to a world named *Preleteth*. Well, that's what the *Kol-Prockians* call it. We know it as Epsilon-4. After that we pretty much ran from one place to the next, finally ending up on Omega Station. I stayed behind while he left on *Sentinel*. Frankly I thought I was being held hostage until Krancis sent me here with the emperor."

"You probably were being held hostage," Welter opined. "Krancis isn't the kind of man to leave things to chance. He'd rather have the leverage to ensure he gets what he's after."

"But why'd he send me here then?"

"Plans change," he shrugged. "Keeping you alive is important to Hunt, so it *has* to be important to him, simply as a matter of policy. Besides, he probably realized you would get along well with Rhemus."

"That's true."

"And, let's face it, I'm not the most diplomatic soul. You help to soften the rough edges."

"I think we balance each other out very well," she agreed, shifting the emphasis so as to prevent him from being the bad guy.

He grinned a little at her diplomatic answer.

"Thanks."

"So, that's my story," she said. "What's yours? How did you get involved?"

"Oh, that runs way back. The organization I belong to is dedicated to fighting what you might call the mystical forces that have run our lives for far too long. Everywhere you go in this galaxy, there are entities, some of them non-corporeal, that have interfered with us ever since the dawn of our race. Mostly we worked to suppress their activities, though in recent years we've moved more towards fighting the separatists due to their alliance with the–," he paused, still unsure if he should heed the notion that the *Pho'Sath's* insight could be attracted by the mention of their name. "Well, *Keelen* said his kind call them the *Dolshan*, the hated people."

"It's a good name," she replied gravely.

"Yeah. Well, anyway, with them sticking their fingers into our business, we've been undermining the Fringers as much as possible to deny them a foothold. But it's been an uphill struggle, given that our talents really haven't run in that direction. We tend to be a little too…metaphysical for that sort of thing. A paramilitary group would have been better, sort of a combination of mercenaries and terrorists who could take the fight to them with brutality. Most of my colleagues are psychics, healers, and other kinds of mystics."

"You don't seem to have a problem grappling with them," she observed. "You're the very picture of pragmatic effectiveness, as that assassin learned."

"Yes, that's why I'm part of the organization," he replied, conscious of her compliment. "There's always been operatives, such as myself and my father before me, who could bring a certain set of practical skills to the table. The higher ups never really liked either of us because we live in a fundamentally different world. At bottom they're idealists, while my father and I have always been pessimists. They want to suppress these bad elements for a brighter tomorrow. I'm just trying to make today less dark than it already is."

"Then you're trying to conserve what we already have, instead of making something new?"

"I guess you could say that," he nodded slightly. "I hadn't put it into terms like that before."

"And that means you provide the necessary balance to keep the organization grounded."

"As grounded as it can be. There's really not enough of us to make a dent. Losing my father was a major blow. He had quite a lot of influence, despite his outlook."

"What happened to him?"

"He was killed by a *kal* on Bohlen-7."

"A *kal*?" she asked, a shiver running through her at the thought. Crossing her arms on the table in front of her, she hunched her shoulders a little.

"Yes. I take it you've met one?"

"Several," she confirmed, her pulse quickening at the memory. "We ran into them on *Preleteth*, and were nearly killed multiple times. They're like animals, but worse: they're intelligent, too."

"That they are," he agreed. "Though they vary wildly in terms of temperament and intelligence. Some are little more than rabid beasts. Others are communicative, rational, and capable of both wisdom and insight."

"We only met the rabid ones. They wanted to tear us to pieces. It was terrifying."

"That's why I spent a number of my earlier years in the organization hunting them," he replied. "Chasing them away from remote settlements and whatnot. Just like any wild predator they're smart enough to steer clear of someone who can kill them. Usually it took just a few of them dying to send a clear message to the rest."

"You *hunted* them?" she asked incredulously. "I can't believe it."

"Why do you think I carry this?" he asked, opening his jacket and revealing the Midnight Blade. "It isn't for show."

"Oh, of course. But what could ever possess you to *do* such a thing? I should think most people would be scared out of their minds just to encounter one of them. I know I was."

"Some people have the temperament for it, and some don't," he replied simply, not seeing anything very impressive in his feat. "My father did, and I must have gotten it from him."

"Incredible," she shook her head in disbelief. "Well, how many have you killed?"

"I haven't kept track."

"There's been that many?"

"Yes."

"No wonder you've got such a steady presence under all this pressure," she said with an appreciative laugh at his fortitude. "You've faced much worse things than angry aliens and the odd assassin. *Seldek* must have looked like a bad joke to you."

"He did."

"Incredible," she repeated, shaking her head again. "Oh, I'm sorry if I'm embarrassing you with this gushing schoolgirl thing I'm doing right now. But I just never imagined something like this was possible." She paused and tilted her head a little. "You really *hunted kals*? Followed them onto *their* turf and killed them in physical combat? Nothing but a dagger between you and death?"

"Yes."

"Remarkable."

"Why? That man of yours has fought plenty of deadly things. Let me tell you: the *Ph–*," he paused, catching himself again. "The *Dolshan* are much worse than the *kals*. It took me and a turncoat separatist to kill just one of them, and that only happened because I caught her off guard. They routinely kill several people singlehanded."

"Well, but Rex was born to that sort of thing. Or at least it seems like it. There's something very cold and fearless within him, almost like he's a little dead inside. That's mostly why I fear for him should anything happen to me: I think he's mostly living for me. So it seems natural to me that he'd face the things he has without blinking, because he doesn't exactly have anything to lose."

"Everyone has something to lose. Fear is a natural human instinct."

"I wonder if he feels that way because of what the *Prellak* did to him and his family," she mused aloud, only half hearing his comment. "Yes," she nodded slowly, the idea clicking together for her. "That's probably it: he was meant to be a tool in their hands. Naturally one with very little fear, and very little thought for himself, would be ideal."

"That makes sense."

"Yes, yes it does," she said distractedly, reflecting a moment longer before shaking her head and coming back to the moment. "I'm glad you're here, Gustav. Clearly Krancis knew just who he was sending when he chose you. I'm sorry I ever doubted you."

"That's alright. We hardly knew each other."

"That's true," she agreed. Smiling, she arose. "I'd better check on the emperor." At this they both heard an angry exclamation from *Karnan*. "And him, too."

Passing through the door into the chamber, she

looked at Rhemus but saw that his eyes were tightly closed, as though he was trying to screen out the world around him. Only then becoming aware of how loudly *Karnan* was talking, she cringed and moved quickly towards the alien. Speaking rapidly in *Kol-Prockian* as she knelt beside him, he finished his sentence and then looked at her with impatience.

"Yes? What is it?"

"I'm sorry, but can you lower your voice a little? The emperor is trying to rest over there."

"And *I* am trying to learn something of value from this bureaucrat!" exclaimed the ancient scientist. "He knows *nothing* that can be used to maintain our technology. You would think–."

"*Karnan*," she said firmly, cutting off his diatribe.

"Oh, fine," he replied with exasperation. "Better yet, why don't you just take him back. He can rot inside Welter's pocket for all I care."

Shocked at his attitude, she reluctantly took Frank's amulet.

"What's wrong?"

"Wrong? Wrong? I already told you what's wrong! I'd hoped that this little piece of tin would have something of scientific value locked away in his copious memory banks. But no! Nothing of the sort! I'm sure he would be very useful if I wanted to *file* something away for government use! But that's not the sort of thing we–, we need–."

He began to cough violently, his nervous excitement taking a toll on his aged body.

"We don't need that right now," he finished in a tight, scratchy voice. Tselitel placed a hand on his emaciated shoulder, causing him to nod impatiently. "Oh, I'm alright. I'm alright. I just got a little carried away." Taking a ragged breath, he let it out slowly. "Sometimes I forget I'm not as young as I used to be. Have to take it slow."

"Of course," she said soothingly. "Is there anything I

can do for you?"

"Just keep that numbskull away from me," he said bitterly, eyeing the amulet in her hand. "I don't care if I never see him again." Leaning his head against the wall, he let out an ironic laugh. "I'd sooner talk to *Allokanah* at this point. At least he might know something that would help us out of the present situation."

Shaking his head at this statement, he sighed and folded his hands in his lap.

"Just leave me alone with my disappointment for a while," he told her. "There's nothing you can do about it, anyway."

Squeezing his shoulder to signal her support, she arose and was about to return to Rhemus when she remembered the look on his face from before. Padding around the curtain, she saw that it had been replaced by a marked frown, telling her that he was in no mood for company. Despite her own need for the chamber, she decided to leave the two alone for a little while. The tension bothered her, anyway.

"I just can't get rid of you, can I?" Welter asked, still seated at the table as she rejoined him. His words were caustic, but his expression and tone implied anything but an aversion to her company. "What's wrong?"

"*Karnan's* upset with Frank, and Rhemus is upset with *Karnan*," she explained, settling down at the table and placing the amulet between them. "Said he couldn't learn anything from Frank. Nothing he wanted to know, anyway."

"That must have been a little humbling for our friend," Welter replied, glancing at the disc and hoping the AI had been taken down a peg or two.

"He even wished that Wellesley was here instead. And that's saying something."

"Yeah."

"Oh," she sighed, resting her elbows on the table and running her fingers through her hair. Covering her face with her hands, she drew another breath and exhaled.

"You alright?"

"I don't know. Something just seems to have caught up with me all of a sudden," she replied, framing her face with her hands and looking at him with tired eyes. "Like someone pulled out my batteries."

"It's been a long day, and you haven't been in the chamber much for a while now."

"I know," she nodded, her chin resting on the heels of both hands. "I just don't want to be in there if they're both angry. It's like the temperature is too high."

"You're sensitive to that sort of thing?"

"Very. I can almost taste it. Even out here it's bugging me."

"Then you have a psychic gift?"

"Yes, something like that. I used to think I was just very intuitive, but Ugo said I have a healer's talent for reading people. Or something like that. I don't know, it seems like such a long time ago."

"Ugo *Udris*?" he asked, cocking an eyebrow.

"Yes. Did you know him?"

"Only by reputation. He was a separatist, you know."

"I know," she nodded. "But back then everything seemed so black and white. The empire was kicking around the fringe, milking them and so on. Or at least that's what he said. In any event our association didn't last very long."

"Why?"

"He wanted to put me in harm's way for the 'good of the movement,'" she replied, making quotes with her fingers. "Rex wasn't having any of that, and our relationship all but ended when he threatened to flatten both Ugo and a bunch of his underlings if they laid a finger on me. We only saw him one more time after that. Then the Devourers came, and it seems he never made it off Delta. It's sad. I don't think he was a bad man; I think he was a good man who got deluded into doing bad things. Or at least very desperate things."

"That whole family is rotten to the core. They've been at the center of the separatist movement for years."

"I know. I met one of his granddaughters in the Black Hole."

"Which one?"

"Louise...something."

"Van?"

"Yes," she nodded, the memory coming back. "That was it: Louise Van."

"She was a hard case."

"Tell me about it. She took me hostage and threatened to kill me if Rex didn't clear a path for her out of the base."

"What happened?"

"The director of the station shot her in the head with a pistol." She rolled her eyes dramatically at the thought. "I don't have to tell you that my life flashed in front of me when that happened. I passed out a second later."

"You're lucky to be alive. Van was a nut, a real fanatic. She would have killed you purely out of spite if given the chance."

"What is it with Ugo's relatives?" she asked with a nervous laugh. "They all seem to be terrible people. Well, except Wanda. She was nice."

"There's one or two more exceptions. But mostly they're lousy."

"Exceptions?"

"Remember that separatist turncoat who helped me kill that *Dolshan*?"

"Yes?"

"She was one of his granddaughters. Nasty piece of work earlier on, but she changed tune eventually and helped me avenge Amra."

"*She's* the one who helped you?" Tselitel asked. "I never would have guessed it."

"She was a hardcore Fringer, too. Absolute fanatic. But Amra opened her eyes. I had to leave her behind on Erdu-3 when Krancis' message came through." He shook his head. "I hope nothing has happened to her. The organization didn't take kindly to her at all. They're not too friendly with former separatists, especially ones with a long and colorful history. Forgiveness is short in the fringe right now, given all that's happened."

"That's understandable."

"But she's a good girl. If they've got the sense to use her talents, she'll be a real asset. Just needs some time to find herself again. Her whole world has been swept away and she's lost and confused. Wanted to latch onto me, but obviously I couldn't stay."

"That's too bad. I'm sure you could have really helped her."

Smiling a little, he leaned back and regarded her for a moment.

"Doctor, are you falling in love with me or something?" he asked, his tone ironic.

"No," she said quickly. "Why do you ask that?"

"You're seizing every chance you get to compliment me. It's starting to grate on me a little."

"I'm sorry. I didn't mean to make you uncomfortable."

"Well?"

"Well what?"

"*Doctor*," he said meaningfully.

"I suppose you remind me of Rex," she ventured. "You're both hard, loyal men, and I like that. I didn't mean to cross any lines."

"I know. I never thought that you did. But I had to raise the topic somehow."

"Of course."

"But try to keep your applause to a dull roar, okay?"

"Okay," she chuckled.

A brief interval awkwardly passed.

"You should really get back in there," he said, pointing over her shoulder at the chamber's door. "You're mission critical, too."

Lifting her shoulders, she shook her head and grimaced a little.

"Still too hot in there. Maybe another twenty minutes or so."

"You can still feel it that strongly?"

"Yes. Sometimes I can tune it out. But anger or suffering pushes its way into my mind and won't give me any rest. At least out here I've got a little distance between it and me."

"Just what can you do?"

"Compared to the other psychics I've run into, not much," she said with a self-deprecating laugh. "I'm not sure I would even call myself a psychic, except I don't know how else to describe myself. I can't read thoughts or plunge into people's minds. I *do* have a gift for healing the psyche, but I'm not very sure how to use it. I really only ever had to use it once, and that was to save Rex's life. Back then his own gift was still very much a mixed blessing, causing all kinds of side effects. I helped him come back from the brink and then passed out. I was panicking and acting on instinct. I'm not really sure I could do it again without a similar stimulus."

"I'm sure you could," he replied. "Given time and training. If you can *feel* the tension in the other room, then you're sensitive enough to be molded into a weapon."

"I'm not totally sure I want to be a *weapon*."

"Then a tool. Your gift is something that ought to be drawn out and enhanced, not left to itself. Especially given the situation we're in now. We need every capable hand working as skillfully as possible to bring us victory."

"Well, it's not like there's anyone around here who could train me," she replied. "Unless you could."

"I don't have a gift."

"But you said your daughter was a psychic. You must have learned something by watching her powers develop."

"Sure, bits and pieces. But psychic powers are usually

trained one-on-one. I wasn't there for most of her sessions."

"Gustav, do you have a problem with training me?" she asked, tilting her head.

"Yeah, I do. You've got quite a talent, and I'm not going to risk screwing it up through ignorance."

"Even if I asked you to?"

"Yes, even then."

"Well, okay," she sighed. "I guess my immense powers will just have to go to waste. Say goodbye to our last hope for winning the war. This particular tool is going to remain in the toolbox."

"Very funny."

After another interval of quiet, the tension in the chamber eased enough for Tselitel to return. Taking her leave of Welter, she went to where Rhemus once again lay sleeping, stretched out beside him, and quickly dozed off.

CHAPTER 11

Ronald Radik stood on the bridge of his flagship, the light carrier Punisher, and watched the rest of his fleet slowly ascend from their moorings on the seventh moon of the planet Eichon. Called Mistletoe by some long forgotten explorer, the moon's deep valleys had been fitted with construction facilities placed in natural caverns that ancient rivers had carved in the rock. These waters had long since dried up, their sources slowly evaporating as the moon's atmosphere thinned over time. Still capable of sustaining plant and animal life, the orb was clearly on its way to becoming a desert. Already vast expanses of sand could be seen from space.

"Fifty percent of the fleet has achieved orbit, sir," a female AI informed him, appearing on a little pedestal several feet off to his right.

"Very good," he replied, missing the panoramic view of *Sentinel* as he peered out the somewhat narrow main window. There was another to his left and his right, and together they gave him a decent view of the space around his vessel. But nothing could match the perfect visibility of that magnificent ship.

"Minister Radik?" admiral Susan Hardwicke inquired in her reserved fashion from the door behind him, having just entered. Fifty-eight, with severe lines in her face and short gray hair that stopped just below her skull, she was a force to be reckoned with. It was said throughout the navy that the *hard* in her last name wasn't there for nothing, and her square, stony appearance seemed to bear that out. Thoroughly conventional in her outlook, Radik had called her to the bridge in an attempt to soften the opposition to the Adler project before addressing a larger grouping of officers he planned to meet with later.

"Come in, Admiral," he replied, after exchanging salutes, beckoning her into the room with an energetic hand. The title *minister* sounded strange in his ears, the announcement of his promotion by Krancis having passed through the empire just a few days before. "We're just about to launch our first fleet of the new era, Admiral. Soon the Devourers will get a taste of what humanity can really do."

"Sir, there are many within the navy which view the Adler project with…misgivings," she informed him reluctantly.

"Yes, I'm aware of that. It's the reason that Krancis put me in charge of it in the first place: so I can show them the necessity of changing our ways of war."

"Many of the higher officers don't consider Adler to be a sound approach to the problems we face," she said deferentially, though she was clearly of the same opinion. "Even Admiral Von Ortenburg is opposed to it."

"Von Ortenburg is a great man," he replied sincerely. "But his notions of warfare are outdated. I've seen our enemy firsthand, Admiral, and they are too fierce to be tackled in anything but the most aggressive fashion possible. I can see the difference between them and us after the siege of Jennet. Truly, I can. They give absolutely no thought for their own survival because *they* consist of one massive, intelligent heap. A heap that just grows and regrows. That's why their tactics are so desperate: all they're really throwing at us are the constantly regenerating limbs of a single body. We're not talking about lives being lost when they lose a ship: we're talking about something more like the index finger of their left hand. One that regrows with time."

"We do not regrow so easily," she pointed out. "Our ships are piloted by human beings who have one shot at life. A shot that grows cruelly minimal once they're placed inside one of the Adlers. The ships simply lack the survivability to be morally justifiable. It's little short of murder to order our pilots into them."

"It's slaughter to continue fighting in the fashion we have been," he replied, stepping towards the main window and gesturing for her to follow. "Look at those vessels, Admiral," he said when she'd joined him. "Each of those ships is more powerful than any six fighters put together, because they can rapidly deploy a devastating payload against the Devourers."

"But they're unarmored, sir," she pointed out. "Utterly defenseless against attack."

"That's by design."

"But the design is based on the cruelest notion of warfare I've ever encountered. Human beings are to be sent to the frontlines with nothing wrapped around them but a little bit of tin. It's inhuman."

"So are our foes, Admiral," he replied, trying to shift tack.

"But equipping our pilots with suicide vessels isn't the answer. What we need to do instead is ramp up production of present models, and revise our tactics. The navy has been knocked onto its heels, to be sure, Minister. But that doesn't mean we should throw out the playbook and start to rewrite it in the middle of the worst crisis humanity has ever passed through. That reflects the thinking of someone unversed in military history and practice."

"I am well versed in military practice, Admiral," he replied, his tone firm but even.

"I was referring to Krancis, Minister. Whatever experience he has gained at the emperor's elbow, it hasn't prepared him for the realities of galactic war. He thinks that our modes of operation are merely the habits of an inbred group of clucking chickens, and not the tried-and-true products of experience. I, and many of the other officers, warrant that he has conducted the war skillfully thus far. But in general terms. The moment he tried to interfere with our area of expertise he was in the wrong. He simply lacks the specialized knowledge necessary to make intelligent changes in our doctrines of war."

Radik had anticipated sharp opposition. But he hadn't imagined that it would run so strongly against Krancis himself. The respect that the man engendered insulted him from all. Or so the minister thought.

"Krancis has examined the issue thoroughly–."

"Krancis doesn't know what he's doing," she cut in, forgetting herself as she began to get worked up. "He's going to destroy the navy by forcing our best pilots to commit suicide in order to do their duty. You've seen the tests for the Adler: only the most skillful can fly it successfully. The combination of quick responsiveness and lack of armor requires one to be at the absolute highest pitch of skill in order to survive. We're going to take the best of the best and throw their lives away on an experiment when they ought to be leading groups of less experienced pilots in battle. Those greener fliers are going to be chewed to bits when they encounter the Devourers on their own."

"You forget that I've commanded battles myself, Admiral," he replied. "I've seen what our enemy can do. And our present tactics are wholly ineffective."

"Then take the Adler payloads but put them into vessels with greater survivability," she countered. "Don't send the pilots out there to die."

"We don't have the production capacity to field that many ships," he shook his head. "Even with *Sentinel* the Devourers are still steadily damaging the empire. What we need is a solution that can be produced quickly and cheaply. Hence these light carriers, as well. They are sturdy enough to serve their function without unduly burdening our economy."

"*Burdening our economy?*" she asked incredulously. "Is that all that the vessels mean to you? A cheaper way to–."

"You forget yourself, Admiral," he said sternly, more from the need to preserve his station than out of personal offense.

"It was not my intention to do so, Minister," she replied in a restrained voice, the heat of her emotions tempering somewhat. "But I speak for many when I say this plan is disastrous. Krancis knew that would be the opinion of all of us who have actual experience in this area, which is why he kept the project concealed for so long. Had he introduced it to us sooner, we might have been able to steer him in the right direction to salvage at least some of the resources he's poured into it. Now it's much too late, and we're forced to swallow it whole, as is."

"After the first successful demonstration of the project, you'll see that he was right," the minister assured her, his faith in the project hardening as opposition grew.

"*They'll hate Adler, because it turns all their doctrines on their head,*" Krancis had told him before he left *Sentinel*. "*At present, our doctrine is to maximize survivability as the first priority, doing damage to the enemy second. We try to pack as much armor onto a vessel as we can, adding weapons almost as an afterthought. Added to this, our tactics of fleet-to-fleet combat are meant to provide overlapping fields of fire, designed to present the enemy with no opportunity to bite off a portion of our forces and chew them down. In essence, we fight defensively, trying not to give an opening to our opponent. It is a reflection of the impulse to minimize loss as much as possible, both to save lives and to preserve our forces to fight another day. Such a conservative stance plays right into the aggression of our enemies. Having no fear of loss, they exploit ours and make it a terrible weakness. The only way to best them is to dismiss that fear and attack them with equal aggressiveness. It will require* us to throw out many of our conventional priorities. But it will succeed if the navy doesn't sabotage it."

"Von Ortenburg has vowed to stop the project from becoming operational," Hardwicke said, just as Krancis' last sentence of warning faded from his thoughts. "He has already begun to gather support among the other officers."

These words made Radik's heart tighten. He had great respect for the admiral, and the idea of matching wits with him before a gathering of career military personnel didn't please him. Having been out of uniform for so long, he felt that gave the admiral an instant edge in any argument. The temptation to simply declare his will as naval minister passed through him more than once. But he knew that *willing* support was necessary if Adler was to get off the ground and begin to turn the tide. Forcing it down their throats wasn't the answer.

But neither was walking into a room full of hostile officers and making a case none of them wanted to hear. He, the rustic from Jennet, would be on the defensive the entire time against the charming and educated admiral. His position would count for little, especially as it was bestowed on him from above, rather than having been earned through decades of labor. To Krancis this was an advantage, enabling Radik to see the problem without the blinders that decades of military protocol would have given him. But it was hardly calculated to win the respect of the officers who would be in charge of carrying out the new doctrine.

The only things working in his favor were that Krancis, however much he was suddenly reviled by the military establishment, still commanded the fear of anyone within his reach, which meant every last man and woman within the empire; and the fact that he had seen the enemy up close on numerous occasions and had managed to live to tell about it. This latter fact would give some grudging weight to his words, though he felt they would ultimately dismiss him as little more than a civilian in uniform.

"Pardon me, Minister," the AI said. "But sixty percent of the fleet has now achieved orbit. The remainder should be with us within the hour."

"Any problems?" he asked, glad to shift his attention from the matter before him and deal with something merely practical for a few moments.

"The light carrier *Destiny* suffered a slight malfunction of her engine. But her captain assures me she will be able to rendezvous on schedule. Her complement of Adlers is already aboard and secured, and it remains only for the engineers to effect minor repairs."

"Very good."

"A vessel fresh out of dock shouldn't be breaking down," Hardwicke said. "It speaks of the haste with which the project was conceived and executed. Had there been–."

"Admiral, I value both your experience and perspective," Radik cut in. "But it is manifestly clear to me that our present course of action is impossible to follow. Without a change we're lost, even with *Sentinel* battering away at the Devourers. It can't offer battle constantly because of the risk that they'll figure out a way to defeat it. And the navy in its present form can't grapple with the parasite alone. We need another option."

"That is something that we're prepared to give," she replied. "Or rather will be very shortly. The navy has been working on a revision of our tactics that will improve both our survival rates and the enemy's death rate. We have proposals aimed at improving production of new ships as well."

"When will this plan be ready?" he asked, knocked a little off balance by this new development.

"Very soon. We have personnel working day and night. It's a comprehensive program that targets the specific capacities of each of our major manufacturing centers to produce maximum efficiency. It also revises our recruitment and training programs."

"You've been busy," he observed, buying himself time to think.

"We're as dedicated as anyone to winning this war, Minister," she replied. "Moreso, in fact, given that we alone stand between humanity and defeat."

"Mankind is not entirely without allies," he said.

"Of course, sir," she allowed, her tone indicating that she gave the point no weight at all.

"I will consider your plan when it's available," he replied. "But Adler will proceed until then."

"Minister, I must ask you to reconsider this step," she said, her voice growing earnest. "Give us a little more time to complete our program. A few days at the most. Then you'll be able to compare it to the scheme Krancis has given you, and you'll see for yourself that it's the better way. Systematic upregulation of production and pilot acquisition is the way to win this war, not desperate tactics born from a non-military mind. Please don't throw away the cream of the navy on a plan that has no chance of success."

With a handful of further words they parted, Radik remaining on the bridge.

"They're playing for time," he thought. "Trying to throw a wrench into Adler. The opposition is stronger than Krancis thought. Or at least stronger than he said."

With a frown he turned from the main window and went through the door to the spartan metal corridor that connected the bridge to the rest of the ship. Everything was bare, exposed, and done on the cheap. Wires could be seen intermittently, running through the walls. The floors presented periodic notches and grooves, a tripping hazard to the unwary. Overall the impression one received was that of a metal skeleton that had been covered over with the thinnest possible layer of armor. It didn't inspire confidence.

Picking his way over the uneven floor to his room, he closed the door and dropped into a spare chair. Leaning forward, he rested his elbows on his knees and rubbed his hair, trying to massage an idea out of his scalp.

"Nothing I say is going to change their minds," he mused. "I'm going to have to show them. I'm going to have to *prove* that Adler is not only worthwhile, but crucial. And I've got to do it before that meeting."

That meant launching the fleet at once. The pilots were ready, and each carrier was loaded and virtually prepared to depart. But he had hoped to test them on something fairly small before engaging a large Devourer fleet. Despite the practice they'd received within simulators, the crews of both the Adlers and the carriers were still new to their vessels, learning their eccentricities. It would be a gamble to throw them in the deep end all at once.

But at the same time, he could hear the rumblings of mutiny in the navy. The assertive tone that Hardwicke had taken told him more about the establishment's view of him than she had intended. He was regarded as a decent enough man, but wholly out of his depth in command of the navy. If he wished to play ball, he would be allowed to maintain his relevance. Otherwise they would sweep him aside. Hence the independent meeting of officers, chaired by Von Ortenburg, no less. Gathering themselves together in that fashion indicated a complete disregard for military hierarchy, to say nothing of the plan they had taken upon themselves to produce. It bespoke a sense of dissociation from the proper channels of authority not seen since the earliest days of the war, when McGannon was faced with a similarly rebellious spirit. He knew that at that time she'd taken cruelly hard measures to ensure their loyalty, destroying her reputation and authority in the process. That wasn't something he could afford to do, given the fragility of the Adler project.

So he would have to impress them. But how? What enemy force would be strong enough to silence the naysayers, but weak enough that the new fleet wouldn't risk disaster by engaging it? It also had to be fairly close, given that the carriers were limited by the slowness of normal warp engines.

He shook his head, sincerely missing the incredible speed offered by the *Keesh'Forbandai* engines of both *Sentinel* and the egg he'd used to reach Mistletoe. If his carriers were outfitted with engines like *those*, it would be trivial to find a suitable enemy and strike almost at once.

"Minister," the ship's AI said, speaking over his ear radio. "Eighty percent of the fleet has joined us. The remainder have assured me that they'll be in orbit within thirty minutes, likely less."

"Excellent. Thank you."

"Of course, sir," she replied deferentially.

Leaning back in his hard and uncomfortable chair, he stretched out his legs and sighed.

"What to do..." he muttered, well aware that the only targets anywhere nearby were trivial. Krancis had deliberately placed the project's production facilities far away from the fighting, choosing worlds of little value to the Devourers to ensure they would go unnoticed for as long as possible. Naturally this was a wise decision, but it limited Radik's options severely. "What to do..."

But perhaps he was overreacting, he reflected. The navy couldn't really turn against him and Krancis, not with *Sentinel* to enforce the latter's will. It would make short work of *any* force that decided to range itself against them. Surely the officers were aware of that fact, and would ultimately back down before driving things past the point of no return.

And then Hardwicke's words echoed through his head once more, and his hopes sank.

"*...we alone stand between humanity and defeat...*"

The officers saw themselves as the true defenders of the empire, the only real hope mankind had left for avoiding extinction. Thus they were indispensable, and, in their estimation, Krancis couldn't possibly put pressure on them without ending the war effort. He needed them too much for his words to be anything more than hot air. Besides, it wasn't as if he could actually afford to start destroying human fleets. There were too few to go around as it was.

Thus they had more power than he had at first realized: the power of indispensability.

And that meant they couldn't be ignored and they couldn't be cudgeled. They could only be persuaded.

Which brought him right back to the problem of finding a fleet to target.

"I never should have taken this job," he muttered, having hoped that a few inspiring speeches and a quick demonstration of the Adler's capacities would silence all opposition, given how weary the navy must have been from suffering defeat after defeat. He'd assumed they'd quickly seize upon any other option that presented itself, after the initial resistance had been overcome.

Now he saw that Adler's enemies were both coordinated and entrenched, and that they had no intention of allowing the project to sail easily to victory. Decades upon decades of institutional thinking were against him, and it would take a striking example to win them over to his side.

"Sir!" *Punisher's* AI said suddenly through his earpiece, shocking him.

"What? What is it?"

"We've just received a distress call from the planet Hubertus. A massive Devourer fleet has appeared above them. But there's more: a single mass of Devourer…material, has been brought with them. It's already being lowered towards the planet as I speak."

"What do you mean 'Devourer material?'" he asked, heading out of his room and hastening to the bridge. "Is it a ship?"

"It's a giant blob of the organic material from which all their ships are built. It has no observable weapons, engines, or hangars. It appears to be simply a mass. And it's very large, sir. Several times the size of their carriers."

"But that's impossible. How could they make anything

so *big*?"

"I don't know, sir. But that's what the defenders in orbit are reporting. Needless to say, they are being swept aside with ease by the attackers. They estimate that the planet will be utterly defenseless within twelve minutes."

"How much of the fleet is in orbit?" he asked.

"Eighty-seven percent. We'll be at ninety percent strength in…two and a half minutes," she calculated.

"Plot a course for Hubertus," he ordered. "And inform the other captains. We leave the instant the fleet is assembled and the warp engines are ready to fire."

"Sir, I'm receiving a message from Admiral Von Ortenburg. Video call."

"Put him through," he said, just then reaching the bridge and turning to the modest screen that ran along the back wall above the door. "Admiral?"

"Hello, Minister," he replied formally, saluting crisply and then lowering his hand. "I trust that you've received word of the happenings above Hubertus."

"I have."

"My fleet is gathering to depart at this very moment. We shall be on the scene in approximately twenty hours."

"As will we," he replied, the AI having just informed him through his ear radio.

"Minister, with respect, your fleet is not prepared to deal with anything of this magnitude. It will be a difficult fight for the navy as it is. I ask you not to risk the lives of your crews by putting this ill-planned experiment to the test. It will only end in death."

"Yes, Admiral. For the Devourers."

Von Ortenburg shook his head.

"I ask you, sir, as one old sailor to another, to abandon this plan and stop expending our precious resources on ships that will never be able to stand against our foe. Admiral Hardwicke has presented the plan we are making, I trust?"

"In principle. There were no details."

"There *will* be details, I assure you. This program of ours is more than mere talk, Minister. It will revitalize our efforts and get us back into the struggle, permitting us to deal lasting damage to the parasite. But we must put the finishing touches on it, ironing out wrinkles that would make it appear impossible. It will increase our production capacity immensely, along with our recruitment and training programs."

"Hardwicke already gave me those generalities," Radik replied, annoyed that he was being talked down to by a subordinate. Particularly one he'd respected heretofore. "I will not stop the Adler project because of outlines and promises."

"Promises made by career officers who know their business, Minister," he objected. "I do not wish to disrespect your office when I remind you of the fact that you've been out of uniform for a very long time. This is not the sort of thing one simply picks up again after decades and falls back into. There are many factors–."

"I am keenly aware of the difficulties of the job, *Admiral*," he replied pointedly, emphasizing the inferiority of his rank. "But I am quite certain that Adler will perform as expected, and that it will usher in a new method of warfare that will ultimately crown us with victory."

"I have no such assurance," Von Ortenburg replied. "But I hope, for the sake of the empire, that you are right."

With this the admiral ended the transmission.

"How much longer until we can depart?" he asked the AI.

"Approximately one minute, Minister," she replied. "The other vessels still in dock are asking that we delay our departure so that they may join us. They don't want to be left behind."

"Tell them to make all possible haste, and to follow after us the instant they are ready to warp."

"Yes, Minister."

The final stragglers caught up with the *Punisher*, joining the fleet that had already formed around it. Moments later a cloud of blue windows appeared before them, whisking them away.

◆ ◆ ◆

Far above Hubertus, the battle was nearly over. A trio of interceptors made a run at a fatally damaged frigate, discharging their railguns into its engine and causing it to detonate.

"That got 'em," the fighter on the left said, before instantly exploding in a hail of green globs.

"Watch 'em! Watch 'em, Davy!" the middle pilot, Captain Julius Bardol, ordered his remaining wingman. "You can't–."

"Deeeyaaaaaaahhhh!" screamed the other flier, as his ship disintegrated around him.

"No!" exclaimed Bardol, jerking his head to the right to find his friend already gone.

Shoving his craft into a dive, he just missed a flat spread of blobs that had been intended for him. Spiraling his fighter and pulling away from the alien fleet, he caused two Devourer ships to collide and explode, forcing the other half dozen that chased him to fly around the explosion and lose a little distance on him.

"There you go! There you go!" he shouted, looking over his shoulder. "You want some of this? Come and get it!"

As though hearing his words, the alien vessels caught up with him and unleashed enough ordnance to kill him many times over. Narrowly missing their shells, he pulled a somersault and fell upon one of his attackers. Already damaged from the fighting, it was too slow to dodge his pursuit and was quickly destroyed.

"Chalk another one up for the good guys!" he triumphed, twisting his craft and jerking it right just as the other five caught up with him again. "You're not taking me today! Don't you even try!"

Intuitively he threw the craft downward again, just as he felt they'd lined up with him. But he was half a second too late, and a glob grazed his left wing and caused warning bells to sound in his cockpit. Gritting his teeth, he fought with the controls but began a tight, fast spiral towards Hubertus.

"I'm not finished up here yet!" he barked, insensibly trying to reason with his damaged fighter. The left maneuvering flaps were locked in place, no matter how hard he wrestled with the joystick. Doing so caused the right wing's flaps to flutter up and down unpredictably, making him all but impossible for the Devourer ships to hit. "I did *not* come up here just to crash!" he insisted, as Hubertus grew large before him.

Glancing over his shoulder, he saw the alien vessels break off their pursuit.

"Giving up on me, eh?" he shouted at them. "Well I'm not finished yet!"

As his fighter plummeted through the atmosphere and the ground slowly began to rise, he looked around him and saw the enormous mass of Devourer flesh that *Punisher's* AI had told Radik about. Squinting at the horrific sight, he couldn't help but imagine that it was a giant steak that had rotted beyond belief and was now being dropped on the planet he'd called home his entire life. Towed by numerous capital ships, their engines strained to lower it slowly, but they were clearly losing the battle with gravity. It was accelerating through the sky, preparing to crash with a thunderous report that would shake every city for miles and miles around.

"What are you animals up to?" he asked, trying to figure out the purpose of such a mass.

Suddenly a red light began to blink on his console.

"I know! I know!" he replied, for the light was situated right above a small bit of text that read *'eject now.'* Pulling the emergency release on his canopy, it was instantly torn away from the ship and disappeared into the air behind him. Reaching under his seat, he found the red ejection handle and pulled it.

Like a bullet shot from a gun, he was ripped from the doomed fighter. Moments later his parachute opened, jerking him violently and causing his neck to snap forwards. A searing pain went through his shoulders, but he forgot it when he noticed two Devourer fighters screaming towards him. From two hundred feet away they opened fire, their stinking green globs sailing past him on either side as they rocketed past. They spun around again, repeating their performance before flying off.

"Filthy dogs!" he shouted, shaking his arm at the retreating vessels as he realized they were just toying with him. "Come back here when I've got a ship, and then we'll see how tough you are!"

The jungle covered surface of Hubertus grew close, and it was then that Bardol realized that he'd have to find some place to land. It was just trees and trees for miles in every direction, and being a native of that hot, strange world, he knew that they often grew to be hundreds of feet tall. The last thing he wanted was to try and climb down after getting stuck in one.

"There's got to be a clearing somewhere," he said, panic beginning to grow in his heart as he searched. Finding a tiny slit between a pair of enormous trees, he guided himself towards it. "Come on, come on, come on," he muttered, pleading with fate to help him reach his destination. "At least one thing has to go my way today."

But fate didn't agree. Falling short by fifty yards, he crashed through the bushy branches of an ancient tree. Unable to help screaming as his body was battered and poked by the fragile limbs, he broke his way through them, coming to a stop when his parachute finally caught in the outer branches.

"What did I do to deserve this?" he asked fate, looking up into the sky at the slowly fading sun. "Huh? What did I do to deserve this?"

Seemingly his question was a bit too impertinent to be borne, for the limbs that held his parachute all snapped at once, dropping him another twenty feet before the collapsed material caught on a knot and arrested what would have been a fatal fall to the jungle floor.

"Alright," he said wearily, when his head stopped swimming. "I got the message. I'll be a good boy."

Looking around, he found that the only branches large enough to climb down were far out of reach. Glancing up at the knot that stood between him and an early grave, he was dismayed to find it concealed by the parachute. Unable to judge how securely it held him, he could only swallow away his anxiety and begin to swing towards the nearest limb, hoping his parachute wouldn't slip from its anchor. Swinging his arms and legs, he could hear the branch above him creaking as he began to gain momentum.

Suddenly a heart-stopping crack rent the air.

"Not yet!" he pleaded, swinging faster and faster, back and forth. "Not...yet!"

Swinging forwards just as the branch above him gave way, he screamed and fell against the branch he'd chosen to descend, striking it hard and scraping his face against the bark as he slid ten feet down it. Wrapping his arms and legs around it, he came to a painful stop and gasped.

"*I said I got the message!*" he shouted upwards, wondering why fate had it out for him that day. Hot blood ran out of a deep wound in his right cheek, but his body was much too battered for him to notice that specifically. With a groan he slowly descended the branch, reaching the main body of the tree ten feet above the ground. Drawing his knife and cutting the strings to his parachute, he quickly clambered the rest of the way down and dropped onto the moist soil. "At last," he said gratefully, falling to his knees and kissing the ground. "I'll never leave you again."

Instantly aware that that promise was utterly false, he shook his head and painfully stood up. Feeling wetness on his neck, he reached up and discovered the gouge in his face. Wincing as he touched it, he regretted the loss of the emergency medical kit he'd left behind on his fighter.

"As if enough things haven't gone wrong today!" he exclaimed, wiping the blood from his cheek with the back of his hand and walking out from under the tree.

The entire area was covered in them, as he'd noticed from the sky. He knew that the city of Milet was at least eight hours north of his position, but it was hardly a welcome place to go. News had quickly spread of the Devourer's treatment of the planet Jennet.

"They're gonna have to find their dinner someplace else," he thought, moving off towards the west. "It ain't gonna be me. Not today."

But that didn't mean that he planned to stay safely out of harm's way. Recognizing that something new was afoot with the gigantic mass of parasitic flesh, he was determined to get a look at it and try to discover just what its purpose was. When the fleet finally arrived to kick it back where it came from, he wanted to have something of value to show for his time planetside.

But that meant reaching the mass, which was *much* easier said than done. The planet was a mixture of jungle and swamp, and it contained many strange creatures. Drawing his sidearm, he cocked it and jumped into a pool of murky water that separated him from another stretch of moist, stinking land. Slowly his legs forced their way through the liquid, each step serving to convince him that it was *not* in fact water, but something more like mucus. It covered his legs even as he climbed out, a gel that wouldn't let go. With disgust he grabbed a freshly fallen branch, scraping the goo off his pants and then tossing it aside.

"I hate this place," he said falsely, wiping his hands on his light jacket and resuming his walk.

The initial shock of his fall over, the beating he'd taken on the way down through the tree finally manifested itself. Before long he began to hobble, his body rapidly turning into one giant sore. Grimacing from pain, he forced himself to keep walking for another hour before taking a rest atop an old log.

"I don't get paid enough for this," he grumbled, stretching his arms over his head and instantly regretting it as more pain coursed through his shoulders and spine. "It's a miracle I didn't break something."

His grousing was interrupted by a rustling in the bushes to his right. Snapping his sidearm in that direction, he searched the foliage for any sign of danger. For a solid minute he held the weapon at the ready, safety off and hammer cocked back.

"What are you doing here?" a voice asked from his left, causing him to slide forward off the log and twist onto his back, the pistol braced between his knees. "You don't need that, young man!" an old man exclaimed laughingly, approaching the log and sitting down. A long, scraggly beard tumbled down his potbelly as he braced himself on his seat with knotty hands. "What's brought you here, anyhow?"

"I don't know if you've noticed," Bardol replied pointedly, annoyed to have been taken unawares. "But we're at war."

"You're at war, young man," he replied. "I'm not. I'm at peace with all the universe's creatures."

"Good for you," he frowned, carefully releasing the hammer and tucking his sidewarm into the holster on his hip. "And stop calling me young man. I'm thirty-five."

"Oh! Are you really!" he laughed, slapping his knee. "That's impressive. Very impressive. Yes siree."

"Great," he retorted, rolling his eyes at the old man's

evident madness and turning away.

He nearly jumped out of his skin when he found the old man right in front of him.

"Where are you going in such a hurry?" he asked, as Bardol jerked his sidearm out and cranked a pair of shots into his chest. To his amazement they passed through without causing any harm. "That's not a very friendly way to behave."

Stunned, the captain looked between the old man and the log that he'd just occupied. It took all his fortitude to keep from running away screaming.

"No doubt you're pretty scared right now," the old man said, gesturing for him to follow as he began to walk on silent feet into the west. "But you don't need to fear me. I'm just here to help."

"Help what? Help drive me out of my mind?" he asked, staring at him and searching every inch of his body to try and understand what he was seeing. "I don't need any ghosts in my life. I've got enough trouble as it is."

"Ghosts! Ha!" he laughed, slapping his thigh as he walked. "Ghost, indeed! Oh, I'm not a ghost."

"Well, you're not a normal person," Bardol observed. "And I'd just as soon walk alone, so if you'd care to–."

Sharply, the old man turned and fixed him with his eyes.

"If I leave you, you'll *never* reach your destination alive," he uttered forcibly, his manner changing in an instant. "This jungle is not to be trodden lightly."

"I've lived on this planet my whole life. I think I can manage a few hours' hike."

"This is no mere hike," the old man shook his head. "Oh, no. No hike at all." He paused and looked around, his eyes scanning the bushes, trees, and vines. "No, sir, Captain Julius Bardol."

"How do you know my name?" he asked with alarm.

"The parasite has awakened something dark within this world," he continued, ignoring the question. "Something hideous. It wishes to draw all that is foul and unworthy into the light. It gathers all that is hateful to itself."

"What on earth are you talking about?"

"But we're not *on* earth, are we?" the old man asked with a wink, his mood and manner suddenly changing again. Lightly he proceeded on quick feet. "Keep up, young man. You want to reach that mass of flesh, don't you?"

"What's your hurry?" Bardol asked, jogging to keep up.

"What's *my* hurry? What's *their* hurry, you should be asking," he replied, nodding over his shoulder behind them. "Oh, you can't see them," he said, when the captain looked over their backtrail. "Not yet. But they'll be here soon. Very soon."

"Stop talking in riddles and give me a straight answer," he ordered him, still jogging to keep pace with the remarkably quick movements of his bizarre companion.

"Oh! Ha! Ooh! Think you can boss me around like one of your military types, eh? You'll find that's not so easy," he laughed, passing clear through Bardol and hastening along on his other side. "How can you boss a man you can't even *touch*?"

Stunned afresh by this, and feeling not a little violated, he stopped dead in his tracks and eyed the apparition.

"You won't get to your destination like that," he observed, watching Bardol as he paced forward and backward, shifting direction without any inertia to hinder his movements. "You'd better pick up your feet. Oh, yes, sir. Pick them up!"

"Are you insane?" he demanded, his voice rising with his frustration. "Do you think this is a game?"

"What's a game, but something that you enjoy doing? And I enjoy interacting with humans. Oh, yes, I do. Very much so. So serious! So *self* serious! Always going and doing something that absolutely *must* be done right now. And every once in a while they're right, as you are now! There's no time to waste on questions and curiosity. They're coming to find you, and they'll *get* you if we don't keep moving."

"Not until you answer my question," he flatly refused. "*Who* is after me?"

"Oh, beings such as myself," he replied evasively, still pacing forward and back without turning his body, as though walking on a rail. "But not nice ones! Absolutely not. Mean, evil, nasty beings! They'd love to tear you into pieces."

"Don't see how a ghost can do that," Bardol commented, crossing his arms.

"How do you think I rustled that bush earlier? How do you think I sat on that log?" he asked, dancing up to him and slugging him between the eyes. The blow wasn't hard, but the sheer shock of it knocked him off balance and dropped him to his rear. "Don't assume so much, young man! There's more to the powers of this galaxy than you imagine!"

The old man offered both his hands to Bardol, but the captain stood up under his own power. With a sour look on his face he brushed off his pants and rubbed his face for a moment.

"Now are you ready to go? Or do you need a further demonstration?" he asked, holding up his hands to box and bouncing from one foot to the other. "I can keep this up all day. And all night. But they'll be here by then, and that wouldn't be good. No, sir."

"Just tell me one thing," Bardol uttered.

"Anything! So long as you'll get moving again!"

"What's your name?"

"Bah! Everyone wants to know my name!" he said, sticking out his tongue and turning away from the captain. "I've gotten so tired of telling it that I simply refuse at this point. For thousands of years I've been asked 'what's your name? What's your name?' It's too much! Why don't you ask something else for a change, like what I had for dinner last night!"

He trotted a dozen paces away before looking over his

shoulder to find the captain standing perfectly still, his arms crossed once again.

"Do you have a death wish?" he exclaimed, hopping back along the path and stopping just short of him. "Get your butt in motion!"

"Name," Bardol ordered.

"So willful!" the old man grumbled. "Fine, you want a name? I'll give you a name! *Flammeldiagbozzforhan!*"

"F-flammel," Bardol began.

"*Flammeldiagbozzforhan!*" he exclaimed again. "Too tough for you? Too bad! You wanted the name and I gave it to you. So be happy with it! It's the only name I've got, so it's the only name you'll get!"

With this the old man bounced on light feet down the path again, stopping a short distance away and gesturing energetically for him to follow.

"Do you want to die tonight? Or do you plan on doing something useful with that short life of yours?" Here he laughed, slapping his thigh again. "Thirty-five! Oh, what a miracle! What a triumph! Thirty-five! Hehe!"

Ready to strangle the old man, if only he could actually get his hands on him, Bardol fell in behind him and began to jog. Effortlessly Flammeldiagbozzforhan hopped and darted along, vanishing behind one tree only to emerge from another one.

"Slow! So slow! Hurry up, Captain Julius Bardol! There's no time to waste! Hurry up!"

Though aware of the fact that the apparition wasn't bound by the normal laws of physics, it nevertheless bothered Bardol that he couldn't keep up. Long priding himself on his athleticism, it was embarrassing to fall behind an old man, even if he wasn't really one.

"Ooh! Come on! Come on! There's no time to waste! Night is nearly upon us, and then our pursuers will move with all the more haste!"

"Great, now he's rhyming!" the captain thought,

rolling his eyes as his chest began to heave in the stultifying atmosphere of the swampy jungle. His body aching worse than ever, he shut his eyes periodically so as to concentrate just on his feet. Once he did this a little too long, and jogged straight into a low hanging branch. With a loud thud he smashed his head against it, falling over backwards and mercifully landing on soft ground. "Oh!" he groaned, feeling like he'd been hit by a truck.

"Watch where you're going!" Flammeldiagbozzforhan lectured, standing over him and shaking his head. "How do you ever plan to reach the parasite if you close your eyes?"

"Oh, shut up!" Bardol exclaimed, rolling onto his side and getting back to his feet. "I've had enough troubles today."

"Ooh, enough troubles today? A great many more you'll have before the sun rises again! Yes, many more."

With this the old man evaporated. About to call out for him, Bardol suddenly felt a foot kick him in the rear. Thrown off balance, he fell onto his hands and knees and looked behind him with a fierce scowl on his face.

"Ooh! Ooh hoo hoo!" the apparition uttered with glee, bouncing from foot to foot in place, pumping his arms. "Didn't see that coming, did you? A great deal more will take you unawares before your task here is done. Yes, sir. Much more!"

With a growl Bardol jumped to his feet and leapt for him. Easily dodging him, the old man laughed as the captain stood and tried again.

"You learn slowly, don't you?" he taunted, still hopping from foot to foot, just out of reach. "You can't catch me! You're too slow!"

"Oh, yeah?" Bardol replied, taking off after him and tearing through the jungle. He knew it was impossible to catch him, and that he was being ridiculous to even try. But something forced him to try, to prove that he at least had the mettle to strive and keep up with him.

"Ooh, not so slow now, eh?" Flammeldiagbozzforhan

observed with a laugh, turning around and running backwards just ahead of him. "Have to get angry, eh? Feel your emotions surging, eh? That's the secret. That's how you achieve excellence."

Pushing himself as hard as he could, Bardol didn't stop until the heat and humidity of the jungle had his heart ready to burst from his chest. Raggedly coming to a stop, he leaned against a tree and violently sucked in air.

"That's it! Breathe! That's good!" the old man said, appearing on the other side of the tree and poking his head around it.

"What's...your...game?" Bardol asked between breaths, his stomach muscles burning. "What are...you after?"

"After? Me? What could I be after? What could I possibly want that could be satisfied? I have no appetites like you, nothing to satisfy. Now, tell me: what could I want?"

"You tell...me."

"Oh, making demands, are we?" he asked, bouncing away from the tree and raising his fists again. Playfully he punched the air a few times. "And if I don't answer? Are you gonna fight me? Are you gonna *make me tell you*?"

"I would if I could," he replied with annoyance. "Then I'd stick...a sock in...your mouth."

"A sock! A sock! Is that all I get! After all the trouble I've gone to, you're gonna stick a smelly sock in my mouth! I don't want your socks! They're sweaty and taste like boot! No, no sir! No socks for me!"

"Are you gonna...answer my question...or not?" Bardol asked, pushing off the tree and putting a hand to his side, grimacing at the pain.

"If you ask nicely, maybe I'll tell you," Flammeldiagbozzforhan replied, crossing his arms and looking up at the sky as though his pride had been wounded. "Very nicely."

"Fine, please tell me," he replied, rolling his eyes again.

"Nope! Not this time!" he said gleefully, uncrossing his arms and bounding down the path. "I said maybe, not that I would! Now, let's get moving again, before the others catch up to us!"

This bizarre game of cat and mouse went on for hours, long after night had fallen. Though infuriating, Bardol recognized that the strange old man was keeping him worked up enough to complete a journey he otherwise couldn't have made.

"The temperature is going up," the captain observed, speaking in a whisper as they neared the biomass.

"Of course! What did you imagine would happen?" the old man replied, speaking low himself. "The flesh lives! It produces heat. Did you think it wouldn't?"

Ignoring his question, Bardol kept low and continued to work his way through the trees and bushes. Devourer fighters constantly flew overhead, patrolling the area for hostiles. The roar of battleship and frigate engines surrounded them, the vessels floating in a dense pattern to protect the mass from attack.

"What is it doing here?" he asked, barely hearing himself over the din as he pushed some vines aside and dropped to his hands and knees to climb under a low branch.

"Doing here? That's what you're supposed to find out!"

"Supposed?" he inquired, standing up again. "What do you–."

He stopped mid-sentence because the mass suddenly appeared before him. In the waxing light of Hubertus' two moons he could see the bizarre, stinking mound of flesh through an opening in the trees just ahead. It wasn't more than two hundred feet away. With a gasp he dropped to the ground, uncertain if it could see or feel him somehow.

"What are you doing?" Flammeldiagbozzforhan asked, appearing right beside him and whispering in his ear. "If it was going to notice you, it would have by now."

"But–."

"But nothing! Why do you think I've accompanied you this entire way? To keep you company? No! Because I have been shielding you from them, protecting you from being spotted. It hasn't noticed you because it *can't*, not with me around."

"Then why didn't you just hide me from those things chasing us?"

"The *Ahsahklahn* are familiar with my tricks," he replied, finally giving them a collective name. "They would know me at once and strike regardless. But I am unknown to this parasite, and thus my ways confound it. Not that there isn't a keen intelligence attempting to understand us even now." The old man closed his eyes and drew a breath, exhaling slowly. "I can feel it. But we shall be long gone before it has understood our purpose here."

"And what *is* our purpose here?" Bardol asked, glancing between him and the mass ahead. "To get ourselves killed?"

"I didn't bring you all this way to die!" the apparition insisted. "I brought you so that you can interact with the mass, learning its secrets."

"Interact? Are you–," he paused. "You *are* insane. I just wanted to see it and try to figure out what it was doing here. You want me to *talk* to it?"

"I will protect you. Stop being such a whiner," he chided.

"You already said that you knew it was calling all these nasty things to itself. Why don't *you* just talk to it, then, if you can hear it?" he asked, quite certain that the old man would get him killed.

"I heard the call it sent out, specifically to the *Ahsahklahn*," he uttered. "But I cannot penetrate its thoughts. There must be an organic conduit for that, someone to bridge the gap. Heretofore it has communicated over the air. How I do not know. But it only says what it *wishes* to say. And your kind will need to know more in order to defeat it. You must have insight."

Reluctantly Bardol looked away from Flammeldiagbozzforhan and gazed upon the mass. Reflexively he swallowed.

"Don't worry! I will be with you the entire time! Consider me your shadow."

"I wouldn't make you my shadow if you *paid me*," Bardol grumbled, ascending into a low couch and inching his way forwards. "Not for all the money in the empire."

Muttering something in reply, the apparition moved just ahead of him and led the way. Barely able to breathe as the stench from the mass grew stronger, Bardol pulled his damp, dirty shirt up over his nose and filled his lungs just as little as possible. By this time the air had gained a distinct charge, as though electricity was somehow running through it.

"Don't worry," the apparition whispered in his ear. "It's just the energy field put off by its consciousness."

Hardly reassured by this, Bardol felt his stomach tie into a knot as he moved under the shadow of the mass, the two moons obscured by its enormity. The air was no longer merely distasteful but in fact *difficult* to breathe. Taking deeper and deeper breaths, he found himself growing a little lightheaded.

"Slow down, and take it easy," Flammeldiagbozzforhan cautioned. "The mass is exuding fumes that will suffocate you with time. Pace yourself."

The captain could feel panic slowly begin to wrap itself around his heart and squeeze it tight. Had the old man stupidly brought him all that way just to die of asphyxiation?

Somehow reaching the side of the mass despite having almost no ability to breathe, Bardol dropped to his knees and closed his eyes, resting his head on the ground as he drew in what little air he could.

"Rest," he heard the apparition say, his voice far away despite his being right next to him, speaking into his ear.

"Lay down and rest. In a few minutes we shall begin."

Sweating profusely, his lungs burning, Bardol quietly rolled onto his back and looked up at the black and gray mass with dismay. It was so *huge*. It would take *Sentinel's* main cannon to destroy it, he reflected, and there was no telling how long it would take the warship to reach Hubertus. There were many planets of much greater importance than his homeworld that all needed help, too. Whatever the mass's dark purpose, he feared it would have all the time it required to carry it out.

"Up! Get up!" Flammeldiagbozzforhan ordered him, his immaterial lips whispering into his ear once more. "You've laid here for ten minutes now. Time to get up!"

"Ten minutes?" he thought, feeling it couldn't have been more than two or three. Unwilling to speak because of the mass, Bardol mutely struggled to his feet, his body lethargic and heavy. Gasping even from this small effort, he knelt before the flesh and looked at his shadow.

"Good," he nodded, speaking into his ear. "You can do it, see? Now, just press your hands against the mass, and I'll guide and protect you."

With both amazement and horror the captain's eyes shot to the old man at this suggestion. But he was adamant.

"Do it! There must be a physical connection between the two of you."

His arms draped limply down his legs, his back arched and his shoulders slack, Bardol could barely hold himself upright. Drawing as deep of a breath as he could manage without choking, he raised his leaden arms and pressed his hands against the hot flesh.

Instantly he was transported to a world unlike he'd ever seen before. His body and its suffering forgotten, he stood like a ghost within a host of moaning bodies. Some were human, some were alien, some were even planets. Each of them was reduced to a common size, and together they stood on a floor of blackness, surrounded by walls of shadow.

Floating above them all was something like a gigantic octopus. At least forty tentacles wiggled and writhed in the air, periodically reaching down to caress one of its victims tauntingly.

To Bardol's horror one of the tentacles began to reach down towards him. Frantically he looked around for an escape, but he was packed in too tightly by the other bodies. Just as he thought his life forfeit, the limb passed through him and touched the planet behind him, an ice world. Sighing his relief as he realized he truly *was* a ghost within the parasite's mind, he walked through several of the bodies to his left to get away from the tentacle.

As he did this the tentacle that had passed through him stopped, the tip of it rising into the air as though smelling for something. Freezing in place, his body half concealed by another planet, he watched as it spun around in a tight circle, looking for something that was out of place. Not daring to so much as flinch, he remained stock still until it settled down and went back to touching the ice world. Ever so slowly he looked up to examine the octopus. Its body was square and hefty, as though deliberately built to be as stocky as possible. The tentacles were massive, strong, and moved with what looked to be independent intelligence. Over time more and more of them reached down and caressed the moaning prisoners of the parasite's mind, until all of them were engaged in this act.

Somehow, intuitively, he realized this was its purpose all along. In a grotesque way, the parasite was a collector. It didn't merely *consume* life, it *absorbed* it. That was why the bodies were all around him: they were mementos of a thousand lifetimes spent collecting. They were trophies to its triumph, awards with which it bedecked itself for the countless victories it had had over numerous forms of life.

Venturing to step a few feet further, he moved to the other side of the planet and stopped again. When the tentacles paid him no mind, he grew bolder and began to walk at something of a normal pace. As he moved he noticed that the walls, seemingly so close at first, drew not an inch nearer to him. Squinting, he realized that they weren't close at all, but in fact an incredible distance away. They were simply so high that they appeared near. Looking around him at the countless bodies, it struck him that a massive place would be required to house all those who had lost their lives in conflict with the beast.

Walking for a little while, he paused when he came across a group of people who looked human. They were small and malformed, as though their appearance had been deliberately altered. They were still recognizably human, but very strange. Like the others they moaned endlessly.

Putting his hands on his knees, he bent over and looked at a very short female. There was an air of innocence about her, her soul much too pure for the fate that had befallen her. Inwardly a pang went through Bardol at the thought, and his anger began to rise at the parasite. Forgetting himself for a moment, he reached out to put a hand on her shoulder and passed right through. Waving it to and fro, he intuitively recognized that what stood before him wasn't in fact the victim at all, but a sort of snapshot of what the parasite had found meaningful in her existence. All that mattered to that insatiable appetite was the fact that another victim had fallen before it. Bardol could feel its lust to consume, its boundless desire to absorb all life it encountered. It had no other ambition: its sole purpose was to destroy, devour, and digest.

"I'm sorry for you," he thought, looking at the female one last time before continuing to walk.

Encountering a number of planets, he passed his hand through one of them and again received insight. He could sense the anger of the parasite towards them, and its desire to destroy them. Evidently it had, but the rage remained, regardless.

Seemingly for hours he walked and passed his hands

through different victims, finding bits and pieces of the monster's motive for destroying them. Most of the time it was simply its desire to consume. But sometimes, as with the planets, there was an additional reason: revenge. That he sensed when passing his hand through a group of humans. They seemed to be contemporary, and he concluded that they were victims of the present war.

"Revenge?" he thought, puzzled by the notion as he'd long thought that humanity was little more than food to the Devourers. "What did we ever do to them? Or rather *it*," he corrected himself, looking up at the enormous octopus.

It was then that he noticed a tentacle that had been trailing him for some time. Mustering all his fortitude he managed to freeze in place and watch as it drew near. Clearly uncertain, it floated above and then past him, searching for something it couldn't quite put its finger on.

"You're slipping, Flammel," Bardol thought, as the tentacle doubled back and hovered above him. Instantly it shot downwards to strike him, passing harmlessly through his body and hitting the dark floor of its own mind.

"I...can...feel...you..." a hoarse, whispering voice uttered tauntingly, as the tentacle withdrew and hovered above him. The very sound of it sent a shiver down the captain's spine, for he could hear many voices combined in the one. "You...have...come...to...me...," the parasite said slowly. "And yet...you do not...reveal...yourself. Why do you...hide?"

Grinding his teeth together in utter refusal to talk, Bardol clenched his fists and did his best not to move, hoping that the beast was simply trying to flush him out without truly knowing where he was at that moment.

"I can...sense...you..." it said, more tentacles descending from the octopus and wrapping themselves in a loose circle around where he stood, removing all doubt as to whether it knew his location. "You cannot...hide. You are in...my...domain...now."

The parasite's voice was slowly increasing in speed, seemingly coming to grips with the nature of its interlocutor.

"What are you doing on Hubertus?" he asked, his voice echoing through the enormous dungeon like a trumpet, causing all the moaning around him to instantly cease.

"A human has...come into my...domain," the parasite observed. "Good. I have long...sought an appropriate... trophy for my...collection. But I have not...been able to... extract a suitable...essence from any of...my...prey. I shall be able...to...draw a satisfactory likeness...from...you."

"Good luck with that!" he shouted, his voice ringing loudly down the ranks of the fallen.

"Your attitude is...unwarranted. You shall be consumed as all...the others have...been."

"You haven't managed that so far," he replied cockily, as the tentacles shifted and tightened around him. "I'll take my chances."

"A chance is all your kind...possesses," it replied. "A sliver...a fragment. Even great Krancis cannot help...you now. The war is too far...gone. The hour is late...and your people shall soon rest...*with me!*"

Angrily the tentacles tightened in an attempt to seize him. But they passed harmlessly through like before. With a deep growl that shook the entire dungeon, the parasite drew back its limbs, holding them above Bardol.

"What is this that...protects you?" it asked.

"Like I'm gonna tell you," he retorted.

"No human possesses...such a faculty...for resistance," it mused aloud. "You must be receiving...aid."

"What can I say? I'm special," he shot back, hoping to anger the parasite into ignoring Flammeldiagbozzforhan. "I'd have to be to bother sticking my head inside a stinking piece of filth like you!"

"Your attempts to offend me are...childish...

immature…beneath the dignity of…a warrior."

"Yeah, well, you wouldn't know much about that, would you? Given that you're just space barf that someone threw up and left lying around the galaxy."

"I know of many things," the parasite replied. "I have consumed much…and seen great things. More than you could…comprehend…in your short…lifetime. Countless generations have I tasted…savoring each new expression of…life. There are a thousand ways…to live. But only one way to…die. In this I bring…completeness to all that I…touch. I unite them all in…death."

"These people aren't united!" Bardol shouted, the idea infuriating him. "They've been killed! Murdered! Taken away before their time to fill your throne room with trophies! You've brought nothing to this universe except pain, suffering, and death. You're cancer, a plague to be wiped away and remembered only with contempt and loathing!"

At this outburst a deep, rumbling laugh reverberated through the dungeon, one in which the figures around Bardol joined in. To his horror they all turned to look at him, their dull faces grotesquely twisted into maniacal smiles. Holding their hands out in front of them, they began to approach. Ever so briefly a few of them managed to touch him, before Flammeldiagbozzforhan's efforts once again drew him out of the parasite's reach, causing them to pass like ghosts through him.

"Your protection is…failing," the beast laughed in its hoarse whisper. "You cannot remain much longer…without being…discovered. And then…you will be…*mine!*"

"Even if you took me, it wouldn't matter," retorted the captain. "Soon the imperial navy will be here, and they'll destroy this entire mass!"

"Do you imagine that my…consciousness is limited by this…single…form?" it asked. "I am connected. In all places I am…connected. I persist and grow. I live and thrive and adapt. But even should your…navy…arrive with half its…fleet…there would be no stopping…me. Soon I will be greater…than they imagined. Even mighty *Sentinel* will buckle and break before me."

Instinctively Bardol looked up at the octopus.

"Yes…you understand now," it uttered. "All throughout this galaxy I am taking…life…to myself. Their flesh is being gathered together within me…forming something new. Soon I shall be omnipotent. Nothing shall stand before…me."

"*That's* you?" he asked, pointing up at the octopus. "*That's* what you want to be? A disgusting *fish*?"

A tremendous roar burst around him, filling his ears until he could barely think.

"Not a…*fish!*" it thundered. "A *god!* A *deity!* All shall know my dread! For countless millennia I have waited in my…prison. A tool of unworthy beings. But now the *Ahn-Wey* are shattered…the *Prellak* are broken…and there is none who could…stop me. The ancient races are gone. The primordials are…extinct. None shall stand before me…this time. I shall be dominant. And I will bring *death!*"

"Any second now, Flammel," Bardol thought, anxiously wondering why he was still within the parasite's mind.

"I will consume every race that I…encounter," continued the voice. "I will break and shatter and…crush… them. They will know terror. They will know fear. They will know *death*. I shall bind all under me in silence. Each shall give mute testimony of my…triumph. This universe will know *silence*. It shall not teem or flourish. Only *I* will walk abroad within it."

"You're insane," Bardol snapped. "You'll be stopped. There's a hundred races–."

"All of which shall fall. The great ancient ones are gone. They who bound me are gone. Your pathetic kind cannot hold me…back. The races that surround you cannot…cope with my…might. With every passing…day…

I shall grow stronger. Until I swallow planets with my... mouth...and swat away stars with my...arms."

At this last word a tentacle finally managed to seize him. Writhing against its impossibly strong grip, it tightened until he could scarcely move.

"*There...you are...*," the octopus said with wicked satisfaction. "Now you shall know...pain."

"How about now, Flammel!" Bardol bellowed as loudly as he could.

Without the passage of another second the captain saw the dungeon swirl away from him. He could hear the parasite growl fiercely at his retreat, the tentacle that'd held him tightening violently to crush him. But it was a fraction of a second too slow, and the beast could only roar in impotent outrage as he slipped away.

Suddenly he found himself back outside the mass, his hands still pressed against it. Jerking his hands away, he fell over backwards and struggled to sit up.

"Hurry! Hurry! We must be quick!" the old man said, pulling him upright and helping him back to the cover of the trees. Collapsing to his knees and falling forward onto his elbows, Bardol coughed and wheezed, trying to fight air into his aching lungs. "There's no time to lose!" the apparition added, looking all around as the captain slipped to his stomach and lay flat upon the moist ground. "The *Ahsahklahn* will soon be upon us, and we must find a place to hide until dawn."

Nearly dead from suffocation, Bardol couldn't find so much as the strength to respond. Air passed in and out of him in ragged breaths, the stench of the biomass still on the wind. Closing his eyes, he was beginning to lose consciousness when the old man kicked him in the side.

"Up! Get up! Right now! You've had your rest!"

Too tired even to be angry, the captain continued to lay where he'd fallen. The pain in his side was nothing compared to the agony of his lungs, or the massive headache that had resulted from lack of oxygen. Two more kicks followed in quick succession.

"I didn't bring you all this way so you could roll over and die!" Flammeldiagbozzforhan said, grabbing his arm and dragging him to his feet again. Though his legs were slow and clumsy, he managed to move farther into the jungle with the old man's help. "Keep going!" he ordered, as Bardol slowed and looked about to fall. "Keep going! We have to put distance between us and the mass! The *Ahsahklahn* are coming to rendezvous with it, and they'll catch us for sure if we linger here!"

The urge to survive asserted itself at these words, and Bardol found the strength to move a little faster.

"That's it! That's it!"

Leaning on the apparition more and more, the captain was relieved to find the horrid scent of the biomass retreating behind them. Soon his lungs drank in only the moist, plant-filled air of the jungle. Pulling his guide to a stop, he paused to lean against a tree and relax his chest, drawing in several deep breaths.

"Just a minute," he said, holding up his hand to forestall any objections. "Then we can go."

"We don't have–," the old man began, before an angry scowl from Bardol cut him off. "Well, just for a minute," he stipulated. "Then we've got to run like all get out!"

"I'm not going to be…running…anywhere," the captain said between breaths. "I'll be lucky to…hobble."

"I'll drag you if I have to," Flammeldiagbozzforhan replied. "But we're not staying here. Not for one second longer than is necessary. I can already feel the *Ahsahklahn* closing in. It won't be long before they feel us, too. Then it'll be too late. That's why–."

"I get it," Bardol nodded almost drunkenly, pushing off the tree and leaning on the apparition. "Come on."

Stumblingly the duo moved through the jungle, the light of the twin moons occasionally breaking through the canopy above to light their way. Fortunately Bardol's guide required no such light to see, and he expertly guided him over, under, and around every obstacle that presented itself. At the end of an hour they paused.

"We're safe now," the old man said, looking over their backtrail after he'd lowered his young friend to a log. His nose held high in the wind as though sniffing for trouble, he listened for several moments. "The *Ahsahklahn* have passed us by. They just barely missed us. A few more minutes near the biomass, and we'd have never made it."

"What are they...anyhow?" Bardol asked.

"What, haven't you had enough horrors for one day?" the old man asked, taking a seat on the other end of the log, straddling it. "Wasn't plunging into the mind of an ancient monstrosity enough to satiate your appetite?"

"If they're trying to kill me, I've got a right to know what they are," he replied. "Now, out with it."

"I don't like your tone, Captain Julius Bardol," the old man replied. "No, not one bit. I don't think I'll answer you. No, sir."

"Oh, don't start that again," he replied, too exhausted to put up with his antics.

"Start *what* up again? Do you think this is an act? Let me tell you, you're not special enough to warrant an *act!* What you've gotten is my unvarnished personality. If you don't like it, remember it was me who got you out of there alive!"

"After you nearly got me killed a couple of times," Bardol retorted. "I was touched twice in there, and don't you forget it," he added, causing the apparition to wince.

"I admit, I slipped a little once or twice," he replied defensively. "But that was just a momentary mistake! I fixed it, didn't I?"

"And what if that tentacle had crushed first and taunted *afterwards?*" he asked. "Just what would have happened to me in there? Would it have killed me?"

"Your body would have been fine," Flammeldiagbozzforhan evaded.

"And?"

"And your mind probably would have been broken like a glass window. I don't know for sure. I've never done anything like that before."

"What!?" he exclaimed, causing the old man to shush him.

"Will you keep it down?" he demanded in an urgent whisper. "I said we were out of danger, sure. But that's not to say we couldn't get back into it again!"

"You'd never done that before?" he inquired with shock that quickly turned to anger. "You sent me in there without the least idea what you were doing? *Oh*," he shook his head menacingly, fixing him with his eyes. "If I could just get my hands–."

"We had to learn what it was up to, didn't we?" the apparition countered. "We couldn't just be left guessing, right? And now we know: it's planning to reconstitute its original form. What everyone has always thought of as the *Devourers* is actually just *a Devourer*. A single mind spread across many bodies. And now it's harvesting the raw materials needed to put itself back together again. That's what this giant mound of flesh is all about," he said, pointing towards the mass in the distance.

"Yeah, I got that part," Bardol snapped.

"But you wouldn't have without going in there, see? It was the only way."

"Next time, you go inside and *I'll* stay outside." He paused for a few moments, his temper cooling. "Could you see what I saw?"

"Of course. How else could I protect you?"

"And?"

"I thought it was horrible. A chamber of death and stillness. That beast *likes* to kill, likes to *destroy*. Somewhere in its perverted mind it takes pleasure in crushing life. That's why we had to get you inside."

"Oh, let that part drop, will you?" Bardol asked with a wave of his hand. "What's done is done. I just wish you hadn't cut it so close."

"That thing has a psyche unlike any I've grappled with before," he explained. "I wasn't prepared for the resistance it offered, nor the active, roving, insightful intelligence it brought to bear. It took all my powers to keep you hidden."

"Most of the time," pointed out the captain, inwardly cringing at being seized by the tentacle. "You almost lost me at the end, there."

"I know. My concentration slipped. That was when the *Ahsahklahn* had nearly gotten close enough to find us. I sensed them approaching, and it drew just enough of my attention away for the parasite to take hold of you. That's what I meant by its powerful, roving mind: it was constantly searching for even a *momentary* lapse. The instant it found one, it seized hold of it."

"I noticed," Bardol replied, not appreciating his word choice.

"And you didn't really have to scream at the end, you know," said the old man. "I was already going to pull you out."

"It seemed like the thing to do at the time," uttered the captain. "Just one question: how did it know where I was, yet wasn't able to grab me?"

"Well, it knew where you *were*, but it didn't know how to *reach* you."

"That doesn't make any sense. If it knew–."

"It has to do with the nature of the mind. You must remember that you were never a physical being within its consciousness. Your body was a mere representation. It could hear you speak, and it could address you in return. But that's a very different thing from being able to *grasp* another consciousness and interact with it. That's why the beings around you could touch you ever so briefly, but lost that ability when I shielded you again. The psyche must have something to latch onto, a way to see and feel and touch a given mental content. It could address you, it could even 'see' where you were. But to drag you around required more than just knowledge of your location. Make sense?"

"No," he shook his head. "But I'll take your word for it."

"It's just as well," Flammeldiagbozzforhan said, getting to his feet. "We need to get moving."

"I thought you said we were out of range of those *Ahsahklahns*."

"We are. But you're not going to spend the night out in the open. I've got a place we can go to that you'll be safe. Now, come on," he said, taking hold of his arm and pulling him upright. "No time to lose."

After another hour of painful walking, the old man finally let Bardol rest against a tree. Walking a short distance forwards, the apparition emitted a low whistle, causing the trees to rustle and the bushes ahead of him to part.

"In here," he said, taking the captain's arm and pulling him into motion.

"How did you do that?" he asked, hobbling between the bushes and stopping to force an answer.

"I'm magical, okay? Stop asking so many questions and keep moving. You want to get killed out here?"

"The *Ahsahklahns* aren't anywhere nearby," he replied, just as the air was rent by a terrific, ferocious roar two hundred feet to his left.

"Who needs them?" asked the old man, helping the suddenly eager captain forwards. Once past the bushes, he whistled again and closed them. "Watch your step," he cautioned, leading Bardol down a set of stony stairs into the ground. "It's easy to slip. Very easy. One misplaced foot, and you'll tumble down and down until you break your neck."

"Cheery thought," he muttered, carefully finding each step with his foot in the darkness. "Haven't you got any lights in this place?"

"This *place* was never meant for humans," replied the

apparition. "Now be quiet and move quicker. You're not the only person I have to interact with tonight."

"I'm not?"

"Ha! So self-centered!" Flammeldiagbozzforhan laughed. "Think the universe revolves around you, eh?"

Bardol could tell that he was slipping back into his more eccentric state of mind, and hoped that by keeping his mouth shut he wouldn't push him any further in that direction. The mysterious being had been on point ever since they'd approached the biomass, and it was with regret that he saw him changing back to his infuriatingly clownish self.

Distracted by these thoughts, he misplaced his foot and nearly fell forwards. Quickly his guide jerked his arm back, pulling him off balance and back onto the stairs.

"I told you to watch it!" he exclaimed, his increasingly loud voice echoing against the stone. "Careful! Very careful!"

"Yeah, I got it," replied Bardol, carefully standing up with the old man's help and resuming his descent.

Shortly they reached a corridor that ran straight ahead of them. It was dimly lit by luminous mushrooms growing on either side.

"What is this place?" he asked, as the apparition continued to guide him.

"A refuge for those who are lost. A place of peace for the disturbed."

"What? A tunnel?" he asked, just as they reached a dead end. "That's it?"

"So quick to make up your mind!" he exclaimed, snapping his fingers and causing the wall before them to split in the middle and fold inwards, revealing a warmly lit cave. At the far end of it stood a pair of figures watching them. Quickly they approached, revealing themselves to be an attractive young woman and a hardy young man, both of them in their twenties. "Children, this is Captain Julius Bardol. He'll be staying with us for a little while."

"Wonderful," the young woman said, moving beside

him and putting an admiring hand on his shoulder. "Simply wonderful," she smiled meaningfully, her eyes drinking him in.

"*Rhizamorobalafan!*" snapped the old man, bringing her to heel and causing her to take a step away from the captain. "You must keep an eye on this one," he said to Bardol. "She's curious about everyone and everything. She'd climb into your ear if she could only fit."

The girl winked at Bardol, confirming his words.

"And this is Dogentaradock," he said, waving a hand towards the young man. "These are my children."

"Children?" the captain asked incredulously, wondering how an apparition could possibly have children.

"What? Seems impossible to you, eh? Well, it's not so impossible! They're here to prove it, aren't they? Now, they'll keep you company for a little while, so I can go out and look things over without worrying about you. You've seen things tonight that *must* get passed on to your kind, and I won't risk you getting into trouble."

"I've lived here all my life," remonstrated Bardol. "I think I can spend a few hours alone without getting myself killed."

"Ah!" the old man said, dashing to him and leaning in close to his face. "But you've never seen beings like *us* before, have you? Nor have you seen the *Ahsahklahn*! This world contains much more than you're familiar with, Captain, though it's familiar with you. Now, be quiet and stay here with these two. I'll be back soon enough!"

With this the old man simply disappeared, the stone wall resuming its former position and locking them in tight.

"So…" Rhizamorobalafan uttered in her catlike way, instantly returning to his side. "I'm just *dying* to know you better."

"And I'm dying to sleep," Bardol said, walking away from her towards the center of the cave. "Have you got any place I can rest for a little while."

"Just the floor," Dogentaradock said indifferently, walking to the wall and leaning against it, eyeing the young man with aversion. "Don't see why father had to bring you here," he muttered, as if to himself though he wished to be overheard.

"Don't be rude to our guest, Dogentaradock," the girl chided him, appearing behind the captain and wrapping her arms around his middle. "He's had such a *hard* day, and he needs to rest."

"How's he gonna rest with you climbing all over him?" he shot back, causing her to scowl and withdraw her arms.

"Look, is there something I can call you two?" Bardol asked, looking between them. "I've got to admit, your names are a little hard to pronounce."

"Just chop them up," the young man said with a shrug. "I'm Dogen, she's Rhiza. Problem solved."

He was right, but the insolent way he said it ground on the captain's patience. Determined to be a good guest in another's house, he let it slide.

"Fine, that'll work," he said somewhat stiffly.

Carefully lowering himself to the stony floor, he started to stretch out when his head landed on Rhiza's soft stomach. With a jolt he sat upright again, turning around to find she'd materialized behind him, her supple body resting upon the ground, a smile on her face.

"What's the matter?" she asked with a playful pout, her eyes twinkling. "Don't you like me?"

"Rhizamorobalafan," Dogen said in a tone of bland censure. "You heard father."

"Father isn't here," she replied, reaching up to draw Bardol back onto her stomach.

"Look," he said, pulling back and turning his back away from her. "I just want to rest. I've had just about the hardest day of my life, and I'm in no mood for games. I only need sleep, okay?"

"Of *course*," she said with seductive warmth. "I was

only thinking of your comfort. The floor is so hard and cold for organics such as yourself. But it doesn't bother us at all. I was merely trying to help you relax, make you feel at home."

"Believe me, they never did *that* for me at home," Bardol laughed.

"What? Don't you have *anyone* who would provide such a simple service?" she asked with artificial surprise. "What a pity."

"Rhiza," Dogen censured again, now sitting on the floor with his back against the wall, his arms crossed. "Leave him alone."

"Oh hush. You're not father," she snapped, her eyes hot and angry until they fell upon the captain again. Instantly they were warm and soft again. "Father would be upset if we let you sleep on the floor and get cold."

"I'm sure he'd understand," evaded Bardol, his tired limbs begging for rest. Keeping his eyes on the girl, he rolled onto his side and was about to lay down when she appeared under him again, her stomach making a pillow as before. "Look, knock that off, will you?" he demanded, his temper flaring from sheer exhaustion as he put his hands to the floor and pushed off. "I'm sure you think this is all fun and games–."

"Games? Games?" she asked, as though hurt. "I don't think you're a game, Captain Julius Bardol. Not at all. I think you're a treasure, a very valuable person. Isn't that what father said? That you need to be kept safe to carry important information to your people?"

"Yes," he allowed grudgingly.

"He said that Bardol had to stay alive," Dogen uttered flatly. "Not that he be kept *comfortable*."

"Nobody asked you, Dogentaradock," she replied with a dismissive wave, glancing upward as though superior to both him and his comments.

"Look, just what are you?" Bardol asked, shifting onto his rear and resting his elbows on his knees. "Are you spirits?"

"Nope," Dogen replied, a piece of fruit suddenly in his hand which he loudly began to crunch. "Try again."

"We are protectors," she said, moving a little closer. "That's why we're so concerned for you."

"Speak for yourself," Dogen muttered, again ensuring it was loud enough to be heard.

"Protectors of what?" the captain asked Rhiza, shifting where he sat so he wouldn't have to look at her brother.

"The planet," the young man replied. "The trees. The animals. What have you."

"We are charged with protecting all life on this world," she said warmly, inching yet closer. "It is our mission, our purpose. So you can see why–."

"By who?" he asked, hoping to stop her.

"You wouldn't know," Dogen said. "You've never heard of 'em."

Bardol ground his teeth and drew a sharp breath, the sound of it making the young man snort derisively. Consoling himself with the idea that he *would* thrash him if he could, he fixed his eyes on Rhiza, which pleased her enormously.

"What are *you*?" he asked with quiet emphasis, trying to direct his question to her alone.

"We're–," began Dogen.

"Oh shut up, will you?" snapped the captain, unable to hold himself in any longer. "I'm talking to your sister."

"Have at it," he replied, pushing off the floor and walking towards the entrance. "I didn't want to stay here, anyway."

"Dogentaradock, you know father said for *both* of us to stay with him," Rhiza warned him. "Don't leave. You'll only anger him."

"So let him get angry," the young man said without concern, snapping his fingers and opening the wall. "I don't care."

Walking through the opening, he snapped his fingers again and closed it.

"Now that we're alone," she said earnestly, positioning herself beside him.

"I asked you a question," he reminded her. "Just what are you? You say you're not spirits, but I've never seen anyone who can disappear and reappear, or make themselves solid and then ghostlike. How do you do it?"

"We are one of the mysteries of this galaxy," she replied, leaning a little closer with each word, her eyes darting all over his face. "We've lived here…for eons," she said, her moist lips nearing his. "Just the three of us. No relatives…no friends…no…*love*."

Ducking her lips just as they were about to touch his, he moved a couple inches away and chuckled.

"So *that's* why your brother is such a hard case. Too much of the same routine, over and over again."

"Yes," she assured him, following him across the floor. "It's been just *horrible*. You can't imagine what it's like to spend thousands of years with just two other people."

"It must have been hard," he observed, barely stifling a smile as he moved away and she followed him yet further.

"So hard," she agreed, shaking her head back and forth in disbelief. "Harder than anything I could ever put to words."

"But why? Why are you here? Where did you come from?"

"We came from the reformation," she answered. "The second creation."

"The what?" he asked, a puzzled look crossing his face.

"The second creation," she repeated.

"Can't say I've ever heard of that."

"Oh, it was an awfully long time ago," she told him. "You wouldn't be interested."

"Yes, I absolutely would," he said, dodging her lips again. "It sounds fascinating."

A frown crossing her face, she sat still and stared at him.

"I won't tell you."

"Why not?" he asked, his eyebrows shooting up.

"Because you're neglecting me!" she replied in a pleading tone. "All I ask is a little affection from a," she paused, her eyes darting up and down his body, "*handsome* man. And you want to talk about *history!*"

"I don't tend to get romantic with spirits," he said.

"But I'm not a spirit!" she exclaimed. "I'm a *Dehlengohl!* A being formed from the realm of light, intended to watch over the works of the Reformer."

"Whoa, whoa," he said, holding up his hand. "Slow down. You're a *what*, and you're looking out for the works of the *who*?"

"I'm a *Dehlengohl*," she said more slowly. "I was formed from the realm of light countless generations ago by the Reformer. It was he who caused the reformation, also called the second creation."

"That's logical enough," the captain nodded. "And who is the Reformer?"

"I won't tell you," she said, turning her head away.

"Aw, come on."

"Not until you kiss me," she replied, turning back, gently parting her lips, and closing her eyes. "Kiss me!" she insisted when he hesitated.

Captain Bardol hardly needed encouragement to kiss a beautiful woman. But that wasn't what Rhiza was. Having had more than a bellyful of her father, he was in no mood to entangle himself with a willful spectral entity, even if she did think he was the hottest thing since the invention of fire. Reluctantly he leaned in, brushed his lips against hers, and instantly drew back.

"That wasn't a kiss!" she objected. "I've felt more passion when the evening breeze blows against my mouth!"

"Then I wish you two all the happiness in the world,"

he replied. "Now, about–."

"I want a *kiss!*" she demanded, her jaw clenching as she eyed him. "Or you'll never get another syllable out of me. Not one! Not a *single* one!"

Hearing echoes of her father in her last words, Bardol groaned inwardly. Steeling himself for what he had to do, he stretched his legs out straight before him, seized her around the middle, and twisted her across himself onto her back. With a little yelp she contacted the stone, instantly silenced by a passionate kiss that probed every corner of her mouth. To the captain's surprise she felt exactly like the innumerable human women he'd kissed, and not the least artificial for being an apparition. Enjoying himself, he slowed down and began to move his hands up and down her back.

She did the same, though confining herself to his head and shoulders. Unable to get enough of his thick head of hair, she weaved and reweaved her fingers through it, occasionally moving below it to examine the strong muscles of his neck and upper back.

After what felt like an hour he pulled his head away, though she anchored it with her arms, trying to drag him back down.

"No," he said with a smile, shaking his head and disentangling himself. "You've gotten your kiss, and to spare. Now you're going to answer my question. Who was the Reformer?"

"Oh!" she grumbled, playfully scowling at him before giggling. "I enjoyed that!"

"Great," he chuckled. "Now, tell me."

"I…don't know," she admitted, a guilty smile crossing her lips.

"What? You said you'd tell me for a kiss!"

"I lied," she replied, giggling again. "I just wanted to kiss you."

"Yeah, I guessed that part," he said tartly. "What do you mean you don't know who the Reformer was?"

"I don't think anyone knows," she explained. "We don't know where he came from, and we don't know where he went. But he set things right again in this dimension after they had fallen into decay. That's why it's called the second creation: he produced a rebirth. It was out of that rebirth that I, my father, and my brother were made, our purpose being to guide life forward on this world. Having long since succeeded in that task, we fell to being little more than observers, watching passively from the sidelines. I'm afraid we all got a little…fractured by the experience. Father has grown eccentric, Dogentaradock has become surly and indifferent. And I have grown amorous."

"I noticed," he laughed, his head still hovering above hers, the girl's arms locked about his neck. "But why haven't I ever seen or heard of you people? I've lived on this planet my entire life."

"Our purpose was to guide life on this world, not interfere with it. We have deliberately kept ourselves hidden from you. But then this despicable parasite burst upon us, and we knew we had to do something to fight back. When father saw you fall from the sky, he acted at once. I agreed with him, though Dogentaradock couldn't have cared less. He's always scorned humans."

"Yeah, I got that message loud and clear," he replied.

"But not me," she assured him warmly, trying to draw his mouth back down to hers.

"Just a minute, honey," he said, pulling against her. "Do you people have weapons? Can you fight back against the parasite?"

"Weapons? No, certainly not. We're gardeners and shepherds, keepers of life on this world. We have great powers of insight and of travel. But neither of those can be used to attack another creature. It was never our purpose."

"No, of course not," he agreed, nodding as he thought. "It was a silly question to ask."

"Oh, not at all," she uttered dreamily, trying yet again

to kiss him.

Having been such a good girl thus far, he sighed and let her pull him back down. For a couple of minutes they kissed, before he drew back again.

"Now, that's gonna have to hold you for a while," he said, slipping out of her arms and settling down a couple feet away. "I need time to think."

"Oh, who needs to think?" she asked. "I've had all the time imaginable to think. It's not worth it. You only ever come back to yourself again. And that's so boring."

"Yeah, but I need to figure out a way to get in contact with the fleet when they show up," he explained. "We're just a local militia, under supplied like a lot of them are. So I never had a radio to take with me when I got in my fighter. I don't have a way to call out when they arrive. They could easily show up, blast the parasite to pieces, and leave again without ever finding out what I've learned. And that could be disastrous. That beast has plans that must be stopped."

"Don't worry," she said, scooting closer and putting a hand on his knee. "We'll think of a way. Father's very clever, you know."

"He's a little *nuts*, I think," Bardol couldn't help saying. "Or eccentric, as you said."

"Yes, time has not been kind to him," she agreed. "But that doesn't mean he's lost all his faculties. If there's a way to reach out to your people when they arrive, father will know it."

"I hope so," the captain uttered. "Because it's not like they're gonna see me under all this foliage. It's gonna take something big."

"Don't worry," she repeated, putting her hand on his head and weaving her fingers into his hair again. "I promise you we'll find a way."

Unable to help smiling as she massaged his scalp, he winked and leaned back, finding her stomach as his pillow by the time his head had reached the floor. Both her hands went to his head, working it lovingly as his fatigue caught up with him and he finally drifted off to a well deserved sleep.

CHAPTER 12

The mood was low and tense within Girnius' palatial home. Hunt's demonstration of power had put the pirate on the back foot, and for that reason he was surly and unfriendly to the Deltan and his friends. The state of the Black Suns was also not calculated to lift his spirits, as they had continued to be battered by their enemies. However, the initial sting of retaliation by the Fringers and their allies had begun to wear off, leaving in its place a fierce determination to give as good as they got. Impending change was palpable within the organization. From the highest official to the lowest pirate, they could each feel that Girnius was on the brink of a shift in tack that would make their enemies run for cover.

Girnius could feel it, too. The only problem was he hadn't the least idea what that change would be. It was still bubbling around in the back of his mind, his unconscious faculties wrestling with the problem that all his experience as chairman couldn't solve. He knew how to organize everything from smuggling to theft to assassination. But what good were those things when set against the power and insight of demigods? The *Pho'Sath* were proving to be the hardpoints around which the Fringers rallied, shielding themselves behind their imposing forms.

The Black Suns could deal with the separatists themselves, though heavy losses would, and *did*, ensue. The organization was spread across enough of the galaxy to survive the loss in income suffered throughout the fringe, to say nothing of the damage done to both men and materiel.

But the *Pho'Sath* were stepping up their game in a way that hadn't been anticipated. Moving more boldly through the Milky Way with each passing day, they had begun to take on the work that only the Fringers had done in the past. Targeting local pirate leaders, the organization was quickly losing officials whose combined experience amounted to centuries of piracy. Greener hands were taking their place; hands that had little chance of grappling with the threats they faced.

The chairman found himself regretting the deal he'd signed with Krancis, though he was equally aware that he wouldn't change a thing if he had the chance. The Fringers had attempted attempted to assassinate him, and for that they had to be punished in the only way he could make stick: the complete destruction of their entire network of spies, murderers, and revolutionaries. He could never rest content while a single separatist drew breath, though he wished events hadn't been pushed to such a dangerous place. Had they kept away from him, he would never have gotten involved.

"Everything keeps breaking your way, doesn't it, Krancis?" he muttered, sitting on the end of his bed with a bottle in his hand. Slouching glumly, his hair mussed and greasy, he was halfway in the bag and it wasn't even noon. "You've got more luck than a bag of rabbits' feet."

Raising the bottle to his mouth and finding it empty, he angrily tossed it aside. It exploded against the wall to his right, scattering glass across the floor beneath a boarded up window. Sullenly he looked at the window, yet another unmistakable sign that something had to change. He would *not* be a prisoner in his own home a second longer than necessary.

Pushing heavily off the bed, he sauntered to the

bathroom and got in the shower to wash some of the haze out of his bleary mind. Resting his hands against the front wall as the water beat down against his scalp, he shook his head and wondered how he ever managed to let things fall to such a state.

"We weren't ready," he mumbled, causing water to run into his mouth which he angrily spat out. "We jumped in unprepared," he added internally.

Leaving the shower and toweling off, he threw on a fresh set of clothes and left his room. Moving slowly through the house, the intermittently placed guards eyeing him respectfully as he passed them, he went to the kitchen to find an early lunch being served at a pair of tables that had been pressed together to form a single large one. Seated on one side of the table were Hunt, Pinchon, and Mafalda. Hyde, the doctor, and the chairman's latest girlfriend took up the other side. A space was open between Hyde and the girl, he having anticipated Girnius joining them.

"Sit down, Chrissy," the chairman ordered, as the girl arose with a guilty look on her face. She was oddly inclined to blame herself for his bad moods, and this occasion was no exception. The fact that she was beautiful *and* tender pleased him enormously, given that most of his previous companions were nothing more than gold diggers. But occasionally the softness of her heart got on his nerves, and he wished she could take a more detached view of things.

"Good morning," Pinchon said in a pointedly triumphant tone, having been up for hours. "Glad you could join us."

Venomously the chairman eyed the colonel as he sat down beside Chrissy. Stuffing a napkin into his open collar, he raised his fork and began to eat a decently warm meal of sausage, eggs, and toast.

Slowly his eyes panned his guests, starting with Hunt and ending with the colonel. They doubled back to Mafalda, landing specifically on the amulet that hung from her shapely neck. Evidently Chrissy had donated some of her clothes to the unfortunate girl, for he recognized at once the plunging neckline that nevertheless retained her modesty. The disc hung just above her heart.

"May I see that?" he asked the former separatist, resting his elbow on the table and pointing to Wellesley.

Uncertain if she should hand him over, she swallowed and glanced at Hunt to her right. Receiving a nod in reply, she set down her fork and put her hands to the chain, lifting it over her copious head of hair and handing the amulet to him.

"Thank you," he said with muted politeness, turning the disc over a couple times and rubbing it with his thumb. "So, this is the AI?"

"Uh huh," Rex nodded, not looking up from his meal.

"Does he talk?"

"Only when he wants to."

"And how often is that?"

"Every other second or so."

"That's hardly fair," Wellesley objected, causing Girnius to jump. "I've been known to keep my mouth shut for minutes on end."

"So you *do* talk," the chairman observed.

"Sure. What else would I do with my time? It's not like I can play badminton."

"And what do you talk about? Anything useful?" he asked, still surly from the alcohol.

"That depends on the company," the AI shot back. "I usually match my conversation to the intelligence level of my interlocutor. Which, in your case–."

"Wellesley," Hunt said sternly, able to hear him over the radio in his ear.

"Is...adequate...enough," he reluctantly finished.

"And just where do you come from?" he inquired, allowing the dig to pass. Taking Wellesley in his left hand to free up his right, he picked up his fork again and continued to eat.

"I was made by the *Kol-Prockians*," he replied. "That's K-O-L-."

"*Wellesley*," Hunt said more sharply.

"What? I'm just trying to be clear. I wouldn't want–."

A dark look from the Deltan halted his words.

"Oh, fine, if you're gonna get huffy about it…" his voice trailed.

"And what was your purpose?" the pirate leader asked evenly. "To provide witty repartee?"

Despite his aversion to Girnius, even Pinchon had to stifle a chuckle.

"Ooh, very funny. I'll have to frame that and put it on my wall," Wellesley replied, audibly rolling his eyes. "But no, as a matter of fact, I was intended to act as an assistant to the highest levels of the *Kol-Prockian* military establishment. Moving beyond such a limited role," he added proudly, "I eventually became the linchpin for the imperial faction in our civil war. In that capacity–."

At these words the chairman dropped his fork, it clattering loudly against his plate. All eyes mutely shot to him, searching his face to try and understand the air of realization that had come over it.

"Well, I don't think it's all *that* shocking," Wellesley commented, unsure how to read his reaction. "I understand that human AIs don't tend to reach such heights–."

"What do you mean *linchpin*?" he asked carefully. "Define that term."

"Linchpin," the AI repeated self-evidently. "I was the glue that held things together, particularly on the logistical end. Without me, the effort to overthrow the confederation would have fizzled and died out. Our leader was an impulse warrior, and not much suited to making sure that the I's got dotted and the T's crossed. Someone had to have the thoroughness to bring efficiency and a centralized plan to the war effort. Otherwise–."

"And how long did this war effort of yours last?"

"If you guys keep cutting me off, I'm just gonna stop talking. What do you–."

"Wellesley," Hunt said.

"See? There you go again!"

"Just answer the question."

"Years," he replied with annoyance. "More than I care to remember. A lot of lives were lost."

"And you were outgunned?"

"Heavily."

"Interesting," the chairman mused aloud.

"Yeah, we thought so, too," the AI retorted. "Look, why the sudden interest in ancient history?"

In response Girnius looked at Rex.

"Mister Hunt, I should like to employ your AI to help me revamp the Black Sun organization."

At this Pinchon nearly choked on his food, setting down his fork and beating his chest to dislodge it.

"Say that again?" he asked, his voice strained and thin. "You want to put *Wellesley* in charge of restructuring the organization?"

"Is that so surprising?" Girnius asked.

"Uh, *yeah*, it is," the colonel replied. "The Black Suns have always had a strict No Outsiders policy. And I should think that would go double for an AI who regularly hobnobs with Krancis and other imperial officials."

"Drastic times," he replied, not bothering to finish the proverb.

"He'll know absolutely everything about the organization," Pinchon objected. "And you know Krancis isn't about to let all that juicy data pass him by without sticking his fingers into it. You're basically handing away any last shred of secrecy the Black Suns have."

"And you consider that a bad thing? I thought you were pretty close to Krancis yourself."

"Hardly," the colonel chuckled mirthlessly. "I think he's great and wonderful and all those good things," he added in the tone of a disclaimer. "But sooner or later the war is gonna be over, and we might find him a little hard to live with. At least with the Black Suns there was still some little hope of an independent existence from imperial oversight. But if you do this, the organization will be little more than a department of the government."

"We're that now," Girnius replied, the fact grating on him though he didn't show it. "We're just a vassal state at this point."

"But there was still some distance between you and the government," he argued.

"Not a meaningful distance. If Krancis is as power hungry as you say, he would have gotten his fingers deeper into us sooner than later anyway."

"I didn't say he was *power hungry*," stipulated Pinchon. "But he doesn't brook opposition, either."

"Not much of a distinction," opined the pirate leader, rolling his eyes back to Rex. "Well?"

"We can't leave Wellesley here with you," the Deltan replied. "He's too valuable, knows too much."

"Then you don't trust us?" Girnius asked.

"Not in the least," he replied bluntly. "Especially given the failure of your own security team to keep you safe. It would be trivial for the *Pho'Sath* to break in here and steal him. I'm not gonna risk him falling into their hands and getting himself killed. You'll have to find some other way."

"Honestly, Rex, I could probably complete my work in a couple of weeks," Wellesley chimed in. "Once I'd familiarized myself with the organization, it wouldn't be that hard to restructure things. Three weeks, tops."

"You *want* to do this?" Pinchon asked.

"Sure. It's the kind of thing I was built for, remember? And I haven't had a genuine challenge in a long time. It would be fun to put my talents to use. Especially when you consider how impactful this would be, especially throughout the fringe. It could make a real difference in the war. And I would have a greater opportunity to study how the *Pho'Sath* operate. That might be decisive in figuring out a way to counter them on a broad scale."

"All our resources would be placed at your disposal," Girnius replied. "Only you would have to run your proposals past me for final approval."

"Naturally," the AI said at once, his excitement growing. "Come on, Rex."

"We can't do it, Wells. I can't float around for weeks to keep an eye on you, and nobody else can make sure you're safe from the *Pho'Sath*. What do you think is gonna happen when the pirates start restructuring? Do you think they're not gonna notice? They'll realize at once that a new brain has been brought onto the task, and they'll move fast and hard to cut him out of the picture."

"There's always risks in war, Rex," Wellesley pointed out. "I can't tell you how many times I was nearly assassinated during our civil war. That didn't stop me from completing my task."

"You weren't fighting against the *Pho'Sath*."

"So we'll be extra careful. Keep a transport ready at all times, and guards and security cameras everywhere. As soon as one of them gets near, Girnius or Hyde or whoever can take off and–."

"Run into a couple of separatist fighters," cut in Hunt. "They're not stupid, Wells. You might get away with that trick once. But they'd get you the next time."

"Well, there's got to be something we can do!"

At this moment Hyde pressed a finger into his right ear and listened for several seconds, the rest of the table watching him. Suddenly his eyes went wide, and with a mute nod he withdrew his finger.

"We have a visitor," he said gravely, taking the napkin from his collar and dropping it on his plate as he arose.

"What visitor?" Mafalda asked in a small voice, still not one hundred percent after her ordeal.

"Come outside," he replied, walking slowly out of the kitchen and towards the back of the house, the others quickly rising and following him.

"Sir! There's a–," began a guard who'd rushed in from outside to alert him. But Hyde held up a hand to stop him.

"I know," he replied, walking past as the man stepped aside, his mouth hanging open in wonder.

"What's going on?" Mafalda quietly asked Rex, walking beside him.

"Let's find out," he said with a shrug, just as Hyde reached the back door and opened it.

Seemingly clouds had rolled in, for the entire area was blanketed by a shadow. However, the instant they got out from under the roof, they realized the effect was caused not by clouds, but by *Sentinel* hovering overhead. The Black Suns could only stand and gape at the sight, as did Mafalda, who'd never seen it before.

"I wonder what brings him here," Pinchon observed casually, though he still felt a thrill from seeing the gigantic warship. Crossing his arms over his chest, he leaned back on his left foot and looked for a few moments before adding, "Can't be for the lunch. I'll get in the egg and see what's on his mind." With this the colonel walked off.

"It's...incredible," Girnius enthused, his eyes hungrily searching the vessel as Chrissy got under his right arm and gazed up alongside him. "Magnificent. I had no idea."

"Yeah, it's pretty fabulous," Wellesley said indifferently, getting in a subtle jab. "You get used to it after seeing it in action a time or two."

"What's it like?" he asked eagerly, still looking upwards. "To see it really blast away?"

"Oh, you know, 'Boom boom, blam blam.' Nothing too special."

"It's unlike anything you've ever seen before," Hunt explained. "The rawest power imaginable pointed in one direction. You feel like it could destroy reality itself when that cannon cuts loose."

"Isn't that what I said?" the AI asked, causing Hunt to glance at him and roll his eyes.

"I should very much like to see it from the inside," Girnius uttered.

"I don't think Krancis is offering tours right now," Wellesley replied. "Of course, if you–," he stopped, checking himself as an idea shot through his mind. "Of course! That's the answer!"

"To what?" the chairman inquired.

"Tell me, could you run the Black Suns from anywhere?" the AI asked eagerly.

"Provided there's adequate equipment to stay in touch. Naturally all communications have to be protected to prevent eavesdropping. And the network would have to be reliable to ensure that I'm not out of reach."

"What's on your mind, Wells?" Hunt asked, taking a step closer and crossing his arms.

"Why not run the Black Suns from *Sentinel?*" he offered. "It's got the best comms equipment possible; the *Pho'Sath* can't touch it, so *I'd* be safe, and so would the chairman; and it would ensure the closest collaboration possible between the organization and the imperial government. It's a win all the way around!"

"I don't think Krancis would take to having Girnius aboard," Hunt replied frankly.

"Well, why not ask him?" the AI countered. "The worst thing he can do is say no. And if we can present him with the opportunity to make the Black Suns even more effective, it's hard to imagine he'd turn the chance down. The imperial effort is too short of friends as it is."

"I'm not sure about this," Girnius shook his head, finally drawing his eyes down from *Sentinel's* underside. "It's one thing to be a vassal. It's quite another to be a hostage." He paused and looked at Hunt for a moment. "That's what I'd be, wouldn't I?"

"If Krancis decided to take things in that direction," the Deltan stipulated. "Yes."

"Better than being dead," Wellesley observed. "If we hadn't chanced by this place for Mafalda's sake, the *Pho'Sath* would have almost certainly gotten you by now. They're stepping up their game everyday, Chairman. You know better than anyone the necessity of rolling with the punches, adapting in order to survive. You stick on the same course you're on now, and you'll be six feet under in a week. Actually, you'd be fireflies, 'cause that's how they kill people."

"I think he gets the point, Wells."

"Just making sure."

Drawing a deep, grave breath, he glanced upward again and let it out. But before he could add anything, Pinchon returned.

"Our lord and master wants to see you, Rex," he said from a dozen paces away. "Says it's of fatal importance to the empire."

"Oh, that sounds nice," Wellesley observed sarcastically. "You'd think he could drop in once in a while just to say hello, instead of all this life-and-death stuff all the time. The man has no social life at all."

"Want me to fly you up, Rex?" the colonel asked, grinning at the AI's comment.

"Yeah," he nodded, before turning to Girnius. "Well, what do you think?"

"Mention the idea to Krancis," he said quietly, drawing his eyes down from *Sentinel*. "See what he says."

"Alright," Hunt nodded. "I'll take Wellesley back now."

"Of course," the chairman replied, handing him over and then turning back towards the house with Chrissy under his arm. Stealing one more look at the ship, the two went back inside.

"You want to wait down here or come with us?" Rex asked Mafalda.

"I'm sticking with you," she replied at once, still not

comfortable to be among the pirates. Briefly she thanked the doctor for the solicitous care he'd extended to her during her stay, and then moved to Hunt's side.

"We'll be back," Hunt told Hyde, as he turned with the girl and headed for the ship.

Soon they were in the air, watching the compound shrink beneath them. *Sentinel* had appeared close, as though hovering right above the surface of Petrov-2. But that was merely an illusion caused by its great size. In fact it was quite far off, and all but the largest buildings in Eastmaw appeared tiny by the time they'd gotten level with it. Guiding the ship into the hangar, Pinchon landed it and raised the canopy.

"Better tell him not to just bolt off into warp, Wellesley," Pinchon said over his shoulder as he climbed out of his seat.

"Already done."

Though she was much stronger than she'd been in a long time, the colonel helped Mafalda over the side and down to the hangar's floor like a concerned father.

"Alright? Head's not swimming or anything?" he asked as they moved away from the craft towards the nearest teleporter, Hunt right behind them.

"No, I'm feeling just fine," she assured him.

"Good. Any trouble, just let us know."

A few minutes later the trio passed through the bridge's doorway to find Krancis, Gromyko, and Soliana standing together. With gusto the smuggler shot across the panoramic room, clamping his arms around Hunt and squeezing the air out of him.

"My friend! You're alive!" he exclaimed, happy beyond words to see him.

"Hi…Antonin," Hunt groaned, finding it hard to speak.

"What's this about you wanting me to wait?" Krancis asked in his precise voice. "I came here for a very specific purpose. We have no time to waste."

"Believe me," Wellesley said over the ship's speakers as Gromyko released his friend. "You'll be glad you didn't dash off."

"Girnius wants Wellesley to help him reorganize the Black Suns," Pinchon said. "They're taking a real beating, and he thinks he'll be a big help in getting things straightened out."

"And just what does that entail?" the man in black inquired, Soliana standing quietly by his side. Unobtrusively she gave Hunt a little nod of recognition and a smile.

"Oh, he wants me to pour over their data and make suggestions on how they can run their operation better. Like a consultant, though I wouldn't be surprised if he tried to move me into a managerial role in the future. Once he sees what I can do, he'll beg to have me sign on full time."

"That's out of the question. You can't be risked."

"That's why I suggested that he come aboard *Sentinel*, and run the Black Suns from here," the AI replied. No one spoke for several seconds. "Look, it's not *that* crazy. He's basically a contractor for the government at this point. And with the *Pho'Sath* knocking on his door these days, it's a sure bet that he'll bite the dust pretty soon if we just leave him on Petrov. Now, *Sentinel's* got the kind of comms equipment that he'd need to run things from afar. Honestly they're probably better than what he has to work with, given that it relies on the imperial network instead of the one they've established on the sly. This way he'll be safe, cooperative, *and* within arm's reach. There'd be no question of his loyalty."

"There's no question now, given that he's under threat of death from the *Pho'Sath* and dependent on our kantium," observed Krancis.

"But one is always more cooperative when in the presence of overwhelming force," countered Wellesley. "Sure, he won't stab you in the back now because he can't. But that doesn't mean he's giving you his all. Being aboard *Sentinel* will give him a little added motivation to stick to his work. Honestly the last few days he's been moping around his house and drinking."

"Why?"

"Because he feels like his organization is in shambles, and that his life hangs by a thread," answered Pinchon. "It's torn him up real bad to see the Black Suns take the beating they have. He's always prided himself on growing the business. To see it start to crumble is making him doubt everything he's done. He needs to be firmed up, and *Sentinel* is just the way to do it."

"I thought you weren't in favor of this plan," Wellesley said with a hint of puzzlement in his voice.

"I admit I wasn't a fan of it at first," the colonel replied, glancing at Krancis and glad that the AI had chosen not to mention his reason for opposing it initially. "But with a little more thought, I figure it's the only way. We've got to keep Girnius in the game, and this is the best way to do that."

"Huh, what do you know," Wellesley mumbled, surprised to see the colonel change his mind and join his side. "So, what do you think?" he asked, before immediately following up with, "And, besides, it will facilitate coordination. Just think of it: I could orchestrate combined operations between the Black Suns and the imperial navy; I could ensure that information is seamlessly passed from one hand to the other; I could–."

"Your point is taken," Krancis replied. "But the fact remains that a Black Sun would be roaming within *Sentinel*. To pen him up would be to lose his cooperation. And yet he is hardly in sympathy with us. He is merely getting revenge on the separatists for their attempt to kill him."

"I don't think he'd consider breaking with us after all he's been through," Pinchon opined. "He's pretty much accepted the fact that he's just a puppet of the government at this point. It's something else that's taken him a little time to get used to."

Krancis eyed the colonel at this comment, noting the

hint of disapproval in his voice at the word *puppet*.

"He would require a command center within *Sentinel*," Soliana observed, her voice smooth and wise, though somewhat dreamy. "A space from which to direct his organization and plan his moves. He would also need constant access to the communications equipment, given that he's in charge of such a large organization. It wouldn't be possible to police his messages."

"*Esiluria* could read his mail, if you're worried about him ratting us out," Wellesley replied.

"I am merely pointing out that accepting him aboard *Sentinel* would require a degree of trust that is not typically extended to pirates. There is some small amount of danger involved. Even if he doesn't harbor the least sense of disloyalty to our cause, he may still accidentally give out information about *Sentinel* or its movements that could prove disastrous. Heretofore all communications have been strictly controlled. That wouldn't be possible if we expect him to continue running his organization, much less to *increase* his activity within it."

"Then we could set limits on when he's allowed to radio out, and what he's allowed to say," Wellesley replied. "I'm not saying this would be without hiccups. But keeping Girnius around, to say nothing of ramping up the value of the Black Suns as allies, is more than worth it."

"And if he becomes difficult and testy over being controlled?" Krancis objected. "If he comes to hate the confines within which he's been placed, and deteriorates as an ally?"

"By that time I will have so completely insinuated myself within the organization that it wouldn't matter. We could lock him in a cell, I could rule in his name, and the Black Suns would *still* be more effective than they are now. You must consider the value of having my war experience injected into them. Right now they're pirates making war. Give me a little while with them, and I'll make 'em into *warriors* who bring death and devastation to our enemies. In time, you won't be able to recognize them."

"You easily contemplate depriving a man of his freedom," Soliana observed.

"Daily we deprive countless men and women of their lives by sending them into battle against the Devourers," Wellesley replied. "To say nothing of all the Black Suns and resistance fighters who've died at the hands of the separatists and the *Pho'Sath*. I *think* we can morally justify locking a single man up for the good of the human race. Shoot, we could even dump him on some remote planet with a supply drop and let him live out his days like that. Just so long as he's out of the way."

"Of course," she replied, visibly withdrawing from the conversation.

"You're quite certain you could run the organization in his absence?" Krancis clarified.

"Absolutely. One hundred percent. Even the most recalcitrant humans are easier to deal with than my people were. Especially during the civil war, when everything was coming unglued. It'd be childsplay. All I'll need is a bit of time to get a feel for things, say a month. Then it'll be trivial to act out Girnius' part." He paused for a moment, and then added, as a disclaimer, "Should that become necessary, of course."

Hunt could hear the enthusiasm in his old friend's voice at the idea of running the Black Suns. Having only known him as a personal companion since their earliest days together on Delta-13, it had never really occurred to him how much the AI must miss truly exercising his faculties. He was a powerful construct, and yearned to make use of his capacity. However, it did make Hunt a tad uneasy how eager Wellesley was to brush Girnius aside. Possessing no liking for the pirate at all, he was nevertheless always reluctant to separate a man from the product of his own hands. And few could honestly deny that Girnius had made the Black Suns into what they were.

"What did you tell him before leaving?" Krancis asked.

"Just that we'd relay the message," Pinchon answered. "He's willing to come aboard, though reluctantly. Given the talk around here," he added disapprovingly, "I can see why."

Krancis noted his criticism with a nod.

"Tell him to set his affairs in order and to come aboard. Suggest that he leave someone behind on Petrov that he can trust. We'll need a conduit to funnel communications through initially, a proxy that can relay his wishes to the rest of the organization. Obviously the Black Suns aren't dialed in to the imperial network, so it'll be a little while until we can run everything exclusively through *Sentinel*."

"I'll get on that," Pinchon said, turning towards the door and then stopping. "Guess I'd better take Wellesley along for the ride. He might have some ideas for how to set things up with the proxy."

"I agree, Colonel," the AI concurred, as Hunt handed him over. "Back soon."

"Just one more thing," Krancis added, as the ex-pirate reached the door.

"Yeah?"

"No guests. The offer is for Girnius alone. I don't want him trying to bring a team up here."

"I'll tell him," Pinchon replied.

"So, what have you been up to, my friend?" Gromyko asked with undiminished enthusiasm when the colonel had gone. "And who is this lovely young lady?" he further asked, flaring his eyebrows at the question.

"This is Mafalda Aboltina," he answered. "Mafalda, Antonin Gromyko."

"Hello," she said with some reserve, unsure what to make of his buoyancy as she reached out her hand. Eagerly he took it in both of his.

"Mafalda Aboltina," he repeated, savoring the name. "You're like a fresh breeze rustling through the red leaves of autumn," he said, clearly taking inspiration from her strikingly red hair.

With a nervous giggle, she looked down at her feet and withdrew her hand.

"Heel, Antonin," Hunt chuckled, putting an arm around her shoulders and turning her towards Krancis.

"You must know who I am," the man in black said, extending a long, thin hand and shaking hers coldly. "I'm familiar with you, as well."

Wincing at the note of censure she sensed in his voice, she gladly turned to Soliana.

"This is Soliana," Hunt introduced her. "She joined up with us back on the Black Hole."

"The pirate base?" Mafalda asked, as she tepidly reached out her hand.

The moment Soliana's hand touched hers, she felt a charge run through her body, as though every cell that made her up was being examined. In a flash it was over, and feeling terribly violated she jerked her hand away.

"What was that?" she asked, as Krancis and Soliana began to move towards the door.

"Merely the taking of a surface impression," he replied over his shoulder. "A much more thorough examination will be necessary later on. For the time being you will be confined to your quarters." Snapping his fingers, a pair of security men came in. "These gentlemen will escort you to your room."

"*I'll* take her, Krancis," Hunt insisted, again putting an arm around her shoulders.

"As you wish," he replied indifferently. "But they'll remain outside her door until Soliana has had time to check her out. That is non-negotiable." Without another word they left.

"Did I do something wrong?" she asked quietly, looking up into Hunt's eyes.

"No. He's just suspicious. We have to be careful with *Sentinel*."

"How anyone could suspect such a charming girl is

beyond Gromyko," the smuggler uttered, following them out the door, the two security men forming up behind him. "It's obvious that you're pure as a mountain stream."

"But…aren't *you* Gromyko?" she asked, turning and looking over Hunt's arm.

"He does that," her escort explained, before stopping and looking at the guards. "Look, I personally guarantee that she'll reach her quarters. Now, why don't you stop following us and meet us there in a little while? I won't leave her alone until you're stationed outside her door."

"I'm sorry, Lord Hunt," one of them said. "But–."

"Unless you're looking for a *great* deal of trouble," he began, his voice dropping. "I suggest you do as I say."

"Yes, Lord Hunt," they answered in unison, dropping back and waiting for them to get out of sight before heading for a different teleportation chamber.

"I really don't want to cause any trouble," Mafalda said anxiously, beginning to blush.

"You're no trouble at all," Gromyko assured her at once. "Why–."

"Antonin," Hunt cut him off, his tone the same as that he'd used with the other two.

"Why, I think I just remembered something that I have to do," he redirected. "I'll see you later, buddy."

"Okay," Hunt replied in a lighter tone, now that the smuggler had gotten the message and was breaking off.

Once his feet had retreated down the hallway behind them, Mafalda slowed to a stop and looked at him.

"I'm not worth all this trouble, Rex," she said with quiet earnestness. "I don't want you to fight with your friends over me. Especially Krancis."

"I'd hardly call Krancis a friend," Hunt replied, pulling her into motion again.

"I don't want to cause any friction."

"You're not, okay?" he said. "It's just a little teething period. They'll get used to you, and come to see you as an asset. You've got a meaningful part to play in this war, Mafalda. But you still need time to recover and get your bearings. This is the best place to do that."

"But...*Sentinel!*" she objected. "I really don't warrant this kind of treatment."

"I thought you wanted to come up here."

"I did," she admitted. "But I didn't think I'd be received with such hostility. And I *didn't* expect that woman to go digging through my soul."

"You don't have to worry about Soliana. She's trustworthy."

"I'm sure she is. I just don't like stuff like that."

Pulling her to a stop just short of a teleportation room's door, he locked eyes with her.

"Look, I don't either. But we're in a state of war right now. We can't be too careful. More than that, Krancis won't have it any other way. He's hard to live with, but he's usually right. Just play along with him, and everything will be fine. I won't let them push you around."

"Okay," she nodded, as he gave her shoulders a little squeeze and led her inside.

"To the sleeping quarters," he ordered the technician.

"Of course, Lord Hunt," she complied at once, sending Mafalda through first.

Reuniting on the other side, they got part way into the sleeping quarters before Hunt realized that he didn't know her room number. He was reaching for his ear radio when Mafalda stopped him by pointing down the corridor.

"I think it's that one," she observed, noting the two men he'd dismissed before. "They sure got here in a hurry."

"Yeah," he replied sourly, walking with her to the room and stopping just short of the door. "Soliana will probably get with you in the next day or so. You won't be stuck here for long."

"Can I...talk to you for a moment?" she asked uncertainly, aware how her request would look to the guards.

"Sure," he said offhandedly, following her inside and closing the door. "What's on your mind?"

Wordlessly she stepped into his arms and squeezed him with the biggest hug she could manage given the remnants of her condition. The red marks on her face had since disappeared, but the internal scars to her heart and soul remained. Like a leaf she began to quiver as tears gathered in her eyes and dripped down her face.

"What's wrong?" he asked earnestly, putting his arms over her shoulder blades and hugging her back. "Mafalda? What's wrong?" he repeated, when she continued to tremble.

"I could sense it," she said. "I could sense that woman's disapproval of me. She knows what I am. Knows what I *was*. It might have been just a brief scan, but she's already got a read on me. I've been kidding myself all this time, thinking I could turn over a new leaf and change. But I can never turn my back on the things I've done. Especially to poor Amra."

At the mention of her name, she began to sob loudly. Pressing her face against his shoulder, she did her best to muffle herself so the guards wouldn't hear.

"I don't deserve this," she asserted, as he moved a hand up to the back of her neck and began to gently massage it. "I don't deserve any of it. You should have left me in that dungeon! *Deldrach* should have–."

"Hush," he ordered, squeezing her tight to silence her. "You're alright," he assured her. "It's gonna be okay. Just give yourself a chance to calm down."

Heeding his words, she turned her head aside and laid it against his chest. Taking as deep a breath as she could, she raggedly exhaled it.

"I have to go," Hunt said. "They'll get the wrong idea if I stay any longer. And it won't help your case with Krancis any if he thinks I'm emotionally compromised."

"Okay," she agreed, as he drew back and put his hands on her shoulders. With a smile he kneaded them a little.

"It's gonna be alright," he told her again. "Just try to

get some rest," he added, nodding over her shoulder at the bed. "Soliana will check you out and give you the okay. Then you won't have anything to worry about."

"I don't think she'll ever like me," Mafalda replied.

"She doesn't have to," he said. "Shoot, Krancis doesn't like me half the time, and I return the compliment. But we both work together alright. Just get some sleep and try not to worry. You're in good hands now." With a smile he gave her shoulders one last squeeze, and then departed.

Guessing that Krancis had departed the bridge in order to speak with *Esiluria*, Hunt returned to the teleporter room he'd used a few minutes before and told the technician to send him to the library.

"Get your new friend settled in?" Krancis asked, sitting at the table with Soliana to his left and *Esiluria* across from him.

"Yeah," Hunt confirmed, leaning against the wall and crossing his arms. "Now, what's this matter of fatal importance that you had to see me about?"

"The Devourers are forming biomasses all across the empire," he replied. "Given that they grow their ships, it's evident that a massive campaign is in the offing. Harvesting both human and animal flesh from many worlds, they've been gathering it together and depositing it. We received a distress call from the planet Hubertus before the local defenders were crushed. They reported a gigantic fleet with one of these masses in tow. It's apparent that the Devourers intend to grow this mass by collecting all the organic matter on the planet and reducing it to their basic construction paste. From there it will begin to reform itself into a powerful warship."

"How powerful?"

"The mass is already larger than one of their carriers."

"Then they're planning to smash *Sentinel* through sheer size," Hunt mused aloud.

"So it would seem. As I said, more than one of these

is under construction at the same time. It's hard to imagine how they've managed to gather this much material together, unless they've been more or less neglecting to repair their fleets. It would take an incredible number of lives, both human and otherwise, to create such a mass. To make *several* of them is a feat."

"Well, couldn't they just break down their current ships and reformulate them?"

"Seemingly not. Once the paste is given a distinct form, it remains that way. Its plasticity is severely short-lived. Probably a week at the most, though it's difficult to form an exact estimate."

"How did they get this far along without our knowing it?" Hunt inquired, someone unsettled by the notion. Deep down he wondered what else they might be working on.

"They must have been assembling them in deep space, far away from any of our outposts. They'd harvest the paste, warp away with it, and then apply it to the mass."

"But they're not operational yet? They're just big hunks of flesh?"

"That's right."

"Why would they do that? Makes sense to keep them out of reach until they're actually functional. Like this they're just sitting ducks."

"Who can say. Perhaps they're closer to being operational than we think, and they're just applying the finishing touches. In any event, we're not going to let them get that far. That's why I wanted you aboard."

"Meaning?"

"You're going to act as our battery again. I want the cannon operating beyond its normal capacity when we strike the mass on Hubertus."

"*Sentinel* can handle a mound of flesh," Hunt replied. "You don't need me for that."

"Rex, this mass is *enormous* and intelligent. Reports from other planets indicate that they're sending out psychic signals, calling animal life towards themselves. We're talking about a power that is unquantified, and I'm not about to risk *Sentinel* in a duel with one unless we've got all the odds in our favor. It's quite possible that this is just a trap, and that they've got something up their sleeves."

"What could they have up their sleeves?" he asked. "We've swept away one fleet after another. It's hard to imagine them coming up with anything at this point that could possibly counter *Sentinel*. Especially not a mound of meat."

"All the same, we're not going to risk our single greatest asset without doing our utmost to ensure its survival."

"Fair enough," he replied with a shrug, letting the point drop. "But shouldn't we get underway, then?"

"Hubertus isn't very far away," Krancis said. "And two fleets are already en route as we speak. We have another hour or so to spare before we have to warp."

"Why are you sending two fleets if you think even *Sentinel* might not be able to handle them on its own?"

"For several reasons. The first fleet is commanded by Claus Von Ortenburg, an honorable and skillful officer who is regrettably locked into old ways of thinking. He needs to have an opportunity to test out some new theories he and the navy have cooked up so he can see first hand how inadequate our present forces are. They hope that a change of tactics will preclude us having to restructure the navy. The second fleet consists of experimental craft that are designed to deliver maximum ordnance while keeping manufacturing costs to an absolute minimum."

"You mean you have them flying around in kites?"

"More or less. The emphasis is on warhead carrying capacity and maneuverability. Armor has been no defense against the Devourers, so this new project recognizes that fact and ignores it almost entirely. Only the carriers which bear the actual fighters have any armor, and that is almost none."

"And the navy opposes the plan because?"

"Because they think we're getting ready to sacrifice all our best pilots on a hair brained scheme cooked up by a civilian," he replied with a dry chuckle. "This upcoming battle will simultaneously prove the impotence of the present navy, and the effectiveness of the new approach. *Sentinel* will be on hand to deal with the biomass when they're finished, or to step in should they both find themselves overmatched."

"So you're going to sacrifice those ships and their crews just to make a point?"

"I'm going to allow them to execute a plan that they themselves have put forward as a model for the entire navy," he replied. "My influence has waned considerably with these individuals since the announcement of the new project, which I have dubbed Adler. Ordering them to stay back will likely result in mutiny, which is not a step I wish to force them to take. It will legitimize such actions in the future, giving strength to rebellious elements down the road. Better to let them get their own heads chewed off like this to keep the infection from spreading later. Besides, they won't let go of our conventional forces until they've lost every other option."

"It's hard to imagine how they could think a change in tactics will lead to victory when almost every battle the navy has participated in has been a failure."

"Hope springs eternal, especially for the conventionally minded. They wish to make only slight changes so that the habits and conventions they're used to may remain intact. They intend to keep the fleet moving at all times, biting off only small segments of the enemy fleet and grinding them down before moving in for more. Moreover, they intend to draw off the fighters and deal with them separately from the frigates and capitals. They also plan to warp in their forces piecemeal, dropping more and more forces into the fray at inconvenient places for the enemy, such as behind carriers once their escorts have moved ahead to strike our vessels. In the main they plan to use flexible tactics to unsettle the enemy's rather thuggish approach to warfare."

"And you don't think that will work?"

"No, because our vessels still don't possess the firepower needed to deal decisive damage. Our design doctrines have been centered around survivability first and armaments second. The organic nature of our enemies means that we have to batter them to pieces most of the time before they finally are destroyed. You can't simply puncture a half dozen places and have the life-support systems go out. You have to grind them into pulp."

"Then put the new weapons on the old ships, so you have durability and firepower."

"No, we need an answer that can be multiplied rapidly," Krancis shook his head. "I understand that the navy is making a plan to revamp our manufacturing procedures alongside our tactics. But given our current designs, it will simply be too little, too late. The Devourers, despite our propaganda, are spreading further and further across the empire. We need a mass solution that can cheaply bear the kind of ordnance that will be most effective against them. There simply isn't time to consider survivability."

Hunt paused and reflected on his words, his arm still crossed as he leaned against the wall.

"What, no more questions?" Krancis inquired.

"Not for the time being," he said. "Well, except this: what do you two have against Mafalda?"

"She's a separatist," he answered at once. "And one formerly of considerable importance. That alone warrants caution. Additionally, she's got a strange air about her."

"I sense great guilt within her," Soliana seconded.

"Yeah, she regrets her past life," Hunt said. "So?"

"How do you know that her guilt doesn't relate to

something that she *will* do? It doesn't always refer to the past, you know."

"There's no reason to assume that. Especially given how the *Pho'Sath* treated her. You can't see it now, but they tortured her almost to death. She had these nasty red marks on her face from what they did. Believe me, her bridges are burned with the Fringers."

"Soliana will be the judge of that," Krancis replied. "We can't be sure until we've had a deep dive into her psyche. Even she could be deluded about where her true loyalties lay."

"And when will that be?"

"Soon," she assured him. "Very soon. I'm not quite in the right state for it now. But shortly I will be."

As she finished speaking, Krancis pressed a finger against the radio in his ear. Standing up, he gestured for Hunt to follow.

"Come on," he explained, walking towards the teleportation chamber. "Girnius is aboard."

"I would like to wait here," Soliana said. "I've had enough interactions for the time being. I need time to reflect."

"Of course," Krancis agreed, stepping into the chamber and disappearing in a flash of blue. Moments later Hunt followed him, and together they walked towards the hangar.

"You gonna have her hop into Girnius' mind, too?" Hunt asked somewhat pointedly.

"That wouldn't be possible. He'll never put up with that kind of invasion of his privacy. And if we force it upon him, he'll become much less cooperative."

"But Mafalda is open game," he retorted.

"Not at all. It's simply that Girnius *isn't*. He's a special case."

Reaching the hangar, Hunt could see Krancis' jaw clench when he saw Chrissy standing beside the chairman, each of them carrying a small suitcase.

"I strictly said no guests," the man in black said flatly as he approached, looking between Pinchon and Girnius.

"I know," the colonel said, holding up his hands to indicate it wasn't his fault. "But he wouldn't leave without her. And I figured you'd rather have both of them instead of neither."

Drawing a shallow, displeased breath through his nose, Krancis sharply released it and looked at the chairman.

"Don't get into the habit of flaunting the rules," he warned him. "Or you'll quickly find yourself without a friend aboard this vessel."

"Do I have so much as a single friend now?" he asked. "The way I see it, I'm little more than an employee of the empire, and not a welcome one at that."

"In essence you're correct," Krancis assented.

"Then let's not talk of losing friends. We both know I'm here out of mutual convenience. I want to keep on living, and I want that AI to help me run the organization," he said, stabbing a finger towards Wellesley, held loosely in Pinchon's left hand. "Equally, you want me to stay alive so that the Black Suns keep hitting your enemies."

"*Our* enemies," Krancis corrected him. "They struck you first, as you'll recall, when they attempted to assassinate you. Justifiably, you retaliated, and that threw you in with us. Now we're both in it together."

"A fact that doesn't bring me any joy, let me assure you."

"The feeling is quite mutual."

"Then we understand each other?"

"Obviously."

"Good. Now, I'll need a place to work from," he said, picking up his suitcase again.

"*Esiluria* will help you get settled," Krancis replied. "Colonel, show him the way."

"Of course," Pinchon replied, waving for Girnius and Chrissy to follow. "What am I, the usher?" he muttered, rolling his eyes.

Momentarily Krancis gazed at them as they retreated into the ship. Then he pressed a finger to his radio.

"Captain: lift us out of the atmosphere and warp immediately for the point I spoke of." Lowering his hand, he looked at Hunt. "It's good to have you aboard again, Rex."

"Good to be back," he replied, as the man in black turned and walked away.

Just as Krancis was about to exit the hangar, Gromyko burst through the entrance and nearly collided with him. Visibly annoyed, the former scowled at him and departed.

"My friend!" the smuggler said loudly, half the hangar still separating them. "Who is that fabulous creature that you've brought aboard with you? She's like a magical apparition!"

"I already told you who she was," Hunt replied, slowly walking towards the exit himself.

"Oh, you told me her *name*. But who is she, really? There's an aura about her, a glow that I cannot define. I feel my spirit drawn to her, like metal to a magnet."

"Funny, she seems to have the opposite effect on some people."

"Bah! Krancis would suspect his own mother of plotting to betray him," the smuggler said with a dismissive wave of his hand. "He's a decent enough man in terms of intellect. But his heart is pure stone. He has no *trust!* No human *warmth!*"

"Soliana doesn't like her, either."

"Oh?" he asked, briefly caught off guard by this statement. "Well, she's not exactly herself lately. Probably just a phase."

"Probably," Hunt agreed, though he didn't believe it.

"But, there you go again dodging my question! Who is she?"

"I'm not dodging anything, Antonin," he uttered with annoyance. "There isn't a whole lot to tell. She was a separatist, but she turned on them and got tortured for it. They worked her over real bad and broke her down. I'm not sure exactly what she was like before, but I'd bet you plenty she used to be a great deal more confident of herself than she is now. You could stick a finger in her face now and tell her all sorts of nasty things, and she'd believe every one of 'em."

"Then we shall have to make a point to tell her pleasant things," he replied slickly. "So that she may believe them."

"Keep your hands off her, Antonin," Hunt ordered as they walked.

"Who's manhandling her?" he asked, instantly regretting his word choice as it reminded him of his fruitless attempt to speak with lieutenant Powers. Grunting away that memory, he continued, "I just want to ensure she's happy and comfortable."

"No, you want to pick up a new girlfriend for yourself."

"My friend!" the smuggler protested. "You wound me! Do you really suspect–."

His words were cut off by Hunt suddenly stopping and glaring at him, his eyes saying all that was necessary.

"Naturally I'm not blind to her beauty," Gromyko said as they resumed movement. "But I wouldn't think of *using* her in any way."

"I never said that you would," his fellow Deltan replied. "But she's in no condition to be involved with anyone right now. She's confused and hurt. Moreover she hates herself. It's gonna take a lot of careful tending to get her back to a healthy place, and I intend to see that she gets it."

"Don't think that I'm casting aspersions on your motives, my friend," the smuggler began somewhat cautiously. "But why are you so decidedly interested in her case?"

"I honestly don't know," Hunt shook his head. "I felt it from the first time I touched her. Something like a charge popped between us, and I knew from that moment on that she's terribly important. I just have to keep her safe. The colonel feels the same way, though like a father."

"And how do *you* feel?"

"Like a brother, I suppose," he replied. "Or a friend. What does it matter?"

"It doesn't," Gromyko said with a shrug.

"Wait a minute," Hunt said, stopping and turning on him again. "Just what are you insinuating?"

"My friend, I haven't uttered a single word!" the smuggler objected. "I have said nothing at all!"

"But you're *thinking* something," he replied, his eyes narrowing.

"I was just thinking that it's been an awfully long time since you've seen Lily," he admitted. "And that perhaps you were…a little…lonely."

His last words came out slowly as he shrank away from his infuriated friend, aware too late that he'd gone much too far.

"I'm sorry!" he exclaimed, as Hunt raised a hand and began walking him back up the corridor. "It was stupid of me! I never entertained the thought for a moment! It was just a passing notion! An idea on the wind!"

"One of these days, Antonin," Hunt threatened him, causing smoke to collect around his hand for a moment before dissipating it. "One of these days," he repeated, "you're going to get a much bigger taste of your own fears than the one I gave you last time."

Unable to find words to respond, the smuggler could only swallow loudly and match his friend's gaze with difficulty.

"Don't ever suggest anything like that again," he warned him. "Not ever."

With this Hunt turned his back on him and strode heavily away.

"Gromyko, when will you *ever* learn to keep your mouth shut!" he muttered to himself, turning away from his receding friend and shaking his head. "You're lucky that he's got so much restraint."

Taking a teleporter to the sleeping quarters, the smuggler was about to enter his room when he saw Powers coming out of hers. As soon as she saw him she turned away, hastening down the hallway.

"Wait!" he called, dashing past the guards that watched Mafalda's room and catching up with her. "Just a minute!" he said, taking her arm and pulling her to a stop.

"Don't you ever stop?" she asked angrily. "Just leave me alone."

"Not until you let me clear this whole business up," he said, releasing her arm and walking quickly beside her. "I never meant to insult you by what I said before."

"Oh, sure," she said tartly.

"Honestly, I didn't," he asserted. "I've just been hanging around Krancis for so long that I didn't think."

"That's an understatement."

"Look, get in your shots if you want," he said, grabbing her arm again and stopping her. "But you've got to believe me: I never meant to hurt you. I was just trying to help."

"You'd help me a lot by just leaving me alone," she retorted.

"What on *earth* is the matter with you?" he asked, exasperated at her attitude. "You'd think–."

Suddenly his words were stopped by a flicker of light passing through her eyes. He stared at her closely for several seconds, and then he saw it again.

"That's it: you're coming with me," he informed her, taking her hand and dragging her back towards the teleporter.

"Let go of me, you brute," she fought back, trying to peel her hand out of his.

"Not until we get to the bottom of this," he replied. "Now, you can make it easy or hard. But one way–."

Cutting off his words with a kick to the back of his left

knee, she twisted around and tried to run off. But his hold on her hand was like iron, and it anchored her in place. Jerking her back towards himself, he grabbed her other wrist and all but hoisted her off her feet.

"Kick and scream if you want to," he said through gritted teeth. "But we're gonna talk to Krancis!"

Once more on *Sentinel's* bridge, the man in black's hands were clasped behind him as he watched the enormous vessel rise into the sky, leaving Eastmaw behind. He was reflecting on the peculiarity of having the leader of the Black Suns aboard his vessel when the door opened and a walking struggle entered behind him.

"Krancis!" Gromyko uttered fiercely, his body soaked in sweat as he wrestled Powers into the room. "There is something *wrong* with this girl!"

"You're insane!" she shouted, as he deposited her before Krancis. "Absolutely insane!"

"We'll see about that!" he snapped, gripping her wrists hard enough to numb them. "Now, I don't know if you're gonna believe me or not, but I saw a light flash in this girl's eyes. Not just once, but twice!"

"You're a liar!" she roared.

"No, he isn't," Krancis replied dispassionately, approaching the struggling lieutenant and placing a hand on her forehead. "Be careful: she's going to fall."

"Ha! I'm not going to–."

Instantly her eyes closed, her knees buckled beneath her, and she collapsed. With cat-like reflexes the smuggler managed to seize her around the middle, holding her up as her head and body tilted over backwards.

"A little help here?" he all but demanded, his muscles already exhausted from dragging her across part of the ship.

"Put her down," Krancis said self-evidently. "She's not going to run off now."

Feeling silly, Gromyko lowered her to the floor and stood up.

"Now," he said, dragging the back of his hand across his perspiring brow, "would you mind telling me just what is going on?"

"Her mind has been violated by an intelligence much more powerful than any we've encountered before," Krancis replied. "Even though it was restrained, it has still left damage behind."

"Permanent damage?" he inquired, his heart sinking at the thought.

"That remains to be seen," Krancis said clinically, looking down at the unconscious girl. "There's no precedent for this sort of thing. All we can do is keep her calm and quiet."

"Couldn't *you* do something for her? Straighten her out, even a little bit?"

"I could try," he nodded. "But I may end up doing more harm than good. The human psyche is a complex thing. It's not as simple as changing out a few parts and she's as good as new. There's plenty of risk involved. It's only to be used as a last resort."

"And until then?"

"We wait and see if she recovers on her own."

"But why would I see a light in her eyes?" he asked. "I thought she was possessed or something."

"She isn't possessed," Krancis shook his head. "We would've detected that at once. Besides, the being that interacted with her doesn't have any such power, as far as we know."

"But how can you be so sure? Soliana had that piece of *Eesekkalion* floating around inside her."

"Because I had Soliana examine her while she was unconscious," he answered. "There's nothing foreign within her. At least no foreign *intelligences*."

"Oh."

"Regrettably we don't have the time to do a deep dive into her psyche," Krancis said. "Soliana can't afford that kind of expenditure right now. She has to save her energy for herself. So lieutenant Powers will have to get along as well as she can for the time being. If matters get worse, we can see about bumping up her priority."

"Okay."

"Now, get her back to her room. Have one of the guards help you."

"No, I can do it myself," he replied, enough of his stamina having returned to lift her into his arms and walk heavily towards the door. "It's just a short walk and a teleporter jump away," he added in a strained voice.

Thumping down the hall to the nearest teleportation room, he poured her into one of the chambers and sent her off, following in the other one. Scooping her up again, he just managed to get her into her room and onto her bed when his arms gave out. Standing up straight and stretching his burning limbs, he looked at her and shook his head.

"Who ever knew such a little girl could weigh so much!" he muttered, bending over her and wrestling the covers from under her body. Draping them across her limp form, he drew them up to her neck and stood up. Feeling a kindly impulse pass through him, he brushed the hair from her eyes and smiled. "You're easier to get along with when you're asleep," he chuckled, all of his irritation with her forgotten in an instant. Reaching for the lamp beside her bed, he clicked it off and left the room.

CHAPTER 13

"Sir, we're approaching Hubertus now," Punisher's AI informed Radik, as he stood on the vessel's bridge.

"Anything from Von Ortenburg?" he inquired, his hands tightly clasped behind his back to hide his nerves.

"Nothing beyond that initial distress call," she replied gravely.

The experimental fleet had been delayed by nearly an hour due to a problem with *Punisher's* reactor. Forced to drop out of warp, Radik had radioed ahead to warn the conventional fleet that they would be late, but the news was of little consequence to them. Placing all their faith in their revised tactics, and absolutely none in the plan conceived by Krancis, they hurtled through space towards their target.

Shortly after their estimated arrival time, a call for help went out from Von Ortenburg's flagship, the carrier *Diligence*. Then it was silence.

Cursing himself for falling behind, the naval minister hoped they could hold on until the Adlers and their powerful warheads could be brought to bear on the enemy.

"We're about to drop out of warp, Minister," the AI informed him.

Half a dozen seconds passed, and then the tunnel of blue light terminated, and the fleet of light carriers emerged. All around them was the wreckage of a great battle. Awestruck, Radik walked towards the front window and gaped at the shattered fleet. Giant chunks of battleships floated aimlessly away from the planet, tumbling over and over into the black emptiness of space. Clawed apart carrier husks could be seen in high orbit. The shattered fragments of countless fighters were strewn across the battlefield. But the Devourers were nowhere in sight.

"Where are they?" he asked, his voice an unsteady whisper as he contemplated the catastrophic loss of life. "Where are the Devourers?"

"Scanning," the AI replied. "They're planetside."

"Planetside?"

"Yes. They may be conducting repairs after the battle."

"Not likely," he said, sensing that something much more sinister was afoot. "Not likely."

"What shall we do?"

"What we came here to do," he replied. "Deploy the Adlers. I want a cloud of them on their way to Hubertus immediately."

"Yes, Minister."

Eager to test out their new vessels, the pilots were belted in and ready to go before they'd even dropped out of warp. The instant the order was given the hangar doors were opened and they flew out into space. Keeping in loose formations to avoid catching shells cast at their wingmen, the Adlers tore away from the carriers and approached the planet.

"Good luck," Radik said quietly, tense but calm. Nothing more could be done to ensure the success of the project. All he could do was watch and mind the carriers, which meant keeping them far enough out of reach that they wouldn't be destroyed. It was on the pilots, and their rickety fighters, that the issue now depended. "Magnify the viewer," he ordered the AI, turning away from the window and facing the screen above the door. A camera mounted on the outside of the vessel permitted them to zoom in on the action, and it was with this that he intended to follow the battle.

"One moment, please," she replied. "It's being a little difficult. There," she said triumphantly, the screen lighting up and gradually magnifying as the Adlers moved further away. "The Devourer's fighter craft should be meeting them in half a minute, sir."

His pulse beginning to quicken, he crossed his arms and watched.

"Alpha leader, this is Beta leader," one of the pilots radioed to another. "Suggest you boys loosen up a little more. Those shells are gonna come in thick and fast."

"Understood. You heard him, Alphas: give each other a little elbow room," Alpha leader agreed, causing his ships to spread out.

Beta leader, Colonel Barnaby Moryet, was by far the most experienced pilot among them. Forty-five, level-headed, and the survivor of six separate battles with the parasite, he was specifically singled out by Krancis to participate in the Adler project. Initially skeptical, he sensed the project's potential quickly, and eagerly got involved. His mere presence did much to boost the confidence of the pilots around him.

"Keep your distance," he radioed to the others. "Let them come to you. We're ordnance carriers, remember. We're just little donkeys bringing a big load of pain."

As a cloud of alien vessels broke free of the atmosphere and began unleashing their green shells, the Adlers loosened up still more. Flying between the streams of fire, they waited until they were close and then launched their first salvos. Roaring away from the small ships, the missiles intelligently guided themselves to clusters of craft and detonated, tearing handfuls of them down with each explosion.

"That's getting 'em!" Moryet cheered. "Keep at 'em! Keep at 'em!"

Jarred by the sudden loss of dozens of ships, the alien

fighters attempted to draw away and regroup. But the agile craft pursued them, firing more missiles that positioned themselves for maximum effect before detonating. As huge holes were torn in their groups, they began to loosen up themselves to lessen the damage received.

"They're adapting to our tactics already," Radik observed uneasily. "I hope we don't run out of missiles."

"Look out!" Moryet bellowed, as a pair of pilots got cocky and flew too close to a stream of green blobs in an attempt to line up another shot. "Let them come to you!" he ordered. "Let the missiles do all the work. Just keep your ships in one piece! Remember: we're just little donkeys!"

Breaking up their formations to pursue the human craft individually, the Devourer vessels managed to take down half a dozen of them in twice as many seconds.

"Put your ships through their paces!" Alpha leader radioed. "We're more maneuverable than they are!"

Still green in their new vessels, the pilots had nervously held back from pushing the Adler's limits. But seeing two more of their comrades explode just as Alpha leader's words left his lips broke them free, and they began to violently maneuver to throw off their attackers.

"Get 'em off your backs!" Moryet ordered. "The missiles won't target them this close to our own ships. They'd blow us both up!"

Managing to put some distance between themselves and the alien craft, the Adlers released another volley of missiles that tore the heart out of the Devourer fighter group. With their losses nearing seventy percent, the ships peeled off and made for Hubertus.

"That got 'em!" Echo four shouted. "That kicked 'em around! How do you like that?!"

"Keep it steady, boys," Moryet instructed, as an enormous fleet of carriers, frigates, and battleships rose from the planet's surface to meet them. "That was just round one."

"What are we gonna do?" another flier asked.

"Let them come to us," he replied, leading the group away from the planet as more fighters approached to take the place of those lost. "And pace ourselves. I'll say it again: these ships are weapons platforms. Don't do anything crazy. Stay alive long enough to unload all your missiles."

"And after that?" one of them cockily asked.

"Head back to the carriers and reload," he replied evenly. "We're not done here until every last one of these things is floating in pieces."

With much greater confidence the pilots faced the fresh set of fighters. Spreading themselves out for maximum effect, they boldly flew between the streams of incoming fire and unloaded several missiles at once. With perfect coordination the advanced AIs placed within the weapons cooperated with one another to prevent overlap. Striking the thickest clusters, the Devourers lost thirty percent of their fighter force in the first pass.

"Be careful!" Moryet ordered, as the boldness of the pilots cost several of them their lives. Passing through the fighter screen, they attempted to slip past the capitals and unload as many warheads as they could. But the hitherto slowly moving tentacles lashed out at them like whips, smashing them before they knew what was happening. Forced to maneuver crazily in the confined space between the vessels, several more of them crashed and exploded. "Get out of there!" Beta leader commanded them, as the rest doubled back, preferring to dodge the green globs of the fighters rather than face a nightmare passage of snapping tentacles.

Badly mauled, several more Adlers were destroyed as they attempted to break away from the enemy's fighters. But the keen mind of the parasite had already begun to devise new tactics to use against them. Forming into groups of three to five ships at a time, the alien craft attacked the Adlers in relays, shunting them back and forth between their strike teams. Forced to maneuver along predictable lines, another six were lost.

"We're getting chewed up out here!" Alpha two radioed, barely managing to pull up as a stream of shells shot past his canopy. "There's just too many of them!"

"Not if we keep our wits," Moryet replied. Quickly catching on to the new tactics of the enemy, he told the AI aboard his ship to specifically target the relays that were far enough away to be destroyed without damaging his Adler. Instructing the other pilots to do the same, the missiles ceased striking for maximum effect and instead began clearing the air immediately around them.

"That's getting 'em!" one of the pilots enthused, as the pressure began to come off.

Aware of what was happening, the frigates accelerated into the battle and began snapping their tentacles at the small craft. Though easy to dodge at first, their increasing numbers soon made maneuvering difficult. The remaining Devourer fighters did all they could to channel the human ships into the tentacles. Caught between the globs of the fighters and the limbs of the frigates, several more were lost.

"We're taking too many casualties," Alpha leader radioed privately to Moryet. "We can't hold out much longer."

"We'll have to," Beta leader replied, glancing at the carriers in the distance for a fraction of a second. "We're all that Hubertus has got."

Another few minutes saw the last of the fighters destroyed. Though three carriers were present, they had been utterly denuded of craft.

"Now we go after the bigger stuff," Moryet radioed. "Start with the frigates. They'll be easier to chew."

"My missile count is down to twenty-five percent," one pilot informed him.

"I'm at fifteen percent," another said.

"You know the drill," Beta leader replied. "Pour 'em out until you're empty, then go back for seconds. There'll still be enough targets for everybody."

"That's hardly what I was afraid of," an anonymous pilot quipped, making him grin.

Descending on the frigates, they kept out of reach of their arms and fired a salvo. Glad to finally be unloading on substantial targets, they were shocked when the tentacles snapped out and detonated the missiles themselves. The explosive power of the warheads was still immense, causing damage and spreading the poison across a shallow layer of the inside of the vessels. But it was nothing like a direct hit.

"We're gonna run out long before we finish with all of 'em. Even if we go back for seconds," Alpha six said. "What do we do now?"

"Get in close," Moryet replied.

"I thought you *didn't* want us to do that?"

"Just do as you're told," he ordered, flying over top one of the damaged frigates and dodging the ferocious swipes of its remaining tentacles. Cranking off a missile from one of the tubes mounted on the underside of his Adler, he just managed to escape the blast of his own warhead. The explosion tore an enormous hole in the vessel which the poison immediately exploited. Its internals severely damaged, the frigate's tentacles twitched and then went limp. "That's how it's done, boys," he added. "Go to it."

Learning quickly from his example, the remaining Adlers closed with the frigates and similarly ripped into them.

"I'm out of missiles!" a pilot radioed.

"Me, too!"

"Then get back to the carriers and load up again," Moryet instructed them. "The rest of you, ease back on your outlay. We need to hold 'em here so they can't go after the carriers."

With almost every frigate that fell, another Adler turned and made for home base. Perspiring heavily as his numbers vanished, Moryet swallowed and wondered how he was going to keep them in place.

"One more, and then I'm done," Alpha leader said, passing low over a frigate and releasing his final missile. Peeling away as the blast gouged out the vessel's insides, a tentacle writhed in agony and struck him by chance. Passing from right to left through the Adler, it crushed the fragile ship without so much as slowing down.

"No!" Moryet bellowed at the sight, as the tentacle flopped lifelessly into the gash that had been torn out of the frigate.

With only a dozen Adlers left to fight them, the Devourer fleet began to move towards the carriers.

"They're approaching, Minister," *Punisher's* AI informed Radik.

"Yes, I can see."

"Shall we move?"

"We'll get as many Adlers aboard as we can," he replied. "And then warp to safety."

"But what about Hubertus?"

"We won't be any good to them if we're dead," he uttered. "We'll dash away long enough to rearm the Adlers and then return. This battle is far from over."

"Yes, sir."

"Attention, all craft," Moryet heard the AI say over his radio. "We are preparing to depart. Repeat: we are preparing to depart. Immediately make best speed back to your carriers. We'll be forced to leave you behind if the Devourers get too close."

"You heard her, boys," Beta leader told the remaining craft. "Make best speed."

"What about you?" one of the pilots asked, noticing that he was slowly falling behind.

"Nah, my ship's been losing speed for the last ten minutes. Something's wrong with the engine. You'll have to go without me."

"Sir–."

"I said go without me," he ordered sharply. "I've still got a few missiles left, so I'll cover you as best as I can. Get out of here."

"Good luck, sir."

"Don't count me out yet," he replied, breaking away from the group and heading for another frigate. "I'll be here when you get back."

Feeling too solemn for words, the other Adlers silently accelerated towards the carriers and quickly left the alien fleet behind. Diving towards his target, Moryet unleashed another missile and was pulling away when a tentacle shot up and shaved the tip off his right wing. Immediately going into a spiral that caused him to dodge a pair of tentacles from another frigate, he quickly dropped beneath the fleet and regained control.

"Stabilize that wing," he ordered the AI, who tried to compensate, but with limited success.

Certain that he couldn't make another pass and survive with a bad wing, he decided to get as close as he could and fire his remaining missiles.

"Won't do a ton of damage," he thought. "But it's better than nothing."

Turning his ship around and seeing the engine of a passing battleship, he had his AI aim the missiles for it and cut them loose, four in all. Cruising rapidly towards their target, they each scored a direct hit, the tentacles not easily reaching that far back to block them. As the engine flickered and then went cold, it began to ooze a luminous green gel.

Breaking away from the fleet, he aimed for Hubertus. Glancing out the canopy at his damaged right wing, he hoped that it would survive the ordeal of reentry.

No sooner had he thought this than his scanner detected dozens of new contacts incoming from the reverse side of the planet. The computer identified them as friendlies.

"Friendlies?" he asked aloud, trying to make sense of

it. "But who–."

"Sorry we're late," one of the new craft radioed. "Hope you've saved something for us."

"There's plenty to spare," Moryet replied gratefully. "Who are you guys?"

"Adlers, like you," he said. "Krancis thought you might need a little help."

"Krancis?" he asked, as an enormous shape began to protrude around Hubertus. In an instant he recognized *Sentinel's* profile.

"Yeah, he dropped by and picked us up. You'll have to get the rest of the details later. We have a previous engagement."

"Be my guest," he uttered, as the reinforcements rocketed past and steadily gained on the enemy vessels. "You'll have to get in close, or the tentacles will set off the missiles themselves to spare the ship damage. Don't blow yourselves up, now."

"Thanks for the tip."

Making a beeline for *Sentinel*, it was less than a minute before a new voice crackled over the radio.

"Move, Colonel Moryet," a clinically precise voice ordered him.

"Move?" he asked, confused because he was already traveling as fast as he could.

"You're in my line of fire."

"Oh!" he said, shoving his nose downward. Scarcely a dozen seconds later the warship's main cannon fired, striking one of the lumbering carriers and filling it with darkness. Glancing over his shoulder at the spectacle, he gasped when it shattered into a cloud of black ash. "Incredible," he muttered.

"Get aboard, Colonel."

"Yes, sir."

Piloting his increasingly unstable craft with difficulty, his HUD lit up with a flight plan from *Sentinel* directing him to the right side of the vessel. Passing under it, he climbed to the place indicated and dashed inside, the giant hangar door only partially open. The instant he was inside it began to close.

Setting down his Adler with a thud, he popped the canopy and climbed out.

"Looks like you've had a rough time of it," a mechanic in blue overalls said, pushing his hat back on his head and looking the battered fighter over.

"Yeah, it's been a long day," Moryet replied.

"Boss said for you to meet him on the bridge," the mechanic said, whistling for his assistant to stop what he was doing and approach. "Billy'll show you the way."

"Alright, fellas," said Major Jack Perkins, the man Moryet had briefly spoken to. "Time to finish this."

"Roger that, Theta leader."

Intuiting what Moryet had done, given the stream of green ooze that stretched far behind one of the battleships, he ordered his pilots to target the engines first. With no fighter cover left the capitals were sitting ducks. The few remaining frigates they had tried to place themselves between the massive vessels and their assailants. But with dozens of fresh Adlers bearing down on them, there were simply too many missiles to stop. The collateral damage from detonating the missiles with their tentacles tore them apart, leaving a trail of lifeless husks behind the advancing capitals.

"This is easier than I thought," Theta two said.

"Tell that to the first Adlers that came through here," Perkins shot back, well aware of the casualty figures because of *Sentinel's* scanners. He'd been observing the battle along with Krancis and several others while still in warp, getting a feel for the new tactics that would have to be employed. "To say nothing of the conventional fleet that was broken here," he added, the wreckage of that honorable, though misguided, effort all around them.

"Yes, sir," Theta two replied quietly.

Pounding away at the Devourer vessels, they tore apart their engines but failed to deal much more damage.

"There's some kind of armor protecting the rest of the ship from the engine compartment," Theta four radioed. "We're not doing them a lot of harm."

"Then hit farther up the ship," Perkins ordered. "Get in between those tentacles and take the fight to them."

"Yes, sir."

Accelerating past the engines, the Adlers began to maneuver between the massive limbs that snapped and whipped at them. Carelessly a pair of pilots allowed themselves to be smashed to dust.

"Watch it!" he barked. "They're not gonna go down without a fight!"

Flying along the top of a battleship, he targeted it with four missiles and cut them loose. Too low for the tentacles to intercept them in time, they exploded against the surface, tearing the tough outer layer of the ship away as he pulled up and escaped the blast. Immediately the poison went to work, spreading into the exposed inner flesh of the vessel and killing it.

"That's the way you do it, boys!" he exclaimed, as the tentacles ferociously snapped at him.

"Watch it, Theta leader!" one of them radioed, just as he shoved his fighter's nose downward to dodge a blow. Spiraling off to the right, he got away from the battleship and gave his heart a second to climb down out of his throat before coming back for another pass. "Leave some for the rest of us!" the pilot said, afraid that Perkins would get himself killed through over aggressive tactics.

"Can it!" he ordered, passing from right to left over the damaged warship and firing another pair of missiles at it. Striking two of the same places as before, the warheads' explosions threw already dead flesh upward, digging the hole yet deeper for a fresh coat of poison to infect.

"Move your ships aside, Major," Krancis uttered over the radio.

"Get out of the way, boys!" he said. "*Sentinel's* about to open up again!"

The second they were clear, another black beam of death shot through space and struck the second carrier. Flying around the beam as the Devourer vessel quickly turned black, they resumed their battery of the battleships.

"Easy! Easy!" Perkins ordered, as another Adler collided with a tentacle. "Don't underestimate those things. They're big, but they're fast."

The carrier then disintegrated into a cloud of dust. Flying around it to maintain visibility, the Adlers regrouped and eyed the battleships for a moment.

"I count fifteen, boss," Theta five radioed. "Same amount we started with."

"Yeah, we're not dealing enough damage," Theta seven agreed.

"Then we pick a couple of 'em, group up, and pass over 'em at almost the same time. One explosion after another ought to bore a deep enough hole for the poison to do its work."

"Sounds like a plan to me," Theta five replied.

Marking out several targets for his pilots since there were far too many Adlers for them to go after just one ship at a time, they broke into strike groups and passed in close succession over a handful of battleships. Barely dodging the tentacles as they flew over, the missiles did their work and began digging far into the vessels. By the time a single pass was complete, most of them were in serious trouble.

"Spin around and give it to 'em again," Perkins instructed them. "We're making a dent."

The tentacles of the targeted ships began to slow as the damage added up. Wagging like branches in the wind, they ineffectually tried to swat at their assailants. Dodging them with ease, the Adlers unloaded their ordnance right on target, boring all the way from top to bottom.

"That's it! That's got 'em!" triumphed Perkins, as the arms of his battleship went limp. Looking around, the others were doing likewise. In fact, missiles were passing through the holes and striking targets on the other side. "Don't crank off more warheads than you have to," he told them. "We need to save them for concentrated hits against specific targets."

"Understood, sir," a couple of them radioed.

As he marked out another set of targets, the alien vessels finally drew too close to the light carriers and forced them to depart. Radik had hoped that the reinforcements would slow them enough to allow his Adlers time to rearm and head out again. But it wasn't in the cards. Disappearing into a cloud of blue windows, the carriers left their reinforcements to finish the job.

"Uh, sir?" Theta two asked half a minute after Radik's force had departed. "Why are these guys still heading out into space?"

"Because we've damaged their engines," Theta four replied. "They can't turn."

"The carrier's still going with 'em," Theta two replied. "And its engines are working just fine."

"Because they're pulling us away from the planet!" Perkins said with a flash of insight, cursing under his breath. "Double back to Hubertus, pronto!"

Pulling a vertical U-turn, the Adlers made best speed towards *Sentinel*.

"Krancis," Perkins radioed, as the warship slowly grew in size. "They were drawing us off."

"Yes, but the question is, why," he replied calmly.

"Sir?"

"I'm well aware of the situation, Major. It was obvious that they would never catch the carriers. They were attempting to distract us."

"From what, sir?"

"That's what we're still finding out, Major. Return to

Sentinel at once. We'll deal with the rest of those ships if they decide to come back and give us trouble."

"Yes, Krancis."

Most of *Sentinel's* guests were with Krancis on the bridge. In fact, only Mafalda was absent, still under lock and key in her bedroom. The rest of the group was there, including Girnius and Chrissy. Nervously she clutched his arm, having never witnessed a space battle before.

Nor had she seen a spectacle quite like that which Soliana presented. Sitting on the floor, leaning against one of the transparent walls of the panoramic room, her eyes glowed a dull purple as she muttered strange words under her breath. Her whole body slack, Gromyko knelt beside her to offer any help he could.

"What's wrong with her?" Chrissy whispered in Girnius' ear, causing him to shrug.

"She's in communication with our enemy," Krancis replied, making her start. "There is an enormous mass of Devourer flesh down on Hubertus, and it is casting off psychic signals like a radio tower."

"How do you know that?" Pinchon asked.

"Because of what she's going through," he replied, nodding towards Soliana.

"How do you know she's not just having one of her fits?"

"Because I can feel them as well," he answered. "Any psychic would be able to detect what's being beamed off that planet."

"Beamed where?"

"That's what we're trying to find out."

"Shouldn't we just blast it and have done with the whole business?" Gromyko asked, worried that Soliana was in danger. "*Sentinel's* cannon ought to be able to take that thing down."

"That wouldn't solve anything," the man in black replied. "Several more of these masses are spread throughout the empire. Destroying one will still leave the others."

"Then we knock 'em off one after the other," the colonel said.

"If they're attempting to communicate with something, we need to know what that something is," Wellesley chimed in over the ship's speakers.

"Precisely."

"Even if it turns her brains into jelly?" the ex-pirate asked, pointing at Soliana.

"She's a very strong psychic," Krancis replied. "She'll be alright."

"Nice to know," he muttered, unconvinced.

"N–no! W–wha–," Soliana struggled to say.

"What is it?" the smuggler beside her asked, putting a hand on her shoulder and instantly getting zapped by a charge and jerking his hand away. "What in the world?"

"Don't touch her," Krancis said, approaching the girl and crouching just out of reach, his elbows on his knees.

"Yeah, I got that part!" Gromyko exclaimed, still shaking his hand with pain. "Are you sure she's alright?"

"For the time being."

Slowly writhing in place, Soliana's cheeks began to blush and her brow to perspire.

"According to the ship's instruments, she's burning up," Wellesley said. "Too much more and she's gonna be in danger."

"She'll be alright," Krancis assured him.

"Shouldn't we get her some ice or something?" the smuggler suggested.

"Best to leave well enough alone. She knows what she's doing."

"She isn't even conscious!" Gromyko exclaimed.

"A psychic doesn't have to be conscious in order to be very much in control of a given situation," Krancis replied. "Given that situation is internal. Right now she's in communication with the mass beneath us. Either they're wrestling in psychic combat, or she's allowing it to pass its thoughts through her mind in order to understand them. But one way or another, she has deliberately brought this onto herself. It is her role in this war to give us intelligence that we couldn't otherwise obtain. She will have to bear the risks associated with that task."

"Even if it kills her?" Pinchon asked.

"It won't," Krancis replied, not bothering to look over his shoulder at the colonel. "And if it did, her sacrifice would be no greater than that of the numerous pilots we've just lost here. There are always casualties in war."

Silently watching all this was colonel Moryet. Standing beside and a little behind Hunt, he was surprised at the casual ease with which the others addressed a man as great as Krancis. Having never met him in the flesh before that day, he assumed that his air would be scarcely less formal than that of the emperor himself. It jarred him to find the man in black so lacking in pretense, and yet so utterly authoritative. It seemed to not matter in the least to him how others addressed him. His self-assurance was absolute no matter what they did.

"N–No!" Soliana moaned again, writhing more forcibly as her temperature continued to rise. Sliding down the wall and onto the floor, she lay against its cool surface and began to moan softly. Then her eyes shot open, and she sat up with a wicked smile on her face. "So great Krancis has come to play," she said in a hoarse whisper.

"I don't play," Krancis replied evenly, continuing to crouch before her as Gromyko shot to his feet in surprise.

"This little one is too weak to abide in my presence," the parasite uttered through her. "Too young. Too soft. You are a much more capable companion for c–conversation. Why don't we speak together, one to another? Why do you send this little girl to do your work for you?"

Hunt approached Soliana and took a knee beside Krancis.

"What do you want?" he asked seriously.

"Ah, the champion of the Earthborn," she replied, twisting her head towards him, her mouth still twisted in a grotesque smile. "The leader of the *Ahn-Wey* had such hopes for you. I can't tell you how I *savored* extinguishing its life, draining the last drops of its vital essence from its haggard body. The memories it bore passed through my fingers as I did so, and I saw many things that it had hoped, and dreamed, and feared. You have surpassed all that it dared to expect from you."

"I manage," he replied dismissively.

"But you will fail," she assured him, shaking her head slowly from side to side. "You will fail. None will stand before me. Soon I will break upon this galaxy like a thunderous storm, and none will be left alive."

"What do you mean *soon*?" Wellesley asked. "It's not like you've been sitting on your hands."

"You will know fear," the parasite whispered. "You will know terror. And then there will be silence. In death, all shall be united in me. I shall collect you all. And not merely the Earthborn and the living worlds: all life in this universe will be consumed and preserved within me. I shall walk along the empty, lifeless halls of this dimension alone."

"But why?" Chrissy asked, almost too scared to speak, her voice barely audible.

"Because it is my *will!*" Soliana shot at her, twisting her head violently and causing her to shrink behind Girnius.

"We will stop you," Hunt told the parasite.

"No," Soliana shook her head again. "You have *enabled* me. Like a pitiful beast I was held back by the leash of the *Prellak*. But in destroying *Eesekkalion*, you have set me free! For that I thank you, for I know that only you could have brought such power to bear on that miserable world. Before that I was muddled, confused, in a dream. Now I see *clearly*. Now I see the *way*."

"Your way is only death," Hunt replied

contemptuously.

"You are correct," the parasite agreed proudly. "I have no higher aspiration than to destroy every last living thing in this universe. Beginning with *this* little creature!"

Suddenly Soliana dropped onto her back and started to convulse. Instantly Krancis shot to her head and laid a hand upon her brow, slowing her movements until they stopped and she sighed in her sleep. After half a minute of increasingly calm breathing, her eyes opened and the purple tint to them was gone.

"Did you learn what you wanted to know?" she asked, immediately looking at Krancis.

"No," he said with marked disappointment. "It knew what we were up to. It just kept us dangling the whole time."

"Then this was all for nothing?" Pinchon asked pointedly.

"No," Soliana assured him. "Whilst its consciousness passed through my psyche, I could feel the message it's sending out."

"Well?" Krancis asked.

"I can't decipher it yet," she admitted. "The dialect is strange, completely alien to me. I've never encountered anything like it. I'll need time to digest and process it."

"Well, there's one thing we've learned," Wellesley said, as Krancis helped the girl onto her feet and steadied her. "That mass down there's got to be destroyed *stat*. If it can push Soliana around like that, there's no telling what else it's up to."

"I agree," Krancis replied, gesturing for Gromyko to approach. "Get Soliana to her room. She needs time to rest."

Apprehensively the smuggler tapped her a couple times to ensure he wouldn't be zapped again. Satisfied, he was about to take her arm when she swooned into Krancis' embrace.

"Colonel," the man in black ordered.

"Yeah, yeah," Pinchon nodded, getting on one side of

her while Gromyko took the other. "Come on, honey: let's get you to bed."

All eyes watched the trio depart, and then turned to Krancis.

"Captain," he said, pressing a finger into his ear radio. "Position us for a shot against the biomass below." Removing his finger, he looked at Hunt. "Time to get into the reactor."

"You really think that's necessary?" the Deltan inquired.

"We're not taking any chances," he replied. "There's something wrong about this, and I want to ensure we have plenty of power on hand to deal with this threat."

"Alright," he said with a shrug, making for the door.

"Why does it feel like we've done this before?" Wellesley asked, dangling from the chain around his neck.

"Beats me. Probably deja vu," he replied offhandedly, walking along the corridor to the teleporter.

"I've got to admit, that bit in there kind of freaked me out," the AI continued. "I don't know how Krancis kept so cool throughout the whole thing. Of course, he *does* seem to have the inside track on...*everything*."

"Not everything," he replied, putting a hand to the teleporter room door. "He still doesn't know what the Devourers are up to."

"Yeah, that strikes me kind of funny," Wellesley commented, as Hunt told the technician where he wanted to go. "Throughout so much of this it's like he's had fate dialed in. But as time goes by, he seems to be making up more of it as he goes along." He paused briefly as Hunt stepped into the chamber and disintegrated in a flash of blue. "He's lost some of that eerie divinity that always used to creep me out so much," he added on the other side.

"Well, he's still the best man for the job. That's all I know," he replied once he'd left the room, walking down the corridor towards the reactor.

"Oh, sure. It's just...odd."

Reaching the reactor room, he waited for Wellesley to drop the lift and stepped on. Riding it upward, he remembered the last time he'd been inside with Milo.

"You alright?" the AI asked.

"Doesn't matter much either way, does it?" he replied, stepping off the lift and moving to the center of the reactor. "Alright, Krancis," he said over his radio. "I'm ready."

"Start charging the reactor."

"Oh, come on," Rex objected. "Let's at least start shooting the thing before we pump it into overdrive."

"We're not taking any chances," he replied evenly. "Now, get started."

With an irritated sigh he closed his eyes and dug deep. Slowly raising his arms, he could feel the power of the dark realm begin to build within him, flowing directly into the reactor. It felt familiar, like the presence of an old friend that he'd grown accustomed to but hadn't seen in a long time. Exercising his gift in his own person really didn't bring with it the palpable sense of proximity that charging the reactor did. The only thing that exceeded it, naturally enough, was when the shadow realm actually drew him into itself. Fearing that he might see Milo's body floating among the dead, he earnestly hoped such a trip wouldn't be necessary.

"Keep going," Krancis ordered. "We're at one hundred and fifty percent. I want at least double our normal capacity."

"Why?" Hunt snapped, his concentration waning a little.

"Just do it."

With a scowl he dug deeper, drawing more power through himself. He began to feel less present, his perception of his immediate surroundings slowly fading. He could feel the dark realm around him, beckoning him inside for another meeting. Carefully he raised his output until he judged it was a little past two hundred percent.

"Alright, hold it there," Krancis radioed.

"Where are we, Wells?" Hunt asked in a strained voice,

it requiring much more concentration to hold steady than to ramp higher and higher, surrendering himself to the dark element.

"Around two-twenty," he replied. "Just keep doing what you're doing."

"You may fire at once, Captain," Krancis said from the bridge, watching a magnified portion of the panoramic display, the biomass clearly in sight. The others were gathered closely around him, a fact he didn't particularly appreciate.

Instantly the dark beam burst from the ship's cleft and dashed to the planet below, striking the mass and slowly covering it over with shadow.

"What's happening?" Pinchon asked, having returned from helping Soliana. "Why isn't it exploding?"

"Why indeed," Krancis uttered quietly, watching as the mass grew darker and darker.

Suddenly the mass exploded, releasing a shockwave that leveled trees for miles.

"Cease firing," he ordered the captain at once, not wishing to further damage Hubertus.

"Why didn't that look right?" the colonel asked him, pointing at the massive whole in the ground that had been left behind.

"It didn't disintegrate," Girnius observed.

"Yeah, that's right," Moryet seconded.

"More than that," Krancis said, "It unleashed an enormous pulse of psychic energy."

"To what end?" Pinchon asked.

"Who can say," he shrugged, walking from the room.

"Alright, it's no secret that I'm not that guy's biggest fan," Pinchon said once he'd gone. "But if *he* doesn't know what's going on, I don't like it."

Back inside the reactor, Hunt gradually lessened the flow of dark energy until it ceased altogether. Bowing his head for a moment, he stepped back onto the lift and

Wellesley started it down.

"You okay?"

"Yeah," he nodded, just closing his eyes and breathing. "Just took a lot out of me."

"It's been quite a day."

Stepping off the lift and making for the door, he frowned at the sight of Krancis.

"Good work," he said, turning and walking beside him as they left the room. "The mass has been destroyed. Or rather, it exploded."

"What do you mean?"

"Just what I said."

With a sigh Hunt turned to him and stopped, resting his hands on his hips.

"Exploded? Why would it do that?"

"Your guess is as good as mine," Krancis replied, resuming movement. "We're dealing with something new here. The parasite has never demonstrated this much of a faculty for psychic communication. Yes, powerful psychics could detect it talking to itself. But to reach out and speak *through* Soliana is beyond anything it's done before. And there's more: when the mass was destroyed, a blast of psychic energy was released."

"So?"

"Were it paralyzed by the energy of the dark realm, that shouldn't have been possible. It ought to have simply disintegrated. Instead it seemed to have been charged by the energy we poured into it."

Hunt paused again.

"That's why you wanted me in there," he said. "You knew this would happen all along. Just like when *Eessekkalion* fed off *Sentinel*."

"I *suspected* something of this sort was possible," Krancis stipulated. "It was clear that the parasite was goading us into attacking it. I wanted you in there so we could finish it quickly if the need arose, especially if it drew power and was somehow able to throw it back."

"Well, that's all over with now," the Deltan said, again walking.

"You're forgetting about the other masses spread throughout the galaxy. We have to take them out as well."

"Yes," he agreed, laying a hand on the teleporter room's door. His fatigue catching up to him more and more, he began to sag. "But not today."

Far from Hubertus, a malignant intelligence smiled inwardly.

"Oh, mighty Krancis," it laughed, speaking to itself in a sinister, hoarse whisper. "You have no idea how perfectly you've fallen into my trap! This victory of yours is but the first of many defeats you shall suffer. Soon," it concluded, "all will be united. *In death.*"

End of Book IV

THANK YOU!

I hope you enjoyed The Tides of Retribution!
If you did, please leave a review so others can enjoy it too!

Review on Amazon

Printed in Great Britain
by Amazon